THE HARLEQUIN CREW SERIES

THE HARLEQUIN CREW SERIES

CAROLINE PECKHAM
&
SUSANNE VALENTI

This book is dedicated to JJ's condoms.
Big, thick, long and wide,
Ribbed and studded with spermacide.
Strawberry, bannana, peaches and cream,
One tossed in a bush, another in a stream.
Trojan, Durex, SKYN and Crown,
Rip it open and go to town.
Double wrapped or ultra thin.
Pick your poison and enjoy within.

Rejects Park

ROGUE

CHAPTER ONE

I'm not dead.

I gasped as those three words resounded through my skull and the memory of Shawn's hands locked tight around my throat threatened to drown me in terror.

I'd seen my death in his eyes, watched as the bright blue colour of them seemed to flare with energy and excitement as he pinned me to the wall and choked the fucking life out of me. *"Sorry about this, sweetcheeks. I'm really gonna miss that ass of yours, but I can't have witnesses. You understand."* Those were his last words to me as I fought for my motherfucking life, thrashing and scratching and gouging at his arms as his grip never faltered. The last words I ever should have heard as he squeezed and squeezed until my ears were ringing and darkness closed over my vision and I fell into the deepest depths of oblivion. I'd thought I was dead. Hell, maybe I was.

But then why did my throat hurt so fucking much? My head was pounding and there was a heaviness to my body unlike anything I'd ever felt before.

I groaned as I opened my eyes but all that escaped my lips was a hoarse croak which felt like fire burning up my throat. Even with my eyes open, the darkness didn't let up. It was pitch black and the air I sucked into my lungs was stale and left the scent of damp earth coating my tongue.

"Shawn?" I rasped, but it barely even sounded like his name and he was the last fucking person I wanted to see anyway. But my mind was a fog of confused, disjointed thoughts and memories and he was the only person my malfunctioning brain could latch onto right now.

I tried to lift my arm to push my hair away from my face, but I found it trapped against my chest.

As I sucked in another breath, some rough, scratchy fabric was drawn against my lips and my heart leapt in fear as I realised the heaviness I felt wasn't in my body – it was *on* my body.

There was a weight pressing down on me, pinning my arms to my sides and trapping me in the dark. That damp earth smell surrounded me, drowning me in it and a croak of fear escaped my lips as a terrifying thought occurred to me.

I wasn't dead. But I *was* buried.

With a cry of alarm which sent more pain through my tender throat, I yanked hard on my arms and I almost sobbed with relief as I managed to drag them up my body until I was shoving hair away from my face and pressing shaking fingertips to the rough material I'd been wrapped in. It felt like some kind of heavy duty sack or sheeting.

Panic dug its claws into me at the thought of being underground and a shiver of fear passed through my skin as I wondered how much air I even had left down here. Every breath I sucked in seemed thin, full of that damp earth scent which made me want to heave. But puking right now seriously wasn't going to improve my situation and I *really* needed to improve my fucking situation, or I was pretty sure this dead girl was about to get a whole lot deader.

I pressed my palms against the sack in front of my face and tried to exert pressure against the weight above it as I began to wriggle my legs.

As the heaviness above me shifted, the weight on my chest suddenly increased and a hoarse shriek of terror escaped me as I started thrashing and kicking with more vigour. I cursed and kicked and clawed at the rough material which was wrapped around me until my fingernails managed to tear through it.

Cold, damp soil poured through the hole the moment it was created and

8

I screamed a broken, shattered sound of pure terror as the dirt spilled over my face.

I kicked harder, clawing huge clods of dirt into my hands and somehow managed to shove myself into a vague sitting position as I tried to hold my breath, and dirt cascaded over me in a never ending torrent.

I scrunched my eyes up tight and fought with everything I had as I dug and crawled and battled my way towards the surface.

My lungs ached with a desperate, urgent kind of need and the fear pressed in on me almost as tightly as the dirt I'd been buried in. But just as my body felt ready to give out on me, my hand thrust through the surface and balmy air washed over my palm.

With a snarl of determination, I kicked harder, clawing the dirt away from me until I managed to push my head free of it and I sucked down a shuddering breath of relief.

I coughed and heaved as I pressed my cheek against the cool earth, still half buried beneath it and suddenly lacking in all energy as I just fought to calm my thrashing heart.

The dim, pale blue light of dawn fell through the trees which surrounded me and I slowly cracked my eyes open as I tried to get my bearings. The sound of gulls calling out to one another and the tang of salt in the air told me I was near the sea and I groaned as I tried to figure out how I'd ended up here.

But it was no good. The last thing I remembered was Shawn's hands wrapped around my throat as he tried to kill me in his club. Then darkness. It had been night then…how many hours had it been? How long had I been underground? How close had I just come to actually dying?

I rasped out another groan as the pain in my neck drew all of my attention for a moment and the pounding in my skull had me praying for oblivion again.

With a curse that didn't even sound like it was me speaking, thanks to the damage that asshole had done to my vocal cords, I dug my fingers into the ground in front of me and dragged the rest of my body up out of the dirt. It took way longer than I would have liked and I couldn't help but think that I must look like some kind of undead asshole right about now. Or I would have if anyone was here to see me. But as I appeared to be slap bang in the middle of fucking nowhere, I guessed there wasn't much chance of that.

When I finally managed to drag my feet free of the shallow grave my boyfriend had gifted me, I fell down onto my knees before collapsing to the ground and rolling over so that I could look up at the canopy of trees above me and lay there panting as tears pricked the backs of my eyes. But I wouldn't let them fall. I'd cried my last tears a long damn time ago and I'd sworn never to let anyone get close enough to hurt me like that again ever since.

The Harlequin boys had broken my heart once and I had no intention of ever giving it out to anyone again.

The dirty, brown material I'd been buried in was still tangled around my legs and I tugged it off of me as I stood, clutching it in my fist as I looked down at it, wondering if I'd ever meant anything at all to the man who had killed me so casually.

I turned the torn piece of sack in my fist, frowning as I spotted a logo stamped across it, hidden within the mud that stained it.

Pappa Brown's Russet Potatoes.

He'd buried me in a shallow grave wrapped in a fucking potato sack. Anger flooded through my flesh unlike anything I'd ever known at the fucking callous disregard that asshole had held me in. The feeling was quickly followed by disgust for the fact that I'd ever let that vile excuse for a man lay his hands on my body. But you didn't say no to Shawn Mackenzie, everyone knew that. I could have just run when he set his sights on me, but I'd foolishly believed that being his girl would offer me some level of protection in these fucked up games I ran in, where men played at being kings and everyone died with a knife in their back in the end.

My mouth was so dry that my tongue felt swollen and the headache was making me dizzy as well as nauseous. I was coated in damn mud, my blue crop top and ripped jeans clearly ruined and my once white sneakers now very much brown. A quick swipe of my hand over my long, brunette hair told me that it was no better.

I swallowed against the lump in my throat and looked around for some sign of where I needed to go to get out of here, but there were just trees everywhere. The ground sloped down to my right though so that seemed like the easiest path to take.

I stumbled downhill, my feet catching on roots as my tired limbs ached and the pain in my body threatened to overwhelm me. But I needed to keep moving. Had to get away from here and find somewhere safe so that I could figure out what the fuck I was supposed to do now.

The sound of the waves reached me and the light ahead brightened before I stepped out onto a white sandy beach, a sigh of relief escaping me at the sight of the ocean. Fuck, I missed it sometimes more than my own mother. I mean, my mother was a total bitch who I barely even remembered, so I missed my period more than her whenever I wasn't on it, but still, the ocean held a special place in my heart unlike any other. I couldn't even remember the last time I'd been swimming in it though, let alone surfing.

I drew in a deep breath of the crisp, ocean breeze and looked out at the horizon for a long moment as I tried to process what had happened last night. But all that came back to me was that one, all important thing. I was a dead girl walking. And Shawn could never find out about that unless I wanted to live to see that fate brought to reality. Of course, if I managed to get to him before he got to me…

I shook my head before I got carried away and started thinking about anything crazy like revenge. I certainly wasn't in any shape to be carrying out hits on gangster assholes right now anyway. And the leader of The Dead Dogs would be a damn difficult target to get close to. First things first, I needed water, food, clothes…money.

I dipped my fingers into my back pocket where I knew I'd had a twenty stashed and closed my eyes for a brief moment with a smile tugging at my lips as I found it right where I'd left it. That was something. Admittedly, not a whole lot. But it was a start.

Any normal girl would have been afraid right now, but every moment since the Harlequin boys had betrayed me, I'd been growing tougher like a rose growing thorns. I knew how to take things in my stride, even my own death. I was either one lucky bitch or the Grim Reaper had been preoccupied tonight and he'd come looking to claim what he was owed soon enough. I was banking on the former.

As I opened my eyes again, I turned first to my right and then to my left, looking out along the horizon for any sign of anything which might tell me where the fuck I was.

"Motherfucker!" I yelled loud enough to startle a couple of seagulls who had been fighting in the sand...oh wait, they were fucking actually and looking rather scandalised at the interruption, but that wasn't the point.

The point, was that beyond the cerulean sea and the long stretch of white sand, far off in the distance lit up by the first rays of the rising sun, I could see a goddamn pier with a goddamn Ferris wheel parked up at the far end of it. Not just any pier and Ferris wheel either, oh no - that right there was what me and my former boys liked to call Sinners' Playground. It used to be my favourite place in the entire world once upon a time. But the thought of coming back here now had me wishing Shawn had done a better job of choking me to death. My gut tightened and a lump of dread rose in my throat.

This place had been my home once. The only one I'd ever known. Where I ran the streets with the Harlequin boys at my side and the world seemed full of endless blue skies and a thousand possibilities. *And look how quickly that had gone to shit...*

Fucking Shawn in his final act of fuck you had driven me out here to bury my still warm corpse in a shallow grave in the one place in this world that I hated above all others.

If I hadn't already wanted to kill him for putting his fucking hands on me, then I sure as hell did now. I was going to go ahead and slap a nice, big post-it note at the forefront of my mind holding a life goals to-do list, and right at the top of it would be the words *kill Shawn Mackenzie.* It would have helped if he wasn't the current leader of The Dead Dogs, the second biggest gang in the state, but I didn't care. He'd bought his death with mine, I'd see to that even if it cost me all I had.

It was just a shame that right now, that was a sum total of nothing. Well... twenty dollars and the key I kept on a leather necklace around my neck.

I sucked in a breath and quickly grasped at my shirt, right between my cleavage where the key always hung and relief filled me as I found it there. I wasn't really surprised. Shawn had always called it my sentimental piece of crap so of course he hadn't taken it. But that was just because I'd told him it was the key to my dead grandma's liquor cabinet which I'd worn since her death to keep her close to my heart. Never had a string of bullshit served me so well. Because this key opened something far more precious than a cupboard full of booze. Even if my imaginary grandma had had expensive tastes.

My gaze strayed to the Ferris wheel in the distance again and I licked my lips, tasting damp soil coating them.

I used to think my life might just have been perfect. The Harlequin boys and me. One big, happy, unconventional, marginally fucked up family.

Maverick told me once that all four of them were in love with me. He said one day I'd have to choose between them and that would be the end of it all. Our happiness dashed to pieces by me choosing one of them and rejecting the others.

Little did I know that the end would come much more swiftly than that. The only kiss my boys had ever given me was the very same one that Judas offered up to the man he was supposed to love.

At least when your heart breaks at sixteen you learn that lesson well. I'd never trust the promises of anyone who claimed to love me. I'd never believe in anything other than myself.

When they'd cut my heart out and left me bleeding and alone, I'd done what any self-respecting runaway brat did best and ran the fuck away. But maybe it was time I stopped running. Ten years was a long time to bear a grudge and I still held the key to their dark, dirty little secrets. Perhaps it was time I claimed what we'd locked away…

My fingers tightened around the key and I strode down the beach to the water. I needed to rinse the grave dirt off of me before I made any decisions. Because if I chose to let the Harlequin boys back into my life again, then I knew that I'd have to bring my A game. No falling for their bullshit, no listening to their sweet talk and no more talk of heartbreak – not even to myself. They could never know how much they'd hurt me that night ten years ago. How shattered my heart still was and how keenly that pain still found me when I thought about them. And over the years, that hurt hadn't dulled a scrap. So it might just be time for me to pay them back for it.

Rejects Park

ROGUE

CHAPTER TWO

I walked down the sand to the waves which lapped against the shore, pausing to find a rock and wedge my twenty under it before striding right on into the water.

It was cold against my already chilled skin, but I tried to take comfort in the fact that I could still feel anything at all.

Dead girls weren't supposed to shiver. In fact, dead girls weren't supposed to do a whole lot of anything. And seeing as that meant there were no expectations weighing on me any longer, I was going to shed every last hang-up I had.

I walked until the water was deep enough for me to dive beneath the waves and I fought off the moment of panic that holding my breath delivered to me. This wasn't going to break me. In fact, I was determined that this was going to be my rebirth. For the last ten years, I'd been treading water, living on the outskirts of power and trying to survive each day as it came. I kept my head down, minded my own business and kept my shit together. But while Shawn had been drawing me closer, I'd kept my wits about me. I'd known what I was doing letting myself get tangled up with him and my eyes had been wide open for every moment of it. Last night wasn't the first time I'd heard or seen something I shouldn't. It was just the first time he'd caught me. And the last. Or so he thought.

I swam away from the shore with confident strokes and a feeling of euphoria which I'd only ever been gifted by the ocean. There was just something so pure about the saltwater which felt like it was washing away my sins, though in all fairness I'd need to scrub a lot harder if I expected to remove those from my flesh.

It might have been ages since I'd been beneath the waves, but my body remembered and as I swam, a lightness filled my soul which I grasped onto with both hands like a lifeline. This was what I needed. Just me and the water. Nothing and no one else. Because people were problems that I didn't want. I'd been alone for a long damn time, even though I'd been surrounded by people. But they were strangers charting their own course to hell. I didn't need any passengers on my ferry. Dead weight just dragged you down anyway.

I kicked up to the surface and gasped as I drew in a deep breath to satisfy my aching lungs. The sun was rising higher now, gilding the tips of the waves as I rolled onto my back and floated there, looking up at the pale sky.

I knew the price of heading back to Sunset Cove would be high. Probably the highest I'd ever paid for anything, even counting my death. If I did this, all traces of the girl I'd once been would be lost. But maybe they already were. I was just clinging onto the idea of them because it made all the fucked up shit I'd suffered through tolerable. But if I wanted out of this life. All the way out like I'd been dreaming of for years, then I needed to go back. I needed to take what I was owed then set my eyes on the horizon and run for my life. Not this sorry excuse for an existence I'd been festering in for years, but for the life I'd always wished for in the darkest corners of the night. The one I'd never really believed I could claim. But it was now or never. I was a dead girl walking and I needed to decide my own fate.

I turned and swam back towards the shore, dipping beneath the waves again and sighing in a stream of bubbles as the water slowly lit with the blue of the sky all around me and I felt like I was home at last.

Once my feet could reach the bottom again, I stopped and started scrubbing at my hair, my face, my body. I needed to get the grave dirt off of my flesh and I refused to flinch away from the sting of my wounds.

The cuts burned in the saltwater, but at least it was cleaning them. I needed it to clean them, to wash away all evidence of what Shawn had tried to do, of the feeling of his hands on my flesh, of his tight grip on my throat.

My heart raced as I remembered that look in his eyes as he'd squeezed the life out of me. That cold, callous acceptance and more than a little excitement too. I knew he'd killed people before me and I'd never even imagined he might love me, but I'd been his girl for almost two years and I thought that I might have meant...something to him. But I guessed not. Even after all of these years, I was still just the girl everyone liked to throw away.

I strode back out of the water, glancing down at the full sleeve of tattoos on my left arm as they glistened wetly, the patterns clear without the grave dirt hiding them, a mixture of ocean creatures and violent things which probably made no sense to anyone but me. But those images were my soul in ink. From the painted skulls dressed in flowers to the stingrays circling my bicep, the pair of angel wings on my back and the other creatures and images which marked my flesh, each of them meant something to me far beyond the obvious.

I wrung the water from my long hair, cringing at the pain in my neck as I tilted my head to do it and looking down at my ruined clothes. I may have been able to wash the dirt from my flesh, but the water had just made the stains on my shirt and jeans stand out more.

I retrieved my twenty from beneath the rock and forced myself to look towards the distant pier again. If I was really going to do this then I needed to get my head in the game. I had to be prepared for whatever this was going to take from me.

I shook off the urge to bitch about my lot in life and started walking.

Big girls don't cry and all that jazz. Or maybe broken girls didn't feel. And dead girls didn't hurt.

In the distance, in the general direction of the pier and the town I'd grown up in, I spotted a few luxury condos lining the waterfront so I kicked my wrecked sneakers off, tied the laces together and slung them over my shoulder as I started walking.

I was in desperate need of pretty much everything, so I was fairly sure I would be able to alleviate at least a few of my desires there. The rest I'd just figure out as I went. That was basically how I'd been living my entire life anyway, so why change the habit of a lifetime?

The sun crept higher in the sky as I walked, cresting the horizon and filling the clouds with streaks of orange that reminded me of just how much I used to love this place. There was beauty here, especially beyond the edge of the town where the water met the land and there were no people to interrupt the silence.

By the time I made it to the first house, my throat felt so raw that each breath caused me pain. I groaned in relief as I spotted the outdoor shower set up within a little wood cubicle right outside the fence that ringed the property, beside a gate which offered the owners access to the beach.

I dropped my shoes and lurched forward, setting the cold water running and thrusting my head beneath it so that I could open my mouth and drink my fill. Every mouthful was like a balm to the aching burn in my throat and I swallowed greedily, trying to fill my belly enough to deny the rumbling that had started up in it. Food wasn't likely to be an option for a while, so there was really no point in my body protesting its emptiness so forcefully.

When I was finally satisfied by the water, I turned back to look at the house, pushing wet hair out of my eyes and trying to gauge whether or not anyone was home. These houses were vacation places for the most part and seeing as we were only just coming into February, there was a good chance a lot of them would be empty. But with the fancy alarms these people had installed, that was actually a bad thing from my point of view.

The house closest to me seemed to be all locked up, so I moved on, squelching along in my wet and ruined clothes with sand sticking to every part of me as I walked towards the next house further down the beach.

The heavens must have been smiling on me today because as well as allowing me to crawl my ass up out of a grave, they'd gifted me the blessing of a lazy bitch who had left her laundry hanging out overnight.

I groaned longingly as I jogged towards the fenced in yard, glancing up at the house which it belonged to to check for anyone looking out this way before hopping over the fence and closing in on the dry laundry which was blowing back and forth in the sea breeze.

Man sock, boxers, bed sheet - bingo! A blood red bikini hung from the line right beside a cute pair of denim shorts which seemed to whisper *slip your ass into me* to the tune of the waves crashing against the shore. And who was I to deny something that wanted my ass that badly?

I dropped my shoes, shed my ripped jeans, panties, crop top and bra and stood there in my birthday suit, letting the dolphins get a nice long look at my ass if they fancied hopping up out of the ocean for a gander. Sadly, there were no towels so I made do with the bed sheet, silently apologising for using it to wipe the sand from between my butt cheeks, but a girl had to do what a girl had to do. And I was sure if the homeowner knew what kind of day I'd had, they'd let me off.

I slipped on the - *oh hello baby* - *designer* bikini and quickly adjusted the ties to secure the girls before pulling on the shorts. They were a little snug. Okay, there was probably more cheek hanging out the bottom of them than contained inside, but beggars can't be choosers and at least they weren't wet. I fished my twenty from the pocket of my ruined jeans and slipped it into my bikini top with a smug grin. Lastly, I hooked a fancy, white lacy kimono cardigan thing from the clothesline and pulled it on to complete my outfit change. The look was a bit boho for me, but I was calling it a win.

I grabbed my wet clothes and headed back out of the yard, hopping over the fence before jogging up the side of the house to the little street which backed it.

I kept my pace fast until I'd left the beach house behind then dumped my ruined clothes in the neighbour's trash further up the street, keeping hold of my sneakers and hanging them over my shoulder again just in case I couldn't find replacements.

I walked about another mile before I came up on a house with a car parked up out front with a hassled looking guy throwing stuff in the trunk while his kid yelled abuse at him from the front porch.

The little brat looked about nine and he was kicking his skateboard into the street and letting it roll back to him with a petulant look on his face.

"I don't want chocolate, I want vanilla!" he screamed, face red, glaring at his father who looked like he was in a rush to get somewhere.

"I told you, Benny, I don't have vanilla," the dad said. "How about we stop for pancakes on the way back? Can you give me a hand grabbing your bags from your room?"

"I hate you!" the kid screamed and the dad threw me an apologetic look without really looking at me before hurrying back into his house with a shake of his head while the brat threw a fit.

Just as I got close to him, a little white dog with a brown patch over its eye scampered out of the bushes, wagging its tail hopefully as it approached the kid like it thought it might get some food or something. The thing didn't have a collar on and it was bony enough that I knew it was a stray. There were plenty of those out here; the weather was always nice enough and in the summer the tourists fed them up so they got good and fat. You didn't tend to get so many in the part of town where I grew up because people could barely afford to feed themselves, so they weren't going to be handing out anything to mutts.

The kid spotted the hopeful pup and grabbed his skateboard from the floor, hefting it over his head as he lurched towards it. "Get out of here you mongrel!"

He swung the board at the little pup which leapt away with a whine of fright and I lunged forward, catching the other end of the board and snarling at him.

"Why not pick on someone your own size, you little asshole?" I demanded, holding onto the board and glaring at him as he gaped at me like no one in his life had ever called him out on being the entitled little prick he clearly was.

I yanked the skateboard out of his hands and smirked at him. "I'm taking this because you're a shit human being," I explained. "And if you cry to your daddy about it, I'm gonna wait until you're asleep in your bed and then come and drag you out into the night and dump you out at sea."

"What?" he squeaked and I realised that I was a grown ass woman threatening some kid. Not my finest hour, but he was a dick and he needed to learn a lesson.

"I want your hat, too," I decided, eyeing the baseball cap on his head which he quickly handed over.

On closer inspection I realised it was a Red Power Ranger cap which sucked because everyone knew the Green Ranger was the best, he was just totally underrated. Either way, the cap was mine and the kid had learned a good life lesson. "Be nice to dogs and I won't have to come back. And go help your dad with the bags you little shit."

He ran off, seemingly too stunned for tears and I grinned down at my new board.

Wait a minute, this wasn't just any old skateboard, it was a motherfucking Element Board, *sweeeet.* That kid really was a spoilt brat and my day just got way better.

I dropped the skateboard to the road and hopped on, kicking off the asphalt for a while to build up some speed then letting the hill take me as I rode it towards the town.

As I tried not to focus too heavily on what the fuck might be waiting for me when I arrived back in Sunset Cove for the first time in ten years, I noticed the sound of hurrying paws trailing me and glanced back to find the mutt chasing me down the street.

"It wasn't an open invitation," I called out to it and it barked back happily.

I pursed my lips but I guessed the two of us were having a pretty shitty day so I couldn't really justify making a fuss. No doubt it would get bored of chasing me soon enough anyway.

It didn't take long for the sound of a car following me down the road to reach my ears and I glanced back, spotting the silver Audi cruising along the road in the distance. I had to assume the dad wouldn't appreciate me robbing his kid, so I quickly turned down a side road which ran towards the beach where there was a sign for a surf and turf beach hut swaying in the wind.

The little bar was open and as my stomach growled again, I decided to give in to its demands and feed it.

I flipped the board up as I hopped off of it, pleased with the fact that I'd clearly managed to retain that skill from my childhood as I strode down to the bar and grabbed a menu from the polished red counter.

I perched my ass on a bar stool in the sun and quickly picked out the cheapest thing on the menu that might shut my rumbling stomach up. A bowl of French fries were two dollars but I could upgrade that with a veggie burger if I pushed to five-fifty.

"Can I take your order, sweetheart?" a peppy voice asked and I looked up to find a woman smiling down at me. "Holy mother of fuck - what happened to you?" she shrieked and I flinched, wondering what I must look like for her to have reacted like that.

"My boyfriend punched me in the face, strangled me and dumped me in a shallow grave a few miles from here," I said blandly, slapping the menu down on the table and pointing out my burger. "I'll have that please."

The woman gaped at me some more then started nodding as she scribbled my order down. "Drink?"

I eyed the milkshakes with longing then groaned, shaking my head. I was on a damn budget after all. "Tap water will do."

The server backed away and I had no doubt that I was about to become the latest subject of kitchen gossip, but there wasn't much I could do about that now.

Once she was out of sight, I surreptitiously lifted the silver napkin dispenser and tried to use it as a mirror. I could make out some purple bruising to the left side of my face which would explain the tenderness and it looked like my throat had finger marks wrapped around it too.

Fuck Shawn. I hoped he got eaten by a fucking alligator. Or a bear. Or a really hungry rat.

The woman returned with my food, the basket of fries overflowing to the point of insanity and an extra heap of salad to go with my burger. She added a chocolate shake to the mix, patting my arm and giving me a wink as she dunked the straw in it.

Well shit, if I'd known that I could get free shakes just by showing up looking like shit places then I would have done away with my makeup years ago.

I sighed as my own joke fell flat in my head and I felt weirdly like crying over that fucking milkshake. People weren't nice to me. I didn't mean that in some self pitying bullshit kind of way either. It just wasn't like that in the world I lived in. No one did shit for nothing; everything was for sale and loyalty was a rarity I'd never come across. The only time I hadn't felt that way was when I'd been tricked into thinking the Harlequin boys were really mine. It was a pretty lie for a while. But the heartache following it had hurt so much that I wished I'd never known that feeling at all.

I picked up my shake and sucked on the straw, my chest tightening with gratitude towards some waitress who didn't know me as the sweet taste of the milky ice cream soothed my throat as it went down.

A sob shuddered through my chest and I gripped the edge of the table so hard that it hurt my fingers as I fought against the urge to just curl up in a ball and bawl my fucking eyes out. I'd almost died. And my life had been nothing. There was no one who would miss me. No one who would care. I would just be remembered as Shawn's girl who took off one day. If that. Fuck, was that really the sum total of the mark I'd left on the world?

I sucked in another breath and focused on the empty feeling in my stomach before grabbing a handful of fries and shoving them into my mouth. They were salty and oily and fucking orgasmic and I quickly grabbed the mayo, squirting a huge dollop on the side of my plate before dipping more fries in it.

A little paw tapped my bare foot and I glanced down to find the mutt there, blinking up at me with those big puppy eyes, guilting me into tossing a couple of fries his way too.

The hopeless feeling in my chest slowly slipped away from me as I grabbed my burger in two hands and demolished it as fast as I could, groaning in pleasure as I filled my aching belly, not caring that I was covering my cheeks in sauce. It was likely an improvement on the bruises anyway.

This right here was heaven. I was never going to forget that. The sun on my back and a burger in my hands with the sweet taste of chocolate milkshake coating my lips.

The mutt got way more food than I think I'd ever willingly offered up to anyone in my life, and when I finally sat back and slurped the dregs from my milkshake down, I genuinely felt like I was going to pop. And it felt really damn good.

"My shift just ended, if you wanna grab a ride back to town?" the waitress said as she approached again. "I'm Candy, by the way."

She held out a hand and I shook it warily. People weren't this nice. It wasn't normal. At least not any people I knew.

"I've got my board," I replied, shaking my head but she just rolled her eyes as she took my twenty and rung up my bill.

"You're grabbing a ride, sweetie, no arguments." She shoved fifteen dollars back at me, letting me off the fifty cents and I tried to push the five back her way, but she just shook her head. "Grab your dog and let's go," she called, turning and heading around the side of the bar and giving me no choice but to follow her.

"It's not my dog," I called after her, but she wasn't listening and the mutt followed me like it didn't agree.

A few cars were pulling in around back and as I climbed into the car, the clock on the dash told me it was only just eleven.

"Is your shift really over?" I asked suspiciously and she grinned at me.

"Look, cards on the table, I was in your position once. I had a boyfriend who used to knock me about when he had too much to drink and I get the feeling you're running. So let me help you run. It's a milkshake and a ride in a car, I'm hardly Mother Teresa. Brian can cope without me until I get back," Candy said, matter of fact.

I opened my mouth to protest and then wondered why the fuck I'd say no to her offer before tossing my skateboard on the back seat and moving to pull the car door shut behind me. Before I could manage it, the mutt leapt into the footwell and curled up by my wet sneakers, giving me a look that said I was stuck with him now.

I probably should have said no. I wasn't in any state to look after myself yet, let alone some mutt, but I guessed I had given him fries and he was kinda cute. Worst thing that could happen was that he'd spot an easier target and ditch me. And I'd been ditched enough times in my life to be a pro at that.

Candy pulled out of the parking lot and I closed my eyes as the balmy air washed in through the window and teased my drying chocolate brown hair into loose curls that shifted in the wind.

The drive to town only took fifteen minutes and Candy dropped me off at the northern end of Sunset Beach where there were already people out surfing, awakening an ache in me for my old life as I watched them.

I'd spent more hours than I could ever count out on the beach here when I was growing up, catching waves, causing trouble and living life to the fullest even though I'd been born into one that should have felt empty.

I thanked Candy as I grabbed my skateboard from the back of the car and the mutt hopped out too, following me as I headed down the once familiar streets of Sunset Cove.

A shudder raced down my spine as I wondered whether anyone had noticed me yet. The Harlequins ran this town and their boss had placed a death threat over my head if I ever set foot back here after all.

But I'd been gone a long time, I looked a hell of a lot different and Luther had no reason to expect my return so I was fairly certain I was safe for now. I'd just have to keep a low profile while I was here, make sure I didn't draw his attention while I did what I needed to then ran the fuck away before he caught onto me slipping into his town right beneath his nose.

I guessed my next problem was finding somewhere to sleep tonight. I needed to spend a bit of time here, checking out my old haunts and figuring out where my boys were now.

No, not *my* boys. *The* boys. Or I guessed they were men now. Either way, I was certain they'd still be here, running the same streets and playing the same dangerous games. Hell, they were likely playing much worse games now. But it didn't matter. I gripped the key at my chest and pulled my Power Ranger cap down low to hide the worst of the bruising on my face as I walked. I just needed to find out where they were, get hold of their keys, take what they owed me, release their most dangerous secret into the world and leave forever. Simple.

If only.

CHAPTER THREE

Older women could be classy and sexy as fuck. But the one I was currently sat across from was trying too hard to be both and failing to be either. Not that my smile gave that away any more than the way I combed my fingers through my raven hair and flexed my bicep every time her gaze drifted down my body. She was picturing me in her bed tonight, her hands itching to unwrap the dirty little gift she'd bought herself. She thought she was the powerful one here. An ex-businesswoman with a whole lot of time, too much money and a thirst for younger men. I fit the bill for her sordid fantasy. Korean-American men got her hot apparently. And luckily for her, I was for sale. But what she didn't know, was that I was going to be the lucky one tonight.

The other fancy ass people in the ocean view restaurant probably thought one of two things. The lie: that I was her grandson. Or the truth: that I was an expensive as shit escort squeezing her money teets for a night with beautiful lil me. But as sweet as five thousand dollars would feel rolled up in my fist after I'd zoned out, rubbered up and made the old gal squeal, I was just one greedy motherfucker who hungered for a teeny bit more than that tonight.

"You didn't comment on my dress, Egbert, I bought it just for *you*," she purred, trailing her hand down her neck, her fingers grazing the juicy diamond necklace at her throat before floating lower to her sun-baked cleavage. Side note: Egbert was not my name. Obviously. I liked coming up with the most ridiculous escort names I could get away with. Like Egbert Dickington. Or Roger McWickly. And my personal favourite Sandy Balls.

I smirked, my gaze lingering on the diamonds around her throat a little too long before I focused on her blue dress. Nope, it was green. My bad. "You look edible, Casandra." *Like an over-cooked lasagne made by a blind hobo.*

First rule of living in the baking pacific town of Sunset Cove; sunscreen. It really wasn't that hard to grasp. But a lot of the pensioners in the upper quarter of town looked like deep-fried chicken after a lifetime here. And not the mouth-watering kind. The kind you suspected might really be deep fried rat. Harsh? Maybe. Rich people deserved a bit of ribbing in my humbly honest opinion though. They lived ten miles from one of the poorest places in the U S of A and those diamonds could've solved a helluva lot of problems for a helluva lot of people. Specifically, *my* problems.

"Get your motherfucking heads down and your wallets out!" a booming voice cut through the air and people started screaming as a guy in a ski mask strode into the restaurant waving a gun. Adrenaline daggered along my veins.

Casandra wailed as the guy strode toward us and I leapt up from my seat, grabbing the back of my chair and hefting it toward him with a heroic yell. He knocked it aside and it smashed to the ground, his gun whipping onto me as his dark green eyes flared behind his ski mask. He came at me like an oncoming storm, grabbing the back of my head and placing the barrel of the gun right between my eyes. My heart hammered madly as I dropped to my knees beneath him, raising my hands in surrender.

"Everyone fill the bag with your cash and jewellery or I blow pretty boy's brains out!" he barked, tossing the linen sack at Casandra and she screamed, flinching full bodily so her sun-baked tits nearly bounced out of her dress. "Do it!" the gunman roared and she shakily took off her rings, dropping them into the bag before throwing her purse in too. The necklace - *my* necklace - followed next and the guy snatched the bag, tossing it to the next table along. Everyone hurried to fill it as the waiters and waitresses urged people to comply. When the bag was fit to bursting, he picked it up, hauling me up by the scruff of my neck and shoving me toward the door.

"No one moves until I walk out of here or I start shooting," he warned and my heart thundered in my chest as he jabbed the gun into my spine and started marching me toward the exit with my hands clasped behind the back of my head.

The second we stepped through the glass doors, a warm breeze whipped around me which tasted of the sea, washed up Hollywood stars and green, green money. The gunman marched me across the street into an alley out of sight of any security cameras and I dropped my hands from the back of my head, glancing over my shoulder at him with a lopsided grin.

"Hey brother."

"Let's go, JJ," Fox said firmly, lowering the gun and we started running side by side.

A wild laugh escaped me as we turned left down the next alley and headlights flashed to draw our attention to the beat-up blue Ford waiting for us. We tore toward it as I whooped and we dove into the back, crashing into one another as Fox slammed the door behind him and Chase put the pedal to the metal. We were pressed back into our seats as we made our getaway and my stomach hurt from my laughter.

Fox tore his ski mask off and his floppy, dark blonde hair fell forward into his eyes. I shoved it out of his beautiful damn face and kissed him on the forehead, thumping my chest in excitement.

Fox scruffed my hair and shoved me back with a smirk, tossing the heavy linen sack onto my lap and crushing my junk.

"*Fucker*," I grunted, but I couldn't be that mad when the weight of that bag meant we'd just scored ourselves a serious prize.

"Did you get it?" Chase called from the driver's seat, the scent of smoke filling the car as he lit up a victory cigarette.

"Yeah, man. And a whole lot more to fucking boot," I said, fishing the diamond necklace out of the bag and moaning as I wrapped it around my neck and clipped it into place.

"Back in the bag, JJ," Fox commanded, ever the fucking boss, but I just pretended to toss fake hair over my shoulder.

"Get it off of me with your teeth, bad boy," I put on my best woman's voice and he snorted as Chase barked a laugh in the front.

"You like it rough, huh?" Fox lunged at me, flipping me up in my seat as he wrestled me and threw a few punches into my sides that I returned.

"It's mine. She was *my* mark," I teased.

"You know the rules," Fox growled, his forest green eyes narrowing on me as he pulled rank like a dickwad.

"Yeah, I know." I shoved him back with a grin. "Just playing, bro."

Fox was the money guy as well as the boss. He'd work out everything we'd earned tonight down to the exact decimal point and make sure half was evenly divided between us three and the other half went toward the Harlequin empire. Those were the rules. And our rules were bound by blood and brotherhood. Nothing could break the three of us because our code was iron. It made us some of the most powerful men in the most powerful fucking gang in Sunset Cove.

We wouldn't see the pay-out from this job for a while though. That shit had to be sold on the black market, but not until the news stories faded from memory and people stopped hunting for their stolen shit. Then once it was sold and cashed in, all the pretty money would be laundered through our businesses. I'd push some through my strip club, Chase would push some through his gym and Fox would divide the rest up through all of the little businesses we had a finger in throughout Sunset Cove. And there were a shit tonne of those.

A cop car raced past us on the street, blue and red lighting up the whole interior of the car for a heartbeat and I whooped as another one followed.

There was nothing like the high of a job and I leaned through the front seats, plugging in my phone and turning on Hot Stuff by Donna Summer, cranking the tune so it pounded in my ears. I rolled my hips, dancing almost as good as I did in my club to this song, grinding my crotch up against the driver's seat.

Chase laughed around the cigarette in the corner of his mouth as I started singing along at the top of my lungs. I placed a kiss on his curly hazel hair which was getting long again before dropping back into my seat beside Fox. He didn't join in singing like Chase did, but a grin played around his mouth that was the only hint he was riding the same high I was. Fox tended to be more highly strung than the two of us, but I guessed when you were the most feared man this side of The Divide and had the blood trail to justify it, that wasn't surprising. We were pretty much the only people in town he smiled at and if anyone else saw him turning anything but disinterest their way, they tended to be a fucking dead man.

"Let's get fucked up tonight," Chase suggested, flicking his cigarette butt out the window in a cascade of sparks.

"Pool party?" I suggested hopefully, bouncing in my chair as I continued dancing, bracing my hand on the roof and thrusting my hips.

"No," Fox growled.

"Oh, come on." I rounded on him, my ass hitting the seat as he killed my dreams dead. "Give me one good reason why not."

"I'll give you two. One, because the whole of fucking Sunset Cove P.D. will be looking for a reason to come sniffing around our end of town tonight, and two, because I fucking said so." He levelled me with a stare that dared me to challenge him on this, but I knew better than to do that. Chase rarely got the message though.

"Ten people max," Chase bargained, swivelling in his seat to look at him and taking his eyes wholly off the fucking road so I got a look at his strong features and bright blue eyes.

"I said *no*," Fox's voice dropped to that deadly growl which usually preceded first degree murder.

"For fuck's sake." Chase punched the wheel as he turned back around and I pouted.

"Well if I'm not getting my dick wet tonight, you guys are gonna have to listen to copious amounts of porn when we get home. I'm feeling me some dub-con anime followed by a spectacular cream pie, you guys in?" I offered.

"Why do you always invite us to your porn parties?" Chase tsked.

"Why do you guys always say no?" I shot back and Fox released a low chuckle, a thing even rarer than his smile.

"You could always head back to that old bird and save us listening to your dolphin sounds when you come. Then you can bring us back five more Gs," Chase joked and I laughed.

"I only made the dolphin noises that one time," I defended myself. "The girl was into it. All kinds of sea creatures actually, but you probably didn't catch the sea turtle impression. They sound like this when they're fucking by the way-" I tipped my head back and started grunting, jerking my hips at the same time as I flapped my hands like flippers.

Fox snorted and Chase roared a laugh as he watched me in the rear view mirror. The car swerved and Fox kicked him between the arm rests.

"Eyes on the fucking road."

Chase flipped him a salute then his eyes whipped back to me in the mirror. "The worst thing is, I know you ain't making that shit up," he said through his deep laughter.

"If there's a fetish for it, I've done it. Just saying," I said, cupping my hands behind my head and spreading my legs wide.

"You're such a shithead, man. I dunno why I love it, but I just fucking do." Chase shook his head at me. "You ever wonder what Rogue would think of us all now?"

A weighted silence slammed into place in the car and I dropped my hands from behind my head, sharing a look with Fox. His hands were fisted tightly and I guessed that meant he'd forgotten about the girl as much as I had. As in, not at all. I swear I could still smell her sometimes, that coconut shampoo of hers I'd woken up to a hundred times on Sunset Beach. After all these years, nothing about her had faded in my mind. I hadn't *wanted* to forget. Even despite all the fucking shit between us. It was an unspoken rule that we didn't talk about her. And I mean we *never* fucking talked about her. So why was Chase bringing her the fuck up?

"You say her name again, I'll rip your tongue out," Fox said in a quiet but deadly tone.

"Easy, brother," Chase said placatingly. "It just slipped out. I dunno why she even came into my head."

Fox was stiff as all hell, like a man-sized boner straining inside a too-tight rubber. I nudged his boot with my shiny loafer, making him meet my eye.

"She's a thing of the past. Who cares what she'd think of us now?" I asked with a shrug and Fox grunted in reply, his jaw pulsing.

I couldn't say I hadn't thought about that exact thing before though. Ten million and one times to be precise. And more specifically, what would she think of *me* now I was all grown up, my muscles filled out, my cock experienced and graduated with a shiny dickplomer. I wasn't some little virgin anymore who didn't know how to kiss right, let alone fuck right. Since a girl had offered me a blowie for fifty dollars when I was eighteen, I'd realised that instead of scraping by to make ends meet, I could make bank off of the one thing my momma had given me. All it took was a little deadening of the soul and voila, earning that kinda cash became easy. But not as easy as stripping which I loved the shit out of. A whole load of girls screaming my name while I thrust my dick in their faces? Yeah, the job was made for me. The escorting just happened to make bigger bucks. And where there was money, there was Johnny James. At least I'd sold my soul for a good ROI.

Then there was the fucking. If eating pussy was an Olympic sport, I'd be a gold medallist. And if there was a dick of the year competition, I'd have a whole shelf dedicated to my winning streak. It was just a shame Rogue had never gotten to see me like this and I was doomed to live in her memory as a scrawny kid who'd once tried to kiss her and failed so spectacularly that it was still one of the most embarrassing moments of my life. *Don't go there, bro.*

Rogue was never a safe subject for any of us. Even Chase had tensed up, despite the fact that he'd been the one to mention her. She was like the Harlequin ghost who haunted us from time to time, summoned by name alone like Bloody Mary. Instead of stabbing you in the back though, she kicked you in the nuts and punched you in the heart simultaneously.

The song ended and Chase unplugged my phone before he lit up another smoke.

Thump.

I stilled at the noise which had definitely just come from the trunk of the car.

Thump, thump.

I swivelled in my seat while Fox sat forward, his eyes pinned on Chase who was acting like he hadn't heard that shit.

"Chase..." Fox said, his tone filled with warning. "Who's in the trunk?"

Chase took a long drag on his cigarette, avoiding the question for a few more seconds while whoever was in there started thrashing and shouting against a gag. "Well...remember that guy Fritz? I happened to pass him by on my way over here and figured, what the fuck? Let's kill two birds with one stone tonight."

"This isn't one stone," Fox snarled. "I had a plan to deal with Fritz, you know we don't double up jobs, especially when they're not fucking planned. That's how shit turns bad. That's how idiots get caught."

I groaned, kicking the back of Chase's chair. Why tonight? When I was riding a high and ready to go to bed with a tube of lube and a smile on my face?

Fritz had raped a girl who worked at my club a few days ago. He was some creep who'd wandered into town last month, but we hadn't taken any real notice of him until he'd shown his true colours and touched one of my girls. His death was written, but even in Sunset Cove you didn't get away with murder without a little planning. The fact that Chase had picked him up without okaying it with Fox was as good as pissing on our code. It wasn't fucking right.

"Jesus, Chase," I muttered. "Are you outta your mind?"

"I saw an opportunity and I fucking took it," Chase argued, blowing out a lungful of smoke as he took a turning at high speed. "I don't see the problem."

Fox was eerily quiet and that wasn't good. Not good at all.

"Next left," Fox bit out after a few more turns. We were taking the cliff roads back to the lower quarter, the winding tracks rarely used since the highway had been finished a few years back. This place was a dead zone and though I just wanted to head home and celebrate our win, it looked like I was gonna have to get my hands dirty tonight.

"Come on, man, we'll just cut his dick off and drive the message home, what's the problem?" Chase asked Fox and I scrubbed a hand over my face. Dumbass was gonna pay for this. He never learned.

"The point is, we do shit by the book for a reason," Fox hissed, his cut-from-stone features twisting into something demonic instead of angelic. "We don't *wing* shit. That's what keeps us out of prison, what keeps your life fucking sweet."

"It's no big deal," Chase growled furiously. "No one's gonna see us out here."

"Well you'd better hope not," Fox said in a low voice. "Pull over."

Chase slammed on the brake and dust flew up behind the car as it skidded along the track a few feet before jerking to a halt. Fox practically flew out of the car and I dove out just as fast, jumping in between him and Chase as Fox bared his teeth, looking ready to teach him a lesson before we even dealt with the guy in the trunk.

Two walls of muscle pressed in on me as Chase didn't back down even though Fox looked like he was about to go all Ted Bundy on his ass.

"Stop," I demanded and they both listened as I looked between them. I was the voice of reason whenever these two butted heads. They were unshakeable brothers ninety nine percent of the time, but Chase liked to test Fox's boundaries on occasion. And if I wasn't there to break it up, blood was inevitably spilled. "We have to deal with Fritz. There's no choice now." I fixed Fox with a glare and his jaw flexed.

I cupped his rough cheek, keeping his gaze on mine and a grunt of irritation escaped him. He shoved away from me, stalking over to the trunk and popping it open. He reached inside, dragging Fritz out by the lapels of his denim vest and throwing him to the ground.

"Please – god – please!" the weedy little bastard yelled.

Fox drew a gun so fast I wasn't even prepared when the first shot was fired. Chase moved to my side, his leather jacket grazing my arm as Fritz screamed, blood pooling out over his crotch from where his cock had just been blown clean off. I cupped my junk as I sucked in air through my teeth. I had not been ready for that dicksplosion.

Fox aimed the gun higher, pulling the trigger with a detached coldness in his gaze and Fritz's screams were cut off as the bullet landed right between his eyes, dead centre. His final scream echoed around the cliffs and my ears rang for a long minute before the sound of the sea reached me once more.

None of us spoke as I walked forward, bending down and lifting Fritz by the arms. Chase moved to lift his legs and Fox leaned back against the car as we carried Fritz to the edge of the cliff, placing him down and shoving rocks into his pockets. I gazed over the edge of the cliff down to the deep, frothing water below and Chase lifted the guy's legs as I picked him up by the arms once more. *Just your average Friday night in Sunset Cove.*

We swung him left to right, building up momentum before nodding to one another and launching him over the edge. He flew like a bird. Like a dead bird with rocks in its pockets, but still. Fritz hit the water with a huge splash then slowly sank into its depths. The sharks would destroy the dickless wonder by morning. Nom nom nom. We should really have been given some kind of medal for feeding the shark population around here. There were a few rare species in these waters, but I liked to think they just became a little less rare tonight.

Bubbles fizzed up from the sea as I watched the place his body had gone in. I hadn't always felt dead inside about killing. The first time hadn't been like this. The first time had changed me. It had been the catalyst to my heart turning black.

I hadn't grown up dreaming of being a murdering psycho or anything, but that didn't mean I felt bad when we wiped people like Fritz from the face of the planet either. I didn't feel guilty. I didn't feel much of anything right now except the warm air winding around me and the feel of my brother standing close to me.

Chase lit another cigarette, and I moved toward him, cupping the back of his head, the scent of smoke rising between us.

"Make it up to Fox," I growled. "Don't pull this shit again."

"Yeah, yeah," he said, smirking, but I knew he would as he clapped my shoulder and we walked back to Fox who looked ready to keep killing tonight.

He strode toward Chase when we got close, snatching the cigarette from his mouth and crushing it in his fist, before punching Chase right in the jaw with the same hand. Chase stumbled back with a growl, then went at Fox like a battering ram, throwing his shoulder into his gut and knocking Fox back several steps.

They started fighting aggressively, cursing and punching one another until Fox went full Fox and knocked Chase on his ass, kneeling over him on the ground and fisting his shirt in his hand. I didn't step in this time, I could see that they needed to fight it out, but it still made my gut knot watching them getting at each other like that.

"For every rule you break from here on out, I'll break one of your fingers until you learn your lesson," Fox warned him.

"*Dude*," Chase balked, but Fox just got up, kicking dust over him before tugging the car door open and dropping into the driver's seat.

I pulled Chase to his feet, dusting him off and a muscle worked in his jaw. He shoved away from me, stalking off down the road and I sighed, getting into the passenger's seat as Fox started the engine.

Fox was as silent as the grave and I released a long breath as I looked over at him then back to the road as the quiet built in my ears.

"He was just trying to take initiative," I broke the silence at last as we watched Chase's broad form continue on down the lane ahead of us into the dark.

"And I'm just trying to protect our asses," Fox growled. "We have the code for a reason, JJ. What the fuck was he playing at tonight?"

I hooked up my phone from where it had fallen into the footwell and twisted it between my fingers. "He doesn't do well being kept to heel. You've gotta let him off his leash from time to time to keep him content. You know what he's like."

Fox's hands gripped the steering wheel, the intricate infinity tattoo on his thumb stretching as his knuckles turned white. "Yeah...I know," he admitted eventually. And for a stubborn asshole like him, that meant a lot.

He'd go to hell and back for me and Chase. We all would for each other. But Fox was so used to running things that sometimes he forgot that Chase had been ruled by his piece of shit daddy for half his life, and he'd never liked being bossed around since he'd gotten away from him. He let Fox take the lead for the most part, but sometimes, times like this, he fought against that power. Even if it wasn't what was best for all of us.

"You gotta let him stretch his little penguin wings," I joked, smirking and Fox rolled his eyes at me, but his mouth twitched at the corner.

"Penguin's don't fly," he muttered and I snorted.

"They do if you throw 'em hard enough."

Fox broke a short laugh then flicked on the headlights and pulled away down the road, gaining on Chase within a few seconds and putting his window down.

"Get in, brother," Fox called, making an effort not to sound like a bossy asshole, not that it particularly worked.

Chase looked to him, scratching at his stubbled jaw before shrugging and pulling the back door open and sliding in.

Silence fell and Fox drove off down the road while I thumbed through music on my phone and picked out It's Nice to Have a Friend by Taylor Swift. Fox shot me a narrowed eyed glance as I started singing along. Loudly. It was totally not aimed to break the tension and get them to make up. Not at all.

As I turned up the volume and Fox tried to swipe the phone from my hand, a low chuckle escaped Chase. I shoved the phone under my ass just as Chase leapt at me from behind and soon the three of us were laughing like nothing had ever happened between us. It was the way it always was. The way it was meant to be. Nothing could ever rock the foundations of the Harlequin boys. We were as invincible as the moon. Rulers of the night. Three kings of the goddamn world. Or at least, kings of one piece of it. But as far as I was concerned, it was the only piece that mattered. Because it was *ours*.

CHAPTER FOUR

Note to self: sleeping in a car is not fun. Especially the heap of shit I managed to steal down by the boat yard yesterday. I mean, it was all I could really manage with my limited resources. I'd grabbed a screwdriver from a plumber's van when I passed it, tossing him a wink as I pushed it up my sleeve and walked on by with him none the wiser. It probably would have been more effective if my face wasn't such a vibrant shade of purple, but I was still taking it as a win because he didn't catch me out. Either way, armed only with a screwdriver, my choice of cars to boost had been particularly limited as they needed to be old enough to have no alarm and a key system that I could bypass with my little yellow friend.

So I'd found myself a nice red Jeep which was older than I was and had plastic windows which I could open with no effort at all. Of course the thing wasn't at all comfortable and the non-windows had let the cold ocean breeze in all night long. It was also seriously low on gas and had made a weird grinding noise when I changed gears, but beggars can't be choosers and all that.

Still, I was going to need to make some serious improvements for tonight. A blanket at the very least. Maybe some clothes too as my cute bikini and short shorts had lost their appeal while I was shivering my tits off in the dark.

I groaned as I pushed myself upright and yelled a half assed curse at the fucking seagulls who seemed to think that this was the perfect spot to stop and screech at each other for hours on end.

The little mutt, who I refused to name because I was still waiting for him to abandon me, sat up happily and licked my hand as I pushed my knotty hair out of my face. A hairbrush needed to make the top ten list of things I had to obtain today. After being buried alive, swimming in the sea and now sleeping on my hair, my ass length brunette locks were most definitely a hot mess. Good thing I had my trusty Power Rangers baseball cap to hide the worst of it, but whatever way we were looking at this, a brush was definitely a must.

I pushed the car door open with some difficulty as the door groaned and jammed up a bit and then finally managed to shove my way out of the damn thing.

I rolled my shoulders back and cursed as I squatted down to get a look at my face in the wing mirror. I looked...fucking awful. I was sporting one hell of a black eye, though thankfully it wasn't so swollen that I couldn't see out of it and the finger marks on my neck had turned a mixture of yellow and blue which I was hoping meant they'd be gone within another day or two. At least they didn't seem to be as obviously caused by choking now that the colours were merging anyway. Small wins and all that.

There was a half open pack of gum in the glove box and I was hungry enough to go for it - not to mention the fact that a toothbrush needed to make the list. *Fuck.*

I'd parked up on the little old road which ran down beneath the pier and I sighed as I chewed on my stale gum and looked up at the wooden boardwalk above my head. When I squinted, I could just make out my name carved into the wood surrounding one of the thick beams which held it up, just beneath the edge of the pier itself. JJ had done that way back when life was peaches and cream and the worst thing I had going on was a neighbour whose eyes followed me a little too often and whose touches lingered a little too long. Back then that had seemed like the end of the world. But give me Axel Phillips to deal with again any day of the week. At least the version of him who hadn't quite decided what to do with me yet. The one who made me uncomfortable when I was thirteen but made no move to take any more than unwelcome looks at me.

42

JJ's name was up there too of course, right beside Fox, Chase and Maverick as always. I wondered if they ever came down here now? To the boarded up boardwalk and the broken down Ferris wheel that used to mean the world to me. Hell, it used to *be* my world. I used to dream that one day we'd figure out how to get all the old rides going again and make a home in one of the abandoned casinos. Simple dreams for a sweet girl with no idea how hard life was going to kick her up the ass. Then again, I didn't think I'd want to be that naive now. At least now I knew what the world was willing to throw at me. I didn't have to wonder what if and I didn't have to waste time on dreams.

I spat the gross gum into an overflowing trash can, ducked beneath the pier to pee like a hobo - which I guessed I was now - then returned to my car, my fifteen bucks, my skateboard and my Power Rangers hat. Nice. Home sweet home.

The mutt was wagging his tail and rolling over on the front seat, seeming to think we had it pretty good, so I was inclined to take his word on it. I had to assume he'd seen far worse than this if he thought this was a step up, and I didn't wish to fall any lower to find out what I was missing.

What I had assumed was the butt crack of dawn was actually mid afternoon if the sun was anything to go by. I guessed dying really took it out of me. Which meant I'd slept in that hunk of shit for fourteen hours or something. No wonder my body was aching and I was gasping for a damn drink. Though the swelling in my throat seemed to have gone down a bit today.

I scrubbed a hand over my face and instantly regretted it as it stung all of my bruises in all the worst ways.

What the fuck was I going to do?

I needed to sort my shit out then work out where the Harlequin boys were now. Maybe once I'd spent a bit of time watching them, I could figure out the best way to get hold of their keys. That was all I needed to do. Five keys and I was set for life. I'd have everything I needed to start over somewhere new and far, far away. Maybe I'd get a flight over to the east coast and find a beach town there. A couple hundred miles had to be far enough to be sure that Shawn would never hear of my miraculous reanimation and I could get away clean and free. Assuming I was cool with letting that motherfucker kill me and get away with it. I was still half certain I wanted to get my hands on a gun and dole out a bit of my own justice to that prick, but right now I'd settle for some freaking toilet paper.

Wow, I really had hit rock bottom. Who knew TP was such a precious commodity? But it was definitely going on the list. I should probably add an actual toilet to the list too, but that seemed to be aiming a little high for today. I was pretty sure public restrooms and living out of my stolen car were on the agenda for the foreseeable.

The obvious place to start was Harlequin House where Fox and Maverick used to live and Fox's dad no doubt still did. But if Luther Harlequin found out I was back in town then I was going to find out how serious he'd been about killing me if I ever came back here. And I was pretty sure he'd been just as serious as Shawn was and was likely more proficient too. He had a reputation for execution killings. Two to the chest and one to the head. Unless he was really looking to send a message and went the mutilation route of course. But I doubted I was worth that much effort to him. Besides, I'd been a skinny kid with way too much fondness for eyeliner when I'd last been in town so I doubted he would recognise me now. I might have spent every waking hour I had with his sons, but that didn't mean he ever paid me much attention.

I was irrelevant to him. Broke, dumb, a girl. Though I kinda took offence to the dumb label because I'd done okay in school. When I showed up. Street smarts were worth more than all that paper learning shit anyway. Of course, killing one of his men had given him reason to pay attention to me, but not for long. I was almost certain he wouldn't know me now.

My boys were another matter. I'd know their souls in the dark from their heartbeats alone...or at least I would have once. Or maybe I thought I would have and it had all just been bullshit.

Whatever. That was why it hurt so fucking much when they broke me.

So as I didn't want to risk Harlequin House or The Oasis – the club where most of the Harlequin Crew hung out when they weren't breaking laws or killing people was just as risky, the next best bet was the bait shop. Everyone in town knew they were selling way more than worms and tackle in there, so long as you knew the right way to ask for it. There would be gang members there keeping watch, girls for sale too assuming nothing had changed. One of them would probably give up something that I could use to trace the boys.

Everyone in Sunset Cove knew who Fox Harlequin was at the very least. They had when he was sixteen anyway, so I was willing to bet they knew a whole lot more now. Daddy's little protégé was probably a major player in the Harlequin Crew these days.

I hopped back into the car, scooping the mutt onto the passenger seat and tussling his ears before twisting the screwdriver which I'd jammed in the ignition and starting her up. The old Jeep gave a whine and a splutter, but she got there in the end. These cars were nuke proof, I swear. I'd bet the thing would out live me - though I was also already dead once over so I guessed it already had.

I forgot about the clutch as I forced it into gear, cursing the stick as I swung the wheel around and headed back up the road towards the busy streets of Sunset Cove.

It was funny really that such a beautiful place could hold such dark secrets. The rich assholes who had their vacation homes up and down the beach for miles around never seemed to notice how fucked up this town was. Or maybe they just didn't wanna look too closely. They certainly never drove down these streets where the graffiti was every colour of the rainbow and the potholes had potholes. The cops didn't come down here either and neither did anyone with any kind of sense. Not unless they belonged. And I wasn't convinced it was a good thing that I did.

I took a road to the edge of town, managing to get the radio tuned just enough to listen to Malibu by Miley Cyrus and with the wind teasing through my hair and the sun shining again, I started singing along and smiling. Because I might have been a dead girl, but it hadn't stuck. So fuck it. I was going to be free.

I rolled the windows down and whooped, earning a strange look from the mutt, but I knew he got it. Life was never as bad when you had the wind in your hair.

Like I'd expected, the bait shop on the edge of the little boat yard was packed when I pulled up in the parking lot. There was a cafe next door to it with plastic picnic benches and colourful parasols filled with people who were eating ice cream and drinking beer. They were laughing and smoking and wasting their lives away in the best possible way. There was a half pipe on the edge of the beach beyond the sea wall where people were giving their skateboards and BMXs a workout and even better than that, the surfers were out in full force on the waves. It was a Saturday so even the assholes with jobs were able to come play today.

The ache in my chest was unreal as I watched them, wondering if I could flirt my way into having a go on some dude's board before remembering the fact that I looked like a train wreck right about now so there was no chance of that. But fuck me. That right there was living. Surfing had once been a part of my soul. I'd been free in this town. A girl who knew the tides, always had sand between her toes and four boys at her side who were a perfect balance of dark and light. We'd spent countless days riding the waves, building bonfires on the beach, laughing and playing and *being*. But nothing good ever lasted. I should have known our life in the sun would eventually be swallowed by the miserable grey cloud called reality.

I grabbed my skateboard, pulled the screwdriver from the ignition and whistled to the mutt as I hopped out. I threw the car door closed behind me, but it resisted and didn't quite shut. I just left it. If anyone here wanted to steal it then a closed door wasn't gonna stop them and I'd just boost another.

I rounded the bait shop, moving to lean against the railings that stopped people from falling into the deep water this side of the sea wall and I cast my eyes over the boats which were bobbing on the waves for a few minutes before turning back to people watch.

It didn't take me long to spot the muscle hanging around. There were a few guys who fit in with the crowd, but there was also like six dudes in leather jackets looking bored as fuck while they chain smoked.

They weren't going to be the right marks for me though. Sworn in gang members were tight lipped motherfuckers at the best of times. I needed to find the working girls and as I looked around, I spotted them. Three girls chatting and laughing, sitting around one of the picnic benches together while flashing smiles at potential Johns as they walked by.

I headed over to them with my board tucked under my arm and a bullshit smile on my face which they saw through instantly.

"What are you, competition or customer?" the platinum blonde asked. She had her hair tied in loose pigtails and a smirk on her face that said she was hoping I was the latter.

"Neither," I said with a shrug. "I'm a broke ass bitch looking for a guy I know who lives around here. I've got fifteen bucks and a dog I didn't ask for, so I was just hoping you'd take pity on my busted face and point me in the right direction."

The girl with dark skin and a bubblegum pink bikini top rolled her eyes and pointed to the empty chair opposite her. "I'll take a favour," she said. "How long you gonna be in town?"

"Honestly? I've got no idea," I replied. "But I'm good for a favour if you wanna trust a girl with a fucked up face."

"Oh good, you know about that. I was worried no one had pointed it out yet," the last girl said, smirking at me as I rolled my eyes. She was a redhead with lips painted ruby red and a glazed look to her eyes that said she was stoned. I guessed she was one of the girls who didn't love her line of work and medicated to forget how much she hated it. It was a shitty kind of life, but there were a lot worse to be had.

"Yeah, I noticed," I replied with a tight smile to let them know I didn't want to go into that right now and they gave me those *been there done that* looks which made my heart ache. "I'm hoping it'll fade fast. Either way, I'd really like to find this old friend of mine."

The girls exchanged a look and the redhead shrugged, pushing to her feet and slapping on a bright smile which contrasted with the deadened look in her eyes. "I've got bigger fish to fry," she said, grabbing her purse and sauntering over to a silver BMW that had just pulled up.

"He's a regular," the blonde explained. "I'm Lyla, this is Dianne."

"Di," the other girl growled, flipping a look at my baseball cap. "I never went in for the Red Ranger much."

"Green Ranger for life," I agreed. "But the kid I stole it from clearly had poor taste. What's a girl to do?"

"I'm pretty sure that a girl is supposed to like the Pink Power Ranger," Lyla put in. "But I was more of a Pokémon kid myself."

"Psh, the Pink Ranger was such a princess. I'm telling you, it's all about Green," I replied, waving her off and Di grinned. I got the feeling me and her were soul sisters, at least when it came to kids TV.

"Girl knows her shit," she said, elbowing Lyla like she should know that too and I laughed.

"You know the trailer park over by the pier?" Di asked and I nodded.

"I grew up around here once upon a time," I replied with a shrug. "What about it?"

"That's us. Everyone who's no one lives there or at least hangs out over there. You wanna come pay me that favour then you'll find me there if I'm not here. During the day obviously - if it's night then I'm wherever the party is happening."

"Got it. I'll be there. I'm Rogue by the way - I know, my mom was stoned like ninety percent of the time so I blame that for the name."

Di nodded like that was good enough for her, which it should have been. Everyone who grew up on these streets knew the only currency any of us could rely on which was really worth a damn was our word. If you kept your word then you were someone worth knowing. If you didn't, then you weren't. Simple as that. Di was willing to offer me the information I wanted to test my worth. If I showed up to pay back that favour I owed her then I was worth her time, if not, no harm done but I'd be best off not showing my face around here again any time soon.

"Shoot then, who are you looking for?" Di asked and Lyla perked up too.

"An old friend of mine. He was in line to be a pretty big player around here back in the day and I can't imagine him ever moving away. The name is JJ Brooks," I said, swallowing the lump in my throat as I spoke his name aloud. Those boys had been nothing but the memories of ghosts to me in all this time and now I was resurrecting them. I hadn't spoken their names in years. I hadn't so much as admitted I'd ever even known them, because I was pretty sure I never had. The boys I'd loved never would have done what they did to me. So maybe that meant the boys I'd loved had never really existed at all.

Di sucked in a breath and Lyla laughed.

"You really have been gone a long time," Lyla said.

"JJ Brooks is like, Harlequin Crew royalty," Di added, raising a brow at me. "You sure you wanna mix it with him?"

"I only need a bit of his time," I replied with a shrug. "So if you can tell me where to find him..."

"He runs Afterlife," Di said. "Amongst other things. But that's the err, legal, side of his business."

"What's the illegal side?" I asked and the two girls laughed again.

"You're looking at us, sweet cheeks," Di taunted. "And JJ is the most expensive of us all. So if that's what you're after you're gonna need more than fifteen bucks and a stray mutt."

"Are you telling me JJ is on the game?" I asked, arching an eyebrow as I tried to marry my memory of the scrappy little brawler with a big mouth and bigger sense of humour with the idea of him selling his body to the highest bidder.

"Only if you can afford him," Di said with a laugh. "And like I say, you most certainly can't. But he makes a killing off of lonely housewives and rich old broads. The rumour is he fucks even better than he dances too and that's saying something."

"Well shit," I breathed, leaning back in my seat and looking out at the sea. "Maybe he'll go down on me for a Red Power Ranger cap? Dude never did have good taste."

The girls both laughed and I smiled as I teased my fingers through my knotted hair. Of course, I had no intention of getting anywhere near that close to JJ. I just wanted to see him, figure out what made him tick these days and try to work out where he might be keeping his key. If I could retrieve it without him ever knowing I'd been back here then that was all the better for me.

"Feel free to tell me to fuck off, but is there any chance either of you girls has a hairbrush?" I asked, looking back to them as I pointed out the bird's nest on my head but they both shook their heads sadly.

"Not here. But you can come down to the trailer park later and borrow some stuff if you like? We'll be having a bonfire on the beach and a few beers once it gets dark," Di offered.

"Speak for yourself," Lyla sighed. "I'll have to work tonight too if I wanna pay my rent on time. And I'm not sucking Joe's cock to cover the rent again - he was way too rough for fifty bucks and the asshole came on my favourite shirt. Fucking savage."

I laughed with them and pushed myself to my feet. "I may just take you up on the offer of a drink by the bonfire later. But I'm gonna need to see if I can track down JJ first," I said.

"See you when I see you," Di said and Lyla waved.

The mutt had been wandering around, begging fries from unsuspecting chumps and had clearly been better fed than me at this point but he showed up as I walked towards my stolen Jeep, yipping excitedly and licking my ankles anyway. I guessed he valued me saving him from death by skateboard over a few throwaway scraps from those other assholes. Lucky me, maybe I should have been flattered.

"I guess it's you and me then, is it?" I asked him and he yipped again. "No accounting for your poor taste, my man."

The dog either didn't agree or didn't mind that I was a shitty kind of owner and he hopped up inside the open door of my new car with his tail wagging. I jumped in too, reaching up to unclip the plastic roof with some difficulty before balling the material on the back seats. With the top down - if I could call it that, was it a convertible if it still had roof bars? Whatever, point was, the sun was shining down on me, the temperature was rising and I was on my way to claim what was owed to me. So it couldn't all be bad.

The Jeep struggled with the up hills but glided down the other side of them easy enough and I wasn't going to make any kind of comment on the level of gas in the tank. All I would say was that the arrow had passed beneath the little red bar and we were playing fast and loose with the dangerous reality of how many miles I could tease out of the dregs.

So far the car was still going though, so I wasn't gonna waste time worrying about that.

Afterlife had been a fairly popular strip club back when I ran these streets but when I finally pulled up outside it, my brows rose. The place was at least four times bigger than it had been when I'd last been here, the businesses on either side of it bought out and merged into it now and it looked...cool.

It was lunch time so it was hardly peak hour but there were a bunch of cars in the parking lot and I pulled my battered Jeep up next to a flashy orange Mustang GT with the top left down.

I wasn't totally convinced that I was going to have enough fuel to get the Jeep started again, so I pulled my screwdriver/key out of the ignition and pocketed it.

The mutt whimpered as I turned to look at him and I shrugged because I wasn't really sure what I was doing here either. Was I going to be conducting a one woman stake out in a stolen bikini with a half starved mutt as an accomplice? Better planning may have been a good idea. But here I was and it seemed silly to back out now.

I huffed and forced the door open before hopping out in my ruined sneakers and weighing my options.

The club looked kinda fancy and I very much did not. It also looked closed which meant the cars parked up around me probably belonged to staff. So maybe I'd get lucky and find JJ here. Then what? If he didn't wear his key like I did then he would obviously keep it at his house, not here. So I could follow him home, but that didn't really help me because I was very much reliant on a beat up car with no gas in the tank. So maybe I needed a new car.

I wandered closer to the GT, admiring the interior and smiling as I spotted a pair of designer sunglasses with black frames and pink lenses just sitting there begging for a new home.

I hooked them up and popped them on with a smirk before spotting a shirt tossed on the back seat and stealing that too. It was a man's white wifebeater with oversized arm holes and a black and orange sketch of the sun setting over the sea on the front of it.

I tossed the boho cardigan thing into the back of my Jeep and tugged on the wifebeater, tying a knot in the side of it to make it fit better and grinning to myself. *Look at me with outfit options.* I was practically a regular rich bitch with my own walk in wardrobe in the back of my car.

With my fresh new look in place, I started around the club, moving into the shade beneath a palm tree at the edge of a wide outdoor bar area with a view of the sea.

There was music playing inside the club and I could hear a man barking instructions, clapping his hands in time to the beat and cursing at someone who was clearly fucking up whatever he wanted them to do.

I slipped closer, using the shade between the palms to cover me as if that made me any less visible in the blaring light of day while the mutt scampered away in search of snacks. I hoped he brought me back some this time because

I was about to blow my fifteen bucks on something carb filled and greasy at the first chance I got, and that didn't seem like the best move for the last bit of money I could lay claim to.

I made it to the glass doors beside the tinted black windows which ringed the club and peeked inside.

There was another large bar area closest to the doors, but beyond that there was a main stage set up with strip poles and cages on podiums. In the centre of the stage were five ripped guys in sweatpants with their chests bare. The four whose faces I could see were a mixture of typically gorgeous dudes, but something about the guy whose back was to me made my skin prickle and my eyes were instantly glued to him as he clapped his hands again.

"You gotta roll your hips, Adam," he snapped. "Not thrust them like you're trying to bang a nail with a hammer. *Roll.*"

He made his point even more clearly by placing his hands on the back of his head and pushing his fingers into his inky black hair while he rolled his hips in a move that seriously shouldn't have been legal. I bit my lip as my eyes stayed glued to the movements of his body like he was some kind of sex god and the blonde guy who I guessed must have been Adam tried to emulate it.

He didn't really succeed and the sex god cursed him out. "I need five minutes to chill out," he barked. "You guys keep practicing while I'm gone."

He turned to look over his shoulder towards the bar and I gasped as I recognised him. Johnny James was not the boy I'd left behind all those years ago. He was...well he'd bypassed man and slipped right on into dirty fantasy material. His black hair was pushed away from his angular face and those honey brown eyes which had always been dancing with laughter now held a primal kind of hunger in them as he searched for something by the bar. His muscles looked cut from glass, each of them perfectly defined to the point of the impossible. He had a tattoo across his lower abs of a flock of swallows which kinda forced my eyes down to his waistband as they disappeared beneath it and my gaze hooked on the bulge within his sweatpants which made me think he wasn't wearing any underwear. I was practically panting at the sight of him and all he was doing was standing there. Fuck me. I hadn't been expecting that.

I ducked back out of sight as a flirtatious giggle met my ear and JJ jumped down from the stage before heading towards a door around the side of it with a brunette girl scurrying after him in a pair of shorts that were way too short for her. And this was coming from me while I currently had my ass cheeks hanging more than half way out of my own shorts. But like, I could practically see what that girl had eaten for breakfast.

The door swung closed behind the two of them and curiosity won out as I slipped into the club. I cast a look at the bar but it was empty now the girl had gone and the four guys on stage currently had their backs to me as they practiced some kind of slow motion grinding thing, so I darted past them and slipped through the door too.

It was cool inside, the luxury of aircon chilling my skin and I moved down a dim corridor until I came to a door which had been left open, letting me see into a large office.

JJ was in there, the giggling girl on her knees before him, making promises about helping him with his stress while he looked at something on his phone.

"Thanks, Jessie," he muttered like she was getting him a coffee instead of taking his dick out of his pants and rolling a condom onto it before sliding it between her lips.

JJ kept scrolling on his phone, muttering a few curses about whatever he was looking at while I watched him in fascination. It wasn't even about him just getting the world's most casual BJ, though that was making my heart race a little if I was being totally honest. But it was mainly just that he was there, right in front of me, this piece of my heart who had once been such an immovable part of my life and had been gone for so long. I wanted to hug him and punch him in equal measures, but apparently I was just gonna settle on watching him get his cock sucked. I mean, he could have shut the door, so I had to assume he wasn't that worried about having an audience, but I probably should have left all the same. It turned out I was a nosey bitch with no boundaries though because I just kept watching.

As JJ typed something out on his phone with one hand, he moved the other to grip the girl's hair and guide her movements up and down his shaft with such indifference that it was somehow weirdly hot. I wondered if he fucked like that too? With a cold detachment that said this was a means to an end and his heart and soul had absolutely nothing to do with it.

He grunted a curse as he came, thrusting his hips forward to plunge his dick deeper into the girl's mouth and his eyes suddenly snapped up to meet mine.

I gasped and he frowned, pushing the girl back and saying something which I didn't even hear because I was already running.

I bolted back the way I'd come, raced across the bar where the guys on stage all stared at me in alarm and I shot out the door. I turned towards the parking lot, but a strong hand locked around my wrist and I cried out as I was yanked back into a hard chest.

"What do we have here then?" JJ asked curiously, whirling me around and pushing me back against the blacked out window of the bar. "If you want to watch me getting sucked off that has a price you know."

"I promise you, I had no interest in seeing that," I growled, tipping my head low so that the brim of my baseball cap hid my face, but of course he wasn't going to let me get away with that.

JJ caught my chin and forced my gaze up to meet his through the pink lenses of my new sunglasses. I gasped, staring at the once familiar face of the boy I'd loved and seeing all the strangeness of the man he'd grown into while trying to figure out how the fuck I was going to escape him.

"Who...is that my shirt?" he asked with a frown as his gaze trailed down me before snapping back up to my face. "And my sunglasses?"

"No," I bit out because of course I'd had to go and steal from him of all people. "We must just have the same shitty taste in clothes."

JJ barked a laugh and then snatched the cap from my head before placing it on his own.

"Hey," I snarled. "That's mine."

"We'll call it a trade. That shirt and glasses cost around two hundred dollars and I'm guessing your cap doesn't come close to that."

"Actually, it cost me the exact same as the glasses," I replied, pursing my lips at him because everything I was currently wearing had been free. "But I'll take that two hundred bucks if you wanna buy them off of me?"

"Wait a second," he said, reaching out to pluck the glasses from my face and staring into my eyes like he was seeing a damn ghost and all of the hostility fell from his expression in a heartbeat.

My heart leapt right up into my mouth, twisting in this pathetic little mockery of all the things I'd used to feel for him before I could lock that shit down.

"Rogue? I…is it really you?" he breathed like he didn't actually believe what he was seeing with his own two eyes. "Fuck me, you got hot in the last ten years-"

My fist snapped out and caught him in the jaw as hard as I could before I followed it up with a swift knee to the balls because fuck him and then I was gone. I turned and ran and growled at myself for ever even considering coming back to this cursed place and the boys who haunted it.

JJ started chasing me while swearing about his bruised junk, but the mutt appeared from nowhere and leapt at his ankles with a furious snarl giving me a better chance to bolt.

I ran for the Jeep, grabbing the screwdriver from my pocket and wrenching the door open as I reached it.

I leapt in behind the wheel, jamming the screwdriver into the ignition and starting the old car up with a whine of protest.

I yelled out for the mutt to hurry his hairy ass up as he raced after me with JJ right behind him and the second the little dog leapt into the car, I slammed it into reverse and swung it out of my spot, side swiping the Mustang as I went and caving in the rear side.

JJ started cursing me but I didn't care, I just needed to get the fuck away from him and this place. I shouldn't have come back here. This had been a terrible idea. I just needed to set my gaze on the horizon and keep driving until I couldn't even see Sunset Cove in my rear view mirror.

I pulled out across a busy intersection, slamming my foot down on the accelerator and the Jeep chose that moment to give up on life. One second I was flying along and the next I was rolling to a stop in the middle of the fucking street as a beat up orange Mustang GT swerved across the road in front of me.

"Stop!" JJ yelled in a tone that said he was used to people listening to him and I flipped him off as I looked around for another escape route.

I cursed my luck, reaching beneath the passenger seat and grabbing my skateboard then yanking it out into my arms.

Horns were blasting as people swore and shouted for us to get out of the fucking road but I ignored them all, climbing over the seats into the back of the car and leaping out onto the street as JJ vaulted out of his own car.

"Rogue, come back here," he demanded but that was a solid no from me.

He lunged at me and I ducked away from him, plucking the mutt from the front seat, lowering him to the floor beside me and dropping my skateboard on the sidewalk.

"Don't you dare!" JJ yelled and I tossed him a smirk as I leapt onto my board, kicked off and shot away down the hill.

I had to focus on where I was going as the mutt raced along beside me and by the time I could look back, JJ was nowhere to be seen.

I laughed to myself as the sea air pulled at my hair and I sped down towards the seafront with victory sailing through my limbs. But I felt sick from seeing him too. Heart sick. Stomach sick. All the sicks.

That was it. I had my answer. Messing with the Harlequin boys was a seriously bad idea and I just needed to get the hell out of dodge before they came looking for me again. I'd grab myself a new ride, steal some cash and be gone before nightfall. It wasn't worth the risk of staying. I'd forget about the keys and the secrets and all of it in favour of just never having to see any of them ever again.

Just as I closed in on the bottom of the hill, an orange Mustang shot out of a side road right in front of me and I screamed as I tried to stop the inevitable from happening before slamming into the hood and tumbling straight over it.

I fell on my ass on the other side, my elbow grazing on the asphalt as I lost sight of my board and my dog too.

"Mutt!" I yelled, five seconds before the little white dog bounded around the hood of the car and started licking my face with abandon.

I scrambled back up to my feet with a curse and came face to face with JJ Brooks who was grinning from ear to ear as he took me in.

"Just like old times, eh Rogue?" he teased. "You never could skate for shit."

He grabbed me before I could turn and run and I kicked and cursed him as he dragged me around to the back of the car and popped the trunk.

"Don't you dare!" I yelled as I tried to punch him again, but he just laughed as he slung me inside and threw the lid closed a moment later.

"Let's go and see the boys," he called cheerily from somewhere beyond my sweltering prison.

"JJ Brooks, let me out of here right now!" I screamed as I kicked and thrashed.

"Yeah, yeah, I will do soon," he replied. "Now quit your yelling or I won't be bringing the dog with us."

I fell silent at that, rage spilling through my veins as my hands balled into fists and I glared in the general direction of his voice.

"Get my board too," I demanded. "And I want my fucking hat back."

CHAPTER FIVE

I stood at the kitchen island with pages of notes spread out on the cream marble, resting my palms flat on the surface. It was hot today and Chase had opened the sliding doors so a breeze blew in from the pool area ahead of me, the high walls around it doing far too much to block that breeze though. Chase was lying outside on one of the sun loungers with a cigarette in the corner of his mouth and a rum and coke in the other one. It wasn't even ten am.

I had a half drunk protein shake beside me made with fresh fruit and soy milk. I'd started looking after my health around the time I inherited my position in the Harlequin Crew from my dad. His legacy defined my blood, my enemies, my status. But I ran the gang differently to how my dad had. And I prioritised protecting the people closest to me from our rivals for as long as fucking possible. So I would make sure I was always fit and healthy to ensure I was the best I possibly could be at that role, but I couldn't do much about my ability to dodge bullets. That's why shooting first and asking questions later was my way of life. I'd seen too many good people hesitate when they were faced with a tough decision and end up dead for it. So I became a bad one to protect those closest to me. I'd take a hundred bullets for JJ and Chase so long as they took none. And I'd fire a hundred into a hundred skulls for the same reason.

My gaze drifted to Chase again as smoke coiled up around him and he rearranged his junk within his black swim shorts. He was making a good effort at pissing me off lately, and it was time to smooth over the tension building between us. I was a strict as shit boss, but I tried to be a fair one too. If he needed to make more decisions to settle this restlessness in him, then I needed to accommodate that. He and JJ were the only people in the world I made allowances for when it came to being a leader in the Harlequin Crew. I didn't take direction from anyone; I gave the orders, and if they weren't listened to, there were consequences. But my brothers were family, so I'd had to work on my limited ability to compromise for years to satisfy them within their roles beneath me in the hierarchy. At the end of the day, I'd be lost without them. And I didn't plan on losing any more members of my family than I already had. So compromise may have been a bitch, but she was a bitch I was willing to be fucked by from time to time for their sake.

I placed down my protein shake and headed to the sliding door, stepping outside where the sun beamed down on my naked chest, making my tattoos gleam. I wasn't covered in them like some of the Harlequins were, I'd chosen each one because it represented an important moment in my life. The good, the bad, the good that had turned bad, the bad that had gotten badder. It was all there. A story only I knew how to read, though JJ and Chase would have had the best chance at translating my flesh. But not all of it. Some of my marks were secrets. And there was only one girl in the world who knew their meaning. Even though she'd never be around again to see them.

"Hey, brother," I called to Chase and he pushed his aviator Ray Bans up onto his head, stirring his dark curls as he lodged them into it. His deeply bronzed chest glistened with factor thirty tanning oil, defining his abs even more than usual and making the ink on his arms look like it was poured over him.

He pushed to his feet, draining his rum and coke in one long gulp, before putting the glass down. "Wanna swim with me, Foxy?" He jumped at me, grabbing my arm and trying to wrestle me towards the pool. Fucker was definitely tipsy.

I smirked, tussling with him for a moment then shoving him off and knocking my knuckles against his cheek. "We've got a job to plan. I thought you could pick the target this time." I gave him a sideways grin, folding my arms over my chest and his brows arched.

"Oh yeah?" he asked.

"We have a list of marks." I shrugged. "Your choice."

He grinned, clapping his hand to my shoulder as we headed back inside and he took in all the notes I'd laid out on the counter.

I pointed to the list we had of possible marks. JJ's club attracted the kind of people that spilled their secrets in his ear easily enough, especially when he was making them come for a good price, so we often got a few leads that way. But I always had our crew listening out for opportunities too, and I'd brought in a few leads of my own this month.

"JJ's been buttering up the daughter of an oil tycoon from Texas. They're going to be in town in a few weeks and word is they're buying a property on the beachfront. They've already put in a few orders for artwork ranging up to ten grand a piece."

"Nah." Chase waved a hand at me dismissively and anger rippled through me, but I held it in check. "Too boring."

"Easy jobs shouldn't be ignored for the sake of a bit of excitement," I growled, frowning at him as he leaned over the worktop, looking down at the list and twisting one of the leather bracelets around his wrist. "We could cash in with artwork. I know a guy who can sell that shit within a couple of weeks."

"Well you said *I* could pick, Fox, so am I picking or not?" He looked up at me, his blue eyes accusing and I fought back the urge in me to force his hand on this.

"Go ahead," I said and he smiled broadly, eyeing the list again before tapping on one. "A ferry?" he questioned, fishing for more info on the job.

"There's a ferry leaving the marina in three weeks which is reportedly transporting a shipment of Cartier watches over to Ballena Island."

"How much?" he asked eagerly and I smirked.

"Eighty grand."

"Wooah fuck!" he whooped, climbing up onto the kitchen island and kicking the notes around with his bare feet.

"Chase!" I barked and he dropped down to lie in front of me, smirking.

"I wanna do the ferry."

"Yeah I can see that," I said, a grin pulling at my lips as I slapped his cheek lightly. "Problem is, boat jobs are high risk."

"I like risk," he purred hungrily.

"Yeah, but risk gets people dead," I warned, my voice dropping seriously as I looked down at my friend. "And I don't like taking unnecessary risks."

He rolled over onto his back, the oil on his skin making some of my notes stick to his body and I shoved him over the edge of the island, making him curse before he landed on the floor on his back with an oomph. I leaned down, peeling my notes off of him and tossing them back onto the counter with a dark smile. They'd end up burned anyway, so I wasn't precious about them.

"But," I said tantalisingly, placing my bare foot on his chest to stop him from getting up. "If we plan it right, I'm sure we can reduce the risks."

"*Yes*," he hissed, grinning as he batted my foot away and rolled over to do some celebratory press ups.

The ink on his back was a treasure map, covering almost every inch of his flesh, and it was a place I knew well. Sunset Cove. Our home. Twisted into art was an X that marked the spot located right here. At Harlequin House. The beach kissed the back door and a security perimeter ringed this whole property. It was like a private resort, but the people living on the inside weren't vacationers looking for their next cocktail, they were three dark princes who ruled this land with an iron fist. I took in a few more of my favourite places on earth as Chase continued his set, from Sinners' Playground with its Ferris wheel on the pier, to JJ's club Afterlife in town, and the boardwalk that passed Chase's gym called Raiders. His ink marked all of our territory up to The Divide. The place where our turf met with The Damned Men's. I wondered if Chase would tattoo our newly conquered land on his ass when we pushed The Divide another few miles back too.

I walked to the fridge across the room, tugging the door open and tossing my smoothie in there for later. Shit got warm real fast in Sunset Cove. You had to eat food quick if you didn't want the sun to ruin it.

I closed the refrigerator door and a breath got choked in my lungs, my body turning to stone, my heart nothing but a heavy lump of heated solder in my chest. Because a real life incarnation of my deepest, most desperate desire was standing right there. Right in my house. My fucking breathing space. The girl I had longed for, ached for, hunted for, shattered for, was here. Impossibly. Fucking. *Here.*

My mouth went slack and no noise escaped me at all as I stood frozen, taking in every inch of *her*. I didn't believe it. My mind wouldn't believe it. My heart wouldn't believe it.

I refused the truth in front of me because it just wasn't feasible that she was standing here after all this time. This wasn't a dream or a nightmare or some fucking vision here to taunt me.

I'm awake and she's here.

I'm awake and she's back.

I'm awake and she's home.

Her hair was a dark sea of hazelnut, tumbling over her shoulders almost down to her waist, her honey brown skin kissed by a thousand suns since I'd seen it last. Her stormy blue eyes were painfully deep, dragging me in and I knew I must be imagining this, but the vision was so fucking real that I didn't care what drug I was on so long as it remained in my blood forever.

She was the girl who'd gotten away. The girl who I'd had to accept would never, ever walk back into my life. Until she had. Right this fucking second.

My eyes kept roaming her features and the shock of finding her before me gave way to horror at the bruises shadowing her face, her neck. Someone had hurt her. Someone had laid their filthy fucking hands on her and *marked* her. Rage and vengeance collided inside me, twisting into a cold and hungry creature which longed for the death of the person responsible for this. It didn't matter if a whole lifetime stood between the last moment I'd seen her and this moment of her return. Nothing changed my desire to protect her. From everything and everyone who sought to hurt her. *I will make them pay.*

"Look what I found," JJ sang from behind her and I realised he was holding her hands behind her back. A prisoner? Interesting.

I schooled the shock on my face as fast as I could, but there wasn't much I could do for my heart which was about to bust out of my chest and give the game away. Her eyes drank me in as deeply as I was drinking in her, like we were so thirsty for each other that no body of water on earth would quench us. But then that thirst in her eyes was gone and a hard wall stood in its place, blocking me out before I'd even had a second to dive in.

"Hey," I breathed like a fucking moron. *Hey? After ten years, that's all I've got to say? Fucking 'hey'??*

"Who are you again?" she asked, her brow furrowing as if she was trying to place me.

I grunted angrily, knowing she was playing with me, but on some level, I feared she wasn't.

"Like you could forget," I growled.

"Rogue?" Chase rasped and she turned, looking at him where he was standing by the kitchen island, an unlit cigarette forgotten in the corner of his mouth.

"Oh right, the Harlequin boys," she said coldly. "Well I'm glad a few of you are here so I can tell you all to fuck off at once. If you can pass the message onto Maverick too? That'd be swell." She tugged at her arms and JJ released her, smirking like he was having the best day of his life. And I should have been too. This was everything I'd wanted for so long, and yet the way she was acting said I was not going to get the warm reunion I'd dreamed of a thousand times. Where she wrapped her arms around me and her lips found mine because she'd missed me as much as I'd missed her. She'd have a reason she never came back. Someone had kept her away, something had happened that meant she couldn't return to us. Why wasn't that happening?

JJ tsked. "We'd rather you didn't mention the prick, pretty girl."

She frowned at that and the crease between her eyes was so familiar to me it made me ache.

Before I realised what I was doing, I'd reached out and brushed my fingers over that tiny crease to smooth it out then ran my hand down to her jaw, tilting her chin up to look at me…making sure that she was real I guessed. Despite those fucking bruises, she was painfully beautiful as a full grown woman. Tattoos adorned her flesh in places and I wanted to examine them all, learn their meaning and have her tell me every single thing she'd done between the last time I'd seen her and now. A deep and unnerving possessiveness filled me over her. A claim I'd laid on her ten years ago awakening in me once more, but it wasn't some kid's dream anymore, it was a man's demanding desire. One that burned inside me like a flame growing rapidly into an inferno.

"Fox," JJ murmured and I noticed he'd moved closer, his fingers brushing her throat where the bruises were. "This is unacceptable."

I nodded firmly and Rogue scowled, batting our hands away from her. "You know what's unacceptable, Johnny James?" She shot a glare at JJ. "Kidnapping people. So as fun as this little throwback isn't, I'm gonna head out and flirt a cocktail out of a bartender at the nearest surf and turf."

Heat tore through my chest and I yanked her away from JJ, pushing her back against the fridge and crowding her in there as she narrowed her eyes at me. Ice spilled from her gaze and my brow pinched.

"Hi, Foxy boy," she said at last, her voice husky and seductive, yet full of rejection and disinterest too. "You got taller."

"You got mouthier," I tossed back, the edge to her voice making my dominant side rear up and take notice.

"My tongue can do a lot of things these days that it couldn't back when we were sixteen," she said, her eyes as sharp as blades. "It's called growing up."

Chase appeared beside me, his muscular shoulder butting against mine and I had the urge to growl at him like a dog. Instead, I forced myself to let one arm drop so he could see the girl we'd all had to let go of a long time ago. *Fuck, is she really here? Am I losing my fucking mind?*

My dick seemed to be particularly happy about her return and even the momentary image of fucking this new, older, smartass version of Rogue had me hungering for her like I hadn't for any girl in a long time (see: never).

"Where the fuck did you come from?" Chase demanded and I was glad at least one of us was managing to form sensible questions. I had so many running through my head that I couldn't choose a single one to demand of her. But my brain was starting to catch up on this headfuck and I was trying to figure out the best way to handle it.

Rogue's eyes shot to Chase and I didn't miss the way they dipped to his sculpted chest before they moved back to his face. We sure as shit weren't boys anymore and it looked like she was living in her own headfuck as she realised that. With the amount of testosterone in this house, I was surprised the kitchen appliances hadn't sprouted dicks yet.

"I blew in on the wind then JJ found me and kidnapped me," she said hollowly, throwing JJ a vengeful look.

Man, she'd always been fiery but this girl looked like she had the devil himself blowing flames up her ass. Did we deserve that? Maybe. But it still pissed me off when she turned those hell flames on me.

"I did do that," JJ said with a smirk, moving up against my other shoulder and resting his weight on me. "And I'd do it again. And again. And ag-"

"Shut it," I snarled and JJ fell quiet as I leaned in close to Rogue, one percent of me just wanting to see if she still smelled like coconut and sea air.

"Are you sniffing me?" she gasped, planting her hands on my chest and that unbidden growl rose in my throat again. The fuck was happening to me right now?

I huffed out a breath, tasting that familiar scent on my tongue and wanting to seek out more of it, bottle it, fucking trademark that shit in *my* name.

"You totally sniffed her, dude," JJ laughed and I turned, knocking him aside and walking away.

I just needed to breathe something that wasn't her, something that didn't make me want to find the nearest set of handcuffs and tether her to me forever. I'd put my love for Rogue to bed a long time ago. I'd lived through the heartache. I'd pined and hurt and my entire chest had hollowed out with the loss of her. My heart had never let another girl in, not even close. But her being back hadn't factored into my new life. I'd let go. We all had. We'd had no fucking choice. But now…now what the fuck was I supposed to do?

I moved to stand on the other side of the kitchen island, facing them all as Chase lifted an arm and rested it above her head on the fridge, drinking her in with a sneer on his lips.

"Who hurt you?" I asked her the question that was baiting me most.

A part of me wanted to believe that this had somehow been an accident, because picturing some motherfucker with his hands wrapped around her throat was about to turn me into an even bigger serial killer than I already was. But those fingerprints were an admission of their own. Someone, some rat, some fucking *scum* had done that to her. And I would not rest until they lay in pieces at my feet.

"Oh this?" she asked sarcastically, pointing at her neck. "I got in a fight with a seagull over an ice cream. The gulls 'round here have gotten *real* violent."

"That's not funny," JJ hissed and I nodded my agreement while Chase's eye just twitched with the rage in him.

"Anyways, this has been *so* much fun," she said girlishly, ducking out from under Chase's arm and dancing past JJ as he tried to catch her.

She made it to the sliding door as JJ moved to block the only other exit and she spun around to look at us, warning us off with her eyes as me and Chase took a step toward her too. "But I'm gonna go and do something even more fun than hanging out with you guys. Like letting that murderous seagull peck my eyes out before ramming a surfboard up my own ass. Ciao!"

She darted out the door and the three of us walked calmly after her, stepping outside and watching as she jogged around the enclosed pool area. She gazed up at the high wall on the opposite side of the pool then hurried up to the stone barbeque, climbed onto it and leapt forward, catching the top of the wall by the tips of her fingers. My gut lurched as she started hauling herself up and I cursed, charging around the pool toward her with JJ in tow.

I leapt up, grabbing the back of her denim shorts in my fist and tugging hard. She clung onto the wall and I half uncovered her peachy ass as her shorts and bikini bottoms slid down, my fingers dipping between her cheeks as she fought to climb up. My dick got a lot of filthy ideas about the feel of her soft flesh against my hand and I held on tighter, refusing to let her go. She shot curses at me as JJ caught one of her legs and the two of us yanked her down off the wall. She kicked and punched like a girl in desperate need of an exorcist, but she could have had ten demons possessing her and I still would have fought to keep this woman in my house.

I caught her waist as we lowered her down between us and her eyes widened at the sight of me scowling at her.

"You're not going anywhere, hummingbird," I growled, using the nickname I'd once given her, the same reason I had a hummingbird with gold tipped wings tattooed on the inside of my left forearm. It held power, that name. And her throat bobbed as I pinned her in my eyes, cracking her façade for half a heartbeat. I leaned in near to her face, my heart pounding and my chest heaving at how close I'd almost come to losing her again. "I used to spend a lot of time thinking about what I'd do if you ever came back, Rogue. And the long and short of it is, baby, that I'm never letting you get away again."

Her fist came at me and I refused to release her to block it, her knuckles slamming hard into my mouth. I tasted blood and anger rippled through me like thunder.

"Shit Rogue, do you realise who he is these days?" JJ gasped just before I tore her away from him, tucking her under one arm and locking her to my side as I strode toward the house.

"I'm getting the feeling he's an asshole!" she called back to him, but I didn't give a shit.

I *was* an asshole. And I also held all the power in this town, so I was gonna do whatever the fuck I liked. Because I'd waited too long for her and spent too much of my life fearing what had happened after we'd lost her. I'd never allowed myself to consider the possibility that she was dead. That something beyond my control had happened to her and taken her from this world. And now she was here, I fully intended to make sure that nothing ever happened to her again.

Chase was looking between us all with wide eyes and one hand clawing into his hair as I stormed past him with Rogue struggling against my hold. I stalked through the house, kicking doors open and sensing JJ and Chase hot on my heels. I knocked open a guest bedroom, striding inside and tossing her onto the bed so she bounced across it, spitting curses at me.

I locked the window, tucking the key into my pocket before heading for the door. Then I stepped outside, slamming it shut half a second before she collided with it and I twisted the key in the lock, pocketing that too.

"Motherfucker!" she screamed.

"Come on, dude, you can't keep her in there," JJ tried to reason with me, but I shouldered past him.

"I need to think." I walked outside so I didn't have to hear her kicking the door and calling me every dirty word in her vocabulary.

I paced outside under the glaring sun and Chase moved to my side, his arm brushing mine.

"We can just drive her back to wherever she came from," he growled.

"What?" I snarled, rounding on him, my heart thundering at the mere suggestion of sending her away again. "Why the fuck would you say that?"

His jaw locked for a moment and lines of tension formed on his brow.

"She's not good for you, man. She's not good for any of us."

I shoved my palms into his chest, my teeth bared in fury. "Don't fucking talk about her like that."

"We searched for her and she nearly broke us because she was gone!" Chase shouted, his muscles flexing furiously. "I'm not watching that shit show again. We need to deal with this *now* before she gets her claws into any of us again."

"She's not going anywhere," I said dangerously, getting up in his face. If he wanted to push me on this, he was going to regret it.

"Agreed," JJ chipped in, but I didn't look back at him. I glared at Chase, waiting for him to back down. And finally, he turned his cheek, tutting under his breath. He knew I'd win either way. This wasn't a debate. And if there was anything in the world I was going to pull my King of the Harlequins card on him for, it was this. I was the boss, and she was staying. No one would tell me otherwise.

I drew in a steadying breath as Chase stood there looking like a wounded animal, then I turned my back on him and looked to JJ.

"Where'd you find her?" I growled.

"She showed up at the club. She was sleeping in a Jeep. Not hers. Looked stolen to me considering she had literally nothing with her but a ratty little dog."

I started pacing again, the fury at knowing she'd been living like that making me too angry to function. But there was something far, far worse than even that gnawing at me. Something I simply couldn't get out of my head.

"Who gave her those bruises?" I hissed, barely able to get the words past my lips. I'd plant every bullet I had in the motherfucker who *dared* hurt her. I would remove limbs, sever arteries, rip out every single organ-

"She won't say," JJ said, planting his shoulder against one of the struts that held up the awning on this side of the pool.

"Oh she'll say alright," I growled, marching forward to head inside again, but JJ held out a hand, pressing it against my shoulder to halt me.

His touch wasn't firm, but I gave him my attention, knowing I didn't always act rationally when I lost my head like this. Maybe I needed his voice of reason right now, because mine was long gone.

"Give her some time to cool off. You already locked her up, she's gonna be as pissed as a caged bobcat right now."

"And you think time's gonna improve that?" I scoffed.

He moved closer, smiling but there was a storm swirling in his brown eyes. "Can't hurt."

I went to shove past him anyway, then paused, a thought occurring to me. "You mentioned a ratty dog…"

"It's out on the porch." He smirked as he caught on to what I meant and he twisted away from me, disappearing into the house in the direction of the front door.

"Don't do this, man," Chase begged from behind me and I glanced back at him. He was tapping a cigarette against the box in his hand, his eyes imploring.

"She's one of us," I said ferociously, daring him to test me on this.

"So was Maverick," he countered darkly and those words drove into my skin like needles.

My lip peeled back to berate him, but JJ reappeared with a little white dog in his arms, scratching its head and making its eyes droop happily.

"Here, give him to me." I took the dog from his arms and it immediately started chewing my hand as I carried him down the hall then pounded my fist on the door to the room she was locked inside.

"What?" she snapped.

"I've got your dog," I said and she gasped.

"Don't hurt him, you fucking bastard!"

I rolled my eyes. "I'm not going to hurt him. I came to give him to you."

She fell quiet for a moment and I reached into my pocket for the key, pushing it into the lock and twisting. I knocked the door open and the devastation beyond it was pretty unfathomable for how little time she'd had in here. The curtains were ripped down, the bedsheets torn to ribbons, the closet doors looked half ripped off their hinges and anything that had been in the drawers was now scattered everywhere.

She reached for the dog demandingly but I lifted him up above my head on one hand. "Come out here and talk to us," I ordered and she glowered at me like she was trying to rip my throat out with her eyes alone.

Her upper lip peeled back for a moment then she schooled her features, tossed her hair and shrugged. "Fine."

She held out her hands for the dog and I placed the little mutt in her arms. She hugged him to her chest as if I was going to snatch him back from her at any second and gut him, but I wasn't interested in the dog. I was interested in her, and who the fuck had laid their filthy hands on her body. Hands I was going to enjoy cutting off in payment for this unspeakable act against her.

I gestured for her to walk ahead of me and she did so, my gaze immediately dropping to her ass peeking out from those tight denim shorts she wore, and I wet my lips with how much I wanted to sink my teeth into that tanned flesh. My cock throbbed like I was a virgin aching for his first taste of pussy and I felt like one again too. A fucking teenager lusting after his best friend. A girl who I would have done anything for. Who I would still do anything for.

JJ stood in the kitchen with his elbows pressed to the island and Chase stood behind him with his arms folded and smoke seeping between his teeth like a pissed off dragon.

I moved up close behind Rogue, then leaned past her, tugging a stool out at the island and gesturing for her to sit.

"Yeah…no, I'm good," she said coolly, moving away from me to stand on her own side of the island, stroking the dog's head while she looked between us all with a casual disinterest.

"Who hurt you?" I growled, the rage in me pooling up to the surface, barely able to be contained.

"A guy," she said lightly, shrugging one shoulder, but I guessed that was progress from the seagull bullshit.

"*Which* guy?" I snarled the exact same time JJ and Chase did. For all Chase's bullshit about getting rid of her, he suddenly seemed seriously interested in getting that answer. We all would have died for her once. That apparently hadn't changed for me. And one sweeping glance at my friends' faces told me it hadn't changed for them either.

"Not your business," she said airily. "Just like the rest of my life isn't your business. Like it hasn't been for ten years actually."

"Why are you back?" Chase bit at her, but I didn't snap at him for his tone because I needed the answer to that as keenly as I needed air to breathe.

"Not your business," she answered in that same light tone as if we were nothing to her. And maybe we were. Maybe she'd moved on a long time ago and we were just a distant memory which she never bothered thinking about. The idea of that pained me in a way I could barely digest.

"Not our business?" JJ tsked, shaking his head. "You have no idea, do you?"

"Pfft, she knows," Chase muttered, glaring at her.

"I know what?" she asked like she didn't really care, but her eyes gave away just enough curiosity that I knew she did.

"You want answers from us? Then you'd better start giving them yourself," I warned and her eyes slid onto me, cutting deep into my soul, reawakening every part of the kid in me who'd obsessed over this girl for his entire life.

"Fine…I'm here to get my asshole bleached, they've got the best beauty salon this side of Sunset Cove. Your turn," she deadpanned and JJ burst out laughing.

He was the only one though, because Chase practically inhaled his entire cigarette and my teeth started grinding as she continued to withhold this information from me.

"Why were you sleeping in a car?" I pressed.

"Because I don't have a fancy house like this one to count fluffy little sheep in when I go to sleep at night," she said, acting like this was all some joke to her.

Was *I* a joke to her? Was everything I'd shared with her long forgotten? Did I not hold any place in her heart anymore? I knew it was stupid to think that she might have missed me, but I'd clung onto the hope that wherever she was she'd at least thought of me from time to time. The possibility that she hadn't was threatening to break me all over again.

"Where did you come from?" I snapped, starting to lose it with her bullshit answers.

"Careful, Foxy, it looks like you're about to bust a vein over wittle old me," she taunted. "Wouldn't want it to seem like you missed me or anything."

"Missed you?" I spat, stalking toward her, gripping her shirt in my fist and yanking her closer so the little dog was pressed between us where it started growling. "Those words are a fucking mockery of what I went through when we lost you. What we *all* went through."

"Poor lost boys, how hard it must have been for you all to forget about me. It wasn't that hard for me by the way, I thought you were called Badger when I arrived until JJ used your real name."

The little dog yapped angrily at me as heated fury slid over me like a second skin. I had so much to say to her and yet all the things I'd pictured telling her over the years that I'd searched for her just faded away now she was really here. I'd never once expected her to look at me like *that* when I finally had her back. She hated me. And it might have been worse than that. Because it looked like she just wanted to walk out of this house and be rid of us for good. But why come back then? Why show up in this town, of all the towns on the west coast? She must have known we'd find her. So why come? Why now?

"I need answers, hummingbird," I said, a threat to my voice. "And I'm going to get them."

"Are you trying to scare me, Foxy? Because you can't scare a girl who's been to hell and back."

Maybe I *was* trying to scare her. But I needed answers dammit. I couldn't understand how she was so calm, so unaffected by being back here after ten years. Like it meant nothing. Like all of it, the lifetime we'd spent together, meant absolutely jack shit to her.

"You know what, Rogue, you don't wanna tell me why you're here yet? Fine. But I'm gonna need a name and address for the dead man who did that to your face because if his blood isn't wetting my hands by dawn, we're going to have an issue."

"Wind your neck in, Badger," she said, fucking mocking me. "Because I'm not giving you shit. Oh, except this..." She held the dog in one hand then reached into her denim shorts' pocket, rummaging around in it for a second while the three of us waited, curious as fuck to see what she had hidden in there.

A beat later, she took her hand out and flipped me her middle finger. I slammed my palm down on the kitchen island in fury and the way she flinched made me even angrier. If some asshole had touched her once like that, then how many times might he have hurt her before this? The finger mark bruises on her neck were enough to make me so far beyond protective, that I wanted to load my pick-up bed with guns and go hunting for the man responsible without even a clue to guide me to his door.

"A. Name," I pushed.

"Give it up, bro, she doesn't wanna tell us," JJ said and I shot him a glare, but as soon as I met his gaze, he cocked his head and gave me that imploring look that always seemed to work on me and I huffed out a breath.

"Can I go back to my car now?" she asked, sounding bored and my eyes whipped back to her.

"You're not sleeping on the side of a road, Rogue. You're staying here," I insisted, and I knew I wouldn't be letting her leave whether she accepted the offer or not.

She was quiet for a long moment then clucked her tongue and shrugged. "Fine." She strode over to the fridge, nudging JJ aside and taking out some orange juice.

She poured herself a glass before heading out onto the patio and dropping onto a sun lounger in the shade of an umbrella, tucking the dog up next to her. Her bronzed legs were in the sun and looked so appetising that I had to drag my eyes away.

At least that was one good thing to focus on. Rogue Easton was under my roof, locked up tight in the place I'd dreamed of bringing her to a million times. She'd been in my dreams since I was eight years old. And she'd laid claim to my soul long before then. Now she was back, I was finally going to do what that little boy had never been able to. I was going to make her *mine*. And I was never going to let her go.

CHAPTER SIX

I closed my eyes and tried to pretend that I hadn't found myself deep in the wolf den with the predators closing in on me as I feigned total indifference to my situation. But on the inside, I was a wreck. These boys, these *men,* were so different to the people I remembered and yet, this aching part inside of me was throbbing with a need to open my arms to them and beg them to take me in.

The worst part of that was how easy I thought it would be if I did. They wanted me here for some reason. They'd taken one look at me and demanded I stay, but that didn't make any sense. I was one of a very few people on a very short list. Fox's dad and the leader of this crew of cutthroat gangsters wanted me dead. I wasn't supposed to be in Sunset Cove. Not now or ever. That had been made terrifyingly clear to me when I left. My return here was a death sentence which was due to be carried out the moment Luther laid eyes on me.

My life, everything I ever had been or ever would be was supposed to end if my ass ever made it back here. And yet, here I was. My ass firmly pressing down on what was very clearly an obnoxiously expensive sun lounger while three assholes circled me like vultures.

"I'm gonna make some lunch," JJ announced loudly.

"Why? We just ate," Chase said in response which was followed by what sounded like someone getting punched in the arm.

"That was hours ago. Besides, I bet Rogue wouldn't mind a sandwich. Would you?" JJ asked and I reluctantly cracked an eye open to look in at him in the kitchen being all domesticated and shit.

My pride demanded I tell him to take his sandwich and shove it up his ass until he could taste it in his mouth again, but my pitifully empty stomach demanded I kick my pride to the curb and tell him *yes please* while worshipping him on my knees and kissing his feet. I settled on a happy medium with a side of fuck you tossed in.

"I've had one meal in the last three days so yeah, I'll take your sandwich and if you've got some chips too, that'd be great," I said.

"Why haven't you eaten for three days?" Fox demanded and I flinched out of my fucking skin as I realised he was standing right over me, casting me in his shadow and just lingering there like a big wall of muscular crazy.

"Because dead girls don't need food," I snarked back at him then instantly regretted it as I got trapped in the penetrating gaze of his deep green eyes.

"What's that supposed to mean?" he growled. Like, actually growled.

"Not a lot as I'm clearly living my best life right now, locked up in your dad's house wondering if he's planning on turning up to kill me himself or if he hands that kind of work over to you now."

Stone cold silence hit me in response to that and I arched a brow as Fox gave me crickets, his jaw ticking.

"Bullshit," Chase called, stepping out of the house to stand beside Fox and pulling a pack of cigarettes from his pocket. "No way you don't know about Luther."

Fox turned to glare at him and Chase arched a brow like he didn't know what he'd said that was wrong.

"What about him?" I asked, sitting up and leaning out to steal a smoke from him without bothering to ask.

I was aiming for rude but the casual over familiarity of the gesture had me mentally sitting in the back of his mom's car while the rain pounded down on the roof and we talked shit about everything and nothing while laughing our asses off for a brief moment before I blinked the memory away.

Chase observed me for a few seconds with a look in his eyes that said he wished I hadn't come back and as fucked up as that was, I actually preferred that attitude to Fox's weird overbearing shit and JJ's casual disregard for what I wanted.

Fox glared at the cigarette in my hand like he wanted to snatch it away from me and I gave him a flat look which dared him to do it.

Chase sparked up and then leaned down to let me light my own smoke from the end of his. As I inhaled deeply, the cherry flared with heat and I watched as it was reflected in his eyes, the scent of sea air, chain smoking and danger coiling around me from his skin as he got too close.

Chase had always been slim and underfed when we were younger, but it looked like he'd gone on a mission to rectify that in the years we'd spent apart. His body was thick with muscle that said he did more with it than just work out in the gym and the ink on his skin was as dark as the soul that peered back at me from within his ocean blue eyes.

"Daddy Harlequin is-"

"Dead," Fox ground out and my gaze flicked back to him as my lips popped open at that piece of lifechanging information.

My gaze slid back to Chase for confirmation and he shrugged.

"Dead as a fucking doornail. Took a bullet right between the eyes a few years ago," Chase confirmed, taking the cigarette from his lips as I took a drag on mine.

"Good," I replied as the shock of that statement sank in and I leaned back in my sun lounger as I tried to feign indifference, but shit, that was big news, huge, enormous, gigantic, fuck you up the ass with a baseball bat news.

With Luther Harlequin dead and buried, I was free - assuming his heir hadn't decided to stick to his decisions and would kill me for him. But as that heir was standing over me looking like he was trying not to blow a gasket as he drank me in with a mixture of so many emotions in his gaze that I couldn't count them, I was going to guess not. Fox could have killed me the moment I was shoved through the front door and yet here I was, lounging by his pool and drinking his OJ.

No one called me out on my joy over Fox's dad's death which said

79

plenty about the motherfucker in question and I lifted the cigarette to my lips, taking a long drag as I bought myself a few seconds to process that shit because it changed…everything. And nothing.

JJ cleared his throat from inside the house and gave Fox a hard look which seemed to hold a question while Fox just shrugged innocently before turning to look back at me. There was a time when I could interpret every look my boys exchanged and send them silent messages of my own, but unless Fox was having trouble holding a fart in, I was lost as to what they were thinking about me in that moment.

I only usually smoked when I was stressed, but I figured this situation met the requirements. Mutt didn't seem to like it much though, hopping up off of the sun lounger and moving around the pool before cocking his leg against a potted palm.

"This is why I don't allow dogs in my house," Fox grunted, his eyes following Mutt with distaste written on his features and I stood up with a saccharine sweet smile.

"Okay, no worries. We'll get out of your hair then."

I turned my back on him and tried to walk away, but his hands grasped my waist and he tugged me back against him instead, his warm, ripped abs pressing to my spine through my stolen shirt as I sucked in a surprised breath.

"No one even breathes in Sunset Cove without my say so, hummingbird," he warned. "So don't go thinking you're doing anything at all without me okaying it."

I jerked out of his grip and turned back to glare at him. "Keep your fucking hands off of me, Fox," I warned, pointing my cigarette at him. "I don't know why the hell you want me here, but I'm not your property so you can keep your paws to yourself."

"Is it a price issue?" Chase asked as he dropped down into the sun lounger I'd just vacated. "Because I'm good for the money if you wanna warm my bed while you're here. Once your face heals up of course. I'm not buying damaged pussy."

Fox whirled on him in the blink of an eye, grabbing the edge of the sun lounger and flipping it up so that Chase was thrown into the pool with a cry of outrage. The huge splash drenched the front of my legs and I took a step back in alarm as Fox stalked towards the edge of the pool and grabbed a fistful of Chase's curly dark hair as he surfaced.

"You call her a whore again and I'll break your fucking nose," he snarled before shoving down on Chase's head and dunking him beneath the water again.

Fox's muscles flexed, the fox tattoo between his shoulder blades drawing my gaze for way longer than I would have liked it to. But Fox Harlequin had always been the kind of guy it was hard to take your eyes off of and now he was like an actual force of nature.

I held my ground as Fox stood up and stalked away from the pool, cutting me an unreadable look as Chase emerged from the water coughing and cursing.

"You were wrong anyway, Chase," I said, releasing a trail of smoke from my lips. "My pussy isn't damaged in the least. So if you wanna make good on that offer you could just bend me over and forget about my fucked up face. I get the impression you're not all that pleased to see it anyway."

I flicked my cigarette into the pool as Chase smirked cruelly and I totally ignored Fox as I moved back into the house where JJ was looking at me with an assessing gaze as he pushed a plateful of food across the kitchen island to me.

"I call bullshit," he announced as I took a barstool and tore a bite from my sandwich. Avocado, cheese and sun-dried tomatoes filled my mouth and I groaned loudly as I chewed, not giving a shit if they knew I appreciated the food. It didn't come close to making up for what they'd done to me and I had no qualms about eating every single thing in their fridge if they were dumb enough to offer it up for free. "You don't carry yourself like a working girl."

"Well, there's a first time for everything and you guys look like you can afford to pay a good price for pussy. So all I'd need to do is close my eyes and imagine you're absolutely anyone else and we'd be good," I snarked back.

JJ smirked like that made sense to him and Fox dropped down into the chair beside me, practically breathing down my neck.

"I'll give you whatever you want. You don't need to earn money," he said in a low growl and I arched an eyebrow at him.

"Why?" I asked.

"Because you're one of us. What's mine is yours."

I scoffed lightly. "No thanks."

Fox opened his mouth to say something else, but JJ placed a hand on his shoulder and gave him a meaningful look as they silently communicated something between each other and I gave my attention to my sandwich. Some things never changed. JJ and Fox still liked having their secrets. I wondered if I could still figure them out just as easily as I once had. But I found I didn't even want to try. Being back here felt like the air was too thin and the silence too loud. I needed to escape the thick layer of Harlequin that was slowly trying to drown me and just focus on finding those keys.

As none of them was wearing a shirt, it was pretty easy to see that they didn't wear their keys around their necks like I did, which meant that I was probably in the perfect place to figure out where they kept them. So I'd stay put for now while I tried to find them. But the moment I did, I'd be gone even faster than I'd disappeared the first time.

"I'm gonna guess sleeping in a car isn't all that restful," JJ said as he moved around to my other side and boxed me in like he and Fox were a pair of bookends. "So if you wanna have a shower and a rest in one of the guest rooms, you can. There's one with an en-suite opposite my room," he offered and I jumped all over that option like a seagull on a French fry.

"You're saying I can escape the overbearing Badger to my right? That would be a hell yes." I hopped up, licking the last sandwich crumbs from my fingers and ignoring Fox as he bristled.

I headed over to the fridge first, ignoring JJ as he led the way towards a corridor beyond the kitchen.

I tugged the fridge door wide just as Chase stalked back through the open doors, scrubbing at his dark curls with a towel while dripping water all over the tiled floor and scowling at Fox.

I grabbed a pot of what looked like freshly made guacamole, a bottle of white wine, a couple of cans of soda, a punnet of raspberries and a second bottle of wine because it looked expensive so why the fuck not?

JJ appeared beside me with a frown so I turned to him and dumped my haul in his arms for him to carry before turning and pulling open the cupboards until I found a family sized bag of Doritos and tossed them into his arms too.

Once he couldn't carry any more, I reached out and stole the pink lensed shades from his face and put them back on mine.

"I want my hat back," I growled as I waved at him to lead the way and he cocked an eyebrow at me like he found me amusing.

"I think I dropped it when I was chasing you," he admitted.

"Of course you did. I literally own five things in the entire world so why would you be careful with one of them?" I replied scathingly, tossing the cupboard door closed as I gave up on my food raid.

"Why is that exactly?" Chase asked me and I flicked a glance his way, refusing to look at the water sliding down his bare chest in lickable beads of moisture.

"Because I haven't had a home for ten years. But you guys know all about that, don't you?" I said icily.

"You had a home," Chase replied without so much as a flicker of remorse in his gaze. "It's not like you were cast out onto the streets."

I gave him a smile that was all venom and shrugged nonchalantly. "It's not like any of you cared either way."

"That's not true," Fox said, gripping the edge of the kitchen island hard enough to dent it if it hadn't been made of fucking marble.

"Isn't it?" I asked sweet as pie before turning and walking off down the corridor that led from the kitchen. I had no idea where I was going, but I cared more about walking out on his bullshit than I did about accidentally wandering into the wrong room.

JJ skirted me and headed off into the depths of the house, taking a set of stairs and saving me from making an ass of myself by walking into a closet by accident. I followed on after him, whistling to Mutt and pretending I couldn't feel Chase and Fox's eyes burning a hole in the back of my head until I turned a corner and left them behind.

He turned another freaking corner like we were in a hotel or something and led me up a couple of steps before heading into another corridor.

"That's Chase on the left, then I'm next and Fox is in the master on the right," JJ explained as we passed by closed doors and I feigned disinterest while drinking it all in. "And you can have this one." He moved to the door beyond Fox's directly opposite the room he'd said was his and used his elbow to push it open for me.

The room was painted white like every other part the house I'd seen so far. There was a queen sized bed made up beside a pair of French doors with floor length white curtains drawn wide either side of them. I trailed inside and found a view of the sea waiting for me beyond them with a large balcony right outside. The private beach was fenced in and a jetty led out to a speedboat where a Harlequin thug was patrolling, his large gun on clear display. I could see another one moving closer to the house and I pouted. Even if I could get down there, I'd never get past those assholes. I wouldn't have been surprised if the place was crawling with security cameras too.

I stepped up to the doors and instantly tried to open them, growling in frustration as I found them locked and gave them a good rattle to make sure.

"Just how long do you plan on keeping me prisoner in here?" I asked as JJ put my snacks on the nightstand and I leaned my forehead against the window, watching the sea so I didn't have to look at him.

"You're not a prisoner, Rogue," he said, sounding kinda pissed about the accusation and I turned back to look at him with a scowl, thanking the rose tinted glasses for giving me some small barrier against this echo of my forgotten hopes and dreams.

"Oh yeah? So I can just go then, can I?"

JJ pursed his lips and sighed. "We just wanna make sure you're alright."

I rolled my eyes at that false sentiment. "Better late than never, hey?"

"It's not like that," he protested. "We couldn't find you Rogue. You were meant to stay in Fairfax and you ran."

"Oh, so it's my fault that I didn't want to stay living with that controlling old bag? And how long exactly was I supposed to stay there? Because it wasn't like I ever heard from any of you on that issue. Let alone anything else."

"Well maybe if you'd stayed put-"

"Then what?" I demanded because I wasn't going to listen to his shit about this. That place hadn't been a home to me. That woman didn't care. She wanted me to sell drugs to the kids I went to school with and when the cops started sniffing about, she was clearly going to throw me to the wolves. I wasn't going to stay there, especially when I had no reason to think the Harlequin boys even remembered me, let alone might be coming back. It was bullshit.

84

They forgot all about me the moment I left Sunset Cove.

JJ seemed to figure out this wasn't going to get him anywhere and turned away with a sigh, heading through a door at the back of the room and the sound of running water soon reached me.

I glanced at the open door behind me just as Mutt leapt up and made himself comfy on my fancy new bed, but it seemed kinda pointless to try and run again right now. Fox and Chase were blocking the exit and I wanted the chance to look for their keys anyway. But what was the deal with Maverick? Because it was seriously starting to seem like the Harlequin boys were down to three and I just couldn't imagine that. The four of them had been utterly inseparable... Then again, I'd thought the *five* of us were once, so maybe none of them cared about anyone and the three of them were only still together out of convenience.

I kicked off my dirty white sneakers and trailed after JJ to the en-suite which turned out to be almost as big as the bedroom. The white tiled walls were accented with little blue embellishments and there was an enormous walk in shower as well as a wide vanity, my own toilet - complete with honest to shit toilet paper, might I add - and last, but by no means least, the biggest fucking bath tub I'd ever seen. The white claw footed beast sat before another floor length window with a view of the sea and looked like the kind of thing you only ever saw in movies.

"The balcony runs along the whole back side of the house," JJ explained as he poured way too much bubble bath into the tub and it frothed up like a cappuccino, filling the air with the scent of coconut. "The door in your room leads out to it as well as the one in Fox's and the one in the den. They're all locked right now though."

I didn't comment on that because of course they were, but whatever, I was staying put for now anyway. And when I was ready to run it would take more than a locked door to stop me.

"I'll go find you some clean clothes and I can toss that stuff in the washer for you if you like?" JJ suggested and I shrugged like I didn't care but I did. I really, really did. Clean clothes sounded like heaven right about now.

He headed out of the room and I collected up a bottle of wine with my chips and guac before tossing them all down on a little table beside the tub.

I hadn't had a bath in...probably as long as I hadn't been in this town. And the only times I'd had one back then was if I'd stayed at one of the boys' houses when their families were away. Never in this house though. We never hung out at Fox's house.

I tugged off the shirt I'd stolen from JJ and dropped it to the floor before shimmying out of the booty shorts with a sigh of relief.

I was just about to tug the strings of my bikini bottoms loose when JJ strolled back into the room like he owned the damn place.

"Don't stop on my account. I've seen more tits and ass this week than you'll see in your lifetime," he said as I stopped what I was doing and narrowed my eyes at him over my shoulder.

"Wow, Johnny James, you really learned how to charm the girls while I was gone, didn't you?" I said. "But as irrelevant as that statement makes me feel, I'd still rather you fuck off before I get naked. 'Kay?"

JJ grinned at me like I'd just asked him to come closer instead of fuck off. He stalked towards me with his pile of offerings in hand, placing a red wifebeater with black skulls all over it down for me alongside a pair of boxers and a fluffy white towel.

"I don't happen to keep any women's clothes here, but Chase thinks a girl might have left her panties around here somewhere the other week if you want me to track them down for you?" he asked, his eyes sparkling with amusement like he thought he knew exactly how I'd react to him baiting me. But it had been a long time since Johnny James had known me and he wouldn't be winning me around with his boyish nonsense either.

I moved right up into his personal space, the scent of sea air seeming to cling to his skin and overwhelming me with a feeling of being home for a few seconds before I shook it off. I didn't have a home, the Harlequin boys had seen to that for me.

I placed my hands on his chest and shoved him back a step, followed by another and another until he was standing outside the door to the bathroom, still smirking like we were playing a game.

JJ reached out and snagged his pink sunglasses from my face while I scowled at him through them and his cocky grin didn't even drop when I swung the door closed in his face and twisted the lock for good measure.

JJ's laughter called to me from beyond the door and I ground my teeth as I turned back to the tub, dropped my bikini and stepped in.

The hot water welcomed me into it like the best hug I'd ever had and I sank low with a groan of pleasure as I let it envelop me. Today had not gone to plan at all. My little recon trip had ended in capture and I was now firmly within the midst of my enemy. But on the plus side, I was in the prime location to try and find their keys. I just had to endure their company while I searched.

In the meantime, I was happy to use them for their luxuries and reap the benefits of that in the form of clean hair, fresh sheets and as much wine as I could drink before I passed out. Which was actually quite a lot. Hanging around with Shawn and his crew had shown me the benefits of drinking with the aim of blacking out and I just so happened to be a pro.

Two hours in the bath later, a bottle and a half of wine, the entire selection of chips and dips and copious use of their fancy ass hair products and I curled up in the big bed they'd given me wearing JJ's shirt but passing on his boxers. Clean or not, he could keep those.

Oblivion was calling my name and I was happy to join her in the dark.

I woke with a groan and a mouth that felt full of cottonwool, blinking up at the unfamiliar ceiling with a rush of panic before remembering where I was.

It was dark, the view beyond the balcony doors showing a crescent moon hanging low over a navy sea and the soft lull of the waves against the shore caressing my soul like no other sound in the world could.

The bed they'd given me was stupid soft and after sleeping in that cold, beat up Jeep, I had definitely reaped the benefits of the upgrade.

A soft whimper alerted me to Mutt as he nosed at the door and I pushed myself to sit up, using the moonlight to take in the room and frowning as my gaze fell on an armchair which I swear hadn't been so close to the bed last night. It was placed in the corner beside the balcony doors, but I could have sworn it had been angled towards the view the last time I'd seen it, not directed at my sleeping place.

I shook my head and dismissed the chair, swivelling around to get out of bed and finding a tall glass of water waiting for me where my half empty bottle of wine had sat the last time I saw it. There was also a couple of painkillers beside a pair of thick socks. I frowned at the idea of one of them coming in here while I'd been sleeping but shrugged it off in favour of taking the pills, draining the water and then pulling the socks on over my cold feet. My feet were always cold, especially at night and one of the things I was saddest about losing back at Shawn's was my collection of fluffy socks. It was a stupid thing to miss, but there was something sacred about finding favourite socks that rivalled the love I felt for my lost coffee mug. Cest la vie and all that, but damn, I wished he'd buried me with a few choice items.

One of the boys had clearly remembered the countless times I'd complained about having cold feet though. And I wasn't sure how I felt about that. On the one hand, it could be seen as kind of sweet, but on the other it just made me wonder even more about all the shit that had gone down between us. If they cared about my feet being cold then how come they'd never cared about where I was or what I was doing with my sorry excuse for a life?

I slipped out of bed and then out of the room with Mutt scampering ahead of me with his focus fixed on the kitchen down the stairs at the far end of the corridor. My gaze skimmed over the three closed doors which housed the sleeping boys and it occurred to me that this right here was the perfect opportunity to start doing some digging.

I slipped along the wooden floor, silent in my socks as I headed after Mutt and padded back into the kitchen. The little white dog had made it to the sliding doors which led out to the pool, but unsurprisingly as I tried it, I found it securely locked with no sign of a key anywhere.

I pouted as I looked about, moving through the house to the front door and giving that a fruitless attempt too before returning to a rather desperate looking Mutt with a frown. I could go and wake one of the guys, tell them to let him out before he took a dump on the mat or...

My lips twitched into a smirk as I spotted a huge, potted fern in one corner of the room and I scooped Mutt up before placing him down in the soil surrounding the plant.

The little fella instantly cocked his leg and relieved himself with what I would have called the doggy version of a contented sigh and I grinned at him as I looked around the open space.

The house was still silent and as my gaze fell on a little white tower of drawers which stood to one side of the room an idea occurred to me. No time like the present, after all.

I slipped across the open space, glanced back towards the stairs where the guys were sleeping then opened the top drawer. There was a roll of money inside. More than I'd seen in a damn long time and it was most definitely whispering my name and telling me to take it with me when I ran. *Not yet, my love, but soon.*

I closed that drawer and found another with random bits of crap including several keys on a ring, but they were big and bulky, not what I was looking for and not the keys to the doors or windows here in the house either.

I moved my search on, rifling through drawers, cupboards, shelves. Anywhere and everywhere that might hold something of interest or most ideal of all, the rest of the keys that matched mine.

I crept from room to room, exploring the house while trying to hunt down anything interesting and coming up short time and again. There was a locked door beyond the kitchen which I couldn't budge and had to give up on with a frustrated huff and another one before the dining room. When I made it to the big tv room at the back of the house, I even checked down the backs of the sofa cushions. Nothing.

"If there's something in particular you're after, you could just ask, you know," JJ said casually and I almost screamed as I lurched upright and whirled on him, finding him standing in the doorway in a thin pair of shorts and nothing else, his muscular arms folded over his chest as he leaned on the door jam and waited for me to explain myself.

"I want to leave," I said defiantly, folding my own arms while trying not to think about the fact that I was only wearing his wifebeater and had just been bent over the couch with my bare ass in the air aimed right at him. The shirt fell down to my mid thigh while I was upright like this but...yeah, there was no denying the amount of ass that would have been hanging out of it while I was bent over like that. Goddammit.

"So you thought we might keep the keys to the front door between the cushions?" he asked, seeming somewhat amused and I just shrugged. "Maybe I should go and wake Fox and Chase up, see what they think about you searching the house in the dead of night."

"Don't," I said before I could stop myself, but I wasn't sure why I was bothering. JJ had no loyalty to me so there was no reason for me to think he'd keep this between us.

JJ's face split into a knowing grin and he pinned me in his gaze as he considered his options.

"Alright. How about we swap secrets then? I won't tell so long as you explain those bruises to me," he offered.

"That sounds like you'll just own two of my secrets. It's not a swap," I pointed out and his smile widened in a way that made my stomach knot.

JJ may have seemed like a nice guy on the surface, but there was something about that look in his eyes which told me that was all bullshit. I'd met enough dark souls to recognise the danger of the ruthless streak in them no matter what mask they presented to the world. This was a man who was used to getting what he wanted by one means or another and I wasn't going to forget that. The boys I'd once run with were living the life they'd always been destined for. One of violence and crime and death. Any sweetness they'd once had would be thoroughly corrupted by now.

"Looks like it," JJ agreed. "So what's it to be?"

I rolled my eyes and stalked towards him, slipping past him when he refused to move out of the doorway and ignoring the way my body had been pressed to his in the tight space for that split second before I made my way back to the kitchen.

I helped myself to a glass of OJ, poured a second for JJ because I was a peach like that then dropped down onto a stool before the kitchen island as he came to sit beside me.

I took a long swig of my juice, placed the glass down and looked into it as I decided to give him the truth. At least enough of it to get him off of my back. They weren't going to drop this now that they'd seen the bruises and it was easier to just get this over and done with.

"My boyfriend turned out to be even more of an asshole than I realised he was when we got together. I guess he just got fed up of me or whatever and we got into a fight..."

It had really been more of a 'him screaming at me for being a dumb, nosy, whore while I tried to escape and then begged for my life when he caught me' type deal, but I didn't really want to explain the agony of Shawn's fist colliding with my face or the way my head had slammed against the wall as he threw me back against it.

"A fight about what?" JJ asked darkly.

"The kinds of things dumb assholes and their even dumber girlfriends fight about. Money, other girls, the usual," I shrugged but it had been something a whole lot worse than that. I should have just left the moment I realised he had company. If I hadn't been a nosey bitch and lingered there like a cocky asshole, expecting him to be pleased to see me if he caught sight of me anyway then I could have saved myself a whole heap of drama. Though that said, despite the fucked up way I'd ended up here, I couldn't say I was sad to be rid of Shawn. I'd been marked as his for longer than I had really liked, but in the life I'd been living, the alternatives had all been much worse. Besides, I couldn't have been the one to break things off between us if that wasn't what he'd wanted. Not without running a long damn way from him so that he could never track me down. That wasn't how The Dead Dogs worked. So in a way, I was just glad to be done with him.

"And then what?" JJ asked, his voice softening a touch, making me glance up at him.

"I'm not telling you his name," I said firmly. "Not his address, the town he lives in or even the state. I'm not even gonna tell you what colour hair he has or what's tattooed on his ass. This is my fight. I don't want some ghosts from my past charging in like a bunch of tough guys and trying to fix my problems for me. When I deal with him, I'm gonna be the one who pulls the trigger. I'm not looking for your help with this or anything else."

"Just tell me, Rogue," JJ insisted. "Tell me what he did to you and if you want, I'll keep my fucking mouth shut and you can just go right on back to bed. Tomorrow we can act like you never said a word and if you really don't wanna tell me who he is then I'll accept that. For now. But I need to know what happened to you, sweetheart."

"I'm not your sweetheart, JJ," I growled, shifting away from him. "I'm not your anything. But if you want to know what he did to me, then fine."

I got to my feet and moved to stand right in front of him, reaching out to wrap my fingers around his throat as he gazed at me.

"He shoved me up against a wall, wrapped his fingers around my throat like this and *squeezed.*" I tightened my fingers around JJ's neck, his Adam's apple bobbing beneath my palm as he looked into my eyes, watching me relive it while managing to hold his tongue. "He squeezed so hard I couldn't breathe and then squeezed even harder while I fought back with everything I had and found it wasn't even close to enough to stop him. Then he told me he was sorry and that he was really gonna miss my ass and I blacked out somewhere around the moment he delivered those parting words. When I came to, I was in a shallow grave not too far from here and I just walked my ass back to the one place in the world I never wanted to see again and the people I hate most in this world."

"Rogue," JJ growled, catching my waist between his hands as he tried to drag me closer but I just blinked away the prickle in the backs of my eyes, hardened my jaw and shook my head as I refused to let him move me.

"You wanted to know," I said in a hard voice. "And now you do."

"I'll kill him," he snarled, his grip on my waist tightening as a monster danced behind his eyes and I could see the bloodlust pulsing within his veins. "I'll make him suffer a thousand times more than-"

I shoved myself away from him with a snort of dismissal. "You got your answer, Johnny James. Don't blame me if you didn't like what you heard."

I turned and walked out on him, heading back to my room as the sound of his stool scraping back across the tiles followed me. I expected him to come racing after me, demanding a name and ranting about all of the things he was going to do to Shawn in my name. But as I made it back to my bedroom door, the distinctive sound of something wooden breaking filled the air instead and I flinched as a smashing sound followed.

Mutt shot past me in alarm, darting into my room with his tail between his legs and I slipped inside as I heard Fox shouting something from within his room. Just before I could close my door, he stepped out wearing nothing but a pair of boxers with a pistol in his hand and a snarl on his lips. He didn't even seem to notice me as he strode away, heading towards JJ and the sounds of destruction without so much as a flicker of fear or confusion, just a determination to deal with whatever was going on. And damn his ass looked good when he was striding away all purposeful like that.

I closed my door and twisted the lock for good measure. Not that I really thought it would keep any of them out if they wanted in, but I wanted them to know I had no desire to see any of them if they came to my door.

The sound of raised voices came from the kitchen a moment later then everything fell quiet.

A few minutes later, the glow of headlights shone in through my window, wheeling around before I heard the car pulling along the drive.

I retreated to my bed, tugging the sheets up around me as I waited for them to come back. But they never did.

CHAPTER SEVEN

Fox pulled his black pick-up around the front of the house while I hit call on Chase's number for the fifth time. *Answer, motherfucker.*

"Yus?" he slurred at last. "That you again, Rosie? I'm up for that BJ now."

"We're going out, you coming?" I growled, my fist curled tightly on my lap. Fox's jaw was pulsing hard and I didn't think there would be much left of his teeth soon if Chase didn't hurry his ass up. We'd grabbed some clothes out of the laundry, both of us in t-shirts and jeans.

"Fuck…my head," Chase groaned down the line. "I'll settle for your lips on my cock then JJ, anything to take the edge off of this oncoming hangover."

"*Chase*," I snapped. "Get out here or we're leaving."

Fox turned the truck down the drive, his patience obviously wearing thin.

"Hold your fucking horses, I'm coming," Chase growled then started muttering, "Just not in the way I'd hoped after a three am wake up call…"

Fox let the engine idle and I lowered my window, leaning out of it and looking back at the house. Chase was climbing out of his window in a pair of boxers and an open blue shirt, a pair of jeans scrunched in his hand with some sneakers and what looked like a bottle of rum.

He used the drainpipe to shimmy down half way before dropping onto the gravel, stumbling a step before jogging toward us and I shoved the truck door open, sliding along the bench to let him in.

Chase leapt inside with his unruly dark hair in his eyes and a stupid smirk on his face.

"Where are we going brothers?" he hollered, slamming the door shut behind him and starting to tug on his jeans.

I swiped the rum from the footwell, taking a long drink as Fox took off down the road.

"You're drunk," Fox deadpanned.

"No, I'm soberly challenged," Chase corrected, laughing and I punched him in the thigh as he buttoned up his jeans. "Shit, I need a top up or this hangover's gonna be as much of a bitch as your momma, J." He swiped the rum back from me, taking a drink before pulling out a box of cigarettes and pushing one into his mouth. He lit it up, leaving the window down so the smoke carried out of it on the cool night air. I let the comment about my momma slide because as much as I loved the woman, his assessment of her was kinda accurate.

"Did you lock your window?" Fox demanded.

"Yeah, I think so," Chase said.

"Well did you, or didn't you?" Fox growled, giving him a death glare, looking like he was about to go climbing up to Chase's room to check.

"Yes," Chase insisted.

The house was locked up tight, so even if Rogue decided to come back out of her room and take off, she was going to find her ass firmly caged.

"So what's the occasion?" Chase asked.

"Rogue," Fox growled, his knuckles turning white on the steering wheel.

He'd about lost his fucking shit when I'd told him Rogue's secret and I was expecting Mount Harlequin to blow its top any second. I really should have been organising a town-wide evacuation. "And you need to sober the fuck up right now so you're not deadweight for this conversation."

"And how do you expect me to do that?" Chase drawled.

I turned to Chase and he frowned at my serious-as-shit expression. I only got like this when I was feeling murdery and even in his half-pissed state, he could recognise the change in me.

"The piece of fucking scum who'd touched Rogue was her ex-boyfriend. And he didn't just beat her around – which trust me, would be more than enough for me to slit the motherfucker's throat – but he also choked her out. He thought she was dead and buried her in a shallow grave on the edge of Sunset Cove." Acid sizzled in my veins as I pictured it.

Chase's face paled and the tipsy look in his eyes dissolved into a killing-spree rage. *Yup, that sure sobered him up.*

"You got a name this time?" he asked hungrily, but I shook my head.

"I need blood in payment for this," Fox growled like fucking Batman and Chase and I nodded our agreement. "I've put a call out to every one of our people asking for information on this guy, but it didn't jog anyone's memories with the little we know. So far they've got fuck all leads."

"She came from out of town," I sighed. "This asshole could be anyone from anywhere."

Chase cracked his knuckles one by one, taking a long drag on his cigarette. "Well if our guys haven't heard anything about some deadbeat putting their girl in the ground, maybe we need to broaden our horizons."

"Precisely my thinking," Fox said dangerously and I glanced at him, adrenaline seeping into my veins as a dark smile curled up my lips.

"The Dollhouse?" I guessed and he nodded firmly, accelerating down the streets that led toward the cliffs.

Soon, we were winding along the ocean view road, the crescent moon hanging low over the water and casting it in silver.

Fox eventually turned up the private road that led to the Dollhouse. Or so everyone this side of Sunset Cove called it. It was a middle ground between the rich and the poor, a huge hotel at the highest point of the cliff that looked like a Malibu Barbie Dreamhouse. It was essentially a brothel on steroids run by Fox's Aunt Jolene and her husband Chester. They weren't part of the crew because women couldn't be sworn in thanks to Luther's rules, but he'd given his sister this land a long time ago, letting her do whatever she liked with it so long as she paid the crew a cut out of her takings.

Jolene didn't meddle with anything on our side of the cliff. I guessed she liked running things her own way because she'd refused to let her husband join the Harlequins unless she was allowed to join too. In my opinion, keeping women out of the crew was bullshit, but Luther's rules still applied here. Especially because the old boys, or the elders as we called them, still had a stick up their asses about women joining. Fox had to pander to them unfortunately, but I guessed they'd die off eventually then he could run Sunset Cove however he liked.

The Dollhouse might have been on our territory, but Jolene and her husband were fit to defend themselves without our help. Chester was ex-military and had their security detail trained up and armed to the teeth. Rumour had it they had this whole cliff ready to blow as and when the notion took them.

We wound up the road towards the property, the floor length windows on the bottom floor giving a view into the never-ending party that was always going on here. A huge pool ran the whole length of the house and was full of bikini-clad girls and Ken doll lookalikes. There were plenty of X-rated Barbies too who had their tits out and were laying on the many sun loungers under the pink glow of the outdoor lighting.

The balconies on the first and second floor were full of dancing, grinding bodies as they moved to an endless beat, high on drugs, sex, or just fucking life. I knew that feeling. Fuck it, I *was* that feeling half the time. But not tonight. Tonight, I was an animal with a thirst for blood. And not the sexy vampire kind. The kind who caused pain for the sake of pain. Because no one hurt Rogue Easton and got away with it. That had once been a cardinal fucking sin in Sunset Cove, and as far as I was concerned, it still was. It looked like my brothers agreed with that too. Even Chase - who had plenty to fucking say about her staying here - would clearly still draw blood for her. He couldn't help it. We'd all loved that girl once, and the mark she'd left on us was everlasting. It was just a fact of life now. Even if she hated us and would gladly watch us burn for her, we'd drag her enemies into the flames as we went.

I opened the glove compartment and took out the three handguns stashed there, checking they were loaded before passing one each to Chase and Fox before tucking mine into the back of my jeans.

Plenty of people noticed when Fox pulled up beside the pool and got out, not just because he'd off-roaded his way onto their front lawn, but because everyone had just realised who had arrived.

We walked around the pool, heading toward a pink Cadillac which had been made into a hot tub. Girls and guys shouted propositions to us, while others cowered away, ducking their heads and having the good sense to drop their eyes. Tonight, was not a good night to fuck with us. In fact, no night was a good night to fuck with us. But especially not when we were out scenting blood like hungry dogs.

"JJ, baby, are you here for a good time?" Jessie called to me from the Cadillac. She worked for me in the club and it was good to see her enjoying herself as she hung one leg over the edge of the tub and some blonde dude went down on her.

"Not tonight, sweetheart," I tossed her way and her eyes widened at my tone, seeming to get the hint.

I was in asshole mode. And when I was in asshole mode, people tended to end up bloody. When Chase was in asshole mode, they tended to end up dead. And when Fox was in asshole mode, they tended to end up obliterated. All in all, someone's fate wasn't looking pretty tonight.

Me and Chase flanked Fox as he headed inside through an open sliding door, the thump of the bass pounding in my ears as we did a sweep of the party-goers then strode up the bright pink staircase to the next floor. People parted for us like the red sea for Moses and a whole lot quicker too.

Upstairs the floor was sparkly and white and a huge bar stretched nearly the entire length of the house ahead of us. This place was a playboy's wet dream; Chester and Jolene had built it after winning big in Vegas. They'd spent every penny they had to bring their vision to life, but I had a very well informed hunch that this place was sitting on a whole lot of debt and hiding one helluva bankruptcy in the pockets of its owners. The Granvilles weren't business people. Their whores were cheap and underpaid, most of them hooked on crack meaning they were semi-functional and didn't inspire repeat customers.

Beyond that, the Granvilles' mantra of living in an endless party meant anyone was welcome here twenty four seven, so the clientele tended to be poor-ass alcoholic losers seventy five percent of the time. The booze was almost as cheap as the whores, and all in all, when you looked a little closer at this so-called dream house, you realised it was a shit heap with cracks in the walls.

I was half waiting for them to sell up so I could buy them out for a pittance and build something really worth having on this cliffside. If this place was run with even half the management of Afterlife, it coulda been something special. But as it was, it only held a decent vibe on Saturday nights and wasn't worth shit any other day of the week. Had they taken my advice when I'd given it though? Hell no. *You can't teach business sense to a drunk horse, I guess.*

Someone stumbled into Fox, spilling his drink all down his shirt and I swear someone else screamed as they witnessed it. The guy backed up, taking in what he'd done as Fox's shoulders tensed.

"Ohhh shit, look what Barry's done!" some helpful little tit shouted from behind the guy and I glared between Barry's sniggering friends.

Fox punched Barry so hard in the face that he hit the ground before he even knew what had happened. It was a kindness really. He could've done a whole lot worse. Anyone who crossed us, accidentally or otherwise, had to be put in their place. But just as I thought this little issue was wrapped up with a tidy ass bow and some confetti, his stupid pack of dudebro friends dove forward to defend his honour.

Fox roared a challenge and started beating the hell out of them with vicious blows. I glanced back to look for Chase and cursed as I spotted him face fucking some girl on her knees in a pink bikini, his hand fisted in her hair as he casually smoked and gazed out the window, seeming oblivious to the fight that had broken out. *Just your average goddamn weekday.*

I leapt forward to help Fox, throwing heavy fists into the faces of the drunk assholes and they fell like sacks of shit at our feet, not getting a single punch in before their asses hit the floor. *Pathetic.*

"Hey! No fighting in my house!" a man boomed and I looked up to meet Chester Granville's gaze, his eyes widening as one final fucker made a brave but pointless attempt to take us down and fell to the mercy of my fists.

Chester was a huge, middle aged guy, built like a fort with spiky blonde hair and his stupid large biceps strained against a too-tight shirt. He cut the music just in time to hear Chase groan loudly and spill his load to a whole fucking audience who broke out into cheers.

I snorted a laugh and Fox cut me a look that said he was not amused. I whistled at Chase, getting the hint to round him up and he jogged over to us, pulling his zipper up while the girl curtsied and ran out of the room giggling.

"Who turned the music off?" Chester's wife Jolene strode into the room in high heeled boots and a skin-tight leopard print dress, her blonde hair falling in waves around her shoulders. All the money in the world couldn't buy good taste unfortunately. Not that they had all the money in the world, but they definitely hadn't spared even a penny on taste.

Jolene was beautiful and a couple of inches taller than her husband when she wasn't in her heels, but in them, she dwarfed him like a tiger next to a kitty cat. A kitty cat with bulging muscles and a fluffy blonde moustache, but still.

She folded her arms as she spotted us, cocking her head to one side. "Are my nephew and his friends causing trouble in our home?" she asked with an edge to her tone.

I sure as shit hadn't missed the armed security lurking in every corner of the room, or the ones that shadowed the lord and lady of the house themselves. I also hadn't missed the fact that not a single one of them had stepped in to stop us putting a pile of drunk idiots on their asses. So long as we were allied to their little mistress and master, we could do whatever the fuck we wanted around here.

"I'm not sure, pookins," Chester said, painting a stern look on his face.

I swooped down on the guy who'd spilled his drink on Fox, hauling him to his feet by the scruff of the neck as his friends groaned and crawled away from the scene of the massacre. The massacre of their dignity that is.

"Here's your culprit." I grabbed the guy's hair in my fist angling his head towards Fox as he started trembling. "You owe my brother an apology."

Fox sneered at the guy and he actually tried to press back into me to get away. I lowered my mouth to his ear, more than happy to let him know I was the least safe place in this room to be. "Do you think I'm going to protect you from him, little boy?"

Chase smirked as he moved to stand beside Fox, releasing a breath of smoke that was directed into the guy's face.

"I-I'm sorry Mr Harlequin," he stuttered at Fox and I shoved him to his knees.

"Now suck his dick," I commanded and the guy actually reached for Fox's belt, making Chase roar a laugh.

Fox smacked the guy's hand away with a growl, stalking past him toward the reason we'd come here. "Evening, Aunt. A word?" he asked of Jolene, embracing her quickly and she pecked him on the cheek.

I grinned at Chase and Jolene nodded to us, turning to lead us from the room. Her husband trotted at her side like a neutered puppy. After Rogue had left town, I'd vowed never to let a woman take my balls again. They would stay firmly between my thighs for the rest of my days to be sucked on and fondled by many a woman. And the odd guy when the occasion called for it. I wasn't into men exactly, but a brother could always use a helping hand from time to time, a finger here, a tongue there. We were all just flesh and bone, and sometimes a hand was going spare that might as well be put to use.

Jolene led us into an office that looked like a Disney princess's headquarters and I dropped into a fluffy pink office chair while Chase threw himself onto a puffy bean bag. Fox stood as rigid as a toothpick as he gazed coolly across the desk at Chester and Jolene.

"So I'm guessing by your expression, Fox, you're not here to party?" Jolene asked.

Chester dropped into a seat and his wife placed her hand on his shoulder, the clear power in their little empire.

"I have an offer for you," Fox said, cutting to the chase.

"What kind of offer?" Chester narrowed his eyes and if I wasn't mistaken, Jolene's long pink nails dug into his shoulder.

"We're looking for information," Fox explained. "If you're able to get it for me, I'll reward you for it."

"How much?" Chester piped up again then winced as Jolene's nails dug in tighter.

"What information?" Jolene demanded, placing a hand on her hip.

"We're looking for someone whose girlfriend recently disappeared," Fox said, choosing his words carefully.

"She would have gone totally off the radar," I added.

"Like a ghost," Chase growled, somehow looking intimidating as he rested his elbows on his knees and sat up on the beanbag.

"She was a brunette, five nine, tanned, twenty six years old with tattoos on her left arm, back and right thigh," Fox said. "That ring any bells?"

Chester glanced up at his wife who was either giving us a seriously good poker face or she genuinely didn't know shit. I could read people like books normally, but Jolene was a master at hiding her real emotions. Just like her brother and his son.

"That's not much to go on," Jolene said at last. "What interest is she to you?"

"That's our business," Fox growled.

I pushed out of my seat, walking to the window and gazing down at the lawn where naked party goers were jumping through a sprinkler. "You know, it would be an awful fucking shame for you to lose this place."

"Lose it?" Chester hissed. "Why on earth would we lose it?"

"Hm, I dunno. Ceilings fall down, someone gets legionnaires disease from your badly kept hot tubs, a drunk idiot falls from one of your balconies and breaks their neck, a couple of assholes get trigger happy because you don't get your muscle to pat people down on their way in." I took my gun from where it was tucked in the back of my jeans and the two of them stiffened as I twirled it in my fingers and fixed them with a dark smile. "Shit happens. So you need a safety net. A nice little money cushion to fall back on during the bad times. And there's always bad times. Are you sure you're prepared for that?"

"If you're suggesting that we don't-" Chester started, turning red in the face at my insinuation, but Jolene dug her nails into him so hard he stalled mid-sentence. I swear there was blood seeping through his shirt. That woman was an animal. And one I would never underestimate.

"Five grand," Fox offered. "If you get me a name by the end of the week."

"It can't be done," Jolene laughed airily.

Chase stood up, lighting another cigarette as he casually disrespected their private office. "You get a lot of clientele here. People from the upper and lower quarters. Even people from out of town. And people like to talk when they've had a few drinks. And I *know* you like to listen Jolene. That's why your paid pussy all wear these." He reached into his pocket, tossing a little microphone down onto the desk so it bounced across it to land under Chester's nose and I smirked. *Trust Chase to take a blowjob for the team.*

Jolene bristled and Chester turned even redder.

"You'd better have paid my girl by the way," Jolene snarled and Chase laughed obnoxiously.

"She was begging for my cock, I think she would have paid *me* to suck it. But I wouldn't have taken the money anyway. I'm generous like that. So you're welcome." He winked and Jolene's upper lip peeled back as her head snapped around to face Fox.

"I won't be disrespected by your men in my home," she hissed. "Your father would never have-"

Fox reached into his pocket, taking out a roll of cash and tossing it onto her desk. "Call that a down payment for the information I want. But Chase really doesn't pay for fucks and I sure as shit don't pay for them for him. Take care of yourself, Jolene." Fox turned his back on them, striding across the room and shoving his way out the door.

I tossed a salute to Fox's aunt and Sergeant Douchenheimer and headed after my boy, my shoulder brushing Chase's as we followed.

Exhilaration buzzed through my veins as I tucked my gun away and the music washed over me. Part of me wanted to stay and get fucked up, but most of me wanted to return home to check on Rogue. At least her being locked up in a house that belonged to the most powerful men in town and surrounded by armed men put me at ease some. But not nearly enough. Not now I knew what she was running from. I wouldn't be heading home just yet though. We were by no means done for the night.

My restless soul settled a little knowing we'd done something in an effort to find out who the asshole was who'd hurt Rogue. But it wasn't nearly enough. I was sure we'd find some of The Damned Men to alleviate our stress and wet our hands in their blood before dawn.

We made it outside, walking over to the truck as people snapped pictures of us on their phones like we were damn celebrities and I booted one right out of a guy's hand into the pool. Chase whooped, flicking his cigarette after it and managing to burn a hole in an inflatable shaped like a giant dick. If I had this place, the pool toys would be flamingos and unicorns, not ride along cocks.

We climbed into the truck after Fox and the silence settled over us as he turned on the engine.

We all knew where we were going without any of us having to say a word. The fight was in us tonight and it needed to be let out. And there was really only one place where it could be truly sated in Sunset Cove.

The Divide.

CHAPTER EIGHT

I was surprised I managed to sleep again after everything that had happened the night before, but when I next opened my eyes, the gulls were calling beyond my window and the sun was rising up into the sky.

I slipped out of bed and immediately spotted a pile of clothes on the armchair facing the bed that hadn't been there last night.

I frowned as I moved towards it, finding my booty shorts and red bikini freshly laundered plus a black tank with a white rose printed on it alongside my Red Power Ranger cap which I was guessing JJ went and found for me. But if he thought I was gonna thank him for it then he'd be waiting a long damn time. I changed into the clothes, frowning as a different scent washed off of the shirt as I dragged it over my head. This was a rich, cedar scent that immediately made me think of Fox. I growled at myself as that thought occurred to me, knowing I was right and hating that I could tell it was his from nothing more than the stupid smell of a shirt that was freaking clean.

I drew in a deep breath and headed for the door, frowning as I found it unlocked and trying to remember if I'd left it that way. I could have sworn I'd locked it when I came back here last night, but then again, it was one of those twisting situations which always turned the wrong way and boggled my brain so maybe I'd just done it wrong.

I headed down the corridor, cutting a glance at JJ's cracked door as temptation urged me to take a closer look, before giving in to common sense and heading on down to the kitchen instead.

The sliding doors were wide open and the scent of breakfast hung in the air, even though I couldn't see any food hiding anywhere.

Chase was lounging beside the pool, cigarette jammed in the corner of his mouth while JJ sat upright on the lounger beside him, leaning in close so they could talk.

Not that they were talking now. The silence in the air was enough to hear a pin drop and more than enough to confirm the subject of their conversation.

I pursed my lips as their gazes fell on me, but before I could say anything, the front door banged and I turned to find Fox striding into the room in a pair of running shorts and no shirt, his skin slick with perspiration and looking good enough to lick.

Not that I'd be licking it. But shit, these boys really had grown up in the past ten years. They'd grown and grown and...*wow I can totally see the outline of his dick through those shorts.* And it was not a small outline either. Damn.

I licked my lips before I could stop myself and when I forced my eyes up and away from the leviathan lurking inside Fox's shorts, I found his green eyes fixed on me. The anger in them was clear enough and it was even more obvious that it wasn't aimed at me. Which meant JJ had spilled. One glance at the treacherous little -okay, not so little anymore - prick was enough to confirm it – that boy had never had a good poker face and he looked guilty as fuck right about now.

"Great. Thanks, JJ. I know who not to trust with any of my secrets in future," I snapped, turning away from Fox and yanking the fridge open as I hunted down some food.

I reached out to grab something, but before I could, Fox caught my wrist and tugged me around to face him, tossing the fridge door closed behind us.

"I want a name," he growled, crowding me in against the worktop until his chest was practically pressed to mine and I was pinned in the intensity of his gaze.

"Or what?" I hissed, my anger over...well, fucking everything in my shitty ass life actually, spilling over as he tried to force me to bend to his will. "Are you going to choke me out too? Or maybe just shove me about a bit until I give you what you want?"

"Fuck you. Don't compare me to that motherfucker," he snapped, pushing away from me as fast as he'd moved in on me and I narrowed my eyes at him as he stalked over to the oven, grabbed a plate out from inside it and tossed it down on the kitchen island.

I eyed the stack of pancakes with my stomach rumbling before Fox pointed at them, giving me a look that demanded I eat them as he placed a bottle of maple syrup down beside them and slammed a knife and fork down too.

It was literally the angriest table service I'd ever seen but I was as hungry as a shark in a cornfield, so I plopped down onto the stool before them and started eating. Fox stalked back to the fridge, grabbed a protein shake out of the door and started shaking it so vigorously that I was surprised the top didn't fly off.

"I hope that's not the way you jerk off," I said lightly, biting down on a fluffy forkful of pancake as he glared at me. "Though if your poor cock is always having to put up with that treatment, I guess it could explain why you go around looking half constipated all the time."

Chase barked a laugh behind me and I smirked into my next bite of food while Fox just glowered.

"I was thinking that I could take Rogue with me to Lucinda's today," JJ said loudly as he walked over to join us, clearly working to change the subject and I tossed him a scowl without replying as Fox considered it. "I think she could do with a bit of pampering," JJ pushed, giving Fox a less than subtle look which said stop-being-a-dick, but I was willing to bet that was a physical impossibility.

"What's Lucinda's?" I interjected. "You're not just taking me places without letting me know what I'm doing there."

"It's a beauty salon in the upper quarter," JJ said, giving me a grin. "I've got some work to do there and I thought you could get your hair done or whatever."

"Pass," I replied. "I've got fifteen bucks to my name which won't buy me shit in some fancy salon and I'd rather save that for food."

"My treat," JJ insisted as Fox scoffed lightly at my lack of funds. "I owe you for being a shitty secret keeper. You can get whatever you want done and I'll pay."

I pursed my lips, glancing between JJ and Fox before shaking my head again. "No thanks. I don't need charity. I can look after myself."

"Oh, so you have a job then, do you? A way to make that fifteen bucks grow?" Chase asked from his sun lounger and I turned to glance at him where he lay in the sun all oiled up and glistening and...not in any way tempting. Fuck him.

"Yeah, I do actually. I can get whatever I want whenever I want it. And I don't want some fancy haircut."

"Stealing shit isn't exactly a job," Chase replied in a mocking tone, seeing right through me and I smirked at him before I could stop myself. He had always been the most likely one of them to get me into trouble and I guessed he was still the most likely to corrupt me if I let him.

"You're going," Fox announced like it was up to him. "If you stay with me today, I'm gonna end up trying to shake that fucking name from your lips. Go get your nails done and stay out of trouble. I'll give you some money for new clothes too. Maybe after a day of relaxing you'll stop being such an unreasonable brat and tell me what I want to know."

I stood up suddenly, grabbed the bottle of maple syrup from the worktop and lunged at him with the full intention to dump the contents over his stupid fat head, but JJ's arms locked around my waist before I could do it.

I cursed him as he hoisted me off of my feet and tried to fight my way out of his grip while he chuckled in my ear.

"Come on, sweetheart, let's get going before you start a riot in the house," JJ said as if he was giving me a choice.

Fox glowered at me as I was carried away from him and I launched the bottle of syrup at his smug face, but he just caught it before it could make contact.

Chase's laughter followed us outside and JJ bundled me over to a black pickup before opening the door and shoving me inside. I scooted across the seats as he followed, moving to the far side of the car and folding my arms as

I glared out the window.

"Where's Mutt?" I asked as JJ slammed the door behind him and my little dog was left behind.

"Chase will watch him. I don't think dogs like beauty salons so much anyway," JJ said cheerily before starting the truck up and pulling us off of the gravel drive.

My gaze trailed over the group of four armed dudes hanging out by the gate, almost looking like they just happened to be there. But I knew well enough that they were on watch, ready and willing to kill any fucker who tried to get close to the house without permission.

The dull click of the doors locking rang out and I huffed irritably as I opened the window and let the warm breeze tease through my hair, turning my attention to the view.

"I thought the orange GT was yours," I muttered as we pulled out onto the road.

"It is. But some asshole in a beat up old Jeep side swiped it, so it's currently in the shop," JJ replied, arching a brow at me and making me laugh.

"I happened to like that Jeep. I mean, a newer model with AC might have been nice, but aside from that I thought it was a pretty sweet ride," I said defensively, though why I was defending that old stolen piece of shit, I didn't know.

"Yeah, well, I think the original owners may have it back now, sweetheart, so you'll have to forget about that one."

I shrugged and let the conversation drop off as I looked out of the windows at the familiar landscape and drank in all the changes that had occurred since I'd left.

JJ took the road which ran up the side of the cliff and I watched the view over the ocean with a deep sense of homecoming filling my chest. Whatever else I had to worry about over returning here, I couldn't deny that my heart belonged to the sea and it was happy to be back by the water at last. I refused to admit that it had anything to do with anything other than the sea though, because Sunset Cove was not and never would be my home again.

As we drove into the upper quarter, the buildings became obviously more expensive. This part of the town was a new addition which the wealthy assholes had claimed for their own, lording it over everyone from their vantage point up on the cliff. They liked to pretend the lower quarter wasn't there at all, forgetting about the people living down in the valley and leaving us to our own devices down there in the dirt. Which was just the way we liked it of course. They could stay out of our business and we could target them for ours.

We passed Afterlife where I'd found JJ yesterday and kept driving until we came up to a boulevard of fancy stores and boutiques called Avalon Row. JJ pulled down a side street and parked up in a spot behind a restaurant that wasn't currently open before getting out and offering me his hand.

I ignored him and tried to open my door, only to find that the damn thing wouldn't budge.

"Child locks, sweetheart. We can't have you running off on us when we've only just found you," JJ explained with a grin and I muttered something about controlling assholes beneath my breath as I scrambled over the seats and hopped down beside him.

Of course, he didn't just let me walk myself wherever we were going, tossing his arm around my shoulders and keeping me close as we walked along behind the stores. I glanced up at him as I tried to maintain my anger despite his casual, easy going attitude and pouted as he grinned back like we were having the time of our lives and I wasn't a prisoner at all.

I reached up and stole his pink sunglasses once more, earning myself a chuckle from him as I pushed them up my nose and let myself relax in his hold just a little. It wasn't like I was looking to run yet anyway. I needed to find their keys and I didn't really have anywhere to go even if I did leave.

"What happened to your face?" I asked, noticing the shadow of a bruise lining the edge of his jaw and reaching out to brush my fingers along it.

"Do you care about me now, sweetheart?" he asked with a disarming smile, meant to make me forget my question.

"Ah, so I'm supposed to tell you where I got my injuries, but you'll keep your own secrets about yours?" I said, not surprised in the least about the double standards. The three of them clearly thought they ruled the fucking world so why wouldn't they be utter hypocrites with their own behaviour?

"It's nothing, pretty girl," JJ said with a shrug, using the name he'd always used to call me as if no time had passed at all. "But we were all a bit worked up after finding out what had happened to you last night, so we went looking for a fight. I wanted to beat some asshole's face in even if it couldn't be the motherfucker who hurt you."

I rolled my eyes at the macho bullshit.

"So some poor innocent idiot had to take a beating to sate your testosterone fuelled crazy?" I asked.

"No. They weren't innocent. I can promise you that." He winked at me but didn't elaborate and I dropped it. Their gang bullshit didn't interest me much anyway.

JJ drew me over to a door at the back of one of the shops and knocked sharply before a perfectly made up blonde opened the door with a wide smile.

"Hey, JJ," she purred, making a show of checking him out as she moved aside to let us in.

"Hey, Lucy, how's business?" he asked, leading me down a short corridor and into a huge salon.

Everything was obviously expensive in a way that screamed *you don't belong* to my broke ass but drew me in at the same time. The walls and furniture were a mixture of pale pink and white with gold fixtures adorning everything.

There were a couple of other girls wearing the same pink uniform as Lucy working around the salon, though there was only one customer having her hair done near the glass front of the building. A row of doors leading into private rooms with words painted on the doors like *facial chamber* and *massage parlour* ran along the wall to my right, and all in all the place looked pretty damn fancy.

"Everything is good here, J," Lucy purred, petting his arm with a wide smile that said she would offer him the full range of services if he asked for it. "Is this Fox's new girl?"

"Err, no," I said, whirling around to look at her in surprise. "Why would you think that?"

Lucy cut a glance at JJ and shrugged a little helplessly. "I just assumed... we were told to expect a pretty brunette who belongs to Fox with JJ today, and here you are fitting the bill-"

"I fit no such bill," I said firmly. "I don't know where his girl is, but she isn't me."

"Right. Yeah, Fox can be kinda caveman about the things he wants. And he's got you living in his cave, so as far as he's concerned you're his girl now," JJ explained, saving Lucy from my glare.

"What?" I asked, not bothering to hide my feelings on that bullshit. "I think I must have just had some kind of brain aneurism, because it sounded like you just said that that asshole told these people I'm his property."

"Not just us," Lucy said, giving me a shrug. "He spread the word last night to everyone within the Harlequin Crew's reach. He said you're his girl and if anyone so much as looks at you the wrong-"

"No," I growled. "Just, *no*. Not me. I'm not his anything."

"Roll with it, sweetheart, it's not worth the headache of trying to deny him," JJ advised.

"Well what the fuck does being *his girl* mean?" I demanded.

"Nothing really," JJ said placatingly. "Just that no one can hurt or harass you, that he's got your back and you have free rein around here to do what you like."

"I guess that doesn't sound that bad," I muttered, glancing around the lavish room again.

"And no other dude can look at you, talk to you, touch you or fuck you unless they wanna get a bullet between the eyes for it," JJ added, winking at me as my mouth fell open and the complete and utter fucked-up-ness of that statement washed over me.

"He's taking control of my sex life?" I demanded. "Who the fuck does he think he is to tell me I can't have sex with anyone?"

"I think the point is that you can *only* have sex with *him*..."

"Fuck. That. I'm out." I turned away from JJ and stormed towards the door at the front of the salon, intending to walk my ass out of here, steal a car and drive the fuck away from this place and Fox Harlequin's bullshit for good. After popping back to grab Mutt of course. But then, I'd be gone.

I pulled the door open but instantly found my way blocked by two big ass guys with bulging muscles and tattoos on their tattoos.

"Move," I snarled, but they just exchanged a look and refused me.

JJ caught my hand and tugged me back into the salon with a sigh. "Just forget about that for now, Rogue," he begged. "Fox has got his boys keeping an eye on you even if you wanted to run and you came here to get your hair done, so why not just enjoy it and you can call Fox out on his shit when you get home later? You could even get your nails painted all nice for when you need to claw his eyes out."

I cursed colourfully enough to draw a gasp from a woman getting her hair styled by the window and Lucy shushed me as she smiled brightly and tugged me over to a pastel pink hairdressing chair on the far side of the room before pushing me down into it.

A display of fake pink and white roses curved over the mirror in front of me and I couldn't help but feel like I didn't belong here one bit. I was like a donkey at a horse market. I almost looked the part, but I just fell short of the line when you gave me a closer look.

"Did you want a bit of colour in your hair?" Lucy asked brightly, clearly deciding to ignore my outburst in favour of doing her job.

"Isn't that like stupid expensive?" I muttered. I'd never really done anything like that with my hair because there had always been better things to spend my money on, but I wasn't against the idea of getting a fresh look. I had come back from the dead after all so if I was going to be re-born then maybe I should do it with fancy new hair.

"I told you this is on me, sweetheart. Get whatever you want," JJ said, taking a seat in the chair behind the reception desk and throwing his feet up as he looked at me in the mirror.

Well, if JJ wanted to make sweeping statements about paying for whatever the hell I wanted done then I was happy to test the limits of his wallet for him. I was really pissed at Fox, but I was happy to take it out on his errand boy if I had to. Fox would get his later.

"What was it Fox called me?" I asked sweetly as an idea occurred to me. "A pretty brunette? Maybe he won't like me so much if I'm blonde then."

"His last girl was blonde," JJ supplied as he began flicking through a magazine on hair extensions. "And the one before that was a redhead. In fact, I'm pretty sure he's hooked up with girls with every colour of hair you can think of, so I doubt you're gonna land on one he's not had before. Not unless you wanna just go all out with rainbow hair." He laughed at his own joke, but my eyes met Lucy's in the mirror and her lips twitched in a way that said we were thinking the same thing.

"Ah, here we go," JJ muttered, but as I looked back at him, I found him ducking down beneath the desk, pushing himself underneath it and disappearing beneath the pink tablecloth.

"What the-" I began but Lucy pressed a finger to her lips to silence my questions a moment before the door swung open and a woman strode in looking like a movie star with three big men flanking her.

Lucy hurried over to greet her and she started making a big fuss of saying hello as the two biggest dudes moved past them and began looking around the salon. They opened the doors to the treatment rooms, checked out the back and generally seemed to be looking for something.

"You see, nothing and no one here besides me and the ladies," the woman said with a frustrated huff. "Honestly, I come here to *relax*, not fraternise with anyone."

"I'll be back in a few hours," the man who I guessed was her husband announced as he leaned in to place a kiss on her cheek. "Ronald and Duke will be right outside if you need them."

"Oh, at least let them go and sit in that little cafe down the street," the woman complained. "They can watch the door from there to make sure I'm not accosted and the ladies here can relax without them peering through the windows."

"Of course, my love," the husband agreed, jerking his head at the two men who dutifully headed outside before he handed a roll of cash to Lucy and left behind them.

Lucy led the woman to the room with the words *massage parlour* scrawled across the door and a few moments later, JJ appeared from beneath the desk.

He caught my gaze in the mirror, tossed me a wink then disappeared into the room behind the woman as Lucy closed the door after them and approached me again.

"I've got a nice selection of pastels," Lucy said like there was nothing weird about that whole situation at all. "Pink, blue, lilac, yellow, we can totally do that if you want?"

"Wouldn't a job like that require me to bleach my hair before beginning on the rainbow colours? That sounds expensive," I pointed out.

"It is," she agreed. "It's the most expensive colour job we do."

"Perfect. I'll have that then." I grinned at her in the mirror and Lucy chuckled, seeming to be onboard with my anti-ownership move. Girl power was alive and well in this place at least.

"I can get Carly to come do you a mani/pedi at the same time if you'd like?" Lucy offered but just as I was about to answer, a lusty moan came from behind the door where JJ and that rich woman had disappeared to.

"What are they-"

"Don't worry about that. Mrs Broadale pays extra for additional services when she comes in here," Lucy explained, winking at me in the mirror as my brain scrambled to keep up with that.

"You mean...he's...with her, in that room, alone-"

"Screwing her brains out? Yeah. She pays top dollar for him too. It's the perfect cover for rich married women to come and spend a few hours at the salon. JJ set this whole place up for me, fronted the cash for the salon to be fitted out and everything and all he does is show up from time to time to give a certain few clients *the special*."

"That's...innovative," I said as Mrs Broadale's moans came again, louder this time and drawing the attention of the woman getting her hair done at the front of the salon.

"Maybe I should come in for what she's having next time," she said with a chuckle and I laughed along as Lucy beckoned to the girl who was going to be doing my nails before heading off to find the hair dye she needed for my new look.

While she was out the back, she turned up the volume of the pop music that was playing throughout the salon and effectively hid the moans of the married woman who JJ was currently servicing.

I frowned down at the choice of nail polishes I had to pick between as I tried not to feel weird about what JJ was doing. It wasn't like I had anything against whores. I'd had plenty of friends who worked the sex trade in my lifetime, but there was just something about trying to marry my memories of the sweet boy who used to blush when I sat beside him with this sex god for sale who I saw in him now. Their confidence and attitudes to their bodies were like polar opposites and yet when he laughed or teased me, I could still see that boy I'd loved shining out from within his eyes. I guessed I just didn't like to think of him as being too different from the boy I'd known because I wasn't sure what that meant as far as who he was now.

I let the girl choose the colours for the nail polish and tried to relax as the two beauticians got to work. I had bigger things to concern myself over than JJ's choice in occupation. Fox Harlequin had drawn a line in the sand today. He'd decided to come at me with far more bullshit than I'd been expecting with this ownership crap and dying my hair a colour he wouldn't like wasn't even a drop in the ocean of the shit I was going to unleash on him if he decided to persist down this path.

I may have stooped to many things in the years that I'd been away from this place, but one thing I had no intention of ever being again was a possession. I wasn't his. Wasn't going to be his. And I was going to teach him a lesson about the woman I'd grown up into. Because they might have all changed in the last ten years, but they had nothing on me. I'd been reborn in suffering, hardship and a determination that could only be won by clawing your way up out of the dirt with nothing and no one to rely on but yourself. So bring it on Harlequin boys. Because if they thought they could force me to fall in with their bullshit, they had another thing coming.

The unicorn hair colour job ended up taking hours which I probably shouldn't have been surprised by, but in the end, I was pretty damn pleased with the results. I looked like a whole new girl and I found that I was glad about that. I wanted to move on from what Shawn had done to me and start a new chapter of my life where I was my own woman, standing on my own feet and daring the world to do its worst, because I'd already survived more than could ever be thrown at me again.

Lucy was super sweet and even though I hadn't been meaning to spill my life story to her, I had managed to give her enough snippets for her to figure out that I basically had nothing to my name and was stuck living in Fox's house until further notice. The complimentary champagne might have helped a little with loosening my tongue if I was being perfectly honest because I'd lost track of the amount of refills I'd had way back when she started adding the pink to my hair. She'd instantly figured out that my situation meant I had no makeup or hair products either and had given me the full works, expertly hiding the lingering bruises on my face and making my lashes look longer and fuller than should have been possible. Then she'd painted my lips a sugary pink colour that looked good enough to lick before putting together a huge bag full of all the products she'd used and more and adding it onto JJ's bill.

JJ had eventually emerged from his job with Mrs Broadale a couple of hours ago, but when he'd realised I was going to be in here for the long haul, he'd left me to it and headed off down the boulevard saying he had errands to run.

Of course, I'd given it five minutes before asking for a bathroom break and had tried to make a run for it out the back door, but I'd come face to face with three Harlequins who were oh so conveniently hanging out there to make sure I didn't do exactly what I'd been aiming to do.

In hindsight that was probably a good thing because I'd been in the middle of a bleach cycle with my hair at the time and I was going to guess that if I'd left it in for too long while I ran, I would have really fucked up my long locks.

Just as Lucy was finishing up on styling my hair into loose curls which trailed down my spine, JJ reappeared looking really damn pleased with himself while carrying a butt load of bags from various stores.

"Fuck me, rainbow child, I really hope you didn't expect this look to turn Fox off of you because I can assure you, you've failed spectacularly. You make me wanna find out what the rainbow tastes like," he said, biting his fist in an over the top way and groaning as he took me in.

"Save it for your clients, big boy," I teased, rolling my eyes as I tried not to get all hot and bothered over the way he was looking at me, but he was making it all kinds of hard. "Where have you been anyway?"

"I had some business to attend to down the street and then I went shopping," JJ replied, moving closer to me and smirking as he placed the bags down beside me and indicated for me to look inside them.

I reached for one at random and found it full of lingerie, pulling out a tiny red lacy thing and arching an eyebrow at him.

"Is this scrap of dental floss meant to be for me?" I asked.

"No need to go overboard on the thanks, sweetheart. I got you everything you might need though - panties, bras, bikinis, shirts, shorts, dresses, shoes, a vibrator, socks, a couple of hats, a-"

"Back the fuck up there, did you just say you got me a vibrator?" I half yelled, forgetting in my ever-so-slightly-inebriated state that the salon had been filling up with clients over the last few hours and drawing more than enough curious looks.

"Sure. You said yourself you don't wanna fuck Fox and he sure as hell won't be letting you fuck anyone else, so I thought I'd provide you the tool you might need to bolster your willpower." JJ's eyes sparkled with amusement, but there was something else he wasn't saying which I couldn't quite figure out. "So come on, don't you wanna get changed?"

"Gah, you're impossible," I growled, rummaging through the bags as I hunted for something to change into. Not because he wanted me to, but because these shorts really were too small for me and they were cutting off the blood supply to my ass. I'd unbuttoned the fly several hours ago and had been dreading forcing it closed again ever since.

I found way too much cute stuff in the bags and mentally cursed JJ for buying me shit I liked before selecting a navy sun dress with a halter strap and a pair of sandals to show off my new pedicure.

I stalked away into the small bathroom to get changed, taking a moment to appreciate my new look in the mirror when I was done. This girl didn't look like some asshole had nearly killed her. She looked strong and determined and damn fierce. And if I could look like her then I sure as fuck was going to *be* her. The Harlequin boys might have been aiming to break down my barriers and be testing me in ways I'd never expected to be tested, but I wasn't going to bow down to their desires. If they wanted to come at me, then I was going to be ready.

JJ was paying up when I emerged in my new clothes and I had to fight a blush at the look he gave me as I walked towards him. Goddammit, I wasn't a blusher. I certainly wasn't sweet enough to get flustered or innocent enough not to know what to do with that look he was giving me if I wanted to. But I was also repeatedly being made into a teenage girl again by these boys as my memories and reality collided in ever more flustering ways. I just needed to be sure I didn't let them know it.

Lucy looked as pleased as pie as she took a crazy amount of money from his hand and I had to fight the urge to let my eyes bug out of my face while JJ didn't even flinch at the price.

"Give me a twirl then, pretty girl," he urged, his eyes light and full of mischief that made me want to play along.

I rolled my eyes then spun in a circle for him, only stumbling a little bit – because free champers and all – then gasping as his hands caught my waist, stopping my movement with my back to him.

"You forgot the tags," he murmured, the heat of his body caressing mine even though he wasn't actually pressed up against me.

I held still as he gently brushed my multicoloured hair over my shoulder, his fingertips dancing across my skin and raising goosebumps in their wake before he found the tag hanging from the tie at my neck and snapped it free.

Instead of releasing me right away, JJ's fingers slid down my shoulder blades, making my breath catch as he caressed the ink on my skin.

"Why angel wings?" he asked in a low voice, his lips almost brushing my ear with the closeness of him.

"I liked the idea of someone having my back, even when I knew I was all alone," I murmured, not entirely sure why I'd offered him that truth, but the large pair of feathered wings which ran down my back always made me feel a little like someone might be watching over me.

I turned my head to look at him as his fingers continued to slip down my bare back and was surprised by the pain I found in his gaze.

"Rogue..." he began, his voice rough like he had something desperately important to say to me and because I was a damn fool, I just stayed there, his hands on my body, my heart thrumming with the closeness of him, my gaze locked on his as I waited for…what exactly? I didn't know, but for one weak moment I wanted it to be something.

JJ glanced away from me, seeming to remember where we were and he offered me a tight smile.

"You look unbelievable." He pressed a swift kiss to my cheek which burned my flesh then stepped away from me, turning to grab the bags of shopping and leaving me breathless as I tried to figure out what that had just been.

I quickly regained my composure, smiling at Lucy as I said goodbye and following JJ to the back door again.

Fox's men all greeted him as we emerged from the salon, their curious gazes taking me in but not lingering too long.

I ignored them and walked with JJ back to the black pickup. He tossed the shopping in the back and opened my door for me like a real gent which we both knew he well and truly wasn't and before I knew it, we were driving back to the lions' den.

JJ was quiet on the way back, though he kept shooting me glances that I was pointedly ignoring while enjoying the fading buzz of my champagne. If he had something to say then he could damn well say it without me forcing it out of him.

A sign for Subway caught my attention up ahead and I groaned, shooting him a pleading look which finally dragged a grin back out of him.

"Fine. I'll get some for all of us," he said, pulling into the drive through and ordering a bunch of subs for us which made my rumbling stomach stupid happy.

The moment we had the sandwiches in the car, I dug mine out and started unwrapping it.

"Fox doesn't really like us eating in his car," JJ said half-heartedly. "And he prefers it if we can all eat together back at the house..."

"Nooo," I groaned, peeling the paper away from my hot sub and inhaling deeply. "I need it now, J."

"I'm sure you can wait five minutes," he said, reaching out to try and shove it back into the bag on my lap but I lurched away from him.

"I need a foot long in my mouth, Johnny James," I warned him in a serious tone. "I need to put it in my mouth and swallow it down good and make sure I lick all of the-"

"Shit, Rogue, you're gonna get me in trouble if you keep going down that road," JJ warned, trying to grab my sub again and I cursed him as I lurched towards the window, losing a slice of tomato in the process which fell down onto the carpet with a wet slap of mayo.

"Whoops," I said as JJ groaned and I took the opportunity to take a big bite of my sub. It. Was. Heaven.

JJ pulled the truck up the drive to the house and turned down into the underground garage while I made every effort to demolish my food in as little time as possible.

"Give that here," JJ demanded as he parked up, trying to snatch it from me and making me squeal as he half dove on top of me. "We need to eat together."

"Leave me alone, J!" I shouted. "I just need it in my mouth. Let me put the foot long in my mouth. Stop trying to sandwich block me!"

The bag of subs for everyone else fell on the floor as I tried to escape, but the damn child locks were keeping me captive once more. I managed to wriggle out of JJ's grip, kneeing him in the side before flipping over and throwing my front half out of the open window where I could hold my sub out of his reach and take another bite.

JJ grabbed hold of my hips as he tried to drag me back and he half climbed on top of me so that he could attempt to steal my sandwich. But no man came between me and a foot long. Ever.

I squealed again as I managed to take another bite of my food, laughing as I felt mayo smear up my cheek but still tasting victory on my tongue as I chewed.

"What the hell are you two doing?" the surly growl of Fox's voice alerted me to his presence half a second before he grabbed the truck door handle and wrenched it open.

Fox caught me before I managed to faceplant the concrete, but JJ wasn't so lucky, rolling as he fell out of the truck and coming to a halt at Fox's feet while I was set down on mine.

"Ah, look who it is," I sneered, my light mood darkening at the sight of this tanned, blonde, super hot, super asshole. "My owner. Did you get me a nice leash yet or am I still going to have to sleep in the doggy cage until I'm house trained?"

"What the fuck are you talking about?" Fox demanded. "And do you know you've got mayonnaise all over your face? And that your hair is like sixty different colours?"

"Well, if your new pet isn't living up to the beauty standards you laid out for me then feel free to set me loose into the wild," I growled, taking another savage bite from my somewhat squashed sub and accidentally taking a bite of the paper it was wrapped in too.

"What the hell is going on here, JJ?" Fox asked, turning his attention to his friend as he got to his feet and giving me a moment to try and pluck the wet paper out of my mouth and wipe away the mayo which was coating my cheek, because it was definitely undermining the seriousness of my anger.

"You know what Rogue is like with food. She went all seagull in the car and I was trying to make her stop so that we could all eat together," JJ explained.

"I did not go all seagull," I growled, but I still had a mouthful of food so it came out kinda muffled.

I chewed and swallowed, tossing the bit of paper away and using the mirror on the side of the truck to check my face for mayo.

"I'm pretty sure you actually squawked," JJ teased and I stood uptight, whirling around to narrow my eyes on him.

"Well I'm not the one who-"

"Fuck off, JJ, I want to talk to Rogue alone," Fox interrupted us and my scowl got a whole lot deeper as I looked up at the blonde asshole as he pulled rank.

JJ looked inclined to argue but I raised my chin, my gaze fixed on Fox as I shook my head. "It's fine, J. I can talk to the dickwad alone. I'm not afraid of him."

Fox practically growled at me and JJ released a low whistle as he grabbed the bag of subs and held a hand out for my half eaten one too.

I cursed beneath my breath and handed it over. I wanted my fists free for punching anyway.

I entered into a glare off with Fox while we waited for JJ to walk away and head up to the house and tension crackled between the two of us like electricity.

The moment the door closed behind JJ, Fox took a step towards me and I instantly stepped back.

"You don't need to touch me to talk to me, asshole," I growled and Fox tsked as his gaze trailed over me from the top of my unicorn hair right down to the tips of my freshly pedicured toes. "Do you like it?" I asked obnoxiously. "It was the most expensive style they did and it had the added benefit of getting rid of my brunette hair which you loved so much."

"Who said I loved it?" he asked, reaching out to shut the truck door so that the sound of it slamming echoed around the garage.

"What was the wording exactly?" I asked, placing a finger on my lips as I faked having to think about it. "Oh yeah, that's it. *The pretty little brunette who belongs to Fox.*"

"You're right," he agreed, taking a step closer to me. "Calling you pretty was a bad move. It doesn't even begin to encompass the way you look, hummingbird."

I raised my chin, swallowing back a lump in my throat at the use of that damn nickname again.

"Good," I said, choosing to breeze on past that minefield. "And I'm five foot nine, asshole, so I'm not exactly little. Just because you tower over me doesn't mean everyone else in the world does. And now I'm not a brunette either. So it sounds like your girl isn't me."

I took a step forward like I intended to walk away from him, but he caught my waist and pushed me back against the truck instead, moving his hands up to grip the roof either side of my head and caging me in as he leaned down to look me in the eyes.

"You came back to me bruised and hurting," he growled. "And you won't tell me the name of the motherfucker who dared to lay his hands on you. You walk into my house with hate in your eyes and venom on your tongue and speak to me in a way that I would kill anyone else for. And then when I offer you the protection of the whole of Sunset Cove knowing that you're mine so that no one in their right mind would so much as dare to look at you wrong, let alone hurt you again, you throw it back in my face like I've done something unforgivable to you."

"I never asked you for a damn thing," I hissed, refusing to blink as he glared at me with those forest green eyes of his. "JJ dragged me back here kicking and screaming. So how about you just let me go and save yourself the hassle of my company?"

"You can keep bullshitting yourself with that line if you want to, Rogue, but it isn't flying with me. You knew you couldn't come back to this city without me finding out. Hell, you thought my dad was alive and you came back here despite the fact that you thought there was an axe hanging poised to cut you off at the neck if you so much as stepped a toe over the border. But you came anyway. You came because this is your home. It's where you belong, and you ached for it the entire time you were gone."

"You're wrong," I replied fiercely.

Fox reached out slowly and tugged on the leather necklace around my neck, drawing the key hanging from it up to dangle between us. "Am I?"

"I don't have to put up with this crap," I growled, knocking the key out of his hand so that the solid weight of it fell against my chest again. "I just need you to understand that I am not, never have been and never will be *your girl*. I don't care if the only reason you spread that rumour was for my own protection - I don't want it. I don't want-"

Fox leaned in suddenly and pressed his mouth to mine, stealing the breath from my lungs and freezing me in place as I gasped against his hard, demanding lips.

For the briefest, craziest second, I almost gave in, almost melted into a puddle and let him prove me wrong in everything I'd just said. But then I remembered standing there in the rain as he took the only things I'd ever cared about from me. Took the only thing I'd ever *been* from me. And left me all alone with nothing and no one for ten fucking years.

I slammed my palms into his chest and shoved him back as hard as I could. He didn't move a single inch, but he broke our kiss, glaring down at me as my lips tingled and a thousand what the fucks danced across my mind.

"Tell me you're not mine again," he growled gripping my chin between his strong fingers and forcing me to meet his gaze, like he thought I couldn't possibly deny it now.

"Dead girls don't belong to anyone, Fox," I hissed, my heart pounding and thrashing with too fucking much of everything which I refused to try and process. "Dead girls don't even have a heart to offer out."

I yanked my jaw out of his grip, ducked beneath his other arm and set my gaze on the door which led back to the house as I stalked away from him.

"You never used to be the kind of girl to run from her problems," Fox called after me, his voice echoing in the underground space.

"Well that's just something else you don't know about me anymore," I called back. "Because running away is my fucking specialty these days." *And you were the one who got me into the trend.*

"There's nowhere to run now you're locked in this house," he pointed out.

I ground my teeth but forced myself not to snap back. That was what he wanted. Fox had always been the kind who angled for a fight the moment the tide didn't turn his way. He didn't like anything to be left unresolved and always wanted to hash it out, or more accurately, force his opinion through so hard that everyone else was left with no option but to cave in.

But not this time. And not this girl. He wasn't going to back me into a corner and force me to resolve shit that couldn't be resolved. What we'd had long in the past was destroyed the moment they broke their word to me. We'd all sworn once that we would always have each other's backs no matter what. And they'd proven at the first test that that wasn't the case.

If he seriously thought he had me beat because he was forcing me to stay in his fancy ass home then he was in for a rude awakening. Fox Harlequin hadn't even begun to understand the girl I was now. And I had the feeling he was in for a real shock when he figured out that his little hummingbird was never going to bend to his rules.

CHAPTER NINE

I worked myself close to a coma in my gym, Raiders, which sat down on the boardwalk fronting the beach, gazing out at the view of the sea and sand.

My muscles burned and sweat poured down my bare chest as I drained a bottle of water and tilted my face towards the air-conditioning so an icy breeze gusted over me. There were a couple of guys sparring in the boxing ring and the rest of the place was teeming with muscle heads pumping iron. All of them were Harlequins. No one else was allowed to sign up here. They paid us the full two hundred dollar membership fee every month, but really they were only supplying us with twenty five percent of that. We topped up the rest, paying them dirty cash to cover the transactions that came from their bank accounts, laundering the money and keeping our hands squeaky clean in the process.

"Aren't you supposed to eat dinner at home on Sundays?" Brandy called from the office, resting her hip up against the doorway and smirking at me. She was as wrinkled as a ballsack but still wore a tight pink mini-skirt and a low-cut top, showing off her fake tits this job had no doubt paid for. Her hair was bleached blonde and curling, cropped short to show off her large hoop earrings.

"Did Fox call?" I asked, swiping up my towel and slinging it over my shoulder.

"No, sweetie, I just know your routine. I'm observant like that." She winked, but I had the feeling she was lying to me. The three ignored texts on my phone from Fox were evidence enough that he would have tried to contact me some other way.

I painted on a crooked smile, slowly walking towards her and resting my own shoulder against the doorway, casual as fuck, dangerous as hell.

"Hey Brandy? You ever lie to my face again and I'll cut you loose. Fox isn't the boss of this place. I am. So you answer to me before him in this gym, got that?"

Her faced paled and she nodded quickly, straightening. "I didn't mean any offence, Mr Cohen." She bowed her head respectfully and I ran my tongue over my teeth then burst out laughing, clapping her on the shoulder and making her wobble on her five inch heels.

"Just kidding, darling." I grinned and she released a nervous chuckle. "But seriously." I let my smile fall flat and her lower lip trembled as she tried to figure out if I was joking or not. I cracked up again, leaving her to work it out as I turned away, heading into the showers.

It wasn't long before I was dressed in my stonewash jeans and a black Ducati t-shirt and I headed out of the gym, spinning my motorcycle key on my finger. I swung my leg over my navy blue bike and drove off down the road at high speed, following the boardwalk everyone called The Mile - because it was, well, a mile long - and racing toward home.

The sun was setting over the ocean and the sky was lit in darkest magenta as it slid away beyond the horizon, seeming to pool into the water.

The last rays of light were draining from the sky as I pulled through the gates to Harlequin House and took the ramp down into the underground garage. I parked my bike beside Fox's truck, taking a smoke from my pocket and lighting it up as I walked through the range of cars, trucks and boats we kept down here. Most of them were stolen - or bought with stolen cash. Any lifted vehicle had to come from at least a ten mile radius according to The Code. Fox's rules, not mine. Though that one I was in agreement with so we never crossed paths with the rightful owners ever again. Others? Not so much.

Especially doubling up on jobs. I was efficient, me. We could've been pulling off ten times the amount of jobs if Fox would just listen to me more often. He wouldn't even let us pull more than one big job a month because he wanted us to 'keep a low profile'. Which meant half the time, we were still living from week to week on petty cash, waiting for payday because it took weeks to launder our prize.

And I wasn't even gonna get started on the cuts we took. Fifty percent split three ways, while the other fifty went to the Harlequin empire, plus paying off assholes left and right for who even knew what, and funding all kinds of shit that I didn't get a say in. We should have been pocketing every last penny if you asked me. But no one ever did.

I took the stairs up into the house, pushing through the glass door into the hallway. I was met with a charging bull who shoved me against the wall and my heart didn't even lurch. Fox was angry. What a surprise.

"We have work to do tonight, asshole. You wanted more responsibility in this job so I handed it to you, and this is how you repay me?" he asked in a low growl, his hand fisted in my shirt.

"Is the ghost still here?" I asked around my cigarette and his eyes narrowed.

"Yeah, she's still here," he said darkly. "Problem?"

I shoved his hand off of me, taking the cigarette between my fingers and blowing out a heavy breath of smoke. "Look, man, don't take this the wrong way, but she's your kryptonite. All of our fucking kryptonite actually. And instead of telling her to get fucked, you offered her a cosy bed in our house. In a house we don't normally let anyone into unless we *all* approve it."

Fox sighed, pushing a hand into his dark blonde hair and turning his back on me. "She's different. She's already one of us."

"No," I growled, striding after him and pressing a hand to his shoulder, making him look at me. His brow was furrowed and I suddenly felt like a jackass for ignoring his texts. I just wasn't in a good headspace lately and now Rogue had turned up, it had sent me into a tailspin. But it came from a good place. Mostly. "She's not the same girl we grew up with. Just like we're not the same boys who grew up with her."

His mouth pressed into a flat line and he took in my expression like he was trying to hear me out, but his alpha instincts were fighting against him too hard. I knew how he felt about Rogue. We'd all fucking been there. I'd cared for her too once, but we couldn't just let this new version of her back into our house without even a single background check. I'd been avoiding the chick like she was lava creeping in my back door since she'd arrived. And my instincts said that wasn't far from the truth.

"I'm not sending her away," he said, his tone firm, allowing no room for negotiation. "I'm not going to let her go when I just got her back." There was a possessive undertone to his voice that got my blood boiling.

"Listen to yourself," I snapped. "She's doing it already, getting in your head, making you *weak*. You wanna be in a position like we were after Maverick got out of prison?"

"It won't be like that," he snarled dangerously and my heart pounded furiously. "We were taken by surprise then, no one can touch us anymore. And you can't tell me you didn't feel something when she walked through that door, Chase. She's part of us. That hasn't changed."

"Well maybe not for *you*," I said, sneering. "But to me, she's just a stray who JJ dragged in off the street who we know nothing about. For all we know she's here to gut us in our sleep. I know you wanna protect us, Fox. You always have our backs. So why are you taking this risk for the sake of some chick?"

He scrubbed a hand over the stubble on his jaw like I was exasperating him. "JJ found her in town and she ran the hell away from him. Not to mention the bruises all over her face that some fucking deadbeat asshole gave her. You think that sounds like she's after something to you?" he pushed, his eyes daring me to keep fighting him on this.

My heart twisted uncomfortably at his words, but I had to stick to my gut. I knew being a stubborn ass wouldn't get me anywhere with my argument, but the thing about being a stubborn ass was that I couldn't even talk myself out of a decision once I'd made it. And when it came to Rogue Easton, I was fully decided that she was trouble with a capital everything.

"She didn't come to Sunset Cove for our help then did she, Fox? So what did she come here for?" I demanded, desperate for him to see reason.

He gritted his jaw, shaking his head then walking away, clearly done with this conversation. "We've got work to do, and the dog had your dinner so you can make yourself something when we're done."

"For fuck's sake," I muttered. Fox cooked every Sunday and his food was like a slice of goddamn heaven on my tongue. Now the girl's mutt was apparently eating better than I would be tonight.

"You made your choice not to be here this evening," he said coolly, reading my damn mind.

He rounded the light wood stairway and led me up to our office on the second floor. JJ was at the desk inside, his bare feet up on the surface, a mojito in his hand, and a cocky look on his face.

He looked to me, arching a brow. "Well look who finally showed up, el gruñón." He kicked out of his seat, smirking at me and planting his drink down on the desk beside the notes laid out on it.

"Did you miss me, el coqueto?" A teasing grin pulled at my lips. A latino chick had gotten drunk and pissy with me and JJ a few years back on Sunset Beach and we mocked each other with the nicknames she'd given us from time to time. I was 'el gruñón' – the grumpy one – and JJ was el coqueto – the flirty one.

"I missed you bad, big boy." JJ jumped on me, hugging me like a damn koala and I slapped his back as I laughed. He released me after an inappropriately long squeeze, encouraging me toward the desk and I gazed down at the papers laid out before me with interest.

"Catch me up then," I said as Fox swept around the desk and dropped into the chair JJ had just vacated. He picked up a diagram of a ferry and tapped a circled area in the hold. "One of our men who works at the docks got us this today. He has it on good authority that all goods travelling to Ballena Island do so on this ferry."

"La Mujer Bonita," I read the name of the boat aloud. "Owned by Carlos Ortiz."

"His wife comes in the club," JJ said. "And woof, let me tell you, she's no pretty lady. She's got hair on the chins on her chins and sweats like a pig in heat when I grind my dick in her face."

"Has she ever propositioned you?" Fox asked, leaning back in his seat and stacking his hands on his stomach.

"Nah, but...I mean she likes what I'm selling, she gets that hungry look in her eyes during the show. I could test the waters. She's usually in on Thursdays for ladies' night."

"Alright, dangle the bait and see if she bites," Fox instructed. "We can do it without her if we have to, but if you can get her talking about that boat then find out what you can. Our guy says Carlos started out the ferry business thirty odd years back after regularly transporting his friends from their home on Ballena Island to the mainland. So I'm guessing his old lady knows a thing or two about that boat too."

"Got it," JJ agreed.

"Are the watches gonna be here?" I tapped on the hold in the ferry.

"Most likely," Fox said. "They're heading to a jewellers out on the island who open in the summer for tourists."

Ballena Island was notorious for its swanky city tourists who wanted the 'real west coast experience'. They showed up with their polished surfboards, ass cheek implants and bleached white teeth every year, ripe for the picking. There was always money to be made off of people like that. The kind that floated through life like their farts tasted like strawberries and money grew on their cocks. Some of them accidentally drifted into our end of town sometimes and they scurried back to their resorts and beach huts pronto, preferring to remain inside their traveller's bubble as they soaked up their oh-so-authentic boho bullshit experience.

"Rumour has it the mayor wants to set up an official ferry that runs that trip by the start of the season. It'll be built like a brick shit house with safes and storage rooms for everything going out there. Carlos's little family-run ferry won't be taking any precious cargo once that happens. So this is our only chance to hit it," Fox explained with that hungry look he got when there was money on the table. "I've been talking with our pawn broker and he says the watches will be travelling in one of these." He pushed his iPad across the desk and I took in the photo of a metal lockbox which had a lock code on it.

"So we steal the box?" I guessed and JJ bounced on his heels, looking to Fox who was smirking.

"No, it's got a tracker and an alarm system that'll get us fifty shades of fucked if we try to force it open," Fox said, but the glimmer in his eyes said he wasn't concerned about that.

"So what's the plan?" I pressed, not liking being out of the loop as the two of them shared a grin.

"We got a tip off that the code was sent to the jeweller yesterday by express mail so he could open the box when it arrived," Fox explained, swinging from side to side in the office chair. "One of JJ's girls works the mailroom on Saturdays." He picked up an envelope from the desk with an express stamp on it and tossed it at me. I pulled out the letter from inside it, smiling at the code staring back at me. Man, I loved being us.

"We sent a forgery in its place. It was seriously quick work on JJ's behalf." Fox tossed him an appreciative glance and JJ's chest puffed out.

A ripple of jealousy passed through me, but I ignored it, placing the letter back on the desk. We all had our roles to play, and I'd play mine soon enough.

"So, what do we need transport wise?" I asked.

"We need a fishing boat. Something old, inconspicuous. Paid for in cash. And clothes to match too. We'll need a car waiting for us when we return to shore as well. Again, keep it lowkey. I want the getaway car parked in a blind spot away from the main beach with a change of clothes in the trunk." Fox looked at me expectantly and a smile tugged at my mouth.

Vehicles were my forte. And I knew exactly how to get my hands on what we needed. "No problem."

"We'll need tools to breach the door to the hold," JJ said thoughtfully, tapping on the diagram again. "If it's a secured door we might need something explosive too."

"We can't force that door," Fox said firmly then leaned forward and rested his elbows on the desk, all cunning like. He really lived up to his name sometimes. "It needs to be picked. So if it's reinforced, you'd better find out from his wife so we can come up with a way to deal with it." He fixed JJ with a stare and he nodded seriously, running a hand down the back of his neck.

"Why can't we force it?" I frowned.

"Because there'll be too many eyes on us pulling this off in broad daylight. There'll be plenty of boats out on the water, not to mention the coastguard keeping watch, but once the ferry is far enough out to sea we'll board it and get hold of the contraband fast. I have a guy who I can pay off to shut down the engine so that we can get on and off, but he says it'll only stay motionless for twenty minutes before they get it going again. But that should be plenty of time. That box will have travelled a hundred miles to get here, there's no way they'll be able to tell at what point the watches were stolen if we're subtle about it, and the least likely place will be on the boat in the middle of the ocean." Fox stacked up the notes as I grinned. The dude really was a genius sometimes. And the thought of preparing for this new job was getting my heart pumping and adrenaline coursing through my veins.

"Who wants a drink?" I asked, heading to the door and they both agreed.

I opened the door and my heart clenched as I found a very suspicious looking rainbow-haired girl scurrying away down the hall. I strode after her at a fast pace, my mood taking a dive as I grabbed her arm and twisted her around to face me.

"Spying on us, ghost girl?" I hissed and she pursed her lips, prising my hand off of her flesh before shrugging.

"I don't know what you mean," she said innocently.

"Don't give me that shit. What did you hear?" I demanded, sensing Fox and JJ moving up behind me.

"Nothing," she said sweetly. "Just something about a boat, a code and a box of watches." She smirked and I grunted in fury, looking back at the others.

"This is why she has to leave, this is unacceptable," I snarled and Fox moved to my side.

I lifted my chin, waiting for him to berate her as I fixed her in my sights. Finally, he had to see what she was now. Trouble. And a fucking sneak. She could be feeding information back to our enemies for all we knew.

My gaze moved down her body, taking in the white tee she wore which showed a pink bikini underneath it. My dick jerked in my pants and my teeth clenched tighter as I tried to ignore that reaction to her. I'd been a fool for her once just like Fox and JJ had been. I wasn't going to make that mistake twice.

"If you wanted in on our meetings, hummingbird, then you'd have to swear in to the Harlequins. Which obviously you aren't allowed to do," Fox warned her and she rolled her eyes.

"Good," Rogue agreed. "I'd rather take the pistol you keep hidden under your coffee table and blow my brains out than join your gang." She tossed her hair and walked away while JJ chuckled, earning himself a punch in the arm from me.

"Great. Now she knows where to get a weapon," I muttered.

"I know where four of your hidden weapons are actually," she called lightly as she disappeared down the stairs.

"See." I pointed after her, staring at Fox who was watching her go like a man possessed. "We can't let this stand."

"Chill out, bro," JJ said, laughing. "It's Rogue. We know her."

"We don't know her." I rounded on him, baring my teeth. "Not anymore."

Was everyone in this house crazy except me?

"I'll move the weapons if it makes you feel better, but she's staying no matter how much you bitch about it, brother. Question me on it again and I'll make you regret it," Fox said in a deadly tone then headed downstairs after the snake in our house and my hands curled into tight fists as JJ followed.

I jogged after them down to the kitchen where Rogue was crouched down petting her dog as he lapped at a bowl of water. I noticed her toenails were each painted a different colour just like her hair and I ground my teeth harder as my eyes followed the curves of her bronzed legs up to the skull and roses tattoo on her thigh. Rogue Easton hadn't just gotten hot in the last ten years. She'd gotten fucking third-degree burns scalding. She'd always been my type, but this girl with her quirky hair and the white band tee tied up over her toned stomach and fitted Billabong shorts was just - *fuck*. No. I had to stop looking.

I walked over to the fridge, ignoring my friends as JJ made a show of spinning bottles in his hands as he fixed Fox and Rogue cocktails. I took a whole bottle of rum for myself, turning around and walking straight out the sliding door onto the patio. I was fuming as I dropped down to lie on one of the sun loungers, not bothering to turn on the fairy lights which hung from the awning. I lit a cigarette and toked on it until my lungs couldn't take any more poison, breathing out the smoke before twisting the rum cap off and swallowing a long swig.

Fuck this shit. Fox was going to walk us right into the same pit trap we'd fallen into ten years ago. As soon as our balls had dropped, that girl had become the centre of a war in our group that had threatened to break us apart for good. When we were kids, it didn't matter. We all loved her as a friend, and what more we felt we didn't understand or know what to do with. But when puberty gifted us raging testosterone and muscles that gave us the power to fight for her, that was when the cracks had started to form. I'd wanted her as much as the rest of them had. We'd all been pushing her to choose, trying to win her from each other, but hindsight was twenty-twenty and when I looked back on it now, I realised we should've sent her packing the second she got between us like that. They were my brothers. And I'd lost one already because of her. I sure as shit wasn't going to lose another. There was no one for me outside of this house. Those two guys were my whole fucking family. And with the way they were both looking at her, I knew it wouldn't be long before the shit started to fly.

Not on my watch.

I picked up the baseball cap I'd left here earlier and shoved it down over my head, pulling it low so I could shut out the world as I laid back on the lounger. One cigarette turned to three and I swear I hadn't chain smoked this much since my momma had died. If there was a god, he sucked ass at choosing the people he took from this world. My dad deserved to go a long time ago, but he'd beaten two rounds of cancer and clung to life like a fucking cockroach.

Apparently I'd inherited the same immortal genes from him. I'd taken two bullets last year and had the scars on my abdomen to prove it. That was why I never bothered to quit smoking. Fox was all about healthy fucking living. But what good was that in the lives we led? I wasn't going out of this world because of the tar in my lungs. No chance. One day, a bullet would get too near to my heart or a knife would cut too deep and that would be that. I didn't plan on wasting the life I did have in the meantime. That was why, when we weren't working a job, I spent my time fucking, smoking, drinking and just fucking *living*. If it brought me pleasure, I made a goddamn habit out of it. And if it didn't, I made sure I had nothing to do with it.

JJ understood that better than Fox. Though the difference between me and him was that he was an optimist who read mommy porn in his free time and always had so many hopeful, sunshine soaked plans for the future. Fox had stopped making plans beyond the next few weeks the moment Rogue had left our lives. He used to be so...full. Now he was like a half drunk can of soda with all the fizz let out of it. I'd tried my best to heal that wound in him when Rogue had left. But I'd had my own wounds to lick, and in the end, we'd all just found the best way to deal with our scars was to stop talking about them. About *her*.

Someone moved the lounger to my left and a soft body dropped onto it. I tipped my hat up, peeking over at the company I hadn't asked for.

Rogue lay with her long legs stretched out and a beer in her hand. I could hardly see the bruises on her face in the dark out here, but as I dragged on my cigarette, the cherry lit them up, making anger burn hot and potent in my chest. Why wouldn't she give us a name? It'd been a whole week and she still wouldn't give us a damn thing. I'd tie the guy to the back of my bike and drag him through the streets of Sunset Cove in payment for this. But I had no way of finding out who was responsible without her input. Besides, why should I care anyway? She wasn't my friend anymore. She wasn't my anything anymore. Still, I'd killed assholes for less than this without knowing the ones they'd hurt. I liked playing karma. All I needed was a good reason to strike and I was the scariest motherfucker in the room.

"You picked the wrong Harlequin to bother, ghost," I muttered, letting my hat drop back over my eyes.

"I'm not here for you." A clicking noise sounded as she turned on the outdoor heater and warmth blazed from the fire at the top of it.

"If you're cold, why'd you come outside?" I growled.

"Well I didn't see you lurking like a fucking shadow out here," she said.

I sat up, leaning close to her and pushing the butt of my cigarette into her beer, making it hiss as it went out. Her lips parted indignantly as I stood up and glared down at her. "Why don't you take your dog and your flowery rainbow hair and get the fuck out of our house? Go back to wherever you came from, ghost."

"This *is* where I came from, asshole," she said coolly and my gaze travelled down to the key hanging around her neck on a leather necklace. I'd clocked it the second she'd arrived here. That key was one of five and all of them held a ticket to something we'd long given up on getting our hands on ever again.

"Is that why you're here?" I asked suspiciously, pointing out the key. "You wanna try your luck and steal the rest of the keys?"

She stroked her thumb over it, shrugging one shoulder. "I don't know what you're talking about, this is my grandmomma's key."

"Drop the shit," I hissed. The girl didn't even have a grandmomma.

She got to her feet, casual as fuck as she pulled her top off and dropped her shorts so she was standing in front of me in her skimpy pink bikini, making my cock harden just like that.

Fuck me. That body.

She was tanned all over her toned flesh and I wanted to pull at the strings of her bikini bottoms to check if that trend continued. And if it did, that meant she liked to sunbathe naked which was a mental image I really wanted to verify the accuracy of.

Damn beautiful ghost tits. She is not getting in my head.

"You should really try chilling out sometime, Nathan." She pressed her finger under my chin to close my slack jaw then sauntered past me.

"Nathan?" I spat, turning to watch her and my eyes immediately fell to her pert ass cheeks before she dove into the pool and disappeared into its depths.

I seized the moment to adjust my swelling dick in my jeans, trying not to be head fucked by this girl all over again. She'd gotten to me before, I knew the taste of her spell. And I wasn't going to fall under it again.

She resurfaced in the middle of the pool and floated on her back, gazing up at the stars hanging above us in the sky, acting like I wasn't even there.

She knows my name isn't fucking Nathan.

I was too stubborn to leave so I just sat back down on my lounger, my elbows on my knees as I continued to watch the siren in the water, her hair shimmering colourfully around her as she tried to lure me in. But I didn't let any girl get under my flesh anymore, none of us did. We'd all built our own type of armour and mine was made of ice and spite. No one had gotten within a mile of my heart since her. But when I looked at her out there, I was painfully aware of the cut she'd left on that ruinous muscle, a wound which was starting to pull apart and bleed.

"Where is he?" she asked after a while, her gaze still on the stars.

"Who?" I grunted, sipping my rum again and figuring oblivion was probably a good friend to hang out with tonight.

"Maverick," she said simply.

His name was a bullet to my chest, a blade in my skull. I swilled a measure of rum in my mouth, avoiding answering, unsure if I even wanted to answer. What did I owe her anyway? But then I thought of the night she'd left and guilt stirred in my gut. We'd abandoned her as deeply as she'd abandoned us. I knew I wasn't innocent in any of this. But I'd also watched my friends shatter over her for years. Fox had never let go, always searching for her, always sure the next lead would take us to her. But all the trails inevitably ran cold.

She had been gone as completely as if she were dead. And I'd figured out we were better off that way a long time before Fox and JJ ever gave up on her. But eventually, they did. And things got better. We weren't completely broken anymore. We had fun again. We built a life, a family. The three of us were stronger than ever. If she'd stayed, we would have lost each other. She would have driven a wedge between us so deep that we all would have been cast adrift.

But I had a dark secret that no one else was privy to. I knew who she would have chosen. My heart had been ripped out a while before anyone else's when I'd learned that fact. But I'd never uttered a word of what I'd witnessed to anyone. Not even to her. But finding out you're not the one to the girl you would have died for was a pretty bitter pill to swallow. I'd swallowed that motherfucker down and moved on eventually though. That was life. It was a soul-sucking bitch.

I let the silence stretch between us, figuring it didn't matter if she knew the truth. Maybe if she knew then she'd realise staying here in hopes of getting her hands on the rest of those keys was a fool's game. It wasn't gonna happen. Even now her key was in plain sight to me, it made no difference. It didn't stir up old desires of what lay beyond the door it opened, because that dream had been put to bed a long time ago.

"The night you left, Luther set the cops on Maverick's ass over Axel's murder," I started and she swam to the edge of the pool, folding her arms on the ledge as she listened. "He needed a fall guy to go down for it, seeing as they already had the body and all, so he picked the one who no one would miss but us. And as our opinions meant shit back then, we couldn't stop him from sending Maverick down."

"He went to prison for what I did?" she gasped, her wide eyes telling me this definitely was news to her.

I nodded stiffly, not feeling bad about that anymore because fuck him. "Maverick wanted us to give him an alibi, but Luther was hanging you over our heads. Said he'd kill you if we didn't do what he said. We couldn't help Maverick any more than we could help you, or ourselves."

I could see her swallow from here, but she said nothing, waiting for me to continue.

"He went down for six years – eighteen months in juvie and the rest served as an adult - and when he got out, he could never forgive us for abandoning him. Then some bad shit happened and...well he's gone now. He lives on Dead Man's Isle, runs his own gang. The Damned Men. We're at war with them every fucking day. We don't go beyond The Divide and neither do they."

"What's The Divide?" she breathed, her voice like velvet and so familiar that a part of me wanted to keep her talking just so I could bathe in the feel of hearing it again. I just wished I could cut that part out of me and drown it in the pool.

"It's where our turf meets theirs. It's a war zone. We claim an inch of their territory and they reclaim it back the next day, it's an endless cycle. A blood bath. Don't *ever* fucking go there," the warning slipped from me before I could even consider it. What did I care if she went prancing off to The Divide? She'd end up dead and that would be my problem solved. But shit, even as I thought that I felt a sickness I couldn't shake. No, even after all this time, I had the urge to protect her. It was why I wanted to destroy the asshole who'd bruised her face and why I'd become a living hurricane since she'd arrived. But that didn't mean I was above sending her away again. I could do that. I *would* do it.

"Anyway, point is, if you've come back to get the keys, you've got no fucking chance, ghost." I got to my feet, moving forward and standing over her so she had to lean back and look up at me.

"I'm not here for any reason that concerns you, dude," she said smoothly, but I tutted, knowing she was lying. I was always good at reading people, I just wished I'd been better because maybe then I would have figured out who she wanted out of us a long time ago and it could have saved me the heartache before I fell for her.

I lowered down to a crouch, swigging my rum as she was cast in my shadow, the light from the house blocked by my body. "Well I'll just spell it out in case you get any stupid ideas. You wouldn't be able to find my key, or Fox's, or JJ's. And if by some miracle you did manage to get your hands on them, then it wouldn't help you anyway. Because Maverick took off with his key and I'm sure it's buried in his fortress somewhere. You'd be shot a hundred feet from the outer fence if you went there. So good luck with the little plan that you think I can't see working behind your eyes, ghost. But I suggest you cut your losses and get out of Sunset Cove. I'll even give you the cash to set you up somewhere else. *Anywhere* else."

"I'm good right where I am, Chase," she said, her upper lip peeling back.

I leaned down, cupping her chin and ignoring the rush of heat that ran to my cock as my gaze wandered to her full lips. "I knew you couldn't forget my name, little one. It's carved on the inside of your skull just like yours is carved on the inside of mine. The five of us did a real number on each other, huh? But it all ended in tears. Did you cry for me, or did you only shed tears for the one of us you always planned on choosing?" The rum made my tongue loose and I brushed my thumb across her lips, unable to help myself.

She sucked my thumb into her mouth and my dick turned to iron, letting me know just how much I still hungered for this girl. She bit down hard and I cursed, yanking it free and eyeing the bloody teeth marks in my flesh. *Bitch.*

"I didn't cry for any of you," she snarled viciously and I got to my feet again.

"Liar," I said coldly. "If you hurt my friends again, I'll hurt you back, ghost. I promise you that. You fucked up Fox so good that I'm already feeling vengeful, and JJ's never been the same since you left. Ten years is a long time, but apparently it wasn't enough to mend what you did."

"What *I* did?" she scoffed. "You were the ones who forced me to run."

"You were the one who kept running," I snapped, my voice echoing off of the walls and she just glared at me with venom in her eyes. "You're the worst thing that ever happened to us, ghost," I said through my teeth. "And mark my fucking words, I'm not going to let you happen to us again."

CHAPTER TEN

"Hey," Fox's voice drew my attention as I lay in the admittedly waning sun beside the pool and I cracked an eye open so that I could look at him.

I had my headphones in and Let You Love Me by Rita Ora was playing, making me feel relaxed for one of the first times since I'd shown up here. And by *my* headphones, I of course meant that I'd stolen JJ's phone from his pocket just before he'd left for the club earlier and had found his headphones in his room when I not so accidentally wandered in there instead of into my own. I may or may not have also had a quick look in his nightstand drawers and closet for his key, but of course I hadn't found it. All that I had found were condoms. So many condoms I had trouble believing he'd ever actually get around to using all of them and was caught between being impressed and intimidated by the hoard.

Luckily me and JJ had always had the same taste in music and it looked like that hadn't changed in the years we'd spent apart, so I didn't even have to bother making up my own playlists. And he still used his own birthday for a passcode too so I had instant access to his cellphone. He wasn't quite dumb enough to leave any information on it though, but I had found an insane number of female contacts listed with descriptions like 'Karen with angry husband', 'Olivia with the perky tits' and 'Backdoor Jennifer'. Looking over them had made me feel kinda uncomfortable so I'd turned my attention to the music and had only read like six of his filthy text convos. There was stuff in those that was enough to make me blush and I'd thought I was pretty sexually diverse in the things I'd tried. Maybe not though.

"We're having a party tonight. I got you a dress to wear. Come on, we don't have long to get you ready." Fox turned and walked away like he assumed I would follow along at his heels. But that would happen exactly never and if he wanted me to play nice tonight then he was about to be severely disappointed.

I pulled my headphones from my ears and dropped them alongside the phone as I got to my feet then turned and walked away around the edge of the curved pool.

Fox looked back over his shoulder at me just as I climbed up onto the diving board and arched an eyebrow at him as he frowned at me.

"I don't want to dress up for some dumb party," I said. "So just open up the front door and I'll be out of your hair."

"That's not how this works, hummingbird," he replied, striking a low blow with that nickname which sucker punched me somewhere just south of my heart. "I say jump, you say how high."

I rolled my eyes at him and dove into the pool. The warm water enveloped me as I sank into it and started swimming, loving the feeling of my body gliding beneath the surface and aching for a taste of the sea even more than I had been before. I'd seen the surfboards the guys kept in the garage when JJ had dragged me out to get food with him again last night and I was seriously aching for some time on the waves. But I wasn't going to ask any of these assholes for anything, so I'd have to figure out how to get my own board once I got my ass out of here.

I swam all the way to the far end of the pool before coming up for air beside the wall and gasping as I found Fox there waiting for me. His green eyes were stormy with anger and his strong jaw was locked tight in a way that told me he wasn't used to not getting his own way.

He didn't even say anything, just reached down, caught my wrists and hauled me straight up out of the water.

"Let me go," I demanded as my feet landed at the edge of the pool in front of his.

Fox kept hold of my wrists, pinning them behind my back and leaning right in so that our chests were touching and water was seeping through his white shirt from my bikini clad body.

"I'm starting to lose my patience with you, Rogue," he growled. "You show up here looking like death warmed up, keeping secrets, telling lies and then you have the audacity to fight against us at every turn. Have you forgotten who I am? I'm not your friend, I'm not some desperate dude with a hard on for you and no fucking hope. I'm Fox motherfucking Harlequin and if you don't start showing me some fucking respect, then you're going to end up seeing the man who everyone in this town fears."

I swallowed thickly and for a moment I wasn't even standing there in front of this man who had grown into the role his father had laid out for him and instead I was looking at a boy with blonde hair and dark green eyes as the rain pounded down on us and I shivered before him.

"We're Harlequins now," Fox growled firmly. "And you're not. There isn't a place for you amongst us. You were just…a way for us to pass the time. A girl we could all try and win, but the game got old. We don't need you anymore. We don't want you."

Those words were like a direct knife to my heart, twisting and squeezing and crushing the life out of me as my gaze skipped between him and the other three boys who had promised to always have my back, always love me, never abandon me. And not one of them said a single word against him.

The pain of the Harlequin boys destroying my entire world and taking the only good thing I'd ever had from me that night was almost enough to overwhelm me and panic welled up within my soul as every muscle in my body coiled with the need to run and run and run until I never had to see this place or these boys ever again.

"Get your fucking hands off of me, Fox," I snarled, trying to yank my wrists out of his grasp but only succeeding in pressing our bodies together even more firmly.

"Get your ass inside and get ready for the party. If you test me on this,

I'll take your little mutt to the shelter and you'll never see him again," Fox threatened.

I yanked on my wrists again and Fox released me so suddenly that I fell backwards with a shriek of fright, crashing back down into the pool and sinking beneath the surface with my heart pounding a frantic beat in my chest.

I sank to the bottom and kept myself there as I tried to fight off the urge to cry over the memories Fox had just brought to the forefront of my mind. If I got lost in them now, I didn't think I'd ever recover again.

By the time I swam back up to the surface, Fox was already disappearing inside and I cursed him beneath my breath as I heaved myself up and out of the water, wrapping myself in the towel from my sun lounger and stalking back inside.

My hair dripped all over the hardwood as I went and I left footprints too, but boohoo. This wasn't my house, so I didn't care about damaging the fittings.

Mutt was curled up on the end of my bed as I pushed open the door to my room and I grunted a greeting at the pup as he wagged his tail and rolled over, hoping for a belly rub.

Fox had left the dress he'd bought me draped over the armchair in the corner of the room and I growled at it as I stalked over to get a closer look. It was tight, short, black and the tags said it was expensive too. I had half a mind to set the fucking thing on fire, but that was too obvious.

I wasn't going to play the little brat throwing a fit because I didn't like what he was telling me to do. I was going to play a smarter game. And that meant Badger needed to think he was winning.

I took a shower to wash the chlorine from my skin then took the time to style my pastel rainbow hair in heavy curls which tumbled down my spine before carefully applying the makeup Lucy had given me when I was at the salon. I assumed JJ had had to pay for it alongside everything else I'd gotten done from my hair to my nails, but he'd offered and it was really the least he owed me.

By the time I'd finished applying it, you couldn't even see the lingering bruises on my skin anymore. The ones on my neck had already faded to next to nothing anyway and the black eye was in its final stages of blue and yellow, but now I looked as fresh as a daisy. Well, a daisy with a preference for thick eyeliner and bubblegum pink lipstick anyway.

Music was thumping from further into the house and the sound of laughter and chatter told me that this fun gathering was well underway, so I slipped into a set of lacy black underwear and squeezed into the dress next.

I was now the proud owner of my own underwear and several outfits thanks to JJ's little shopping trip, so at least I didn't have to worry about clothes anymore. It still didn't make a lick of difference to the way I felt about these assholes, but every little win needed to count at the moment because I was seriously short on good news.

Lastly, I slipped on a pair of chunky white heels JJ had bought me and assessed myself in the mirror with a critical eye as I rearranged my boobs within the dress to give maximum appeal to my admittedly modest chest. The short dress showed off the tattoos on my legs and found I quite liked this look even if Fox had been somewhat responsible for it.

A knock sounded at the door just as I was about to head for it and I moved to open it with a sigh of irritation, expecting Fox to be there demanding my presence like a caveman wanting to show off his shiny new club.

Instead, I found JJ leaning against the wall looking fucking edible in a pair of stonewashed jeans and a white linen shirt which had a deep V-neck to show off just enough of his defined pecs to make me drool a little bit.

"Well look at you," he purred, his eyes dragging over me in the black dress and drinking in everything from my tattoos to my black fingernails with the little skull decals. I was pretty certain I'd never spent the amount of money it had taken to put this look together in all my life, but I wasn't going to complain about spending their cash. It looked to me like they had more than enough to spare anyway. And the least they could do was clothe the girl they'd kidnapped. "But you're looking a little tense, sweetheart. Do you want a bit of help relaxing?"

JJ let his gaze dip to my chest and it wasn't hard to pick up on what he was offering.

"I'm pretty sure I can't afford you," I replied coolly, refusing to show so much as a hint of interest in his offer.

"First time is on the house," he replied smoothly. "Besides, I work so damn much I hardly ever get to fuck anyone I really want to."

"That's...either an oddly flattering statement or a desperately sad one," I said, my brow pinching.

"Do you feel sorry for me, Rogue?" he teased, stepping closer and dropping his mouth to my ear. "Because you can make me feel better about my lot in life if you wanna let me eat you out before we go and join the party."

I tried to ignore the heat which ignited in my veins at that suggestion and laughed him off as I placed my hand on his chest and forced him back a step.

"Maybe next time, asshole. Right now, I need a drink."

JJ laughed and followed me as I left the room, closing the door behind me so that Mutt could have the space to himself and avoid everyone downstairs.

"No one will come up to our rooms," JJ explained. "Fox would fucking kill them if they did. The party will stay in the main part of the house and around the pool, maybe it'll even spill down to the beach if anyone can be bothered to walk down there in the dark. But Fox has the gate locked up tight right now to make sure you can't slip away from us, so probably not."

"You guys can't just keep me locked up here forever you know," I growled but JJ only laughed like this was all some big joke as we stepped out into the kitchen and found the place full of people who were drinking and dancing and generally enjoying the party.

"You wanna dance, pretty girl?" JJ asked, swiping a can of beer from the counter and cracking it open.

He took a long sip then held it up to my lips, making my stomach dip with the memory of him doing that exact thing to me a hundred times when the five of us used to hang out beneath the pier and have our own private parties in the dark. Back then we hadn't wanted anyone else to be around. But I guessed everything changed eventually.

I took the drink he was offering and his gaze stayed hooked on mine while I drank, mischief sparkling in his eyes that said he knew something I wasn't allowed to know.

"Come on then, let me see your best slut drop," I teased, walking away from him to the middle of the room where a bunch of girls were grinding together to the beat of Ice Cream by Blackpink and Selena Gomez.

I started dancing as soon as I made it to them, closing my eyes and tilting my head back as I tried to drown myself in the music. I needed to be free of everything tonight. Even if it didn't last and I was going to come crashing back down to reality with a bang the moment I opened my eyes again. For this moment, this dead girl just wanted to feel alive. I'd made a speciality out of letting go of all the shit I had going on and living in the moment so it was easy for me to give in to the pull of the enjoyment that was waiting to be had here. It was the only way I'd found to survive the cesspit of my life and it was working out pretty damn peachy so far. So long as I kept my focus on the shallow things I had going on, I never had to worry about drowning in the darkness of the deep.

Someone moved up behind me and an arm curled around my waist as he drew me back against his chest. I knew it was JJ even without the scent of him making my senses prickle as the mixture of almond oil and sea air wrapped around me as tightly as his arms. There was just a part of my soul that was always going to ache for the boys these men had once been and would recognise them even in the dark.

JJ tugged me close so that my ass was pressed against his crotch and our hips fell into this impossibly perfect rhythm together as we both moved to the beat of the music. I reached my arm over my shoulder, gripping the back of his hair as I held him close and he kept his hands on my hips. I knew I shouldn't have been doing it, but there was something about the fact that I couldn't see him that made it feel like I was buying myself a little freedom to pretend that there wasn't an uncrossable divide between us now. Like I could pretend I didn't know him and didn't feel the ache in my heart which throbbed a little harder with his arms around me.

The more we moved like that together, the more heat began to build in my core, the aching, needy part of me wanting to take him up on the offer he'd made and just use him to take away some of the hurt and fear I'd been feeling ever since I'd woken up in that grave.

The songs merged from one to the next, JJ's hands slipping to caress the hem of my dress as my breath hitched and temptation did its best job to lure me into its trap. I wanted to feel wanted. To believe I wasn't disposable. But I also knew this man who was holding me close had proved that he had no issue with throwing me away once before.

"What part of *she's mine* did you fail to grasp?" Fox's cold voice snapped me out of my less than ladylike fantasies about JJ and my eyes popped open as I found him standing before us, his face a deadly mask and murder in his eyes.

"Chill out, man, we're just dancing," JJ said, but his hands slid from my body all the same and he took a step back. "Besides, this is *Rogue*. We've been waiting a long time to see which one of us she'd pick. I think it's only fair that she gets a chance to see-"

"The last time I checked this was *my* crew," Fox snarled. "My house. My gang. My money. And *my girl*. Don't go thinking that just because I love you, you don't have to play by the fucking rules JJ. You know exactly who you're fucking with right now. So either back the fuck off or I'll make you."

JJ tsked like he wanted to say something else then flicked a glance at the crowd of people watching. I knew how this play went. I'd been running with these kinds of men for way too long. When it came down to it, Fox was the boss and his word was law. If JJ didn't fall into line then the shit was going to hit the fan and a point was going to have to be made, especially with this many people watching.

"I'm not your anything, Fox," I said loudly, drawing his attention back around to me. "I don't know what it is that you think gives you the right to lay claim on people, but I'm not your property or anyone else's. If you seriously wanted me to be your girl, you might wanna try a little harder at winning me around. Because right about now, the idea of tying myself to you makes me wanna gouge my eyes out with a rusty spoon."

I shoved past JJ and made a move towards the pool, but Fox's hand latched around my wrist before I could escape and he tugged me towards him, his eyes burning with fury.

All around us people had scurried away, but I could feel the eyes of every single person at this party on us all the same.

JJ stepped forward like he intended to get between us, but Chase appeared and caught his shoulder, yanking him back and leaning in close to say something to him that I couldn't hear.

Whatever it was seemed to be enough to make JJ back down though as he turned and headed away without another word.

Fox didn't release me, tugging me after him as he started walking and the crowd parted like the tide to let us through. He kept going until we reached the door opposite the tv room which was always locked. He produced a key and opened it before shoving me inside where I found a set of stairs leading down into the dark.

"Get your ass moving Rogue before I change my mind about punishing the two of you publicly," he growled and something about the raw anger in his voice made me obey him for once as I took hold of the bannister and headed into the shadows at the foot of the stairs.

Fox flicked a light on which illuminated the space at the bottom of the stairs and I quickened my pace as I headed down.

At the bottom of the stairs I found a basement with grey couches filling the open space and a picture of the Harlequin Crew's symbol of a snarling skull wearing a harlequin's hat painted onto the wall behind a large mahogany desk. All three of the guys had that fucking thing tattooed on their bodies and I hated looking into its dead eyes, feeling like it was mocking me with the fact that they chose it over me.

"What is this place?"

"This is where I do business with the members of my crew, when we're not at The Oasis," Fox said and I scrunched my nose up as he mentioned the huge bar the Harlequins owned and used as their clubhouse. When we were kids we'd always avoided that place like the plague but I guessed now he was a fully fledged leader of that bunch of psychos he must have spent a lot of his time there.

"Well I'm not a member of your crew, so why the hell am I here?"

Fox moved around me, opening a wooden cabinet by the rear wall and pulling out a bottle of rum. There were no windows down here and I shifted uncomfortably as his gaze remained locked on me like I was the only thing in the world that he cared about. But he'd proved that that wasn't the case when he ruined my life ten years ago, so I wasn't buying it.

"You're here because this is where you belong. Because this is where you should have been for the last ten years and because I'm never going to make the mistake of letting you run from me ever again," he said in a low and deadly tone that didn't allow any room for argument and made me feel all hot and riled up.

"Fuck you, Fox. You have no idea where I've been or what I've been doing for the last ten years. You don't want me. You don't even know me. And if you've forgotten, you were the one who told me to fuck off and never come back."

Fox's upper lip curled back and he moved to take a seat on a big, leather chair as he took another long swig of his rum. "Come here."

"No."

"Don't test me tonight, Rogue. I'm not the kind of man who people say no to."

"And I guess that means you think I'm the kind of girl you can just boss around until I'm falling to my knees at your command? Well, sorry to burst your bubble, asshole, but that is not and never has been me. But I'm sure there are plenty of keen bitches up there for you to pick between, so how about you just leave me out of your plans and let me go? I'm getting really over this whole knight in shining armour role you seem to think you're playing at. I didn't ask you to lock me up in this house and I sure as hell didn't ask you to rescue me, so I have no intention of falling down and weeping in gratitude for any of it." I folded my arms and glared at him as he pushed up out of his chair in a motion so sudden that I almost flinched.

"This isn't about me rescuing you, hummingbird," he growled as he stalked towards me and I refused to move so much as an inch. "And it's not about me looking for you to ride my cock in thanks for giving you a bed to sleep in and putting food in your belly. This is about you and me."

Fox came to a halt right in front of me and I raised my chin defiantly as I held my ground. The four inch heels put me closer to his height, but Fox Harlequin was a beast of a man and even with the extra inches, he towered over me by almost a full head.

"You and me have been written in the stars for a long fucking time, Rogue. I know you used to feel it too. We're inevitable. Always have been, always will be." He leaned in closer and cupped my face in his hand, making me look at him as my heart thrashed and I had to fight against the desire to scream at him that he was full of shit and I didn't have any intention to be his anything now or ever.

"You don't get to decide my life for me, Fox. Maybe around here you're used to having that kind of power over people, but not me. Never me."

I shoved away from him with my heart racing and he let me go, watching as I hurried up the stairs and back to the party.

"Well that didn't take long," Chase's voice caught my attention as I made it to the top of the stairs and I turned to look at him with a frown.

"What didn't?"

"I'm assuming you went down there to suck his dick just like Fox decided you would. No one can say no to the boss man after all. Am I right? I have to say that I'm impressed with how quickly you managed to get him off though. Maybe when he's bored with you, I can take you for a ride?"

"Fuck off, Chase. I'm not gonna suck your dick any more than I'll be sucking Fox's. He may have it in his head that I'm his but I'm not buying the bullshit he's selling. I never have and never will belong to anyone. I may have fuck all to my name and I might even be a dead girl walking, but the one thing I will always have is my own freedom. No man will take that from me. Not even the great Fox Harlequin."

"Is that so?" Chase asked, pushing off of the wall and closing in on me with much more interest in his eyes than he'd held before. "I wouldn't have minded being a fly on the wall for that little conversation. Did his head explode? Or did he just ignore your point of view on things entirely and assume you'd change your mind soon enough?"

"I didn't hang around to find out. Either way, I'm not his so I'll suck whatever dicks I want to. But don't go getting any ideas about that including yours, because I hate you too," I said, tilting my chin up to meet his gaze and stare at him in defiance.

Chase plucked his cigarette from the corner of his lips, stepped so close to me that we were practically pressed together aside from the thinnest slice of space dividing us and then exhaled to engulf me in a cloud of smoke. "Ditto."

He stepped around me without another word and I turned to scowl at his back as he headed down into the basement where Fox was presumably still raging out or pouting like a bitch.

Before I could look away from the stairway, another guy headed down there, then another. I moved aside as more and more people started heading down there and looked around in confusion, wondering if I'd somehow missed an announcement or something when JJ reappeared with a smile just for me.

"You survived the Fox then?" he teased, taking my hand and drawing me away from the basement door and back through to the kitchen.

"I'm not afraid of him," I scoffed, though that wasn't entirely true. The Harlequin boys frightened me because they were the only people I'd ever known who had tried to break me and succeeded. I wasn't afraid of any threats Fox might make to try and force me to get into line with his plans. I was more afraid of getting sucked back into their world and falling into their arms, only to be tossed aside when they got bored of me again.

"Good. You have to know he'd never hurt you. But he is a bit...intense when he wants something."

"I picked up on that," I muttered.

"All the more reason to keep your head down then. Fox is easy enough to please, just so long as you don't push back against his rules."

"Psh." I waved him off and he smirked as he leaned in close to speak in my ear.

"Or at least make sure you only do it in secret," he whispered, turning his head and pressing a kiss to my neck right beneath my ear that made my pulse skip and heat race across my skin.

JJ leaned back just as fast as he'd drawn close and winked at me.

"Now be a good girl and enjoy the party while we're talking downstairs," he advised. "Just stick to making friends with girls and Foxy won't have any reason to get pissy about it."

I ignored his suggestion and narrowed my eyes at the juicy worm he'd just offered me. "Why don't I just come downstairs with you?"

JJ shook his head and backed up a step, a clear refusal in his dark eyes. "No can do, sweetheart. Official Harlequin Crew shit. Members only - and you are definitely not sworn in."

"Well then why don't I swear in?" I offered, mostly because I wanted access to their secrets and I didn't actually care about keeping my word to any of them. So if I had to promise to be in their gang for life then I didn't mind breaking my word and running for the hills the moment I had what I wanted.

"That's not up to me," JJ said, his eyes twinkling with some dark humour. "And there's no women allowed in the crew anyway. But if you wanna ask Fox to make an exception for you then be my guest."

I pursed my lips as I considered it. I'd just told Fox in no uncertain terms to get fucked. Was I really going to turn around and beg for a position in his crew? Then again, did I care about preserving my dignity when all I really wanted from this place was the contents of that crypt?

"Fine. I'll go ask him." I tossed my rainbow hair like a My Little Pony with an attitude problem and started towards the basement once again, but JJ caught my arm to stop me.

"He won't want to talk to you about that in front of all the other members. If you're determined to ask him then I'll get him to come up here." He took his phone from his back pocket and quickly shot Fox a message before I could object and I rolled my eyes at the dramatics involved with asking a simple question before grabbing another beer from the kitchen island and starting on it.

When Fox entered the room it was kind of like that part in Jurassic Park where the T-rex makes his appearance and every other fucker in the vicinity can't help but turn to look in terror. I was surprised my beer wasn't rippling to mark his approach. He definitely had an aura about him that bred fear. Even if I hadn't known he was the leader of the Harlequin Crew, it would have been painfully obvious that he was someone to be afraid of.

He strode towards us with his black shirt half unbuttoned to reveal the beginnings of the artwork on his chest and the way the fabric strained across his broad shoulders forced me to look at him in all the wrong ways. But fuck that. Being pretty didn't excuse his bullshit.

"What is it?" he asked as he came to stand in front of me, looking down at me with narrowed eyes that said I was in the doghouse. *Dickhead.*

"I wanna sign up to your little crew," I demanded. "I don't like secrets and I figure the only way you're going to let me in on what you have going on here is by signing up."

"No," Fox said simply and for some pathetic, unmentionable reason, that reaction actually stung.

"Why not?" I growled.

"Firstly, because there's no women in the Harlequins, it's in the code. Secondly, because I don't want you running jobs with us and putting yourself in danger. And thirdly, because you're still lying to us about a lot of things.

159

Either way, you're perfectly safe here in the house and you have no need to earn any money, so I don't see any reason to initiate you even if I did decide to bend the code for you."

"Maybe I don't want to live off of your charity," I growled.

"Tough." He folded his arms and gave me a flat look that said I was trying his patience even though his eyes burned with the kind of hunger that said he wanted to eat me up.

JJ stood watching this entire exchange like it was a reality tv show he was engrossed in and clearly had no desire to leave us to it.

"I want to be able to come and go from this place as I like," I pushed. "If I'm a member you'll know you can trust me and-"

"No."

"But if you-"

"If you want to be able to come and go, then you should give my offer more consideration," Fox said in a low voice, taking a step closer to me so that I was distracted by the pure, hard wall of muscle standing before me. "If you're my girl then you'll be safe wherever you go. No one will dare touch you. You could leave the house as and when you please and take the time to remember exactly why you fit here so perfectly. This is where you're meant to be, Rogue. Always has been. There's a space for you at my side that you've been waiting to step into since we were just a bunch of dumb kids running the streets. Just stop fighting it and you can have whatever you want."

"No," I growled, moving closer to him myself as I refused to be intimidated by him. "I'm not some whore you can command into your bed and I won't let you blackmail me into it either. You don't even know me anymore, Fox. So stop basing your fantasy on the version of me you think you remember and take your head out of your fucking ass. I'm not your girl. I'm not anyone's girl."

"Fine," he replied with a shrug. "But until you realise that you're wrong about that, I think it's best you stay here where we can keep an eye on you."

Fox turned and stalked away from me, leaving me feeling like he'd just sucked all of the air from the room as he went. He barked an order at JJ to follow him and he tossed me a smirk before turning and following his boss back to the basement like a good little grunt.

I waited for them to head through the door and downstairs, taking note of the two big dudes who moved to stand before the door and block the way down there once Fox and JJ were inside. They were both carrying guns which they'd jammed into the backs of their jeans and the dark expressions on their faces said they meant business. There was no way I'd be snooping in on that little boys' club meeting.

I cursed Fox beneath my breath, finished up my beer and headed back into the thick of the party, glancing around for a likely looking drinking buddy to take my mind off of the bullshit. I recognised a few people from when I'd lived here before, but none of them were offering up the friendliest of vibes and I was kinda inclined to avoid all of them. I'd only been tight with four people in this town before I'd left and I didn't want to try and reconnect with people I'd never connected with in the first place.

"Rogue?"

I turned at the sound of my name, grinning as I spotted Di through the crush of bodies in the middle of the kitchen, she was wearing a figure hugging blue mini dress and had half the guys in the place staring at all of the dark skin she'd left on show.

"Hey!" I called with a real smile as I made my way over to her and I found the two other girls who had helped point me in JJ's direction down by the bait shop on my first day back in town with her too. I remembered the blonde was called Lyla, but I wasn't sure I'd caught the redhead's name. "What are you guys doing here?"

"The Harlequin Crew throw the best parties," Lyla shrugged. "Everyone knows that."

"I like your hair," the redhead said as she reached out to tug on one of my rainbow curls with interest. "It looks good enough to eat."

"Just ignore Bella, she's off her tits," Di explained, smacking Bella's hand away from me before she could get any real ideas about having a taste of my cotton candy hair.

"I'll be careful to make sure she doesn't take a bite out of me," I agreed with a laugh.

"I can eat you for fifty bucks if you like?" Bella slurred. "I haven't had a client with a pussy for a while. Make's a nice change from all the D."

161

I barked a laugh and Di and Lyla joined in.

"I don't have the fifty to spare," I said with a sigh. "But thanks for the offer."

Bella just shrugged then stumbled away from us, heading towards the kitchen island and the booze.

"I guess you found JJ then?" Di asked and I nodded, not offering up any more info on how that bullshit had proceeded.

"You girls wanna drink with me?" I begged. "I'm seriously low on people I like in this place and you guys seem cool. I'm on the hunt for friends in a desperate and needy kind of way, but I'm hoping you'll overlook that flaw because I'm actually pretty cool when I'm not begging people to like me."

Lyla started laughing and Di grinned. "We were just gonna try and drag Bella's ass home before she starts puking and gets herself beheaded by the Harlequins for ruining a rug or something. But there's gonna be a bonfire on the beach tonight which we could hit after we dump her ass back in her trailer. Where are you staying anyway?"

"I'm actually between beds right now," I replied with a groan. "I'm staying somewhere, and I kinda hate it, but I have no other options so I'm stuck."

"You can always crash at mine tonight if you like?" Lyla offered. "Or if you've got two hundred bucks to put down, there's a trailer going just down the row from mine. You could probably get away without paying the deposit if you don't mind sucking Joe McCreevy's dick though. That said, he's pretty rough and kinda gross so I wouldn't really recommend it."

"I'm gonna sweep right on past the part about sucking gross dick and land on a trailer I could call my own. Because that sounds fucking perfect," I said. I really needed some space from these assholes and I was already giving up on finding their keys just lying about somewhere. I was going to have to think smarter about how I was going to get my hands on them and that was impossible to do with the three of them breathing down my neck at all times.

"Well, I dunno about perfect, but the trailers are pretty decent - they don't leak anyway - and the park fronts the beach. There's always someone to hang out with too because the whole place is populated with runaways

162

and rejects so we've all built this weird kind of family. I think you'd be the perfect fit," Di said.

"Alright, I'm in," I agreed, not least because it made serious sense to me to make my escape while the three guys were locked up in the basement having their secret club meeting. I just wished I'd be able to see the looks on their faces when they realised I was gone.

"Perfect," Lyla said. "Let's go grab Bella and get out of here then."

I followed the two of them as they went in search of the redhead, my mind whirling with how I was going to be able to grab all of my shit and the mutt without the girls realising that I'd been staying here. They were being seriously cool by trying to help me out, but I got the feeling that if they realised they would be going against what the Harlequins wanted by helping me then I'd be tossed to the curb faster than a used condom.

Bella was leaning up against the fridge when they found her, her face smooshed against the door and her eyes half shut as she hummed something beneath her breath.

Lyla sighed dramatically and Di rolled her eyes as they moved to wrap her arms around their shoulders and started towards the exit.

I followed behind them, but as the front door came into view, I spotted three guys hanging out around it who looked way too serious to be taking part in the party. And as one of them narrowed his eyes in my direction, I became certain they were there to guard the door. More than that, they'd been told not to let me out of it either.

"Where are you guys parked?" I asked as I hesitated. "I stashed some of my shit outside when I got here, so I can just run and grab it then meet you at the car?"

"We're parked down the street. Turn left out of the drive and just keep walking. It's a blue Chevy," Di said and I nodded as I filed that info away.

"Okay, great. I'll be there in a sec." I turned away from the doors just as one of the big guys took a step towards me and I scurried away to make sure he didn't get any ideas about warning me to stay here in front of the girls. This was my passport out of this place and I wasn't going to fuck it up.

I headed back through the kitchen, stopping at the drawer where I'd seen the wedge of cash on my late night search of the place and grabbing out whatever was in there. One quick look said it was a couple of grand and I smirked to myself as I folded my arms to hide it. I probably should have been terrified of what the guys would do to me for stealing from them, but I'd already faced death and won once, what was a few pissed off douchebags in comparison to that?

I quickly moved through the house, passing another less than subtle dude who was making sure no one headed up to the bedrooms. He clearly knew me too though as he gave me a vague nod when I passed him and made no attempt to stop me.

I ducked into JJ's room and upended his gym bag all over his bed then shoved my stolen cash into a side pocket. I glanced around and spotted the pink shades I liked sitting on his nightstand. I grabbed them followed by a couple of his tanks and hoodies to sleep in before taking it all with me back to my room.

Mutt ran at me, wagging his tail and licking my ankles with glee as I appeared and I tickled his ears before racing around the space and tossing the clothes, makeup, wash products and shoes the guys had bought me into the bag. It wasn't even half full by the time I was done and I whistled at Mutt, pointing him at the bag and wondering if he'd do what I wanted or not.

The little dog hopped right in then turned to give me a conspiratorial look which I took to mean *let's do this bitch.* Dude definitely had my back.

I zipped the bag up, leaving a gap at the end for him to poke his nose out of, grabbed my skateboard then slipped back out into the corridor. I paused as I reached the door to Fox's room then headed inside with my heart pounding and a smirk on my lips.

His room was massive of course, the view out over the balcony even better than the one from my room and everything laid out all neat and tidy. I could still remember coming over to this house and sneaking in through his window while he kicked dirty socks under the bed, thinking I hadn't noticed them, so this perfect layout seemed all wrong to me. But never mind, I wasn't here to figure out at what point in the last ten years the asshole had worked out how to use the laundry hamper.

I hurried into his bathroom and grabbed a pink lipstick from my bag before quickly writing him a goodbye note on the mirror. It was short and sweet, but I was sure he would appreciate it.

Nice.

I shoved the lipstick back into the bag, gaining a lick from Mutt as I went before heading out of Fox's room and jogged back downstairs to the party.

The guy watching the stairs wasn't looking my way as I descended and I managed to slip back into the crowd without him noticing my bag.

I circled the party as fast as I could without all out running and headed to the pool area where a large group of guys were chugging from a keg like this was a frat house or something.

I passed them and the bikini clad girls who were lounging around the pool, showing off the goods as they eyed potential hook ups and made it to the brick barbecue beside the wall.

I cast a quick glance around and the moment I was certain no one was looking my way, I climbed up onto it and eyed the top of the wall beside me.

I tiptoed up to slide my bag onto the top of the wall, followed by my skateboard then leapt for the wall myself.

I grunted with the effort of heaving myself up onto it, which was made even harder by the tight dress and heels I was wearing. After a few attempts, I managed to hook a leg over the top of the wall but I was pretty certain my dress slid up high enough to flash my lace panties at anyone behind me. Ah well. I'd never claimed I was graceful.

I cursed as I managed to wriggle up onto the top of the white bricks but then my balance shifted and suddenly I was pitching too far to the other side, my gut lurching as I began to fall.

A strong hand caught mine before I could topple down onto the dirt on the other side of the wall and my heart leapt in fright as I looked around at my saviour.

A guy was grinning at me as he stood on the barbecue, holding onto me with an iron grip which made me think he was about to drag me right back into his arms and ruin my escape attempt.

"Let me guess, you're running from some asshole who isn't good enough for you?" he teased, releasing my hand once he was sure I wasn't going to fall and making me frown as I realised this wasn't an arrest. Or, *capture*, I guess. I wasn't sure what the term was, but either way, this dude didn't seem to be trying to stop me, just saving me from falling on my face.

"Something like that. Thanks for saving my ass and all, but I've really gotta go," I said, giving him a tight smile and swinging my leg around so that I could lower myself down the other side of the wall.

I dropped down onto the dirt, wobbling a little in my chunky heels before cursing as I realised I couldn't reach my bag or board anymore.

"Umm...a little help?" I called out hopefully and the guy's laughter reached me before he popped his head over the wall and looked down at me. He had that surfer vibe going, messy blonde hair and a Hawaiian print shirt hanging open over a white wifebeater.

"I'm Carter, by the way," he said as he took hold of my skateboard and tossed it down to me.

"Rogue," I replied, reaching up to grab my bag as he lowered that down next.

"Nice to meet you, runaway girl."

Mutt barked happily as I set him loose and I swung the bag over my shoulder before glancing back at the guy who'd helped me.

"I owe you one," I called with a grin and he laughed as I turned tail and ran off into the dark.

I jogged up through the trees and made my way onto the road without being spotted.

Just as I turned to start looking for Di's car, she rounded the corner and the glow from her headlights spilled over me as she pulled up to let me in.

"Do I wanna know?" she asked, eyeing my slightly ripped dress, bag of shit and dog curiously.

"Not really," I admitted and she laughed as I opened the door and slid in beside her. Mutt jumped in by my feet and I tossed a greeting back to Lyla who was nursing Bella on the backseat.

"If you puke on me, I'm gonna kill you, carve you up into little pieces and feed you to the dolphins," Lyla said to the near comatose girl while stroking her hair and I laughed as we took off down the street, leaving the Harlequin boys and their bullshit behind.

We took the back roads through town with the balmy evening air blowing in through the windows and I leaned back in my seat, enjoying the feeling of the wind in my hair and the taste of salt on the air.

Di drove us through the roughest part of the lower quarter and down towards the sea until we reached a trailer park with the trailers all crammed in close together and a thick wire fence ringing the complex. There was a faded old sign with the name Royal Park written on it, but someone had spray painted the word Rejects over the top of the Royal part.

"Welcome to Rejects Park," Lyla announced as she saw what I was looking at. "Where the people no one wants gather to feel a little less alone."

"That sounds pretty fucking perfect," I admitted, exchanging a grin with her that accepted our shitty lots in life and said *fuck it, let's make the most of it anyway.*

We parked up in a dusty lot and I jumped out of the car, turning to help drag Bella out too as she slurred something unintelligible and practically hung off of Lyla's neck.

"Whoever came up with the concept of never leaving a bitch behind clearly never had to put up with this shit," Di muttered but she dutifully helped us to drag Bella's ass into the trailer park all the same.

Ride or die clearly meant something to these girls and I was here for that. Loyalty was always hard to come by in the kinds of places I found myself and when I saw someone showing signs of it I wanted to be a part of it, even if I'd never found anyone to even come close to what I'd once had with my boys.

We headed between trailers until Lyla pointed out one with a red door and a half collapsed set of stairs and the three of us hauled Bella towards it.

We made it inside and Di cursed at the mess all around the place as we managed to get Bella into her bed.

"I'll stay here with her while you two go sort out that trailer," Di offered. "If I can be sure she isn't going to choke on her own tongue then I'll come down to the beach in a bit."

"I'll gladly take that deal," Lyla agreed as she snatched my hand and tugged me back out the door, grinning conspiratorially.

Once we were outside she groaned and threw her head back. "I love that girl, but she's gonna kill herself taking all of that shit one of these days," she said as we started walking.

"Does she get fucked up that bad regularly?" I asked as Mutt ran around my feet, wagging his tail excitedly as he sniffed everything.

"More and more often," Lyla admitted. "She's not like most of us here. We're all outcasts and runaways, but for a lot of us this place is way better than whatever we left behind. Bella wasn't like that though. She came here after she lost her mom and the house she'd grown up in was taken from her when she was just seventeen. She fell into the sex trade because she didn't really have any other choice if she wanted to buy food and shit, you know? But she could find a way out of it if she wanted to bad enough. If I'm honest, I just don't think she cares about herself enough to try and save herself."

I frowned sympathetically at the idea of that and gave Lyla's fingers a squeeze. It wasn't like Bella's story was all that unusual around here, or anywhere that I'd been over the last ten years, but it didn't make it suck any less. Sometimes I felt like the world had forgotten about people like us. The big fish just swam on by while the sharks circled the tank and the little fish like us had to fight every day not to end up eaten.

"So, err, Joe McCreevy is a decent enough landlord," Lyla said as we started up a hill towards the only actual building I could see around here. It was a wooden beach house with a wide porch and faded white paintwork. Nothing too fancy, but nice enough. "But he's a bit...I don't wanna say creepy-"

"But he's creepy?" I put in and she laughed.

"I mean, there's a reason people 'round here call him Joe McCreepy. Let's just say, if you ever can't make the rent, he's *more* than happy to take payment in flesh. To be honest, I think he prefers that half the time. Some girls just fuck him regularly instead of ever paying and that's cool if it's what they prefer, but it's just worth knowing that he'll be thinking along those lines when we show up. So if you don't want that-"

"I prefer to keep financial transactions out of my sex life," I agreed with a laugh. "But don't worry. I'm good for the money so he'll have no complaints."

"Okay, cool." Lyla moved up the steps and rapped her knuckles against the door as I came to stand beside her.

There was some loud cursing from inside and some thumping and banging before the door was finally tugged wide and I found myself face to face with a big guy who was probably in his fifties with slicked back black hair and the kind of stubble that said he was just too lazy to shave it often. He was wearing a white wifebeater with a ketchup stain on the belly and a pair of ill-fitting cargo pants above a pair of well worn sandals...and socks. Shudder.

"Hey, Joe, this is Rogue. She needs a place to stay and I was telling her about the trailer you've got available," Lyla said with a smile way too bright for this particular specimen to have earned.

"That so?" Joe asked, his gaze sliding over me like butter rolling over a bagel - slow and kinda greasy. "You got the money for the deposit, or..." He rolled the toothpick which was stuck between his teeth back and forth with his tongue, making it clack against his canines as he gave me an appraising look.

"I've got the money," I said firmly, sticking my hand into my bag and grabbing a couple of hundreds out for him.

Joe reached out and took the cash, his fingers sliding over the back of my hand and making me snatch my fingers away fast. Yup, he'd definitely earned the name McCreepy and I'd only just met him.

"How much for an hour of your time then, sugar tits?" he asked me, his gaze raking over said less than sugary tits and making me want to cover them up to stop him looking.

"Err, I'm not actually in the trade, sorry," I said, trying not to sound as grossed out as I clearly was. I mean, I was a big girl who'd had her fair share of questionable conquests in my twenty six years, but I really wasn't much of a fan of being leered over. Especially after what had happened with my neighbour Axel when I was sixteen.

"Well, alright then. You'll find I'm a very amenable landlord," Joe said, turning back to his house and leaning in through the door, seeming to accept my refusal as easy as that and I really hoped that he had. "I don't like to play hard ball, and if you ever have trouble coming up with the rent then I prefer to come up with *alternatives* rather than kicking folk out. Rent is due every Saturday – a hundred a week, I like cash and you can either push it through my hole in an envelope with your trailer number on it or hand it over direct."

Lyla pointed at a hole in the door as I gave her a horrified look and I blew out a relieved breath.

"Okay, sounds good," I agreed.

"You're number twenty-two. Here you go." He handed me a key with a blue surfboard keychain on it and the number twenty-two painted on the base. "You got money to put on the electric meter? I can get you running with all the facilities like water, propane, etcetera if you got another hundred to start you off?"

"Yeah. Facilities sound good," I agreed, rummaging for another hundred in my bag and handing it over.

Joe eyed me like he was wondering where I'd gotten all of that cash then seemed to realise he didn't give a shit. "Come on then, I'll get all your needs filled."

Lyla gave me an excited grin and we turned to follow Joe out into the park.

"You gotta watch out for rattlesnakes gettin' beneath your trailer," he said casually as we walked. "The fences keep the coyotes out but there ain't nothin' I can do for a snake."

"Great. I'll keep an eye out," I assured him with a shudder.

"I got some anti-venom up at my place if you do get bit, but I gotta charge a pretty penny for it. That stuff ain't cheap, you understand?"

"I bet not," I agreed.

"That's me," Lyla said, pointing out a trailer with a pink door and cute fairy lights hanging all around the little porch that was constructed out the front of it. "Come over any time - but if only the blue lights are lit then I'm with a client."

"Got it," I agreed as Joe approached a trailer a few down from hers and gestured for me to unlock it.

I moved forward with way too much anticipation as I looked at the blue and white trailer, stepping up onto the wooden deck in front of it and imagining getting my own set of lights to string up outside - *probably better check that there isn't some signal system in use for the hookers here first.*

I unlocked it and tried to tug the door open, but it got stuck.

"You gotta jiggle it," Joe grunted, leaning around me to grab the door handle and jiggling it as his chest pressed to my back.

I cringed away from him but the door burst open before I needed to deploy the elbows, which was probably for the best as he was my new landlord and all.

"Gimme a sec to get the electric going," Joe said, heading around the side of the trailer while I stepped inside.

Mutt shot past me, racing around the dark space excitedly, his little tail wagging as he went.

There was a faint smell of shea hanging in the air and I could just make out the kitchen cupboards and sink in front of me.

I squinted around as I tried to figure out the layout and the lights suddenly blinked to life as the power came on.

I sucked in a sharp breath as the inside of the trailer was revealed to me. The whole thing had been decorated in a retro style with pale blue cupboard doors and white surrounds. The oven was baby pink and there were blue cushions on the chairs either side of the table to my right. The whole thing was seriously cute and about a million times better than I'd been expecting.

A few doors led off of the main space at the far end of the trailer to my left and I moved down to open them up, finding a shower room, toilet and finally a bedroom. I stepped into the small space, grinning at the unmade bed which took up almost the entire space with the little blue curtains hanging by the window.

I'd never had a place that was entirely mine before. I could actually see myself liking it here.

"You gotta watch for this window," Joe said suddenly, making me shriek in alarm as he pushed the window at the foot of my bed open from outside and stuck his head through. "The lock is dodgy and folk can see right in here and get a look at whatever you're up to if you don't make sure to pull the curtains."

"Noted," I said, reaching out to slam the window as he retreated and laughing breathily as my racing heart began to slow.

I headed back out into the main part of the trailer, finding Lyla smiling at me in the kitchen. "Cute, isn't it? A girl named Dotty used to rent it and she did it up like this. But then she went and got knocked up and moved out to live in a house with bricks with her baby daddy."

"I love it," I admitted.

"You're all set up," Joe called from the doorway. "Don't forget. I need some kind of payment on Saturday." The look he gave me let me know what kind he was hoping for but that would be a hell no. Cash in his hole would be my go to method, thank you very much.

Lyla laughed at the look on my face and headed out after him. "I'll give you some time to get yourself settled. If you wanna come down to the beach with me in a bit, we can go see who's hanging out by the fire down there tonight. There's some pretty hot guys living here if you look hard enough." She winked at me and I grinned back. "Welcome to the neighbourhood, sweetie."

The moment she closed the door, I turned the lock and looked around at my own little space. I dropped down onto the blue couch and breathed out a laugh.

Mutt jumped up and snuggled into the couch beside me with what I could have sworn was a doggy smile on his face.

Tonight I'd managed to escape the entire Harlequin Crew with hundreds of dollars worth of clothes and shit they'd bought me as well as around two grand in cash without them even seeing me run.

I was set up in their town with my own place and no way for them to figure out where to find me and on top of that, I was freaking loving my new trailer. I wasn't sleeping in a car or wondering whether or not I was going to get caught peeing in a bush.

Shit, I bet they're freaking out right about now.

A laugh tore from my lips as I imagined it and Mutt jumped up, barking excitedly.

"Home sweet home, boy," I said to him. "I think we're gonna like it here."

CHAPTER ELEVEN

"**T**he Damned Men claimed the old Sailor's Eye Lighthouse last night," Draper told me.

His name was actually Dirk, but everyone called him Don Draper on account of the stupid ass suits he insisted on wearing about town and his quaffed dark hair. He fancied himself a businessman because he swindled tourists in the upper quarter to take his overpriced tours to locations in Sunset Cove that had featured in movies. Which of course, they hadn't. The closest Sunset Cove had ever gotten to fame was the alleged time the Beach Boys had visited back in the seventies and Carl Wilson had gotten food poisoning at the Squid Shack. Suffice to say, if the story even was true, the band had never come back. But the Squid Shack was still a popular as shit destination thanks to Draper's tours and the cordoned off toilet where Carl had supposedly shat a lung.

"We'll make a move to claim it back," I growled, irritation prickling along my skin as I turned to Kestrel who was my best eyes and ears in the cove. He wasn't much to look at with his small build and washed out looks and he tended to blend right into the background, but that was what made him so good at his job. "I want a report on how many men Maverick is stationing there and how often they come and go."

"No problem, boss," Kestrel agreed.

"We won most of Palmview Street at least," Draper added and a murmur of excitement rippled through the room. The elders were nodding enthusiastically, the old folks my dad had worked with since back in my day including a few of my uncles. My Great Uncle Nigel always had a lot to say, but before he could pipe up about how we should announce our victory by painting the houses on Palmview Street in the Harlequin colours or some other pointless vanity endeavour, I spoke.

"Not good enough," I snapped and silence fell instantly. I looked to Chase and JJ who were sat to my right, their expressions as dark as mine. "How much more territory have we won this year?"

JJ sighed. "Practically nothing. Whatever we win, they take back. And whatever they win, we take back."

"The Divide's always been a push and pull," Merkle reasoned across the room, the muscly bald guy one of my best arms smugglers. "So long as they're not gaining territory, it's serving some purpose as a barrier at least."

"We should be gaining territory," Chase snarled and I nodded my agreement as others in the room nodded theirs.

Uncle Nigel tutted, pushing his fingers into his grey beard. "We should be celebrating our victory, splashing the news across town, reminding the people of Sunset Cove who protects them in their beds at night, who keeps the streets clean of Damned Men filth."

"What good will that do?" Chase rolled his eyes.

"It will bolster the people," Nigel pushed. "And without the town's support, what are we but heathens? The Harlequins are great, so let it be known!"

I suppressed an internal sigh, waving Chase down as he opened his mouth to argue. I nodded to my uncle, knowing I had to keep the elders content. "We'll organise a rally. But I want The Divide pushed back a mile by the end of the month, and I want the fucking lighthouse back by the end of the week," I demanded. "Merkle, triple our weapons supply. And I want new recruits." I stood from my seat, sweeping a finger around to point at everyone. "You'll all sign up fresh blood or I'll question your value as a

Harlequin. We're done here."

I strode toward the stairs, feeling Chase and JJ close on my heels as I made it to the top and knocked twice to let my men know we were coming out. They stepped aside as I opened the door and I nodded to them, my eyes skimming across the party goers down the hall as I instinctively hunted for Rogue.

Unease filled me as I headed through the house, failing to spot her anywhere.

"Where is she?" I growled as we made it to the kitchen and Chase grabbed a bottle of rum off the island.

"I dunno, man. Let's just have a good time. We haven't even celebrated our last job. Who cares where the ghost is?"

"You're always fucking celebrating," I pointed out, ignoring a shot glass as he held it out to me. JJ downed one and I walked out onto the patio, hunting the pool, the loungers. But she wasn't among anyone there.

The uncomfortable feeling I was getting only continued to grow and I headed back inside, feeling my friends following me again as I made it to the stairs and my man stepped aside to let me pass. I jogged up to the first level and hurried along to her room, pushing the door wide and stepping into the space. Empty.

I turned back into the hall, my heart beginning to thump unevenly as I noticed my door was ajar and I strode through it as JJ headed into his own room.

I swear I could smell her on the air. She'd been in here. And the bathroom door was wide open so maybe she was *still* fucking here, snooping into my private space.

I crossed the room in a few furious strides, switching the light on as I entered the en-suite and came face to face with a lipstick message written in curling letters across the mirror.

Bye, Badger X

My hands curled into tight fists and I gritted out the only word I could manage right then. *"No."*

I stormed back through the room and into the hall, sure she couldn't have gotten out of my house. There was no way. I had a man on every door. Wherever she was, she had to still be here.

"She took my fucking sunglasses again," JJ huffed as he stepped out of his room.

Chase was leaning against a wall down the hall, drinking rum like he gave no fucks, but as he took in my expression, he stood upright and frowned.

"What is it?" he asked.

"She's trying to leave," I hissed, shoving into her room and starting to check that all the balcony doors were locked. There was no way she'd gotten out. No fucking way.

JJ helped me search, his brow creased in concern as we worked from room to room, stalking her, hunting her. All of her stuff was missing from her closet. Everything we'd bought her. Fuck, that girl was going to be in trouble when I found her. People didn't disobey me without consequences. I'd offered her fucking everything here and she was throwing it back in my face.

"No joy?" Chase asked as I headed back to the stairs and I bared my teeth at him.

"Start looking, asshole," I commanded and his eyes darkened.

"If she's gone, I say good fucking riddance."

I lunged at him, locking my hand around his throat and pinning him to the wall as a deadly energy burned through me. "She's mine. And if her presence upsets you, then you don't have to stay here, Chase. But she is staying either way."

His lips parted indignantly, but I didn't hang around for his response, storming downstairs while JJ murmured something to Chase which soon got him following me. I strode outside again where the music had been turned up and people were grinding against one another by the pool.

I stuck two fingers in my mouth and whistled, causing everyone to look my way and stop mid-fucking dance as they realised who wanted their attention.

"Who's seen my girl?" I demanded and several people shook their heads in answer.

But one shirtless guy with a joint in the corner of his mouth pointed to the wall, seeming nervous.

"The rainbow haired chick, right?" he asked in a drawling surfer way and I nodded, my hands curling into fists. "She scaled that wall about an hour ago, boss. Jumped right up from the barbeque and I was like *woah*, that rainbow chick can fly."

Fireworks burst through my skull and I grabbed the nearest sun lounger, tossing it into the pool with a bellow of rage. "The party's over, get the fuck out of my house!" I roared, taking my gun from my waistband and firing a shot into the sky. People screamed and ran like they were under attack as they grabbed their clothes and sprinted for the exits.

Chase and JJ shared a look that said they were fucking concerned, and they should have been.

An hour. She'd been gone for one whole hour. She couldn't have gotten that far on foot, but what if she'd jacked a car again? Or hitch-hiked? Or-

I rounded on JJ and Chase. "Split up. JJ, search the beach. Chase, head to the west side of town, I'm going south. Call me if you find her."

I stalked into the house, a possessiveness filling me that wouldn't quit. Losing her wasn't optional. I wouldn't sleep until I found her. She'd walked back into my life and hell if I was going to let her run from me again. She might have hated me, but I didn't give a fuck. I'd figure that out just as soon as I got her back. I couldn't think beyond that. I just needed Rogue Easton in my home, in my life. She had to stay here or I'd fucking break. *And I will not break for her again.*

I fetched my keys from upstairs then unlocked the door that led into the garage and ran down to it, jumping into my truck. I started her up and tore out of the garage, racing along the drive and flashing my lights at the men on the gate to let me out. There were plenty of party goers walking on foot in flip flops, wearing bikinis and shorts with drinks still in hand. I beeped my horn and they scattered faster than fucking ants as my headlights lit them up.

I tore through the middle of them and the wheels of my truck bounced as they hit the road and I burned up the tarmac as I turned south, speeding along the streets. I took the backroads, sure she'd try and outsmart me if she was out here looking for somewhere to hide for the night. But there was nowhere in Sunset Cove that she could hide from me. This was my domain. I knew every shadowy corner, every darkened door, every fucking back alley. But the size of the town was against me. Especially if she had a vehicle, she could be anywhere. She could be on the fucking highway to the next city by now, in any direction.

"Fuck!" I roared, punching the steering wheel, my pulse pounding too loudly in my ears.

I pulled up the display on my car dash, tapping on JJ's number and hitting call. He answered after one ring. "Anything?" I demanded, speaking before he could.

"Nothing yet. Just relax, brother. We'll find her."

I hung up on him, calling Chase instead.

"Give me good news," I growled down the line and he sighed.

"Look, man. She's gone. Face it, we're all better off without her. Don't you remember the fucking dark days after she left? Better we deal with it now than go through that again."

"How can you say that?" I hissed. "You know why she left. Because of *us*. And I'm not going to make the same mistake twice."

"It's her fucking choice. She doesn't want us anymore. She wants our cash, or our keys, or all of the fucking above," he pushed and my teeth snapped together as I refused to believe that.

"It's more than that," I growled. "She's one of us."

"She stopped being one of us a long time ago. Why can't you accept that?" he demanded and it was only because he was my lifelong friend that he could get away with speaking to me like that. I'd destroy anyone else for it. But I wasn't pig headed enough not to listen to the closest men in the world to me.

"Because I fucked up with Rogue and I'm going to make it right this time," I snarled.

"By keeping her as your prisoner?" he scoffed.

"If that's what it takes," I hissed then jammed my finger on the button to kill the call.

Fuck him. I didn't care what he thought of my behaviour over Rogue. It didn't make a whole lot of sense to me either, but she'd awoken a beast in me who was nothing but a feral creature with one, single need. And that need was her. I couldn't fight that part of me any more than I could cut off my own head.

So I was going to find her, bring her home and make her mine. I didn't care what price I had to pay for that. Rogue Easton was not getting away a second time.

Dawn broke through the sky like gold paint spilling across a canvas. I was up on Carnival Hill, gazing down at the glistening water from the seat of my truck, my phone as silent as the grave.

Gone.

She was gone.

She'd slipped through my fingers like sand, silent and inevitable. Yet my heart refused to let go this time. There was no choice in it like there had been before. When I'd stood on Devil's Pass as a sixteen year old boy and told her to run. I could still feel the cracks in my heart that were left there from that day.

I wished I could reach into the past and rip that fucking day from existence. I wanted to change the thread fate had spun for us and spin us a new one. A life where we'd all just stayed together and none of the fucked up shit had happened to us.

But I was stuck in this new reality where Rogue hated me, where my brother had become my sworn enemy, where so much blood had been washed from my hands that I'd long since forgotten the moment I'd become a monster just like my father.

There'd been a time I'd tried to fight that. I'd never wanted to end up like him. A man I hated. Who had forged me in his image and handed me the baton to run his crew in his place. I had vowed to be better. But I wasn't. I'd done just as many dark and twisted things as he had. And now I knew why he'd done them too.

I curled my hands around the steering wheel as tiredness gnawed at my brain and I scraped through every option I had left to me. There was one thing I knew wasn't an option though. Because it hadn't ever been an option in all the years since Rogue had been gone. I wouldn't give up searching for her.

Even after JJ and Chase had finally stopped looking and I'd sworn I had too, I'd never really meant it. I may have called off my men from the hunt. But I'd still sought her out in every woman I'd claimed. I'd found something in them that reminded me of her, a piece I wanted to carve out of them and keep. The way they smiled or laughed, the shape of their eyes or nose, the way they spoke their mind, or gazed at the sea like it held a million possibilities in its depths. I had tried to find my Rogue in fractures of all of them. But all along, I knew I was fooling myself. And by the time I'd had my fill of them, they lost their appeal. I could no longer see the pieces of Rogue I thought I'd found in them. She was an illusion, always alluding me, tempting me into a stranger's eyes only to leave me high and dry when I tried to dig her out of them. So to lose her again when I had found the real thing after all this time was unimaginable.

I was well aware I wasn't thinking straight, let alone acting straight since she'd been back. But I'd always known the sacrifices would be high to hold onto her if she ever returned. My mind was the least of my worries.

I sat there until the sun had fully risen and scrubbed at my eyes, starting the truck and turning down the dusty track that led up here through the trees. I'd walked this path a thousand times in my youth. We'd hung out on Carnival Hill all the time, played in the woods, watched the sun set over the water. In a few months, the carnival would come with a circus and music, games and rides. I'd once won Rogue a hummingbird keyring just like the tattoo on my inner arm on the miniature rifle range. I remembered laying with her on the beach after, her fingers wound between mine as we gazed up at a moon which had seemed impossibly large.

"Do you prefer the night or the day?" she asked and my thumb skated across her knuckles.

"The night," I answered.

"Why?" She rolled toward me, our fingers becoming unclasped. I took the cigarette from her mouth, smirking as I toked on it.

"Because anything seems possible in the dark," I answered as I released a line of smoke and it coiled away on the wind.

"What would you do if anything was possible, Fox?" she whispered

conspiratorially, leaning closer so her coconut scent reached me.

I'd keep you as mine.

"That's a secret," I told her, falling down onto my back as she tried to wrestle the cigarette from my hand while I laughed.

My secret hadn't changed. Only I didn't care to keep it quiet anymore. Maybe if I'd been brave enough to say it back then, everything could have been different.

I wouldn't be shy about my intentions for her now. We'd already lost too much time together. My heart had been too hollow for too long, and now she was slipping away again right under my watch.

I drove down to the main road and headed back toward Harlequin House, but before I got there, JJ called.

"Did you find her?" I demanded as I answered, my heart thundering against my ribcage.

"Yeah, get down to Sunset Beach, just off the end of The Mile," he said and relief crashed through me like a fucking tsunami.

"On my way," I said, hanging up and speeding through a stop sign.

She hadn't left town. She may have run, but she wasn't gone. And that surely had to mean she was staying regardless of what she thought of me or the others.

Maybe she wanted to put down roots in the soil she'd grown up on. And maybe that meant I had time to change her mind about being mine. Not that I was gonna give her a whole lot of fucking choice in the matter. And the girl was in serious trouble for being an ungrateful little brat right now. But first, I just needed to see that she was okay before I went volcanic on her ass.

She was turning me into one hell of an unpredictable bastard and it made me feel all kinds of uneasy. My ways were set in stone. I had systems and rules and the fucking code to think about. But with her, it all just went tits up. She'd only been back in my life a week and I was already losing the plot, trying to hold onto her with all I had. But the fear of losing her was just too fucking raw. It didn't matter if it was ten years ago, nothing had healed the loss of her. She'd owned my heart this entire time and it didn't matter if it was just a bloody lump of meat that had been carved up by a butcher because of her absence. It was still beating, so it was still hers. And even after it stopped it would remain hers until it was nothing but ash in her palm.

I started to stew as I raced along the roads, the morning brightening up all the dark spaces in this end of town, but it couldn't chase away the monsters that lived here. We were always in plain view, night or day, bad deeds trailing in our wake. Mine were miles long and painted a picture of me which had children and adults alike cowering in their beds. I was a living nightmare that reminded everyone to fall in line with my crew or they might just find themselves as bait for the sharks out in the deep blue sea with a fishhook in their thigh. My enemies were those who disobeyed the laws I laid out. For no empire was great without order. And this town was mine to rule. So I ruled it well.

I headed down The Mile and turned off the road down a track that led onto the beach intended for emergency vehicles, the unmade road making my truck jostle as I took the bumps at speed, anxious to reach my girl. I was getting more angry at her by the second, furious that she'd show me up like this.

My worry that she was gone was fast fading into something I knew far better. Rage. And when my temper took me, I tended to be a savage asshole who took no fucking prisoners. But I planned on making an exception this time. Because I sure as shit was going to be leaving this beach with one prisoner. It was time Rogue learned that there were consequences for messing with the king of this town.

The wheels of my truck hit sand and I slowed to a halt, gazing out at the surfers on the water catching the morning tide. There was a smoking bonfire in the distance and a bunch of passed out people lying around it. Among them was a girl with rainbow hair sitting with her knees pulled up as she pulled off her shirt to reveal a tiny baby blue bikini top.

I slammed my foot to the accelerator, my focus pinned on her as I drove across the beach like a fucking maniac. Some of the surfers had to leap out of my way and they got a face full of sand as the huge wheels spat it back at them. A few of the people sleeping near Rogue woke up, spotting the oncoming vehicle and scrambling to their feet, running for their fucking lives. Rogue looked to me, her lips popping open, but she didn't move. Not a fucking inch.

I pulled the parking brake, half doughnutting the truck as I spun the wheel and coming to a firm halt several feet from her. I shoved my door open and got out before tossing it closed behind me, taking in a deep breath of the morning air as I marched toward her.

She gazed coolly up at me as I came to a stop in front of her, my shadow consuming her as her little dog yapped furiously at me.

"Good morning, Badger," she said airily, reaching into a sports bag beside her and calmly taking out a bottle of sunscreen. "Help a girl out? I don't wanna burn." She reached behind her back and I choked on my own breath as she yanked on the bikini string, undoing it so the bikini top slipped forward. Half a second before her tits spilled out, I did the only thing I could think of and leapt on her. I crushed her down onto the towel she'd apparently slept on, baring my teeth in her face.

"Hey!" she yelled.

"What the fuck do you think you're doing?" I demanded, so close to her that I could count every eyelash framing her large navy blue eyes. The curves of her near naked body pressed to mine and I could feel that the bikini top had slid down so her bare breasts were crushed against my chest. Her nipples were hard and her widening eyes told me she'd noticed it too. So I smirked, gripping her jaw in a tight hold as my cock jerked to attention in my pants.

"Get the fuck off of me," she growled and I reached between us, my fingers grazing over her soft flesh and getting me rock hard for her as I searched for the bikini top.

"You don't get your tits out in front of strangers," I ordered her and her lips popped open indignantly.

"Firstly, I wasn't. I was making sure you could put the sunscreen on my back and not miss the fucking strap line. And secondly, I can get naked anywhere I want because I'm not your damn property. But I wouldn't get naked for *you* if you paid me."

My fingers grazed over her flesh as I ignored her and her palm crashed against my cheek. I growled irritably before finding the slips of material and manoeuvring them up over her breasts, keeping her concealed as I did so. I tied the knot firmly behind her neck as she continued to struggle which only meant she was grinding on me harder and was getting a feel for every inch of me.

I was seriously fucking satisfied when I returned my gaze to her face and realised she was blushing. She clenched her jaw though and anger pulsed in her eyes while I took in her pinking cheeks with a thirst that would never be sated.

"Well enjoy standing up and showing everyone your boner for me, asshole," she said in a sharp tone that contradicted her blush and I rolled my eyes.

"As if I give a fuck that everyone knows my girl turns me on." I got up and headed back to my truck in search for some clothes I could put on her, but when I came up short, I pulled my own shirt off and turned back to her. Finding her fucking gone.

I clutched my shirt in a death grip as my eyes fell on her ass hanging out of the bikini bottoms which were apparently a fucking thong as she walked past the smoking bonfire. She started talking to some of JJ's girls from the club as they returned from the water with their boards under their arms. She took a long purple board from Diane and jogged towards the water, giving me no option but to wait here for her.

Her dog sat on her towel, looking like it was guarding it from me, especially since the little bastard was glaring right at me.

Did she sleep here all night like a fucking hobo? What did she expect me to do, just let her live on the streets? Maybe a night sleeping rough had knocked some fucking sense into her and she'd gladly dive into my truck and come home with me just as soon as she was done surfing. I took out my phone to call JJ, wondering where the fuck he was, but was saved the bother when he came running out of the water with Chase, their boards tucked under their arms.

"Nice to know you've been enjoying yourselves," I gritted out. "Did you just pop back home for your boards and shit before you even bothered to call to let me know you'd found her?"

"Chill, bro," JJ laughed. "I got Piston to grab our shit and bring it down here for us. We never took our eyes off of her, I swear. We kept an eye on her from the ocean."

"What if she'd run off again?" I growled.

"Then we'd all be back to living the good life," Chase muttered, walking on past me and I watched him go with a scowl as he reached the edge of the beach where Piston's truck was parked up with the man himself smoking behind the wheel as he watched the surfers.

Chase rested his board against the truck, pulling off his wetsuit and leaving it to dry on the hood so the artwork of Sunset Cove on his back gleamed wetly in the morning light. His dark red trunks were soaked through and more than one girl was staring at him as he took his pack of smokes from the car and walked back toward us, lighting one up.

JJ stripped out of his suit too, hanging it to dry on my truck before he moved to stand beside me, looking out to the water where Rogue was diving under the waves with her board to get beyond the break. My teeth ground in my mouth as I watched her round ass disappear.

She turned her board around and started paddling as a wave built up behind her, her arms carving through the water as she fought to catch it and as it pushed her forward, she jumped up, her knees bending as she rode the wave, looking like a fucking dream as I just stood and stared at her toned body tensing and flexing, forgetting everything as I just fucking watched.

She was smiling so brightly that I swear it made my heart skip a beat and I couldn't help but wonder if she'd been able to get out on the water much wherever she'd been for the last ten years. We'd all used to joke that she should have been born a mermaid because she was so obsessed with the sea, and I really hoped she'd at least had this wherever she'd been.

Her little bikini was garnering her a lot of attention and my eyes flipped over to the assholes she'd been out here with last night as several of the guys elbowed each other, pointing her out in the water.

I stuck my fingers in my mouth, whistling for her and as her eyes met mine, I beckoned her in, my possessive anger raking bloody claw marks across my insides. I itched to put a bullet in the skull of every man staring at her. And as I started striding toward the water with the intention of dragging her ass back into my arms, she flipped me off with both fingers.

"Rogue!" I bellowed, my head snapping around to take in the wolf whistling guys as my brain came close to combusting. Anyone who saw me promptly shut the fuck up, but my gaze locked on one asshole in particular who had his phone out, *recording* her.

Carter Jenson. The hippy junkie douchebag with his harem pants and cuntbag attitude.

I tore my attention away from him and waded out into the sea, swimming for Rogue as soon as I got deep enough. She wasn't fast enough to escape me. I upended her board with a sharp tug on the nose of it and she screamed as she fell under the waves. I shoved the board behind me, letting it sail back to shore as I caught her waist and clutched her against me to shield her body from view.

"Let me go you psycho!" she shouted, clawing at my back as I flattened her against the plain of my chest. She wasn't nearly strong enough to fight me off as I waded back to shore and caught her wrists, pinning them at the base of her spine. She sank her teeth into my shoulder and I groaned, unable to help liking that as I walked her up to my truck and JJ helpfully opened the door for me. I dumped her inside, climbing in after her and JJ tossed my shirt into the footwell, laughing his fucking head off.

I grabbed it and dragged it over her head while she kicked and screamed and writhed, but I wasn't letting her go anywhere until she covered herself the fuck up.

"If you wanna stay here with your friends then put the fucking shirt on or I'm taking you home this second," I snapped and she stilled in shock.

"You can't treat me like a child," she hissed, her body writhing beneath me and the scent of sea salt clinging to her flesh.

"I can if you behave like one," I shot back. "What the fuck kind of stunt was that? You were trying to bait me."

She narrowed her gaze then her eyes became hooded and she wet her lips. Her legs curled around me, drawing me flush against her body and my breathing came heavier as I considered how she might like being fucked on the bench of my truck. No one would question who she belonged to ever again if they heard her screaming my name.

"No Fox, I didn't want to bait you," she purred and my throat thickened as my gaze fell to her full lips, my dick grinding into the thin material of her bikini bottoms through my jeans, but it was all too much material for my liking. "I wanted to remind you that I'm not yours. And you can't tell me what the fuck to do." She slammed her forehead into mine and I cursed as I reared back while she tried to wriggle free and open the door behind her.

But she wasn't getting away that easily. I clutched her hair in my grip, just tight enough to restrain her and she unhooked her legs from my waist, though the panting breaths leaving her were an obvious giveaway to how much she wanted me. So why couldn't she just fucking admit it? Who cared if she hated me? She'd get over it once I was inside her making her scream.

"Do you wanna stay here and play with your friends?" I asked again and she locked her lips tight together. "Then I guess I'm taking you home." I got off of her and she sat up, shaking her head, looking just as agonisingly tempting in my shirt as she had without it.

"No," she blurted. "I wanna stay."

I pressed my tongue into my cheek, stepping out of the truck. "Test me again and you'll regret it," I warned and she nodded, though I didn't trust that innocent look for shit. I guessed I was soft for this girl though. I didn't give second chances to anyone, let alone third or fourth chances. I mean, I was still considering a mass killing spree on this beach for anyone who had looked at her out on the water. But as I didn't fancy spending the rest of my life in prison, I only had one particular asshole in my sights right now.

I gestured for Rogue to step past me and she scowled as she slid out of the truck and did so.

"Morning, sweetheart." JJ smirked at her and I didn't miss how her eyes dipped to his naked chest before she gave him a smile with actual warmth in it before heading over to sit back on her towel with the mutt.

Chase shook his head at me, muttering something to himself and I glowered at him.

"If you've got something to say, spit it out. Don't mutter under your breath like a little bitch," I snarled and he pushed a hand into his wet hair, taking his sweet time to answer as he sucked on his cancer stick.

I'd tried getting him off the things, but then he just turned to harder shit, so this was my way of compromising. Telling Chase what to do led to him acting out like a pissed off toddler. In fact, him and Rogue had that in common.

"The whole beach just saw how weak you are for that chick," he said coldly, jerking his chin in her general direction. "You wanna fuck her? Go nuts. But keeping her long term…" He tutted, toking on his cigarette again. "It's gonna get you dead."

I moved forward and squared up to him, lifting my chin to emphasise the half inch of height I had on him but he stared right at me, not backing down like he should. "I don't give a fuck if everyone on the planet knows she's my girl. In fact, I'd gladly send them all a fucking warning individually. If you think a single motherfucker in this world could use her against me, you're wrong. Because no one will get close to her without ending up dead at my fucking feet for it. When I'm done driving the message home, everyone in this town will treat her like she's a live bomb fit to fucking blow." My eyes shifted over his shoulder, landing on the back of Carter's head as he walked up the beach toward the public restrooms. "Now if you'll excuse me, I'm gonna go and hand out my first warning."

I caught JJ's eye and silently communicated for him to watch Rogue to which he nodded his agreement. Then I walked away up the beach, my boots kicking up sand as I went, my fingers flexing as my thirst for blood grew to a tangible taste on my tongue.

I slowed my pace as I entered the restroom, the sound of Carter pissing reaching my ears and I folded my arms as I came to a halt behind him, waiting for him to finish.

"There's another urinal right there, bro," he said without looking over his shoulder. If he had, he would have realised that not only was I not his bro, but I was a goddamn predator out for its next meal.

He finished pissing, shaking his junk and tugging up his stupid fucking harem pants before heading over to the sink and washing his hands. I followed silently and he stilled as his eyes met mine in the rusted mirror on the wall.

"What part of mine do you not understand?" I asked in my deadliest voice and if the guy hadn't just relieved himself, I was pretty sure there'd be a wet patch growing around his crotch right now.

He turned around to face me, the blood draining from his face drop by glorious drop. "Look man, I d-dunno what's upset you, but-"

"What's upset me, *man-*" I moved closer to him and his ass hit the sink as he backed away and I continued to advance on him with slow and measured steps. "Is that not only did you stare at *my* girl-"

"She's hot and I'm only human," he gasped and I sneered, hatred slithering through my veins as I got close enough to smell the sweat on him.

"You recorded her for your dirty, pathetic little spank bank." I stuffed my hand into his pocket, wrenching his phone out and dropping it onto the floor. I slammed my heel onto it repeatedly until it was nothing but shattered glass and broken metal. I never took my eyes off his while I did it and his lower lip started to tremble, the cogs working behind his eyes as he tried to come up with some excuse that would save his pathetic ass from what was going to happen next.

"She's y-yours," he stammered. "I get that now. I won't go anywhere near her again."

"No," I said, reaching out and calmly taking hold of his throat. "You won't."

I cracked his head back against the mirror before throwing him to the floor. He screamed like an infant as I started kicking him, my mind going to the darkest, most twisted place it held as I kicked and stamped and made this asshole hurt for daring to even *think* about touching my girl.

Footsteps pounded into the room and Chase appeared, his eyebrows arching for a second as he took in the guy I was beating the living shit out of. Then he continued walking over to a urinal, whistling as he relieved himself and I reached down to grip Carter's hair in my fist, pointing a finger in his face.

"This is your one and only warning, do you understand me?" I growled.

"Y-yes," he sobbed and I released him, my upper lip peeling back as I headed outside and Chase appeared a second later, his shoulder brushing mine as we walked back down the beach together.

"Look, if she means that much to you, I won't say another word. I just care about you, brother. I remember how fucked up we all were after she left last time. I just…don't want that shit to play on repeat. I've lived it once. We won't survive it again."

I looked to him, finding a frown etched into his forehead. I wasn't stupid enough not to realise JJ, Chase and even fucking Maverick had loved Rogue once. But I didn't know exactly how deeply that love had run. We'd never spoken about it. All I knew was that we'd all fought over her enough times to make it clear she was under all of our skin. But it was obvious Chase had moved on and JJ wouldn't step on my toes when it came to her. He didn't do relationships anyway. For him, it was all about sex. But he wouldn't cross any lines with Rogue now I'd claimed her. That didn't mean her return wasn't a headfuck for both of them though.

"I know the risks," I told him.

"You're always trying to convince me not to take risks, asshole." Chase smirked at me, toying with one of the leather bands on his wrists.

"Yeah well, when it comes to her, I have no fucking boundaries," I said with a shrug. "I'll do anything for her. And anything to keep her."

"I'm guessing that's why you just laid out hippy McGee back there?" he asked.

I blew out an amused breath and he raised his eyebrows knowingly.

"Come surf with me, headcase," he asked, grinning at me like a fucking idiot, but I shook my head.

"I'm gonna go and...not be an asshole to Rogue," I said and he laughed, throwing his damn head back.

"Good luck with that." He jogged over to JJ who'd attracted a little group of fan girls and I made a direct path towards Rogue.

She was lying on her back with JJ's sunglasses on, her dog curled up in the shade of her gym bag which she'd propped up with some old cola bottles.

Yeah...no.

I headed past her and her apparent new friends to where a couple were sitting under a large parasol. I ducked under it, plucking it out of the ground and the girl yelped in surprise, clinging to her boyfriend as I walked away from them.

"That's Fox Harlequin," the guy gasped as I headed back to Rogue and planted it in the ground, meaning her and the mutt were shaded properly.

"Who the fuck is sun-blocking me?" she asked without opening her eyes beneath the glasses and I snatched one of her friend's towels, laying it down beside her and dropping onto it.

She finally opened her eyes and huffed out a breath. "Come to badger me, Badger?"

I tried not to let that petty little nickname annoy me, but it did. "I came to talk."

"Great, could you do it somewhere else though, you're kinda killing my vibe."

"Rogue," I warned.

"Badger," she sighed, pushing JJ's glasses onto her head. "Why don't you go surfing with your bros or something?"

"So you can run off again?" I arched a brow and she stared me down for half a second, all poker face before she cracked a smirk.

"You think you know me so well, don't you, asshole?"

"I *do* know you so well," I said simply.

"You don't know this new version of me. She plays dirty. You won't like her very much."

"I like her so far," I mused and she frowned at me like I was dense.

"Why?" Her nose wrinkled and it was so fucking familiar and cute and one of the million things I'd missed about her, I couldn't help but smile. "I hate you. So what part of my attitude towards you is turning you on? Because if it's the challenge, you need to get your head out of your ass because I am off limits to you. That is not an invitation to try harder. It's an invitation to fuck off and take the Brady Bunch with you."

Her fiery tone was getting me hot and I realised I didn't really give a shit how much she ran her mouth at me. So long as she was still fucking here, I'd take anything on offer. "I can read you just like I could always read you, baby. It's why I call you hummingbird, remember?" I reached out to place my hand over her heart, but she slapped it away before I could get close.

"I'm not your hummingbird. That little nickname doesn't mean shit to me anymore. You're really not getting the message, are you?"

"Nope." My gaze dropped to her mouth which was parted with panting breaths then to her chest which was heaving, the way her thighs were pressing tightly together and I just fucking smirked. Because I wasn't deluding myself. She wanted me. Maybe just to fuck right now, but it would be more than that in time. It would be just like it was when we were teenagers and we were always so close to crossing that fucking line. But when I got my shot again, I wasn't going to pussy out this time. I was going to claim her as mine so deeply, that she'd never dare deny to the world who she belonged to ever again.

"You should put some sunscreen on," I said.

"And you should get some sleep. You look like shit, Badger." She looked at my eyes which were no doubt heavy with dark rings, but I'd have gone a whole fucking year without sleep just to be sitting next to her here in the flesh again. I had no intention of closing my eyes anytime soon in case fate dared to steal her from me once more.

I reached for the bottle of sunscreen beside her dog and the mutt jumped up, growling at me. I pointed at him and barked, "Sit," in my sternest voice and the beast whimpered as its ass hit the sand, but it still glared at me like it was considering mauling my hand.

I swiped up the bottle and Rogue pouted at me. "So you want me to lie under a massive fucking umbrella, in a t-shirt *and* put sunscreen on? Are you into pasty vampire ass or something?"

"I'm into you not getting skin cancer," I deadpanned, opening the bottle and squeezing some lotion into my palm. Then I grabbed one of her legs, rubbing it into her flesh and she only kicked once before she fell still and let me continue. I worked up her calves, my heart pounding hard as I reached her thighs and dipped my hand between them, making sure she was covered all the way up to the hem of my shirt. Though I was seriously tempted to reach further. But even as I thought it, her thighs clamped shut on my fingers and her eyes narrowed at me.

"I don't need your help." She snatched the bottle away from me and my palm tingled with the warmth of her flesh.

It started off a chain reaction in my skin as I hungered for more. I wanted to touch her everywhere, examine all of her tattoos, seek out her scars and mark her with my tongue and teeth. I always grew bored of the women I'd pursued in the past. But I'd pursued her in my dreams for year after year. I would never grow tired of her. Would never be fucking sated.

"Stop looking at me like that," she snipped.

"Like what?" I asked in a low tone and goosebumps spread across her leg as my fingers brushed her flesh once more.

"Like you want to drag me back to your castle and lock me in a tower."

"But I do want to do that." I smiled darkly and she bit her lip for half a second before her expression turned to stone.

"I'm not coming back to your house, Fox. I have a new home."

"Where? The fucking beach?" I snarled, my anger rising quickly again.

"No," she said. "Somewhere I like. Somewhere that's mine."

I tsked. "Harlequin House is yours. And you'll grow to like it."

"I don't want to live with you. I didn't come back here to be enslaved by my enemies."

"*Enemies*," I scoffed.

She scowled then pushed to her feet. "You know what, Fox? You wanna sit in the shade. Go the fuck ahead." She grabbed her bag then kicked sand at me before walking off at a fierce pace down the beach. Her dog bounded after her and venom poured through my veins as I shoved myself upright and took off after her.

"I warned you, Rogue!" I called after her and she raised her middle finger in the air in answer, but her pace noticeably quickened.

Her friends were calling out for her to stop, but she kept walking, then broke into a fucking run.

I cursed, taking chase as she sprinted down the beach at full pelt and the girl was fucking fast. I ran after her with a growl of frustration, locking her in my gaze like a damn missile as she turned towards a little group of beach huts and darted between them.

I was two seconds behind her, racing between the huts and silence met my ears as I delved into the shadows.

"Rogue," I snapped. "Come out here."

There was no answer as I slipped into a cool space behind the huts beside a rocky wall and I moved along, glancing down the little alleys between the wooden buildings as I searched for her.

I walked from hut to hut, swearing under my breath as my heart started to pound with the worry of losing her again. Why did she have to keep fucking running?

I made it to the final hut, finding the last alley void of life and my teeth snapped together as I strode down it back onto the beach. I gazed along the sand, but she wasn't anywhere in sight. So I turned back to the huts, narrowing my eyes. The window of the closest one was ever so slightly ajar and I smirked as I walked up the steps onto the little porch, resting my ear to the door.

"Shh, Mutt," her voice reached me and I threw my shoulder against the door, sending it flying open.

Rogue screamed dramatically and I launched at her, grabbing her around the waist and throwing her over my shoulder. She kicked wildly, thumping me in the back as I strode out of the hut and the dog barked and nipped at my heels as I headed off down the beach, yanking her shirt down over her ass to make sure no one got of view of what was mine.

She fought me all the way back to my truck and I was glad when I noticed that JJ and Chase had returned to the water so I didn't have to bother explaining to them why I was kidnapping Rogue. But if she hadn't run, I wouldn't have had to.

I walked around to the back of my truck, reaching into the bed and taking out a length of rope before dumping her into it face down and climbing in to straddle her.

"You fucking prick!" she screamed as I bound her wrists behind her back and tied her ankles for good measure. Then I stood up, lifting her again and jumping out of the truck before planting her in the passenger side of the cab. The dog bit deep into my ankle and I swore, dropping down and grabbing him by the scruff, lifting him up so he was on eye level with me.

"Are you and me gonna have a problem?" I snapped at him and he growled, his eyes flicking to Rogue with a desperate plea in them.

Call me fucking crazy, but I kinda related to the lovesick little creature in that moment so I tossed him into Rogue's lap while she continued to curse me with every colourful word she knew before I shoved the door shut in her face and strode around to get in the driver's seat.

I yanked my door shut and she fell silent at last, glaring at me in all her sandy, rainbow sweetness and she looked so fucking hot I leaned over and crushed my lips to hers. She bit my lip so hard I tasted blood and I laughed as I drew away and started the engine.

"You taste like sunshine, hummingbird."

"You taste like a dead man," she growled.

"No, I taste like your new roommate. Get used to it." I drove down the beach, beeping my horn at JJ and Chase out on the water and they waved goodbye.

We were soon out on the road, heading home. And I didn't care if Rogue was as pissed off as a bobcat in a bees' nest. She was my fucking bobcat. And I would find a way to tame her until she was purring in my lap.

"I am always, *always* going to hate you, Fox Harlequin," she said in an icy tone aimed to scold. And it did. I just didn't believe her. Because there was too much between us. Too many days in the sun, too many secrets shared, too many memories that were etched into my heart as deeply as they were etched into hers. She just needed to remember why we still belonged to each other.

CHAPTER TWELVE

I refused to talk to Fox again the whole way back to his house while the taste of his blood lingered on my tongue and the heat of his kiss left my lips tingling. Fuck him. Fuck his stupid washboard abs and his fucking beautiful tattoos and his carelessly perfect hair and his I'm-the-king-of-the-world bullshit.

My wrists were tingling from the tightness of the rope that bound them behind my back and Mutt kept whimpering softly as he nuzzled against me, like he was trying to apologise for not taking down the big bad wolf for me. But I didn't need any help taking on this asshole. I was perfectly capable of doing that all by myself.

We pulled into the underground garage and Fox hopped out of the truck, rounding it to open my door and smirking at me as he hoisted me into his arms again without so much as a *do you mind?*

He threw me over his shoulder like I was a sack of potatoes and I had to fight the urge to scream over him treating me like some fucking possession that he could just haul around at his whim.

We headed up into the house with Mutt following close behind and Fox tossed me down on the white couch, my face smooshing into the cushions while my ass was left sticking up into the air.

I cursed him out, but my voice was muffled by the fabric beneath me as I tried to wriggle upright and I mostly just succeeded in thrusting my ass up even higher like I was a baboon looking for some action.

"If you want me to fuck you, you could just ask, baby," he teased, grabbing my hips and yanking me backwards so that I was tugged upright and fell back into his lap as he sat down on the couch.

"Why are you doing this to me?" I demanded. "Why can't you just get the hint and leave me alone? You do realise that claiming me like some caveman out for a mate isn't an acceptable form of courting, don't you?"

"If I was going to claim you like a caveman, my cock would be inside you right now and you'd be begging for more while hating yourself for it even more than you claim to hate me," Fox growled.

I tried to lurch out of his arms, fighting like a tomcat to escape while ignoring that teeny tiny bit of my brain - or no, it was more like a direct thought from my vagina who had rather ironically gone rogue on me - which wanted him to do that and prove his damn point.

"Untie me," I demanded as Fox's hands curled around my waist.

"You know, we could have a lot of fun with you tied up like this. And then you could just pretend to yourself that you'd had no choice but to go along with-"

I threw an elbow back into his gut as hard as I could and shoved myself upright, trying to hobble away with my feet tied.

Fox got to his feet behind me, catching the back of my bikini bottoms as I pitched forward and almost face planted the grey floorboards. He yanked me upright by them then half lifted me off of the floor as he swung me around towards the dining table where he pushed me face down over it.

"I can feel the way your body reacts every time I touch you," he said, cockily stepping up so close behind me that the hard ridge of his cock pressed to my core as he ground himself into me and a shiver raced down my spine as a moan almost escaped me but I bit it back hard.

"Fox," I hissed, trying to deny the heat in my body that was all hate and lust and fucking rage. I was wound so tight and so worked up that I was pretty sure I'd come all over his cock the second he pushed it into me, but I refused to give in to that desire.

"Yeah, hummingbird?" He swept my hair off of my face so that I could see him better as I looked back over my shoulder at him and his fist tightened in it just enough to let me know how rough he liked it.

"Get your fucking hands off of me and untie me right now," I growled, forcing aside any and all desire in my body with all the grit and determination I had. Because this wasn't why I'd come back here and I wasn't about to let him call the fucking shots on me.

Fox groaned like I was seriously testing his patience then stepped away from me, heading over to the kitchen and grabbing a knife. He slit through the ropes holding me, releasing my ankles first then my wrists and I whirled on him, punching him in the jaw the moment I could.

He was on me in a heartbeat, upending me and throwing me down on the dining table on my back before moving on top of me and forcing his hips between my thighs.

His green eyes darkened to pitch and I knew I was looking at the man everyone in this town feared as he glared down at me, the knife still in his hand and my heart jackhammering in my chest as he raised it.

"You think you really hate me that much?" he taunted, finding my hand and pushing the knife he held into my grip. I watched him in fear as he turned the blade in our combined grip and pressed it against his throat before removing his hand and just staring down at me. "So do it, then. Take your vengeance and rid the world of a monster while you're at it. My heart only beats for you anyway so if you want to carve it from my chest then you can. It's yours whatever way you want it."

I gritted my teeth and glared at him, my mind racing over every single reason I'd had to love this man once and realising they'd become the motivation for my hatred instead. He'd promised me the world and then taken it away again oh so fucking easily.

"Please don't do this," I begged, looking between all of them.

Fox was like a statue, cold and distant, his mind made up, the decision already dealt with.

I actually felt my heart shattering as I looked into his eyes and found nothing of the boy I'd loved there anymore. Just a Harlequin through and through who was done with me now.

The memories threatened to drown me and the ache in my fractured heart sharpened to a blinding pain. I'd let these boys get close enough to break me once before and I was never going to make that mistake again.

I exerted pressure on the blade, forcing Fox to lift his chin as a bloody line appeared on his throat and I swear his cock bulged even more keenly between my thighs.

But as I tried to force myself to push forward, to end this eternal suffering and take payment for everything they'd stolen from me, I found myself immobilised by all the reasons I'd once had to love them. It was just an echo of a thousand memories now, but it was the foundations of who I was. Who I had been. And no matter how much I hated the man above me, I knew a small, stubborn, foolish part of me would always love the boy he'd once been.

I pulled back and dropped the knife so that it fell off of the table, releasing a shaky breath as I accepted my own limitations where it came to hurting him.

"We're like the tide and the shore, hummingbird," Fox said in a low voice, leaning down to brush the words against my lips. "No matter how far the tide retreats, it can never stop itself from coming back for more."

He moved forward like he was going to try and kiss me again but I got the horrible feeling that I might let him if he did, so I twisted aside, scrambled out from beneath him and hopped down off of the table.

Every inch of my skin was living with this painful kind of desire and my pulse was skyrocketing as I backed away from him step by step and he watched me go with a confident kind of certainty that said he knew I'd be back again soon.

"If you're the shore in that analogy then you can consider this gap between us to be a sea wall," I ground out. "And no matter how many times the tide draws close to you, it will never cross that barrier."

Fox's jaw ticked and I turned away from him as I darted up the stairs to the room that was supposedly mine with my heart thundering and my body aching with a desperate desire which I refused to give in to.

When I made it into my room, I twisted the lock behind me then moved straight into the en-suite. The moment I closed that door, I pressed my back to it and slid my fingers straight inside my damp bikini bottoms to caress my aching core.

A soft moan of relief escaped me as I teased my clit and dipped my fingers into the wetness between my thighs.

My eyes fell closed and I refused to think about that blonde motherfucker or the way he'd taken control of my body. I didn't think about how hard and thick his cock had felt as he ground it against me and I gave no attention to how fucking lickable that V which dove beneath his jeans had looked while he reared over me.

The scent of him sailed up to surround me from the shirt he'd forced me to wear and I moaned loudly as I came hard, tumbling into oblivion with a pair of piercing green eyes staring back at me from the confines of my own mind.

Fuck Fox Harlequin. Fuck him for everything he could have been and everything he'd ruined. Fuck him for making me angry and hot and so fucking worked up that my own body had betrayed me. But most of all fuck him for thinking he could have me. Because if there was one thing in this world that I was willing to swear to above all others, it was that that would never happen.

Fox Harlequin might have been the ruler of this little slice of hell, but he was never going to own me.

I lay on my front by the pool in Fox's stupid house wearing nothing at all so that I could tan my ass while I played games on JJ's phone and listened to Riptide by Vance Joy with his headphones. I'd turned the volume up loud so I couldn't hear anyone calling my name while I lay there and pouted... and plotted. Because there was no fucking way I was staying here like some goddamn possession locked up safe and sound where no one could play with me.

I was currently not hearing a word Fox was saying as he tried to get my attention by standing over me and shouting my name really freaking loud. He could talk to my ass for all I cared.

When he finally gave up on that and reached out to touch my shoulder,

I flinched away from him, slapping his hand away and scowling as I dragged the headphones from my ears.

"You may enjoy treating me like a dog, but I don't need to be reminded of when to pee," I growled, narrowing my eyes as I looked up at him while making sure my tits stayed very much pressed to the sun lounger beneath me so he couldn't get a view of the goods. I was gonna need to figure out a way to sunbathe front up without them seeing me soon though or I'd have to just give in and let them look. It was weird that I cared really, because I wasn't precious about my body, but there was something about these boys seeing me naked that seemed sacrilegious or something. I'd spent way too long worrying about that as a teenager to just go full frontal without any kind of fanfare.

"We're going out," Fox said, jaw ticking as he fought to reign in that temper of his while his eyes kept skipping from my face to my body and back again.

"No thanks," I replied, moving to slide the headphones back up onto my head, but he snatched them off and tossed them aside.

"It wasn't an invitation. Chase is at the gym and JJ needs to go to the club. I've got a job to run, so you can't stay out here. I need you to come inside so that I can lock up."

"Wait...you're telling me that *you're* going out and you intend to lock me in the damn house while you're gone? I can't even sunbathe?" I made no effort to hide the disgust in my tone and Fox shrugged.

"Well, you've already proven that you're a flight risk. After that shit down at the beach, I'm inclined to think you're best off behind locked doors where I can be sure you're safe." He flexed his fist, glancing off to my left like he always used to when he was trying to hide something and I narrowed my eyes suspiciously.

"I can look after myself, Badger," I hissed. "I've been doing it for a hell of a long time."

"And look where that got you - half dead in a shallow grave. You do understand that, right? You're literally only alive because that asshole you were fucking didn't do a better job of finishing you off." Fox looked seriously pissed off at the thought of me screwing someone else and for once we were in agreement because fuck Shawn. But also, fuck Fox, so whatever.

I wanted to get right up in his face, but I refused to flash him my bare body, so I was stuck glaring where I was, but that wasn't going to hold me back.

"Oh I'm perfectly aware that if the great Fox Harlequin wanted me dead, I'd find the job much more thorough. No doubt you'd take me out on your boat and toss me to the sharks when you were done too. Just like Daddy used to."

"Don't knock it until you've tried it, love. I have the practice down to an art form now – the key is plenty of chum. And don't go thinking that I'm going to keep letting you get away with your shit. You're on lockdown until further notice. Unless you wanna give me that name so that I can eliminate the threat against you?" He cocked his head like he was waiting for an answer and I reached out to snatch the shirt I'd worn to bed from the floor beside my sun lounger so that I could get to my feet and rip him a new asshole.

Fox smirked like he thought he'd won something and strode away from me to let me get dressed. I yanked the shirt over my head, forcing my arms through the holes and ignoring the rich, cedar scent of it which marked it out as his. He was so freaking big that I could wear the damn thing like a dress, so as I stalked inside behind him, my ass was at least covered.

"Don't walk away from me, asshole," I yelled as I strode after him and JJ looked up from the lunch he was eating at the kitchen island.

"Guys," he said placatingly. "Can we just try to-"

"Did it ever occur to you that I want to off that motherfucker myself?" I demanded of Fox's muscular back as he opened the fridge and grabbed his protein shake out of the door.

"If you wanna be the one to pull the trigger then fine," Fox said. "Give me a name and I'll have fun with him for a couple of days. Then when I'm done, you can come on in and blow his brains out. You can even wear a tiara and play the part of the vengeful queen."

"You know, I still remember when we were fifteen and I punched you hard enough to give you a black eye and made you beg for mercy while I pinned you beneath me," I hissed. "I've beaten the great Fox Harlequin before now and I sure as fuck can go after my ex without needing him served up on a fucking platter."

"If you're referring to the time that you fought me for the right to pick what movie we were gonna sneak into down at the plaza, I think you're remembering it wrong. Did I let you jump all over me and pin me to the ground between your thighs? Yeah, but I'm pretty sure that little encounter served a far greater purpose than letting you pick a dumb movie. I'd been aching to get between your legs for a long time and I was perfectly happy to let you think you'd beaten me in exchange for that little bit of wrestling."

"True story," JJ agreed while my lips popped open in outrage. "The rest of us were pissed as fuck over that and I'm pretty sure Fox used it as inspiration material for a long time, if you know what I mean." He mimed jerking himself off as if I might have been too dense to pick up on that and I snarled internally.

"Whatever. I'm still perfectly capable of fighting my own battles," I said stubbornly.

JJ caught my hand and tugged me to sit on the stool beside him with a look that said *back off*, while I gave him a returning look that said *never*.

"If you wanna agree to be my girl, then you can have more freedom," Fox said as he leaned back against the work surface and looked over the kitchen island at me. "Every Harlequin in the city will watch your back no matter where you go."

"That sounds like hell on earth. I don't want to be watched," I snarled and JJ's hand landed on my knee beneath the worktop as he gave me a squeeze that could have been a warning but also sent warmth warring beneath my skin.

"Is that the only reason you're saying no?" Fox demanded. "The public recognition of your position if you're linked to me like that? What if I'm just asking because it's what I want?"

"I don't see why you would. We've done nothing but argue since the moment I was dragged through your door." I opened my mouth to go on, but JJ shifted his hand on my thigh beneath the table and the only thing that escaped my lips was a surprised breath as he gently caressed me with his fingertips and little zaps of electricity raced right to my core from his touch.

Fox tsked as he took a long swig from his shake before striding out of the room in the direction of the stairs.

My gaze moved from his retreating form to JJ's honey brown eyes and the moment they did, he smirked at me and pushed his fingers beneath the hem of the t-shirt I was wearing.

"What are you doing?" I hissed.

"You seem stressed, sweetheart," he replied in an equally low voice. "I'm just trying to help. Besides, I'm pretty sure you aren't wearing any panties under here, but I need to make sure."

My lips parted to tell him to stop, but as he continued to shift his fingertips along the sensitive skin on the inside of my thigh, I found myself momentarily lost for words. The last hands I'd had on my skin were Shawn's and as much as I was attempting not to give that asshole much thought, I felt weirdly dirty for knowing he'd been the last man to claim my body. Like I wanted to feel someone else possessing me to wipe away the stain his hands had left on my flesh.

Fox reappeared with a black shirt on and a gun jammed into the back of his pants. I'd once watched a documentary that happened to mention how doing that put you at risk of accidentally shooting your butt cheek off, but as this was Fox, I wasn't going to warn him about that. Although I did have to admit that it would be a damn shame to fuck up an ass as nice as his.

"For the record," Fox said as he strode back to the counter where he'd left his protein shake and picked it up again. "The only reason we are arguing is because you want to act like everything the four of us used to share means nothing to you now."

"*Five,*" I growled. "I don't care if you all hate Maverick now, you can't just deny that he was a part of us too. But I guess you don't care about making things up with him because he doesn't have a pussy. And as far as I can see it, Fox, the only reason you wanna fix things with me is because you've cooked yourself up a little fantasy about owning mine."

JJ moved his hand right up to the apex of my thighs and I stifled a gasp as he very nearly touched my core, my heart leaping with the thrill of the idea of him doing so right under Fox's nose.

"That's where you're wrong," Fox snarled.

"Oh yeah?" I taunted while trying not to pant with how much I wanted JJ to close that last little bit of distance between us and I tipped my thigh to the side to give him better access.

"You're mine, Rogue," Fox said in that takes no prisoners tone of his that said he really did believe he owned the entire world. "Always have been.

Always will be. It's why you came back to me, whether you're ready to accept that or not. So what I'm gonna need you to do, is stay put in the house while we go out. And when you're ready to give me the truth, we can talk about you going out again."

He strode around the kitchen island and I almost groaned in disappointment as JJ took his hand off of my leg, letting the t-shirt fall back down to cover me up before Fox could see what he'd been doing. Of course, I still hated him too. But letting him finger fuck me beneath the counter while Fox was being all you-belong-to-me, would have been the perfect secret up yours to that asshole.

Fox locked the door which led out to the pool and pocketed the key before turning and striding away like we were done here.

"You coming, J?" he called back and I looked at the man in question as he shook his head.

"I'm still eating. I'll head off in a few," he replied.

"You're going to be late," Fox grunted like that pissed him off, but JJ only shrugged.

"Can the boss really be late? I'm pretty sure they're all just early until I show up."

"Whatever." Fox headed out to the garage and silence fell as the door banged behind him.

"What was that about?" I demanded as JJ took a bite of his grilled cheese like nothing at all had happened.

"You mean the bit where I tried my luck with you or the part where you spread your legs and got nice and wet for me?" he asked casually before lifting his heated gaze to mine.

"*Please*, you were the one desperate to get a feel of me," I scoffed, ignoring the ache between my thighs that I really would have liked him to deal with as thoroughly as possible.

"Oh yeah?" he taunted.

"I thought Fox's word was law? Doesn't his claim on me mean you shouldn't be touching me?" I asked.

"I thought you said you weren't his girl?"

"I'm not," I replied fiercely.

"Well then. Sounds like there's everything to play for to me." JJ got to his feet and headed for the stairs, leaving me wondering what he'd meant by that.

"Where are you going today?" I asked as I leapt up and chased after him. "You can't seriously be going to leave me locked up inside on a beautiful, sunny day like this."

"Boss's orders," JJ shrugged as he made it to the top of the stairs and headed for his room.

"Well, the boss also claimed I was his property and I'm pretty sure you almost sampled the merchandise downstairs. So maybe you can just take me with you and it can be our little secret?"

"Oh, so it's come to blackmail has it?" JJ asked with a laugh. "Are you sure you're not just following me up here so that I can fuck that wet pussy of yours and help put out that fire in your veins?"

"Dead certain," I assured him coolly, ignoring the way everything in my body tightened at his words and the blatant confidence in his ability to fucking destroy me and holding firm as he stripped out of his shirt. Christ, why did I have to have self respect right now? His body was like...super high maintenance edibility. I needed to lick it. Slooooowly.

"How about this then, I'll bring you to the club with me if you pay for it with a kiss," JJ suggested.

"Seriously?" I asked, my gaze dropping down over his sculpted muscles and caressing those swallow tattoos which dove beneath his waistband before I could stop myself. I had an urgent kind of need to see the full extent of that tattoo, but I was pretty sure if I asked to see it we would be entering the point of no return. Shit, he got crazy hot while I was gone. This was not a problem I'd been expecting to face when I'd made my choice about coming back here.

"One kiss. At a time of my choosing. I've got a point to prove with you, runaway." He pinned me with an honest to shit smoulder and I practically had to cling to the doorframe to stop myself from begging him for it right now.

I was starting to think I needed to make use of that vibrator he'd bought me whenever I could escape to my trailer again to relieve some of this ache in my flesh. The last thing I needed was to drop my guard around the three men I'd come here to screw over and end up screwing them instead.

"Deal," I said, shrugging like I wasn't bothered either way and JJ gave me a panty melting smile.

"Fine. Get dressed and let's go. I picked you up some more clothes this morning, seeing as you won't tell us where you left the rest of the shit we got you." JJ grabbed a paper bag by his bed and tossed it to me, making me grin as I looked inside at what he'd bought. Damn straight I wasn't giving up the location of my trailer though. I intended to be back in it asap.

I headed to my room and chose a black bikini with a cute white shirt that tied in a knot to leave my stomach bare and a pair of figure hugging denim shorts that had been cut to leave threads trailing down to tickle my thighs.

I hurried back out to find JJ and he led me to the front door with a smile playing around his lips. "I'm going to be in the doghouse for taking you out," he grumbled but the playful look in his eyes said he was looking forward to Fox finding out as much as I was.

Fox had always been the leader of their crew even before he'd taken power officially. It was what he'd been born to do, but it seemed like the boys still enjoyed testing him. Of course Maverick had always been the one who butted heads with him the most, never really accepting him as the leader, so I guessed in a sense I wasn't surprised to find that he wasn't here taking orders like a good boy. But it still seemed weird to me that he wasn't here at all. He and Fox may have clashed at times, but they'd been adopted brothers and the closest of friends. Their loyalty to one another had run deeper than blood. What the hell had happened to break something that should have been unbreakable?

"Well, if you actually manage to keep a secret this time, maybe he won't find out," I said lightly. Of course, I had every intention of running again the moment JJ took his eyes off of me, but that wasn't the point.

The orange GT was sitting in the sunshine, looking as good as new, clearly back from the shop without any sign that it had been half wrecked by me and my stolen car a few days ago.

JJ held the door for me and I whistled to Mutt as we left, ignoring the eye roll JJ gave me as my little white dog joined us. I slipped inside and JJ rounded the GT so that he could drop down behind the wheel.

He started up the car and by the time we pulled out of the drive, I assumed he wasn't going to respond, so when he did, it came as a surprise.

"Some secrets are harder to keep than others," he said darkly, his grip on the steering wheel tightening. "I want you to know you can trust me, Rogue. You've always been able to trust me, even when you thought I betrayed you... but sometimes trust means doing what's right instead of just blindly keeping secrets. And what's right is wiping the piece of shit who laid his hands on you off of the map. If betraying my word to you is what it takes to do that, then I will."

I pursed my lips and looked out the window as I decided not to respond to that. He made a few good points even if I didn't want to admit it.

We drove through Sunset Cove and began climbing the hills towards the upper quarter until we finally reached Afterlife perched about halfway up the cliffs with a view of the cove below. Around here was about as far as the rich folk would come down the cliffside before turning back from the lower quarter and pretending they'd never even noticed its shadow looming on the horizon.

The atmosphere in the car was thick with the words neither of us wanted to speak to each other yet, but I knew I was going to have to face up to my shit with these boys sooner or later.

"You know, it's all well and good you claiming to be so concerned for me now. But when I really needed the four of you, I was all alone," I said just as we pulled up at the club. "And it doesn't really matter how much you try and convince me you want me back now, because everything we used to have is gone. It's broken beyond repair. Maverick is gone and Chase doesn't even want me back, Fox seems to think he owns me and you..."

"What about me?" he asked.

"You seem to think we can just start right back up where we left off. Maybe add a bit of sex to the games we used to play. And sometimes I let myself forget for a few moments because it really is tempting to let you do that. But then I remember the nights I slept rough, the men who abused me, the times I went hungry and I just...don't even think I'm the girl I used to be anymore. In fact, I know I'm not. And I don't want to be either. So stop treating me like you know me, because you have no idea what it took to bring me back here, and you never will."

I got out and lifted my chin to the heat of the sun as I stepped out of the A/C inside the car. Mutt headed off to pee on every available surface and I was glad to give him a new stomping ground to mark out.

JJ got out a moment later and stalked around the hood to face me, his gaze dark as he pinned me in it.

"You're not the only one who changed in the last ten years, Rogue. And believe me, I've survived my fair share of shit over that time too. After you left and Maverick was...gone, Luther forced the three of us to become fully fledged members of the Harlequin Crew officially, getting us to run jobs and follow commands and all of it. The price of membership had to be paid in blood more than once and he made sure we paid in full. The kid you knew died when he made me into a killer and believe me, that's not even half of what I've done in the years since. You already know what my mom was like and...fuck, I can't even begin on what made me decide to get into the sex trade. My mom is a prime example of why I never wanted that life. But shit doesn't always go to plan. So no, I don't think we can just pick right up where we left off and yeah, I know that messy doesn't even begin to cover what happened to all of us over the last ten years. But I do know that the moment I saw you back here, my heart leapt right up into my throat and I swore to myself I'd never let you go again. The bond we have can't ever be undone. Ride or die doesn't come close. We're more than family, more than anything tangible. Our fucking spirits are entwined. So you can keep trying to run and we're gonna keep coming to catch you when you do until one day, you realise you're right where you're supposed to be."

JJ's words made my thrashing heart squeeze with feelings I wasn't supposed to be having and I had to fight against the urge to just accept them and throw myself into his arms. It didn't matter if they'd been dealt their own shitty hands. We were where we were. And the scars time had left on us couldn't be erased.

"If that applies to me, then why not Maverick too?" I asked in a low voice.

JJ's face darkened and I could practically see him locking me out. "We don't talk about him."

He caught my hand and started tugging me towards the club and I let him because it seemed pretty pointless not to.

As it was the weekend, the place was open even though it was only lunchtime, the glass doors which fronted it drawn back to allow the tables out on the terrace to become part of the club. People ate and drank and enjoyed the sunshine while being served by gorgeous guys and girls in tight fitting uniforms that were really just swimwear but somehow managed to look classy with the beach vibe.

"There's a few things I need to sort, but some of the boys will be able to keep an eye on you if I have to step out," he said, releasing me as we stepped into the bar. "If you wanna earn some money you can pull a shift serving drinks, or-"

"No thanks," I said simply, glancing around at the mainly wealthy clientele and hunting down a few likely marks. "I have other ways to make money."

"Well, if they involve stealing from rich assholes then I'm gonna have to say no to that. You can rob them blind anywhere else, but we don't want this place getting a reputation for thieves. And believe me, I'm getting more than enough money from them in other ways."

"You're no fun," I groaned, dropping down onto a bar stool as I prepared myself for a long wait with not a lot to do.

"Bullshit. I'm all fun. You just can't afford to play with me right now."

"I'm never gonna pay for your dick, JJ," I warned him.

"Nah. I might just give you a freebie for old times' sake though," he replied with a wink, acting as if we hadn't even had that awkward moment over Maverick and I took my lead from him too as that seemed like the simplest way to deal with it.

"No thanks," I replied, damn near convincingly too. "I'll just take a free drink or two instead."

JJ grinned like that deal was acceptable to him and waved the bartender over. "The beautiful girl here eats and drinks for free. Okay?" he said and the girl nodded, offering me an intrigued look.

"I'll have one of those fancy ass cocktails with the cherries in it," I said, pointing at a woman who was drinking one beneath the shade of a palm while eyeing the wait staff.

When I looked back around at JJ, I found two men standing with him, eyeing me with interest. They were both of the heavily tatted, scowling, gangster variety and were kinda hard to tell apart aside from one being blonde and the other being dark. But they shared that same, low ranking gangbanger vibe that said they never stepped a toe out of line. Snooze.

"Rogue, this is Dan and Piston. They're gonna make sure you don't get into any trouble or accidentally run off while I go and deal with that special client I told you about," he explained.

"You got me babysitters?" I groaned as the two admittedly hot dudes gave me appraising looks. "And you didn't tell me about any client."

"Oh yeah, that's right, I didn't." JJ smirked and strode away from me without another word.

I silently seethed as he approached an older woman with a bright blue sundress on and dropped down into the seat beside her to talk, laying on the charm thicker than syrup.

"So," I said, taking a long sip of the cherry...thing and quite liking it. "Do you guys wanna get fucked up with me?"

"We can't really get shit faced while we're supposed to be looking after you," Piston said, shrugging apologetically and pushing a hand through his blonde hair and flexing his bicep. Dan just kind of glowered which seemed like code for I'm-a-miserable-fucker-so-don't-even-bother-asking.

"Great," I huffed, turning back to the bartender and ordering three more of the cherry things plus a shot of rum. No. Two shots of rum. And some cheese fries.

I tapped my foot impatiently as I looked around at the other people here who seemed to actually be having fun and envied them. Their lives seemed so gloriously boring.

After three cherry cocktail things, the two shots and the arrival of my cheese fries, I watched as JJ led the woman in blue out of the bar area and through a side door.

My stomach dropped as I watched them go and it took me a moment to realise that it kind of stung. He'd just been flirting with me, touching me, making me look at him in a way I hadn't meant to and now...he was just on to the next?

I knew I was dumb for caring about that and if it had been any other guy, I absolutely wouldn't have given a shit, but for some reason, I did. Just a little. Really, I should have been relieved to know he wasn't getting any ideas about something I absolutely didn't want to give him though, so I just turned the other way, grabbed my drink and got to my feet.

Mutt appeared, licking my foot before joining me as I headed off.

I strode out into the sun with my silent, brooding guard dogs following me and squealed with delight as I spotted Di standing off to the side of an open stage area right near the view which looked out over the cove. I wasn't normally a squealer but what could I say - cherry alcohol thingys.

"Oh my god, I'm so glad you're here. I've been lumped with this pair of silent clowns and I'm bored to tears. To. Tears. Please save me from the nightmare of fun-sucking company," I begged, making a mental note to organise a fun night out for her some time soon because if she saved me for a second time now I was really going to be in her debt.

"We're just doing our jobs," Piston complained, looking a bit pissed.

"Oh really? Is JJ paying you to watch me then? Because I got the impression he just said jump and you said how high." I replied scathingly as Di looked between us, biting down on her lip to hide a laugh.

"Well, he's the boss, so-"

"Nu-uh, Fox is the boss. And JJ never said you had to be the fun police while you watch me. You just decided on that for yourselves."

"Oh, if you wanna have fun, you should join in with the contest. You look like you're dressed for it already and the winner gets five hundred bucks," Di said with a grin. I glanced down at her and noticed she was wearing the same swimsuit and shorts combo the other waitresses were wearing.

"Are you working?" I asked, blaming the booze for the slow uptake.

"I pull a few day shifts when they've got them going spare. JJ likes the working girls and guys to have at least a few nights off a week so that we can give our sexy bits some down time. So I'm usually working here in the evenings dancing, but I get a few waitressing shifts in where I can. So what do you say? The staff will take part too, but only members of the public can win and you're easily the hottest girl entering. Your main competition will be that dude." Di pointed to a drool worthy specimen in a clingy white t-shirt and I checked him out while biting down on a cherry from my cocktail stick.

"Umm, okay," I agreed. "But I don't really know what I'm agreeing to."

"Wet t-shirt contest," she said with a smirk. "It's a totally perverse pastime that relies solely on the willingness of the men and women in the crowd to wanna bang you. But JJ made it a contest that men and women *both* enter to at least take the utterly sexist vibe off of it. We do them once a month and they always pull in a big crowd." Di grinned and I found myself nodding.

"I'm in," I agreed. My say yes attitude drove my decision making because I'd long since learned that the best way for me to enjoy this unpredictably shitty life was to grab every opportunity by the balls and squeeze until I was laughing.

"You're not," Dan said.

"What?" I whirled on him with a glare, brandishing the last cherry on my cocktail stick and ignoring the way the world spun a bit as I moved too fast. Those drinks were strong. "JJ said to make sure I didn't run off. He said nothing about me being unable to take part in competitions being held in his club. He clearly approves of this contest or it wouldn't be going ahead, so sit down and watch the show, because I'm about to win me a prize."

I whirled away as the two of them exchanged a look and I had to guess that I'd won because neither of them tried to stop me as I took Di's arm and walked away.

"That was badass," she commented with a grin and I smirked to myself as we headed over to the area that was set up like a stage.

Di grabbed a microphone as a couple of scantily dressed guys moved to the front of the stage with hoses and got into position to soak the contestants.

I moved to stand amongst the group of people waiting to go on and sought out tall, dark and drool-worthy, giving him a flirtatious smile as I moved up beside him.

"I figured I may as well come at my most worthy opponent head on," I said to him as he looked me over.

"Game on, girl. But stop giving me the come to bed eyes, because you don't have enough D for me," he replied with a wicked smirk and I beamed at him.

"Fine. How about the winner gets to have their pick of the hot guys in the crowd then?" I offered.

"You've got yourself a deal - I don't mind beating your little ass twice in a row," he replied, making me laugh.

"My ass is perfectly round, thank you very much," I objected, tossing my rainbow hair. "There's nothing little about it. I do a sets of squats like... every few weeks."

"Oh girl, you should up your routine if you wanna be able to crack a nut in those cheeks."

"What?" I laughed, but Di had finished announcing us and was calling everyone onto the stage one by one to take their soaking and we were both distracted by watching.

I moved to the back of the queue with my new friend, laughing at the ridiculousness of this game. If I won, it would seriously be the easiest five hundred bucks I ever made.

"Girl, do you happen to have a tall, blonde, jealous type boyfriend who wouldn't want you participating in this contest?" my new friend asked me, pointing through the crowd.

I turned to look and spotted Fox storming across the terrace with his gaze locked on me and murder in his eyes. Oh hell no. He was not gonna cash block me.

"I'm next!" I yelled as a blonde girl finished getting drenched and moved off of the stage.

I hurried forward - stumbling a little but not too much thanks to the cherry things - then pushed the next guy in line aside and moved out onto the stage.

The crowd all started cheering as I put my hands in the air, my white shirt riding up to expose my midriff as I locked eyes with Fox who had made it half way towards me.

"Rogue," he snarled, a clear command in his tone.

"Come on then boys!" I called loudly, smiling at the two men holding the hoses. "Make me all wet."

I bit my lip as I looked at Fox again just as the two hoses were turned on and aimed at me. I made a good show of squealing and bouncing about, flicking my rainbow hair like I was making a noughties music video and thought I was Rihanna with that Umbrella or Usher singing U Got It Bad. I probably looked like a total jackass, but the crowd were cheering and I had a nice buzz going so

I was pretty much living my best life.

Or at least I was until I was attacked by a mad man who lifted me off of my feet, flung me over his shoulder and yelled something about heads rolling when he figured out who had let this happen before carrying me away.

Mutt was barking and Fox cursed in response to what I was fairly sure were little dog teeth in his ankle which made me love the little critter more.

The crowd cheered even louder as I was hauled all the way around the side of the club to the parking lot and out of sight while I laughed and enjoyed the ride.

Fox dropped me down to sit on the hood of his truck and placed his palms flat either side of me so that he could snarl in my face.

"Oh, hey Badger, I didn't know you were here," I said brightly, winding a finger through a strand of wet, pink hair as I looked up at him innocently.

"Are you purposefully trying to make me angry?" he demanded, glaring at me with fury in those green eyes of his.

"Why would you think that?"

"Because you're actively going out of your way to draw the kind of attention I don't want on you. I don't like other men looking at you like that. I don't want anyone to see-"

"Do you remember when we went down to Sinners' Playground and climbed all the way to the top of the Ferris wheel during that lunar eclipse?" I asked him, leaning back onto my elbows and looking up at him with my wet shirt sticking to my skin and showing my black bikini top though it.

"What about it?" he grunted, but the way his eyes lit said he knew exactly what I was talking about. They lit even more as his gaze slid down over my transparent top with a fierce hunger that made my breath catch.

"You brought me a rose."

"I found that on the pier," he muttered, almost exactly the same way he had when he'd given it to me. But I'd known it was bullshit even then.

"I left that thing in a vase until it dried out and turned all crispy. I didn't even throw it out after that. I kept it between the pages of a book by my bed," I mused. Of course, I'd lost it alongside pretty much everything else I'd ever owned when I'd been dragged away from my home and tossed away like last week's garbage but I wouldn't have wanted to keep it then anyway.

"Why are you telling me that?" Fox asked, seeming to have been thrown off of the tirade he'd been about to embark on by my story which was what I'd been aiming for. I was so over the lectures already and I always had been the best at making him break away from them.

I shrugged. "I had the strangest idea that you were going to kiss me that night," I said in a low voice, my gaze dropping to his mouth for a brief moment.

"Did you want me to?" he asked, seeming way too keen to hear the answer to that question.

"Yes. And no."

"What does that mean?" Fox demanded.

"That you used to make my heart race and my skin tingle whenever you touched me. That sometimes I dreamed about what a kiss from you might taste like."

Fox made a low noise in the back of his throat, shifting closer to me so that his legs pressed to mine and I parted my thighs to let him move to stand between them.

"But I used to be so afraid of that too," I added. "Because if I kissed you - any of you - I was almost certain everything would change. And I was more afraid of that than anything in the world. The four of you were everything to me."

"Rogue." Fox's throat bobbed and I watched the movement like I was hungry for it, just the way I had that night sitting up in the little carriage watching the moon turn deepest orange above the waves.

"Maybe I shouldn't have held back," I replied. "Maybe I should have found out if a kiss from you would have been as sweet as I dreamed it would."

"I copped out," he said. "I got you up there all alone, didn't tell any of the others, brought you a flower and then when it came to it...I guess I wasn't man enough yet. But I don't have that problem now."

He leaned towards me with intent but I shook my head. "The problem is, I'm not that girl anymore. And you're not that boy. I wanted you then because that was when I thought that you and the others were my whole world. It was when I could look past every shitty, crappy thing in this place and see all of you and know it was going to be okay because I'd always have you. So I guess I should be thanking you really. You opened my eyes to the reality of my life. My worth. You taught me not to live on prayers and wishes and to accept the shit that was thrown my way. You taught me not to rely on anyone."

"We need to talk about what happened when you left," he growled, gripping my arms and pulling me upright so that we were nose to nose. "There are things I don't think you understand. Reasons-"

"Excuses, you mean," I interrupted. "Because that's all they are. But if you want to try and plead your case with me then I'm all ears. I'd just *love* to hear what made my boys throw me away like last week's trash. I'd love to understand why I never heard from you again. Why you sent me to that woman. Why none of you ever even tried to come look for me-"

"We were trying to protect you," Fox said in a low tone. "We were trying to-"

"I hate you, Fox Harlequin," I hissed right in his face, almost close enough to touch my lips to his and let him drown me once and for all, but that wasn't going to happen. "I hate all of you unlike I've ever hated anything. And you know why that is?"

"Why?" he asked, his voice rough, fingers curling tight around my waist, gripping the bare skin beneath my dripping wet shirt like he never wanted to let me go. But it was too late for that.

"Because you were all I had. And you knew it. When I killed Axel, you wiped the blood from my skin and promised me you'd make it right. All of you did. And then you kicked me to the curb and forgot all about me."

"We never forgot you, Rogue. We lost you. We-"

"You took away the only chance I ever had to be happy when I needed you most. It doesn't matter how you justify it. There were a hundred ways that whole thing could have gone and you chose to destroy me when I was at my lowest. And now you stand here telling me what I can or can't do, laying claim to me like I'm some sort of possession and expecting me to forgive you when you haven't even tried to apologise? Please. You might have ruined me, but I'd take a thousand years of misery over a single moment as one of your toys."

The look Fox gave me made my heart twist in a way that had my eyes prickling with memories of the tears I'd cried over him and the rest of my boys, but I fought them back with fierce determination. I would never cry for them again.

"Let's go back to the house and talk about this," he demanded. "Maybe then you'll understand how we-"

"I hear the hot girl with the unicorn hair won the wet t-shirt contest and somehow I missed out on the show," JJ called as he rounded the side of the club and approached us.

I looked over at him just as he tossed me a roll of cash and I caught it automatically.

"Thanks," I said, pushing forward so that I was pressed up against Fox and making him back up to let me stand. "Can we get the fuck out of here now?"

"I'm not done talking to you," Fox demanded. "We need to discuss this. And I'm not letting you get away with this little stunt either. It's past time for us to set some fucking ground rules and I'm done with playing nice about it."

"Fine," I snapped. "Let's all lay our cards on the table and find out where we stand."

"I'll text Chase and get him to meet us back at the house," Fox replied, moving to open the door beside me. "Get into the truck, Rogue."

"I'll ride with JJ," I replied coldly. "He was always my favourite anyway."

JJ grinned broadly at that and moved forward to wrap an arm around my shoulders as he steered me towards his orange GT. Mutt got the hint and leapt inside with a happy woof.

I slipped into my seat wordlessly, only looking back at Fox once I'd clipped my seatbelt into place and was reclining in the plush leather. He was already in his truck, shades on and his mouth set in a firm line as he backed out of the space and shot away towards the road.

"Well," JJ said as he slid in behind the wheel and gave my wet shirt an appreciative look. "This is going to be interesting."

CHAPTER THIRTEEN

Fox messaged me to meet him and JJ back at the house and I left the gym in my grey wifebeater and jeans, walking over to my Suzuki motorcycle and swinging my leg over the saddle. Call me an asshole, but I didn't always bother with my helmet. The pavement would break my fall if I came off today and I'd lost the will to give a shit a long time ago. I was pretty sure that was around the time Rogue had ripped my heart out, Luther made me into a killer and my life got turned on a dime.

I wasn't suicidal, obviously. But I drank in the pleasures of this world like they were fast going extinct because now I knew how quickly the good stuff could be torn away. From the moment I'd realised I should have told Rogue how I felt about her before it was too late, I swore to never fucking make that mistake with anything ever again. So nowadays if I wanted it, I took it. And if it gave me a thrill or made me hard, I took it even quicker.

I tore down The Mile, the wind rushing over me and carrying the scent of the sea and the latest fishermen's catch as adrenaline pumped through my blood. I loved this fucking town. I loved the waves and the pier, the cliffs and the fishes. I even loved the blood spilled at night and the danger lurking in the shadows. Sunset Cove was a dreamer's paradise and a coward's nightmare.

And it was my favourite place on earth.

I sped past Sinners' Playground, my gaze drawn to the Ferris wheel out on the end of the hulking pier as the sun glinted off the metal. There'd once been talk of the mayor demolishing the whole thing and me and my friends had begged Luther Harlequin to save it. He'd said it was on us to deal with it, and that had led to our very first high end bribe. It felt good to have rich assholes in my pocket. I'd once had nothing but sand in there and now I was keeping a whole collection of powerful motherfuckers alongside a wad of cash. I'd once have traded every penny that had passed through my hands in the last ten years to make Rogue Easton mine. Not anymore though. Now she needed to return to wherever she came from before she fucked up the good thing we finally had going here.

I'd thought my wounds had turned to faded scars when it came to her, but now I was faced with her again and it turned out those wounds were pulling open, starting to bleed. And I knew the longer she stayed, the worse it was going to get. I wasn't going to have my heart broken a second time and I sure as hell wasn't gonna watch as she broke Fox and JJ's again either.

I pulled up at the main gate to Harlequin House and Rodriguez and Piston nodded to me, opening it up. I accelerated along the drive and into the garage, kicking down the stand as I dismounted and combing a hand through my curling hair to flatten it a little. I jogged upstairs, pushing through the door and voices reached me from the kitchen.

I walked down the hall, stepping into the room and my jaw locked at the sight of Rogue there. And not just because she looked fucking breath taking, but because she was back in this house. Again. In the heart of our home. Our group.

JJ was making Margaritas like this was some kind of women's book club and my teeth started to grind. I folded my arms, raising an eyebrow at Fox for an explanation.

"We're going to tell Rogue the truth," he said in that bossy tone of his then pushed a Margarita across the island toward me.

I looked to Rogue and she stared back, waiting for me to make a fuss. But I wasn't going to this time. Because that idea actually made a lot of sense, so I grabbed the drink and took a long sip, unable to take my eyes from her in that tiny black bikini top. Rogue waved off JJ's offer of a drink and poured herself a glass of water before Fox jerked his head and walked outside onto the patio. Obviously expecting us to follow.

JJ headed outside with the pitcher of Margaritas and his own glass and I was left with Rogue for a moment, realising her cheeks looked slightly flushed. I knew that sight from the past and exactly what it meant.

"You've been drinking," I deadpanned.

"And?" she asked in that give-no-shits tone which was fast working its way under my skin.

"And are you sure you can face this conversation without a clear head?"

"My head's crystal clear, Chase, don't you worry your little socks about it." She tossed her hair and headed outside with her glass of water and her little dog at her heels, leaving me scowling at her back. And her ass in those short shorts. And then her back again where my gaze drank in the view of the angel wings she had tattooed down either side of her spine, right the way down to her ass again. *For fuck's sake.*

I stalked after her, my heart thumping unevenly. I was more than happy to tell her about the night she'd left and diffuse her attitude problem. And I was hoping it would do us all a favour and remind Fox and JJ of just how torn up they'd been and make them remember the shit we'd had to face because of her.

Fox was sitting at the circular table under the large cream umbrella with JJ at his side and Rogue sat opposite them with the mutt curled up under her chair. I dropped smoothly down on Fox's other side and took my smokes from my pocket before lighting one up.

JJ hooked the packet off the table, lighting one up too and I frowned at him.

"I'm gonna need one for this conversation," he answered my questioning look and I couldn't really argue with that. Though he didn't often smoke anymore, so I guessed he really must have been worried about how this was gonna go. Not me though.

"So what do you want to know?" Fox asked Rogue and I immediately sat up straighter, shaking my head.

"No," I growled before Rogue could answer. "This conversation isn't on *her* terms. She needs to know what we went through."

"Oh yeah, how hard it must have been for you to cut me off and ignore me while settling into your new life as Harlequins," she said icily, her glare just as cold as her tone.

Fox cut me a shitty look and I stared right back, my temper starting to rise.

"Let's just lay out all of our cards," JJ said, trying to diffuse the tension in the air. "This doesn't need to be a who-got-butt-hurt-the-most contest."

I pressed my tongue into my cheek and Fox inclined his head.

"Fine," Fox said, leaning back in his chair and taking a sip of his Margarita. "You'd better start then Chase, as you clearly have so much to say."

I fought the urge to bite back at his pissy tone, taking a long drag on my cigarette before pointing at Rogue with it. "You only see things one way. And I get why. I'm not an idiot. You think we cut you off and left you to rot in whatever new world you ended up in. But it wasn't like that."

"So what was it like?" she asked, not sounding annoyed at me for once just curious, her eyes narrowing as she pinned me in those baby blues.

"It was like...hell." I thought back on the events that had led to her leaving town, my heart bunching up into a fist at the thought of the secret I still held inside. What I'd seen, what I knew and no one else did. Because if I'd ever breathed a word of it, I would have broken my friends further. So instead, I'd just broken in silence, eventually realising that her leaving town was probably the best thing that ever could have happened to us. But that didn't change how I'd felt back then. How fucking cut up I'd been over everything that had happened.

A day before we kicked Rogue out of Sunset Cove, she'd been in serious trouble, attacked by some asshole called Axel who worked for Fox's dad and lived along the street from her group home. He'd dragged her into his house and tried to rape her, but our brave girl had hit him with a fire poker. One clean, hard fucking shot to the head and that had been it. She'd killed him. And we'd all gone running to help clean up the mess the moment she'd called.

I remembered the fear of that night, of peddling on my push bike all the way to that motherfucker's house, picturing the worst, that by the time she'd killed him, he'd already gotten his hands on her. But thankfully, it hadn't been like that. So me, JJ, Fox and Maverick helped get rid of the body, dumped it in the ocean, having no fucking clue what we were doing, but just trying our best to keep Rogue out of trouble. Because Luther Harlequin had an unwavering rule when it came to anyone who killed members of his gang; those responsible died in payment for it. And our Rogue was responsible. My little one, my fucking girl. Back then, we all would have done anything for each other, but for her we would have fought the devil himself and placed his head at her feet.

So we fed that rapey bastard to the sharks and hid her secret as best we could. But we were dumbass kids who'd dumped his body just as the tide was coming in, not weighing it down, not leaving chum for the damn sharks to find. Nothing. So the fucker came back to bite us in the dick when the corpse washed up in the cove the following morning and when Luther heard about it, he was out for blood.

Maybe we still would have been in the clear too, only a guy from Rogue's group home had seen her with Axel. Watched through the fucking window as he pushed her down beneath him, almost fucking destroyed her. He'd seen it all and done nothing to help. And when Luther's men went sniffing around for answers about Axel's death, he'd coughed them up without so much as a threat to his life.

When Fox and Maverick found out that their dad knew the truth, we all planned to run. To meet at the Rosewood Crypt, take our stash and run for the fucking hills. All of us together. But life was never that easy. I'd learned that the first day my sweet old Daddy had given me my first concussion. I should've known better.

"What happened that night?" Rogue demanded. "After Luther figured out we were planning to run, what the hell did he do to you all?"

My throat thickened at her words and I dropped her gaze for a second, sharing a glance with JJ who was working through his second Margarita already. Fox's sat untouched since his first sip and there was a darkness in his eyes which we all shared. Okay, so maybe telling her this stuff wasn't as easy as I'd expected. Now I thought on it, it was starting to hurt like a bitch. I'd suppressed that shit for so long that I wasn't remotely prepared for still feeling like this about it after all this time.

"After Luther spoke to Fox and Maverick, he summoned me and JJ to meet him at his house and took us all to the fucking woods in the back of a goddamn van," I started, a chill running through me at the memory. I would never forget it. In all my years, after all the bad shit I'd done since, that night still defined me in too many ways I wished it didn't.

"There were shovels in the back of it," JJ said, a hardness to his voice. "And when we got out in the pissing rain, he made us all bring one with us."

"For what?" Rogue whispered, but her eyes said she already knew. She'd seen the blood on us afterwards. She knew what we'd become.

"The kid from the group home you used to live with, Clive Anderson," I said. "He was on the ground, just waiting there like a lamb for slaughter in the rain."

Fox raised his chin as her eyes narrowed. We'd given her the bones of this story that night, but with everything else that had gone on, I wasn't sure how fully she'd understood.

"And then?" she asked, a knowing look seeping into her expression but she clearly wanted to hear this.

"Like we told you back then, Clive saw you with Axel, saw him hurting you in his house. He stood there watching while that piece of shit attacked you, tried to rape you," Fox growled, disgust in his tone as his upper lip peeled back. "Then he gave you up to my dad's guys when Axel's body was found."

"Luther told us to kill him," JJ said, his jaw pulsing. I'd seen the hesitance in him that night. He hadn't wanted to become a killer. More than any of us, he'd resisted what we'd done. But in the end, Luther had said we either all did it, or he'd kill Rogue. And when it came down to it, she was always our priority.

"And you did," she said, her eyes shifting between us, her expression unreadable.

We all nodded and I took another drag on my smoke.

"It was you or him. Dad said he'd let you live if we proved ourselves," Fox said firmly, sitting up straighter in his chair. "It's not something I'd hesitate over now for a second, but Clive was our first. I guess that made it harder. It was still the right thing to do in hindsight."

"But you were just kids," Rogue growled, her eyes flaring protectively like she was angry at Luther for forcing that on us.

"Not after that we weren't," JJ said darkly before draining his drink.

"We were Harlequins. Sworn in by blood."

"So then what? You were scared, so you told me to leave town?" Rogue guessed, her eyes watering and making my heart squeeze.

But I couldn't let her affect me like that anymore. I may have regretted the things that had happened between us, but whether it was right or wrong, her absence had fucked us all up so badly that her being here again was simply never going to be okay with me. The past was the past. And she needed to go back to it for all our sakes.

"Luther would have killed you if we'd gone after you. He threatened us, promised he would butcher you right in front of us if we ever dared search for you," JJ said, dipping his head as if he was ashamed. But fuck that. We hadn't had a choice.

"Fine, I get that. I'm not stupid, I know he threatened you, I knew it would be bad, but..." She blinked furiously a few times, forcing back her emotions. "But the way you went about it, how fucking cold you were with me, the way you destroyed my phone so I couldn't even contact you while you all just watched me breaking right before you wasn't necessary, was it?"

"Maybe we could have handled it differently," Fox began but she just snorted derisively.

"You think? I had nothing. No one. Never fucking had aside from the four of you and you knew it. But I don't really wanna hear you trying to excuse that bullshit because it's far too late for that. So why not just explain to me what happened after?" she demanded, her expression hard and unreachable like she'd retreated behind a wall and had no intention of letting any of this touch her.

"After?" JJ asked, inching forward in his chair like he wanted to go to her before seeming to think better of it.

"Yeah. Because after a while, surely you could have found a way to message me? You left me. Abandoned me like you all swore you never, ever would. It was months before I even dared to give up on all of you, but when I did, I..." She shook her head, the pain in her eyes twisting into hate as she glared at us. "Luther's power resided here in Sunset Cove. You could have left. You could have found a way. And we could have run as far away from him as fucking possible. He never would have found us."

Her words burned through my veins right to my heart and I clenched my jaw. I'd found my true place in Sunset Cove after she'd left. It may have hurt like a motherfucker, but when it came down to it, I hadn't really wanted to leave this town behind. And it may have cost me my heart, but I had a life worth living now. Back then, I'd had nothing, no future. I'd been dirt poor and that never would have changed if I hadn't joined the Harlequins. As fucked up as the way it had happened was, I couldn't change it now. And we were all finally in a good place. So why did she have to come back here and screw that up after ten fucking years? When we'd all put it to rest.

"We tried," Fox swore, leaning forward and gazing at her with desperation. "We couldn't do it right away, my dad was watching our asses constantly. And after what he did to Maverick..." I cringed at his name and felt JJ do it too. He was almost as much of a ghost as Rogue had been. Only he was the kind who haunted us on a daily basis even now and made sure to royally fuck with our lives like a psychotic poltergeist. Sometimes I could hardly even remember that we'd loved him like a brother once.

"Tell me what happened with Maverick," Rogue demanded. "Tell me how the hell that even happened."

The three of us shared an intense look and JJ took the lead to explain as Fox seemed ready to punch something at the mere mention of him. I had to share the sentiment. And for more reasons than one.

"Axel's body was with the police," JJ rasped. "They were looking for a culprit. So when Maverick took it upon himself to run away from home and try to go after you, Luther caught him and sent him to juvie for Axel's death."

"He wanted to set him straight, stop him from going after you again," Fox muttered.

Rogue stared at us in horror, her eyes wide and her lips parted. "He came after me?"

"Yeah," Fox snarled. "And risked your fucking life by doing so. My dad told us he'd kill you if we followed you, and he just- just-" Fox slammed his fist down on the table, making his drink spill everywhere but he clearly didn't give a shit. "He could have cost you your life because he was too selfish to just wait. Wait until we had a plan, had given some fucking thought to how we were going to reach you."

"But you didn't reach me!" she yelled, rising from her seat and her dog leapt up with a bark of fright. "You never came. At least Maverick *tried*."

"Don't stand up for that piece of shit," I snarled, getting to my feet too as anger coiled through me. "Your precious Maverick is a nutjob who's killed our people, who's tried to kill us on multiple occasions."

"What?" Her brow creased as she tried to comprehend that and JJ nodded to drive the point home while Fox just sat there seething, his hands curled into tight fists on the table.

"We were there for him when he got out of prison," I clipped. "Waiting to take him home, to forgive him for fucking you over. He'd been through enough, we were well aware of that. He spent six years incarcerated between juvie and prison. So despite the fact that he ignored every single attempt at us contacting him during that time, we were still there waiting on the outside when he was released. And do you know what he did?"

Her throat bobbed as she shook her head and I walked around the table, gazing down my nose at her.

"Your Maverick spat at our feet and walked away. Then that very evening, he showed up at Harlequin House with a gun." I yanked on my wifebeater, pointing to the scar on my shoulder. "And took a few pot shots at us." I rounded the table to Fox, twisting his head to the side and making him growl in annoyance as I pointed out the scar running just below his ear. "And when we managed to run him out of here with a few wounds of his own, he soon made it clear he was never going to give up."

"He killed three of our men the next day," JJ chipped in grimly. "Strung them up on Gallows Bridge in what is now The Divide. Then he set up shop on Dead Man's Isle, started up his own gang called The Damned Men and changed his fucking name too. He's not even Maverick Harlequin anymore. He goes by Maverick Stone now. And the war began not long after that."

Rogue was shaking her head, backing away as she clawed her fingers through her hair. "This isn't right, none of this is right. There has to be more to it than that. Maverick wouldn't, he wouldn't-"

"He would, he did, and he still does," I snarled. "You'll figure it out soon enough if you stay in town." I started walking toward the house, figuring this conversation was more than done, but slowed as I passed her by, lowering my voice to talk just to her. "Which I suggest you don't do, ghost."

I continued towards the doors, but she apparently wasn't done with me yet.

"Why do you hate me, Chase?" she snapped. "What did I ever do to you? Because from where I'm standing, it makes no fucking sense."

I paused by the door, not looking back at her, my teeth grinding to pulp in my mouth. "Every bad thing that's ever happened to us, is because of *you*. You're a plague on our lives. And now you're back, I'm just waiting for the shit to start raining down on us again."

I walked away, done with her. Done with all of it.

Dragging up those memories had torn deeper wounds through my chest, new ones that were tainted by perspective. If I'd just dealt with it all differently, we all could have been saved a world of heartache and loss. Maybe it was selfish to blame her. Maybe I didn't have a right to. But I was going to anyway, because it was the only thing that made seeing her again bearable. And I'd done enough suffering over her to last a lifetime.

I waited for Fox and JJ to arrive, sitting in a stolen Honda Civic on the corner of Tide Street. The rest of our men were already closing in on The Divide where they'd be waiting on our signal to move in.

Maverick had taken the Sailor's Eye Lighthouse, but tonight we were going to take it back and fucking more. We couldn't let him push the boundaries of The Divide back any further. And it was time we stood on the front line and ensured our territory was immovable.

Fox opened the passenger door and dropped into the seat while JJ dove in the back. They were dressed in black, ready for war, guns strapped to their hips and no doubt more concealed weapons hidden across their bodies.

I started the engine, taking off down the road and driving towards The Divide. My heart beat a mile a minute, but it was with excitement as much as apprehension. Merkle had reported there were ten of The Damned Men in position at the Sailor's Eye. And their gang name was more fitting tonight than ever. Because they were soon going to be painting our lighthouse red while we damned them right to hell.

"Did you tell Rodriguez to man the back door at the house?" Fox asked JJ, twisting in his seat to look at him.

"Yeah, man. Don't worry, Rogue's not getting out tonight," JJ replied and I fought an eye roll. "But like...maybe she should be able to come and go as she pleases, because you can't just keep the girl prisoner like you're some caveman with a club."

"So you think I should just let her run off again?" Fox scoffed.

"Yeah," I said the same time JJ did, though there was a harder edge to my voice than his.

Fox stiffened in his seat and I received the brunt of his glare seeing as I was right beside him. "I'm not gonna let her go."

"I get it," I said and he frowned at me, clearly surprised those words had come from my mouth when I'd made it clear the stance I'd taken on this. I refused to meet his eye and could feel JJ's gaze on the back of my head as they waited for me to go on. "We all wanted her back. But you can't lock her up in the house. Frankly, I think we should drop her off in the next state and never speak of her again, but I'm aware you guys aren't going to go in for that, so at least let her make the goddamn choice to be here."

"But-" Fox growled, but JJ piped up in the back.

"She *wants* to be here, dude. She came back. You don't need to lock her up. But maybe she'll reconsider staying at all if you keep forcing her to do whatever you want."

"On second thought maybe she *should* stay at the house," I said with a smirk and Fox punched me in the arm.

"What's your problem with her?" Fox demanded of me and I locked my lips, shaking my head. "You were heartbroken when she left just like we all were, so what is this really about?"

I didn't answer and the silence pooling between us became insufferable. I didn't know why I couldn't voice what I'd seen the night before she'd left. We'd been such idiots, fawning all over her, begging to be chosen. Well fuck being chosen. Being chosen meant gutting everyone else in our group, and

233

that's what she'd been planning to do. She'd been on a path to destroy us long before we'd banished her from Sunset Cove. And with a little time, that had become as clear as day to me.

"Chase," Fox snarled. "Speak your damn mind."

I gripped the steering wheel tighter. "I just don't wanna see you all getting hurt. That's all."

"That's clearly not all," JJ said, shoving me in the shoulder. "Come on, what is it dude?"

"I don't wanna make shit worse for you," I muttered.

"We don't keep secrets from each other," JJ said in outrage.

"I know...but I kept this one," I said, kinda ashamed of that fact. "I just didn't wanna hurt you both more than you were already hurting back then."

"What is it?" Fox pushed, giving off his king-of-the-world vibe.

I sighed, grappling with telling them this. But it had been a decade. Maybe it was time to set it loose into the world.

I snatched a cigarette from the packet sitting in the cup holder and lit it up, needing the nicotine to get through this. The weight of this truth had hung from my heart for ten years. I'd never breathed a word of it, hoping if I just ignored it, the pain would finally go away. But it never had. And maybe letting it out was the only way to really let it go at last. I just hated to think how it might hurt my friends, but maybe it would make them see that she had never been meant for us. That her being back here most likely had nothing to do with us three.

"She never wanted any of us," I expelled in a wave of smoke. "The night she killed that asshole Axel, I saw her. Before any of that happened. I saw her doing something...with someone."

"If you don't spit it out right this second-" Fox growled and I spoke over him, just blurting it the hell out.

"She fucked Maverick. I saw them together. They were naked at Rosewood Manor in the summer house."

"What?" JJ gasped but Fox's stony silence was worse. I could hear my pulse in my ears and my cigarette was getting a quick death as I toked it practically down to the butt.

"You saw them fucking?" Fox hissed.

"No, but...the way they were looking at each other, I could tell. They either had or they were about to. And I got the feeling it wasn't the first time." I shook my head, stealing a glance at Fox's expression and finding his eyes full of the endless kind of hurt I'd desperately wanted to save him from. It made my heart yank and I felt like a shitty friend for giving in and telling them.

"She chose him?" JJ asked in a tight voice.

"Yeah," I murmured, trying to swallow down the ball in my throat. "So, if she came back to town for any of us...I'm guessing it was him."

Quiet fell, but it was weighted with a thousand thoughts as Fox stared out the window like he was looking for his next murder victim.

JJ sighed at last. "Well it was ten years ago, bro, even if she did fuck him, it's not like she never cared for us."

Fox was descending into a dangerous silence that was making the hairs on my arms raise to attention. I was fully aware I'd just awoken the apex predator in him, but he'd pushed me and this was what he'd gotten for himself.

I switched off the headlights and rounded onto Cooper Street which would bring us up close to the lighthouse, driving alongside the far end of Sunset Beach which led into Maverick's new territory

"I'm sorry," I said heavily.

"You should've told us," Fox gritted out.

"I thought about it, but she was gone and it just seemed like the wrong thing to do. You guys were so...fucked up."

"So were you," JJ said gently. "You didn't have to carry that alone, Ace."

I shrugged one shoulder, glad to have least gotten it off my chest after all these years. And I hoped it would make them see things clearer at least. "So maybe we should send her off to the asshole she really wants."

"No," Fox snapped furiously, turning his murderous gaze on me. "She's not *his*," he growled like he was trying to make it so.

"She was," I tossed back, opening my window and flicking the cigarette butt out. "She made her choice."

"No!" Fox barked, refusing to accept my words.

"It was ten years ago," JJ reasoned. "Even if she did-"

"She didn't," Fox snarled ferociously. "She wouldn't have. I refuse to

235

believe that fucking asshole took her virgi-"

A car slammed into the side of us and I cried out as we spun violently sideways and I jerked hard against my seatbelt as we were forced off of the road. My heartrate skyrocketed as our car whipped around onto the beach and I was already undoing my seatbelt and grabbing my gun before it came to a stop.

Bullets ripped into my car door and Fox shoved my head down as a few sailed in through the window.

Shattering glass cascaded over us from Fox's side and I cursed, popping Fox's seatbelt as I turned my head to check JJ was okay in the backseat. The sound of return fire split through the air painfully close by and I saw JJ peeking out of his now shattered window, firing his hand gun with a continual pop of bullets.

Fox pushed off of me, shoving his door open and I crawled out after him, dropping onto the sand and tugging open JJ's door to give him an exit route.

"Fuck, how did they know we were coming?" I snapped.

"Maybe they got lucky and a patrol spotted us, I don't wanna consider the alternative just yet," Fox growled, moving to sit behind the wheel at the front of the car before returning fire over the hood. I took my phone out, dialling Merkle and he answered on the first ring.

"We're already coming up behind them!" he called in my ear and a split second later a rattle of more gunfire carried from the road.

"Hurry," I demanded and killed the call, peering through the Honda with my gun raised and shooting at a big asshole with a machete on his hip.

He hit the ground with a cry and the amount of blood that poured from him said he was a goner. Merkle and our guys were shooting from the alley behind them and the final assholes fell under their assault.

The night air rushed around me and I stood, peering through the battered car as JJ hurried to scramble out of it beside me. Three men lay dead on the street and Merkle and our guys were moving to sweep the area for any others.

"Come on." Fox looked toward the lighthouse, his shoulders tense. "They'll know we're coming. We have to switch to Plan B."

"Hell yes, I love Plan B," JJ whooped and I smirked at him, happening to agree on that.

JJ ran around to the trunk of the car, popping it open and taking out a rucksack then slinging it over his shoulder before tossing a pack to me. Fox reached into the trunk and took the huge assault rifle, shouldering it and nodding to me. I grabbed the three plastic oars and Fox whistled to Merkle across the street to signal the change of plan.

Merkle nodded and started running up the road, taking his men with him while we hid in the shadows on the beach, waiting as they made a charge for the lighthouse. Gunfire soon echoed back to us from up near the looming Sailor's Eye. The light no longer worked on the top of the huge structure since the boat yard down this way was no longer used for commercial goods. But this marked the very edge of The Divide and if Maverick claimed this territory it would make it easier for The Damned Men to push further as they'd be claiming the best fucking lookout in the area.

"Come on," JJ encouraged, pushing me to get me moving and we all started running across the sand towards the waves.

It was pitch black out here and we had to make sure we weren't fucking spotted or the moon didn't decide to give us away. But so long as Merkle was keeping The Damned Men busy at the lighthouse, no one would be looking for us anyway.

JJ dropped his pack, taking out the folded black dingy and me and Fox stood back as he yanked the cord on it. Air filled it fast and as soon as it was full, I passed ski masks out from my bag and we tugged them on to hide our faces in case any lights flashed our way while we were on the water. JJ pushed the boat into the waves and we all grabbed onto the sides of it then ran into the sea.

I jumped in behind Fox while JJ dove in behind me and I tossed them an oar each before pushing my gun into the holster on my hip. We started rowing hard against the waves, totally silent but in complete synchronicity. We'd practised this a thousand times and knew each other to the depths of our souls and back anyway. We'd learned to communicate without words a long time ago and that was what made our unit so unwavering.

We were soon out in the open water, moving fast towards the lighthouse as we circled around to the rocky outcrop it sat on, coming up behind our enemies in the shadows. The waves were calm tonight and we made steady progress towards the dark rocks ahead of us.

Shouts of pain sounded out from somewhere ahead but it was impossible to tell if it was one of our men or Maverick's. We just had to grit our teeth, stick to the plan, keep moving. Reclaim our fucking land.

We finally made it to shore and Fox leapt out, tugging the boat up the rocks as we dove out too to help. Then we ran across the rocks towards the smooth stone wall that rose up high above us, the darkness thick and giving us good coverage as we reached it. We pressed ourselves to the cool wall and I took my handgun out, raising it as I moved behind Fox who had his assault rifle ready to fire.

We reached a back door which was firmly locked and I unzipped my pack, tossing Fox a small pack of explosives. He stripped the tape off the back and used the adhesive backing to stick it over the lock.

Fox stood well back, aiming the gun at the doorway and JJ snatched the trigger from my hand just as I was about to blow it, winking at me before pressing the button. *Asshole.*

A bang sounded that echoed through my skull as stone and a chunk of the door scattered at our feet. I forgot to curse JJ as Fox kicked the remains of the door open and swung his gun left and right, hunting for enemies. But none showed their faces.

We moved after him as he led the way into an icily cold stairwell and shouts and cries of agony sounded from somewhere above us. Merkle had had plenty of time to make it through the front entrance, but as I checked my phone, I found we had no message from him confirming it. It didn't mean a whole lot; if he was facing Maverick's men he'd have had no chance to text us.

Fox started moving up the winding stairs, his back pressed to the wall as he tried to see as high as possible, but the stone steps just kept circling tighter and tighter. I clutched my gun harder, adrenaline making my ears train onto every sound around us. The cries of pain, the gunfire, the waves crashing against the shore.

We kept climbing, moving ever up through the lighthouse as we sought out the fight and hoped to get the jump on The Damned Men.

A scream carried from far above us then cut off abruptly, the sudden silence making my gut constrict. People were dying for sure, but on whose side?

A small amount of light fell on us from above and Fox paused to peer out of a narrow window in the wall, the lights from the town illuminating his eyes. I stepped up beside him, frowning down at the empty street below where Merkle would have approached from. He'd had seven guys with him. Where the fuck were they?

"Something's wrong," JJ whispered as another scream rang out from above.

Gunfire suddenly roared down below us, bullets ricocheting off the walls and sparks flying as what sounded like an army of men pursued us on the stairs. "For The Damned!" they bellowed and I swore, my heart thundering as we did the only thing we could do and ran the fuck onwards while JJ shot blindly behind him.

"Here!" Fox tossed him the assault rifle and JJ caught it mid-air, slamming it to his shoulder and firing wildly.

I couldn't see the men falling as I ran after Fox, the steps circling too sharply for me to catch sight of them. But blood sprayed up the walls and gunfire kept returning as I held onto JJ's shoulder and half dragged him after us as he continued to shoot. Fear and adrenaline surged through me and I thrived on both, hungering to spill the blood of my enemies.

My feet suddenly hit flat ground and a shadow lunged at me in my periphery. My heart stopped. A gun went off. I swore as fire blazed across my right arm and wheeled my handgun around, not hesitating a single second as I pulled the trigger and the asshole who'd shot me fell dead at my feet.

There was no time to check the wound, but my left arm was still working, so I figured I wasn't on the verge of bleeding out just yet. The huge light stood at the heart of the room and men were coming at us from all sides of it. It was a fucking ambush.

I roared in defiance as I fired shot after shot, taking out every motherfucker that came at me, while bullets flew past me by a hair's breadth.

"Take cover!" Fox bellowed, catching my wrist and dragging me against the railing that circled the huge light.

JJ was still firing mercilessly down into the stairwell with the rifle and

I pitied any asshole daring to come after us from that direction. The heat of blood poured down my arm but with the adrenaline still coursing through my veins, I could barely feel the pain. That would come later. If I survived this shit. Which currently seemed like a toss of a coin.

Shots were still being fired at us by the remaining fuckers on the other side of the light, none of them daring to come closer as we sent return fire back at them.

Fox drew a knife from his hip before lowering down to a crouch and making a signal with his fingers which told me to distract them.

I nodded, taking a deep breath before crouching down and moving around the light in the opposite direction to him, reaching into my bag and taking out a smoke bomb. I ripped the pin out of it, shouting loudly to get their attention as I threw it around the light. Smoke poured from it, filling the space fast, the burning scent catching in my throat. They ran from it and blood curdling screams filled the air as Fox gutted them with his blade.

I pulled my ski mask off and tugged my shirt up to cover my nose instead as the smoke raked the back of my throat.

Fox stepped through the smoke splattered in blood as he tore his ski mask from his face and used it to wipe the gore from his knife.

My ears were ringing so heavily that it took me a second to realise JJ had stopped firing and quiet came from the stairs.

"You okay?" Fox asked J and he nodded, pulling his own ski mask off.

"You know I love surprise parties," JJ panted and I chuckled, though I wasn't letting my guard down yet.

I took a long breath, looking around at the carnage, spotting a trail of blood that led up to the glass door which gave access to a large balcony outside.

Fox walked over to it and pushed it open, raising his handgun as he stepped outside, his eyes ablaze as he followed the trail and I hurried along after him with JJ.

"Hey, Fox!" a familiar voice boomed which made my blood chill.

As we rounded the corner, we all raised our weapons at the man who'd once been a brother to us.

Maverick stood up on the edge of the balcony, the motherfucker holding a bloody head in his hand and a grenade in the other, the pin sticking out the corner of his mouth. He spat it over the edge of the lighthouse the second we slowed before him and he ran his tongue across his lips which were stained with blood.

Tattoos crawled up his neck and coated his muscular arms right down to his fingertips. Every piece of skin I could see was covered in ink aside from his face. His dark hair met with equally dark stubble on his jaw and his strong features were set in callous amusement.

My gut knotted as I realised it was Merkle's head in his grip, his face twisted in pain, fixed there forever in death.

"You fucking asshole," I snarled, pointing my gun directly at Maverick's head as hatred coursed through me, but Fox held up a hand to stop me and JJ from firing.

"Clever boy, Foxy," Maverick said with a smirk. "You always knew how to follow the rules, huh?"

"Your men are dead," Fox snarled. "Surrender, asshole."

Maverick laughed coldly. "So are yours, *brother*." He gestured with his chin to the edge of the balcony and I side stepped towards the edge apprehensively.

A railing stood on top of the stone wall to stop anyone from falling over the hundred foot drop beyond it. I forgot to breathe entirely as I saw the butchered men hanging by their necks from lengths of rope tethered to it. Blood ran from their wounds, painting the white wall in red splashes that poured down towards the ground.

"You fucking piece of shit!" JJ roared, raising the assault rifle to point at our enemy.

"This grenade is going off one way or another, Johnny James," Maverick warned. "Pull that trigger and you'll take us all with you. Is my death worth all of yours?"

"What do you want?" Fox hissed, his gun pointed at Maverick as his upper lip peeled back.

Maverick casually tossed Merkle's head away from him and a sickening thump sounded as it hit the ground a moment later. "I wanna piss on your lighthouse." He lowered his fly, taking out his goddamn dick and pissing on the fucking floor in front of us. As he was still holding that fucking grenade, all of us just had to wait for him to finish.

He sighed as he tucked himself away, transferring the grenade from one hand to the other and making us all shift nervously and raise our weapons higher.

"I never wanted this heap of shit anyway." Maverick shrugged. "I just like the taste of your men's blood. Do you three taste as sweet, I wonder?"

"If you want us dead, then throw it, motherfucker," I dared him and Maverick met my eye with his midnight black ones. There was something inherently wrong in him now. It was impossible to see the boy I'd once loved. Whatever had happened to him in prison had fucked him up good.

"How's your catch these days, Chase?" Maverick asked, then threw the fucking grenade at me before diving over the goddamn ledge.

I dropped my gun with a yell of alarm, catching the grenade and throwing it off the balcony with shaking hands. The whole thing exploded in the air with a deafening bang that made us all drop down to our knees and cover our heads.

"Please tell me he just committed suicide," JJ grumbled as we pushed ourselves upright and hurried to look over the edge. Maverick was nowhere in sight, but a long rappelling rope hung all the way down to the ground where he'd jumped.

"Fuck!" Fox roared, scraping a hand through his hair as the wind tore around us. He'd orchestrated this whole fucking thing. Ruthlessly killed eight of our men. "He's dead," Fox promised, like he'd done so a thousand times before. And I knew that this only ended one way. It was Maverick or us. And it was time we made sure it wasn't us.

CHAPTER FOURTEEN

When the boys stumbled back into the house in the early hours of the morning bloodstained and dark-eyed, I watched them in silence from the top of the stairs with my heart in my mouth.

I knew where they'd gone tonight, even if they hadn't wanted me to know. It was a turf war with Maverick's gang and I could tell from one look at them that they'd paid the price for it in blood.

Chase stalked across the kitchen and grabbed a bottle of rum from the cupboard before heading away again with a curse.

"Do you want me to look at it?" Fox asked, though I couldn't see him from my vantage point.

"Nah. I'm a big boy. A few stiff drinks and a smoke and I'll forget all about it," Chase replied dismissively.

"I'm going to wash the blood out of my hair," JJ said a moment later. "I can't sleep with the stench of death in the air anyway."

My heart leapt at that suggestion and I chewed on my bottom lip as I wondered who had been killed, my mind moving to Maverick, the one piece of my past I still hadn't laid eyes on since returning here. They were fighting his gang and had clearly been on the front lines themselves. Had he been there too? Was he somewhere washing blood from his skin or was there a possibility that I'd just lost any chance to see him ever again? My heart dipped at the idea and I was suddenly breathing far too heavily. I didn't wanna admit I was panicking, but there were a bunch of kamikaze butterflies in my stomach right now who begged to differ.

I scurried away as JJ approached the stairs, slipping back into my room a moment before I heard him step onto the landing.

My mind scrambled with the need for answers and I tried to decide what I was supposed to do. Should I just get back into bed and pretend I'd never heard them come home? Or let them assume I had and didn't care to find out whether any of them had been hurt or not?

My gut twisted at the mere suggestion of that and I was struck with the desire to check.

I pulled my door open just as JJ closed his and I hesitated, looking towards the stairs where the low murmur of Chase and Fox's voices carried to me. Between the two of them, I was certain Chase wouldn't welcome my concern and Fox would read too much into it. But JJ was different. I knew I should have been just as angry at him as the others, but somehow it was harder to maintain that rage with him. Plus, I trusted him to be straight with me. Or at least just outright refuse to give me an answer instead of placating me with half truths or complete lies.

I crossed the hall in my oversized red band tee which I was pretty sure actually belonged to J anyway and knocked softly on his door.

There was no response and as I leaned closer to the wood, the sound of running water called to me from beyond it. I pursed my lips, knowing I should probably turn back, talk to one of the others instead or at least wait for him to finish showering, but instead I twisted the handle and slipped inside.

JJ's room was dark, a single lamp switched on beside the open door to the bathroom. His curtains were drawn over the view of the mountains and the almond oil scent of him enveloped me as I pressed the door closed behind me and tried to decide what I should do.

The lights weren't on in the bathroom either and for a moment I was almost certain I heard a heavy sigh over the sound of running water.

I padded across the carpet on bare feet and paused in the glow of light from the lamp, my toes just touching the tiles beyond the door which led into the en-suite.

The way the door opened meant I couldn't see the shower from my position beside it. I could just turn back and leave, ignore the heavy pounding of my heart or the weight in my chest and ask him when he was finished. But I didn't leave.

"J?" I asked softly, moving to stand right at the edge of the door so that only a tilt of my head would gift me a view of him in the shower behind it. "Are you...alright?"

There was a silence that followed filled with nothing but running water which made me question whether or not he'd even heard me and I almost called out again right as he replied.

"Come here."

I should have refused, told him I'd wait in his room or just left altogether, but for some unknown reason, I found myself stepping out from behind the door and looking at him as he stood there in the dark in the black tiled shower cubicle with water cascading down his bare skin and his eyes full of demons.

He held a hand out to me and I stepped forward to take it, my gaze taking in the sculpted muscles of his abdomen and the swallow tattoos I'd fantasised about before landing on his cock which was hardening at my attention. But as I snapped my gaze back up to his, it wasn't lust I found waiting for me in his eyes. It was hurt.

JJ pulled me towards him and I stepped into the shower without questioning it. The hot water drenched me the moment I moved beneath it, plastering his shirt to my frame and making me gasp.

"I missed you so much, pretty girl," he breathed as he curled his arms around me, one hand sliding up my back and pushing into my wet hair.

"I worked every day to make sure I *didn't* miss you," I admitted in reply, pressing my cheek to his chest and hearing the solid rhythm of his heart beating beneath it. Relief spilled into my veins at the solid, unmovable beat of it and I had to admit that I wouldn't have been able to cope with it if he'd died tonight.

"And how did that work out for you?" JJ murmured.

I didn't reply but I wound my arms around his waist and held him close, forgetting all the reasons I had to hate him for just a little while as I let myself bathe in the fact that he was here in my arms. If I closed my eyes it was like no time had passed at all. I could pretend that we were just holding each other because of something that one of his mom's clients had done or my foster carer, Mary Beth, hadn't bothered to do. We could be the whole world to each other and fill the gaps that the abuse and neglect we'd got at home left in our souls.

"Was Maverick there tonight?" I whispered, almost afraid to ask, knowing that JJ didn't like to speak about him.

"Yeah," he said roughly. "He hates us even more than you do, pretty girl."

"And is he still... I mean, I heard you talking about people dying downstairs and I just-"

"It would take more than some turf war to kill that motherfucker," JJ reassured me, leaning down and pressing a kiss to my hair. "I'm not even sure he bleeds at all. The devil took that from him when he sold his soul."

I frowned against JJ's chest, not liking the sound of that and aching to hear the full story of what had happened between them. Chase had given me the bones of it, but they'd been brothers. Maverick had been raised in this house with Fox. A bond like that was damn near unbreakable...but now they were fighting on opposite sides of a war over a town we all hated as least as much as we loved. I felt like I'd stepped out of a dream when I'd left this place and I'd returned to a nightmare now.

I tilted my head back and looked up at JJ, meeting his gaze in the dark as water spilled from his face down onto mine, splashing against my lips, my cheeks, my eyelashes, bridging the divide between us as we lingered there.

He moved his hands to cup my cheeks, his thumb tracing my lips as he drank me in like he was trying to see every change in me alongside everything he remembered, and I was sure I was looking at him in the exact same way.

"I've always wondered if you really were the most beautiful girl I've ever met, or if I'm just biased because I've seen how deep that beauty runs," he said, his voice full of grit and regrets. "And now that I find myself looking at you again, I've realised it doesn't matter if I'm biased. You're everything I've always been missing Rogue. And I'm so sorry about what happened between us. I can only promise you I thought it was the best thing at the time and I've regretted it every single day since."

Something cracked and split apart deep inside me at his words as I looked into his dark eyes and tried to think of the right words to give him back. I should have been telling him it was too late, I didn't care about his apologies or regrets or any of it. But I didn't think I'd ever actually expected any of them to say sorry for it. I'd never believed they could feel that way at all. And definitely not as deeply as JJ clearly felt it.

My gaze slipped from his eyes to his lips and I found myself aching for something I shouldn't have been. Something I needed to save myself from before I fell too deep and couldn't ever come back from.

JJ swallowed thickly, leaning back an inch and looking down at our bodies, the shirt I was wearing showing the hard press of my nipples through it as clearly as the thick length of his cock which was driving into my thigh.

"Will you stay with me tonight?" he asked in a low voice.

"JJ, I-"

"I don't want sex. Despite what my dick might have to say on the matter and how much a part of me might ache for that. But I'd just sleep better with you in my arms tonight, like we used to do at Sinners' Playground and the summer house. If you want to?"

Water slid down my cheeks like tears and I should have been refusing but instead I was nodding, letting him draw me out of the shower and peel my wet t-shirt off to reveal my body to him. I should have been covering myself up, refusing to let him see me like that, but somehow the rules seemed different tonight and I didn't feel like questioning that.

He looked at me with a savage hunger in his gaze that made my pulse race and every muscle in my body clench with anticipation before quickly wrapping a towel around me to cover me up once again.

I dropped my gaze as I focused on drying myself and he grabbed a towel for himself, the two of us looking away from one another as we fought off the heat that was building in the room.

JJ headed back into his bedroom and by the time I followed him, he was wearing a pair of grey sweats and had a fresh black tee and sweatpants ready for me too.

I took them with a slightly uncertain smile and dropped my towel to put them on. JJ didn't turn away from me, but I didn't do anything to hide my body and the way his gaze trailed over me had my stomach knotting. This was something I'd thought of and been afraid of and hungered for in a warring cycle ever since I was a kid and despite my insistence to myself that I wasn't going to let any of these boys see me like this, I just didn't care tonight. There was an innocence to this sin that made it feel too right to question.

"You're gonna make it fucking impossible to spoon you without me getting all excited over it," he commented as he bit his lip in a way that I'd only ever seen guys do on tv. It was way too sexy for any normal man to pull off, but Johnny James was no normal man.

"You mean like you did when we were hiding out at Sinners' Playground before…" I trailed off because that had been right before he'd ripped my heart out of my chest and stomped on it for good measure. It was one of the last times that I'd truly believed I had everything in the world that I'd ever need because I had my boys, and nothing could ever change that or take it from me. But I'd been oh so fucking wrong about that.

JJ's brow pinched as he seemed to notice the change in my mood, clearly remembering that morning as well as I did. The last time I'd woken up believing I had a place in the world. But neither of us said anything more on it. What was there to say anyway? It was history, dead and buried even deeper than the bodies we'd left in the ground.

He moved to his bed, drawing back the covers for me and I slipped into the cool embrace of the fresh sheets as the bed flexed beneath his weight hitting the mattress.

We both moved to lay on our sides, looking at each other in the dark as we rested our heads on the pillows.

"You remember that time I snuck into the group home through the window because my mom had company and the dude kept yelling at me? And you threatened the other girls under pain of death if they ratted you out so that I could sneak into your bed?" he asked with a smile playing around his lips as he scooted closer to me.

"And Mary Beth heard me laughing with you and came to check what was going on?" I added. I'd hidden him beneath my blankets and Rosie of all people had actually covered for me by saying we'd been laughing together –

only because she knew she would have been punished too if we were caught, but still. Rosie had been my roommate in the group home for years and she was honestly the most irritating fucker I'd ever met in my entire life. She was always sniffing around my boys like a bad smell while ratting me out to Mary Beth at every opportunity.

"This feels like that. Sneaking into your bed, wanting to touch you while knowing I shouldn't. Staying quiet to make sure we don't get caught out." JJ reached out to tuck a lock of my damp hair behind my ear and I couldn't help but smile at him. I didn't know how he found ways around my barriers so easily, but it was seriously difficult to stay angry at him all the time.

"You wanted to touch me then?" I asked him curiously.

"I always wanted to touch you, Rogue. You were always the only girl for me," he murmured and I chewed on my bottom lip as I tried to decide whether I believed that or not.

"What would Fox do if he found us here?" I breathed, a little thrill dancing along my spine at the idea of us going against his regime. I was like a fearless protester, flying my flag in the face of a twisted dictator while secretly undermining him. I just had to hope I wasn't caught and executed for my crimes.

JJ's gaze brightened for a moment before narrowing. "Well we aren't doing anything he could object to, are we?" he said slowly and I shrugged.

"He seems to object to pretty much everything I do, so I'm gonna guess that we are." I reached out and caught the drawstrings which held JJ's sweatpants in place, tugging on them lightly as I started fiddling with them. "But let's say, *hypothetically*, we did do something he would absolutely object to. Then what?"

"Are you asking if you're worth risking a bullet for?" JJ teased.

"You think he'd shoot you?" I asked in surprise.

"Anyone else? Maybe. But me? I like to think he'd just try and kick my ass to make me back off. Who knows though? I've never seen him get crazy over a girl the way he is for you. Maybe you're destined to be the death of me, Rogue Easton."

I laughed lightly and JJ caught hold of my leg, hooking his hand around the back of my knee and dragging me closer.

"I can think of worse ways to go," he murmured as he pulled my thigh over his hip and moved to press his forehead to mine.

"I still can't forgive you, J," I whispered as the look in his dark eyes made the fissures in my fragile heart quake.

"I know, pretty girl," he replied sadly, wrapping his arms around me as he let his eyes fall shut.

I frowned to myself, wondering if I should just go. But then I remembered that I wanted something from these four demons, and I wasn't going to let anything get in my way. Not even this sinfully tempting creature in my arms.

"Do you miss Rick too, JJ?" I breathed so low that it wasn't even really a whisper.

"Only in the dead of night," he replied. "When no one else can touch how I feel. And really, what I miss is who he *was*. Who I was. And you and the others too. I miss it being the five of us and the world seeming a whole lot brighter than it does these days."

I woke to a solid dick driving into my ass, a mouth pressed to my neck and a hard, warm body pressed up against me in the most delicious way.

JJ was breathing heavily, the almond scent of him surrounding me and the weight of his arm laying over me making the shadows which normally pressed close to me in the mornings back off for once.

I made a noise that was supposed to be some form of good morning but came out like a moan of pleasure. Maybe it *was* a moan of pleasure though, because JJ's bed was really freaking comfortable and being held in his arms left me feeling kind of...safe.

The noise seemed to rouse him and he flexed his fingers, drawing my attention to the fact that he'd slipped them beneath the waistband of my sweats, his hand seriously close to crossing that line we kept flirting with.

"Johnny James, get your damn hand out of my pants or I'm gonna kick your ass," I growled.

"Mmmm, that sounds fun. Or we could see how much fun it would be if I dropped my hand an inch or two lower..."

I sucked on my bottom lip, glad he couldn't see me or how tempted I was by that offer. Sometimes it was seriously hard to remember all the reasons I didn't want this asshole doing anything like that to me.

"I don't think you could handle me, JJ," I teased, wriggling a little just to make his dick ache as it ground against my ass.

"Don't challenge me, pretty girl, fucking is my speciality. I can make you come like no man you've ever known," he growled in my ear, making the hairs raise along the back of my neck. I laughed in what was intended to be a derisive way but it came out more like a freaking giggle and I died a little inside as JJ pushed his fingers a bit lower, taking the noise as encouragement.

"J..."

"I've never slept with a girl in my bed," he murmured. "You popped my cherry, Rogue."

"You've never had a sleepover with any of the girls you've fucked?" I asked dubiously as he shifted his fingers lower again and I had to try and remember that I was supposed to be telling him to stop.

"They don't want to pay my hourly rate for cuddles, silly," he teased. "Once I've made them come a few times I pack up my shit and go. But now I'm thinking I've been missing something. Although I get the impression this just feels so good because it's you..."

"Johnny," I breathed but my resolve was starting to shatter and I was shifting to part my thighs for him even though I hadn't really decided to yet. But this just felt so-

"For the love of fuck, she's gone again!" Fox roared from the hallway outside and I gasped in alarm as JJ yanked me close and threw the covers over my head half a second before the sound of the door crashing open filled the room.

"What the fuck, Fox?" JJ snarled, sounding all sleepy and angry and cute as shit as he crushed me against him and hid me from view with his dick driving into my ass.

"Rogue," Fox growled. "She's not in her fucking room. I swear if she's hanging out with those losers at the beach again-"

"Isn't that her dog?" JJ asked and true to his nature as the most badass dog in town, Mutt was barking somewhere downstairs. "She wouldn't have run off without him so she must still be here. You'd better go let him outside before he shits in the potted palms again."

Fox swore and stomped away down the corridor, his footsteps retreating as I released my breath and started laughing, a rush of adrenaline surging through my veins.

JJ whipped the covers back off of me and grinned down at me conspiratorially.

"You wanna see if I can make you come before he comes back to look again?" JJ whispered.

"Oh my god, J, no," I laughed, rolling towards him and slapping his arm to tell him off.

JJ caught my wrist and pinned it to the pillow above my head, leaning down towards me and making my breath catch as he gave me a look designed to set panties on fire. Not that I was wearing any, which was clearly a good thing as the smoke alarms would have brought Fox running right back up here.

"You're right," he agreed wistfully. "I could totally do it, but I'm thinking you're a screamer, so he'd hear us. In that case you'd better run or he's going to flip his lid when he finds you here trying to seduce me."

I narrowed my eyes at him but he ignored me, hoisting me up in his arms and placing my feet down on the carpet beside his bed before slapping my ass to tell me to get moving.

I threw a scowl over my shoulder as he flopped back onto the bed with his hands behind his head, grinning like an idiot and giving me a good view of those beautiful abs of his which I really should have spent more time checking out up close when I'd had the chance.

"Hurry up, pretty girl," JJ said in a low tone. "Unless you wanna get caught by Mary Beth again."

I snorted a laugh at the comparison of my shrill old group home owner to Fox. That woman had damn near flayed me alive when she'd caught JJ in my bed the next morning and it hadn't mattered that I'd screamed in her face to tell her I was still a virgin and that he wasn't my boyfriend.

I slipped out into the hall and pulled JJ's door over behind me before heading down the stairs to seek out some breakfast.

Fox was just storming back into the kitchen from checking out the rest of the house with a face like thunder and his muscles all tense and shit as I appeared. He looked kinda like one of those silverback gorillas storming about and flexing his muscles to remind the whole jungle that he was the king and no one stole from him. A seriously hot, tattooed, green eyed, blonde haired gorilla. Not that I found gorillas sexy or anything.

Fox's eyes about bugged out of his face as I casually wandered over to the fridge and started looking through my breakfast options.

"Where were you?" he demanded.

"When?" I replied disinterestedly as I hid my smirk behind the orange juice.

"I came into your room a minute ago and you weren't there," he said, gripping the fridge door and pulling it wide so he could get a look at me.

"Why did you just casually let yourself into my room?" I asked, folding my arms over JJ's shirt as I looked up at him.

"Because I...found your door open and I was worried that-"

"That your little pet had escaped again? Poor Badger, that must have been terrifying for you."

I grabbed a couple of slices of bread and headed away to jam them in the toaster, feeling him stalking after me like a predator on the hunt.

"I'm just looking out for you, Rogue," he growled as I grabbed a butter knife out of the drawer. "Someone tried to kill you before you came back to me. I don't want anything to happen to you if I'm not there to-"

"If you wanna give me a gun and a car then I can go drive by that motherfucker's house and return the favour. What's your preferred method again? One to the head, two to the chest? Seems simple enough." My grip curled tight around the butter knife as I considered that option and found I liked it a whole hell of a lot. Fucking Shawn. I'd look him dead in the eye and let him see the ghost of the girl he'd buried before I showed him how to kill someone a whole lot more effectively.

My free hand brushed against my throat at the memories of him squeezing the life out of me and I shivered before I could stop myself.

Fox's arms closed around me and he dragged me against his bare chest, crushing me in his arms like that was the safest place in the world for me to be. And maybe a tiny piece of me wanted to believe that, but I also couldn't forget what he'd done. What they'd all done.

"Just give me a name, hummingbird. I'll make him scream for hours for you. I'll make him truly regret what he did before you end him," he said in a low rumble that seemed to vibrate right through my chest.

"I don't want your help with this. I don't want your help at all," I protested firmly, pushing against his solid chest until he released me then aggressively buttering my toast. "And you can't keep me locked up in here forever either. I might not have run this morning, but I will again soon. You can't just cage me like some wild animal you've decided to tame."

The softness in Fox disappeared quicker than I could even register, and he ground out a curse as he turned and strode away towards the garage with his muscles all tense again.

I finished buttering my toast and took a savage bite from a piece before turning around to watch as Fox returned from the garage with a sledgehammer in his grasp.

Mutt appeared from the courtyard surrounding the pool, scurrying closer to me with a wide-eyed look that said he thought Fox was fucking crazy. Smart dog.

"What are you doing?" I demanded, my gaze slipping to the garage door which Fox had left slightly open with the keys jammed into it.

"Making sure you can't run off on me the same way you did last time," he snarled as he stalked out of the patio doors to the courtyard which held the pool and strode straight towards the barbecue which I'd used to climb up over the wall during my escape.

I sucked in a gasp as Fox hefted the sledgehammer in his grip and swung it at the barbecue as hard as he could.

Bricks shattered and the crash of crumbling masonry filled the air as a huge chunk of the barbecue was smashed off, flying into the pool with a splash that sent water flying all around before he swung the sledgehammer again.

"What the fuck is going on?" JJ demanded as he jogged down the stairs and I tried to get over the shock of Fox losing his shit as I pointed through the glass doors and he hurried over to get a look at what was happening.

Mutt was getting seriously freaked out by the destruction and he scurried over to me, slipping behind my legs and peeking out just as JJ jogged by.

"What the fuck, Fox? I wanted to cook burgers later!" he yelled as another chunk of barbecue was sent crashing down on the tiles and Fox's muscles bunched and flexed in a way that was giving me serious construction worker fantasies. *Come smash down my walls, builder boy and pound my... drain in?* Ew, no, I'd lost it, maybe I'd let that fantasy go just as fast as it had surfaced.

"I'm solving a problem," Fox snarled defiantly as JJ got closer to him and the two of them began arguing over whether or not the prospect of burgers for dinner was more or less important than the possibility of me using the barbecue to escape again.

My eyes fell to the sun lounger where I'd been parked yesterday afternoon and my lips twitched as I spotted a pair of my shorts still sitting there alongside my Power Rangers cap where I'd taken them off to sunbathe.

I silently snagged the shorts and cap, blew the guys a kiss which they couldn't see as they continued to argue then turned and ran for the garage door with Mutt on my heels.

I grabbed Fox's keys out of the door, slipped through it and locked it again on the other side before eyeing the rack of car keys hanging there whispering my name with sweet promises of freedom.

JJ's ride was probably the most fun to drive, but there was just something poetic in taking Fox's truck that I couldn't resist.

I grabbed the key from the hook then grabbed all of the other keys too so that they wouldn't be able to follow me and ran down the stairs to the garage before leaping into his black pickup, tossing the other keys into the footwell beside me and waiting for Mutt to hop in too.

The moment he made it inside, getting his little white ass comfy on the seat beside me, I turned the key in the ignition and hightailed it out of there.

The grin on my face quickly became all out laughter as I sped up the ramp, opened the garage door with his snazzy little button and headed out along the drive. Fox's boys who were parked up on guard at the gate recognised his truck and because the douchebag had blacked out windows, they even opened the gate for me, assuming I was him. *Fuckturds.* I pumped the gas and sped out onto the street in Fox's fancy truck and I imagined his face going all red and that sledgehammer finding a hole in the fucking wall when he realised that I was gone again.

Mutt yipped excitedly and I had to agree with him - it did look like it was going to be a beautiful day in Sunset Cove.

I drove quickly, knowing full well that Fox would have his gang of miscreants on the hunt for me soon enough and they'd be looking out for his truck too, so I set a course for the water and took advantage of the early hour as I sped through quiet streets.

I made it to the road that ran along the beach and turned left along the boardwalk known as The Mile, the pier in the distance catching my eye and bringing back all kinds of memories as I looked at it. That had been our favourite place in the world once. This abandoned little paradise where five kids who wanted to escape from reality made time to live the way we wanted to even if it never lasted as long as we would have liked.

I made my decision without even thinking about it and drove towards it at full speed, the Ferris wheel catching the rays of the rising sun and seeming to call me home.

I pulled the truck up in the middle of the street a few blocks away from the pier and quickly gave it a sweep, finding a handgun in the glovebox alongside a pack of gum.

I shimmied out of JJ's sweatpants and into my shorts sans panties before tying a knot in his shirt so that I looked somewhat respectable. Well, not respectable but like, not totally as if I was wearing a dude's clothes and hadn't had a chance to shower this morning. Then I took a stick of gum to counter the lack of tooth brushing that had taken place this morning, fixed my hair in the mirror as best I could before hiding it beneath the hat and decided to leave the gun where it was. I didn't really have anywhere to hide it and aside from my overdue visit to see Shawn, I didn't have anyone to use it on either. Though as I thought about Shawn, I considered just turning and driving away again. I could do what I'd said, roll up on him and open fire. Assuming none of his men saw me coming. And none of them noticed the truck of a well known rival gang leader cruising into their turf.

On second thoughts that was probably another death sentence. Besides,

I'd already made my decision about Shawn. I was going to get what I'd come here for first then swing by his place to put a bullet between his eyes right before I ran off to start my new life somewhere far, far away. Simple. And it wasn't worth fucking with that plan now no matter how tempting it might have been to lay that motherfucker out for what he'd tried to do to me.

I hopped out of Fox's truck, ignoring the fact that I had no shoes on and whistled for Mutt to follow me as I headed across the street and hopped the low wall that bordered the beach.

The feeling of the golden sand between my toes made me sigh with happiness and I set a track straight for the waves, walking until they were racing up and over my toes and then turning left towards the pier where my childhood would forever reside in my memories.

My gaze fell on the long wooden structure which ran out into the water and I couldn't help but wonder how long it had been since this place had been open to the general public. It had been firmly locked up and chained off ever since I'd been a kid and the amusement park really wasn't in great shape. But at some point it must have been somewhere that all kinds of people had loved to hang out, full of life and laughter instead of nesting gulls and delinquents.

It didn't take me too long to walk to the pier we'd christened Sinners' Playground with Mutt charging in and out of the waves happily beside me and the sun steadily increasing the temperature as I went.

By the time I made it to the pier, my gut was tightening and a nervous kind of energy was prickling beneath my skin. I didn't know why I was feeling so strange about coming back to our old haunt, but something told me my heart might break all over again if I got up there and found the place ruined.

I drew in a deep breath and forced away my hesitation as I headed up the beach. I made it to the wooden support beam where the guys had carved hand holds all those years ago so that we could climb up there easily. It meant we didn't have to try and climb over the heavy metal gates which had been chained shut and rusted over years before we'd ever come here.

"Wait here, boy," I instructed, reaching down to scruff Mutt's head and he licked my hand before he dove into the shade beneath the pier and started chasing his tail.

The instant I started climbing, it was like I'd been transported back in time, my muscles remembering this climb like it was an old friend, my hands and feet finding the handholds without me even needing to look for them.

When I reached the top, I caught hold of the chain we'd left hanging over the side of the pier for this very purpose and used it to haul myself up and over the edge.

I grinned to myself as I made it, scrambling upright and drawing in a slow breath as the ghosts of my past surrounded me.

The pier had been laid out with an amusement arcade and an assortment of fairground rides, little huts meant to sell ice cream and cotton candy lining the boardwalk with brightly coloured facades which had long since faded beneath the heat of the sun.

I moved between them with déjà vu prickling at my skin and so many memories that I could hardly even breathe with them all pressing in on me.

I glanced back over my shoulder at the heavily chained and boarded up gates, smiling as I saw the spray paint still there from the day the five of us had claimed this place as our own. Our own piece of turf in a town carved up by gangs. Sinners' Playground. The words were still clear, the paint seeming vivid amongst everything else, our initials all marking the board to the right of the bold words, trapped inside a heart I'd painted around them myself. Because back then I'd believed my love for those boys could never falter and we'd all be together forever.

I turned my back on the sign and started walking, heading for our favourite places at the far end of the pier like I just couldn't help myself.

This pier held so many good memories that it was somehow harder to be here than it was to be anywhere else in the cove. But I pressed on regardless, my eyes on the top of the Ferris wheel that I could see above the arcade which barred my way on.

I slipped inside the arcade, enjoying the silence in the shadows and remembering the nights we'd all camped out in here, sleeping between the Pac-Man and Space Invaders consoles and laughing our asses off the whole damn time.

I crossed through the silent space quickly and moved out on the boardwalk again to my favourite part of the pier where the old rides lay dormant and waiting.

My gaze slid over the teacups, the carousel, the bumper cars, all of them holding a host of laughter and joy in my past and I almost smiled at the memories, but it was too hard. They hurt too much in the light of what had followed them, and I wasn't sure I'd ever truly be able to take joy in any of them again.

"Are you looking for me or just haunting somewhere new?" Chase's voice made me flinch and I sucked in a breath as I looked up and found him sitting in one of the Ferris wheel carriages. He was about a quarter of the way around to the right of where I was standing, looking down at me over the baby blue door and arching a brow like I was pissing him off just by existing.

"Shouldn't you be out looking for me?" I replied, glancing behind me and wondering if I should try to run. "I assumed Fox would have set all of his guard dogs on the hunt by now."

Chase grinned like a shark but the deadly look in his eyes promised me there was no joy in it.

"I did wonder why my phone was blowing up. I just hadn't gotten around to checking it yet," he replied with a shrug. "Besides, I'm not in the mood to chase your ass around town. In my opinion, if you don't wanna stay locked up in our house then that's fine by me. I never asked you to come back anyway."

His words stung a little, but they were also kind of a relief. Somehow I found the fact that Chase didn't want me here easier to deal with than the other guys trying to force me back into the fold after everything that had happened. At least with Chase it was simple. Hate I could do. I'd been hating the Harlequin boys for a damn long time. It was the bullshit the other two kept trying to feed me and lure me in with that was too much of a mind fuck.

They wanted to open their arms, hug it out and just pretend that nothing had changed in the last ten years. Well, news flash, assholes, a whole lot had changed. The innocent girl they once knew had to figure her shit out without four boys at her back and soon came to realise that most people in this world only valued you based on what they could take from you.

I'd been used and learned how to use people. I'd sold everything from my morals to my soul and only managed not to sell my body out of pure determination. That was one line I wouldn't cross. Not after Axel. But that wasn't to say I'd exactly been treated like a princess in the bedroom. I'd just rather be used on my own terms than in return for dollar bills.

"Move over, asshole. I'm coming up to bum a smoke." I approached the Ferris wheel and quickly grabbed the familiar hand holds as I began to climb the framework.

"You're absolutely not invited to join me, you know?" Chase muttered, but he shifted over all the same.

"I never wait around for invitations," I replied dismissively. "I don't make many guest lists. It's been suggested I'm lacking decorum."

Chase snorted what could have been a laugh as I reached his car and he opened the slightly rusting door before offering me a hand.

I took it and he hauled me inside, making the thing rock wildly and I stumbled onto one knee, half falling into his lap.

"If you came to suck me off you coulda just said that," he joked but there wasn't really any humour in it and I shoved myself back to sit on the bench opposite his before reaching out to pluck the smoke from his lips.

I took a long toke on it, turning and hanging my legs over the edge of the carriage through the bars.

"So we're just hanging out are we?" he asked scathingly.

"Looks like it. You wanna tell me why you're scowling up here, like an angry crow or..."

"You know why," he growled, reaching over and making a move to steal the cigarette from me but I plucked it from my lips then held it out away from him.

Unperturbed, Chase dropped his hand to my bare thigh instead and brushed his fingers over the tattoo I had there of a skull with pink roses.

"Why the skull?" he asked, shifting his hand so his fingers slid around my thigh and I huffed as I batted him off.

"Because I'm dead inside," I murmured which sadly, really was the reason I'd gotten it.

"Since when?"

"You know the answer to that," I said, looking out over the sea and releasing the smoke from my lungs.

Chase took a minute to think on that and I just looked down at the water, smiling slightly as I watched a few surfers out catching waves. I was desperate to get back out on the water. That tiny little go I'd had surfing with Di's board was nothing, especially as I'd had the dreaded Badger watching me and had been too distracted to really enjoy it, let alone take my time.

I wanted to buy my own board, get up at dawn and just lose myself in the surf like I used to. I wanted to immerse myself in the sea every morning and taste salt on my lips while eating breakfast on the beach the way we had done too many times to count when we were kids.

"Were you by the sea where you were living before you came here?" Chase asked, noticing what my attention was on.

"No," I said, the sadness sneaking into my voice on that single word.

I glanced at him and noticed the little green box he had shoved beside his thigh as if he was trying to hide it. My gaze caught on his arm next and the way he was sitting at just such an angle to try and hide it from me. I knew that behaviour all too well from the times he used to show up with new bruises his dad had given them and try not to let us see them. I guessed old habits died hard.

"Let me see it," I said, pointing at his arm and he narrowed his eyes at me.

"It's nothing," he muttered.

"Nothing doesn't require a first aid kit," I pointed out. "Stop being a little bitch and let me see."

Chase stole his smoke back as I moved towards him, rolling his eyes as he let me see the cut on the side of his bicep while taking a drag.

"I can do it myself," he said as I picked up an antibacterial wipe and swiped it over the deep wound. He flinched the tiniest bit at the burn and I smirked at his pain like a grade A cock sucker. That said, I liked to think I knew my way around a cock with my mouth, so maybe that was exactly what I was.

"Yeah, but then I wouldn't get to enjoy causing you pain," I replied with a dark smile. "What was this anyway? Looks too thick to be a blade-"

"Bullet skimmed me. Stings a bit, but I've had worse."

I reached up to touch the site of the bullet scar on his shoulder through his shirt which he'd shown me before they'd headed out last night. Chase stilled as he met my gaze with his blue eyes and for a moment I was sure he could see how glad I was that he hadn't died. I didn't want him to think I cared and I didn't really, I just…didn't want him dead. That was it.

We fell silent as I cleaned up the wound, checked it for dirt and shit then patched him up with a waterproof dressing and some antibacterial ointment.

"I hope you're not expecting me to thank you," Chase muttered as I hesitated with my hand on his elbow, my skin prickling at the contact.

"To what?" I asked with a frown like I hadn't heard him.

"Thank you."

"You're welcome," I replied with a smirk before shifting back to resume my lounging position in the seat opposite him. "But I only did it to stop your bitching, so don't go getting all soft on me, Ace."

Chase narrowed his eyes at me, but his phone started ringing and he shook it at me so that I could see Fox's name on the ID.

"What are you waiting for then, Chase?" I asked. "Tell your boss where his prisoner ran off to."

"This game is getting old," he said irritably. "If you don't want to stay then why don't you just run further?"

"I never said I don't want to stay. I said I don't want to stay in that house. Funnily enough, I survived ten years without anyone looking out for me, so I don't feel that the twenty-four hour surveillance is required. Besides, I don't enjoy being stuck in the company of three of the people who ruined my life."

When he didn't reply right away, I turned to look at him and found him stubbing out the cigarette with a contemplative look on his face.

"See that's where you're losing me. If you hate us all so much and have no desire to spend time with us, then why stay in our town? Why force yourself to deal with it day after day and just be miserable over it?" he asked.

"I've got unfinished business here," I said with a shrug. "Ghosts I want to put to bed."

"I only see one ghost around here," Chase replied, his gaze crawling all over me like he was searching for something, but I didn't know what and I hoped he wouldn't find it.

"Perhaps you need to get an exorcist in then."

His cell started ringing again and I sighed, holding out my hand for it.

Chase passed it over with an amused look on his face and I answered it.

"What's up, Badger?" I asked casually, shifting my weight to make the carriage swing a little beneath us.

There was a beat of stunned silence before he recovered his composure. "Where the hell are you? And why do you have Chase's phone?"

"We're secretly hooking up and he's currently between my thighs trying his hardest to get me off. But I have to say, he's seriously bad with his tongue, which isn't that surprising for a selfish motherfucker like him, but I'll probably just fake it in a minute to make him stop. How are you?"

"That's not funny," Fox ground out and it actually sounded like he was grinding his teeth to dust at the mere suggestion of it.

"What's the matter, Badger? You don't like the idea of me getting fucked? Because I hate to break it to you, but I'm not the little virgin girl you ran out of town and I've had plenty of D in the time we've been parted."

"Stop that," he snapped. "And tell me where you are."

"What if I don't want to?"

"I don't care what you want."

"Didn't think so," I said bitterly and he paused.

"I didn't mean it like that," he said with a groan of frustration. "Why do you have to make this so hard?"

"Why can't you grasp the fact that I don't want to be locked up in a house with a bunch of murderers who I don't trust, let alone *like?*" I hissed back and Chase released a low whistle.

"Put Chase on the phone," Fox snapped, his anger back just as fast as it had faltered.

I tossed the phone to Chase and got to my feet.

"This isn't working, dude," he said as he held the phone to his ear. "You can't keep locking her up like a prisoner and expecting her to thank you for it. She's an ungrateful little brat who isn't going to stop pushing back against you every time you push at her. This situation is fucking toxic."

Well, at least the asshole had a good grasp on reality.

I smirked at him as he continued to argue his point with Fox, opened the carriage door and climbed out of it, grabbing hold of the frame and shimmying back down off of the Ferris wheel.

I climbed down quickly, the sound of the gulls and the waves drowning out whatever Chase was saying to Fox and I didn't really care to hear it anyway.

When I made it to the foot of the ride, I headed down the little set of stairs that led up to it and started walking back towards the arcade and the way out of here.

Just as I reached the door to the squat, white building which filled the central section of the pier, Chase called out to me.

"Oh, so you're taking the chicken shit way out of here, are you?"

I turned back to look at him, the familiar words making me pause as I found him tugging his shirt off and looking at me expectantly. He was stupid ripped, like maybe these guys had spent the last ten years working out in all the time they would have hung out with me. Or maybe they were hocked up on steroids and had eenie weenie peenies hiding beneath their shorts in payment for it. My gaze slid down his golden skin to that V dipping beneath his waistband as if I wanted to check that out, before I caught myself and snapped my eyes back to his face instead.

"You want me to jump off the pier with you?" I asked, wondering why the hell he'd wanna do something like that.

"Unless you're not the chick I used to remember showing us up all the damn time?" he asked, moving towards me with a cocky swagger that he never used to have before. That look in his eye said he wasn't afraid of a damn thing and the way he held himself said he always got what he wanted, no matter what it took to achieve it.

"I can still show you up any day of the week," I promised.

"Give me a second to ditch my shit then," he said, brushing past me and snatching my cap off of my head before heading into the arcade.

I really should have just been leaving his ass here and running again, but for some reason I wanted to prove to him that I was still the girl who dared them all to do crazy shit and played on their macho bullshit to force them into it. I wasn't afraid of anything. Least of all, the Harlequin boys.

Chase returned, no longer wearing his sneakers and I was willing to guess he'd tossed them down into the sand alongside his shirt, cigarettes, my baseball cap and his cellphone. I didn't have anything else that the water could ruin, so I just walked back down the pier to the Ferris wheel with him and climbed over the railings that ran around behind it at the foot of the pier.

The tide was high and the water was deep beneath us. I'd done this a thousand times as a kid, so it shouldn't have been a big deal, and yet my heart began to gallop as I looked down at the drop below.

Chase snatched my hand into his and smirked at me, but there wasn't any kindness in it.

"On three?" he asked and I nodded. "One-" Chase jumped, dragging me with him as he kept hold of me and a scream tore from my lips as I fell towards the water and my heart leapt in panic.

We crashed into the waves and sank beneath them, a stream of bubbles escaping my lips as I descended and Chase released me.

I swam for the surface the moment my descent stopped, laughing as I breached the waves and catching Chase's eye for a moment as we exchanged the first real smiles we'd shared since I'd come back.

"I guess you're not chicken shit after all then, little one," he growled, his blue eyes seeming to brighten beside the water.

My gut tightened as he called me that, a piece of me I was longing to forget hurting over him and the boy he'd once been.

I turned away quickly and started swimming beneath the pier, keeping within its shadow as I headed back to shore with Chase beside me.

When the water got shallow enough for me to stand, I began wading up the sandy incline, spotting Mutt running back and forth and barking happily at the sight of me.

Just as we drew close to the beach, Chase caught me by my hips and shoved me back against one of the thick wooden beams which held the pier up, his eyes so dark down here in the shadows that they almost looked black.

"I've gotta take you back with me," he said roughly, holding me still with his muscular biceps flexing and water spilling down the golden skin of his chest.

"Because Fox said so and he's got you running around like his little bitch boy these days?" I taunted and Chase's grip on my waist tightened painfully as he pushed against me, his hard body pinning me in place as that hungry look in his eyes intensified.

"I think you're forgetting that you're talking to a Harlequin, babe," he said, his tone dangerously low. "I could drown you here and now and no one would even question me on it."

"Fox might have a thing or two to say about it."

"I'm not afraid of him." Chase stared me down for a long minute as our breaths came heavily between us and neither one of us backed down.

"What now then, big man?" I taunted as the waves crashed over our legs and Mutt barked furiously from his position on the beach. "You've got me at your mercy. So what are you going to do to me?"

"You should be thanking me," Chase said, licking the salt from his lips and drawing my attention to his mouth briefly before I looked away again just as fast. His jaw was lined with stubble this morning and the combination of that with the way his dark curls were slicked back by the water was attracting my gaze way too much. I shouldn't be looking at him like that. But there had been a point in my life when I'd fantasised about all of the Harlequin boys from time to time and what it might be like to kiss them, touch them... "Aren't you going to ask me what for?"

"I assumed you were just going to tell me anyway," I snarked back.

"Fine. I'll let Fox tell you. But when you're thinking about sucking his cock to thank him for his generosity, maybe you should suck mine instead because it was my idea."

"What the fuck are you talking about?" I demanded, my gaze dropping to his waistband as his suggestion got my mind going down all kinds of cock infested paths.

Christ, I really needed to get laid. Maybe I'd convince Di and Lyla to come clubbing with me the next time I escaped and have some dirty alleyway fuck with a guy I didn't know to clear my brain of all this toxic curiosity. I looked back up at Chase, licking my lips before I could stop myself and his gaze heated too.

"For the record," he growled, his hand moving from my hip to my waistband as he pushed his fingers beneath it right below my naval. "If you got me between your thighs you'd be wetter than you are right now and you wouldn't be faking a damn thing." His hand pushed lower and I gasped as his eyes lit at the realisation that I had no panties on.

"I'll believe it when I see it," I hissed, glaring at him and yet somehow not making any move to stop the descent of his hand. Not that I wanted him to keep going or anything, because I freaking hated him and I had no intention of fucking his hand right here in broad daylight. But for some reason I was playing chicken with him again and I refused to be the one to blink first.

Chase ran his gaze down my body, taking in my hardened nipples pressing through my borrowed shirt and the way my chest was rising and falling heavily. His gaze met mine and he cocked his head as if to say *game on,* despite the hatred raging between us.

His hand pushed lower and a gasp escaped my lips because he was about two inches away from finding out that the sea water wasn't the only reason I was wet right now and I was, for some unthinkable reason, getting really turned on by the idea of him flipping this hatred into lust and doing exactly what he was threatening to do.

I moved my own hand to his shorts, grasping the thick, hard length of his cock through the drenched material and daring him with my eyes to do his damn worst while appreciating the fact that there definitely wasn't any dick shrinking issues from steroids going on with him after all. He sucked in air through his teeth and I got the reaction I wanted as all that hate in his eyes melted into a liquid pool of desire.

"Is this your dog?" a woman's horrified shout came from somewhere to my right and I snatched my hand back as I turned to look at the V blocker in question while she pointed at Mutt and glared at me.

Chase withdrew his hand too, grabbing my elbow and making me walk with him towards the shore. "What of it?" he called back angrily.

"He just took a dump by my sandcastle," she said angrily and I couldn't help but laugh.

"So clean it up, bitch," Chase tossed back at her. "I don't give a shit about that."

I snorted to myself. *Give a shit. Nice.*

The woman looked furious and turned to glare at Mutt who promptly turned and ran from her to start digging through a bag of trash that had been left beside the garbage can at the top of the beach, but not *inside* it. Some people really were animals.

"If you won't get it under control then I'll call my boyfriend up and he'll come drown it," the woman squawked and fury lit in my veins.

"You what?" I demanded, but Chase had already released me and he strode out of the water straight towards the bitch, muscles tense, water dripping and fury lining his features like a freaking vengeful god of the sea.

Maybe I could call up Poseidon and get him one of those giant fork thingymajigs and he could play out a fantasy where I was a mermaid and he was – *wait, where would he stick his dick if I was a mermaid? And how do mermaids poop?* I shook my head to dispel the nonsense taking part in it in favour of paying attention to the dog-hating bitch getting put in her box.

"Do you know who the fuck you're talking to?" Chase demanded as he stalked closer to her. "I'm a fucking Harlequin. Which means that mutt is a Harlequin too. So guess what, you drown him and I'll be coming to collect that debt from you in blood. And I won't make it quick either. I'll sneak into your house at night and cut your boyfriend's throat so that you can watch him bleed out and then I'll play pin cushion with your ugly ass. Do you know what that means?"

The woman shook her head as she tried to back away, her whole body trembling with fear.

"It's a game where I see how many holes I can stick in a person before they bleed out on me. You know, like you're a pin cushion. My current record is seventy four, but I think if I take my time with you, I could hit triple figures," he purred and save me Lord for I have sinned because fuck me Jesus, that was the darkest, hottest thing I think I'd ever heard someone say.

I was damn tempted to drop to my knees and suck his cock in payment for that. This dude, this total fucking asshole of a dude, just went to bat for my Mutt and all of a sudden I wanted to worship him on my knees.

But no, he was still a mega prick of undeniable proportions, so I wasn't gonna be doing that. But kudos to him for making me consider it.

"I'm sorry," the woman gasped. "I didn't mean it. I-"

"How about you fuck off then before I make good on that threat?" Chase suggested and the woman turned and fled towards her stuff where Mutt had just arrived to pee on her purse.

Best. Dog. Ever.

"Come on, ghost. Fox will be shitting a brick right about now," Chase said, beckoning me after him as he strode up the beach and collected his shit from where he'd tossed it from the pier. As I followed him, my gaze ran over the treasure map inked on his skin with every place I'd ever cared about marked out in the black strokes. I took my cap from him and put it on backwards over my wet hair.

I considered running, but one look at his thick thighs said he'd be fast enough to catch me and I was like three percent curious as to what this mysterious idea he'd given Fox was. And I could just run again easily enough. I was a professional runaway after all.

I whistled for Mutt to follow us as we walked up and off of the beach and Chase led me to the street where he'd parked his midnight blue motorcycle.

"Where is Mutt supposed to go on that?" I asked as Chase kicked his sneakers back on and shrugged into his shirt. I could have suggested we go and get Fox's truck but I kinda liked the idea of it just sitting there in the street abandoned so I didn't mention it.

"He can just run along behind us," Chase said dismissively and I folded my arms in a refusal as Mutt started growling like he'd understood that.

"No," I said firmly. "He's only little and it's too far."

"What do you want me to say to that?" Chase asked irritably, reaching out like he intended to force me onto the bike.

Mutt leapt forward and tried to bite his ankles and I smirked as Chase was forced to step back.

"My dog doesn't like you and he's got exceptional taste, so I trust his judgment. And I don't think I'll be taking your offer of a ride after all."

"I literally just watched him eat something out of the trash and then pee on that bitch's purse," Chase accused. "He has terrible taste."

"It was a *burrito* and that purse was fugly. You're only proving my point." I folded my arms and waited him out and he cursed as he looked back at the bike.

"Fine. I've got my gym bag in here. He can go in that," he snapped. "But if you don't get on right now, I'll hog tie you to the seat and leave him here."

"Fine," I replied, mocking his tone and lifting Mutt into my arms while Chase opened the storage compartment beneath his seat and emptied his gym stuff out into it before handing me the bag.

I took it and let Mutt get in before zipping it up so only his head poked out then put the strap over my body and tightened it up so that he was secure.

Chase rolled his eyes at me then got on the bike and I dutifully hopped on behind him, wrapped my arms around his waist and clung on tight as he accelerated away up the hill. What I hadn't considered about this little ride was quite how it might feel to wrap my thighs around him, cling onto his muscular torso and feel the deep purr of the engine vibrating through my body. Safe to say, I was having trouble not dropping my hands a little lower and…dick punching him because he was an asshat who I hated. Clearly.

We wound through the familiar streets and were soon pulling onto the drive at Harlequin House where the asshole in chief stepped out of the door before we'd even parked up.

I noticed the guys who had been posted at the gate all looked kinda pissed at me and one of them had a bloody nose, but I didn't feel bad about it. It wasn't my problem if they sucked at their jobs and hadn't made sure Fox was the one driving his truck.

I got off and set Mutt free before striding right up to the man in charge, swaying my hips like I was on a runway wearing something stupidly hot instead of squelching along in a dude's shirt while looking like a half drowned rat.

"Hey, Badger," I said lightly, brushing past him and heading through the front door.

I didn't stop as I walked inside, heading straight up to my en-suite for a hot shower, tossing my wet, borrowed shirt aside followed by my shorts and cap before stepping in.

I took my sweet time getting dressed in a cute blue sundress and drying my hair before I emerged from my room, And when I made my way back downstairs, I found Fox waiting for me in the kitchen, his jaw ticking and posture tense as he twisted a cellphone in a shiny pink case between his fingers.

I hopped up to sit on the breakfast bar in front of him, smiling sweetly as I crossed my legs and balanced my toes on the stool beside his.

"This isn't working," he said slowly, his gaze staying fixed on the phone in his hands as I reached out and took an apple from the fruit bowl.

"Don't tell me you're dumping me again, Fox?" I asked with a pout. "Though I can't say I'm surprised."

"Don't talk like that," he muttered.

"Why? Because you've decided you want me back in your life now,

272

so I'm just supposed to forget how disposable I was to you the last time you decided I was too inconvenient to keep around?" I took a bite of my apple and he watched me like he was dying to take a bite too.

A knock at the front door interrupted our glare off and Fox pushed away from me before heading off to answer it.

"We found your truck down by the beach, boss. It's back in the garage," a gruff voice said while I stayed where I was, eating my apple and kinda wishing I'd driven his stupid truck straight into the sea.

"Good," Fox replied before slamming the door again and stalking back in to resume his place sitting beside me at the breakfast bar.

"You're not even gonna thank that dude?" I questioned and he gave me a flat look that said I was crazy.

"If anyone else stole from me like that I'd cut a piece off of them to teach them a lesson," he growled and I had no doubts that he meant it.

"Well please don't take a boob. I'm pretty fond of them and-"

"Do you take anything seriously?" he snapped and I just shrugged, taking another bite of my apple.

"It'd be pretty serious if you cut off my boob."

The corner of his lips twitched the tiniest bit and I smirked as he huffed out a breath, twisting the pink phone in his fingers again.

"I guess if you chop me up it'll be even easier to throw me away than it was the last time. You could put me right in the trash and let the garbage guys take me and then-"

"Stop," he commanded.

"Why? Because it makes you uncomfortable to talk about the time you ruined my life and then forgot all about me?" I challenged.

Fox leaned back in his chair, swiping a hand over his face as it looked like he was choking back against the desire to turn this into a real argument and I had to wonder why.

"I...got you a phone," he said, shoving the shiny pink thing at me, clearly deciding against plunging into that minefield.

I took the cellphone and inspected the pink case. There was a mermaid on it in a seashell bikini top with a little purple dolphin beside her.

"Did you steal it from a twelve year old?" I asked, arching a brow.

"That was the only case they had in the shop," he replied, his lips twitching. "I bought it after I spoke to Chase and he told me that you were okay and you were with him. The guy in there set it up for you. I want you to take it and check in with me regularly so I know you're safe."

"You're letting me go?" I asked in surprise.

"No," he snapped. "I'm just giving you some more freedom. Apparently, it's not okay for me to lock you up all the time." He scowled like that made no sense to him and I couldn't help but stare at him, wondering where the hell he got off thinking he could just do whatever the fuck he liked all the damn time.

"Wow. You're actually insane, aren't you?"

Fox shoved his stool back so hard it crashed to the floor and stood in front of me, pinning me in his glare.

"Don't push me right now, Rogue," he growled, making the hairs along the back of my neck stand on end.

"I'm curious, Fox, do you want me to be afraid of you or are you just trying to make me bow to you?" I asked, narrowing my eyes over my apple at him. "Because you really shouldn't forget that I'm a dead girl walking. I've survived the worst things life has ever thrown at me and I'm still here. There's not much left that I'm afraid of these days. Least of all you."

Fox frowned at me and then swiped a hand down his face like he was trying to scrub the anger right out of his body.

"Chase and JJ seem to think that if I keep on trying to protect you the way I am you're gonna run for good one of these days and I...well, I don't fucking want that. So, if you promise to check in and stay close then I'm not gonna keep locking you up and forcing you to run from me," he said, watching me closely to gauge my reaction.

I was so surprised by that that I just lowered my apple to the counter and gave the phone another look. "So it's a leash instead of a cage?" I asked with a frown, trying to decide if I should be jumping at this and clinging on with both hands or ramming my new mermaid phone up his ass.

"I've got you a car, too. It'll be here tonight or tomorrow."

"I didn't ask you to get me anything," I pointed out and he huffed irritably.

"Just decide Rogue. The car and the phone or locked doors?" he snarled like I was the one being unreasonable here. *Psycho*.

"I'll take your shit then," I said, hopping up and forcing him to move back to let me escape. "Better that than being stuck here with you twenty-four seven."

He scowled, his eyes like a dark and dangerous forest I kinda wanted to explore, but I also knew I'd end up eaten by a tiger if I did.

I moved around him to go sit out by the pool and the shattered remains of the barbecue and he didn't object. This was either a win or a cleverly disguised trap and as I sat flicking through my new phone in the sunshine, I quickly figured out which.

There was some pretty carefully disguised tracking software installed on the device which probably explained why the phone was out of the box. I almost hit delete on it before getting a better idea. If Fox wanted to know where I was at all times, then he could have fun chasing me around town and wondering what the fuck I was up to.

Game on asshole. I'm gonna make this fun.

CHAPTER FIFTEEN

It was ladies' night at Afterlife and a crowd of women were currently drinking in the bar, waiting for the show to start as they fiddled themselves under the tables at the thought of seeing their favourite stripper dancing just for them. Well, at least that was what I assumed they were doing.

I sat in my seat in the dressing room, my feet up on the surface before the mirror which was ringed with bright white lights.

"I'd face fuck you with a balloon so good baby," I spoke on the phone. "I'd work that air-filled latex fucker down your throat again and again until it popped, do you think you could handle that?"

"Yes," she moaned. "I could take it all the way, Bobby."

"Say my full name," I growled, nodding in thanks to Estelle as she placed a coffee down in front of me.

"Bobby Inflatable," the woman purred in my ear and I groaned loudly, drawing the eye of my co-dancer Adam beside me who looked confused as fuck.

She started moaning louder and louder and I cursed internally, needing to draw her back and long out this call. My voice was too damn sexy for my own good.

"When you've got my balloon good and wet, I'll flip you over beneath me, and push the bouncy little devil up your as-" A click sounded on the line and I stopped talking as the automated message rang in my ear.

"This caller has used their ten minute package. Please stay on the line."

I pressed the speaker phone button as some weird ass orchestral music sounded and I tossed my cell down beside my coffee, stretching my arms above my head as I yawned. *Come on Juicy Latexdream351. You know you wanna pay for those extra minutes.*

But it looked like I'd finished her too fast and the call died a moment later. *Damn, I'm too good at fetish phone sex to make decent money out of it.*

"Is your girlfriend into balloons?" Adam asked, his brow pinching like he'd never heard of such a thing. I'd heard of all the things though. Nothing surprised me. I'd once had a girl pay to baste me like a turkey and tickle my giblets. The gobbling part was weird, but I was kinda getting into it by the end.

"No, man. First rule of Stripper Club, you don't have girlfriends. But you make sure every girl in the room thinks they're your girl." I smirked. "I was just making some quick phone sex cash."

"Oh right...I don't think I could do all that phone sex stuff," Adam said, rearranging the army pants he was wearing which matched mine. It was his first night dancing in the show and the sweat on his brow said he was nervous as shit. But the kid was a natural if he could just get out of his own way. And I'd trained him up personally, so obviously he was going to be a fucking star.

"Yeah well, dirty talk is my second language," I said with a shrug. "Sadly they don't teach it on Duo Lingo, but I'm a self taught master. If you ever want some lessons, give me a shout."

He chuckled, flattening down his wavy blonde hair and I pushed out of my seat, knocking his hand away and shoving my fingers into his thick locks. "Oh Adam, the girls here don't want you looking put together. You're not going on a date with Nancy Drew. You're going to tease a bunch of horny women and you need to live on in their fantasies after tonight so they come back next Thursday, and the following one and the one after that." I messed up his hair and he eyed me in the mirror with his large grey eyes which were going to get a lot of seats wet in the club tonight. Estelle was going to be working overtime to clean them after.

I handpicked my dancers and the moment Adam had walked in to audition, I'd gotten dollar signs in my eyes. The problem was, I hadn't been banking on him being such a holy Joe. Pretty boys like him usually had experience with teasing women, but from what he'd told me, he'd only gotten really hot in the last year. He was twenty two and had broken up with his girlfriend who he'd been with since he was sixteen. So I was dealing with a one pussy wonder who'd had his self esteem ripped out by a rich bitch who'd replaced it with a whole lot of doubt. She was from the upper quarter and he was from the lower. It was all that star crossed bullshit I had no time for, and oh-what-a-surprise, she'd chosen Daddy's trust fund over him in the end. So he'd shown up here because the guy had nowhere else to go and had experience in dance because said bitch girlfriend had encouraged him to learn so she had someone to practise her Latin ballroom bullshit with. Bitches were nice like that.

Now he had no money and his parents lived in Mexico and called once a year so I'd taken him under my wing because well, ker-ching. But also, I knew what it felt like to be kicked to the curb and have your whole life pulled out from under you. I'd also hooked him up with a room in an apartment that my girls Cherry and Kitty shared. It was only a matter of time before one of them showed him the art of decent pussy and he forgot all about Miss Too-Good-For-Him. I'd suggested he invite her fancy ass down here in a few months' time and watch him lead a show where a hundred girls screamed his name and begged to suck his dick. Karma was a cunt. And I was her wily sidekick.

"So what's rule number two?" Adam asked, looking hopeful.

"Huh?" I frowned.

"You said rule number one was no girlfriends, so what are the other rules?"

"Oh right." *Definitely hadn't been making that shit up on the spot. But I guess I could share my own rules.* "Well, rule number two is no fucking the clients in house. This isn't a brothel, but..." I leaned in close to whisper in his ear. "You wanna make a little extra cash on the side then you can make arrangements in the bar."

He gave me a nervous look in the mirror. "I dunno if I could..."

"Trust me, when the offers start rolling in and you get hungry enough for the money, you'll be tempted. So it's best to set your limits now."

Texas dropped down into the seat on his other side, his dark skin glinting with baby oil and his huge muscles straining against the military uniform he was squeezed into. "We talking rules?" He grinned like a puppy dog. "I don't fuck anyone over forty five."

"That's because you're an idiot," I pointed out, rubbing some almond oil onto my arms – it cost more but I preferred the smell of it and it made my skin all kinds of soft too. "The older the gal, the more money they have."

"I think with my dick, you think with your bank account," Texas said with a shrug.

"So you just do it for fun?" Adam asked Texas curiously.

"Yeah, when you realise hot pussy will pay for good dick, you'll also realise you might as well spend all your free time fucking for cash."

"Yeah and when you realise hot pussy will pay more for better dick, you'll be stealing Texas's clients out from under his nose just like I do." I winked at the big guy and he glowered at me, saying nothing because he knew it was true.

Adam laughed, smiling at me and I swear there were little stars in his eyes. "So what's the third rule?"

I snorted, clapping him on the shoulder. "Always wear a condom, bro. Always, always. Double wrap, triple wrap if you have to. Just never take one of those bad boys off. If you need one, I keep a stash here." I reached over to my dresser and pulled out the drawer, revealing the organised rows of condoms of every variety.

"So you never take one off?" Adam asked and I guessed Miss Money Tits had probably been on the pill.

"Never," I said seriously. "You can catch an STI on the breeze in this place. Especially when Texas is sitting this close."

"Fuck you," Texas drawled, but he was smirking.

The music dropped to a low, thundering beat out in the bar and the audience started screaming. That was our cue. Adam and Texas got up and we met Ruben and Olly by the stage entrance, handing us our hats and I put mine on. The Saints by Andy Mineo started playing and I gave Adam an encouraging nod before leading the way out onto the stage, pulling my hat low as screams rang in my ears.

The stage extended out into the audience and I marched out to the very front of it to the music while the guys lined up behind me in perfect synchronisation. As the beat dropped, we all saluted and tossed our hats into the crowd to a round of screams. The green lights swung around, illuminating the eyes of every thirsty girl in the club and I grinned cockily as I danced, loving the feeling of being the centre of attention.

My body moved to the music, every grind and thrust of my hips bringing more girls closer to the stage until they were crushing one another to try and reach me. On the next beat, we all tore our shirts off and Adam's got stuck on the final button so I ripped it off for him, serving us screams of approval. *Note to self: play up to that shit.*

The other dancers all started pulling girls up from the crowd and I hunted for my own victim, my gaze catching on rainbow hair beyond the swarming women at the stage and my heart pounded harder. I smirked as my eyes locked on Rogue who'd apparently shown up to watch me dance. *How the fuck did she get out of the house again?*

I lifted a finger, beckoning her from the back of the room. She wore a ripped denim skirt and a hot pink tee that was tied up to show off her midriff. She was talking with Di who was bartending tonight in a sparkly bikini and she rolled her eyes at me, sipping her beer. I jerked my head in a command and she shook her head in refusal, but bit her lip in a way that got my dick hardening.

I grabbed the hand of a girl in the front row, tugging her onto the stage and flipping her around in front of me while I wrapped my arms around her waist. I didn't even notice if she was blonde, a brunette or fucking bald as she squealed in delight. My gaze was locked with Rogue's as I ground against Miss Nobody's ass in time with the music then pushed her back down into the audience.

Another girl grabbed my hand and I tugged her up onto the stage, lowering her to the floor face down and falling over her, grinding on her body to the beat. She laughed as I rolled her over, rolling my hips into hers so she could feel every inch of my hard on which currently belonged solely to Rogue. My eyes snagged on hers again and I wanted to claim that it was lust and maybe a hint of jealousy pouring from her eyes, but it also could have been me hoping for that.

What did she think of me now I was all grown up and could have every woman in this room sighing my name in less than a minute? I'd always wanted to be a man, but back when I was a kid that was because I'd wanted to have the balls to claim Rogue, kiss her right, fuck her right. I'd just been a virgin who'd failed hard when I'd actually built up the nerve to try and kiss her. It was still one of the most embarrassing moments of my life and I wasn't sure if she'd even realised what I'd been trying to do.

I leapt back to my feet, waving the girl off stage as I backed up to join the line up of dancers and we moved in perfect time as the beat built to a warring crescendo. The audience wouldn't be getting the full package this early in the show, but as we finished the routine, all of us tore off the Velcro secured trousers to reveal the tight fitting American flag underwear beneath that did nothing to hide our boners.

Women screamed and my gaze hooked on the big guy sitting at the bar with dark rimmed glasses on his face while he was clapping enthusiastically. Everyone just called him Tom because he only ever drank a Tom Collins. I guessed he was gay as he was only ever here when me and my troop were dancing, so I made sure he was let in the door because his bar tab could probably have put a few of my girls through college. Not that most of them had any plans for that. But they could definitely buy themselves a top-of-the-range shiny vibrator or ten courtesy of Tom.

I saluted in time with my co-dancers and we jogged backstage, my head buzzing with the high.

I clapped Adam on the shoulder and he beamed at me. "Fucking perfect," I called over the still screaming crowd back in the bar as we headed into the dressing room to change for the next dance. Jessie's voice carried over a microphone as she filled in the time with some dirty jokes and a spin the wheel game where the top prize was a hundred dollars.

My heart was pounding wildly and I realised for the first time since I'd started this line of work, I was actually feeling one percent nervous about dancing out there, knowing Rogue was in the audience. There was still a piece of that too-nice little kid living in me that I needed to suffocate with a pillowcase and kick in the head. I wasn't a boy, I was a fucking man. And I wanted more than ever to prove that to her.

So as I donned the cowboy outfit for the next bit, I caught my own gaze in the mirror and made a promise to myself. *She'll know I'm not a kid anymore by the end of the night. It's time I put my demons to rest.*

I had a shower after the show, washing off the oil, the glitter, the sweat. A bachelorette party had poured into the club half way through the show and I had the scratch marks to prove it plus more than a few contact cards tucked into my briefs.

I stepped out of the shower, grabbing a towel as Texas walked past me with his cock out and I swiped a dollar bill from between his butt cheeks, waving it in his face. "You missed one."

He lunged for it and I jogged away with a laugh. "Finders keepers!"

"Asshole," he laughed and I smirked as I added it to my pile which I'd tucked into my dresser drawer.

Adam was counting his out, now dressed in a white tank and black sweats, his hair damp from a shower.

"What did you make?" I asked.

Every dancer in my club kept the tips stuffed into their clothes and anything left on the stage was divided equally. I paid my guys well, but the real money was in the tips. I sometimes found hundred dollar bills chilling with my balls after a show and if that wasn't the best way to meet Benjamin Franklin, I didn't know what was. Adam had his best days to live for.

"Just over three hundred," he announced, beaming and I grinned. "I got this too. From the bridal party." He waved a contact card at me with the number four hundred and a question mark scrawled on it.

"Escorting's not for everyone," I said, suddenly feeling protective of my little one pussy wonder as I snatched the card from his hand. "Which one was it?"

"I think it was the mother of the bride." Colour touched his cheeks. "But four hundred dollars…"

I shook my head, dropping into my seat beside him. "Firstly, four hundred dollars is selling yourself short. Secondly, fucking for money costs more than sex."

"What do you mean?" He frowned.

"Leave the kid alone," Ruben called over, his copper hair gleaming wetly from his shower. "Stripping is a warm up to the fucking. He's gonna end up doing it anyway."

"Shut up, Ruben," I snarled. "Not everyone wants dick rot like you."

"Coming from the Escort King." He smirked.

"I keep a clean house," I tossed back and his smirk fell away. "Unlike you who has a surcharge for going in bare. You know when I'll go in bare? Never. Because I'm planning to still have a dick by the time I'm forty."

"Condoms right?" Adam said and I nodded seriously.

"Yeah, always, always, *always*," I pressed. "But just remember, if you wanna start chasing the big money, it costs you-"

"There's a hot unicorn here to see you, JJ," Texas boomed and I looked over to where he was standing butt naked, scrubbing his wet hair with a towel while Rogue stood beside him, casually inspecting his dick. Which was still rock hard. A demon rose its head in me and I flew out of my seat, grabbing my sweats and personal shit before I jogged over to her.

"See you later!" I called to everyone, grabbing her hand and guiding her toward the back door.

"I wanna say hello to your friends," she complained as I towed her along then dropped my towel to get dressed and her eyes fell straight to my cock, killing her line of thought. And most likely any line of thought she'd been having about Texas's cock. Because mine was a work of art, perfectly aligned, girthy, long, smooth and everything was shaved. It took a fair amount of work to keep it this well groomed, but its looks were all genetic and I guessed I had to thank my sperm donor for the great DNA combo he'd gifted me. The more she stared, the harder I got, especially when she wet her lips and my dick twitched hopefully. *I wish, Johnny D.*

Remembering I was supposed to be getting fucking dressed, I tugged on my boxers, grey sweatpants and a black AC/DC tank before kicking on my sneakers, pushing my shit into my pockets and grabbing her hand again.

"Did you enjoy the show?" I asked teasingly and she twisted a lock of blue and purple hair between her fingers as she met my gaze.

"The one I just had a private viewing for or the one in the club?" She smirked.

"Both." I pushed through the back door and led her out into the parking lot, the moonlight washing down on us.

"The strip show was crazy good," she said, grinning at me.

"And the private show?" I quirked a brow as her shoulder brushed mine.

I didn't even know where we were walking to. Where the fuck had I parked? This girl fried my head. Whenever I looked at her it was like looking directly at the sun. Totally dangerous but so, so fucking beautiful. I'd let my eyes melt in my head before I stopped staring.

"You're gonna have to start charging me for those, J. That's the second time you've pointed your dick at me for free," she taunted, not giving me my answer.

"Why does it feel like I should be paying *you* for that?" I murmured and she laughed, poking me in the ribs.

I loved when she touched me. It reminded me she was really fucking here, not just some figment of my imagination. I'd woken up thinking she was still in my life a thousand times after she'd left. Over the years, that had happened less and less often, but it never went away altogether. It was cliché, but losing her had been like having a limb amputated. It was a part of me I always expected to be there instinctively, but as soon as I tried to pretend it was, I couldn't function the same. Because she had been gone. And in some ways, I understood Fox and why he was acting like she was treasure and he was a dragon with the sole purpose to hoard it. But I also knew if we held onto her too tight, she'd run away again. And I would never forgive myself if that happened.

"How did you get here?" I asked. Fox was picking up her new ride tonight so it wouldn't be much longer before she had something road worthy and I hadn't realised he had actually decided to let her leave the house alone before then.

"Chase was meant to be watching me but he said he needed to go to

Raiders Gym and gave me the option of coming to see you rather than going with him. He dropped me off on the way. I think he just wanted an excuse not to have to stay in my company," she said with a shrug.

"Well...I've got some laundry to do for the club," I said. "It's not much fun, but you'd make it miles more interesting. Do you wanna join? I'll drop you home after, like a good date."

"Oh you're dating me now, are you Johnny James?" she teased. "What would your boss think of that?"

"He'd think...I'm making sure his girl is looked after real good." I flashed her a grin, twirled her under my arm then jogged toward my GT, tugging her along after me as she laughed.

I opened the door for her and she frowned at me like she wasn't used to that while I smirked. "Don't go getting any ideas about me being a gentleman."

"Oh, I wasn't. I'm trying to work out your angle." She moved smoothly into the seat and I shut the door, heading around and dropping into the driver's seat.

"Alright, I'll come clean." I turned to her, giving her a serious expression. "There's an alien living up my butt called Al who makes me do weird shit sometimes." I lunged at her, pinning her to the seat and tickling her sides.

"JJ!" she screamed, fighting back as I slid my hands under her top and tickled bare flesh while she writhed beneath me. I'd been hard before, but now I was going to have some real issues departing boner city.

"It's not me, it's the butt alien!" I cried, my fingers skimming her bra and her screams turned to gasps as my dick dug into her leg.

My hands fell still against her skin and I gazed down at her with my heart pounding harder than it had all through the show. God she was beautiful. Her lips were parted and wet and begging me to just-

"Al's a pervert," she said breathily, her eyes sparkling and with her colourful hair tumbling everywhere around her she looked like some kind of mythical creature. I wanted to tame it, catch it in a jar and keep it forever.

"Yeah, he's a real dirty fucker," I agreed then pushed off of the seat and dropped back into mine, rearranging my hair just so I had something to do with my hands. I started the engine while Rogue sat upright, straightening her little denim skirt and drawing my gaze to her tanned thighs before I focused on driving.

"I need to make a stop on the way to the launderette," I told her. "That cool?"

"Sure," she said lightly like my cock hadn't just been making itself known about how much it had wanted to join in with our game. If anyone was a dirty alien pervert, it was him.

I drove away from Afterlife, leaving the lights of the club behind as I headed into the hills that rose up on the west of town. I needed something to take my mind off of where I was headed so I glanced over at Rogue and started up our old favourite game. "Would you rather be as small as my thumb or as big as a tree?"

Rogue snorted. "Well how big's your thumb?" She reached over, taking my hand and her soft fingers wrapped around my thumb. The amount of blood that sent to my dick was unbelievable really. Who needed Viagra when Rogue Easton was gripping their thumb? Sure as shit not me. But I didn't think turning into a walking boner was a great idea right now considering our destination, so I pulled my hand free and rearranged my pants while she sniggered.

"Big enough for you, Easton?" I demanded.

"Nah, I'd be the size of a tree. Then I could squish my enemies. Squish squish squish." She stomped her feet in the footwell.

"Who would you squish first? Fox or Chase?" I asked, 'cause obviously she wouldn't be squishing me. She might have been angry at me, but she also liked cuddling me naked in the shower and letting me spoon her in my bed.

"I wouldn't squish either of them first," she said and my heart jolted as her lips pressed together. I knew she was thinking of the asshole who'd tried to kill her and I dropped my hand to her knee, squeezing and figuring I was a goner for the boner anyways.

"You got a name for me yet, sweetheart?" I growled. I might have been a smiley, approachable bastard most of the time, but I'd spilled as much blood as my brothers in my time in the Harlequins. And I would happily put someone in the ground who'd hurt Rogue. Better yet, I'd chop him into tiny pieces and make a day of it, take Rogue out on a boat trip and feed the pieces of him to the sea life like breadcrumbs.

Chester and Jolene had come up fucking short too, even after Fox had offered to double the pay out for a name. I didn't get it. Rogue wasn't the kind of girl to go unnoticed so why weren't there even whispers going around that could lead us back to the motherfucker who had hurt her?

"No, and you're not getting one. Would you rather eat a dog turd pie or a pile of Rosie Morgan's toenails?"

"How well baked is this pie?" I asked and she chuckled.

"It's really well baked."

"And is there apple sauce?"

"Sure, but you can have that with the toenails too," she said.

I mimed gagging. "Dog turd all the way."

"Glad we still agree on something."

I wondered what she'd think if she found out that Chase was hooking up with that bitch these days and decided not to bring it up. There probably wasn't a good time to mention that one of her former best friends had been doing the dirty with a girl she freaking hated. Not that he would ever have something official with Rosie. But I couldn't help but wonder how Rogue would have felt about it if she'd come back to find one of us shacked up with a girl.

"Rosie asked me out once, you know?" I said, smirking at the horrified look on her face. It was the truth, but I hadn't been interested. I think for a while she'd hoped to take Rogue's spot as the girl in our group but that had never been on the cards.

"Ew, gross, what did you say to her?" she demanded.

"That she couldn't afford me. Would it have bothered you to come back here and find us playing house with girlfriends though?"

"I can't really picture that somehow," she said thoughtfully, scrunching her nose in the cutest fucking way. "Have there been girlfriends then?"

I shrugged. "Not really. Fox has kept the odd girl around for a month or two from time to time. I prefer to keep my sex life financial for the most part and Chase doesn't put effort in to girls since…" I wracked my brain over that. "Well, since never. You were the only one he ever really wanted." I shrugged, thinking of what Chase had said about Rogue picking Maverick. Had he taken her virginity? Had she loved him? I couldn't say those thoughts hadn't been haunting me, because as much as I wanted to write it off as something that happened ten years ago, it still stung.

But back then, I guess I knew I'd never really had a shot with her until I had a growth spurt and managed to grow at least a few facial hairs. And those things were like a bare minimum. What I'd really wanted was to time jump forward to a place where I was a grown ass man who could offer Rogue the world, and I guess I'd finally gotten my wish. So was I really gonna let some doubts over Maverick hold me back? I mean, I probably should have been more worried about the fact that Fox had explicitly told the whole world Rogue was his girl. And as my boss, I definitely should have respected that wish. But as my friend, I was saying fuck no with a spiky dildo. Because I'd loved her just as much, missed her just as much. He didn't get to swoop down like some possessive eagle and whisk her away before I'd barely said so much as a hello. I'd done my time missing her too, hating myself over what we'd done to her, going over every single thing I'd do if she ever came back. And fuck if I was going to miss my shot because he called dibs. Of course, the element of danger helped. Because I liked the rush of doing something bad, of how fucking good it was to have her this close and have her look at me like I really could fulfil her fantasies these days.

"Would you rather fuck a stripper or a gang leader?" I asked, biting down on the inside of my cheek to hold back my grin.

"Hmm…I'd rather fuck a butt alien called Al," she said and I roared a laugh, my stomach knotting as I looked at her. I swear I was gonna crash if I didn't tear my gaze off of her pretty face. But I couldn't stop.

"Man, I really fucking missed you, Rogue," I sighed and she smiled sadly at me before turning to look out her window. I didn't expect her to say it back. Maybe she had, maybe she hadn't. I was always going to be one of the reasons she'd left, and maybe nothing would ever fix that.

"Did you ever blame me for what Luther made you do?" she asked after a stretch of silence. My throat constricted and I scrubbed at my jaw as I thought over my answer.

"No," I said at last. "I was angry at what happened. And it took me a while to…accept who I was. After a year in the Harlequins, god this will sound fucking crazy, but I realised there had never been any other life for me anyway. We could have run, but there's nothing in the world I'm made for better than what I do now. Shit was bad for a long time, but I know I'm where I belong.

I just wish things could have been different. That we could have lived out our dream here, got some apartment together, grown together."

"Yeah, I used to wish for that a lot too," she said coldly. "But then reality bit me in the ass and it's made a habit out of doing that ever since."

"I'm sorry."

"Doesn't matter," she said and I slowed the car as I turned onto Little Street. I parked up at the side of the road beside a palm tree and killed the engine.

"It matters," I growled, leaning over and gripping her chin to make her look at me. "But I can't change it, sweetheart."

"I know," she said bitterly, pushing my hand off of her. This wasn't going how I'd planned, though I dunno what the hell I had planned. I just wanted to spend time with her. I wanted to prove, fuck, I wanted to prove so much to her and yet now I realised how fucking selfish that was. Who cared if I'd grown up and knew what to do with a girl these days? She didn't want me anyway because I'd hurt her too deeply, thrown her life off course and was in some way responsible for all the shitty stuff that had happened to her since. And I didn't need her to spell it out to know there had been a lot of it. I could see it in her eyes, and I knew that she blamed us for throwing her out into the world all alone. Hell, I blamed us too.

I wished she'd had faith that we'd come for her, but we'd had to make sure she left and never looked back until we could figure out what to do. We'd been so fucking afraid for her that it had seemed like the only option. But now I looked back on it, maybe we could have handled it better. I just didn't know anymore. The rift between us was so wide, so full of dark memories that had passed since, that I wasn't sure it could ever be crossed. She was never going to trust me like she once had. She was never going to lie on the beach with all of us and slot smoothly back into our lives. I'd been fucking kidding myself hoping that that might have been the case. Her heart was currently pounding inside a fortress built there because of us. So what right did I have to want anything from her?

The problem was, as my eyes travelled across her painfully familiar, painfully beautiful face, I knew I wasn't good enough to walk away. I did bad deeds for a living, there was no hope for me when I was off the clock.

"I'll be back in a minute," I muttered, opening my door.

"Where are you going?" She frowned.

"I just need to drop in on someone," I said evasively.

"Who?" she asked.

"My mom," I gave in. "Stay here." I stepped out, shutting the door and Rogue immediately got out too and pouted at me.

"Don't you dare boss me around, Johnny James. Your momma was always a sweetheart to me. I want to see her."

I groaned, hovering on the street as I pictured Mom's face when she saw Rogue after all these years. "Alright, but only if you promise to tell her you're my girl." I folded my arms, not willing to negotiate on this.

"Are you channelling Fox tonight or something?" she laughed and I grinned, happy the tension had broken between us as I walked up to her on the sidewalk and tugged her toward me by the pockets of her skirt. My mom had always said Rogue wasn't gonna pick me out of my friends. According to her, I was too short, too skinny, too chatty. It seemed like a prime opportunity to prove to her that none of those things mattered anymore.

"Just think how angry it would make him," I purred in her ear and she shivered. "He'd be red in the face if he knew I'd brought you here, taking you home to my momma."

"You're really convincing when you're rebelling against the supreme canine," she purred back in a husky voice that would have made a killing in phone sex. But I didn't want her talking to anyone else like that. Just me while she straddled my cock and rode me like a damn cowgirl.

"Come on then, pretty girl." I headed along the road past the apartment blocks which were the most up market homes in the lower quarter. Unlike most moms, mine had been so proud when I'd joined the sex trade. She'd always put a positive spin on being a hooker, but I'd never wanted to follow in her footsteps. Dreams and wishes didn't put food on the table though. And I'd fast learned that earning real cash in this town was only achieved through crime or sex. I'd opted for both, seeing as I was ambitious and all.

When we'd first signed up to the crew, Luther had paid us for jobs, but starting at the bottom in the Harlequins meant we were given the smallest cut. Even his own son didn't get a bigger sum than us. King Harlequin wanted us to earn the money in our pockets and that was something I was actually grateful to him for. And I'd learned the value of my body after I'd shot up to over six foot before I was seventeen, and by eighteen I was armoured with all the muscle I'd longed for as a skinny runt. Girls had started noticing me and I'd started realising the potential in that.

"These apartments are cute," Rogue cooed, taking in the little coloured properties. My mom lived in the pink one at the far end which had one of the best views down to Sunset Beach in the whole town.

"Yeah they built them about five years back. I nudged the mayor into it with a few pennies in his pocket." I grinned triumphantly.

"You fucking gangster," she laughed.

I winked at her then snagged her hand and tugged her up the steps to the front door, banging my fist on it. There was loud music sounding from inside and smoke seeping out of the nearest window, the scent of pot sailing under my nose. It reminded me of my childhood. Which was kinda sad really when I thought about it. But the smell was weirdly comforting.

The door opened and Mom stood there in a too-tight blue boob tube and tiny black hot pants. She was as skinny as a rake and barely came up to my chest. Her dark hair fell around her and a joint was smoking between her fingers. She may have been getting older, but she was still beautiful as hell. And a fierce protectiveness gripped my heart as I looked at her.

I'd always wanted to shield her from her shitty life choices, but somehow I'd ended up following in them too. And as much as I understood it more now that I lived it myself, I would join Satan in hell itself before I let her go back to that life. She hadn't been the best mother admittedly, but I still loved her. Even if she was a queen bitch sometimes.

"Johnny James!" She hugged me tight and I had to bend forward to properly embrace her. She was always doing overly touchy huggy things these days, like she was trying to make up for all the hug time we'd missed when I was a kid. When I was seven, I could clearly remember asking Mom if hugging naked made it better, because she was always doing it with all her guy friends who came to visit. I'd taken off all my clothes, opened my arms wide and she'd started crying into her cornflakes. Hindsight really was a dipshit sometimes.

"Hey Mom." I let her go and grabbed hold of Rogue, yanking her against my hip. "Remember Rogue?"

Mom did a theatrical gasp then lunged at Rogue, dragging her in for her own hug.

"Oh hey, Mrs B, how are you?" Rogue squeezed her back and Mom leaned away, gripping her arms as she looked her up and down.

"Love the hair. Where'd you get to all these years? My Johnny hasn't stopped talking about you."

"Well that's not exactly true," I ground out, my neck heating at her words.

"It is true!" Mom insisted, towing Rogue inside by the hand and she shot me an amused look over her shoulder. *Goddammit.*

"So are you and my boy together?" Mom asked hopefully.

"Ha, no way," Rogue answered and I glowered at the back of her head. *I'll get you back for that, pretty girl.*

I headed inside, kicking the door shut and following them through the hallway which was full of potted plants and into the lounge which was teeming with even more potted plants. It was Mom's new favourite hobby. And to be honest, so long as she wasn't sucking dick for cash, she could grow a jungle in here for all I cared.

My jaw ticked as my gaze fell on the sweaty old man currently taking up residence on my mom's couch. I folded my arms, stopping dead in my tracks as fury started coursing through me.

"Who's this?" I boomed at Mom and the guy took a joint from his mouth, his throat bobbing. He was all moustache, I swear to fuck. It was the biggest ass tash I'd ever seen. His head was lacking in the hair department though so maybe he was making up for what he was missing on top. And maybe I didn't give a fuck, so long as he took his moustache out of my momma's house.

"That's just Greg." Mom rolled her eyes at me, encouraging Rogue to sit in an armchair and offering her the joint.

I snatched it from Mom's hand before Rogue got any ideas about getting high with her and Greg's moustache. The cherry burned my palm as I squeezed it up in my fist and tossed it in the vague direction of an ash tray.

"Who the fuck is 'just Greg'?" I growled.

"Oh JJ, you're such a buzz kill. We're just friends, aren't we Greg?"

Mom dropped down beside him, crossing her bronzed legs and Greg sat up straighter, having the courtesy to at least look rattled. He knew who I was. I could see it in his beady little eyes. And in his moustache. I could see it there too.

"If you want friends, you can have girl friends," I clipped.

"Johnny James, do not take that tone with me," Mom growled and Rogue looked between us awkwardly.

"I'm gonna make some coffee." Rogue got to her feet and I wrapped my arm around her waist, pulling her close and speaking in her ear.

"Go back to the car, sweetheart."

"Kiss my ass, douchberry," she said in a sugary voice and I gave her a flat look.

She booped me on the nose and sashayed out of the room as she hunted for the kitchen and I didn't know if I was turned on or fuming as hell.

"Greg." I rounded on him. "Fuck off. And keep your moustache away from my mother. If I find one prickly hair in this house from this day forward, I'll hunt you down, rip that monstrosity off of your face and feed it to a starfish. The starfish won't like it Greg, but so help me, it will eat every scrap because no one defies me in this town." I pointed to the door and his eyes widened as he leapt to his feet. I ushered him on by when he froze like a deer in headlights and I bared my teeth at him. He started scampering from the room while my mom wailed in anger and the front door slammed a second later.

I arched a brow at my flesh and blood. "Da fuck, Mom?"

She rolled her eyes, slumping back in her seat theatrically. "So I'm not even allowed male company now? Greg is a nice man!"

"What's his surname?" I demanded.

"S-starfish," she stammered, then turned bright red.

"That's very coincidental," I deadpanned.

"It is," she squeaked and I picked up a cushion, tossing it at her.

"If you're fucking for cash again, I'll-"

"I'm not Johnny, I swear!" she cried, blinking back tears then falling forward and cupping her hands in her face as she sobbed loudly.

"Stop it with the guilt tears," I insisted and she sniffed loudly as she pulled herself together. I took a wedge of cash from my pocket and those tears dried up just like that. Funny how that worked. Fucking magical.

I tossed it at her and she caught it. I guess I knew who I'd inherited the dollar signs in my eyes from. That and my Korean looks with the splash of Malaysian on my dad's side was the extent of the heritage I knew. My daddy was some guy whose condom had split, or so my Mom told me and that tiny little fact was all she could remember about him. She hadn't even asked his name. I was conceived with the words *oh fuck no* slipping from good old pa's mouth. Then he'd hightailed it out of town, left zero contact details and left even less fucks behind. *Oh well, at least I grew into a respectable stripping escort who's part of the most powerful gang in the state. Daddy would be so proud.*

Rogue returned empty handed. "The milk's off."

"I think we've overstayed our welcome anyway," I said with a shrug. "I've got shit to do. Be good Mom."

She was busy counting dollar bills that had been between my butt cheeks earlier on tonight. *Ah life.*

"See you later, Mrs B," Rogue called and Mom actually looked up.

"Don't run off on my boy again, Rogue. He won't survive it a second time," she said casual as fuck and I dropped my arm around Rogue's shoulders, steering her out of the house.

When we were outside, I released her, walking off ahead of her toward the car and fighting down the twisting, uncomfortable emotions inside me. I opened the passenger door for Rogue as she approached and her fingers grazed mine on the handle as she paused and looked up at me.

"What did you tell her?" she asked accusingly.

"I didn't tell her anything. The whole town presumed you'd run off to find a better life." I shrugged and she huffed.

"So everyone thought I'd just bailed on my best friends? Nice." She dropped into her seat and I shut the door behind her, resting my hands on top of the car for a second as I drew in a long breath. Then I walked around and got in beside her.

Tension sparked like a livewire hanging between us and I toyed with the car key in my hand as I decided what to do.

Fuck it.

I took my wallet from my pocket, flipping it open and rummaging in the back of it, finding a folded photograph and feeling the hard lump of the item I kept within it. I unfolded the picture, the paper worn from how many times I'd looked at it over the years. But I'd stopped doing that eventually, tired of the pain, tired of missing her. I'd printed this photo off at Luther's house a week after Rogue had left town. It was the five of us standing beneath the Ferris wheel at Sinners' Playground. Rogue stood at the front of the photo, her arms outstretched where she held her phone and me, Fox, Chase and Maverick crowded around her possessively. None of us were even looking at the fucking camera. We were all staring at her as she smiled this wild, untamed smile that had always gotten my heart racing.

I passed it to Rogue and she took it with a pained expression as her eyes travelled over the memory. I'd scrawled words at the bottom, a promise to myself as much as her.

I'll find you, pretty girl.

"What have you got there?" she asked, eyeing my hand which was balled into a fist around the stupid thing I'd made for her that day.

"Nothin'." I tried to tuck it into my pocket, but she lunged at me, grabbing my hand and trying to force it open.

"No chance, sweetheart," I taunted and she half crawled into my lap, her knee pressing down on my dick until I sucked in air between my teeth.

"Motherfucker," I growled, grabbing her hair and yanking, making her yelp and look up at me. Her eyes were alight with the game and she slid her hand down my arm to my wrist, curling around my closed hand, leaving goosebumps in her wake.

"Give it to me, Johnny James," she purred and I sucked my lower lip.

"I really want to, sweetheart. But you'd have to pay big bucks for it."

She snorted, punching me in the chest and I gave in, opening my palm and letting her take the gift from it. It was a shark tooth Rogue had found on Sunset Beach and gifted to me when we were eleven years old. After she'd left town, I'd engraved her name on it and made it into a bracelet, attaching it from a leather band I used to wear around my wrist. Even at sixteen, I'd been a fucking chump. Apparently I'd thought making her jewellery was gonna win her over after we ran her out of town. But now it just seemed juvenile and embarrassing.

"Is this the tooth I gave you?" she gasped and I couldn't believe she actually remembered that shit.

I shrugged, realising my heart was beating like a war drum and I was unable to blink as I watched her.

"I had this 'really cool' plan of giving it to you when I found you. I had a whole speech planned as well." I snorted derisively at my idiot younger self. There was a reason that kid was a virgin.

"What was the speech?" she bounced in my lap and I groaned as she ground over my dick.

"I don't fucking remember." But I did. Every stupid word. Because I'd gone over it a million times in my head, practising it as if that would make it any more likely she'd decide to be mine once I found her.

According to Chase, she'd already picked Maverick back then anyway. And I'd been so far out of the running regardless, I'd probably never been in the race.

"You do," she insisted, but I grabbed her ass, squeezed it hard then dumped her back in her seat.

"I don't," I said, tossing her a smile.

"Liar, liar," she sang but I ignored her. She wasn't gonna get those words from my mouth ever. If I could erase them, I'd do it in a heartbeat.

I started the engine and turned the car around, heading back down into town. We were soon pulling up alongside The Mile and I parked up outside the Whirlpool Launderette. I jumped out and Rogue followed as I popped the trunk and took out the two sacks of laundry from the club. Kitty was supposed to be doing it tonight, but she was off sick – *cough chlamydia cough* – and I didn't mind getting the job done.

Rogue followed me through into the brightly lit launderette. It was a twenty four hour place run by a Mexican family who didn't mind me and my girls bringing all kinds of dirty outfits down here to launder. Ana Maria even dry cleaned anything that couldn't go in the washing machine like corsets and outfits with sequins and tassels.

"Hola, Ana Maria!" I called out toward the back room, but there was no answer.

I shrugged, heading past the row of dryers that ran down the centre of the place to the wall of washing machines on the left. I filled two machines and set them running, turning back to find Rogue sitting up on the dryers, her golden legs hanging down, her sandals discarded on the floor.

A radio was playing pop music and as the song changed onto a slow one, the sound of Past Life by Trevor Daniel and Selena Gomez filling the air, I smirked at Rogue and pulled her to feet.

"Dance with me," I demanded, looping her hands around my neck and brushing my fingertips down the length of her arms, running them along her sides until I was gripping her waist.

"How'd you get so confident, J?" she asked as my fingers slipped under the hem of her shirt circled against her warm skin.

"Practise." I shrugged, letting my hands fall from her back and dropping them down to cup her ass.

I tugged her tighter against me and her fingers pushed into my hair as her hips rocked to the music and the denim of her skirt chafed against the crotch of my sweats. My cock was jerking happily as I pulled her even closer, letting her feel how hot she got me and her fingers knotted in my hair tight enough to make me growl.

"How did the whole escort thing start?" she questioned and I chewed on the inside of my cheek as I thought about that.

"Well, I guess I got hot before I realised I was hot. And when I was eighteen, Mrs Blackwell who runs the bait shop offered me fifty dollars to suck me off and I figured it was easy money. So I said fuck it and let her. After that, I guess things just kinda escalated. I realised I needed the practise if I was ever gonna get a girl off, so I just started finger fucking girls at parties until I'd figured out how to make them come in less than a minute. Rumours spread of how good I was until I had girls approaching me for it. And I said sure, so long as they paid me."

"That's so fucked up," Rogue said, frowning.

"Nah," I said. "If it wasn't transactional, I don't think I coulda done it. And I needed to get over…well, you."

"JJ…" Rogue's brow creased and I squeezed her ass to try and get a smile out of her, but it didn't work.

"Don't pity me, pretty girl," I growled. "I would have been a virgin forever waiting for you if I didn't just rip the band aid off eventually."

"Who was it?" she asked, looking like she half wanted to know and half didn't.

"Some rich chick from the upper quarter," I said, chewing the inside of my cheek again. That night had been a special kind of fucked up.

"Was she someone we knew?" Rogue asked, her fingers still in my hair and giving me the good kind of shivers.

"Nah," I said. "She was like forty so it's not like we would have mixed with her."

"What?" Rogue gasped, stopping dancing and gazing at me in horror. "How old were you?"

"Nineteen." I didn't like her looking at me like that and I turned away from her, heading over to the washing machines as if to check if the load was done. But I really just needed to avoid the horror in her eyes.

"J, please tell me she didn't pay you for it," Rogue implored like she cared. But why would she care? It was a long time ago. It didn't matter. Dead and buried. Just like Axel and Clive and our dreams.

"Alright, I won't tell you," I said lightly, leaning back against the machines as I turned to her, keeping my expression neutral.

"Jesus, fuck," she spat. "Why would you do that?"

"Why are you so angry about it?" I laughed, but she scowled, shaking her head.

"Because your first time should be-"

"Special?" I scoffed. "Yeah, and there's a pot of gold at the end of every rainbow, and Santa Claus exists."

"Don't be a dick." She walked towards me, capturing my hand and I realised she'd put the fucking shark tooth bracelet on. And man, it looked stupidly hot on her.

"Was your first time special?" I asked, thinking of Maverick with a knot in my chest.

"No," she said, her eyes turning cold. "It was awkward and fucking uncomfortable and I did *not* expect the blood by the way, so thanks for that Mother Nature."

I frowned and she did too, and I realised I didn't want to know if it was Maverick. The past was the past. Right now was all that counted. And right now, I didn't want Rogue frowning for a single second longer.

Suga Suga by Baby Bash and Frankie J started playing on the radio and I jerked my chin toward the row of dryers down the centre of the room. "I gave you a show tonight, how about you give me one up there?"

She arched a brow. "And why would I do that?"

"Because I dare you to, and as far as I remember, Rogue Easton never backed down on a dare."

She ran her tongue across her teeth then shrugged lightly, twisting away from me and climbing up onto the dryers. I walked over to the radio, turning the music up and she laughed, flexing her arms above her head. Then she started to dance. Like holy shit, this girl can dance, dance. She had that thing I always hunted for in my dancers, that I-don't-give-a-fuck-who's-watching-but-this-makes-me-feel-good way of moving her body that couldn't be taught. You felt music in your soul like that or you didn't, and Rogue really fucking did.

I walked to the end of the dryers and rested my hands on them, watching with a lump in my throat as she pushed her own shirt up, nearly giving me a glimpse of her bra beneath then dropping into a squat that had my dick rock hard and my pulse skipping.

She was so fucking hot. And as she turned, bending forward to give me a view of her ass and a glimpse up her skirt, I knew I couldn't fight this need in me anymore. I had a failed first kiss to rectify. I'd sucked a fucking blanket instead of finding her mouth in the dark, but I wasn't going to miss this time. That moment still haunted me.

"Just a couple more years and we'll all be free to do what we want," I said firmly. "We'll get jobs and shit and become respectable people." I snorted at my own joke and she chuckled.

"I don't ever want to be respectable. If you ever see me doing my taxes and wearing some ugly ass pant suit, shoot me in the head. Just a clean shot. No warning. It's already too late for me."

I breathed a laugh then reached out and brushed a lock of deep brown hair behind her ear before I could overthink it. "I couldn't kill you, Rogue."

"Not even a pant-suit wearing, tax-filing, ass-eating version of me?"

she asked, her eyes dancing with light.

"Well you didn't mention the ass eating before. Is that literally or metaphorically?" I teased and she shivered as my fingers grazed down to her neck though I wasn't sure she even noticed it.

"Hmm, literally ass-eating my boring accountant husband." She mimed puking

"At least your sex life is lively," I said. "You sure you'll still want to die then?"

"Yeah, because there's only one love of my life." She beamed and my heart beat harder and harder.

"Oh yeah?" I breathed. "Who's that?"

I leaned closer to her, my tongue heavy as I gazed at her mouth, a crazy part of me wondering if maybe it was me she wanted. And after all that had happened tonight, I just wanted to get over my fucking fear and show her how I felt. I was so tired of craving her, watching her, never having her. I wanted to be brave like she had been. I wanted to prove I was as manly as any of my friends, and that in another year I'd be able to put all of them on their asses. And if I kissed her like a man then she'd know I was one.

I got closer, almost nose to nose while she grinned.

"The sea," she said but I couldn't remember what the question was that she was answering.

I just nodded, mumbling something that sounded like dolphins before figuring fuck it and just lunging at her, mouth half open, eyes sort of closed but not quite. My mouth hit blanket and I opened my eyes fully in surprise, finding her yawning, her head dropped back onto the pillow and my whole body burned with shame. Did she just reject me? Or did she not notice? Oh god, what's worse?

Rogue walked up right in front of me on her tip-toes on the dryers and I caught the backs of her ankles, running my hands up her legs and she bit her lip as my fingers slid beneath her skirt. I leaned forward, biting down on her knee and she gasped as I dragged my tongue up her thigh. She tasted like coconuts and fucking poetry. I wanted to taste her everywhere and show her what this grown ass man could do to her body.

My fingers grazed her panties and I looked up at her, my gaze locking with hers as I pinged the elastic against her flesh. She pushed her fingers into my hair and I withdrew my hands from her skirt, grabbing her hips and lifting her down, sitting her ass on the edge of the dryer.

I stepped between her thighs, making her skirt bunch up toward her hips. I grazed my fingers down her jaw as she fisted her hands in my shirt, her breaths coming heavily and making me wonder if she'd let me fuck her right here.

"I tried to kiss you the night we dumped Axel's body in the sea," I told her, picturing that moment all too fucking clearly. "When we were curled up together in the arcade at Sinners' Playground."

"When?" she asked, frowning like she had no idea and I cursed, gripping her chin between my finger and thumb.

I sure as hell wasn't going to fuck it up a second time. And she was going to remember this for the rest of her damn life.

I crushed my mouth to hers and she gasped, her back arching as I spread her out over the dryers like butter over bread and tangled my tongue with hers. My cock ground between her thighs, her skirt hitching up over her waist and I groaned as she rocked her hips, grinding her pussy against me.

I fisted one hand in her hair as she met the furious movements of my tongue with her own. My heart was thumping to a hungry tune and every fibre of my being was on fire as I kissed away every asshole who'd kissed her before now. I erased every memory of them with this single one and proved to her how good I could make her feel.

She moaned into my mouth and I devoured the sound, knowing I could do better than that. I pushed one hand between us, finding her soaking panties between her thighs and rubbing my knuckles against her clit. She bucked against me, wrapping her legs around my waist and clawing at my shoulders as I laughed into her mouth.

"Asshole," she panted, but I didn't let her get another word out as I kissed her again, continuing to tease her clit through her panties as my cock demanded I take more of her.

"Mr Brooks!" Ana Maria's voice cut through my thoughts and killed my little fantasy dead.

Rogue shoved me away and I pulled her off the dryer, tucking her behind me as she tugged her skirt down.

"Lo siento, Ana," I chuckled, cocking my head to one side with a puppy dog expression.

She planted her hands on her wide hips, scowling at me. "No traigas tu trabajo aquí!" she reprimanded. *Don't bring your work here.*

"Ella no trabaja, Ana," I promised her Rogue wasn't work. "Ella es mi novia."

"I'm not your girlfriend." Rogue punched me in the arm, stepping around me and I wondered when the hell she'd learned to speak Spanish. "Lo siento, Ana. JJ es un manwhore." She shrugged innocently and Ana Maria laughed wildly.

"I like this one," Ana said, then planted her ass on a chair, giving me a firm, cock-blocking look and I rearranged my sweatpants before heading over to the washing machine with a sigh.

My heart was still beating out of control and I couldn't stop fucking smiling. I probably looked like Anastasia after she'd just been spanked by Christian Grey. Only instead of a red ass, I had blue balls and a hard on that wouldn't quit. The sweatpants were doing zero to hide it and the way Ana Maria and Rogue were now murmuring and giggling together in Spanish, I had a feeling it was the current topic of discussion. But my dick liked the limelight these days. And with Rogue's pussy sweet scent still coating my knuckles, nothing could banish my good mood. Because I'd just shown Rogue how hot I could get her in under two minutes. So she was going to be left wondering what I could do to her in ten.

CHAPTER SIXTEEN

It was rent day for my trailer and yet here I sat, stuck in Fox's house, just as much of a prisoner as ever. I mean, okay, I had a bit of freedom now because technically I was allowed to go out and shit, but he also always assigned either himself or one of the others to go with me if I did, so I wasn't basking in this new supposed freedom much yet. And with the tracking software he'd placed on my cellphone, I had to make careful consideration about where I went and what I did even if I did head out alone.

I wondered how much attention he could even be paying to it anyway. Was it recording the places I went, or would it just ping back the information to him if and when he looked?

I groaned at the thought of trying to out-fox a Fox and rolled over in my sleep. It wasn't even time to get up yet. I swear, it was some ungodly hour like nine am or maybe even eight. Yuck.

But I needed to get out of here today and give my rent to Joe, go visit my poor, sweet, lonely little trailer and assure her that I wasn't abandoning her. And more importantly than that, I was going to head on up to Rosewood Manor and see if Miss Mabel remembered me.

The old lady who owned the sprawling Manor House out to the east of

Sunset Cove, just on the edge of the town limits had been one of, if not the only, adult I'd ever known who actually seemed to give a shit about me.

My mom was a distant, faded memory who I had been informed favoured her drug habit over her kid which was what had landed me in the system. I'd bounced from place to place a lot between different foster families before ending up in the group home down on the shitty side of town. Which in a town like Sunset Cove was saying a lot.

Mary Beth who ran that fine establishment for teenagers had done me the solid of setting a nine pm curfew which she was insanely strict about, providing bland and boring meals which there was never really enough of to fill the ache in my stomach, and yelling as a form of communication. Safe to say, she hadn't made me feel all loved and gooey inside. I guessed the odd teacher had been kind over the years, but not enough to really do anything about my situation or get to know me at all. But Miss Mabel had actually found me and Chase squatting on her property one night and instead of calling the cops, she'd been sweet to us.

We used to be allowed to hang out in the summer house in her sprawling grounds and if we went over there during the day, she'd offer out treats and lemonade. And the five of us had actually managed not to be little assholes about it either - we'd done jobs around the place for her when we had the time and I used to love just sitting on the sprawling porch that fronted her home and shooting the breeze with her about everything and nothing. She was...nice. Like probably the only truly nice person I'd ever known. Lord knew Sunset Cove didn't attract many fine upstanding citizens, especially in the lower quarter.

I needed to stop trying to cling to sleep and accept that the day had begun, so in a sudden move, I threw the blankets off of me and sat upright.

A scream of terror escaped me as I found a man sitting in a chair to the right of my bed. My brain only computed the fact that it was Fox after I'd lunged for my nightstand and yanked the gun I'd been keeping there out of the drawer and pointed it at him.

"What the fuck, asshole?" I shouted half a second before Fox dove on me, grabbing my hand holding the gun and throwing it back against the pillow.

My finger curled against the trigger automatically in fright, but the safety was on so there was just a dull click in the silence that fell between us as he pinned me to the bed.

Adrenaline, anger and a healthy dose of hate was warring through my body, so I blamed that for my other fist snapping out and clocking him in the jaw.

"What the fuck are you doing, Rogue?" he snarled, catching my other wrist and pinning that above my head too.

The blankets were gone and Fox was only wearing a pair of shorts while I'd slept in one of JJ's wifebeaters and my boob was getting dangerously close to slipping out of it.

"Me? How about you tell me what you're doing in my room in the middle of the night like some freaking creep?"

"It's almost eight am," he snapped. "I've been out for a run and I came in to wake you up for breakfast." Now that he mentioned it, those sculpted, powerful muscles of his were all gleaming with a fine layer of sweat, the kind that was fresh and sexy and made me consider the prospect of giving him another workout seeing as he was camped out on top of me right now. But no - he was a super douche. Le sigh.

"Get off of me," I demanded

"Where did you get that gun?" he tossed back.

"Your closet is a terrible hiding place for a weapon," I replied with a taunting look. "Now answer my question about why you were sitting there watching me sleep."

Fox's green eyes narrowed the smallest amount. "Because I miss you," he said roughly. "I've been missing you for as long as I had you and it fucking hurts, Rogue."

My throat tightened up with all the words I wanted to hurl at him, all the insults and curses and hatred and I just stared at him instead.

Fox leaned forward slowly and my frown deepened as he closed the small distance between us. I scowled as I got the feeling he was about to try and-

He turned his head to the side, pressing closer still before his mouth found the hollow of my collar bone and he placed a kiss against my skin which was rough with stubble and made a shiver run right through the centre of my being.

"Stop," I gasped though my back arched of its own accord, my nipples grazing his bare chest through the thin shirt I wore.

"When we were seven, I punched Turner Forbes for pushing you off of the monkey bars," he said before moving his mouth a little further up my neck and making my breath catch as he kissed me again. "And when we were ten, I took Ronnie Thomas's school workbook and made him burn it because he'd written down your initials with his and circled them in a heart."

"Fox," I growled - not a sexy growl because the heat in my veins was rage without any lust at all.

He kissed my neck a little higher again, his knee pressing to the mattress between my thighs and drawing way too much of my attention.

"When we were twelve, I heard a rumour that Colten Baxter was going to ask you to go to the movies with him and I slammed his face into a wall hard enough to knock one of his teeth out." His mouth moved up again, pressing to that deliciously sensitive skin beneath my ear as I tried to pull my wrists out of his grasp and failed. His stubble raked over my skin, followed by the hot press of his tongue and a breathy absolutely-not-a-moan escaped me.

"When we were fourteen, I pushed Oscar Falkner off of his bike and broke his arm so that I could take his place as your lab partner," he growled as he moved his mouth over my jaw and for some reason, even though I'd never known he'd done any of these things, I knew they were true, I just had no idea what I was supposed to think about them.

"I'm warning you, Fox," I gritted out, stealing myself to fight him off as my anger with him grew while he tried to dominate me.

"When we were fifteen, Mike Gaskall was going to ask you to go to the winter formal with him, so I broke his nose," he murmured, his mouth drawing dangerously close to mine as he kissed his way along my jaw.

"Why?" I demanded, his stupid stories making me curious despite myself.

"Because you're mine, hummingbird. And I was never going to let another guy near you. The only ones I made allowances for were the boys. And even then, I would have done whatever it took to keep them back if I thought they were trying to cross that line with you." He said it so seriously, so matter of fact, like he didn't sound like a fucking psychopath and it was perfectly acceptable for him to have just decided that I belonged to him without ever asking me what I thought of it. And that was like a fan to the flames of my fury over everything he'd done to me. "Once you stop trying to fight it, you'll see. We fit, Rogue, always have. It's you and me, hummingbird."

His lips made it to the corner of my mouth and he clearly took the growl that escaped me as encouragement as he pressed his mouth to mine in a hot and urgent demand.

But he was fucking deluded if he thought he was going to win me over that easily and just bend me to his damn will however the hell he pleased.

I recoiled into the pillows, then swung my head forward to crack his nose with my skull.

Fox jerked back with a curse, narrowly avoiding the blow and I drove my knee up into his balls for good measure before scrambling out from beneath him as he rolled off of me with a groan of pain.

"As much as those stories made me feel all warm and fuzzy inside, Badger," I growled as I backed away from him. "You forgot the most important one of all. When we were sixteen, you pushed me down in the mud and told me I was nobody. You looked me in the eyes and tore my fucking heart from my chest and let that motherfucker drag me away like I was nothing at all to you and never had been. So you can keep your bullshit declarations. I don't want them. And the girl who might have cared to listen has been dead a long damn time."

I turned and stormed out of my own room, throwing the door closed in his face as he got up and started chasing me and I hurried away down the stairs to the kitchen.

JJ was there, looking like he'd been out running too as he dished out a couple of plates of toast and moved to take a seat at the breakfast bar. I hopped into the empty seat at his side, flashed him a smile while I thought about the way Fox had grunted when I kneed him in the balls and started on the toast sitting beside him.

"You're up early, pretty girl," he commented.

"I had a badger problem in my room," I explained, taking a savage bite out of my toast just as Fox prowled in, rearranging his tender junk and his green eyed glare fixed on me. "Did you know he's been sneaking in and watching me sleep like a freaking creeper?" I demanded.

"Seriously?" JJ questioned and Fox just levelled him with a flat stare.

"Mind your business, J, I can take care of my own," he snapped.

"And what's with the pained expression?" JJ inquired and I smirked over my toast at the junk in question, which I could see outlined through Fox's shorts again. And it looked swollen. Or, no that was just as big as it had been the last time I'd gone all shorts stalker on his D. *Goddammit.*

"I said mind your fucking business," Fox snarled. "And is that my fucking toast?" He pointed a finger at me accusingly and I glanced down at the food I was half way into demolishing. It actually made a lot more sense for it to be his than mine.

"No?" I questioned and JJ snorted a laugh.

Fox huffed angrily and turned away to grab some bread to make more toast. The moment he did, JJ caught my chin, turned me towards him and captured my lips with his, making the foundations of the building freaking shudder as my heart catapulted out of my chest and heat seared me hot enough to burn me up from the inside out.

I hadn't realised that last night's earth shattering performance on top of the dryer in the laundrette hadn't been a one off and that maybe this was going to be a regular thing, but as his tongue pushed into my mouth I found that I had no objections to that idea whatsoever.

It was far too brief and over too soon as he released me again and we both glanced Fox's way a moment before he whirled back around to face us with a grouchy Badger scowl again.

"I want to go out on my own today," I announced, deciding that I might as well get this over and done with while Fox was already pissed at me.

"No," he snapped.

"You said if I used the stupid phone then I could have more freedom. So stop acting like you own me and let me go out," I demanded.

Fox opened his mouth with the clear intention to argue some more, but JJ beat him to it.

"Just let her go, man. You promised her. Plus her car is here so there's no reason not to let her-"

"Where do you want to go?" Fox demanded.

"To the pharmacy for condoms," I said with a shrug. "And then I'm going out to find someone to fuck, preferably in public."

"Hilarious," Fox deadpanned.

"Are you letting me go or what? Because I'm getting seriously sick of the bullshit, Fox. You promised me freedom, so set me fucking free."

"I actually promised you a phone and a car and a bit of time out of the house-"

JJ threw a crust at him and gave him a demanding look and Fox blew out a frustrated breath.

"Alright, fine. But I want you back at a reasonable hour tonight," Fox said irritably. "Go get your shit together and I'll show you the car."

I smirked like a triumphant bitch, fighting back the desire to call him out on the 'reasonable hour' bullshit because it actually suited me just fine. Reasonable was a vague concept I was happy enough to decide on for myself and I was pretty sure that I found it reasonable to come back at some point tomorrow. Or maybe the following day.

I hurried upstairs and hunted down some clothes, settling on a cute skater dress with black skulls printed on white fabric paired with some white tennis shoes then left my rainbow hair in waves that ran down my spine and tossed a shade of bubblegum pink lipstick on last.

When I made it back downstairs, the boys had finished up with their food and I practically skipped towards the garage door with Mutt on my heels.

"Have you got your cell?" Fox demanded and I held it out, flashing the pink device at him with a sarcastic eye roll.

"I remembered to put my panties on too," I snarked back and he glowered at me before heading to the garage door.

JJ moved up beside me, his hand slipping beneath the hem of my skirt and making my breath catch as he skimmed his fingers up the back of my thigh before cupping my ass in his big hand, his fingers toying with the edge of my lace thong. "Just checking," he breathed, making a laugh escape me as we followed after Fox where he'd headed down into the garage.

My heart stuttered as we made it down to the open space beneath the house and my gaze fell on the red Jeep Wrangler convertible parked there with the top off, ready and waiting for me.

"That's mine?" I asked, my lips parting in surprise as I stared at it.

"Yeah, pretty girl, all yours," JJ confirmed as Fox just stood and watched.

I squealed a little bit - okay, maybe a lot - then raced forward and opened the door before hopping in and whistling for Mutt. I ran my hands over the steering wheel, breathing in that new car smell and wondering if I should be throwing this back in their faces. But fuck it, I'd never had a new car in my life and they owed me far more than this anyway.

I glanced over my shoulder into the back and sucked in a sharp breath as I spotted the surfboard there, my entire body falling totally still as I stared at it with its pale blue design with a white palm tree.

I scrambled into the back, standing up to get a better look at it with my heart racing as I tried not to get all emotional about a stupid surfboard, but shit, I felt that gift like a sucker punch to the heart. And not in an entirely bad way.

"You like?" JJ asked, moving to stand right beside the Jeep and I grinned broadly, leaping at him and forcing him to catch me as I wrapped my arms and legs around his waist and laughed. Because this had to be him, he was the one who had seen me with the Jeep and he was the only one I'd told how much I missed surfing.

"I freaking love it, J," I said, squeezing him tight and he laughed a little awkwardly.

"You should probably be giving this hug to Fox then, because this was all him," he said and I let him set me down on my feet before glancing at Fox who was standing there with his arms folded, watching me with an unreadable expression on his face.

"Oh." I released JJ and moved to Fox slowly, his gaze shifting down my body and causing a ripple effect along my skin. "Thanks, Badger," I said with a grin, reaching up to pat him on the head before snagging the keys from his hand and skipping back to the Jeep.

"Are you shitting me right now?" Fox demanded as JJ cracked up laughing and I hopped into my shiny new car.

"If you don't like being treated like a dog, Foxy boy, then maybe stop treating me like one, 'kay?" I blew him a kiss, started the engine and drove off up the ramp to exit the garage with the memory of his scowling face making me feel all warm and fuzzy inside.

I flipped off the Harlequins who were stationed at the front of Fox's property and they frowned at me as they opened the gates. I laughed to myself as I flicked through radio stations until Stolen Dance by Milky Chance caught my ear and I started singing at the top of my lungs.

It had been a long time since I'd realised that I was broken inside, but I'd quickly figured out that I could still enjoy myself if I focused on it hard enough. It had given me a say yes attitude, so whether it was taking part in wet t-shirt contests or drinking with people I barely knew or singing at the top of my lungs while I drove, I threw myself into it until the smile on my face became real. And for the most part it worked out pretty damn well for me. I could almost believe I wasn't miserable.

I wound through familiar streets, heading east towards Rosewood Manor and leaving the coast behind as the houses began to thin out and the trees began to thicken.

It didn't take long to reach the gates leading up to the huge estate, but as I pulled my Jeep up before the shiny black metal, my heart sank. On the drive, way up by the house, I could see a flashy silver sports car. Aside from that, the grounds looked better kept, the porch had had a fresh coat of paint and there was an expensive looking intercom system beside the gate. I ignored the sense of foreboding that built in my gut though and slipped out of the Jeep to go press the button.

A low buzzing sounded on and off for a few seconds before a curt sounding man answered. "Yes?"

"Hi. I'm an old friend of Miss Mabel's and I'm back in town after a long time. We didn't really keep in touch while I was away, but-"

"I'm sorry, but Miss Mabel died over eight years ago now. I'm her nephew and I inherited the property after she passed. You can't have been a very good friend if you were unaware of that."

"Oh, I'm sorry to hear tha-"

"If that's all, I have things to be getting on with."

"Okay, right, yeah, sorry for your loss-"

The guy cut the connection before I even got to finish that sentiment and I was left standing there feeling like a sack of shit for not even knowing the only decent person I'd known in this whole town had died without me ever saying goodbye.

Miss Mabel had been crazy old, so maybe I was dumb to have believed she might still be here but the knowledge that she wasn't still stung.

I sighed as I headed back to my Jeep, hopping in and pulling out onto the road again and I wrapped my fingers around the key that hung from my neck thoughtfully.

I pursed my lips and started the car up again as a tear slipped past my defences and rolled down my cheek. Mutt hopped into my lap and snuggled against me like he knew I was hurting and wanted to help and for some reason, that just encouraged a few more tears to fall.

I took a deep breath and gave him a squeeze before forcing myself to focus on the task at hand.

I pulled away from the drive and turned up the road, frowning as I realised the fence that surrounded the property had been completely replaced by a ten foot wooden monstrosity with an electrical wire along the top of it which I couldn't even see through. There were security cameras too, enough to cover the entire perimeter as far as I could see which meant I had no way of knowing whether or not the crypt was even still standing or not. But surely it had to be. Whoever her fucking nephew was, he wouldn't have destroyed the old family graveyard, would he?

My gut tugged with concern about that but there was nothing I could do to check it out unless I wanted my ass to be seen on camera. I just had to hope for the best so that once I got my hands on all of the keys, I could come back here, break in to the crypt, take what I needed and go. At that point it wouldn't even matter if I was caught on camera because I wouldn't be hanging around in town to have to worry about being caught anyway.

I swung a U-turn in the middle of the road, let out a breath of frustration and headed back towards town. There wasn't anything else that I could do about the crypt right now and that surfboard was whispering sweet nothings in my ear which I just couldn't ignore any longer.

I was going to drive down to Rejects Park, pay the rent on my trailer then spend the day on the beach and in the surf with my new friends if I could find them or make some more new friends if I couldn't. And after the last couple of weeks, I had to say that sounded like its own little slice of paradise.

A day on the beach enjoying the surf and laughing with Lyla and Bella did wonders for the tension I'd been carrying around with me. This was what I needed. Just some down time away from the ghosts of my past and the dominating auras of the Harlequins where I could relax and talk shit over a couple of beers with the sun warming my skin.

"A bunch of guys are going to The Dungeon tonight," Lyla said as we were gathering up our shit and making our way up the beach with the sun setting at our backs. "You wanna come party with us?"

"Where's that?" I asked curiously.

Ten years was plenty of time for new clubs and bars to have opened up in town and though I knew this place like the back of my hand, there were more than a few additions that I didn't recognise.

"It's beyond The Divide," she said, tossing her blonde hair and glancing over her shoulder like she was concerned about being overheard. "Obviously none of the Harlequins can come because it's in Damned Men territory, but it's one of the best clubs in town and they have a band playing tonight."

My pulse picked up a little at the mention of crossing through that tensely fought over strip of turf, but did I really have any reason to worry? I wasn't in the Harlequins, I had no real affiliation to them aside from Fox's dumb claim that I belonged to him. Besides, the leader of The Damned Men was one of my old boys. No matter what else I might have thought of Maverick, I didn't think he'd actually hurt me. And I was way overdue in my need for a night out.

"Okay, I'm in," I agreed decisively.

"Great, make sure you wear something hot and we'll head out at nine. Lyla walked off up the beach but I stopped, grabbing my cellphone from my bag and glancing over the messages I'd received while I'd been surfing.

Fox:

It's been hours now. Where are you?

Fox:

If you expect to keep hold of this new freedom of yours then I suggest you get your ass home soon.

Fox:

Answer me

Fox:

If you don't let me know that you're okay, I'll come find you myself.

JJ:

Can I get your opinion on something? x

JJ:

Also, can you text Fox before he flips out again x

It was extra irritating because I knew that he knew exactly where I was thanks to his stupid tracking software, but I was also fairly certain that he'd be showing up here soon if I didn't reply. I sighed dramatically, sent Fox a quick message to tell him to stop riding my ass if he expected me to ever come back then asked JJ what he wanted my opinion on.

Several messages demanding my immediate return appeared from Fox but I ignored them in favour of opening up the video attachment JJ had sent.

The sound of Put Your Records On by Ritt Momney poured from the speakers of my cellphone as I was shown a video of JJ dancing on stage with four other dudes, grinding his hips in a sinfully slow and torturous rhythm before tearing his shirt off to reveal his seriously ripped body which seemed to gleam a little beneath the lights overhead.

He threw flirtatious looks at the camera as he moved towards it, unbuttoning his fly with a dramatic flourish while doing that crazy hot lip bite thing that shouldn't have been legal. Just as it looked like his cock was about to spring free of his pants, the video ended and I found another message from J.

JJ:

Made you look ;)

I swallowed thickly, my gaze raking over JJ's body in the freeze-frame as I got some seriously bad ideas about one of the dudes I hated. Not to be outdone though, I raised my cellphone in front of me to take a video, licking my lips slowly as I traced my hand along the edge of my red bikini top, tugging on it so that my nipple was almost revealed before cutting the recording and sending it to him in reply.

Rogue:

If you wanna play with me, J, then make sure you're ready to bring your A game

I decided that was more than enough interacting with Harlequins for the night and quickly switched my cell off, pulling the SIM card out for good measure to make sure Fox's tracking bullshit couldn't give him the location of my trailer. Then I grabbed my surfboard, whistled to Mutt and headed up the beach to my shiny new Jeep where I stowed my board then drove the short journey around to Rejects Park where I pulled up in the lot outside the trailer park and tried to ignore the fact that my car was worth more than every other vehicle here combined. It didn't really matter - if it got stolen then that was more of a Fox issue than mine. I very much doubted the thing was registered in my name anyway.

I grabbed my shit and me and Mutt headed back to my little slice of freedom together, pausing to shove this week's rent through Joe's hole - *shudder*.

When I made it into my retro trailer with its little blue cabinets, I grinned to myself. It had been a long damn time since I'd had somewhere I felt I could truly call my home. When I'd lived in Granshaw, I'd had a room in an apartment with a couple of other guys but it hadn't been my space alone and it was the kind of place where people came and went so I never even got to know my roommates all that well. But this right here was all mine. And no one could take it from me.

A shower, outfit change into a hot as hell little blue dress JJ was responsible for, plus the full works with my hair and makeup later and I was ready to go out and get fucked up.

I was painting my lips a deep plum colour when a bang made me leap half out of my skin and Joe's head popped through the window at the foot of my bed.

I shrieked in alarm, hefting the blowdryer into my grip and wishing it was a damn pistol as I whirled around to glare at him.

"Told ya to watch for this window," he drawled, clacking the toothpick he had wedged in his mouth across his teeth then ducking back out of the window and disappearing again before I could do any more than thank all that was good in this world for the fact that he hadn't done that before I'd gotten dressed.

What the fuck was with him? A shudder raced down my spine as I remembered being sixteen again, walking down the street that led to my group home while that dirty old bastard Axel called out compliments which made my skin crawl.

I quickly crossed over to the window and locked it up tight, making a mental note to get some freaking nails and a hammer and do an even more permanent job of it as soon as I got the chance. And a can of mace. A big one. Anything to keep Joe *McCreepy* out of my personal space.

Mutt seemed perfectly content to curl up on my new bedding, so I stuffed a couple of twenties in my bra, tossed my shiny pink cellphone and SIM card in my closet then kicked on a pair of chunky heels and headed out.

I locked up, hid my key in a little plant pot on my porch then got my ass moving as I headed to meet Lyla and the others.

"Yo, Green Ranger!" Di's voice made me turn towards her with a wide grin and she jogged to my side looking hot as hell in a white figure hugging dress that made her ass look seriously good.

"I was hoping you were coming," I said with a grin as we started walking together. "How are we getting to the club anyway?" Of course I had a car, but I was the kind of selfish asshole who wanted to drink tonight so I wasn't gonna offer to play the designated driver.

"A bunch of the guys will drive," she said dismissively. "They know it's pretty much a guaranteed way for them to end up getting laid tonight when they taxi everyone home anyway and if they do end up too wasted to drive, we can all just stumble off and catch a bus."

We made it to the gates which fronted the trailer park and found a group of around fifteen people waiting to head out. I recognised a few of them, but most were new faces to me.

"Holy shit, is that you Rogue?" a vaguely familiar voice called out and I turned, finding a guy leaning against the hood of a slightly beat up looking green Chevy as his eyes ran over me. He was a pretty big dude with thick arms crossed over his broad chest, his muscular frame straining against the fabric of his grey shirt.

"Jake?" I asked in surprise, suddenly recognising the guy from my old group home and moving over to him with a grin.

"You still owe me a pack of jelly beans," he said accusingly, a smile playing around his lips. "The night you and Clive ran off you promised to bring me some."

My gut lurched at the mention of Clive's name. I knew exactly what had happened to that motherfucker but I guessed it made sense that the other kids in the group home assumed we'd run off together seeing as we'd disappeared around the same time, but I'd hated that creep and they all knew it. Either way, after all this time, it didn't make much sense to correct him and I let him drag me into a bear hug which almost drowned me in his cheap cologne.

I fought a cough as I stepped back and he grinned. "You wanna ride over to the club with me?" he offered.

"Sure," I hedged, taking note of the way he was looking at me and wondering if I had any interest in getting to know him with a whole lot less clothes involved. Maybe he could be the perfect remedy to my Harlequin habit.

I made a move to get into his car just as a girl with a pile of bleached blonde hair piled up on her head and about four inches of makeup caked on her skin moved into my way and dropped into the seat I'd been about to claim.

"Well look what the cat dragged back," she said, her eyes scraping over me in a totally judgemental way.

"Do I know you?" I asked coolly, refusing to rise to her bitch bait. Cat fights were seriously overrated and I didn't waste my time putting basic assholes like this one on their asses unless I had to.

"Err, I'm your foster sister," she said with a flinch of anger at the fact that I hadn't recognised her. "But I guess I'm not surprised the great Rogue Easton doesn't remember anyone aside from the Harlequin boys. I bet it stung to hear about me and Chase."

"Rosie?" I asked in surprise, squinting through the layers of foundation smothering her skin and finally recognising the girl I'd once shared a room with back in the home. She was the only bitch who had ever tried to say we were all foster brothers and sisters and it looked like she hadn't stopped being an annoying little fuck. "And what are you talking about, you and Chase?"

"Oh please. I know he would have told you all about me the moment you came crawling back to town, begging to suck their cocks again. But guess what? He chose me, not you, so go slobber over another guy because my big Chasey isn't interested in your sloppy pussy."

My lips popped open as I processed that. *Chase and Rosie? Rosie??* The little troll who used to sleep beneath my bed and rat me out to Mary Beth at every given opportunity? Ew. Fuck no. How could he-

I stopped myself short as a stab of pain hit me somewhere deep in my gut and I knew she wasn't lying. Of course he'd fucked the girl I used to hate. Those boys had delighted in my fucking destruction so why not just drive the knife in a little deeper after taking everything from me and casting me out to be forgotten?

"You're welcome to Chase, Rosie," I said coldly. "I'm not to his taste anyway. I heard he has a preference for girls who base their make up on clowns and who like being fucked up the ass in exchange for smokes, so you're clearly his type. I wish you every happiness."

I turned and walked away from her outraged expression, spotting Di and Lyla climbing into the back of a blue Ford and waving me over to join them.

I forced a smile as my heart raced with the hurt of that little nugget of shit and climbed in with them, finding Bella already inside so the four of us were crammed into the back.

Two dudes were sitting in the front of the car, but I didn't pay them much attention as I focused on squishing my ass into a comfortable position while the girls giggled and passed about a bottle of vodka.

"Hey, Rogue," the guy in the passenger seat said as we rolled out onto the street and I looked up at his seriously bruised face, taking note of the nose straps, black eyes and curly blonde hair before I even recognised him.

"Holy shit, Carter, what the fuck happened to your face?" I asked because I had no tack and I seriously needed to hear that story.

"It's nothing," he said with a shrug.

"Girl, don't you know who did that to him?" Bella asked with a cackle of laughter which made me realise she was clearly on something stronger than vodka again. "Fox Harlequin fucked. Him. Uuuuuuuuup."

Di slapped a hand over her face to hide her laugher as Carter scowled at the redhead and Lyla reached forward to pat his shoulder sympathetically.

"Why?" I asked, wondering what he'd done to enrage the Badger.

"Errr, he seemed to think I'd been looking at you too much, so..."

"What?" I balked. "When?"

"The other day when you were surfing. I just saw you catch a sick wave, that's all. But he said that you were his girl and I was overstepping by looking at you, and he just wanted to drive the message home I guess. It's fine, looks worse than it is." Carter shrugged as his friend who was driving muttered something about the Harlequins being psychopaths and not wanting to die for letting me ride in his car.

"I am not, never have been and never will be Fox Harlequin's fucking girl," I said loudly, making Bella cackle again. "Just to make that clear. And I'm gonna be having words with that asshole for laying his hands on you, mark my fucking words."

I stewed over the king of the cocks as we drove the rest of the way to the club, taking my turn at swigs of vodka while I worked to forget about the asshole in question and focus on having a good night tonight. No doubt I'd be having a row with him when I saw him again anyway after I'd blocked his tracking attempts on me for the night, but fuck him for thinking it was okay to be monitoring my whereabouts at all fucking times.

We made it to the north side of the city, speeding through The Divide without any incidents. But a prickle ran down my spine as we crossed through that area of fought over turf like there were eyes on the car for every second that we spent occupying it. I even spotted the lighthouse between the buildings as we passed it by, still cordoned off with yellow police tape. I'd seen the stories on the news about the massacre that had taken place there and the boys had been laying low while the heat blew over, sticking to mostly legal pastimes for a while. I had to wonder if they really all believed the place was worth the fight and bloodshed or if it was just a dick measuring contest at this point.

The club was away from the beach and when we pulled up on a side street, I looked around in confusion as I was left wondering about where the hell it could be. The buildings all around us were quiet, just some shops which were closed up for the night and a general quiet in the air which said nothing at all was going on here.

"Move your ass bitch or we'll miss the band," Di teased, giving me a shove so that I opened the door and we could all spill out onto the curb.

The cars with the rest of our group of rejects were all parking up too and we were soon walking down the street giggling in anticipation and grouping together as we headed for the club.

I made an effort to ignore Rosie's existence and found it easy enough in a group this size. The way she was clinging to Jake was making me think that Chase's wasn't the only dick she'd been sucking, but if she seriously thought I was going to be running after her sloppy seconds then she had another thing coming. Stupid twat. I bet she still had that teddy bear I was always threatening to decapitate. Maybe I'd sneak into her trailer and do it one of these days.

Di nudged me as we came up to an inconspicuous looking door which was set into a white wall sprayed with countless graffiti. I noticed the name The Dungeon amongst it a bunch of times as well as spotting The Damned Men tags more than once and my skin prickled as I looked them over.

Was I freaking idiot for coming here? Maybe. But it was too late now and at least I knew Fox and his cronies couldn't rock up here and drag me back to his cave. The Damned Men's turf was off limits to him and his little pals.

Carter banged his fist against the door and a slot opened up in it as someone peered out. "How much sausage and how much bun?"

"What?" I asked with a laugh and Di grinned at me.

"Half and half," Carter replied, and the guy inside glanced at our group before shutting the hatch again and opening the door.

"They like there to be an even number of guys and girls in the club," she breathed in explanation. "Though they usually let girls in whatever."

"Come on then," he said, his gaze roaming over us as he ushered us inside and I followed the others down a short stone corridor before we reached a wide staircase that led down into the dark, lit with purple lights.

The girls were all tittering and giggling together and the buzz of the vodka had me grinning along with them, walking between Di and Bella as we descended into the club and the sound of the band called up to us from below.

As we reached another door at the base of the stairs, two more bouncers opened it for us and the music washed over us. The sound of a deep beat and the rough voice of the singer on stage embraced me as I realised this place had been built in an underground parking lot which had been totally converted to create this club. They didn't ID us which I was going to assume was because this place clearly wasn't legal and not because I didn't look young enough to warrant it anymore. Because I looked young as fuck. Although I guessed all the shit I'd suffered through might have worn on my features a bit. Crap, maybe I should have been worrying about getting crow's feet.

I forgot about checking my face for premature wrinkles as we stepped through into the club and my lips popped open as I took in the full scope of the place. It was huge and absolutely teeming with people.

A large bar built out of cinderblocks ran around the right side of the room, topped with a wooden counter and under lit with a strip of more purple lights. The wall and concrete pillars had been painted black but the floor still held the white boxes intended to mark out spaces for cars to park. Despite the fact that this place was literally some abandoned parking lot, it was somehow stupidly cool - like it had been re-claimed for a rave. Or maybe a modern day speakeasy was more accurate.

To the left of the space, a stage had been erected where the band was playing and my gaze moved to them, drinking in the raw energy with which they embraced the stage. The lead singer had a deep, throaty voice like all the best country and western singers and the music was all grit and energy.

Most of the people packed into the place were dancing and I was more than happy to follow as Di caught my hand and dragged me into the throng.

We started dancing with Bella and Lyla, the four of us moving to the music and letting it sweep us away into the beat as we were submerged in the crowd.

Time slipped past as we danced and drank and laughed and I bathed in song after song while the music filled my soul and made me feel lighter than I had since before I'd come back here. Not that I'd often felt light while I was running with The Dead Dogs and Shawn Mackenzie either.

Fucking Shawn.

My skin got all hot and prickly just thinking about that motherfucker and I cursed beneath my breath, deciding that another drink was probably the best solution I could come up with to that particular shit fest of a line of thoughts.

But before I could turn away to the bar, a large hand traced a line right down the centre of my spine and I fell still as my skin prickled with heat for a much better reason than rage at Shawn.

The mystery man slid his arm around my hips and I looked down, finding tattooed skin covering him from his fingers to his hand and up his forearm where a charcoal grey sleeve had been rolled back to his elbow.

The guy's grip tightened, drawing me back against a hard, broad body and I fell into the movements of my dance again as I let him move me.

The scent of wood and leather surrounded me as we moved together, his other hand moving to brush his fingers against my thigh just beneath the hem of my dress and a breathy moan escaped me as I closed my eyes and tilted my head back to lean against his shoulder.

This was what I needed. An outlet for the tension in my body to help me look at the Harlequins without any unwanted lust clouding my vision. Someone to touch and caress me and wash away the feeling of Shawn's hands on my skin.

I didn't want flowers and kisses. I wanted a man who saw what he wanted and took it. I wanted to use him and be used by him and feel the most perfect kind of dirty in the morning. Because dirty suited me best. I was a fucked up, imperfect creature and I liked to act the part so that I never forgot it. Never again.

The guy I was dancing with moved his hand up my thigh, his thumb lifting the material of my skirt and making my breath hitch as he drew a line of blazing fire right the way up to my panty line with that single digit before allowing the material to fall down again.

I hadn't even seen his face yet and I knew he was the type who could destroy me. This one ate virgin souls for breakfast and feasted on a diet of sex and danger and I wanted to feast with him the next time he dined.

His left arm kept my back locked to his front so when I tried to turn to face him, I couldn't and my pulse hitched as he slid his right hand up the front of my body, his fingers carving a line over my flesh until he made it to my neck.

As his large hand slipped around my throat, I sucked in a gasp of fear, momentarily thrown back into that moment with Shawn as he tried to squeeze the life from my body and I found myself helpless to stop him.

I tried to jerk away but the guy's grip tightened on my throat, his fingers digging in hard enough to make my pulse spike as he tipped my chin up. His other arm tightened around my waist and he drew my ass back hard against his crotch and the solid swell of his cock.

He dipped his head over my shoulder, the rough scratch of stubble grazing my neck right beneath my ear.

"Hello, beautiful," he growled, his voice deep and dark and even more painful than I would have thought possible.

My lips popped open in surprise, my heart thrashing like mad and a soft whimper escaping me that I couldn't even interpret.

He squeezed my throat tighter, his mouth still pressed to the side of my neck just above his fingers and as he bit down on my skin, sucking hard, a moan of surprise slid from my lips and my thighs clenched involuntarily as my needy body reacted to his touch.

It shouldn't have turned me on, especially with his hand squeezing my throat like that, but before I could even really get started beating myself up or telling him to get the fuck off of me or allowing myself to investigate the suspicion I was feeling for his identity, he released me.

I stumbled forward a step in surprise and by the time I whirled around to demand - I didn't even know what - it didn't matter because he was already gone, the throng of dancing idiots around me covering his tracks completely.

I looked back and forth, but between the dark and the crowd, I couldn't see him and I cursed as I wondered if I was just imagining things. Surely that wasn't who I'd thought it was. But the way my heart was racing told me it had been. And if Maverick really was here then there was no way I was going to let him leave without speaking to me.

I'd been listening to their warnings about Maverick, but I'd also heard them loud and clear when they told me he was the only one of them who tried to find me.

Besides, dead girls didn't feel fear. Right?

I glanced back around to let the girls know where I was going but I couldn't see them amongst the crowd of dancers who had closed in tight around us and Maverick was getting away.

I cursed beneath my breath and pushed into the throng of bodies, taking a punt and heading for the bar instead of the seating area to the rear of the club. The Rick I'd known would always choose the party over sitting in a corner and if there was any part of that boy left in the ruthless murderer he'd apparently become then I knew he'd be getting a drink.

The crowd thinned as I moved away from the band and I looked back and forth, hunting the bodies around me for any sign of familiarity. I hadn't laid eyes on Maverick in ten long years and if the tattoos I'd caught sight of and the thick muscles I'd felt pressing against my body were any indication, then he had changed in more ways than one. Just like all of my boys had.

I hurried on, shoving and cursing and feeling like a fucking idiot as I chased a memory through the darkness of the club until I finally came up to the bar and found nothing in the place of the man I'd been hoping to find.

My brow pinched and I kicked the bar before remembering it was built from cinderblocks and cursing as my toes throbbed through my heels.

"Where's the Green Ranger when I need him?" I muttered to myself, drawing an odd look from the guy beside me who I promptly flipped off.

"What's the matter, beautiful? You lost something you were looking for?"

I whirled around with my lips parting as I found Rick standing over me, his almost deep brown eyes devouring and dark presence consuming.

"Shit," I breathed, having no real answer for him as I dragged my eyes over his body. Maverick had been tall when I'd last seen him but he towered over me now and the breadth of his muscular chest made me feel small in all the right ways.

He was wearing jeans and a shirt with the buttons spilling open around his throat to reveal just as much ink as on his forearms and I wondered how far they went beneath his clothes.

Dark hair was pushed back on top of his head with less care taken than he'd used to bother with but still something about it that said he liked it just so. The mouth I'd seen smile a thousand times was set into a hard slash across his face and the way his brows lowered over his dark gaze seemed far too natural to be out of the ordinary for him.

"I heard that Fox had a girl who no one was allowed to touch," he mused as he looked at me, the feeling of his intense gaze on my body making goosebumps rise along my skin. But I couldn't tell if they were from fear, lust or something far more worrying. "I guess I should have known it was you right away. He always was obsessed with you after all," Maverick said in that, deep, sinful voice of his.

"I'm not anyone's-"

"I see you had your first without me too," he said, ignoring me and reaching out to graze his fingers over the tattoos which covered my left arm. "Which one was it?" His hand moved to the skull on my right thigh, his rough fingers grazing sensitive skin in a way that made me ache for more. After all this time, it seemed stupid to be discussing tattoos, but he'd gotten his first ink without me and I'd complained about it at the time, so I guessed I could give him an answer to that.

"The wings on my back," I replied evenly, not knowing how I was supposed to react to this brutal creature before me. When I'd come here it had been with hate in my heart for the Harlequin boys because I'd believed that each and every one of them had left me to rot. But if what the others had told me was true then that wasn't the case with Rick. He'd tried to come after me. He'd served six years for that attempt. And by the time he was released, I would have been long gone even if he had tried to find me. "I got them because I-"

My explanation was cut off by Rick whipping me around, grabbing a fistful of my rainbow coloured hair and driving my face down against the bar as he bent me over it. I gasped in shock, cursing at him as he pinned me in place with his overwhelming strength then yanked the zipper on the back of my dress right down to the base of my spine.

"Maverick!" I yelled, trying to fight out of his grip as his fingers ran down the tattoos on my back and he growled something I couldn't make out.

I threw an elbow back at his gut but before I could land the blow he'd released me again, stepping back so that I could push myself upright and turn to glare at him. He'd left my damn dress undone but I was more concerned with breaking his fucking face than zipping it up in that moment.

"What the fuck was that about?" I demanded, stepping up to him as he just looked me over impassively, almost like he didn't care if I punched him. Or maybe like he wanted me to.

"I'm figuring you out," he replied as if that meant a damn thing and I took my chances with punching him.

He either didn't expect it, or let me land the blow because he didn't even flinch before my knuckles slammed against his jaw and he only moved at all because I hit him so damn hard.

Rick recovered slowly, smirking as he took a step closer to me so that I had to back up, my ass pressing to the bar before he turned and spat a wad of blood from his mouth then pinned me in his dark gaze once more.

"What do you want?" I ground out, forcing myself not to punch him again while my knuckles stung from the hit to his face.

"Straight to the point I see."

"Unlike you, apparently. What's wrong, Rick? You used to be the one I could rely on to give it to me straight. Or was that bullshit too?"

He smiled at me but there was no kindness in it, no fondness over the memories we'd shared of the life we'd once lived. Something had happened to him in the time that I'd been gone. The boy I once knew didn't peer out through his dark eyes anymore. And the man in his place was as cold and callous as any of the worst people I'd ever known.

"I want what Fox wants," he said, moving close so that he could run his knuckles down the side of my face, the ink there seeming to stain my skin with heat I had no intention of feeling. "But don't go thinking I'm sweet on you, beautiful. I want you sweating and panting beneath me. I want you broken and begging and crying because you want it so much that you hate yourself for it. I want to take you and use you and ruin you and then lay you back at his feet and laugh in his face when I do it."

"Good luck with that," I sneered, knocking his hand from my face. "Because I don't want you any more than I want Fox. I never did. So why don't you keep your right wrist nice and limber because I get the feeling your hand will be getting more action from you than I will."

Maverick's hands suddenly grabbed my waist and he lifted me up, driving me back onto the bar and knocking glasses flying as people scrambled to get out of our way. He shoved my knees apart and stepped between my thighs, looming over me as I leaned back, his chest pressing to mine and that rich, masculine scent of his enveloping me as he moved right into my personal space.

I slammed my hands into his chest to try and force him back with a snarl of anger, but he just caught my wrists, his fingers tightening around them hard enough to bruise as he held on firmly and immobilised me.

"You seem to be under the impression that I'm waiting for permission," he growled, his lips brushing mine as I stared up at him with wide eyes. He wasn't the boy I used to know. This was a monster in the flesh of a man. The kind who took pleasure in the pain of others. The kind I'd sworn to stay well away from after waking up in that fucking grave.

"Get your fucking hands off of me, Rick."

Maverick scoffed, leaning forward and taking my bottom lip between his teeth before biting down hard enough to draw blood. "Make me," he growled, his grip tightening on my wrists until I cried out then suddenly, he was gone.

He shoved away from me, turned and disappeared into the crowd, leaving me perched on the bar, panting and bleeding and wondering what the fuck had happened to him. Because I didn't know that man. Not even a little.

But that wasn't good enough. He owed me answers. He'd been the only one of them to come after me, to even try to go against what Luther had wanted and followed me like I'd needed all of them to once.

I licked the blood from my lip, feeling the imprint of his teeth in my flesh and reaching behind my back to force my zipper up again before using my position on top of the bar to watch Maverick as he stalked away through the crowd.

He didn't go the way we'd come in but headed for a door on the far side of the wide open space where a group of scary looking individuals with Damned Men tattoos prominently visible on their skin grouped around him and followed him out.

It was probably a terrible idea to follow him, but despite what I'd heard, despite what I'd seen or even what I'd just felt in the roughness of his touch, that man had owned a piece of my soul once. And I intended to find out if he'd ever deserved it.

I dropped back down to my feet and spotted Bella stumbling towards the exit with Lyla half carrying her. I ducked between the crowd towards them, my gaze half fixed on the exit Maverick was slipping through as I made it to them.

"Ain't no party until Bella pukes a lung, am I right?" Lyla joked as I gave the swaying redhead a concerned look.

"Are you okay with her? I just ran into a guy I used to know and-"

"Say no more, bitch," Lyla said with a wicked grin. "Go get lucky. I'll tell the others you're finding your own way home tonight - or tomorrow if he's got the right amount of stamina."

I forced a laugh, deciding that was the easiest thing to let her believe then left her and Bella to beg a bottle of water from the bar staff as I took off after Maverick.

I made it to the small door with no issues and pushed through it, squinting as I stepped into a brightly lit white corridor with a metal staircase and signs telling me there was access to the street above.

There were no sounds to say that anyone was nearby so I took off up the stairs as fast as my chunky heels would carry me, climbing up and up until I reached the exit to the street.

I shoved on the thick bar which released the door and came face to face with a guy and a girl who looked less than pleased to see me.

"What the fuck are you doing using the private entrance?" the girl sneered at me as the door swung shut with a loud click.

"Don't mind me, I just need to find-"

She threw a punch at me out of nowhere and I barely managed to flinch back as it glanced off of my jaw.

I cursed, spotting The Damned Men tattoo of a grim reaper on her neck as she came at me again and she grabbed hold of my arms, shoving me back against the brick wall of the building hard enough to make the back of my head bounce against it and pain splinter through my skull.

"Hold her down, Onyx," the guy said from behind her, pulling a flick knife from his pocket as he advanced on me with an evil little scowl on his face. "I'll teach her a lesson about who runs this town so she doesn't make a mistake like this again."

The girl grinned wickedly as she increased the pressure of her hold on me like she thought I was just going to stand there and let her pin me down while that motherfucker cut me.

But I'd been playing these games for long enough to know that going easy never won anyone any favours and I wasn't the type to take their shit lying down.

I let him advance and the moment he was holding the knife out close enough to us, I lunged forward with a snarl of fury, shoving the girl back so that the blade ended up slicing along her forearm instead of meeting with my flesh and she howled in agony and rage as she dove at me again.

I took a punch to the cheek and threw one right back into her stomach just as she grabbed a fistful of my hair.

She swung me around towards the wall again and I slammed into it, grazing my arm before stomping on her foot with my big ass heels.

The girl released me then swung another punch as the guy moved back a step with the knife still in hand, clearly waiting for her to incapacitate me again. But as he moved, the light from the far end of the alley caught on the pistol he had jammed into the back of his jeans, letting me know that they could do a hell of a lot more than just cut me if they got the upper hand here.

I went for the low blow, tit punching the girl in a move that would have had the Green Ranger shaking his head in disapproval before taking advantage of her stumbling back and launching myself at her.

My shoulder caught her in the chest as I threw my weight at her, making her lose her balance and fall back against the guy. He dropped the knife in his attempt to catch her then promptly shoved her away from him as he lunged after it, clearly thinking I'd go for it too.

But the moment he lurched down to pick it up, I ripped the gun from the back of his pants, flicked the safety off and backed up several steps as I held them both in my gaze.

"Keys," I demanded in a low snarl, ignoring the wet trickle of blood I could feel running down from my hairline onto my temple.

"What?" the asshole spat like he couldn't understand plain English.

"I'm guessing you didn't walk here, motherfucker, and I find myself in need of a vehicle," I growled. "So give it up."

His gaze scraped over me and he slowly lowered his hands, smirking as he took a step towards me. "You're not gonna shoot me," he said with all the confidence of some big bad gang banger who believed he was immortal. "You look like some kind of rainbow princess, you clearly don't have the balls to-"

I lowered the gun and fired off a shot into his thigh.

The guy fell to the ground screaming in pain and the girl scowled at me so hard it kinda looked like she was trying to take a shit.

"You'll pay for crossing The Damned Men," she hissed like I should be afraid. But I was already dead and all I felt was cold, empty nothingness right now.

The last of my boys had finally shown up and our reunion may have been the most bitter of all.

"Keys, bitch," I demanded. "Or the next bullet is going between your eyes."

Was I going to kill her for being a royal cocksucker? Probably not. But would I shoot her to stop her coming after me? Yeah. I was down for that.

The guy on the ground was sobbing and gasping and praying to a god who wouldn't have helped him even if he was listening. Deities didn't care about scum like us. If they existed at all, they saved their mercy for people far more worthy of it than we were.

The girl reluctantly pulled a set of keys from her back pocket and tossed them at me.

"You wanna tell me where you parked? Or am I shooting your buddy again?" I asked, making no move to retrieve them.

"About a block that way," she jerked her chin to the right. "Black Honda."

"Thank you, sweet pea," I mocked, stooping down to claim the keys.

As I expected, she lurched at me like she seriously believed I was dumb enough to take my eyes off of her and I fired a shot that smacked her straight in the thigh too.

Instead of screaming like her buddy, the girl just howled curses at me as I grabbed the keys, calling me as many names as she could think up while swearing at me with promises of death that I ignored. The Grim Reaper had already come for me once after all. And it turned out even that dude didn't want me. Rejection had never felt so good.

I turned away from the bleeding, cursing, crying assholes and fell still as I found a man watching me from the back of a matt black motorcycle.

Maverick didn't say a word, but the corner of his mouth lifted into a dangerous smirk as his dark eyes lit with some decision that made my already pounding heart race.

He lifted a gun of his own and my heart stilled as for some unknown reason I failed to raise mine. Maybe it was because I knew in my heart that killing him would destroy any lingering fragments of the girl I'd once been. Or maybe it was because death at his hands sounded like the sweetest offer of oblivion I'd ever been given.

Two shots rang out, the sound of them echoing right through my body as my eyes closed automatically and I waited to feel the pain of those bullets ripping through me. But instead, silence fell heavily, followed by the roar of a motorcycle. And by the time I peeled my lids open again, I found myself standing alone in an alley with two corpses and the scent of Maverick's exhaust fumes tainting the air.

MAVERICK

CHAPTER SEVENTEEN

I lived between two eternal fields of grey with a black sky above. Nothing surprised me anymore. I'd learned a long time ago to expect the unexpected. And when life gave you lemons, you'd better not bust your ass making lemonade. You needed to squeeze the acid out into your enemies' eyes and gut them while they were blinded.

Rogue showing up in my life again had been unexpected. But I didn't run to her like the pussy whipped prick I'd been ten years ago. Instead, I inspected her like a cup of poison left on my porch. I'd been thirsty for a long time, so I had to take a sip.

It seemed she was the kind of poison that left me wanting more though and as I drove deeper into Damned Men territory, my tongue felt like a dry lump of tinder in my mouth.

She was Fox's girl. Of course he'd claimed her the second she'd drifted back into town like a seed looking to plant itself in the dirt of our lives. She'd gotten under his skin just like before and now he owned her. But not for long. The girl was ripe for the picking. And if she didn't come knocking at my door for a taste of my cock soon enough, then I'd take her myself. It was tit for tat after all. *You fuck my life, I'll fuck your girl, brother.*

I didn't care to lay a claim on her beyond that. My days were filled with a sole ambition to eradicate every single Harlequin from the earth, then I'd walk into the arms of death with a smile on my face and my purpose fulfilled. The nothingness beyond this life was welcoming to me. The only reason I hadn't tried to catch a bullet with my skull before now was because there were still Harlequins drawing breath. And I'd be damned if I'd die before I saw them all fall.

I'd been curious to see if Rogue Easton had handed her soul over to their crew already, but I'd seen the devil in her eyes looking straight back at me, and I knew what that meant. She was still a lost girl, outcast from even Neverland. And Fox could lay claims on her all he liked, but it was clear she was never going to belong to anyone ever again. Didn't fucking matter though. Fox was a stubborn asshole and if he'd convinced himself he owned her, then the pain would be the same when I left her ruined at his doorstep.

When I'd gotten out of prison, I'd made a vow to never let that bastard be content. And the only thing that allowed me to sleep at night was knowing he wasn't. My so-called brother was living on borrowed time. Time lent to him by Luther who'd handed him the world, his crew, all he needed to surround himself with an army of worthless men who'd die for him. But every one of them I cut down got me another step closer to him. And I hoped Luther was there when the light went out of his precious boy's eyes. Just before I finished daddy dearest himself.

I spat over my shoulder at the thought of them, turning my bike down onto Fishhook Street and racing toward the boatyard. The boat was ready to go and I drove up the ramp onto the catamaran where my men were waiting to leave.

"Let's go!" I hollered as I parked up, swung my leg over the bike and headed to the front of the boat, watching the moonlight bleed into the waves.

It was only a fifteen minute journey and I was soon driving my bike off onto Dead Man's Isle, racing up the curving road that led to the compound. The guards let me in and I sailed toward the front entrance, parking my bike up alongside the few trucks we kept here.

I headed into the huge abandoned hotel I lived in. The word home held no meaning for me, but this was where I resided until I walked into the arms of death. And lately, I felt I was drawing closer to that inevitable day. But that only sent a lick of excitement up my spine, because if my death was near, so was Fox and Luther Harlequin's.

I walked upstairs to the suite I occupied on the top floor, the air cool as I moved into the huge room and stripped off my shirt. I headed across the tiles into the wide bathroom with silver taps and a walk in shower. I stood in front of the his and hers vanity unit and took a switch knife, a lighter and a bottle of antiseptic from the drawer. I ran the blade through the flame of the lighter, eyeing the tattooed tally marks on the left side of my chest and reaching up to cut two thin lines into it. Blood trickled from the shallow cuts and I soaked a pad of cotton wool in the antiseptic, cleaning it before picking up the bottle of tattoo ink by the sink. I used another cotton wool pad to bathe my wounds in ink, marking them on me forever. Most of these cuts represented Harlequins, but occasionally the wrong asshole crossed me and ended up among them. Tonight, two of my own had earned their places on my body. Rogue had done half the work and I'd done the rest. Seeing those marks they'd left on her had awoken my bloodthirst, and I always fed that hungry devil. If she thought it meant more than that, then more fool her.

I might have been obsessed with the girl once, but obsession was an ugly friend. And I'd cut off his head many years ago when I'd been incarcerated.

Juvie had been bearable, but prison had been insufferable. At least until I'd learned to detach and feel nothing but the hollow space in my chest. But it didn't come without sacrifice. That void in me had deepened, devouring all the good until there was nothing left but darkness and rot. My morals had always been thin, but now they were non-existent. It was funny how quickly love turned to hate. My adopted brother had disposed of me like decaying fruit, but instead of disappearing like he'd hoped, I'd festered and festered in the dark.

I wiped the excess ink from the wound and returned to my room, finding Mia coiled in my sheets, her naked body painted in ink, her short, dark hair messed up against the pillows.

I growled in irritation, stalking toward her and snatching a fistful of her hair to wake her. She gasped as I yanked her head back to look at me, a sneer on my lips that made her throat bob with fear.

"You don't sleep in my bed unless I tell you to. Get the fuck back to your own room."

She whimpered as I tugged her hair tighter, but she liked that, her eyes brightening at the pain. I yanked her to her feet and she moved into the cage of muscle my body created, pressing her large tits against my chest.

"Are you going to teach me a lesson, Maverick?" she asked, her long, dark lashes lowering to frame her eyes.

She had my name inked on the inside of her lip and I leaned down to drive my teeth into it, amused by her worshipping me like that. If I was a god, I was the dark kind. The kind who drove fear into monsters' hearts and ate virgins for breakfast.

There was only one girl I was in the mood to fuck since I'd seen her at The Dungeon, but Mia was a decent substitute. I pushed her onto the bed, turning her over and smacking her bare ass so she cried out for more. I grabbed the back of her neck, forcing her down into the sheets as I dropped over her and spoke in her ear.

"If I find you here again without my permission, I'll kill you. Don't fucking test me," I snarled and she quivered, grinding her ass into my cock needily.

I freed my dick, running my hand up and down the tattooed length of it, a vision of rainbow hair wrapped in my fist making me even harder. I put on a condom and fucked Mia in the ass until she was screaming and begging for mercy, planning not to make her come, but she enjoyed this too much. Pain was pleasure to her. And that was fine by me. Because inflicting it was my fucking forte.

I let her stay when I was done, mostly because the girl was valuable to me and if I drove her away permanently, I'd shoot myself in the foot. She was the stepdaughter of Kaiser Rosewood, a man who currently inhabited a tightly locked down property which I wanted to get into. My first issue was that the manor was on Harlequin territory, so I couldn't just stroll up there, even if I brought an army of my men with me. It had to be done more subtly than that. If I went to that house, I was leaving with the contents of the crypt. I couldn't botch the job and risk alerting Kaiser to the value of that place. It was too precious. Because what lay in there could destroy the Harlequins. And help me get my revenge once and for all, even if it took me down with them.

Mia fell asleep beside me and I turned my back on her, closing my eyes in a bid for sleep to come. But it was never that easy. The nights were where my demons lived. And all that waited for me in the dark was a meeting with them eye to eye.

"I'll break you down and build you up into a real man," Officer White whispered in my ear.

I was in the trench, or so they called it. It was a maintenance level in the prison where there were no cameras. A place where there weren't any laws, nothing but me and four animals in the dark.

"Are you sure you wanna mess with Luther Harlequin's boy?" Reed chuckled.

"I'm not his boy," I bit out.

"See, I told you," White said.

"Is that why you never answer his calls, never see him when he comes to visitation?" Officer Hughes asked. "What happened to make you hate the big man, kid?"

"What are you, his fucking lap dogs?" I snarled.

They all laughed. All four of them. I'd thought the other inmates were bad, I'd feared what waited for me when the guards weren't looking. I'd never even thought to fear what would happen when they were.

One of them spat on the ground near where I was kneeling and I flinched. I hated that I flinched. I wouldn't do it again.

"Yeah, I'm a Harlequin just like your daddy," Boyd growled and the others laughed again. It was always a cold sound, no humour in it really, just cruelty. They goaded each other until it became a game. And I was their favourite plaything lately.

"He's not my father," I growled, tugging against the handcuffs locking my arms behind my back.

White kicked me in the jaw and pain splintered through my mouth until I tasted blood. Rage and hate and fear burned a hole in my chest and I cursed them, goading them myself because I knew they wouldn't stop until they'd had their pound of flesh either way.

"Hold him down," White commanded, smoothing back his shiny blonde hair that reminded me all too much of Luther and my brother. He pulled his

belt free of its loops and curled it around his fist. "Let's see how long it takes to break the skin."

I reached for my nightstand with a grunt, trying to force back the flashes of memory in my mind that sliced through my head like a knife. I took out the revolver that lay in the drawer and slipped out of bed, heading onto the balcony where the warm night air wrapped around my flesh like it was drawn to the cold in me.

I emptied the rounds into my hand, placing just one bullet back into the revolver, spinning the cylinder and loading it with a jerk of my wrist. Then I drew in a long and ragged breath before placing the barrel against my temple. The metal was bitingly cold like death itself.

My heartrate didn't increase, my breaths coming evenly as I gazed across the water in the direction of Harlequin territory. My old home. My enemies.

I pulled the trigger with a blind confidence and the click confirmed everything I already knew. Like it did every night. The odds were always the same. Six cylinders, one bullet. I'd done this every night since I'd left prison. And death hadn't taken me yet. So I knew with an unfaltering certainty that life would reside in my veins until I'd ripped every Harlequin from this world. Death was my only friend. And he'd given me another day. Another chance to make them bleed. And bleed they would.

CHAPTER EIGHTEEN

It was late and I was distracting myself from thoughts of Rogue by messing around with my boys. JJ had made sangrias and I swear him and Chase were trying to drink each other under the table. I'd decided to remain sober since Rogue's tracker had gone offline and she hadn't responded to any of my texts. If it wasn't for JJ and Chase insisting I give her space, I'd have tracked her ass down by now and she'd be firmly in my sights. But as I was trying this new thing called being 'reasonable', I'd promised myself I'd give it until two am before I went hunting. Just fifteen more minutes though and I'd be out looking, so she'd better hide well if she didn't want me to find her. I had the willpower of an army of men, but when it came to her I was rendered weak. Because it was her. And that was really all there was to it.

Chase's phone kept blowing up and I finally swiped it up and muted it. Rosie Morgan kept calling and Chase kept ignoring her. It was irritating as fuck.

"At least text her to shut her up." I tossed the phone at Chase who sat across the table from me on the patio.

He caught it and switched it off. "Problem solved."

"You're such an asshole," JJ said as he dropped down beside him.

dripping wet from his dip in the pool. "Just cut her off if you don't wanna fuck her anymore."

"Yeah, the girl annoys the fuck out of me anyway so you'd be doing me a favour," I said. I'd already banned her from being around when I was there. Her voice made my brain hurt.

"She's less annoying with my cock in her mouth," Chase reasoned, lighting up a cigarette. "And I kinda enjoy seeing how long I can keep her quiet for. Though when she comes it's like a siren going off."

"I know, man, I heard her when you fucked her in the restroom at that club on New Year's." JJ tipped his head back and started doing an impression. "Chasey, Chasey-pie! Oh surf and turf me!" He made a noise like a sealion, clapping his hands and bouncing in his seat and Chase roared a laugh while I chuckled.

"Dude, I thought she was right in front of me for a second," Chase said. "But you can't exactly complain about the noise after that fucking sex contest you held in the room next to me in that hotel we stayed in in Lantern Bay. It sounded like you were fucking a whole pod of dolphins."

I chuckled. I had a strict no orgies rule in the house which had had to be implemented because when JJ and Chase got drunk together, shit got weird. But so long as they kept their weird elsewhere, I didn't give a fuck.

JJ smirked. "I just had to know if I could make an entire bridal party come in under an hour. The bride was a squealer. And I did her twice 'cause I'm generous like that."

I swiped up my phone, checking it again, my mind stuck on the only girl in the world I gave a fuck about. And I happened to give all my fucks about this one.

"Still haven't heard from her then?" Chase asked me and I shrugged, tossing my phone from one hand to the other. "She's probably gone forever then."

"Shut up, man," JJ shoved him in the face as I glared at him.

My phone rang and I answered it before I even checked the caller ID. "Hey, where are you?"

"What's it to you?" a deep male voice came down the line and I cursed internally, jamming my thumb on the speaker phone so JJ and Chase could hear.

"Shit, hey Dad," I said.

"Who were you expecting?"

"Just a girl," I muttered, pushing a hand into my hair as I shared a look with the guys. Telling Rogue that Luther Harlequin was dead hadn't exactly been the smartest move, considering she was gonna find out we'd lied one way or another. But I couldn't have her running off again because of him. I could handle my dad. I just needed to figure out how to unfuck the situation first. Because by Harlequin law, he was bound to kill Rogue if she ever came back to town. But I wasn't some kid anymore. He'd left me in charge of Sunset Cove. It was mine to rule. So my word meant something to him now. But that didn't mean he was going to forget about the code either.

"How's it going in Sterling?" I asked to change the subject.

Dad rarely came back to town these days. He was running a bigger division of the Harlequins up in Highbridge County, claiming new territory and pushing back our rivals The Dead Dogs. We'd brokered peace with them several years back, but since some asshole Shawn Mackenzie had taken over, he'd started fighting to claim territory from us again. I'd thought he was just some redneck nobody up until the day he and his gang had killed eleven of our men, ripped out their goddamn insides and written his gang name in their blood right on the fucking street. Dad was dealing with the brunt of his shit. He hadn't attempted to claim any of my turf down here yet, but we were ready for when he did. I had my men recruiting left, right and centre, and if he wanted a war, he'd picked the wrong fucking crew to come at.

"Shawn took a hit last night. We drove the message home good, but the fucking scumbag isn't giving up easy. If he moves south, I need you on standby," Dad said.

"We can handle him," I growled. "Do you want me to come up there?" I asked, though the thought of leaving Rogue behind pained me. But I had duties I couldn't ignore, and if Dad needed more men on the front line, I'd be the first to fucking volunteer.

"No, boy," he growled and I hated that he still called me that. "How's Sunset? Has Maverick cooled off yet?"

JJ rolled his eyes and I had to agree with that. My dad did not get the fucking message that Maverick was a turncoat psycho who was never coming home. He still held onto the hope that I could bring the asshole to heel, whatever the fuck that meant. Maverick had never been tame, but Dad didn't seem to remember things right.

"He's our enemy," I hissed. "Him and his gang killed eight of our men the other day. He cut off John Merkle's head."

"Ah shit," Dad sighed. "Merkle won't easily be replaced."

"Is that all you give a shit about?" I demanded.

"Maverick's just having a tantrum. He was always like that as a kid."

"It's been ten years," I said in exasperation, biting down on my tongue. "One of these days, either I'll end up dead or he will." I could taste blood in my mouth and realised I'd bitten too hard.

"Yeah, which is why I'm getting tired of how long it's taking to broker peace with him," Dad said in a gruff tone that made my heart pound. Luther was the scariest motherfucker in the pacific west, but I wasn't some child he could boss around anymore. My reputation was as fierce as his these days and I wasn't going to listen to this bullshit.

"He's a dead man," I snarled.

"He's your brother," Dad pushed. "We're fucking family. Harlequins don't kill Harlequins."

"He's a Damned Man," I snapped, my blood heating. "He started this war, but I'll put an end to it with a bullet in his skull."

"Watch your mouth, son," Dad warned. "You kill him and there'll be consequences."

"You're fucking delusional," I snapped. "He's not the kid you brought up, why don't you come on down here and see how quickly he points a gun at your head?" I said heatedly, while JJ and Chase shared a look. But I knew my dad wouldn't really come down here anytime soon. And even if he did, I'd have good warning. I'd hide Rogue before he got within ten miles of Sunset Cove.

"He's lost his way," Dad pushed, his sharp tone saying he wasn't going to be talked around on this. I'd already tried a hundred times anyway, I didn't know why I still bothered. But sooner or later, he was gonna have to face a dead Maverick or a dead me. I couldn't see it ending any other way.

"God, if that fucking girl hadn't messed up all your heads, I wouldn't have to deal with this bullshit," Dad muttered and a blade of ice twisted in my chest.

"Well I could say the same about you sending Maverick to prison," I spat and arctic silence fell on the line.

I remembered the day Rick had been taken away as vividly as if it was etched behind my eyes. I'd thought losing Rogue had broken my heart as deeply as possible, but it turned out there had been more pieces waiting to shatter. My adopted brother had been sent down for killing Axel and I'd had to tell him I couldn't help. Look him in the eye and let the cops drag him away. I'd been angry at him for risking Rogue's life by searching for her even after Dad had threatened to kill her if we dared try. But that anger would have passed. He had still been my brother back then. And I knew I'd let him down, but fuck, there hadn't been another option. Even if I'd given him an alibi for Axel's murder or offered to take the fucking prison sentence myself, my dad already had every cop in town in his pocket. The deal was done. I couldn't have changed it any easier than I could have torn down the sky that day. I knew he'd be angry when he got out of prison, but I'd never expected…

I pressed my fingers into my eyes, banishing the ghosts of my past. It was far too late for regrets and guilt now. Maverick had changed. He wasn't my brother. He was my enemy. And I had the scars to prove it.

"Well maybe that bitch of yours shouldn't have killed one of my men," Dad scoffed and the word bitch made my hackles rise and my teeth grit. "Anyway, I don't wanna talk about some long forgotten ghost, I'm calling about the Torres deal. They wanna run a trial with us. We need to shift a hundred kilos in the next couple of weeks and I want the shipment to come into the marina. I want you to make arrangements to collect it. You'll need a van and a few strong men there next Thursday at three am."

"Got it," I said curtly, shifting my mind onto business. "I'll get Pascal to store it. Have you got buyers?"

"Not yet, I'm working on it. I'll call soon."

"Alright."

"Love you, kid." He hung up before I replied because I never said it back and he hated that. I'd stopped saying it the same day he sent Rogue away.

Sometimes I was pretty fucking sure I hated him, other times I was indifferent, and once in a blue moon, I missed him.

"Rogue is gonna castrate us when she finds out we lied about Luther being dead," JJ said, miming chopping off his own balls.

"I don't think we can piss her off any more than we already have," Chase commented with a shrug.

"She'll get over it," I said firmly. "We have to figure out how to handle it first."

"And what if she like...I dunno, asks anyone in town about him?" JJ frowned.

"Why would she?" I asked, though I'd be lying if I said I hadn't considered it. It hadn't exactly been planned, I'd just spur of the moment lied and that was that. "Just keep it locked down until we can figure out a way to deal with it." I pushed out of my seat, tucking my phone into my jeans' pocket.

"Where are you going?" Chase frowned and JJ cocked his head.

"He's going Rogue stalking," JJ said with a knowing smirk and I shrugged as I headed past them.

"Night assholes," I called.

"Bring her home safe," JJ laughed.

"Or don't," Chase added and I shot him a scowl before heading to the garage and grabbing my truck keys on the way down.

Chase talked a big game about sending Rogue out of town again, but the way he looked at her when he thought no one was watching told a different story. He was happy she was back, even if he wouldn't voice it to anyone, not even himself. It was the only reason I hadn't beaten his ass for his shitty behaviour. We all had history with her. We'd all had our hearts ripped out. And I knew Chase; this was how he dealt with his emotions. He blocked them out and pretended they didn't exist until they came crashing in on his head.

He was gonna have to deal with them one way or another, because the girl was mine and she wasn't going anywhere. If she ran, I'd find her. This time, no one could stop me.

I slid into my truck and checked my phone again. Her cell wasn't giving me any location, but I had another way to track her. I brought up the app on my phone and waited for the location to show up from the tracker I'd installed in her new Jeep. My jaw gritted as the location appeared. It was at fucking Rejects Park. She must have been hanging out with some of the girls who lived there. And I didn't see the harm in a quick drive by to check she hadn't gotten any homicidal ideas about cosying up to some trash in his trailer. Because if she had, he was dead. I'd plant two bullets in his chest and one between the eyes for good measure. Then I'd string him up at the heart of the trailer park as an example to anyone else who thought it was a good idea to hit on my girl. I pressed my foot down on the gas pedal as I closed in on her. *She wouldn't dare.*

I soon turned into the park which sat on the edge of the beach down near the pier. I drove my truck down the track which was definitely not intended for vehicles and did a circuit of the park, looking out for her, but the place was dead quiet. I located her Jeep in the parking lot beyond the park between a group of trees and my blood started to burn. What if she was fucking some cunt in one of these trailers just feet away from me? I knew for a fact Carter Jenson lived down here and if she was rubbing shoulders with him again I was going to cut his fucking head off.

I clutched the steering wheel tighter, my pulse thumping at the base of my skull. I drove back into the park, slowing as I approached a white cabin with the words Park Owner painted on the door. I pulled up, stepping out of my truck and hammering my fist on it. There were grunts and groans coming from inside and I scowled impatiently as I continued to bang on the door.

"Just a second!" a man said breathily.

I ripped the door open, nearly taking the thing off its hinges and I came face to face with a hairy ass crack.

"Jesus," I muttered, backing up and the guy hurriedly pulled up his pants, ushering a scantily dressed woman out the door.

"What the fuck?" he rounded on me, but paled the second he set eyes on my face.

"Yeah," I said. "That's the fuck. Have you seen a rainbow haired girl around here? She's got tattoos, real pretty, belongs to me."

His eyes widened and he cleared his throat. "Oh er, Rogue, isn't it?"

"Yeah," I said urgently. "You know her?

"She rents a trailer here."

Acid seeped into my blood and made my head spin like crazy. "Well I'm gonna need a key to that trailer," I gritted out. She lived here? In this dump full of deadbeats and dangerous assholes? The only dangerous asshole she should have been sleeping within ten feet of was me. She seriously preferred the idea of being here than in my house with a private pool and en-suite and everything else she could ever fucking need?

The guy gaped at me, smoothing back his greasy black hair and mopping sweat from his brow. "Oh, well...that's not really the park policy, see?"

I took my gun from the back of my pants and pointed it at his head. "I don't live by other people's policies."

"Right, of course. Mind my manners." He wiped his hand down his jeans and held it out to me as if I might be tempted to shake it. "I'm Joe McCreevy, owner and caretaker of this fine park."

I ignored his sweaty hand and placed my finger on the trigger. "The key," I growled and he nodded quickly, turning away and disappearing before returning with a bunch of keys and shimmying one off of the ring. He handed it to me and pointed down the track. "All the way to the end and turn left. It's number twenty-two, the little blue one. But um...she's not there, ya know?"

My pulse roared in my ears. "Where is she?" I asked in a deadly tone.

"Well I don't know exactly, but she and a bunch of the Rejects headed out to town somewhere. I dunno more than that."

I was about to leave when I paused and turned back. "Was Carter Jenson with them?"

"Er yeah, now I think of it. He was."

Anger rolled through me like a dark sea. "What trailer is his?"

"Third one on the right up that ways." He pointed and I nodded, stalking back to my truck and driving it toward Carter's trailer. I got out of the car, stepped up to the door and twisted the handle. It was locked but one hard kick sent it flying open and I walked inside, gazing around his little shithole from the dirty boxers on the floor, to the washing up in the sink.

I spotted a wad of cash on his nightstand and grabbed a zippo lighter from beside the cooker, humming as I carried the money to the sink and lit it up in a mini bonfire. I dropped it into the sink, letting it burn until it was thoroughly fucked up then ran the water on it so little pieces of green floated in it, just enough so he could tell what it had once been. Then I rummaged through his kitchen drawers, took a steak knife out and plucked a chicken from the fridge. I left it on the side and stabbed the knife into it before grabbing a sharpie from a table and writing on the surface beside the butchered bird. *What part of stay away from my girl did you not understand, dead boy?*

I tossed the sharpie onto the floor, left the fridge wide open and headed back outside, tucking the zippo into my pocket. Maybe I should have just killed the guy, but I guessed he could have one more chance. Assuming he hadn't laid hands on my girl of course. *Look at me all reasonable and shit. The guys would be so proud.*

I was about to get back in my truck when chatter reached me from behind the next trailer along and I wouldn't have given it a moment of my attention, only I heard my girl's name being mentioned. So I slipped into the shadows, creeping around the side of the trailer and throwing a glance out behind it where two guys were sat around sipping beer beside a smoking barbecue.

"-those tits man. They look juicy as fuck," one of them said, miming squeezing and licking some fake tits in front of his face and anger raced beneath my flesh.

"I'd wrap all that unicorn hair in my fist while she sucked my dick good," the other replied and I ran my tongue over my teeth then stepped right out into their little fiesta.

"Evening boys," I said in a dangerous tone that had made bigger men than them shit themselves.

"Oh fuck," the long haired one gasped, his beer almost comically held under his mouth as he forgot to drink it. The other one stood from his fold-out chair, his eyes wide and horrified. "Y-you're, y-you're-"

"Fox Harlequin," I supplied for the speechless idiot, snatching a beer from the ice bucket beside his chair.

I cracked it open and took a long swig, letting them squirm as they waited to find out what I wanted. They weren't gonna like it though.

I drained the beer, tossed the can and shoved chair boy back into his chair. It folded up on him and he hit the ground with a yelp of fear. I turned towards the other guy and smacked the beer out of his hand, grabbing his shirt in my fist and yanking his bearded face close to mine. "You ever speak about Rogue Easton like that again and I'll cut your dick off and force feed it to your mother."

"I'm sorry, m-man," he stammered and I grabbed his long hair in my fist, making him scream as I hauled him over to the barbeque, flipped it open and slammed his cheek down on the grill. He wailed like a little bitch and I shoved him to the ground just to make him shut the fuck up. His friend was running into the trailer, slamming the door shut and I took the zippo from my pocket, strolling over to it and lighting up the dry grass underneath it.

Oh wow that shit goes up like tinder.

I wedged a broom I found lying on the porch against the door so that he wouldn't be getting back out again too easily and headed back to my truck, slipping inside and checking my phone for any calls from Rogue.

Nothing. *For fuck's sake.*

I revved the engine and drove up the track, finding her blue trailer. I drove past it and parked up between a few trees at the end of the track where the shadows concealed my vehicle.

Someone was shouting "Fire!" in the distance and the scent of smoke was carrying to me. Not my problem really.

I walked up to Rogue's trailer, frowning at the tiny size of it then banging my fist on the door, pushing my fingers into my hair to straighten it out. Mutt started barking furiously inside, but no answer came from Rogue so I took out my new key and pushed it into the lock, opening the door and stepping inside. The sweet, coconut smell of her surrounded me and I pushed the door shut, breathing her in. Fuck. She was everywhere in this place. I'd missed this smell for so fucking long, I'd forgotten how good it was.

Mutt suddenly rushed me, attempting to maul my leg and I swooped down and tucked the little bastard under my arm. "Hush it, shitbag."

I flicked a light on, assessing the place, moving through the tiny kitchen and finding some treats for Mutt which immediately stopped him gnawing on my arm. I investigated the area as I left him to eat. There was a busted knob on the cooker but the place was generally in good condition apart from that. I pushed open the door to the bathroom which was barely big enough to turn around in and a had a tap missing on the sink. I tutted then sought out her bedroom and frowned at the sight of her empty bed. I'd been expecting it, but it was still frustrating. *Where are you, hummingbird?*

I considered searching the streets of Sunset Cove, but chances were she'd end up back here eventually. So my best option was to wait until she showed up.

She couldn't seriously want to live here over living in my fucking house.

I clenched my jaw and walked over to her nightstand, pulling the top drawer open and finding a pile of condoms, a vibrator and a notebook. I scooped out the condoms with a growl in my throat, walking back to the kitchen, finding a pair of scissors and cutting them all in half before tossing them in the trash. The idea of her using those with some fucking worthless asshole got my blood hot again and I cursed under my breath, wishing I knew how to make her see that I was the only guy for her.

Mutt finished his treats and returned to growling at me, but I ignored him.

I killed another few minutes before I realised I was gonna go insane just waiting here, so I pushed out the front door again, the sound of a fire engine drawing close as I walked along to the next trailer that looked empty and forced the door open. I stole a knob for the cooker and a tap for the sink then returned to Rogue's trailer and started fixing the cooker first. I twitched the curtain aside as flashing red and blue lights appeared in the park, a plume of smoke illuminated by them where the fire was raging. It didn't take them too long to put it out, so I guessed it hadn't spread. Seemed like a lesson well learned to me.

When I'd fixed the cooker and the sink, I headed to Rogue's bedroom again, kicked my shoes off and laid down on the patchwork quilt that adorned her bed. Fuck, that scent. I turned to smell her pillow like a crazy person and was glad I didn't have any witnesses to that shit. I'd accepted that Rogue made me insane a long time ago. My mind was lost and I didn't care to look for it. Because she was back. And that was all I'd wanted for so long that it'd been hard to remember what it was like before the last ten years had happened.

I think I'd been happy once. Now I only existed, did what had to be done, looked after my boys and just survived. For all the sunshine in this town, it had been as dark as winter for me since Rogue had left. But my light was finally back and I feared it going out again more than anything in the world. I was empty without her, soulless. I'd become a monster in the time we'd been parted and maybe she was never going to want me like this. But I had to try. I couldn't be a good person for her, but I could be someone who always

353

protected her, who gave her fucking everything. I'd carve a slice out of the moon if that was what my girl wanted. I'd figure out a way to get it done. She just had to say the word.

I pushed out of bed again in frustration. Where the fuck was she? It was almost three am now and there was no sound of any partying assholes returning home from their night out. I took my phone out, shooting her another text, but I was starting to think it was pointless. Was she always going to hate me like this? What the fuck was I supposed to do to make it right?

I'd dated a sum total of zero girls in any real way since she'd left. And before she'd left I'd dated zero girls period. I didn't want anyone but her, I'd known that at a preciously young age. I'd been one intuitive fucker, I guess. But I knew the value of people like her. People who made everything worthwhile. People who listened and cared and gave their whole heart to you. I'd fucking ruined that when I was supposed to hold onto it no matter what. I just hadn't had a choice. But this was my fucking second chance. So maybe I wasn't going about it the right way, but I just couldn't fucking give up.

I took Rogue's vibrator from her drawer, envious of the damn thing. Better this than other men, but still. The asshole had been inside my girl without my permission, and I had some rage to vent. I dropped it to the floor, stamping on the smug little bastard, cracking it open as it took the full force of my rage. It started vibrating angrily and I stomped harder on the defiant rubber dick, booting it to death until the batteries rolled out. When it was in pieces, I kicked it under the bed and smiled satisfactorily. If the machines rose up and took over the world, I'd officially be naming myself the Vibratornator.

I walked over to Rogue's closet again, flipping the door wide and pausing as I spotted her new cellphone sitting on the shelf, switched off with the SIM card laying on top of it. That was almost enough to make me crack a fucking tooth, but I guessed I knew she wasn't actually ignoring my messages – she just wasn't getting them because she'd disabled the fucking phone and left it here.

I blew out a frustrated breath and opened her panty drawer. There was a sparkly little thong amongst the mix of sexy shit and panties with childish pictures on like ponies and rabbits, even a few with the Green Power Ranger. Apparently she wasn't over her little obsession with him and I kinda wanted to burn his face off of my girl's panties, but I knew she loved this shit so I guessed I could let it fly. I was being reasonable after all.

I pulled out the sparkly thong and was even more pleased when I realised it was rainbow coloured. I ran my thumb over the inside of it and found myself getting hard. Seriously fucking hard. I hadn't gotten laid since, ergh, fuck only knew. It was either the dancer chick or the nurse. But she'd definitely been brunette because I vaguely remembered fisting her hair while I bent her over something and pictured her as Rogue. *Story of my life.*

I wrapped Rogue's panties in my fist as my cock strained against my jeans and a groan escaped me. Where the fuck was she? Why wasn't she here? Was she out fucking some asshole in a club restroom?

I swore, fury bubbling under my flesh and I clenched her panties tighter. *No, she's mine. She wouldn't. She's fucking mine.*

I unbuttoned my jeans and squeezed the head of my throbbing cock through my boxers before figuring fuck it and dropping down onto her bed. I freed my dick and wrapped her panties around it in my fist, jerking myself off as lust and fury and possessiveness coiled inside me, desperate for an outlet. I rubbed my hard length in furious strokes, the feel of her little panties wrapped around it so good that it made me groan.

I was just a teenager in her goddamn bed, fucking my hand, wishing I was fucking her. Was I gonna live in torment like this forever? Was I really never gonna feel her riding my cock, her tight, wet pussy wrapped around every inch of me like I'd imagined for too many years?

"Fuck," I hissed as I squeezed the base of my dick and rubbed myself harder. Picturing her. I always pictured her. The real twenty six year old Rogue was even better than the version I'd concocted in my head. So much fucking better. Her tits were fuller, her tan more golden, her ass-

I groaned as I came into her panties, using them to soak up every drop of my cum. Mutt barked and I lifted my head, finding him watching me from the doorway, looking indignant.

"Don't judge me, you little asshole," I muttered and he scampered away.

I balled the panties in my fist, tucking my dick back into my boxers and buttoning my fly just as the front door banged open. I shoved the panties into my pocket, pushing a hand into my hair as my breaths came unevenly.

"Fuck, why are the lights on, Mutt?" Rogue's voice came from beyond the room and I got to my feet, walking to the door, but she pulled it open before I could.

She screamed bloody murder, diving at me with a fucking frying pan and I snatched her wrist before she could hit me over the head with it.

"Drop it," I commanded and her eyes went wide as she realised who was in her trailer, but I swear her grip on the frying pan tightened rather than loosened.

It took me one second to absorb the bruises and cuts on her and terror ripped through my core. She had bite marks on her damn throat and her lip was red and swollen. "What happened? Where the fuck have you been?" I wrenched the frying pan from her hand, tossing it behind me then caught her face in my grip to examine her closer. Concern coiled in my chest and I pushed past her, dragging her after me toward the bathroom.

"Get off of me, you psycho!" she cried, trying to peel my hand off of her arm.

I pushed her into the bathroom ahead of me while Mutt yapped and I followed her into the tiny space so she was basically tit to chest with me and there was no way out. "Who. Hurt. You?" My hands were curled into fists and murder was calling my name.

"It doesn't matter, because they're dead," she said and the breath went out of me in relief, but that didn't mean I was any less confused or angry. And it certainly didn't explain the bite marks on her throat.

"Tell me where you've been. How the fuck did you end up in this state?" I grabbed a towel, wetting it in the sink and tilting her chin up as I started dabbing at her split lip.

She winced but didn't pull away and I was glad as she let me work from cut to cut. It reminded me of the night she'd killed Axel, standing in his restroom as I checked her over for wounds, gave her clothes to get changed. It made me want to wrap her in cotton wool and never let her go.

"So you remember how you were all like 'don't go to The Divide'," she said in a terrible impersonation of me.

"You went to the fucking Divide?" I roared, crowding her in against the door to the shower, her body pressed flush to mine.

"I mean, I went to *a* Divide. Can't say for sure if it was *the* Divide. But Rick was there so I'm guessing-"

"Maverick?!" I bellowed in her face, panic pounding through me. "Did he do this to you?" I'd kill him. I'd take a boat, cross the fucking water to Dead Man's Isle and not stop shooting until he was bleeding out at my feet.

"He left the bite marks but not the rest," she growled defensively. For that asshole? Why? Why would she defend him? "He shot the pricks who did this to me. For a second I totally thought he was gonna shoot me too, but he didn't so…yay." She smiled, but then it fell away again.

"Why did he bite you?" I snarled.

"I dunno, because he's gone cuckoo?" she said and I had to agree with that statement.

"You didn't ask for it?" I asked in a tight voice.

"No," she scoffed.

"Who brought you home?" I demanded. "Was it Carter?"

"No. But I saw what you did to his face. Why the fuck did you do that?" She scowled at me, but I knew she didn't really give a shit about that little prick.

"Because he looked at what's mine."

"You mean me?" she scoffed.

"Yeah."

"I'm not yours."

"I asked you a fucking question. Who brought you home?" I demanded angrily and she huffed as she dropped the Carter bullshit and gave me my answer.

"No one. I took a car but it choked out and died several blocks after I got it and I had to walk back. Then one of my heels broke and I had to have a funeral for my shoes on the side of the road. A racoon came, but honestly I think he was just there for a mouldy bit of tuna sandwich someone had left on a-"

"Rogue," I growled, pinning her in place and pressing my forehead to hers. My heart was beating too hard like it was trying to fight its way out of my body into hers. "Why would you go there?" I rasped, the pain of it too much. Of all the places in all the fucking town, why there? Why towards him? Maybe

357

Chase was fucking right. She'd come back for Maverick.

My world started crumbling and I turned away, leaving her there, unsure how to handle this. I could keep her from everyone else. Anyone else. But if she went to him, if she chose him-

I threw my fist into the wall and carved a hole right through it into Rogue's bedroom and she gasped in surprise. This would break me. I couldn't fucking handle it if she was back in town for him. My adopted brother, the man I'd betrayed and who'd betrayed me right back. The man I was at war with, who'd tried to kill me, JJ and Chase.

I was shaking, the bloodlust inside me like a hungry beast that was desperate to be fed. Rogue's hand landed on my back and I couldn't look at her. I couldn't hear what she was going to say.

"It's okay, Badger. I'm home now. And I'm also like dead tired so I'm gonna be pissed about that hole in the morning instead of now," she joked, clearly trying to lighten the mood but I couldn't shake off this rage. Her hand slid further up my back and I didn't know if I wanted to hear the answer to my next question or not. But I had to know. Not knowing was worse than knowing. It had to be.

"Do you want him? Is that why you came back?" I asked gruffly and she took her hand away, her warmth, everything. All of her receded and it left the most hollow feeling in my chest. *Please don't leave again.*

"Rick?" she questioned and I nodded stiffly, my gaze fixed on the hole in the wall.

"I came back because my ex dumped me here in a grave," she said bitterly and if she was trying to calm me down, she was doing one hell of a job of it.

My back tensed and I shut my eyes as I tried to tame the possessive beast inside me that wanted to burn down the whole world so only she and I remained. It seemed like the only logical way to keep her safe in that second.

"Answer the other question," I prompted in a growl, every muscle in my body rigid as I waited for the axe to drop.

"I didn't come back for him. I didn't come back for any of you. I don't know what I'm really here for, or how long I'll stay, but…"

"But?"

"But I'm here now. At least for a while."

I opened my eyes, dragging in a deep breath and nodding. She was here for now. And I'd do whatever was within my power to make sure she remained here. I half turned, catching her hand and drawing her into the bedroom, pushing her toward the bed before tugging off my shirt.

"What the fuck are you doing, Badge?" she balked, but her eyes dropped to my abs, to the tattoos adorning my flesh then moved back up to my face which was set in a hardened, impenetrable, unnegotiable wall that said she was going to get nowhere refusing this. "I'm staying. End of discussion."

"You're so fucking bossy," she snapped. "Maybe I don't want you to stay, did you ever think of that?"

"No, and I don't give a shit." I grabbed her shoulders, turning her around and undoing the zip of her dress. It ran all the way down to her ass and she shivered as my fingers grazed the angel wings tattooed over her shoulder blades and running down the length of her back. I leaned down, kissing each of them and a little gasp escaped her as I tracked my finger down her spine. "I'd ruin you, baby. I'd prove there's no other man on earth who can make you feel the way I do. You deserve to be fucking worshipped. I'd show up at your church every day and get down on my knees for you. Every. Fucking. Day."

"How about you start by turning away while I get changed, because my church is closed," she said breathily and I watched her as she strode to her closet and picked out a pair of pyjamas which were a pale blue shorts and cami combo.

She let her dress fall to her ankles and my throat tightened at the sight of her ass framed by the lace of the black frenchies she wore. She had no bra on and it was the most tempting sight I'd ever seen in my life. I dropped my jeans, kicking them off with my socks and dropping down onto her bed.

"You don't sound like a person who's not looking," she said irritably but then she dropped her panties and I had to bite down on my damn fist to suppress a groan.

"What does a person who's not looking sound like?" I asked, my voice coming out rough and full of desire. I swear I could see the goosebumps spreading across her flesh from here, so why wouldn't she just admit she wanted me like I wanted her? Sure, I was an asshole, but at least I didn't try to hide that shit. I was genuine to a fucking fault. Wasn't that what girls were always demanding guys to be?

"I dunno, less watchy." She pulled on her pyjamas and turned to me, her eyes falling to the huge bulge in my boxers and her lips popped open. "You looked," she accused.

"Yeah, I looked," I growled. "Now get into bed."

I pulled the covers back and she shook her head.

"This is insane. I just wanted to come home and curl up in my bed and relax after the night I've had. But how am I supposed to do that when you're here making demands of me in my own fucking home?" She went full on pout lip and I shoved out of bed, lifting her into my arms and tossing her down onto the mattress.

"Hey!" she squealed.

"You can do those things with me," I insisted, dropping down beside her and drawing the covers up over us before switching the light out. My eyes quickly adjusted to the darkness, a crack in the curtains allowing the moonlight to filter in and I sighed, my heart beginning to slow at last.

"Don't go back to The Divide," I said firmly.

"I can look after myself," she insisted.

"I know," I admitted. "But if you wanna defy me, do it with your smart mouth and your ballsy attitude. Don't go there. Please Rogue."

She sighed. "Why are your possessive ways cute sometimes?"

I smirked. "I'm anything but cute, baby."

"I disagree."

"Did you go through my things while you were lurking in my house?" Rogue asked suspiciously and I was glad she'd decided not to fight this any harder.

"Yeah," I admitted, because she was gonna find the destroyed vibrator and condoms sooner or later.

"You're such a fucking dick," she said through a yawn and I shifted closer to her, seeking her hand out and brushing my thumb across her busted knuckles. I hated that she'd been fighting tonight but there was something hot about the fact that she'd won too.

"I know," I said. "But you missed me, right? Ten years is a long time, you must have thought about me. I thought about you every fucking day. You know it's not normal for a girl your age not to have social media? I searched every girl with a name that even sounded remotely liked yours. I even checked out a profile for a man called Raul Esteban."

She laughed and the sound lit me up from the inside. "Well like Chase says, I guess I'm a ghost."

"Aren't you going to tell me anything about where you've been?" I pushed. "Anything, Rogue. Just give me something."

"You don't deserve something," she said bitterly and I shifted closer, the heat of her body radiating against mine.

"I know, hummingbird," I said in a low tone. "But I'm asking anyway."

Silence pooled between us, then she spoke in a quiet tone that had my utter, rapt attention.

"Okay, I'll answer one question."

I opened my mouth and she spoke over me before I could ask who the fuck had hurt her.

"But not about the guy who buried me," she said firmly and I huffed.

"Fine. Tell me about your first boyfriend then."

"That's not a question," she sing songed and I clenched my fist.

"Was he good to you?"

"Well…he was okay at first, I guess. He took me out for meals which was like a serious appeal as I went hungry a lot back then. And he was nice sometimes I suppose. Especially before we erm, got serious… He had a nasty streak though. It was just a shame I didn't realise it sooner because I ended up kinda dependent on him, sleeping at his apartment and stuff. Because, you know, I had no home and all. But then one day we got into a dumb fight and he hit me. I punched him back and all, but that was it for me. So I took my shit and ended up sleeping in a bus stop for a week. An old lady bought me a ticket to another town eventually, so I guess it all worked out."

"Worked out?" I snarled, my blood pounding furiously through my veins. "That's not working out, baby. Jesus. What was the fucker's name?"

"Cody," she said.

"Surname?" I growled and she laughed.

"Hell no."

"He's dead, there won't be any traces back to you. Just give me a surname, age and-"

"Fox!" she smacked my arm. "You're not killing him, what's the matter with you?"

I tried to calm myself down, but I felt like a rhino about to charge. Rogue's fingers brushed up and down my arm and the sensation drew all of my focus until I could finally think clearer again. Clearer about his imminent death, that is.

I pulled her into my arms, just holding her and she actually melted into my body, her breath skating against my chest. When she finally pulled away, I trailed my fingers along her jaw and down to her throat where her pulse pounded wildly. I smirked at feeling her reaction to me. She could fight me all she wanted, but her heart wanted me. And I'd find a way to win it somehow.

"Your body's a traitor, hummingbird," I purred and she smacked my hand away.

"You've obviously been the big bad Harlequin in this town for a while, Badger, and it's gone to your head. Not every girl wants you, and I'm one of them."

I clenched my teeth in irritation. "But you want Maverick?"

"I never said that."

"He killed my uncle a few years back, you know? Dragged him to Gallows Bridge, cut deep wounds into his thighs, bound him by the arms and threw him over the bridge to hang there on a rope while he bled out. By the time we arrived, it was too late. That's no fucking way for a good man to die. For *family* to die."

She remained quiet and I sighed.

"I'm only telling you because I care about you," I said seriously. "If he ever hurt you-"

"He wouldn't," she said like she really believed that.

"You don't know him anymore," I growled.

She reached out, seeking the scar on my neck Maverick had left there with a bullet and grazing her thumb over it. "Maybe it's a miracle I came back to find you all alive," she breathed.

"Would you have cared if we weren't?" I asked, my throat constricting.

"Yes," she gasped immediately then hurried on. "But that doesn't make anything okay."

"I know. So let me make it okay. And stop fucking lying to my face about how you feel."

"I hate you," she growled, but there was no bitterness in it like usual.

"But you want me too," I pushed. "The rest is minor details."

I ran my hand down her neck, waiting for her to catch my wrist, to tell me no, but as my fingers brushed her hardened nipple through her top, a breathy noise escaped her that told me all I needed to know. I grabbed her hips, swinging her up to straddle me and she yelped in surprise. I ground her against my cock and she gasped then slapped me hard across the face. I swore, rearing up and biting her nipple through the thin material of her pyjamas, making her claw at me and hiss in pain.

"Ow – asshole!" she shouted and I started sucking through the material instead as her hips rocked over my rigid length, making me groan. "*Fox*," she snarled, locking her hands around my throat and pushing me back.

I looked up at her darkly, my patience wearing thin with this shit. She was quivering on my cock, so why couldn't she just give in to this fire raging between us? I had anger in me too over everything that had happened. It wasn't her fault, but I could be angry at the world. I could be angry at the injustice of it all.

She squeezed my throat tighter as she glared at me and I frowned, reaching up and locking one hand around hers in response.

"You're mine," I demanded and her thighs clenched, her hips rocking so her pussy ground against my dick and another curse fell from my lips.

"I'll never be yours," she hissed.

I forced her hands away and leaned up, clutching her ass and holding her in place against me.

"Tell me no then," I whispered, my lips brushing hers. "Say it."

I teased her full lower lip between my teeth and she moaned, her back arching as she pressed into me. "I hate you," she reiterated, a shudder running through the whole length of her body as she rolled her hips again, sending pleasure sparking through my cock.

"It gets harder to believe every time you say it, baby." I smirked against her mouth and her fingernails dragged down my back, my muscles flexing under her vicious touch. "I want anything you have to give me, hummingbird. Fight me, cut me, leave your mark on me. Whatever makes you feel better, but I'm not going anywhere. I've laid my claim and you'll have to summon an army of demons from hell if you want any chance of keeping me away from you."

"I don't need an army of demons, Fox," she said breathlessly, grinding on me again and drawing a deep noise of pleasure from my throat.

She abruptly swung her leg over me and got off the bed, scooping up my clothes and marching out of the room.

"Hey!" I barked, jumping to my feet and stalking after her with testosterone clouding my fucking head.

I found her tossing my shit out the front door and spat a snarl, lunging at her and catching a fistful of her hair. I wheeled her around, driving her against the wall and slamming my mouth against hers. She clawed at my shoulders, fighting me back, but I hooked one of her legs over my hip and drove my rigid cock between her thighs, rubbing it against her clit through the thin clothes parting us.

She moaned loudly, her head falling back against the wall and I pushed my tongue between her lips. She kissed me as fiercely as she clawed at me, tearing bloody marks across my flesh as I laughed into her mouth.

Rogue yanked her thigh free of my grip, kicking off the wall and sending me stumbling backwards until my ass hit the kitchen counter. I clutched her against me, lifting her up and forcing her thighs to wrap around my waist as she bit my tongue then kissed me hungrily, her hands locking in my hair one second before tearing at me the next. She tasted like she belonged to me and I was going to make sure I was branded on her so thoroughly tonight that she'd never question who owned her ever again.

She broke our kiss with a face like thunder. "Fuck you, asshole."

I shoved her back against the wall hard enough to bruise, ripping her hands off of me and pinning them above her head as I dropped my mouth to her throat. Her thighs squeezed my waist like she was trying to hurt me and she wriggled one hand free of my hold as I forgot to care, lost in the presence of her. Nothing she did could hurt. I'd craved her touch for too long, and I didn't care if she wanted to burn me at the fucking stake, I'd still enjoy her fucking company while I went up in flames.

I sucked her throat, wanting to brand her skin and wipe away the marks Maverick had left to her. She cursed, trying to force my head away from her while she continued to grind her pussy on me. I left a bright red hickie on her throat before lowering my mouth to do the same to her breasts and she shoved my head back, fighting to get her other hand free as I tightened my grip on it. She caught a picture frame from the wall, smashing it over my head and I swore as I dropped her, shaking the glass from my hair. Mutt barked loudly and I knocked the box of chicken treats onto the floor so they scattered everywhere and he fell on them with a yip of excitement.

"Those are expensive, motherfucker." Rogue threw a fist at me and I knocked it aside, capturing her face in my palms and kissing her once more.

"God you're a piece of shit," she growled against my lips, but continued kissing me as I smirked, drowning in the perfect taste of her. She started backing up and I followed her in the direction of the bedroom, knocking something over as I went and Rogue pulled away to look at what it was.

"What the fuck?" she balked and I glanced down at our feet where a bunch of chopped up condoms had been knocked out of the trash can.

"We don't need one, I'm clean," I promised, pushing her back towards the bedroom and her eyebrows shot up. *And you are too considering I took blood from you while you were sleeping and had you tested to make sure.* The numbing cream had worked like a dream and she slept like the dead anyway so I probably could have managed without it.

"Excuse me?" she hissed, folding her arms as she stood in the doorway to her room and covered up her peaked nipples through her top.

"What?" I demanded, placing a hand on the doorframe, gazing down at her with the very last few seconds of restraint I had. I was going to go full caveman on her and she was going to find out exactly what being claimed by me felt like.

"Er, firstly, you don't get to make choices like that for my body, dipshit. And secondly, what right do you have coming in here and cutting those up? This is my home."

"It's not your home. And I'm not fucking you with a condom. I've waited too long to-"

"Get out," she snarled, pointing at the door. "I'm not fucking you. I was never planning on fucking you."

"Liar," I growled and she stepped forward and shoved me in the chest. Mutt lifted his head from the treats, barking at me and I released a noise of fury. "You're not kicking me out."

"Yeah, I am actually. Because if you don't leave right this second, you're never gonna see me again, Fox."

A painful lump rose in my throat and I shook my head, refusing to accept that she was playing that card. "Don't do that."

She pointed at the door and I bared my teeth. She lifted her chin, daring me to defy her and I cursed her for being my damn weakness.

"Fine," I hissed. "But if you don't come to the house tomorrow, I'm moving you out of this shitty trailer park and you'll never see any of your trashy friends again. You're dating me whether you like it or not."

I stepped out of the door and she slammed it in my face, shouting through the door. "I'm not dating you, asshole. I have a perfectly stable, no-drama relationship going with my vibrator!"

"Not anymore you don't," I snapped then her footsteps pounded through the trailer.

"Argh!" she roared. "You monster. Why would you do this to Vlad?!"

RIP Vlad. I gathered up my clothes, smiling in satisfaction, though it didn't last long considering my aching dick and the fact that I'd just been turfed out on my ass. This was my punishment for what I'd done ten years ago. Having her back had been my only dream for all that time, but I'd never considered having her back and not being able to actually have her. It was a whole different kind of hell. And if I didn't claim her soon, my dick was going to fall off from lack of use. But my lips still tasted of her and as pissed as I was, I had felt her grind on me, heard her moans, felt her desire as it shook the foundations of her body. Maybe she only wanted to fuck me, but that was a start. So I was calling it a win.

I reached my truck, unlocking it and dumping my shit in the passenger seat before climbing into the driver's side. I pulled on my jeans and shoes, carving my fingers through my hair as sexual frustration made me want to go on a killing spree. I could just see the news headline now. *Ten men found dead with their dicks cut off because Fox Harlequin had blue balls.*

I sighed, starting up the truck and pulling it round to park up in front of Rogue's trailer. Then I dropped my seat back and started plotting out where exactly I was going to install the secret cameras outside this place. I needed to make sure I could keep her safe when I wasn't here. Because I couldn't always be here to watch her, especially when she was making it so fucking hard to be her boyfriend. But Rogue was worth the effort. I had zero experience in this shit, but I was going on my gut instincts and that was to protect her, keep her, and never let her go. So that was exactly what I planned on doing.

Rejects Park

ROGUE

CHAPTER NINETEEN

I woke up with a groan, pressing my tongue to my busted lip and flinching away from the pain of it. Kissing that asshole had clearly been a bad idea so far as that injury went. And so far as bad ideas went too. Because Fox Harlequin was a very, very, bad idea.

If he got his dick inside me, that was it. He would never ever get the message that he didn't own me. And I didn't want to be owned. Especially because, despite the big game I talked, I knew in my heart that I'd never really been free in any other place than this one before. And here in my little trailer with my little dog, I actually had something that was just…mine.

Sure, I might have been willing to cut and run from any and every situation I'd found myself in before now because I kept my emotions out of any and all connections I'd formed with people. Especially boyfriends.

But in my heart, I knew that Shawn had been the one who had come closest to owning me before. I hadn't even wanted to get close to anyone high up in the gang hierarchy, but the problem with being criminally addicted in my occupations was that it meant that wherever I found myself, I always ended up tied to the less than legal rulers of the place. And for anywhere around here for miles and miles, that meant falling in beneath one gang or another and having to bend to their rules.

It turned out that in the town of Sterling where I'd rocked up a few years back, The Dead Dogs ran everything. And everyone with a criminal inclination was expected to pass their takings through them if they expected to be allowed to continue to operate.

That was how I'd met Shawn and I couldn't deny that he'd drawn me in right away. He was just one of those dudes with the biggest balls in the room and the hardest glare. His aura made everyone look his way and when I found him looking back, I'd made the dumb decision to encourage it. Call it dick blindness, but every girl craved powerful cock from time to time, right? And it turned out that once he'd had a taste of me, he'd decided that he wanted another and another until somehow, I became his.

Not that he'd ever stopped fucking other girls apparently, as I'd found out the night he'd tried to kill me. But I was the one he claimed publicly, the one he wanted most often and the one who was dumb enough to think that was a sweet enough deal at the time.

But sweet and Shawn really weren't combinations that mixed and I had been an idiot to fool myself into believing that he was more hooked on me than he clearly was.

I'd been with him for over a year before I realised I wasn't ever going to be allowed to leave on my own terms. And it had been more than two years when he decided to kill me and dump my ass back here.

Fucking Shawn.

Thinking about him hurt. Not because I'd ever loved him - he was too cold for that, too unreachable and I dunno, depraved, I guessed. He had that piece of him missing. There wasn't a heart beating in his chest, it was just a cold, dark, power hungry void. And that had been just fine by me until I'd realised that meant I was yet again disposable.

I probably should have run long before it got to that point, but I was dumb enough to think he liked fucking me so much that he'd keep me around long term and I really didn't have anywhere else to go. So now here I was. A dead girl walking, thrown away once again.

I pushed out of bed, showered, made coffee then headed out onto my tiny deck to drink it in the light of the rising sun.

But the moment I pushed the door open and Mutt shot out to go pee, I froze.

There, parked up right in front of my trailer in a space that was not big enough at all, down a path absolutely not intended for cars, was a big ass black truck with a big ass blonde asshole asleep behind the wheel.

What. The. Fuck?

I placed my mug of coffee down and stalked back inside with my eyes narrowed and fury in my veins. Who the fuck did he think he was to just dominate my fucking life like this?

I stormed to my room, yanking open the door to my little closet and quickly dressing in a pair of denim shorts, a bikini top with an oversized blue tank over the top of it and a black baseball cap. I topped the look off with the pink sunglasses that had formerly belonged to JJ and a pair of white tennis shoes.

I glanced in the mirror at the various scrapes and bruises I'd acquired, taking a moment to look at the hickies on either side of my throat.

As my gaze slid between the two of them, a blush heated my cheeks and I had to fight it off as I thought about the fact that both of them had had their mouths on me last night. It was a damn shame they were both assholes though because I was starting to feel the need to get laid with a quiet kind of desperation that I was seriously going to have to work on soon.

I shoved those distracting ideas aside and focused on the task at hand, releasing a harsh breath.

Then I strode back to my little kitchen, poured a glass of water and headed outside to clear out my Fox problem.

It was too hot to be sleeping in freaking trucks, so Fox had left his windows down before leaning his chair right back and kicking his feet up onto the dash. It looked uncomfortable as fuck and I wished him a cricked neck for his troubles. He had a pistol in his lap, his hand curled loosely around it, but I was willing to bet the cocky motherfucker believed no asshole would ever dare try and sneak up on him in his own turf. More fool him.

I stalked towards him, lifted the glass and dumped the contents in his lap with a wicked smirk.

"What the fuck?" Fox bellowed, shoving himself upright and glaring around like he was hunting for a head to rip off while raising his pistol.

"Morning, asshole, time to go," I said as he opened his door to leap out of the truck.

I smirked at him tauntingly as water dripped down his bare chest making me think about the way he'd pressed those muscles against me last night, the way he'd kissed me, ground his hard cock between my thighs and-

Damn, that backfired fast.

I worked to fight off the oh so tempting thoughts of this particularly pushy motherfucker and turned to jog back up onto my porch to escape him.

"Where are we going?" Fox demanded as he stalked after me. His heavy footsteps making my little wooden porch tremble as he closed in on me.

He clearly hadn't realised that I'd meant it was time for *him* to go and I wasn't planning on joining him, but one look into his psycho eyes told me I wouldn't get rid of him that easily, so I came up with an alternative on the spot.

"Shopping," I said sweetly, turning around to smile at him over the rim of my coffee.

"Why do you look so freaking happy?" he grunted. "Isn't this the part where you start yelling again?"

"I don't think so," I replied with a shrug. "I think that's what you want. To get me all hot and bothered and fired up. So I've decided to play you at your own game instead."

"What's that supposed to mean?" he asked, reaching out to take my coffee from me and drinking the half of it I hadn't gotten to yet. Motherfucker.

I wanted to dick slap him for that alone, but I sucked in a deep breath and blew it out through my nose, forcing myself to stay calm.

"First of all, I think you should know that I'm celibate," I began, my gaze raking over his body slowly before I licked my lips. "I'm waiting for marriage, the white dress, Cinderella carriage, the lot."

"Fine," Fox replied, not even blinking as he set the empty coffee mug down. "Then I'll book a church and have you pinned beneath me in a white dress by the weekend."

My lips popped open in surprise and I just shook my head. "No. Fuck, your level of crazy is out of control. I was just saying that to make you back off."

Fox gave me a dangerous look that made butterflies go to war in my stomach and before I really knew what was happening, he'd grabbed me by the waist, tugged me flush against his body and had lifted my chin so that I was forced to meet his green gaze.

"How about I back off when your heart stops beating like that around me?" he suggested, sliding his hand from my jaw to press down against my thundering heart which was being a damn traitor again alongside my libido.

I swallowed thickly, closed my eyes and pictured a whale doing a hula dance with starfishes covering his nipples. The damn whale was doing a good job at being sexy though, so I gave up on that and just focused on the day that Fox had ruined my life instead and that helped me to shove him back a step.

"I said we're going shopping, so what are you waiting for?" I demanded.

I sidestepped the big asshole, whistled for Mutt and headed over to hop into his truck before rearranging his seat back into an upright position again.

Fox scraped a hand over his face in an attempt to wake himself up or maybe in a display of frustration then followed me, shoving me along the bench so that he could get in behind the wheel.

"No. I'm driving," I demanded, climbing on top of him and trying to get him to shove over, but it was like trying to move a stack of bricks and I just ended up straddling him with the steering wheel digging into my ass.

Fox's hands landed on my thighs and he huffed as he leaned back against his headrest, looking at me seriously enough to make me pause in my attempts to make him move. There was a darkness in his soul that was all new and should have been terrifying. Yet sometimes, I felt like I wanted to crawl right into it and live there with him too.

"Nobody tells me what to do, hummingbird," he growled and I knew that that was the god's honest truth. This man didn't bend for anyone and I was treading a thin line with his temper, but I just couldn't help myself.

"Is that why you fuck girls without a condom?" I sneered, pushing off of his chest to climb back out of his lap, but he dug his fingers into my thighs to stop me.

"Not girls. Just you. When we come together, I want to feel every single piece of it. I want your hot pussy tight around my aching cock and for there to be nothing in this world left to divide us," he said roughly, making my thighs squeeze together in an attempt to block out that visual.

"You're delusional," I said, my voice coming out unintentionally breathy.

"One of us definitely is."

"Just drive already," I growled, climbing off of him with pure determination and choosing to sit on the far side of the cab, leaving the middle seat empty between us.

Fox did as requested for once and when he managed to force his truck back out of Rejects Park, I directed him up the roads towards the high end boutiques on Avalon Row beside the salon JJ had taken me to to get my rainbow hair.

We pulled up outside a lingerie store and Fox looked as happy as a fox in a chicken coop as I jumped out and led him inside with Mutt on my heels.

"No dogs allowed!" a perfectly presented woman cried as my little monster scurried in and she gave my less than pampered outfit a look that said I didn't belong here either.

"Well then why are they letting you work here?" I tossed back at her, smirking as she clutched her imaginary pearls and heading deeper into the store to the section beyond the red curtain at the back.

Rich people made me laugh doing shit like this, trying to hide their sex lives away like it was something shameful or bad. Personally, I'd hang a display of floggers in the window alongside an artfully laid out selection of butt plugs, but I didn't run the store, so what did I know?

Fox moved up close behind me, looking around at the sex toys lining the wall and leaning down to speak into my ear.

"What are you trying to achieve by bringing me here?" he growled, the lust in his voice all too clear, but no, this was not a couple's toy shopping excursion.

"I trust you brought your credit card? Because I'm seeking reparations for Vlad the Impaler," I replied sweetly.

"You gave that thing a full title?" he asked arching a brow at me.

"Yeah. And he lived up to his job description nicely. But now he's been vanquished so I need a replacement."

"I'm not buying you another vibrator," Fox growled. "If you want to feel something long and hard inside you then I have everything you need right here."

I scoffed dismissively and moved over to the shelves holding the vibrators, raising my eyebrows as I looked at the top end models sitting proud at the end of the row. Some of those things cost over two hundred dollars. That shit had to be good.

I reached up and grabbed the three most expensive ones, arching a brow at the oral vibrator which was said to mimic the tongue unlike any other. *Yes please*. Who needed a man when I could have hundreds of dollars of drama free silicone?

"I'm not paying for these," Fox growled as I dumped them into his arms.

"Well, if you don't then the next time you let me out of your sight, I'm gonna go and find a bar and I'll pick out a big blonde, tattooed asshole and let him go to town on me without a condom while I call him Badger and let him plunder my fox hole."

"Then I'd kill him," Fox said darkly and I had no doubt that he meant that.

"That won't erase the fact that he would have had his cock deep inside my-"

"Fine," he snapped, his jaw ticking with rage. "But when you're getting yourself off using one of these things, and panting my name into the dark, just remember that I can do it a hundred times better in person than some piece of plastic."

"Whatever you wanna tell yourself, Badger." I turned and walked away from him, sauntering up to the checkout and smiling at the bitch who had now gotten a bitch friend to come join her in scowling at me.

But when Fox dumped the collection of crazy expensive vibrators down in front of them, they instantly perked up, batting their lashes and becoming all smiles as they got that dollar sign look in their eyes.

"Looks like you two are in for some fun," the new one teased, giving Fox a lingering look that made me wanna punch her.

"Nah. Fox here just can't get me off, so we had to call for reinforcements," I replied with a shrug. "Meet Vlad the Impaler the second, Jack the Licker – you know, like Jack the Ripper but with more tongue and Alexander the

Great…big dildo."

Instead of losing the plot like I expected, Fox just tugged me close and smiled like a shark. "Don't be shy sweetheart," he said. "There's nothing wrong with wanting me to have something to fuck your ass with while you're riding my cock."

My lips parted on an angry retort as the girls tittered excitedly and Fox tossed a roll of cash down before they even told him how much it came to. He grabbed the paper bag full of my new friends and steered me out of the store with his arm around my shoulders.

"Now," he said in a dark tone as he led me back to his truck. "I think it's time I get you home before you go getting into any more trouble."

"Trouble is pretty much my standard. But I have a good few hours' worth of playing with my new toys to occupy me. So if I have to do that in your spare room then that's fine by me."

"Okay," Fox said lightly. "But just remember when your body is trembling and you're aching and panting with one of those things deep inside you, that I'm the one who bought them. Which means I own them, and every time one of them makes you come, I own that too. So whether you're using one of them or finally ready to give in to what the two of us have coming, it doesn't matter, because your body is mine already. And it's only a matter of time before you come begging for the real deal."

A few days, an overly attentive and protective Badger, and a slightly thicker layer of foundation was all it took to hide evidence of The Damned Men laying their hands on me outside The Dungeon. And in that time, I'd been a good little lost girl, staying in Fox's fancy spare room even though he'd agreed that I could stay back at my trailer some nights too.

But with the way he'd been since, and after some strategically worded pleading from JJ, I'd agreed to spend a couple of nights here to stop him from going full psycho. Which actually concerned me - because if I hadn't seen the depths of his insanity yet, then fuck knew what I was in for when I did.

Thanks to his taunting about my new vibrators belonging to him, I'd ended up playing with them a grand total of zero times. And that was becoming a serious issue while I tried to maintain my never ending indifference towards the three stupidly hot men who liked to wander around this house half naked all the damn time.

Chase stalked past me where I was lounging by the pool in a sea blue bikini, his gaze meeting mine for a second before his upper lip pulled back and he moved to pick a lounger on the far side of the pool with his back to me. I checked out his ass while mentally calling him an asshole and cursed my hormones for making my life even more complicated than it needed to be.

He, Fox and JJ had been planning something in hushed tones inside the house all afternoon, tossing glances my way to check I was still listening to music while pouring over a map and talking money. I wasn't dumb - they were planning a job. I just hadn't decided if I cared about that or not. I was perfectly capable of running my own jobs when I needed money, but as of right now, my funds were still topped up enough by what I'd stolen from them.

Annoyingly, none of them had mentioned the pile of cash that had gone missing with me the night of the party and I had quickly realised that they were happy to fund me for whatever I wanted. Fox had even 'left' cash lying around more than once and it pissed me the fuck off. I wasn't some kept little woman. So I wasn't going to be taking another dime of their money. The clothes and shit were up to them, I didn't care about wearing their crap or driving Fox's car because when it came down to it, I could survive without them. But as far as money for my rent or anything else I might need went, I was going to be earning it elsewhere. In the criminal sense of the word earning. 'Cause fuck the nine to five. My tan was not going to suffer for the sake of becoming respectable. Although it was currently suffering for the sake of not flashing the entire household of douchebags, which was why I'd opted for the micro bikini. But I was still going to get tan lines soon if I didn't head back to the beach to sun my naked ass in peace.

"Time me, J, I need to clear my head," Fox's voice interrupted my internal pout and I looked at him through my pink shades as he stripped his tank off and walked out onto the patio.

His gaze fell to my body as he strode out, and I tried not to look back at him even though he was tempting me in with his beach blonde surfer dude vibe with a dollop of ink and psycho. There was a guy who needed climbing like a tree. Shame about the coconut he kept in his skull in place of a brain though.

I let him look, drinking in the feeling of his eyes on my flesh as I lay there before he dove into the pool like a freaking pro and started swimming.

JJ came to sit beside me, dragging another lounger close enough to touch mine before sitting up on it with his feet on the floor and looking down at me with a wicked glint in his eyes.

He took my hand in his and slowly began to paint a pattern over my palm and up my wrist which made fire burn within my veins everywhere he touched.

I opened my mouth to ask what he was doing, but at that, moment, Fox made it back to the edge of the pool and surfaced, drawing in a deep breath.

"Not fast enough," JJ said casually, flicking a glance at his watch which he definitely hadn't been looking at while Fox swam his lengths.

His fingers were still moving over my wrist, hidden from Fox's view by my body and though it was somewhat innocent, my heart leapt at the thrill of it all the same.

Fox cursed, turned away and started swimming again.

JJ gave me his panty melting smirk and slid his fingers up my arm, dancing them over my shoulder, down my collar bone and grazing his thumb right over my hardening nipple with a look in his honey brown eyes that promised the best kind of trouble.

I sucked in a sharp breath, glancing over at Chase's lounger where he still had his back to us, smoking and scrolling on his phone without even an inkling of what JJ was doing.

A moment before Fox surfaced again, JJ lifted his hand away and pushed it back through his ebony hair and I bit my lip to try and quiet the raging hormones he was awakening in me with his game.

"Still not fast enough," JJ called, barely even looking at Fox who snarled in frustration and took off again.

Dude would probably get a PB and never even know it because JJ absolutely wasn't looking at his watch.

The moment Fox's head ducked beneath the water, JJ leaned over me, gripping the back of my neck and pulling me up to meet his lips.

My lips parted for him as his tongue sank into my mouth and my heart raced with the thrill of this game. It was fucking crazy. And it shouldn't have even mattered - if I wanted to kiss him then why should I hide it? But there was something insanely hot about doing so.

I had no idea how J was keeping an eye on Fox's progress, but he pulled back half a second before Fox emerged at the edge of the pool again.

"Dude, that one was even slower," JJ said, glancing his way and Fox snarled loudly as he dove beneath the water and started swimming again.

I pushed myself up on my elbow and caught the front of JJ's shirt, tugging him in for another kiss and barely suppressing a moan as I tasted the sweetest form of temptation on his lips. This was something I'd once fantasised about way more often than I would ever admit. I used to wonder what kissing one of my boys would be like and now I was getting to know the answer to that, I wanted to find out what the rest of him might feel like too.

JJ broke away again and I flopped back on the lounger with a groan that made Chase glance over his shoulder just as Fox surfaced again.

"Maybe just call time on it today, man," JJ said, tearing that sin filled gaze away from me for a moment to look at Fox once more. "You're just getting slower and-"

"Shut the fuck up and keep timing me," Fox snarled, turning away to swim off again.

JJ leaned over me once more, his hand moving between my thighs as he kissed my neck, his fingers toying with the edge of my bikini bottoms before tugging them aside so that his fingers could slick through the wetness at my entrance and I had to choke back a moan.

I was panting as he tugged my bikini back into place and a frustrated growl escaped my lips as I sagged against the sun lounger, aching for more than I could get in the time it took Fox to do his freaking lengths.

"What are you two muttering about over there?" Chase grouched from his sun lounger just as Fox surfaced.

"I'm hungry," JJ said, touching his fingers to his mouth in a gesture that could have been nothing more than a random brush of his hand over his face, but as he licked the taste of me from them, my pulse turned from a gallop to a thunder. "I'm gonna go grab a pizza from Lou's for dinner. Anyone want in?"

"Just get it delivered," Fox said, leaning his muscular arms on the edge of the pool and turning his dark glare on me, his frustration shifting to something a whole lot more carnal as his gaze drank me in. I wondered how much darker it would have gotten if he'd surfaced to find me and Johnny James all over each other?

"Nah. I'm too hungry to wait around for it," JJ said, getting to his feet. "So if you want in then-"

"I'll get my usual," Chase said, looking back to his cellphone with disinterest.

"Fine. Me too," Fox agreed, his gaze staying on me. "Can you time me while he's gone, hummingbird?"

He looked so freaking cute for a moment, holding out his innocent olive branch that I almost felt bad about turning him down. Then I remembered him shoving me in the mud and telling me to fuck off out of his life forever and it got a whole lot easier.

"I feel like going for a ride, sorry Badger. Can I come, Johnny James?" I bit my lip as I looked around at JJ and the grin he gave me in return should have been freaking illegal.

"Yeah you can come," he said, the double meaning so clear in his voice that I was surprised the others didn't catch on instantly.

I was possibly going to regret this in the morning - but I was pretty sure I'd be screaming his name enough times to make up for any shame. Anyway, if I was going to feel shame over screwing anyone then it would be over Shawn. *Fucking Shawn.* I didn't wanna think about him now though. That asshole had always left me wanting, but the look JJ was giving me promised he wouldn't.

"I guess I'll time you then," Chase said, turning to sit facing the pool as he addressed Fox. "But I won't go easy on you if you're training with me."

"Good. Because apparently I'm sucking ass tonight," Fox growled in frustration, turning away to swim on.

I gave JJ a heated look as I got up and pulled my white sun dress over my head before kicking on my sandals and following him into the house.

He took my hand as he led me through the kitchen, exchanging a look with me that was all sex and had my toes curling as I fought not to give it away in case Chase looked after us. We moved out of sight of the others and practically broke into a run as he dragged me towards the garage door, making a laugh spill from my lips.

JJ tugged me through it and shoved me back against the wall behind the door the moment we were inside, his mouth finding mine as he kissed me breathless and I melted for him, my hands shifting up his chest and over his broad shoulders as I started tugging at the material of his tank.

He pulled back forcefully and took his phone from his pocket. "I'm ordering the pizza in," he grunted, stepping back with a determined look in his eyes and dialling Lou's Pizza Place.

I wasn't really in the mood for waiting though, so I shifted into his personal space, kissing his neck and pushing my hand inside his shorts as I sought out the hot flesh of his hard cock. He grunted, rattling off an order for our food to be delivered between his teeth while trying not to react to what I was doing.

I began caressing him, my thumb smearing the bead of moisture from the tip of his dick over the head as I teased him.

JJ cursed beneath his breath as he tried to make the order, muttering something about the guy adding whatever fucking toppings he wanted and calling him once he was outside the gates to the house as I moved my mouth to his chest and began kissing a line down his hard abs.

Just as he was about to hang up, the sound of footsteps came from inside the house and I snatched my hand back out of his pants, jerking upright. The two of us moved away from the door quickly, jogging down the stairs just before it flew open behind us.

"Can you get extra barbecue sauce?" Chase called as he looked down at us.

"On it," JJ assured him without turning back. Most likely because of the huge bulge in his shorts which was aching for more of my attention.

"And maybe grab some more beers while you're out? *Someone* keeps drinking all of them," Chase added with a pointed look at me.

"Well you leave me to sit about in this dumb house all day, so I decided to take up day drinking. If you have an issue with it, you can bite me, asshole."

"Be careful what you wish for, ghost," Chase warned and my skin prickled at that idea.

Shit, I really needed to get laid. Lucky for me, I was already on the case.

Chase closed the door again and JJ hooked an arm around my waist, sweeping me off my feet and making a surprised shriek escape my lips.

He carried me across the underground garage and dropped my ass on the hood of Fox's truck.

"You wanna fuck me on his car?" I asked with a laugh. "What did Fox do to piss you off so much?"

JJ smirked at me, gripping my knees and shifting them apart with a purposeful slowness that made my pulse jackhammer.

"I love Fox like a brother. But I have an issue with him laying down a claim on you like me and Chase have no right to try and win you for ourselves. You were our girl ten years ago, we all wanted you just the same. I'm not gonna roll over like a little bitch and let him play the boss card when it comes to you. So if I get to be the one you've picked then I'm not gonna back off."

"I haven't picked shit, Johnny James. This isn't me making any choice beyond hoping you can get me off," I said firmly and I meant it too. "You aren't going to be my boyfriend just because you put your dick in me. Don't go talking like a psycho."

JJ's grip on my knees tightened, making my flesh ache for more as he pushed my legs even wider.

"Casual sex is pretty much my expertise, pretty girl. Now let me show you why people pay so fucking much for a piece of me."

"I'm not a client, JJ," I growled.

"I know, sweetheart. First time is on the house." He winked at me as he tugged his shirt off one handed and I followed his lead by yanking my dress over my head and tossing it to the floor too.

JJ growled this carnal noise which made a shiver run through my entire body as he moved his hands up my thighs, caressing my tattoos and catching the strings which held my bikini bottoms in place.

He looked me dead in the eye as he tugged them undone and I leaned in to kiss him, running my hands over his abs and the perfectly defined ridges of his muscles before finding that V which dipped beneath his waistband and carving my fingers down the lines of it.

JJ broke our kiss before I could take his cock in my hand again though, moving his mouth down my jaw, my neck, my collar bone, finding each and every nerve ending as he went so that heat built between my thighs, desperate for him to sate it.

His hands slid behind me, tugging the strings of my top and freeing my breasts from the blue scraps of fabric. His mouth found my nipple and I moaned as he sucked and licked and drew it between his teeth in the perfect way to drive my entire body wild.

I tipped my head back as he wound his hands around my waist, squeezing tightly to keep me in place as he pushed me back to lay on the hood of the truck.

"Fuck, I feel like a teenager again," JJ growled as he began moving lower.

"Every single thing you're doing to me says you're not one," I panted, shivering a little at the coldness of the car beneath me and the feeling of his mouth on my skin. Teenage JJ had not had this confidence or expertise as far as I was aware, but this man before me knew exactly what he was doing and what he wanted to do.

"I wanted you so much back then," he said, kissing down to my navel and making my hips buck as he kept using his mouth for all the wrong things. I needed him to get to the point and fast, no more of this teasing bullshit. "So fucking much. And I never stopped. Even when you were gone you were still the fantasy I always pictured. Still the one I thought of first every time I felt turned on."

"Then fuck me like you wished you could back then and stop wasting time on words," I demanded.

We didn't have long and I needed this so fucking much that I almost felt like I was coming undone already and he hadn't even done anything to me yet.

JJ laughed darkly, hooking my thigh over his broad shoulder and dropping his mouth onto my clit without any need for directions.

A throaty moan escaped me as he dragged his tongue over my aching core, licking me slowly as his grip shifted to my hips and he pinned me in place while I tried to writhe beneath him.

He moved his mouth lower, his tongue driving inside me, running a circle around the inside of my slick opening and groaning at the taste of me.

He moved back up to my clit, licking and sucking and making me beg for more as my flesh prickled and tingled and I closed my eyes to focus on nothing but the carnage he was wreaking between my thighs.

I kept bucking my hips against his hold and he gave up on trying to force me to stay still, moving one palm to press down hard on my lower stomach before bringing the other around so that he could push two fingers straight inside me.

A cry of pleasure escaped me and he pushed a third finger in on the next thrust, driving them in deep and hard while sucking on my clit like he was as hungry for this orgasm as I was.

I thrust up against him, fucking his face and his hand and gripping his silky black hair between my fingers as my climax built and built until I was screaming for him and he was slapping a hand down over my mouth even while my pussy clamped tight on his fingers.

"I knew you were a screamer," he said in a smug ass tone which had me aching to prove to him that I could make him scream my name too.

JJ stood over me, the garage light behind him casting his features in shadow and for a moment, all of the smiles and jokes were gone and I could see the lethal gangster who killed men who crossed him and drove fear into the hearts of his enemies. This was a man who saw something he wanted and took it. And right now, the thing he wanted most, was me.

He pulled something from his pocket and dropped his shorts and my gaze fell to his thick, hard cock as it sprang free, making my mouth water with anticipation. JJ wrapped a hand around his dick, slowly pumping it as he drank in the sight of me brought to ruin beneath him.

"Fuck, Johnny James, don't make me wait," I demanded, pushing up onto my elbows as I made a move to reach for him.

But the look in his eyes just darkened as he shifted back, tearing open the condom wrapper between his teeth.

I watched him roll the condom on and I swear a rubber had never looked so fucking good. I wanted his cock inside me unlike I think I'd ever wanted any man before him. He was a fantasy I needed to see play out and I was seriously hoping he could live up to the hype in my head.

JJ moved over me where I lay on the hood, gripping my hips while he remained standing upright and pressing the head of his cock to my entrance.

His gaze met mine and the smirk he gave me was fucking sinful.

"I'm gonna make you scream for me, pretty girl," he promised before driving into me with a savage thrust that gave him his wish instantly.

JJ glanced towards the door as I arched my back, wrapping my legs around his waist and panting at the feeling of his thick cock fully seated inside me. It was almost overwhelming, making my back arch as I reached out for him, aching for him to move again.

"You're gonna get me killed for this," he teased, looking seriously okay with that being the way he died and drawing back slowly, gripping my hips so tight I was certain he was going to bruise me and I really hoped he would.

The next thrust was impossibly harder, deeper, my cry of pleasure followed by another as he began to drive himself into me faster and faster, making it hard for me to even catch my breath as I moved my hips up to meet his.

The angle he held me at drove his cock into the deepest parts of me and I curled my hands into my hair as he watched me, pawing at my aching nipples and running my fingers everywhere.

"Don't forget your clit, sweetheart," he ground out, fucking me harder and making me pant and moan.

I did as he said, moving my hand down to rub circles against the tingling bundle of nerves as he fucked me so hard I could barely breathe.

I couldn't take much more of it, my pussy tightening around him already as he watched me with a feral hunger that made me feel like the most desirable woman in the entire fucking world.

He thrust in again and I swear I saw stars as I came for him, his cock filling me perfectly, deeply and his mouth coming down over mine to devour the sound of my screams as I fell apart for him.

JJ dragged me upright in his arms, his tongue in my mouth, tasting my ecstasy as he pressed my body flush against his.

I gasped as he started moving again, unable to believe he was still going, his cock still thick and hard inside me even as my pussy had clamped tight and begged him to follow me into oblivion.

His mouth stayed on mine as he kept kissing me while he fucked me, growling hungrily every time his cock thrust in and one of my moans slipped between our mouths.

My nails were gouging lines into his shoulders and I felt like I was only just managing to cling onto him when he finally came, his cock swelling deep inside me and my name spilling from his lips in some mixture of a curse and prayer.

I tightened my thighs around his waist as the tension ran out of his body and our frantic kisses slowed into something deep and powerful which made some long-forgotten piece of my soul hum with satisfaction.

He moved his hands into my hair, breaking our kiss and looking at me with that devilish glint in his dark eyes that had always spelled trouble and now held this secret in them too.

The buzz of his cellphone in his discarded shorts saved either of us from speaking and he drew his cock out of me slowly, making me whimper as I dropped back against the hood of Fox's truck to catch my breath, every inch of my flesh buzzing with pleasure.

JJ pulled the phone from his pocket to tell the pizza guy he was on his way out before removing the condom and tying it off, his eyes never leaving my naked body and making me feel appreciated in a way I wasn't sure I ever had before. Sure, I'd fucked plenty of guys, but whether they were hook ups or boyfriends, they'd always turned their attention to something else once they'd gotten what they wanted from me.

In Shawn's case I was left to finish myself off while he headed for a shower. Every. Damn. Time. *Fucking Shawn*. Why the hell had I put up with that asshole and his bad sex? Oh yeah, because I had nothing else thanks to the Harlequin boys and at least being his girl had made me into someone. Or I thought it had until he'd disposed of me without a second thought.

I got up and found my clothes, turning my back on JJ as a prickle of unease ran through my skin and I mentally chastised myself for my taste in men. Sometimes I thought I was purposefully self destructive like this, making bad choices because I feared trying to make any good ones. If the things I did could only lead me into shitty situations, then I didn't ever have to waste time on hoping for something better.

"Look at me, pretty girl," JJ said in a low voice, reaching out to touch my shoulder as I shrugged my dress back on.

"Don't you need to go grab those pizzas?" I asked in a flat tone, refusing to turn towards him as I combed my fingers through my hair to hide the just fucked look I was no doubt sporting.

"Is something wrong?" he demanded, turning me around whether I wanted him to or not.

"Nope," I lied, giving him a fake smile that he saw straight through.

His phone started ringing again and he glanced at it as the pizza place called.

"Don't look at me like that," JJ growled.

"Like what?" I asked.

"Like I'm some bad decision or mistake you made."

"I never said-"

"I get paid for sex, sweetheart. Do you think I don't know regret when I see it in a woman's eyes? I just thought I might have meant something more to you than that."

The hurt in his voice made me pause and my expression softened as I looked up at him.

"I don't regret it, Johnny," I said. "I just..." I blew out a breath as the pizza guy started calling again.

JJ answered it with a snarl of annoyance, his gaze staying pinned on mine. "You'll wait there until I get to you or you'll be getting a blade between the ribs as a tip," he snapped before cutting the call again and I raised my eyebrows at his tone. "Just what?" he asked me.

"I just should know better than to screw a guy who broke my heart before," I admitted, forcing myself to hold his gaze and hating the way those words struck him. But at the same time, I was glad he felt a taste of my pain. I really was a fucked up kind of creature these days.

JJ sighed and leaned in to kiss my lips softly and I let him because apparently I was a glutton for punishment.

"It's just a bit of fun, pretty girl. That's all I'm good for anyway. So don't beat yourself up about it. Okay?" He turned and walked away before I could reply and I got the feeling something I'd said had upset him or pissed him off, but it was clear he had no intention of telling me what.

I waited while he headed up the ramp out of the garage to collect the pizzas from the no doubt terrified delivery boy beyond the gates and bit my swollen lip as I decided he was right. We were having fun, playing out a fantasy and giving each other something mutually beneficial. I didn't need to think into it any more than that.

I probably needed to be more concerned about Fox noticing my swollen lips or the scratches I'd left on JJ's back which were peeking out around the shoulders of his tank. And whatever way this played out, I really just needed to stay focused on my goal. I wanted those keys and it was time I figured out how to get my hands on them. Because the Harlequins were starting to pull me back into their net again, and I refused to get myself tangled up in it.

CHAPTER TWENTY

The bumfuck of a pizza order we received had Fox and Chase ready to burn down Lou's Pizza Place and I only warded them off by calling up the restaurant and getting us free pizza for the next year. Funny how a few friendly threats of murder could open up gateways like that.

Rogue had disappeared upstairs to shower and hadn't returned since and I was just praying she didn't spiral into regret and stop this thing between us before it had even started. I didn't date girls, never had and never would. But I'd also never expected Rogue Easton to walk back into my life. Because if there was one girl I would have dated all the way to the altar, it was her.

My dick was still buzzing from being inside her, but instead of riding the high of fucking the girl I'd fantasised about since the moment my balls had dropped, I was feeling like a prime asshole. I couldn't get the way she'd looked at me out of my head. Like I was just one shitty mistake in a string of shitty mistakes. And I despised that. I didn't want to be a regret to Rogue. I just didn't know how to make it right.

Chase was picking olives off his pizza which was layered with eggplant and anchovies. Like, what the fuck pizza guy? I may have given him the green light for any toppings, but Jesus. This was taking liberties. No one in the history of the world liked eggplant. Not even eggplants liked eggplants.

"At least he remembered the barbeque sauce," Chase muttered.

Yeah I totally ordered that. Oh no wait, I was too busy getting balls deep in our favourite girl.

Fox snatched the pizza box from Chase and dumped it in the trash with the rest of them. "I'll cook."

"Really?" Chase asked hopefully and my ears pricked up too. Fox usually only cooked dinner for all of us on Sundays, but it was the best fucking food ever and I was so here for it.

"Yeah." Fox shrugged, heading to the fridge, taking out some tomatoes and started chopping them. Chase caught the fridge door before it shut then turned to me with a scowl.

"You forgot the beers," he accused.

"Oh shit." I pushed my fingers into my hair. "Totally slipped my mind."

"I'll pick some up in the morning," Fox said. "I've got to head over to Pascal's warehouse to make sure he's got a secure place for the shipment coming in tomorrow."

"I can come with you to check it's all in order," Chase offered.

"No," Fox said simply and Chase cursed.

"Why not?" Chase grabbed some rum and started making Cuba Libres for all of us.

"Because I don't need you," Fox said offhandedly, but I could see Chase taking that to heart as his eyes narrowed.

I checked the time and frowned. I had an hour before I needed to be at the club and I was feeling all kinds of weird because I had two escort jobs booked in tonight.

"I'm gonna get changed for work," I said then headed out of the room, jogging upstairs and slowing as I approached Rogue's door. It was quiet in her room and I chewed on the inside of my cheek as I hesitated there, unsure what exactly I was planning. The door yanked open and I swallowed a curse, looking like a fucking idiot as her eyes landed on me hovering there like a damn creeper.

"Oh, hey," she said, glancing down the hall to check for the others. "I was just about to go on a snack hunt."

"Fox is making food," I said then ran my hand down the back of my neck.

"Well that's…good," she said, smiling awkwardly and I fucking hated that, but I just didn't have the right words to say, so I brushed my knuckles over her cheek instead and walked away to my room.

I headed inside, shutting the door and drawing in a long breath. *Douchebag. What the fuck was that? I have all the game in the world and yet I just choked like a hooker with an asphyxiation fetish.*

I showered, hating that I was washing my pretty girl off of me, then dressed in my best jeans and a fitted white shirt that showed off my biceps. I tucked my phone, wallet and keys into my pockets alongside a few condoms and scrubbed a hand over my face. Why did I feel so…fucked? Not the good kind of fucked either, the bad kind. Which was extra irritating because I should have been on cloud nine partying with rainbows and unicorns and shit. It wasn't like I hadn't had the time of my life, fuck I really had. But now I had to go back to my normal life. And my normal life was clear cut. Sex with Rogue should have been too and yet it just fucking wasn't.

I headed downstairs again and slowed as I found Rogue sitting at the kitchen island. Chase was playing a card game with her, trying really fucking hard not to smile as she made jokes and I had the urge to lean down and kiss her, lay my claim and show my brothers that she was mine. But she wasn't mine. She'd said it herself. But that didn't make the urge go away. It was just a bit of a headfuck because it made me feel like a teenager with an obsession again. And that was a scary ass place to go back to. I'd moved on, grown up.

Fox laid out the pasta for us and I sat down beside Rogue, picking up my fork as Fox dropped down opposite me beside Chase. I wolfed down my meal, figuring it was best to just get the fuck out of here as soon as possible and fix my head. When I was finished, I got to my feet and said my goodbyes.

"See ya, dude," Chase said. "Enjoy the pussy."

My gaze locked on Rogue's for far too long as those words fell between us like an axe. It was something Chase often said when I was heading to work, he didn't even think about it, *I* didn't even think about it. Until now.

Rogue's eyes hardened but she gave me a carefree look which I really hoped was bullshit. "Go get it, JJ."

My throat tightened and I nodded, trying to laugh it off, but it actually hurt. *What's the matter with me?*

"I want you with me in the morning, J," Fox said and Chase's mouth popped open indignantly.

"Why him?" he demanded.

"Because he can get up before seven am without bitching about it," Fox said and Chase's jaw flexed furiously.

"I'll be there," I said and Chase looked even angrier. "Come on man, you hate mornings."

"I'm kinda with Chase on the ungodly hours. Who wants to function before ten am anyways? Fuck em', Ace. We can have brunch together," Rogue said in a way I wasn't sure was entirely a joke. Why would she want to have brunch with Chase? He'd been nothing but a dick to her since she'd gotten back.

"You wanna do brunch?" Chase questioned, though there was a flicker of hope in his eyes that got my back up.

Great, now I'm a possessive asshole just like Fox. Chase had a right to fight for her too, not that he'd win, but I still wouldn't block him when he was ready to shoot his shot because all of us deserved that much after the hell we'd been through over her.

"Sure, if you cook it," Rogue said. "I'll make mimosas."

"What the fuck is happening right now?" Fox grumbled.

"We're making brunch plans," Chase said, throwing a smirk at Fox. "Aren't we, little one?"

My brows arched at that old nickname and I clapped him on the shoulder way harder than was really friendly. He glanced back at me with a confused frown and I fought a scowl.

"Well, have fun with that. Don't kill each other." I managed to force out a totally chill smile.

"No promises," Chase said darkly, looking to Rogue and she lifted her chin, giving him an equally murderous look. The way that shit was going, they were either going to kill each other or end up hate fucking. And I guess I had to hope for the latter if I was cutting my losses. But I'd only just gotten my hands on her and I wanted more of that, more of her. Had I not fucked her good enough? Was she gonna look elsewhere now? *Nah, can't be that. I'm the best fuck in Sunset Cove, if not the entire state.*

I headed to the garage, jogging downstairs and grabbing my GT keys on the way before dropping into my car. I accelerated out onto the drive, heading up to the gate and Rodriguez opened it for me. I revved the engine, sailing past him with a wave and heading down the road. I was soon pulling up in the parking lot of Afterlife, my car drawing the attention of some teenagers loitering there.

I headed in through the back door, finding Diane and Lyla in spangly outfits for the show tonight, both of them crowded around Bella who was sobbing in a chair.

"What's going on?" I asked, striding over to them and nudging Di and Lyla aside so I could step between them.

"Olly called her a dumb slut," Di murmured in my ear.

"For fuck's sake." I hunted for Olly around the dressing room, but he wasn't there. He'd been dating Bella on and off for the past few months, much to my fucking disapproval. It wasn't like I wanted to stand in the way of love's young dream or whatever, but a hooker dating a stripper who took issue with her fucking for cash was asking for trouble.

"He said I d-drink too much as well," Bella sobbed and I shared a look with Lyla which said *well you do, honey.* But I knew how to handle my girls individually, and trying to call Bella out on her drinking habit while the tap was currently busted on her waterworks was a terrible idea.

"Alright, sweetheart, I'll talk to him. Dry your eyes. Let the girls fix your makeup," I said.

"Thanks JJ," Di murmured and I nodded to her, heading off to hunt down my little bastard of a co-dancer who was going to cost me money tonight if Bella didn't dance.

"Olly Sanchez!" I bellowed as I stepped out into the bar which was currently closed.

Olly was sitting at the bar shirtless while Estelle put body paint on his chest. We were having a UV party and all the bartenders were coloured in ultraviolet paint. I always put at least one of my boys behind the bar during the week because there were plenty of women, and men, in town who came here to drool over the guys as much as the girls. Each of us had our own little fan club, but none was as big as mine.

"Take a break, Estelle," I commanded her and she scurried behind the bar. She was the oldest member of staff here and I didn't ever ask her to dress up like my other girls.

She was invaluable to me in other ways though and I didn't give a shit that she wasn't here to give people an eyeful. I'd taken her in five years ago when her husband, who was a regular here, beat her black and blue. I'd kicked the asshole out of town with a broken arm and a few missing teeth and given her work until she could get back on her feet. Turned out, she'd not only loved the job, she was fucking good at it too, keeping all the staff in line and running a seriously tight ship. A lot of the staff called her Momma Stelle because she'd been so good to them and I had no plans of ever letting her go.

"Olly, you piece of shit," I snarled and he rolled his eyes at me. He was as broad as me and his face was cut from stone, but I had the height on him.

"Come on, boss," he groaned.

"Don't fucking *come on boss* me. We're opening in less than fifteen minutes and I swear to fuck, if Bella isn't smiling her tits off when the first customer walks through that door, you're gonna pay me every dollar I'll lose because she's walking around sniffling and sobbing while she takes her clothes off. It's no way to do business, man."

Olly ran a hand through his long, wavy black hair. "I don't want her selling her pussy anymore," he growled, pouting at me like it was *my* fucking fault. Like I was some sort of vag troll who forced girls to get on their knees for men in his creepy cave. But I let no such fucking thing happen in Afterlife.

I spammed him on the forehead in irritation. "It's her choice. I don't make her suck cock, but she sucks it good, so I'm gonna take my cut so long as she keeps choosing to do it, just like I'll kill any motherfucker who tries to hurt her too." Plenty of my dancing girls chose to fuck for extra cash, and I offered them protection and escorts to and from jobs to keep them safe. They were going to do it anyway, so I let them and took my cut. I wasn't a pimp exactly, but well, alright I was a pimp. But one who actually gave a crap about the people who worked for me and made sure they got health care and shit, so at least I was a nice pimp.

A muscle worked in his temple as he continued to pout. "I can't handle it, bro. I see her with other guys and I just wanna – *argh*." He clenched his fists and I sighed.

"You knew what her job was when you started fucking her," I said. "What do you want me to do about it?"

"Put her on the main stage so she can get bigger tips. If she earns more here, she'll stop."

"Bella's not a good enough dancer for the main stage. If she wants more money then she can pull shifts behind the bar or show up to the fucking dance classes instead of being too hungover or high to attend all the time."

He grunted angrily and I grabbed his chin, forcing him to look up at me. "Whatever you do, don't ever call one of my girls a dumb slut again or you'll be out on your ass. I don't need the drama and I certainly don't appreciate the fucking double standards. You work in a strip club with escorts. You wanna date a fine, upstanding girl who worships your cock on a monogamous basis, then find one outside of Afterlife. If not then go make that girl smile, asshole."

He nodded, pushing out of his seat and bowing his head obediently as he darted off towards the dressing room. I headed out of the bar down the corridor that led to my office and pushed inside, shaking my head at Olly.

Jessie appeared a few moments later, biting on her sugary pink bottom lip. Her long brown hair was streaked with UV paint and she wore a tiny silver outfit that showed off a lot of toned skin, all of which was covered in painted hearts and stripes.

She pushed the door shut behind her, smiling coyly at me as I leaned back against my desk. "You looked stressed, baby."

"Olly's being an asshole again," I sighed as she closed in on me and immediately reached for my dick, rubbing my crotch to try and get me hard.

I swallowed what felt like a razor blade in my throat as she dropped to her knees and produced a strawberry flavoured condom from her bra. Her favourite.

She lowered my fly and I continued to force down razor blades in my throat as I watched her, my cock about as active as a dead fish. Not even one out of water, vaguely twitching. It was as dead as a Dodo. *What the fuck Johnny D?*

I thought of how hard I'd been inside Rogue, the way she'd panted and moaned, how she'd felt coming on my cock and I cursed as I abruptly stepped past Jessie, almost kneeing her in the face.

"Not right now," I muttered, helping her to her feet and doing up my fly. She stared at the pink condom she'd taken out of the wrapper with a frown.

"Oh, but it will never fulfil its destiny now," she said sadly as she gazed at the rubber and I snorted, turning her towards the door. She only had a few braincells, bless her heart, but what came out of them when she rubbed them together was pure magic.

"Texas should be here soon. Why don't you go get yourself a piece of him?" I suggested.

Her face brightened at that and she nodded eagerly, bounding away down the corridor. The girl just loved sucking dick.

I dropped down behind my desk, knocking my head back against the chair and gazing up at the ceiling, swivelling from side to side in my seat. *What the fuck was that? I was refusing blowjobs now? Why?*

I thought of Rogue and cursed, shaking my head. I'd obsessed over that girl for too long, she was too deep under my skin. Maybe it was totally reasonable that I couldn't stick my dick in another hole right away. But shit, I had escorting jobs booked tonight. Two regulars. I needed to get it together.

I stayed in my office – okay hid in my office – for an hour after the club opened, trying to figure out what the fuck to do as I busied myself with some paperwork – alright, fantasised about Rogue. I went over every second of claiming her body, committing it to memory and smirking to myself like an asshole.

A knock came at the door and I sat up straighter as Estelle walked in. "Sorry to disturb you, Mr Brooks, but your first client is here. She'd like to have a drink with you at the bar."

I nodded, pushing out of my seat and mussing up my hair as I followed her into the corridor and through to the club.

The place was already filling up nicely and I smiled as I spotted Bella giving one helluva lap dance to a guy in one of the booths with a big ass grin on her lips. *That's my girl. Game face on.* Whatever Olly had done, it had worked a treat.

I rounded the bar to where my client was waiting and ignored my violently pounding heart. "Evening sweetheart," I purred, leaning in and kissing Lilith on the cheek. She was in her forties, her body in good shape and the tight fitting clothes she wore did her every kind of favour. But the idea of making her scream tonight didn't appeal, especially when I recalled Rogue screaming beneath me. No one could top that sound. And I didn't wanna forget it when Lilith started squealing like a pig in heat.

Olly poured me a whiskey and I knocked it back as I took my seat beside my client, rapping my knuckles on the bar for another one as I swallowed.

"You look tense, baby, what's the matter?" Lilith ran her hot pink nails up and down my arm and I fought the urge to withdraw.

I palmed off the question, laying on the charm thick and going through the motions. I could do this. I just had to stop thinking about Rogue and then it'd be simple. The only problem was, stopping myself from thinking about Rogue was as easy as stopping the wind blowing.

A group of men entered the bar and my gaze narrowed as I spotted Kaiser Rosewood amongst them. Kaiser was a big guy who liked wearing pin-striped suits like he was some sort of nineteen twenties gangster. His hair was thick and silver and I guessed he was some sort of businessman, but God only knew what kind of business he dealt in. The asshole had inherited the Rosewood Manor after his old Aunt Mabel had died. She'd been good to me and my friends when we were kids, and that piece of shit hadn't visited her for years so far as I could tell back then. I hadn't even known she had a son until he came out of the woodwork when she died, sniffing around her corpse for scraps. But there hadn't just been scraps, there'd been a whole fucking feast waiting for him.

Miss Mabel hadn't had a will so her entire estate had deferred to him. The fucker hadn't even been at her funeral. Only me, Chase and Fox had been there to say goodbye. And it had been one of the most miserable days of my life. It had happened a few years after Rogue had left and Kaiser had promptly moved into the property and started renovating the place. There was no chance of sneaking onto the grounds after that. And with Rogue and Maverick's keys long gone, we had no way of getting into the crypt again to get the stuff we'd stashed there either. It had been a shitty little cherry on top of an already shitty sundae.

Kaiser didn't just have a new fence put in and cameras all around it, he'd had a bunch of armed guards stationed there too. The guy was shady as shit and whatever he had going on in that manor couldn't be good. He didn't mix with the crew so we never had any reason to go up against him, but there were a few rumours circling that he was banished from town by the Harlequins a long time ago. He'd been allowed to come back by Luther apparently. Fuck if I knew why though.

I still floated the idea of breaking in there and blasting our way into the crypt from time to time with Fox. If Kaiser ever decided to force his way into it, it wouldn't be long before we heard about it. But I didn't imagine a guy like him had any interest in dusty old tombs. And so long as he had no reason to go looking in there, we were safe. I just hoped the notion never took him to knock it down and develop on the land. Because so help us if he ever did.

Whenever he came into my club with his guys, they tended to splash cash around the place like it was as common as water, so I didn't mind his visits. I also had my girls feed back any information to me they heard about his business dealings because one, I was a nosy fucker, and two, Fox had me listening in on plenty of my customers anyway because Afterlife attracted the kind of dangerous people who could one day be a threat to us, or who would make a perfect asset to our crew.

Kaiser took over a booth with his men and a few of my best girls were soon surrounding them, including Di and Lyla.

Lilith caught my cheek, turning me towards her with a slanted smile. "What's got you so distracted tonight, baby?"

"Am I?" I asked, painting on a smirk and she bit her lip, running her hand up my chest possessively and leaning close to speak in my ear.

"Do you wanna get out of here? I can take your mind off of whatever's bothering you."

I should have said yes. Or at least avoided the question, tried to get her to stay at the club tonight instead. But no. I didn't do either of those things. I blurted the first thing that came to my head in an urgent whisper. "I've got the clap."

I've. Got. The. Clap.

That was what I went with apparently. Lilith gasped, lurching away from me like I was contagious and I gave her an apologetic smile.

"Oh um, okay," she said, getting to her feet. "Well perhaps we can rearrange something when, you've, um, dealt with that. Okay?"

"Yeah, sorry sweetheart." I shrugged innocently. "I could see if Texas is available?" I took out my phone, but she waved me off, already heading for the door. *Great.*

What the fuck was I thinking? I'd just flushed five grand down the shitter just like that. And for what? Because my dick had decided it only wanted one pussy right now? *Well I have news for you Johnny D, this is non negotiable. We need the cash.*

It didn't even twitch in response. *Fucking stubborn asshole.*

I know she felt like a dream wrapped in a wish dipped in melted chocolate, but fucking her can't mean we don't fuck anyone else. It just can't.

Nothing. My dick was a dead weight between my thighs, declaring a silent protest in an attempt to make me agree. But it wasn't a choice. Didn't he see that? I literally needed him for my job. Stripping might have made bank on a good night, but it was never going to bring in the big bucks like escorting did.

Fine, you can have one moody bitch fit tonight and that's it. Then we're back to work tomorrow.

I caught Estelle's attention over the bar, beckoning her closer.

"Everything okay, my love?" she asked and I leaned in to whisper in her ear.

"Can you cancel my next appointment tonight. I'm not feeling so good."

"Oh no, is everything alright?" she asked.

"I've got the clap," I blurted. Again.

She nodded seriously, patting me on the shoulder. "Okay, I'll handle everything, you just do what you need to do."

"Thanks," I said with a sigh then drew away from her and headed through the club to the dressing room, taking the back exit out into the parking lot. I'd just head home, jerk off in the shower and give my dick a good talking to about going all monogamous on the pussy he had a crush on, then tomorrow it would all be straightened out. It wasn't like I couldn't continue to fuck Rogue if that was what she wanted too, but I couldn't write off my clients for one girl. Even if she was *the* girl.

I drove home with the windows down, the sea air whipping through the car and clearing my head. I wondered if Rogue was in her room and if I could sneak in there while Fox and Chase were busy and - shit. I was fucked. I was already craving her like candy dipped in ecstasy. I needed more. And I needed to get it right now. Fuck it, I wasn't going to beat off to a Taylor Swift song while crying in the shower, I'd spend a whole night ruining her for other men and fulfilling the desires I'd had about her for endless years. Why shouldn't I do that? I wanted her, she wanted me. It was easy math.

My dick was bouncing in my pants like an excitable puppy dog and I probably should have realised I was a goner the moment Jessie had stepped into my office and my cock had tried to hide behind my balls.

I revved the engine as I sped up toward the gates, but slowed again as a dark lump on the ground drew my attention. My heart thumped wildly as I slammed on the brakes and my headlights illuminated the gates, the blood, the fucking horror show waiting there for me. Rodriquez and Piston were dead on the ground, their heads cut off and laying there with their eyes rolling back in their sockets. Painted in blood across the gates was one blazing red word. WAR.

I leapt out of the car, typing in the code to open up the gate and cursing as I dragged their bloody bodies and heads inside before driving my GT up to the house with the engine roaring. I drove down into the garage, wiping blood off my hands onto my shirt as I ran up into the house. We'd have to cover that shit up later to keep the cops out of our hair but for now I just needed to know that everyone else was alright.

"Fox! Chase!" I bellowed and they came running in from the patio as I made it to the kitchen.

Fox took one sweeping look at the blood covering me and his eyes flared with fear. "What's happened?'

"Where's Rogue?" I demanded, panic clutching my heart.

"She's upstairs," Chase said and relief filled me though I still wanted to see her for myself to be sure.

"What the fuck is going on?" Fox demanded.

"Our men are fucking dead," I snarled, fury bubbling through me. "Rodriguez and Piston. Some asshole cut their heads off and wrote war on the front gate."

"Maverick," Chase spat and I nodded, my teeth gritted tight.

"That fucking asshole, he won't get away with this," Fox hissed.

"What's going on?" Rogue appeared in the doorway with Mutt at her heels and I had to fight the urge to pull her into my arms and make sure she really was okay.

"Get back to your room!" Fox barked and she frowned, looking to me for an explanation.

"JJ, what is it?" She took in the blood coating me with worry in her gaze.

"Our men have been killed at the gate," I said and her eyes widened.

Fox took out his phone, starting to make calls, summoning our club members to the house instead of The Oasis. I guessed he didn't want to take any risks leaving Rogue here alone right now.

"Take her upstairs," he shot at me and I nodded, catching her hand and towing her out of the room.

"We have to hit him hard this time," Chase started saying to Fox as we left. "We have to gain the upper hand."

Rogue tried to tug her fingers free of my grip. "Let go. I'm not going to be sent to my room like a naughty fucking kid."

I leaned down, picking her up and tossing her over my shoulder as Mutt barked angrily. I jogged upstairs as she thumped my back, heading into her room and dumping her on the bed. She glared up at me, but I didn't care, pulling my shirt off and tossing the bloody material aside before leaning down and kissing her. I clutched her cheeks and she gasped against my lips as I stole a fast and desperate kiss from her mouth before drawing away. "Sorry, pretty girl. You gotta stay here. It's crew business. I'll come see you later."

"I'm not your whore, JJ," she snarled and I paused in the doorway as she scowled at me.

"I know, sweetheart. There's no price on earth that would ever be enough to pay for a girl like you."

Her features softened just before I shut the door between us and I headed into my room, washing my hands of the blood and pulling on another shirt.

I jogged downstairs, finding club members already pouring into the house and it wasn't long before everyone was here.

We went down into the basement after Fox sent a few of our men to deal with Rodriquez and Piston's bodies. I sat between my brothers as Fox's uncles, cousins and the rest of the main crew took seats around the space.

"I want to strike back *tonight*," Fox growled. "We can't wait. Maverick has walked right into the heart of our territory, been at our front door. Tell me how he crossed The Divide without our scouts seeing?" he demanded, his tone calling for blood.

"I don't know, boss," Kestrel said. "The lookouts haven't reported anything. But maybe he came hidden in the back of a van or-"

"I want our CCTV footage gone through. Every scrap of it. And when we have the vehicle he came in, I want footage tracked through town until we know the path he took and which asshole let him slip through the net," Fox growled and everyone assented. "In the meantime, we'll head to Gallows Bridge in The Divide and fight The Damned Men until they've paid for daring to do this."

"It's not enough," Chase snarled. "Maverick needs to pay. He needs to be hit hard. Blood isn't what he cares about. Our informants have told us that he's still working with the cartels, storing and helping them transport their cocaine. If we could get into his warehouses beyond The Divide, destroy every ounce of product he has there then he'd be in debt to his suppliers who'd be down hundreds of thousands of dollars. The cartel might finish him off for us, or at least take out a healthy portion of his men for us."

"There's too many eyes there, they'd see us a mile before we got close," I reasoned. "If Maverick is calling for blood, we'll answer with it."

"There must be a way," Chase insisted and a few of the crew nodded their agreement.

Fox considered our brother's words, rubbing his hand over his chin.

"Unless we could half the number of men he has at the warehouse or more, we'd stand no chance of getting close," he sighed. "I want that too, Ace, but I don't see how we could pull it off while The Damned Men have all the advantages like that."

"Well what if we could trick him somehow?" I suggested. "Draw his men away from there by attacking somewhere else?"

"We could hit The Dungeon?" Draper suggested.

"He wouldn't pull men from the warehouse unless it was for something more important to him than that. He's not gonna risk all of that coke for some shitty illegal nightclub," Fox muttered distractedly.

"So we hit him where it hurts," Chase said firmly.

"Where?" I asked, with a defeated sigh. "The only place he cares about that much is Dead Man's Isle itself. And short of us pulling an armada out of our asses and sailing over there to conquer his personal island, there's no way we could pose a big enough threat to it to make him pull men from the warehouse."

"Who has he left guarding the warehouse anyway?" Uncle Nigel asked. "If it's someone we could outsmart-"

"It's Eckles," Kestrel said with a shake of his head. "And that bastard won't take his eye off the ball for anything. Short of a direct order from Maverick himself, we won't be getting him to leave that place unguarded."

"So basically, it's fucking impossible," I groaned, slumping back in my chair as everyone around the room muttered their agreement and disappointment.

"Fine. We forget the warehouse then," Fox said and I could tell how much that pissed him off even though he was trying to hide it. "But if he wants a war then I'll give him one."

A creak sounded on the basement stairs and I jerked my chin at Draper who was nearest to them. He stood, leaning over to look up the stairs then shrugged and sat back down. I was on edge tonight and with everything that had happened, I'd half expected Maverick to be walking down the fucking stairs. But he couldn't get in here. He could throw blood at the walls, but there was no way for him to break down the gates without a tank. He still never should have gotten that close though.

An argument broke out over where was the best place we could hit back, the elders all agreeing that targeting The Divide and cutting down as many men as we could – like in the good old days – was a swell idea. While others suggested places in the The Damned Men's territory we could hit like stores, boats or businesses until my head was hurting and we still didn't have a clear plan.

"I'm done with this conversation," Fox growled at last, rising from his seat. "We'll head to The Divide and hit them as hard as we can. Gather our men, I want to be heading there in the next thirty minutes."

The elders all cheered as we strode through the basement and me and Chase followed Fox up to the main house. My heart beat erratically as he continued up to the next level and knocked on Rogue's door.

He was probably going to chain her to an armed guard tonight to keep her safe in this house and I was all for it for once.

She didn't answer and I glanced at Chase beside me as Fox pushed into her room.

My gut clenched as I followed, finding it empty apart from Mutt on the bed who cocked his head with a whine.

There was no rainbow haired beauty to be seen.

And I knew from the emptiness in my chest, Rogue was gone.

CHAPTER TWENTY ONE

This was, perhaps, one of the dumbest plans I'd ever come up with in my entire life. But on the plus side, I was the dead girl with nothing to lose already, so how much worse could things really get?

It had been a long time since I'd captained a boat, but it turned out it was like riding a wave on my surfboard – muscle memory had my back. Though the small speedboat I'd picked out may have been a little less than ideal in hindsight. But I couldn't resist taking the keys from the jackass who owned it when I saw him swaggering down the dock, thinking he was the shit while they dangled from his back pocket oh so temptingly.

I'd had to leave Mutt behind for this, knowing my little pooch would be okay enjoying the A/C while hoping he wouldn't get the blame for what I was about to do.

The wind tossed my rainbow hair around my shoulders and I tugged my white lace kaftan close to my body as I stood at the helm of the speedboat and directed her across the silver crested waves in the moonlight towards Dead Man's Isle.

My gaze raked over the once familiar outline of the small island. The compound at the heart of it was backlit by the starry sky with the lights which were on in and around the buildings giving me a little more to go on. I scoured every inch of it hungrily, taking in what I could see of the compound that Maverick had claimed for his own, the huge building at the heart of it housing him out here like he was some high end drug lord. And if the whispers about his links to the cartels were right, then maybe he was.

It had been a beautiful day in Sunset Cove and even out on the sea, the air was still balmy tonight. There wasn't a cloud in sight as I looked up at the star filled sky and the crescent moon far above and the waves rolled beneath the boat with ease as I cut a path straight into trouble.

I was playing one hell of a gamble right now, but after my bruises had faded from the night at the club, a couple of things had stuck in my mind. Firstly, that if Maverick had wanted me dead then I would currently be lying in a morgue somewhere alongside those assholes who'd attacked me. And secondly that he had killed two of his own people - I just couldn't decide what he'd done it for. Was it to protect me from them? Or was it to punish them for letting me get the upper hand? Then there was the third theory, the one I would only whisper to myself when I was alone, because it sounded dumb as shit even to me. But what if he'd killed them for hurting me?

There was certainly a time when Maverick would have done absolutely anything to protect me. When we were eleven, I'd had this dumb glittery rainbow pen that I freaking loved and Tommy Banks had stolen it from me in class. I'd hunted him down after school and punched him in the ear for it, but the asshole had just taken the pen from his pocket and snapped the thing in two like a spiteful little bitch. While I'd stood there with my mouth hanging open in outrage as the bastard laughed at me, Maverick had snatched the sharp end of the pen from him and stabbed him straight in the arm with it. He'd managed to hit a vein too and it had bled everywhere.

Tommy had screamed so freaking loud that we'd had no option but to run for it, and when we'd made it off campus to a dark alley down the street, Maverick told me that he would never let anyone get away with hurting his girl. And I'd told him that next time I could stab the prick myself. But I'd still kinda loved the fact that he'd had my back.

So whether I was being utterly delusional or not, I couldn't totally strike the idea of Maverick killing those assholes for me from the list of possible reasons. Which meant two of my theories suggested I would be safe in Maverick's company. And those were better odds than I'd often gone up against in my life, so I was willing to take the risk.

As I drew closer to the island, my gaze caught on the old shipwreck which lay on the shore, lit up by pale moonlight and surrounded by golden sand and nesting gulls. It had been one of our hangout spots once, where the five of us could run off to when we wanted to be alone. Not that we'd come all the way out to it too often, but if we wanted to put some sea between us and the people on the mainland then we'd had this. Of course, back then the compound Maverick was now living in had been an old hotel which had gone out of business. But the place had clearly undergone a lot of renovations since then.

The white building was surrounded by a circular grey wall which was tall enough to be unscalable and I could make out a couple of men walking along it with guns in hand backlit by the bright lighting within the buildings. Inside the compound, a huge building dominated the centre of the former resort, the balconies and terraces making it look like a palace if I hadn't known it was a hotel. There was a huge swimming pool lit up in blue in front of the building with palm trees planted all around it and a bar set up right beside the water in case you didn't want to get your ass out to order a drink. In short, it was the kind of place that people like me didn't belong. And yet Maverick had chosen to make his home there.

I killed the engine as I got within range of the island, crouching down as I opened up the fuel tank and poured a cup of seawater into the tank before screwing it up and starting the engine again. I shrugged my kaftan off too because as much as it was total bullshit, I knew the dudes guarding the dock would be more likely to fall for my shit if they could lay their eyes on a nice helping of flesh for their troubles. But there was power in objectifying myself for my own gain and I was willing to wield whatever it took to get the upper hand in the world I lived in.

For a few minutes the boat carried on quite happily as I weaved across the waves, making sure I didn't appear to be heading for the island and just seeming like I was out for a leisurely boat ride as I moved close enough to be spotted from the shore.

The moment the acceleration faltered and the engine stuttered I made a show of flapping around and fussing like I had no clue what was happening. Once I'd spent a few minutes doing that, I turned my boat towards the island and started waving as I closed in on the little dock which sat to the right of the beach before Maverick's compound. There were bigger boats docked off to the right of my destination, but I was just a poor, mechanically challenged girl with boat difficulties, so I ignored the scary men who were shouting at me from the jetty, telling me to turn away and just kept going until I was pulling up right beside them.

"You can't dock here," the gruff looking bald dude growled as my boat bumped against the wooden boards beside his boots. Who the fuck wore boots in this heat? Oh right, super scary criminal types. Got it.

"Sorry," I said, flashing an apologetic smile at the dark haired dude who stood a little behind him and seemed less inclined to tell me to fuck off right away. "I'm having engine trouble and I can't get a signal to call for help." I waggled my pink mermaid phone at them and the bald dude huffed in frustration.

"Hop out then, let me take a look," the bald guy said, seeming less than happy about it.

I gave him my brightest smile and raised my hand up to him so that he could pull me out. He'd clearly been expecting me to clamber out on my own and grunted in frustration as he tugged me up onto the jetty, not seeming to fall for my charms one bit.

I gave up on him as he jumped down into my boat and moved over to start the engine to figure out what was up with it.

I turned my attention to the other guy who was checking out my white swimsuit and shorts combo with interest and I had to say, this outfit did do wonders for my rack, so I couldn't blame him.

"Can I be a pain?" I asked him, slipping closer and biting my bottom lip.

"What is it?" he asked with a slight edge of suspicion to his tone and I took note of the gun tucked into the front of his belt.

"I really need the restroom," I said with an apologetic smile. "I was about to head back to shore when the boat started acting up on me and-"

"Come on then," the guy said, making a move to lead me away, but the bald guy looked around with a scowl before I could get more than a step.

"Frisk her first, Billy. Make sure she's not carrying any weapons," he grunted.

"Frisk me?" I asked, blinking up at the guy I now knew as Billy. "Do you think I'm hiding something?"

Billy smirked at me and took a step forward. "We have some important people on this island, can't be too careful."

"Is it celebrities?" I asked, giving him the wide eyes and looking all dumbly ignorant as Billy took his sweet time running his hands over me, cupping my ass and even skimming his hands up the sides of my swimsuit like the clingy material could possibly be hiding anything. Did he think I had a gun stashed up my ass? Maybe, because he certainly gave it a good squeeze to make sure.

"That's a secret," Billy replied with a wink before jerking his chin to get me to follow him and we left the bald dude trying to figure out what was up with my boat.

I made small talk as we circled the pool and its perfectly blue water, taking note of the armed men and women moving around the compound. Some of them seemed to be on watch, but most were just chilling out, enjoying the warm evening, having gangster down time I guessed. It felt kinda like seeing Kim Jong-un on a pool vacation, but I guessed the Harlequins were no different in that regard. If blood didn't wash off so easily, then the whole of Sunset Cove would be painted red by now.

Billy led me past the guys guarding the main entrance and into the building. There were more armed men and women sitting at the desk which I guessed was a reception area once, their gaze following me and Billy as we headed past them. I looked around at the white walls, potted palms and tiled floors with interest, taking care to just look like some dumb girl not worthy of their attention.

Billy led me down a side corridor, all the way to a heavy wooden door with a restroom sign on it.

"Here you go, sweetie," he said, his gaze trailing over me as I leaned back against the door and bit my bottom lip.

"You know...I really should thank you properly for helping me out," I said, dipping my voice seductively and letting my gaze move down his muscular body. He actually was pretty hot, with messy brown hair and plenty of ink on his arms and I might even have seriously entertained the idea of hooking up with him if this was some other situation. As it was, I was just hoping he'd fall for my line so I could get him alone.

"I'm not the one fixing your boat," he said with a smirk and I shrugged.

"You can always thank your friend for me later..." I backed up, pushing the restroom door open behind me and as I'd hoped he stalked in after me, catching the door as I moved inside the fancy restroom.

Billy's eyes lit with lust as he closed in on me, boxing me in against the wall and leaning in to kiss me. I placed a hand on his chest to stop him, giving him a heated look before slowly sinking down to my knees with a filthy look on my face.

"Fuck yes," he groaned, leaning a hand against the wall above me as my knees pressed to the tiles and I looked up at him, licking my lips slowly. "Sweetie, your boat can break down around here any time you like."

I smirked up at him as I reached out and rolled his fly down before unbuckling his belt.

Billy groaned with lust, his eyes closing for a brief moment which gave me the opening I needed to snatch the gun that had been jammed into the front of his jeans, flick the safety off and press it to his cock nice and hard.

"Hey, *sweetie*," I mocked as he froze solid, gawping down at me like his brain couldn't quite catch up with what was happening right now. "Be a lamb and take me to see Maverick. Let's take a quiet route, yeah?"

I rose to my feet again, keeping the gun pressed to his dick and losing a whole hell of a lot of the sweetness from my smile as I let him see exactly the kind of girl I was. And that was not the type to offer out thank you blow jobs to strangers. Was he really dumb enough to believe that girls liked to offer up shit like that on the regular? Or maybe he'd just gotten caught up in the idea of it and accidentally let himself think with his dick instead of his head. Either way, I was now firmly in control of this situation.

I'd actually figured this trick out a few years back and had been using it ever since gangsters like this motherfucker didn't fear death enough to buckle at the threat of a gun pointed at their head. But point it at the dick and threaten them with life as a eunuch and funny enough they lost their balls - figuratively speaking.

"Even if I could get you to him, he'll kill you for this," Billy ground out, seeming afraid to move so much as an inch with his junk in the balance.

"Don't play chicken with me, asshole," I said. "I can always start by taking one ball out as a warning. I know you can get me to him, and I know you can do it without anyone else spotting us. As for him killing me, I'll take my chances. I was dead long before I walked in here anyway."

"I'll enjoy watching him gut you, you crazy bitch," Billy snarled as I exerted pressure on his rapidly shrinking manhood to get him moving. Turned out threatening to blast it off was a turn off, who knew?

"Well, the sooner we get to him, the sooner you can find out if he'll grant that wish or not. My money is on me escaping with my life though, so if you want to make a bet out of it, I'm in." I wasn't sure why I was so certain that the man who I had only seen once in the last ten years and who was clearly at least somewhat deranged if not wholly psychotic, wouldn't kill me, but I was. Our bond may have been broken now, but there was enough of it lingering in the air to at least make me certain of that much. "Now take your belt off and make a loop in it like a good boy.

Billy glowered at me as he did as I'd instructed and I made him slip his wrists through it behind his back before cinching it tight for him and then realigning my gun with his cock for our little walk.

Billy cursed me as he headed out the door and I kept the barrel of my gun pressed tightly to his left ball as we took a route which led even deeper into the old hotel.

We passed through a side door and then took narrow corridors which I was guessing had been designed for staff use instead of guests and we were soon heading up a flight of stairs before emerging on the third floor.

We walked down another corridor with arching white walls and came to a set of closed double doors with the words, *gym and spa* printed on them.

I cocked a brow at Billy, but he didn't hesitate before shoving the doors wide and leading me into a huge, state of the art gym with all kinds of equipment filling the space which opened out onto a sweeping wooden balcony with a view of the sea beyond.

There were around ten people working out in the space, most of the muscular men making use of the weights, but my gaze caught on the biggest of them all.

Maverick was in the middle of a set of pull ups, his shirtless back to me as he hoisted himself up and over the bar again and again, sweat gleaming on his inked skin and highlighting the myriad of tattoos covering his body. A huge cow skull with curving horns dominated his back, the dead eyes seeming to look at me knowingly as I locked my gaze on them.

The silence that fell around the gym in response to the rainbow haired girl marching one of their men in with a gun to his cock was palpable, and suddenly I was faced with a room full of Damned Men drawing weapons and aiming them my way.

Maverick dropped from the pull up bar and turned to face me as he caught on to what was going on, his cold mask of indifference flickering for the briefest of moments as he took everything in and I was pleased to see that I'd managed to surprise him.

"Hey, Rick," I said sweetly, purring like a cat for him while secretly sharpening my claws.

"Out!" he bellowed suddenly, making my heart skip a beat. "Everyone but her."

"But, boss-" some poor fool began, and Rick turned his glare on him with no more than a shift of his eyes that promised violent retribution for questioning him.

The guy balked and dropped his gaze even faster than his protests before falling into line.

Everyone scampered past me after that, more than one of them casting me hateful looks as I kept my gun trained on Billy's balls. Once he was the last one left, I took the gun away from his dick and waved it at the door behind us to indicate that it was time for him to fuck off now.

Billy cut Maverick an apologetic glance then took his opportunity to run while I twisted the gun between my fingers thoughtfully.

It seemed kinda dumb to lose hold of my only weapon, but I wasn't going to shoot him whatever happened. So I flicked the safety on and pushed the pistol into the back of my shorts. *Please, Lord, don't let me shoot my ass cheek off by accident.*

Maverick didn't say anything else, stalking towards me slowly while I remained rooted to the spot, drinking in the changes in him and trying to figure out what was going on behind those dark eyes of his.

"You never did know what was good for you, did you, beautiful?" he growled, stopping before me, so close that I could smell the scent of wood and leather on his skin with the underlying roughness of man.

"It's been a long time since anything was good for me," I tossed back and he arched a brow.

"What do you want?" he asked, no sign that he was pleased to see me, no flicker of anything but this cold, detachment that had my bravado cracking at the seams.

I opened my mouth to reply but he took another step towards me suddenly, making me back up and bump against the heavy wooden door at my back. His hands grasped my waist and I sucked in a sharp breath as he ran them up the smooth fabric of my white swimsuit, his grip tight and unyielding as he felt down over my hips, dipping his fingers into my pockets and tugging my cellphone free, dropping it into his own, followed by the gun. His hands explored every inch of my shorts, even pushing between my thighs for a moment that stole my breath from my lungs.

Then he continued, feeling up the length of my spine over my shoulders, even pushing his fingers into my hair, all while I just stared at him and let him do it. The sensation of his hands on my skin had me frozen and I felt like I was caught in a snare, unable to break free and not wanting to for some reason either.

I wasn't sure what he was looking for, because the gun and cellphone clearly hadn't been it as he continued his exploration of my body and I just took the time to study his.

His tanned skin was heavily decorated with tattoos which seemed to each tell a story I was desperate to hear. I looked between the tattoos, unable to stop myself from drinking in the curves of his powerful body too as he stood there fresh from his workout.

My heart was thundering with a mixture of fear and exhilaration as he touched me, dragging his hands back down my neck and making me suck in a sharp breath as he ran his hands over my breasts without any warning.

"What are you-"

His finger dipped between my breasts and he tugged the key I always wore up to hang between us, giving me an unreadable look before moving to tug it over my head.

I snatched his wrist before he could, glaring up at him as I stopped him from taking it.

"You have one of your own, Rick," I growled. "You don't need mine."

A cruel smirk which was all new to this version of Maverick curled up his lips and he leaned in close without releasing my key.

"You come into my house, threaten my men and stroll in here with something this valuable and you really believe I'm going to let you keep it?" he asked, tugging on the key so that I was forced to step forward as the leather necklace it hung from dug into my neck.

"You don't even know why I'm here," I growled.

"I know why you're here. Question is, do you?" His eyes were so dark and full of a void I was aching to dive into. I felt like I could see so much hidden within them, hurt and pain and suffering that he'd endured since we'd lost each other all those years ago. It was a mirror image of the endless emptiness in me and I craved it in a way that I knew could be my undoing.

"Rick," I breathed, but that seemed like the wrong thing to have done because he tugged the leather necklace securing the key around my neck and yanked it over my head before dropping it around his own neck and stalking away again.

He pulled the door open beside us and walked out, leaving me no choice but to follow.

I practically had to jog to keep up with his fast pace and I cursed beneath my breath as he forced me to scurry after him, taking a set of stairs up two more levels until we reached a door marked *Penthouse* which Maverick shoved through.

The door almost smacked me in the face as he dropped it again and my fists curled with anger as I chased him into the enormous suite.

I was momentarily distracted by the place I found myself in. It seemed like this suite took up the entire top floor of the hotel, the luxurious furniture looking decedent and comfortable in tones of white and blue everywhere I looked. A huge balcony, complete with a narrow pool and hot tub opened out beyond the glass wall ahead of me and gazed over the moonlit beach below where I could see the old shipwreck laying on the sand like it always had.

I followed Maverick through the open space to a large dining table which was laid out with drinks and bowls of food and watched as he poured a pitcher of iced water into a tall glass and lifted it to his lips. He tossed the gun and my cellphone down on the wooden surface without a second thought, not seeming interested in whether I was going to pick them up or not.

"Take your clothes off then, beautiful, I don't have all night," he said as he placed the glass down, his gaze trailing over me expectantly as I glared at him.

"What?" I balked.

"I told you that I was going to take Fox's little plaything and break it for him. So I assume you came here because you want me to do just that."

"You think I came here to fuck you?" I asked incredulously. "I don't even like you, Maverick, why the hell would I want your dick in me?"

"I don't like anyone, but I've put my dick in plenty of them. It doesn't have much to do with it," he replied coldly.

"Fuck you."

Maverick's eyes lit with anger and he advanced on me quickly, snatching a fistful of my hair before shoving me down to my knees as I cursed in surprise. "You're forgetting whose house you're in," he growled. "I could just take it from you, and no one here would give a fuck about your screams. So how about you be a good girl and open wide?"

"And *you're* forgetting what happened to the last man who threatened to rape me," I snarled before throwing a fist straight at his balls.

Maverick shoved me away from him before my punch could land and he strode back towards the table with a humourless laugh.

"Believe me, I can't forget about Axel," he promised as he turned around to face me once more and he pointed out a tattoo on his pec which was made up of a tally with so many struck through sections that I had no chance of counting them all.

I glared at him as I scrambled back to my feet, trying to figure out what he meant by showing me that.

"Babe?" a sultry female voice called and I fell still as a girl appeared from a room beyond Maverick wearing nothing but some seriously transparent black lingerie and the ink on her skin. She had a black pixie cut and looked like a freaking model or something prancing around in next to nothing. "Who's this?" she purred, prowling towards him and winding her arms around his neck as she tiptoed up to place a kiss on the corner of his lips.

"No one," he said dismissively, turning to meet her mouth and kissing her until she moaned breathlessly.

Ice ran through my limbs and my gut bunched as I watched her pawing at him, her hand sliding down his powerful body before slipping inside his shorts as he tugged her bottom lip between his teeth and his gaze slid to meet mine.

I refused to flinch, despite the way my pulse was pounding and my gut was knotting. It wasn't like I wanted him anyway, so he could do whatever the fuck he liked. But why had he just shoved me down beneath him and acted like he'd been expecting me to fuck him if his girlfriend was in the next fucking room? Had he even meant any of that? Or was that just something he did and she didn't mind?

"Is she just going to stand there and watch us?" the girl asked, looking at me again with thinly veiled dislike, like she was wondering what I was doing here just as much as I was wondering about her. I narrowed my eyes on her as her hand began to move back and forth inside Maverick's shorts and he just kept his gaze pinned on me like he was drinking in my reaction to this fucking show.

"Fuck no," I snapped. "I came here because I actually thought you might hate the Harlequins as much as I do, Maverick. And I have information that might help you rid me of them for good. But if you don't want it then I'm just gonna go."

I grabbed my cellphone and the gun and turned away from him and his scantily dressed evening appointment, trying to fight off the flush that was crawling into my cheeks. It wasn't like I gave a shit anyway. The days when I'd hated the idea of my boys touching other women were long gone and they certainly weren't my boys anymore.

"Stop," Maverick commanded and for some fucking reason, I did.

I looked back over my shoulder at him with my eyes narrowed, my gaze instantly zeroing in on the way his fingers were biting into the girl's ass as he held her close. She was still pumping his cock in her hand and had started kissing her way down his body.

"I'm not having a conversation with you while your girlfriend plays with your dick," I growled.

"Well give us a few minutes and she'll be done," he taunted.

"If you come that quickly then it's no wonder she's using her hands. No point getting her pussy wet for thirty seconds of disappointment," I shot back before turning and walking away again.

Heavy footsteps followed me across the room and Maverick's hand landed on my shoulder as he whirled me back around to face him.

"Fuck off, Mia," he said, without looking around at the girl he'd left looking confused by the table.

"But baby, I want your cock in-"

"I said, fuck off," he demanded, his mood utterly shifting yet again as darkness and warning filled his tone.

Mia glared at me as she strode for the door, not even bothering to cover herself up before storming out and slamming it behind her.

Maverick moved closer to me and I backed up until I was pressed against the wall. I didn't know why I was so on edge around him, but there was something seriously disconcerting about how unpredictable he was.

He rested his forearm against the wall above my head and leaned in slowly, pinning me in his dark gaze.

"Speak," he commanded and I wondered if I was really going to go through with this, but as I looked at my key hanging around his neck, I knew that I'd already made this decision.

I reached out and caught the key in my fist, tugging him even closer to show him I wasn't afraid and tilting my chin up towards his so that our lips were almost touching as I shared this secret with him.

"I know where the Harlequins are going to strike tonight. Do you think that's something that might interest you, Rick?" I asked seductively, knowing this would tempt him far better than any half naked girl.

His eyes lit at my words and they roamed over my face as if he were hunting for a lie.

"Tell me," he demanded and a smile tugged at the corner of my lips as I tugged on the key with a sharp jerk, breaking the knot securing the leather necklace and returning it to my possession.

"I will," I promised. "Just as soon as you give me your key."

CHAPTER TWENTY TWO

My back was to the wall in an alley as we closed in on our target location, breathing steadily as I waited for one of The Damned Men to walk by. The moment he was in sight, I yanked him off of the street, clamping my hand down over his mouth and wheeling him towards JJ who was ready with a blade. He sank it deep beneath his ribs and the guy died in my arms before I laid him quietly on the ground.

Fox was shrouded in shadows as he stepped past me to the edge of the wall and threw a look around it.

"How many more?" I hissed.

"Two," he breathed, shifting the knife in his grip so that it flashed red in the moonlight.

My phone buzzed in my pocket and I took it out, checking the group chat. "Draper's in position with the others," I murmured as I read the message.

"Good," Fox growled. "Let's get to the end of this street then we'll be able to see what we're dealing with."

He slipped out onto the road and we followed, hugging the walls as we stuck to the shadows, our dark clothes keeping us covered. Maverick was going to take a serious fucking hit tonight. He wouldn't see us coming when we landed it. And I was goddamn here for it.

Fox shrank back against a boarded up store as voices sounded somewhere ahead and he ducked down behind a dumpster while we hurried to do the same.

"-nah it's all quiet this way," a guy's voice carried to us. "I'm gonna do a sweep though, see if I can find him. He's not answering his phone."

"Alright, I'll come with you."

Heavy boots moved our way and I drew in long breaths to prepare myself for the attack. If we fucked it up and too much noise was made, we were dead meat. So we had to keep it covert for as long as fucking possible.

The second the first guy stepped into view, Fox lunged upwards, stabbing him straight in the throat to silence his scream. In the same moment, me and JJ dove on the second guy and J clapped a hand over his mouth, muffling his cry as I finished the job this time. We hauled them behind the dumpster and I wiped the blood off of my knife onto my jeans. It was dirty work, but someone had to do it. And if I was being totally honest, it got my damn heart pumping. After what Maverick had done to our men tonight, I was ready to go full attack dog on these assholes. No one killed our guys and got away with it. Least of all Maverick fucking Stone.

We made more progress along the street, not meeting any more guards as we made it to a tall fence and started following the edge of it. It swung around into a thick group of trees and we made our way through them, keeping close to the fence until we finally reached an area where we could climb over. On the other side was a little stone building that hid us from view so we could slip inside the perimeter without being spotted. I dropped the pack from my shoulders, taking out the blanket I'd stashed there and throwing it up to lay over the barbed wire topping the fence.

I gave JJ a boost up while Fox freestyled it, the two of them dropping onto the other side a beat later before I climbed up the bars and clambered over. I dropped to the ground and we all took a moment to swap out our knives for guns. Adrenaline crashed through my veins and I smiled at my brothers as I prepared for what was coming.

Then we moved up a small hill that overlooked the large building ahead of us and lay down in the long grass side by side, waiting, ready to strike.

"I love spending quality time with you guys," JJ whispered and I snorted.

"Nothing like stabbing up some assholes to warm your cockles, right?" I murmured.

"Focus," Fox hissed and I rolled my eyes the same time JJ did, but we both turned our attention back to the building in front of us and the many armed guards who were standing around it.

A few trucks stood in bays near the gates and a couple of guys were smoking near them, making me crave the kiss of nicotine in my veins before I dove into the fray. I couldn't risk the cherry giving away our position though and I kinda wished I'd had one on the way here. Because if this plan went to shit and bullets ripped through my body and tore me to pieces, I at least wanted the taste of tobacco on my tongue and a buzz in my veins. And as it happened, I found myself wishing I'd had another last indulgence before we'd headed off on this mission too. I should have looked at Rogue harder, studied every inch of her, brushed my fingers over her heated skin and remembered what it was like to love the girl instead of hate her. The two emotions were so sickeningly similar sometimes I didn't know which I was feeling at any given moment. But if I ended up dead tonight with nothing but blood and metal pouring out of me, I kinda wished I'd stolen a kiss from her. Just once in my life. And if I was lucky enough to stand in front of her again after this, I'd steal the dirtiest, filthiest kiss I could and make sure she never forgot the name Chase Cohen. Dead or alive.

Dead Man's Isle

MAVERICK

CHAPTER TWENTY THREE

I led Rogue through to the bathroom in my suite, catching her arm and pulling her after me when she stopped following. As if I was gonna let her out of my sight.

I grabbed a towel where I'd left it slung over the shower door and twisted her around, yanking her arms behind her back and tying them tightly together.

"What the fuck are you doing, Rick?" she growled and the passion in her voice sent a ripple of heat along the length of my dick.

"Making sure you stay right where I can see you," I growled in her ear, tugging the towel hard and making her stumble toward the shower door. I flipped it open and tethered her hands to the handle while she watched me with irritation.

"Is this getting you off or something, because I'm super not interested in some weird ass shower voyeurism so feel free to blindfold me too."

I ignored her, kicking off my shoes and socks before dropping my shorts and giving her an eyeful of my solid length. "Just like old times, huh beautiful?" I sneered and she determinedly looked me in the eye for several long seconds with an expression that said I'm-not-interested-in-your-nine-incher.

I stepped back into the shower, turning the knob so the rush of water fell over me, waiting for her will to shatter as I squeezed shower gel into my hands. As I gripped my cock and ran my palm up and down it, her eyes dropped and she cursed as she lost the game, looking it dead in the eye.

"Fucking hell, did it get bigger?" she balked, feeding my ego and I gave her a rare smirk as I thought of the last time she'd seen it.

"I think your tits got bigger too. You always had nice tits," I commented and she shrugged like she knew that these days. *They'd be even nicer sucked raw in my mouth.*

I thought back on the last time I'd been naked with her, a time I used to think on a lot, but not anymore. It had been years since I'd let my mind drift to that piece of my past.

"Come on, before the cops show up," I teased Rogue as she stared at my new tattoo on my bare chest. We were covered in spray paint and Mary Beth was gonna fry her ass if she showed up at the group home like this.

She continued to ignore me and I grabbed her shirt, ripping it off of her impatiently. Ho-ly fucking tits.

She had tits. Perfect, full, bare tits. *And it was all too late for her to stop me seeing them as she shrieked and threw her arms around her chest to cover herself up.*

"Shit," I breathed as I stared and stared at her. I'd been hoping to see those since the moment they'd started growing. My dick liked thinking about them a lot. And I mean a lot.

"Do you just go around ripping people's clothes off all the damn time as well as getting secret tattoos?" she demanded as she looked around as if searching for a hole to swallow her up.

The blush on her cheeks was cute as hell, but it was making heat rush all over my skin too. I wanted to ask to touch them, but I didn't know how to phrase that exactly. It put me in a weird ass position and suddenly I decided this shit was kinda her fault anyway.

"Why the fuck aren't you wearing a bra?" I balked.

"I didn't know I had to run my underwear choices by you, asshole," she snarled. "You didn't see anything. Right?"

"Err, I kinda saw everything. And I hate to break it to you, beautiful, but you've got really nice tits and I'm not going to be able to forget them. Ever.

Like on the day I die, I will probably have a flashback to this moment and be like, damn-"

"I hate you," she growled and I frowned, not liking her saying that even if she didn't really mean it.

"Alright, alright, I'll make it fair," I said, raising my hands in surrender as she narrowed her eyes on me.

I grinned at her as I committed to this idea, kicking my shoes off, unbuckling my belt, dropping my jeans and boxers, before stepping out of them and revealing my most prized possession to her. It had gotten big in the last couple of years. Especially when I got a boner, and I was currently in boner town. Because, well, tits.

Her mouth fell open as she stared at it and my chest puffed out with pride. I waited for her to tell me how perfect it was, but she didn't.

"It's kinda rude if you don't say anything," I teased and her mouth snapped shut.

"Are they always that big?" she asked, seeming concerned and my chest puffed up even more.

I grinned, shrugging casually, but no, obviously not. I'd Googled that shit. And I knew I was well above average. "Well, like I said, beautiful, you've got really nice tits and I can't say I've really seen all that many in person so..."

That night was stained on my memory. A lot of shit had happened, some good, some bad, some fucking life changing. It would always bind me to Rogue. But fuck if it had a hold over me anymore.

"I see you still crave my cock as much as the last time you saw it." I gripped my shaft tight, relieving the pressure in it as her eyes worked across it with far more confidence than she'd once had. "I've got your name tattooed on my balls, I'll untie you if you want to come and have a closer look."

"No thanks," she said lightly. "Is this shower show gonna last all day because I've got things to do, people to see, keys to take from psychos." Her upper lip peeled back and anger twisted in her eyes.

I finished up washing while she tried to ignore me yet kept watching me out of the corner of her eyes the whole time. Then I walked up to her dripping wet and hard as stone, reaching around her back and making her breath catch.

I untied the towel, yanking it free and using it to dry my hair and chest before wrapping it around my waist. "Enjoying the tour so far?" I deadpanned.

She rubbed her wrists and I noticed a shark tooth bracelet wrapped around one. I twisted the tooth between my fingers and she tried to smack my hand away from it as I almost ripped it off.

"Is this the same one JJ used to carry around everywhere like it might make him grow taller if he kept wishing on it?" I scoffed and she shrugged.

"Well it certainly worked. And on more than just his height."

I absorbed that nugget of shit, picturing cutting JJ's dick off and breaking his legs so he could never claim to be tall again. "I didn't realise you were fucking all of them, but it makes sense I suppose. You should make the most of his herpes riddled cock while you can though, because I plan on smashing his head in with a brick and watching his eyes pop right out of their sockets. I don't think he'll be much of a lay after that."

Her jaw pulsed furiously and I released a derisive breath. So she cared about him, did she? Then why was she fucking them over? There was clearly more to this than she was letting on.

I brushed past her, catching her hand and towing her along again.

"I thought you liked to cut people's heads off?" she said icily, yanking her hand free of my grip. If I cared about her escaping me, she wouldn't have gotten away. But as it happened, I was sure little miss lost girl was going to trail around after me through my house until she got what she wanted either way.

"Not always." I shrugged. "It's a lot of effort to cut through all that flesh and bone, you know? Sometimes I prefer to choke the life out of them. It's quieter. More personal too. So I'll make sure the next one I do that way is Foxy boy. I'll give him a goodbye kiss for you."

"You obviously thought it was worth the effort to cut off Rodriguez and Piston's heads though," she said darkly and I frowned over my shoulder at her.

"Who?" I muttered, not really giving a shit.

"The guys whose heads you chopped off tonight outside Harlequin House before writing 'war' on the gate," she said with a tut.

"I didn't do jack shit, I've been here all night. Is that why you showed up here, beautiful, to tell me off? Because it sounds like a wasted journey."

"I told you why I'm here," she said firmly. "And can we get the fuck on with the trade because this place smells like bullshit. Or maybe it's just the words coming out of your mouth."

I wheeled towards her, shoving her up against the wall and baring my teeth in her face. I could feel her heart thundering against my flesh as my cock drove into her thigh and she started panting like a bitch in heat. "Why the fuck would I lie? I'm proud of each and every Harlequin death I've delivered. I declared war on Fox and his little crew a long time ago, I wouldn't waste the journey to declare it again. And trust me, if I got that close to his house, I'd be sneaking in the back door and gutting each of them in their beds."

"Seems like an unfair fight." She lifted her chin, all snark and defiance. It was making me wanna force her to her knees and make her choke on my cock until the fight went out of her. I had the feeling it would take a bit more than that though from the look in her eyes.

"You don't know what an unfair fight looks like, beautiful," I growled and her throat bobbed.

"Wanna bet?" she snarled and I cocked my head, my curiosity piqued.

"Who hurt you?" I demanded, darkness seeping into my blood and settling there.

"It would be quicker to list who didn't," she bit at me and the devil in me leaned closer.

I got nose to nose with her, breathing in her coconut scent and the desire pouring from her eyes as keenly as her pain. "Well do me a favour, lost girl. Remind me to fuck you before you take a razor blade to your wrists. It would be a damn shame for that body to go to waste before I could get my fill of it."

Her fist came up to hit me and I caught it with a smirk, pushing my tongue between the middle of her fingers then shoving away from the wall and hearing her trail after me. "Great, well book me in for that next week. I'm free on any day that doesn't end in a Y."

I grunted.

"You would have laughed at that once," she muttered.

"The next time I laugh it'll be over a Harlequin's corpse."

"Wow, savage, Mr Stone. You should really consider a career in kids tv."

I turned my head to hide a smile. *Damn beautiful bitch.*

"Why'd you choose Stone anyways? You sound like some sort of British detective. *Maverick Stone*, fights crime by day, giggles over corpses by night."

"It was the first name in the surname book." I shrugged.

"The surname book?" she snorted and I shot her a sharp look. "And surely that would have been like Aardvark or some shit. Maverick Aardvark, I actually kinda like that. Did you know aardvarks can eat up to fifty thousand ants in one night? That's like, so many ants. Can you imagine eating that many ants?"

"No."

"I once saw a colony of ants carrying a whole corndog. A *whole* corndog, Maverick."

"What's your point?" I rounded on her, my eyes narrowing.

She shrugged. "It's just a lot of corndog to carry for all those tiny ants."

I frowned, seeing so much of the girl I'd once laughed with, laying on the beach while the sun melted into the sea and we knew it would rise again and again, believing our time together would never end. *How naive.*

Fuck it, I could dangle my key over her head all night. And I'd get her to jump through as many hoops as I could before she realised I was never going to give it to her. By the time I'd fucked her and left her spent with a permanent ache between her thighs, I'd take her key for myself. And it wouldn't be long before I squeezed the location of the others from one of her boyfriends' lips while they watched their brothers bleed out around them. Because the contents of that crypt was mine. And no long lost girl was going to take it from me.

Rejects Park

ROGUE

CHAPTER TWENTY FOUR

"They told me you were the only one who tried to come after me," I said in a low voice as Maverick opened a safe that was hidden in the wall, unlocking it and taking his key from within.

I'd given him the information he'd wanted about the Harlequins and now it was his turn to pay up with that little piece of metal in his fist.

He'd made a song and dance about putting on a pair of grey sweatpants before leading me out of his room and back downstairs to a huge office that had once been intended for the resort manager, but Maverick had claimed for his criminal dealings. I wondered what deals he'd struck in here, sitting behind the big, oak desk and making arrangements with all kinds of unsavoury characters. The thought of him sitting there at all seemed too refined for this wild man before me. I couldn't imagine him holding meetings or discussing business dealings in a calm and civilised way. So maybe he didn't. Maybe all of his deals were sealed in blood and paid for with stolen things and illegal acts.

He fell still at my words, the key I'd come here for locked in his fist as he looked into the safe and let me see the stacks of cash and several guns inside.

"Ever since they told me that, I can't help but wonder how different our lives might have been if-"

"Luther might as well have shot me that day," he growled, turning back to me with shadows dancing in the depths of his dark eyes.

He left the safe open and moved towards me, his gaze running over me, drinking in my tattoos again like they fascinated him more than any other change in me.

"Why do you say that?"

"Because the boy I was died that night. I lost everyone I'd ever loved," he ground out. "Every single one of them chose to abandon me and show me my true worth."

"Not me," I breathed, his words sounding so familiar to my broken heart that they could have been my own. "None of it was my choice."

Maverick moved into my personal space again, reaching out to brush a lock of pastel coloured hair behind my ear before fisting a handful of it and forcing me to tip my head back. Pain dug into my scalp and I gasped at the sudden change in him.

"Rick," I snarled, grabbing his wrist and digging my nails in as I tried to tug him off of me.

"It doesn't matter," he growled. "What you were, what I was. Those kids died a long time ago, didn't they? And from where I'm standing, it looks like those years corrupted you almost as deeply as they did me. You're just a fucked up little lost girl, back here in hell searching for boys you remember loving and finding demons in their places. How much does it hurt to come back and see how thoroughly destroyed all of it is? I know that when I got out of prison and came back here it felt like a veil had been lifted. And once I could see all the dirt that coated this place, I forgot about any beauty it might have ever held."

"We were happy once," I breathed, giving up on fighting him off and reaching up to cup his stubble coated cheek in my hand.

Maverick fell deadly still at the contact, still gripping my hair tightly, still leaning over me and yet something bigger than this fucking power play passed between us that made my heart squeeze with the force of it.

"Nah. We were just dumb. Living in a lie about a dream, waiting for reality to come and fuck us up good and proper like every other motherfucker in this place. Tell me, Rogue, when it fucked you did you cry? And how long before you stopped crying and just learned to lie back and take it?" His words were dark and harsh and dug deep into the cracks in my heart, but there was a bleak and hopeless kind of truth to them that I couldn't deny.

"I still would have been happy," I protested weakly. "If I'd had you. All of you."

"If you'd had the boys you thought we were you mean. Because the men we are now aren't the same people. The things we've done to each other, to you, to countless miserable fuckers and innocent assholes alike can't just be scrubbed clean. The night you killed Axel was the night our dreams died too." His words were harsh and meant to cut, but it was a double edged sword which I was certain was making him bleed too.

"You're blaming me for killing the man who tried to rape me?" I snarled.

"No." Maverick released me suddenly and stepped back. "He was just the key to removing the blinkers from our vision. For exposing each of us for who we really are."

"So all I ever was was the girl no one wanted?" I asked, my throat thick as I fought against showing him how much those words killed me. Even now I hated to admit that to myself. But it was true, I'd never once had a person in this world who had chosen me above all else. No one at all aside from...him. He was the one person who hadn't thrown me away, who had tried to follow me, tried to keep his word to me-

"And I was the boy no one wanted," he replied bitterly. "The fall guy. The one it was so easy to forget. Who fucking cares? They won't forget me when I gut the lot of them and hang their corpses from Gallows Bridge but I'll sure as fuck forget them."

"I wanted you," I breathed, unable to stop that truth from slipping past my lips even though I knew what I'd get for it.

The smallest flash of something other than all of the darkness and hatred in him flashed within his eyes before he shook his head like he was refusing to believe it and I felt that rejection like a sucker punch.

"Yeah? Well more fool you. I'm just dead weight, beautiful. I'm a sinking ship drowning in blood and anyone who gets close to me now gets dragged to the depths sooner or later. I suggest you run far and don't look back. Sunset Cove is going to burn. All I have to do is kill Luther and the rest of the dominos will fall right behind him-"

"Wait," I gasped, standing up and grabbing his arm. "What do you mean *kill* Luther? They told me he was dead, that I was safe here now. If he's still alive then being here is a death sentence for me-"

Maverick stared at me for a long moment then burst out laughing, clearly catching onto some joke I was missing. "Dead? You seriously think that motherfucker is dead? Sounds to me like the Harlequins are playing you for a fucking fool, beautiful. Though I don't know why you'd be surprised to hear they're a bunch of fucking liars. They always were after all."

I felt like the wind had been knocked out of me, my lungs compressed and burning. I just stared at him with my lips parted as I tried to process that. Luther Harlequin was alive? Fox's father, the man who had been behind me losing everything I'd ever loved and suffering every day since, the man who had placed a death sentence over my head that expressly forbid me from ever returning to this town or seeing the boys who had once been my entire world again, was alive? What. The. Fuck?

Maverick's phone started ringing and he answered it, tugging his arm out of my grasp.

"Are you in position?" he demanded, dark eyes flicking to me as a smirk tugged at his lips. "I've got it on good authority that the Harlequins are coming. The moment you get eyes on them, call me. I'll be heading over soon. I'll text you with any more instructions."

He cut the call and I was still so full of rage over the fucking lies the others had told me that I just stared at him as he tossed his cellphone down on the desk and tilted his head to look at me.

"Shit, you seriously thought they gave a fuck didn't you?" he asked cruelly, a dark kind of humour glinting in his eyes. "You were starting to think that maybe you could have everything you'd once had with them. Please don't tell me you came here hoping to find the boy you once knew in me too." Maverick laughed at me and I swung my fist into his jaw before I could think any better of it.

He grabbed me by the throat and slammed me down on his desk so fast that I could only gasp as he leaned over me, pinning me down as my heart thrashed in my chest and I grasped his wrist, trying to force his hand off of me.

"Tell me, beautiful, how many of them have fucked you since you got back here?" he asked.

"What?" I gasped, looking into his eyes as he leered down at me, his face right above mine. His grip on my throat was just enough to hold me in place without cutting off my air or really hurting me, but after what Shawn had done it still fucking terrified me.

"Well Fox is telling the whole world that he's got exclusive access between your bronze thighs, and seeing as he knows Daddy will be home any day now to cut your pretty head off, I'm guessing he's been making full use of your pussy. But I also know how much Chase and JJ used to ache for a taste of you. And after your little boast about Johnny James's cock, I have to assume he'd made good use of it with you. Hell, I wouldn't even be surprised if they had a bet running to see which one of them could fuck you first." Maverick snorted a laugh but it sounded false on his lips. I just didn't know what that meant. The mask he wore was so tightly fixed to his features that it was impossible for me to get a true read on him.

"Let go of me, Rick," I growled, thrashing beneath him and he just smiled as I fought and punched, looking like he was actually getting off on seeing me panic.

"Don't start letting yourself believe in dreams, Rogue," he said, dropping his cellphone and the key on the desk beside me as he reached out to smooth my hair out of my face before trailing his thumb over my lips. "I made that mistake once and I'll never do it again. If something seems too good to be true, then it always is. So tell me, why the fuck are you here? Because you sure as fuck didn't come here just to sell out those assholes for that key. There's something else you want from me."

A loud knock came at the door and Maverick sneered angrily as he pushed himself upright, leaving me laying on the desk, panting in fear with my heart thrashing and the most utterly fucked up feeling singing in my veins. Because as much as I didn't want to, on some level I'd relished in that. I liked him showing me the worst of him because there was no bullshit to it. I didn't want to pretend that these men were the boys I'd known once because they'd proved a long time ago that I'd never known them anyway. And they sure as fuck didn't know me anymore. So I wanted to look into the depths of his darkness and figure out whether I could survive the fall into it or whether it would drown me if I tried.

Maverick ripped the door open and I pushed myself to sit up, glancing at his cellphone and key which he'd left beside me.

He threw a look over his shoulder at me then stepped outside to speak to whoever had interrupted us.

My lips parted in surprise as I realised he'd just given me the perfect opportunity to do what I'd come here for. I'd been planning on trying to trigger some kind of alarm or somehow making it seem like this place was under attack, but stealing his cellphone was like a thousand times simpler than that.

Though I was starting to seriously regret this plan. Why was I putting my damn neck on the line for people who wouldn't do the same for me?

Fuck the Harlequins.

But fuck Maverick too.

And fuck Shawn while I was at it. Always.

I picked up Maverick's cellphone, finding it still unlocked from his call and I quickly checked the caller ID to find the contact details I needed.

I pushed my tongue into my cheek as I considered my options. I could forget the fucking plan, let the Harlequins go to hell and leave them to deal with their own problems. But if I did that then I was burning my bridges there and then what? Just stay here on the isle of psychos and let Maverick keep tossing me about like a rag doll? No thanks.

Besides, I had unfinished business with that trio of lying motherfuckers. So I'd stick to the plan then I was going to go and wring their fucking necks, get my hands on their keys and blow up their goddamn world before running the fuck away like I'd been planning all along.

I tapped out a message to Eckles on Maverick's phone, telling him that the island was under attack and that he needed all of his men back here asap to defend it. Then I pocketed the phone, grabbed my own cell too and threaded Maverick's key onto the leather necklace around my neck alongside my own.

I ran for the safe, grabbed two of the pistols inside it then snatched a handful of cash, throwing it around the room like a savage before darting for the window.

It was already wide open to let in the breeze and I hopped up onto the thin ledge outside it, looking down at the three floor drop below with a lurch of fear. Then I crouched down, gripped the windowsill and hung from it, sucking in a sharp breath before dropping onto the balcony of the room below.

I landed on my feet but dropped into a roll to stop my ankles from taking the full force of the fall then scrambled upright again and ran inside.

The room I found myself in was a suite and luckily it was empty, so I dashed for the door, checked the peep hole to make sure there was no one beyond it and then let myself out into the empty corridor.

There was a sign for the pool pointing right so I ran that way, flinching as I heard Maverick's bellow of anger as he found me gone upstairs.

I sprinted for the stairs, skidding as I heard men racing up them towards me and yanking open another door instead before slipping inside. I found myself in a supply closet which was thankfully big enough to warrant its own window. I pressed the door closed behind me and held my breath as running feet pounded by outside.

The moment they moved on, I ran for a stack of white sheets, pulled them aside and dove in to hide between them.

The scent of fresh laundry and citrus engulfed me and I fell utterly still as I waited for the searching men to pass me by. I had what I'd come for, I'd drawn Maverick's men away from the warehouse and now the Harlequins would have the opportunity they needed to strike at The Damned Men.

I just had to hope that I could get my ass out of here before Maverick or one of his men got their hands on me. Because if not, I was pretty sure I was fucked.

CHAPTER TWENTY FIVE

My phone buzzed and I tugged it out of my pocket, finding a message from Rogue.

Rogue:

Maverick's men are heading back to the island. You're welcome.

"She's done it," I told the others with a grin and Chase hissed a yes while Fox smirked darkly.

A signal was already going up around the place and we watched as men piled into the trucks at the edge of the warehouse. We might have all been hella pissed at Rogue for sneaking off to Maverick's fucking compound, but she'd also offered us a chance to strike back at him hard, texting us on her little trip over to Dead Man's Isle to lay out her plan.

Fox had nearly busted his fist when he punched it straight into the wall then he'd shouted a load of angry threats and curses before finally calming down enough to accept the fact that the best thing we could do was go along with it now that it was already underway. There was no chance of us catching up to her and stopping her, so we were gonna make the best of it. But I was willing to bet Fox would be chaining her to him once he got her home safe and never letting her out of his sight again.

This warehouse was storing a shit tonne of cocaine and we were shortly gonna blow it sky high. Just so long as the remaining guards didn't shoot us into the afterlife first, but I was feeling pretty invincible tonight. From the glint in Fox's eye, I reckoned Rogue was gonna be put in the naughty corner when she got away from that fucking island though. *If* she got back.

Fucking hell.

I was torn between being impressed and terrified for her life. But I had faith in our girl. She'd make it back. And all we could really do now was trust her and hope for the best. I shot her a text quickly in reply.

JJ:

Get home, pretty girl. Be careful.

The trucks filed out of the gates and I did a quick headcount of The Damned Men remaining.

Seven. *Easy peasy.*

Fox had his gaze set on the scope of his assault rifle. He was the best shot of the lot of us, so we knew the drill.

"You're gonna miss all the fun up here, Foxy," I teased and his mouth hooked up at the corner.

"I've got my eyes right on it, J. Now get into position."

I crawled back down the hill, shifting into the shadows by the fence as Chase joined me.

"Bet I get inside before you do." Chase smirked.

"A thousand says I get there first," I wagered and his eyes lit up with the game.

He snatched my hand, shaking it firmly. "Deal, brother. Don't die." He turned and ran off in the other direction and I started following the fence, jogging along in the dark as I circled around to the west side of the warehouse. From there, I waited until the nearest guard was looking the other way, gripping the straps of my pack to make sure it didn't jostle before darting quietly across before you stopped crying and just learned to lie back and take it?" His words were dark and harsh and dug deep into the cracks in my heart, but there was a bleak and hopeless kind of truth to them that I couldn't deny.

"I still would have been happy," I protested weakly. "If I'd had you. All of you."

"If you'd had the boys you thought we were you mean. Because the men we are now aren't the same people. The things we've done to each other, to you, to countless miserable fuckers and innocent assholes alike can't just be scrubbed clean. The night you killed Axel was the night our dreams died too." His words were harsh and meant to cut, but it was a double edged sword which I was certain was making him bleed too.

"You're blaming me for killing the man who tried to rape me?" I snarled.

"No." Maverick released me suddenly and stepped back. "He was just the key to removing the blinkers from our vision. For exposing each of us for who we really are."

"So all I ever was was the girl no one wanted?" I asked, my throat thick as I fought against showing him how much those words killed me. Even now I hated to admit that to myself. But it was true, I'd never once had a person in this world who had chosen me above all else. No one at all aside from...him. He was the one person who hadn't thrown me away, who had tried to follow me, tried to keep his word to me-

"And I was the boy no one wanted," he replied bitterly. "The fall guy. The one it was so easy to forget. Who fucking cares? They won't forget me when I gut the lot of them and hang their corpses from Gallows Bridge but I'll sure as fuck forget them."

"I wanted you," I breathed, unable to stop that truth from slipping past my lips even though I knew what I'd get for it.

The smallest flash of something other than all of the darkness and hatred in him flashed within his eyes before he shook his head like he was refusing to believe it and I felt that rejection like a sucker punch.

"Yeah? Well more fool you. I'm just dead weight, beautiful. I'm a sinking ship drowning in blood and anyone who gets close to me now gets dragged to the depths sooner or later. I suggest you run far and don't look back. Sunset Cove is going to burn. All I have to do is kill Luther and the rest of the dominos will fall right behind him-"

"Wait," I gasped, standing up and grabbing his arm. "What do you mean *kill* Luther? They told me he was dead, that I was safe here now. If he's still alive then being here is a death sentence for me-"

Maverick stared at me for a long moment then burst out laughing, clearly catching onto some joke I was missing. "Dead? You seriously think that motherfucker is dead? Sounds to me like the Harlequins are playing you for a fucking fool, beautiful. Though I don't know why you'd be surprised to hear they're a bunch of fucking liars. They always were after all."

I felt like the wind had been knocked out of me, my lungs compressed and burning. I just stared at him with my lips parted as I tried to process that. Luther Harlequin was alive? Fox's father, the man who had been behind me losing everything I'd ever loved and suffering every day since, the man who had placed a death sentence over my head that expressly forbid me from ever returning to this town or seeing the boys who had once been my entire world again, was alive? What. The. Fuck?

Maverick's phone started ringing and he answered it, tugging his arm out of my grasp.

"Are you in position?" he demanded, dark eyes flicking to me as a smirk tugged at his lips. "I've got it on good authority that the Harlequins are coming. The moment you get eyes on them, call me. I'll be heading over soon. I'll text you with any more instructions."

He cut the call and I was still so full of rage over the fucking lies the others had told me that I just stared at him as he tossed his cellphone down on the desk and tilted his head to look at me.

"Shit, you seriously thought they gave a fuck didn't you?" he asked cruelly, a dark kind of humour glinting in his eyes. "You were starting to think that maybe you could have everything you'd once had with them. Please don't tell me you came here hoping to find the boy you once knew in me too." Maverick laughed at me and I swung my fist into his jaw before I could think any better of it.

He grabbed me by the throat and slammed me down on his desk so fast that I could only gasp as he leaned over me, pinning me down as my heart thrashed in my chest and I grasped his wrist, trying to force his hand off of me.

the open stretch of ground. I flattened myself to the wall of the warehouse, drawing in a slow and silent breath as I raised my gun higher. Because chaos was about to descend from the sky.

Make it rain, Foxy.

A loud shot went off and the sound of a body hitting the ground reached me as men started shouting.

I hurried to the edge of the building, throwing a look around it and my gaze slammed into a guy's three feet away. *Shit!*

He started firing, shouting out for back up and a chunk flew out of the wall beside me as I lurched back to take cover. Shots went off everywhere and a heavy thud told me Fox had dealt with my attacker.

I threw another look around the wall, finding the way clear and I started running like James Bond, my arms pumping back and forth at my sides as I sprinted towards the front entrance.

A guy had his back to me, shooting at a truck I guessed Chase was taking cover behind. I drop kicked the asshole to the ground and shot him in the head then the whoosh of a bullet rushed past my ear.

A thud sounded behind me and I turned, finding a woman dead on the ground with a bullet between her eyes, a massive hunting knife clutched in her hand. *Nice one, Fox.*

I ran for the entrance, gripping the bottom of the shutter and yanking on it hard so the metal slid up and over my head. I ran inside just as Chase flew in behind me, but before I could celebrate, a shot was fired at us and we dove behind a large pallet filled with blocks of cocaine.

Holy fuck, Maverick's not exactly hiding this shit.

White powder exploded around us as more shots were fired and my heart thundered with adrenaline as I crawled around the side of the pallet with Chase at my back. The gunfire had quieted outside so that must have meant the last of our enemies were in here. And from the sound of the intermittent gunfire in the warehouse, there could only have been a couple left.

I felt Chase reaching into the bag on my back and smirked as I realised what he was gonna do. There were a couple of Molotov cocktails stashed in there because I moonlighted as a deadly bartender.

Chase lit them up and hissed in my ear. "I'll distract them."

I nodded and he went fucking kamikaze about it, leaping to his feet and running away from me as he shouted loudly and threw the cocktails. A smash and a roar of flames followed by screams told me he'd pulled it off and I leaned up over the pallet, setting a guy in my sights and gunning him down with a few well-aimed shots. The last guy was on fire and frantically trying to put himself out, rolling on the floor while Chase ran forward and silenced him with a bang that echoed on eternally throughout the warehouse.

I smelled blood, cocaine and alcohol sifting through the air and breathed in the taste of victory. Fox jogged into the warehouse, shouldering his rifle and smiling darkly at our prize.

I released a low whistle, climbing up on top of a pallet and gazing around at the huge stash of coke here. This was serious shit. Maverick was in deep with the cartel and boo-fucking-hoo because whoever he was dealing with was gonna be as pissed as a coyote with a cactus up its ass when he found out that all of his precious supply was burned to the ground.

It was damn tempting to steal it and sell it on ourselves, but that would just place a target on our backs with the cartel too and that was the last kind of trouble we needed.

Chase took out the bottles of gasoline stashed in his pack and me and Fox did the same, moving around and soaking as much of the product in it as we could.

"You owe me a grand, Ace," I called as I leapt from one pallet to another, throwing gasoline around like pixie dust. A murderous, hot as shit pixie who was hung like a horse. A dicksie perhaps.

"You wouldn't have gotten in without Fox taking out half of your opponents. I took out four single handed on the east side," Chase argued, ever the sore loser.

"Alright, I'll reduce the price to five hundred dollars, but you have to give me a victory blowie on our way home in the car."

"Only if you've got a chocolate flavoured condom with you," Chase snorted as he played along.

"Sorry babe, I've only got banana or passionfruit. You'll have to pay the full grand."

"Come on assholes, let's finish up here," Fox said, but there was a ghost of a smirk dancing around his lips.

We laid a trail of gasoline up to the door then Chase took out his lighter. I snatched it from him, dropping down and lighting the fluid before he could stop me and he aimed a kick at my head, missing as I jerked away. I laughed wildly as the blaze went up, the fire shooting away from us before tearing out around the whole warehouse.

I tossed the lighter back to Chase and he caught it while we all stood there warming ourselves on the flames of glory. The smoke was soon too toxic to hang around and we definitely needed to be high-tailing it home right about now.

I was hoping Rogue would be back at the house by the time we got there and my heart drummed at the thought of seeing her. I was gonna find a way to steal a kiss before Fox spanked her ass red or whatever the fuck he no doubt had planned out in his mind. Because with Fox, no bad deed went unpunished. And even though this had worked out seriously well for us, Fox hated half-cocked plans. And he especially hated plans that put the people he cared about at risk. Rogue had walked beyond enemy lines into the house of our arch nemesis. And now she was coming home to the wrath of a demon. *You really like defying the big man, don't you pretty girl? It's lucky you're worth the trouble.*

CHAPTER TWENTY SIX

O nce the sound of pounding footsteps had faded away from the halls and I'd managed to go unnoticed when one guy stuck his head into the room to check for me, I crept out of my hiding place again.

I glanced around at the closet I'd used to take shelter in and weighed my options. I didn't know this building and I was guessing there were only a few staircases so if I tried to head down any of those, I was willing to bet I'd be spotted. So the window was my best bet.

I was still on the second floor so I needed to figure out how I was going to get down, and as my gaze fell on the sheets I'd knocked from their neat stack, an idea caught in my mind.

I hurried back over to them and quickly started tying them together to make a rope. Two more floors to go and I could run for my boat - which I was hoping that bald dude had fixed.

My fingers were shaking as I tied sheet after sheet into my makeshift rope and I heard more than a few people charging up and down the corridor outside. But it wasn't fear coursing through my limbs, it was adrenaline, the thrill of the job, the one thing I fucking thrived on and lived for.

I'd been so caught up in getting my head around being back in Sunset

Cove, surrounded by the ghosts of the life I'd once lived that I'd hardly run a single job while I'd been here and I was just now realising how much I missed it. Fuck taking hand outs from the Harlequins, I was a self sufficient woman with a doctorate in stealing shit and an honours degree in getting the fuck away with it.

I cracked the window open and looked down at the drop below which led to a little courtyard in the shade with a couple of tables and parasols set up in it. I couldn't see anyone down there, but I could hear them around the front of the building, calling out to each other while they hunted for me.

Maybe Maverick would have let me go anyway. But I wasn't counting on it. Especially not with his key. But I'd been prepared for that and perfectly happy to accept the risk when I came here. Who didn't love getting into the kind of trouble that could easily get you killed and then having to figure out some insane way out of it anyway?

I opened the window wider, tied off my makeshift rope then climbed up onto the ledge. I grabbed the top of it then lowered myself over the side, clinging on as my sandals slipped against the brick wall.

I cursed them as I flailed about, managing to kick them off one at a time and wondering why the fuck I hadn't worn sneakers. Rule number one of this shit - make sure you were ready to run the fuck away. Well, doing it barefoot would make it interesting I guess.

I shimmied down the rope and dropped to the floor with my pulse jackhammering like mad before running across the small courtyard. I grabbed one of the wrought iron tables and dragged it towards the outer wall, flinching at the sound it made and moving my ass faster as someone yelled something from around the corner.

I hopped up onto the table, leapt for the top of the wall and just managed to catch hold of it before heaving myself skyward with a grunt of effort.

I made it to the top, glancing over at the man standing on the lookout post that had been erected at the far end of the wall and breathing a sigh of relief as I found him watching the beach to the east of the island. That was where the boats were kept after all, so it made sense for them to be expecting me there.

I looked down at the slightly rocky terrain beneath me on the far side of the wall and cursed my luck as I lowered myself over it then had to drop down with bare feet onto it.

I landed awkwardly, my ankle twisting and I fell back on my ass, my elbow slicing open on the sharp rocks.

"Motherfucking dick rock," I cursed it as I got up and started running, the pain in my ankle thankfully easing as I went.

I darted between the shadows beneath the palm trees and took a mostly hidden path that I remembered from my youth which cut down between the rocks to the shipwreck on the north coast. From there, I'd be able to get a look at the docked boats and figure out how the hell I was going to get out of here.

I sprinted down the little track between the scrubby plants and rocks and raced out onto the little cove where the wreck sat. Thankfully the tide was high so the water was up to my ankles the moment I leapt off of the rocks and the soft sand beneath the surface caressed my bare toes.

I splashed my way to the shipwreck, climbing in through the hole in the hull and sighing with relief as the shadows engulfed me and I paused to catch my breath.

I scrambled over rotting wood and barnacles and sent the odd pissed off looking crab scuttling away as I moved to the far end of the wreck. As I made it to the other side, I looked out through a smaller hole that gave me a view of the boats.

I cursed as I spotted Maverick charging down the closest of the two jetties, barking orders and looking really freaking raging as he hunted for me. I didn't want him to catch me. No freaking way. He looked like a pissed off troll who might wanna eat a unicorn haired girl for breakfast. And not in the perfectly acceptable, head between my thighs way of eating either. Oh no, he was out for blood and guts and brains. So I was good staying away from his teeth for now.

I bit down on my bottom lip as I tried to think up a way out of this shit and flinched as a phone started buzzing in my back pocket.

I pulled Maverick's cell out and looked at the unknown number before glancing back at the jetty and spotting him with a phone pressed to his ear. It was utterly insane to even consider answering the super psycho. But then again, I'd never claimed to be sane in the first place.

"Hey, baby," I taunted, answering the call and smirking to myself at the sound which followed because I swear to shit I could hear his teeth grinding.

"You'd better hope I don't find you," Maverick snarled, making a shiver run down my spine and my heart thump harder.

"No chance of that," I agreed. "I'm already half way back to the mainland, but thanks for the key."

"I'm gonna give you one chance to give that key back to me," he growled. "Or I swear-"

"Sorry, big boy, gotta go - there's a seagull taking a dump off the side of my boat and I need to shoo him away. Ciao." I cut the call, laughing my head off as I clapped a hand over my mouth to stifle the sound before taking a selfie of me pursing my lips like a basic bitch while flipping him off. I set the phone to loud and popped it on a little wooden ledge for him to find later and hoped he enjoyed the photo.

While that was fun and all, I still needed to get my ass off of this damn island before one of his goons found me and hauled me back for a spanking. Which would be bad. Obviously. Only straight up crazy bitches would like the idea of some big, muscular tattooed guy bending them over his knee and slapping their ass until they screamed.

So that left me with one question which I needed to answer if I had any hope of getting away from said terrible fate.

What would the Green Power Ranger do?

Red Ranger would run right in guns blazing and try to take on the lot of them. But Red Ranger would also be Dead Ranger if that were the case. Let's not get started on what Pink Ranger would do either because that bitch was not the one to follow in a crisis. No. I needed to think Green.

And as Maverick turned and stalked away again down the jetty, I had an idea that had me feeling all kinds of shades of green from moss to grass.

I slipped back through the wreck, heading for the big hole so that I could climb back out again and pausing to check the coast was clear - literally.

When I was certain it was, I took off running toward the deeper water, wading out as fast as I could before diving into the cerulean blue depths and swimming into deeper waters as I began to circle around towards the jetties.

The cut on my elbow stung as my blood tainted the water and I got to experience the joy of wondering whether or not there were any sharks nearby as I swam on and fear crept up on me at the thought. Kinda like a shark would beneath the waves. Fuck.

I rounded the rocks and paused, glancing between the few guys I could see still patrolling out here as a boat load took off to hunt the sea.

When I was sure they weren't looking my way, I took a deep breath, dove beneath the waves and swam hard and fast, thankful for my years of spending time in these waters every day as I powered towards the closest jetty.

My lungs were burning by the time I surfaced beneath it and I had to fight against the inclination to gasp down a huge breath as I clung to one of the wooden beams supporting the structure.

I took my time moving beneath the boards, eyeing the feet of one of The Damned Men as he walked right above me without even knowing it and I headed for a boat at the end of the dock.

Once I reached it, I swam beneath it before pulling myself up and into it as quietly as I could manage. The small speedboat bobbed beneath me and I stayed low as I headed for the driver's seat.

I had in fact stolen a boat or two in my lifetime and hot wiring was pretty much standard practice across all engines. So it didn't take much for me to grab a knife from a box of fishing tackle, prise open the plastic cover beneath the wheel, strip a few wires, connect wire A to wire B and Bob's your uncle, Talulah's your aunt, the engine came to life with a growl.

A shout of alarm went up and my pulse leapt as I hurried to complete my plan before any of the men on the shore got close enough to see me.

I quickly spun the wheel towards the mainland, pushed the throttle to full speed and dove over the far side of the boat before the water settled and any of The Damned Men could spot me.

I swam fast beneath the surface as the boat tore away, completely empty but drawing a whole lot of attention.

I surfaced beneath the jetty once more and tried not to laugh as the guys all leapt into the only other boat remaining moored up with Maverick at the wheel before they sped away after my decoy.

The moment I was certain they were far enough away, I pulled my cellphone from my back pocket and quietly thanked Fox for spending stupid money on getting me the waterproof model before texting JJ to tell him to use Fox's stalker skills to come find me. I made sure the tracking software was working, shoved the phone back in my pocket and turned my attention towards the horizon.

I steeled myself for a long swim, prayed the sharks weren't hungry today and headed off into the blue.

I wasn't sure if I was happy to be heading back to the Harlequins, especially after finding out they'd been lying to me this whole time. But I was damn proud of myself for my little escape and I was pretty sure the Green Ranger would have been proud of me too.

CHAPTER TWENTY SEVEN

I stood steering the speedboat out across the dark sea, my heart in my fucking throat as I hunted for Rogue in a boat somewhere ahead of us. JJ stood beside me, my phone clasped in his grip as he held it up to track the signal. Chase was waving a heavy duty flashlight out ahead of us as we searched for her.

"She should be right in front of us, where's her fucking boat?" I snarled.

I'd gone from raging to full on panic mode when we'd received her message. I didn't know if she was being pursued or what, but the little dot in the ocean had kept moving toward us, so I'd prayed to fucking God she was still free. She was moving slow enough that she had to be having engine trouble and worry clawed at me as I hunted for her out here, desperate to find her before Maverick or his men did.

The bottom fell out of my stomach as the flashlight swung onto her. In the fucking sea.

"Rogue!" I roared, cutting the engine.

I kicked off my shoes and dove from the boat, crashing into the water. I swam toward her through the cool waves, tugging her against me and she clung on without complaint, panting heavily.

"Wow," she said breathlessly. "I didn't know badgers could swim."

I'd never thought I'd be glad to hear her calling me that as I hugged her against my chest and kissed her forehead. "Any creature would figure it out to save you, baby."

She chuckled. "Even a pigeon?"

"Even a wingless, legless pigeon."

She grinned at me and I smiled back, my heart pounding out a happy beat as I remembered swimming in the ocean with her when we were kids. We'd been thirteen when her board had once gotten pulled out to sea on a riptide. I swam the fuck after her and waited with her until the coastguard had picked us up. We'd gotten one asshole of a sunburn, but it was still one of my favourite memories. She'd held onto me like it wasn't her surfboard keeping her afloat, but me.

"I think we're still drifting out to sea," Rogue said, gazing towards the endless horizon as she bit her lip in concern. The shore was becoming smaller and smaller, but the coastguard would get to us soon. We just had to hang on.

"I'd drift right off the edge of the world if that was where you were heading, hummingbird." I clutched her hand and she wound her fingers between mine.

"Is it weird that I don't care what's out there beyond the horizon? I just want to stay here in Sunset Cove. With you and the others."

"It's not weird," I said firmly. "Too many people think travelling the world will make them happy, more fulfilled or some shit. But the real stuff happens right here. On the dirt we grew up on. This place will remember us when we're gone, nowhere else will. So I want to keep making it ours, brand our names in the earth itself. I like belonging here. And I like that you belong here too. Nothing can ever change that."

JJ directed the boat over to us and Chase reached over the edge and lifted Rogue out of the water, hauling her up into it. I caught the edge of it and dragged myself up, moving to the storage box at the back of it and taking out a blanket.

"Get us back home, J," I commanded and he took off across the water, turning the boat around. I pulled Rogue down beside me on the bench, helping to pull her shorts off.

"Always looking for an excuse to get me undressed, aren't you, asshole?" she said as she shivered in the cool air. I wrapped her in the blanket, locking an arm around her shoulders. Chase watched her from the bench opposite, his brows pulling tight together like he had a thousand thoughts on his mind. I had twice as many and it was giving me a fucking headache. But the one that rang out clearer than any other was that she'd been with Maverick. My fucking adopted brother. What had she said to him? What had he said to her? Why was she still breathing? Did his psychotic tendencies not extend to her? The thought of that made me angry. There was nothing redeeming in him. Especially nothing to do with *my* girl.

"You don't need to hug me, Badger," Rogue said sourly and I frowned at her.

I had a lot I wanted to say to her considering what the fuck she'd done tonight. But after swimming this far to the mainland, she had to be exhausted. I was biting my tongue as hard as I could. I was just relieved she was back in my arms. The reprimanding could wait.

She tried to shove me off when I didn't let go and I gritted my jaw, holding on tighter.

"Is this because you didn't get enough hugs as a kid? Or because you miss your sweet *dead* Daddy hugging you nowadays?" she asked bitterly.

I frowned at the odd question, narrowing my eyes at her before sharing a look with Chase. *Oh shit. She knows.*

"Rogue," I growled.

"Don't *Rogue* me, assbag." She elbowed me away again and I snarled in annoyance, not letting go. "You're all a bunch of liars and you can go to hell. Did you really think I wouldn't find out the truth?"

"Well, personally I was planning on you being gone again before you figured it out," Chase said callously, his hard mask back in place again.

"Shut up," I growled at him and he gave me a frustrated look. "We just needed some time to-"

"To what?" she cut me off, glaring up at me. "To tell me more lies? Is Maverick really your BFF too and you throw cuddle parties together at the weekend?"

"Don't be petulant," I snarled in her face and she snarled right back at me like a wild animal.

"I had a right to know Luther is alive," she hissed.

"So you could run for the hills?" I snapped.

"I'm not afraid of him," she said seriously.

"No, just like you're not afraid to run off to Maverick's island and put your life in danger," I said heatedly. "Just like you're not afraid to push me and act like no rules apply to you in my town."

"They don't apply to me," she bit at me. "Because I don't belong to anyone, I don't follow anyone's rules or laws or demands. I rose from the fucking dead and I'm not ever going to make the mistakes I made in the past by letting assholes like you control my life. But what's worse than you trying to do that is the fucking lies. I should've known I couldn't trust a thing any of you say."

"Don't be like that, pretty girl," JJ implored, looking back at her over his shoulder.

"She'll get over it," I muttered.

"Don't speak for me." She rammed her elbow into my gut and I cursed as she wriggled away from me, getting up and heading over to sit on the opposite side of the boat a good foot away from Chase.

"Maybe we should have left her in the water for the sharks to eat," Chase chuckled and I stood up, striding towards him and shoving him half over the edge of the boat with my hand wrapped around his throat.

"Enough. What did I tell you about talking to her like that?" I snarled and he cursed, gripping my arm and ripping my hand away.

He slammed back into his seat and I glared down at him before shifting my gaze to Rogue.

"We lied to protect you," I told her.

"You do a lot of shady shit to 'protect me' that I never ask for. And it always ends up hurting me worse, so how about you go fuck yourself, Badger. Or each other."

"A thank you would be nice for picking your ass up out of the sea with a hoard of The Damned Men after you," I growled, dropping back into my seat as we closed in on the shore. My temper was rising and teaching her a lesson tonight was starting to appeal again. She was a brat who needed to understand her place was at my side and following my orders.

"A thank you would be nice for giving you an in to hit back at Maverick too, but I don't hear you singing my praises." She turned her gaze out to the water.

"Thank you, pretty girl," JJ said and I scowled at him.

"Don't enable her," I snapped before fixing her in my stare. "You could've gotten yourself killed."

"But I didn't." She shrugged.

"That's not the point," I gritted out.

"Isn't it?" she sang. "Oh and FYI, Rick didn't kill those guys of yours. He said he was sitting pretty in his castle. So it sounds like you have another enemy knocking at your door. You really have a lot of those, Badger, don't you?"

I tsked, shaking my head. "He's lying."

"Why would he?" she asked and I frowned, sharing a look with my boys. "He said himself that if he'd done it he'd happily take the credit."

"She's got a point," JJ said and Chase pushed his tongue into his cheek.

"Bullshit," Chase said coldly. "He lied to her face because he wanted to make out he's not a psycho, most likely to get into her panties."

"Right, 'cause that makes sense," Rogue deadpanned but it did to me. Maverick had wanted her as much as we had. And he would have said anything to try and take my girl from me. I fought a smirk at the thought of her rejecting him and his head exploding when he found out what she'd helped us do.

"Well we'll know for sure once our guys have finished going through the CCTV from tonight," I said and Rogue shrugged.

JJ reached the shore, pulling the boat up alongside the small jetty that led out from the beach which backed our property. There was a guard standing on the end of it who helped us moor up then I led the way to the house as JJ and Chase flanked Rogue, marching her inside behind me.

Mutt came running up to greet us as I opened the door, yapping excitedly, diving past me and licking Rogue's ankles. I turned, whipping him up into my arms and cursing as his teeth sank into my thumb.

"Hey, get off of my dog!" Rogue snapped, but I ignored her, heading upstairs and hearing her running after me.

I walked straight into my bedroom and the second she entered, I turned back, tossing the dog out into the corridor and shutting the door with her inside. I twisted the key in the lock and stuffed it into my back pocket.

"What the fuck?" She gazed at me incredulously and I yanked the blanket off of her, steering her into my bathroom.

I caught her elbow as I pushed her along, running my thumb across the cut there with a grunt of annoyance and she hissed in pain.

"Sorry baby," I murmured. I hated seeing her bleed. It wasn't deep, but that didn't matter. "Did he touch you?" I asked in a growl, inspecting her in the bright light of the room, hunting for more marks.

"Only in ways I liked," she purred and I spun her around to face me, my teeth snapping together.

"Did you fuck him?" I demanded, suddenly drowning in a sea of panic. *Please fuck no.*

"Contrary to what you think of me, Badger, I'm not fucking every man I come into contact with," she said wearily. "I pissed him off good though."

I grinned, hounding her into the shower as I pulled off my own clothes. When I reached for her bikini strap, she slapped my hand away with a feral noise and I rolled my eyes, stepping in behind her naked.

She continued to slap my hands away as I tried to wash her, keeping her back to me the whole time. When we stepped out again, she didn't even let me wrap a towel around her.

"Just let me help you," I commanded, but she ignored me, wriggling out of her bikini within the towel and tossing it into my laundry basket by the sink. Then she pushed past me and lunged for my jeans on the floor. I caught her around the waist, nearly dislodging her towel and she bit into my arm like a savage.

"God, you're infuriating," I snarled, carrying her back to my room and dumping her there before grabbing my jeans and taking the door key from the pocket.

"Oh, *I'm* infuriating?" she laughed humourlessly, her colourful hair hanging wet around her shoulders. Fuck, she looked appetising. I walked slowly toward her, a predator closing in on my prey and she started backing up toward the bed.

"Yeah, you're a stubborn, pig headed, reckless little brat," I said, insulting her with every step I took forward.

Her legs hit the bed and she looked flustered for a second before she schooled her expression, straightening her spine. "Well you're a bossy megalomaniac, so how do you expect me to act?"

I got up close to her face, breathing in the scent of my body wash on her skin as my cock started to throb. "I expect you to do as I say."

"That's never going to happen. Not in this lifetime, not in the next, not in the one after-"

I kissed her to shut her up and she jerked her head away from me with a growl of fury. She drove a knee toward my balls and I shoved her back onto the bed before she got close. Her towel slipped loose and she hurried to close it up before I got a look at her bare pussy. While I watched her with a wild hunger, I wasn't ready for the heel of her foot to slam into my dick and I groaned in agony, lurching away as I cupped my junk. She ran past me, unlocking the balcony doors and running away with the bunch of keys in her hand. I cursed, racing after her but she'd already used the keys to get her own balcony door open by the time I stepped outside. I ran flat out to try and catch her before she got into her room, powering up behind her.

She yelped as she slipped inside and slammed the door. I crashed into it, the key turning in the lock a second later. She smirked victoriously, pressing her middle finger to the glass and I scowled at with my heart thrashing against my ribcage.

I watched as she hurried over to her door, opened it to let Mutt in then twisted the lock on that too. I smacked my palm on the glass in anger.

"Rogue!" I barked. "Open this door."

She walked calmly back over to the window, taking hold of her towel and biting down on her lip as she teased it open just a little, barely holding onto it. My breathing became shallow as I waited to get the show of my life. A voice in the back of my head was shouting red alert, but the boy in me couldn't stop staring and hoping that she'd decided to give me a look at her body for some unknown reason.

"Who's really got the power here, Badger?" she asked, arching a brow then yanking the curtains shut and I smacked my palm on the glass again with a roar of frustration.

Damn her. And damn my dick for being so easily misled by her.

I strode back to my room, slamming the balcony door so hard that the whole house rattled before I grabbed some clothes and pulled them on. Fuck knew what I was even dressed in as I shoved out of my door and jogged downstairs on the hunt for my brothers.

It was late, but my boys always celebrated after a job and especially after we'd struck such a serious blow against Maverick.

I found them in the lounge arguing over playing music or porn on the tv. JJ wanted the porn obviously.

They both fell quiet as they noticed my arrival, looking past me as they sought out the fourth member of this household.

"Where is she?" JJ asked, giving up on trying to get the tv remote from Chase's hands and giving me a kicked puppy dog look. "Did you piss her off again?"

"And why are your sweatpants on backwards?" Chase snorted.

I shrugged, dropping into a chair and picking up the bottle of rum left there, taking a swig of it.

"For fuck's sake, Fox," JJ growled, marching toward me and I quirked a brow at the display of aggression.

"What?" I barked, the alpha in me rearing his head.

Chase flicked some music on, falling down onto the couch and planting a cigarette between his lips.

"You know what," JJ said, his eyes narrowing.

"I don't get it." I drank another measure of rum. "Why's she acting like this? She doesn't snap at *you* like that."

"That's because she actually likes me," JJ said cockily and I sat up straighter, anger seeping through me at the insinuation. "Hear me out," he went on before I could strangle him. "If you spent some time with her like I do, talked to her, listened to her, maybe she'd get along with you better. You know, like you always *used* to get along with her when we were kids?"

My lips pressed tightly together, but I *supposed* I could see his point. "So like...a date?"

"I didn't say that. Why don't you just be her friend and see how things go from there?" JJ suggested, but I ignored him, already planning out a date I could take her on. I could win her around. I just had to channel my inner whipped teenager. I used to love taking her places and giving her cute and pointless shit. If I wasn't so caught up in her running out on me again, maybe I would have thought to do that sooner anyway. But then again, my dense teenage ass hadn't won her either. So I needed to up my game. Combine future and past, become her perfect fantasy of me.

My phone buzzed in my pocket and I found an update from Kestrel waiting for me with a clip of the CCTV footage at the front gate when Maverick had attacked.

Kestrel:

No joy, boss. The assholes were covered up and the van they came in had fake plates.

I sighed as I watched the recording, the men in ski masks jumping out of the back of their van and killing our men fast before setting to work with leaving their fucking message.

I tossed my phone to JJ and he sighed as he watched it before passing it to Chase.

"Do you think there's anything to what Rogue said?" JJ wondered aloud. "It's definitely Maverick right?"

"Who else?" I gritted out.

JJ shrugged and Chase ran his tongue across his teeth.

"No one else would get this close," Chase said and I nodded the same time JJ did, putting the matter to rest. "Have you told your dad?"

"Nah," I said. "It's not his business, besides he'll only defend Maverick again. He's fucking delusional."

"Can we talk about what the fuck we're gonna do when he comes home?" Chase asked. "Because if he finds Rogue back in town, let alone sleeping under our roof he's not going to hesitate to kill her."

"Do you think he'd recognise her?" JJ wondered. "We could give her a fake name?"

"Dad's too savvy for that. If he didn't recognise her right away, he'd figure it out fast."

"Especially with the way you two are acting like she keeps your balls in her purse all the time," Chase muttered and JJ picked up a pillow, whipping him around the head with it before falling into a seat of his own.

"Dad isn't coming home anytime soon," I said. "We'll have warning before he does and then we'll hide her."

"Right, and is that your long term plan too?" Chase snarked. "Because if you insist on keeping her then sooner or later Daddy Harlequin is going to find out. And he'll be even more pissed if he knows we all hid her and lied about it."

"Well what do you suggest Ace?" I demanded.

"You know what my stance on this situation is," he said, releasing a cloud of smoke up into the air.

"I'm tired of you acting like she doesn't mean anything to you," JJ said with an arched brow. "We've known you your whole life, and ever since she left, you act like your heart is a dead lump of flesh in your chest just so you never had to have it broken again."

"Did you make that inaccurate assumption because you read it in one of your mommy porn books?" Chase smirked, but JJ just shrugged.

"To become every woman's fantasy, it helps to do some research on what every woman's fantasy is. You'd get laid more often if you took a dip in my library."

"Yeah, but did you really need to buy that special cover edition of Fifty Shades of Grey on Ebay?" Chase snorted and I cracked a smile as JJ scowled.

"It's a classic, man," JJ defended himself.

"Did the description mention whether it had been dried out since the last owner fingered herself over it?" Chase asked and I smirked, enjoying the game.

"When was the last time a girl fingered herself over you, Ace?" JJ pushed his hand through his hair. "Because two days ago a girl had to be kicked out of my club because she tried to get herself off over me while I was dancing on stage. I didn't even have to lay a hand on her. The idea of me is hotter than you'll ever be. And romance books earn their keep in this house because of that."

"You didn't have to buy that special bookcase for them though," I jibed and JJ shrugged.

"Or that Team Jacob poster you hung above your Twilight collection," Chase added and I barked a laugh.

"Dude, as if I'm Team Jacob, if you're gonna rib on me over Twilight at least get your facts right. Edward was always the one," JJ said, raising his chin as he refused to be embarrassed about this shit. I secretly respected J for the absolutely no shits given attitude he had towards anything and everything he enjoyed. If he wanted to sip a bright pink cocktail out on the patio at one of our parties, dressed in a sparkly bikini and a full face of makeup, he'd still get laid before nine pm. Maybe there really was something to his mommy porn hobby. I had absolutely zero experience with getting a woman to actually like me beyond a mindblowing fuck. I could jerk my chin and have two girls fighting over my cock in under a minute because of who I was. But maybe that had spoiled me. Because the only girl I ever wanted to date was finally back in my life and I had no idea how to make her want me for something serious.

Ah shit, I'm gonna have to read JJ's dirty books, aren't I?

"And while we're on the subject, calling them mommy porn is a guy's way of belittling a billion dollar, female dominated genre which outsells any other genre in the world. And if you respected it a little more, maybe you'd have girls falling at your feet like I do. Just a thought." JJ smirked.

"Thanks for the memo, I'll tuck that right up my ass with the rest of your handy advice," Chase said. "I don't need help getting laid, J."

"If you're talking about Rosie, you need to broaden your horizons because that chick is hard work with minimum returns. And I know you don't need help, dude. You're a solid nine point five for looks, but you're a three for game."

Chase scowled.

"I could build that up to a seven and a half, no problem," JJ added.

"You're an asshole," Chase growled.

"I'm talking specifically related to girls, bro. Don't take offence. This is my job. I have tonnes of hot guys walk into my club off the street wanting to join my troupe. But I only pick the ones who have the potential to be the whole package. And you could be that. Then I could get you *so* fucking laid Chase

Cohen," JJ said. "I could make you into a thousand girls' filthy fantasies. And you'd get premium pussy for that."

"Are you trying to recruit me?" Chase laughed.

"Not for the club. For my entertainment. So pick a girl, any girl, preferably the hottest fucking girl, and I'll get you her," JJ said.

Chase opened his mouth and I talked over him before he could pick.

"Not Rogue," I said, because that glint in his eye said trouble.

Chase scratched the stubble on his jaw. "I wasn't gonna say Rogue," he scoffed and I narrowed my gaze.

"Better not have," I warned.

"I know you're a stubborn fuck, Foxy, but my door's always open if you wanna learn how to make girls like you too," JJ offered and I pushed out of my seat.

Chase stood too as he caught my eye and JJ looked between us with his head growing bigger by the second.

"Hold him down," I told Chase and JJ laughed as Chase ran behind his chair and grabbed JJ's shoulders to keep him in place. I punched JJ in the gut and he wheezed, laughing as he fought Chase and tried to kick me. I continued hitting him playfully until the three of us were wrestling and JJ went full savage, sinking his teeth into my fucking arm.

Irritatingly, JJ was the only one of us who Rogue actually seemed to like. So by the time I was done beating his ass, I was also ready to listen to his advice. Because I was willing to do anything to win Rogue over.

I woke to my alarm buzzing at four am and drew in a long breath as I pushed out of bed, yawning as I got up. I dressed in a pair of surfer shorts and a tank before shouldering the pack I'd filled last night, kicking on my sneakers and heading out of the room with a few chicken treats in my pocket.

I knelt outside Rogue's room, jimmying the twist lock until it clicked open. Then I took the chicken treats out and pushed the door open a crack, holding them up as Mutt's nose appeared in the doorway, sniffing furiously as he hunted for the bribe I always brought here whenever I wanted to watch her sleep. I loved doing that. Partly because she wasn't scowling at me when she was sleeping. And the girl slept seriously heavily so she never noticed. The first time I'd come in here and Mutt had yapped at me, she hadn't stirred. But she would have if he'd continued that shit, so I'd smuggled him downstairs and fed him some kibble. Since then, I made sure I had the finest chicken treats added to our grocery list and he was putty in my hands. Never thought I'd have to bribe a street dog, but here I was, making a damn accord with one.

I stepped into the room, moving to her closet and filling my bag with a little lilac bikini, a kaftan, some hot as fuck booty shorts and a cami.

Then I shouldered my pack and moved to her bed, gazing down at her snuggled in the sheets, her beautiful face perfectly still.

I leaned down, brushing my lips over hers, savouring her taste and she moaned sleepily, the sound making my cock perk up. I slid the sheets back, eyeing her bare legs, her little black panties and the Green Power Ranger tank she was sleeping in. I swear that motherfucker on her top looked smug as hell and I pursed my lips before gently sliding my arms under her and scooping her up against my chest.

Mutt growled and I tossed him a few more treats as she mumbled something about angry badgers then snuggled into my body. The heat of her made my heart pound and I grinned as I stole my girl away, heading out of her room and downstairs to the kitchen with Mutt on my heels. I carefully opened the fridge as I held her against me with one arm and took out the bowl of cooked chicken I'd prepared last night. Then I carefully dropped down, placing it on the floor and Mutt came running over to devour it.

"There you go, little bastard," I murmured before standing and carrying Rogue to the back door and unlocking it. I headed outside, nodding to Raul who lifted his gun at my movements, then nodded to me, eyeing Rogue in my arms for a second before promptly averting his gaze.

Don't mind me, I'm just kidnapping my girl on the date of her life.

I headed down the porch steps to the sandy beach, the waves lapping softly against the darkened shore. There was the barest hint of dawn in the sky and I wanted to get moving to see it rise at our destination.

I headed along the jetty and climbed onto the speedboat, laying Rogue in the nest of blankets I'd put there last night before I went to bed. I brushed some hair away from her face as her eyelids fluttered, but she didn't wake. There wasn't much I could about waking her in a second, but if I didn't get the boat moving before she did, she was gonna try to run. So I'd rather be well underway and have the inevitable argument which was coming once we were at sea.

I stood before the wheel and turned the ignition on, the engine blaring to life and Rogue screamed as she woke. I took off across the waves, throwing a glance over my shoulder as she stood up among the blankets, taking me in with wild, tempestuous eyes.

"What the fuck are you doing, Fox?!" she yelled.

"We're going to spend the morning together," I called over my shoulder.

"Er, no, we're fucking not. Turn the boat around. Take me back this second." She came at me, trying to grab the wheel and I pushed her down to sit on a bench beside me. I dropped the pack from my shoulders, unzipping it and taking out a fresh pastry I'd made at midnight. I handed it to her wrapped in paper, wafting the scent under her nose and she gaped at me like I was crazy.

"Fuck your croissant," she snapped.

"It's a pain au chocolat," I corrected then looked out to sea. "But if you don't want it, I guess a seagull will have it."

"Wait," she gasped because destroying good food had always been blasphemous to her. She snatched it from my grip and I fought a smirk as she bit into it then groaned like I'd just thrust my dick into her. My dad had left me to cook my own meals when I was teenager and around the time I was eighteen, I'd decided I didn't want to live off pizza and microwave meals anymore. And once I could make decent food, JJ and Chase had conveniently shown up for meals most nights. We weren't often on the same schedule these days, but they'd made me promise I'd cook every Sunday for as long as we'd lived together.

"Oh God, why did it have to be so good?" she moaned, taking another large bite and sending flakes of pastry tumbling all over her knees. She had a smear of chocolate by her lips and I reached down, wiping it away with my thumb and sucking it off. Everything tasted better dipped in Rogue Easton.

"Where are we going?" she demanded as soon as she'd devoured the whole thing and started eyeing my pack hopefully like there might be another pastry hiding in there. I made a mental note that the girl was as easily bought with food as her Mutt. Though I didn't think even the best pastry in the world could stop her being angry with me. It seemed to make her slightly more complicit though.

"We're going on a date," I announced, looking to her for her reaction. Which was a pout. *Great.*

"You do realise that normal guys ask girls if they actually *want* to go on a date with them? Which, if you'd bothered to do, I would have refused."

"Hence why I didn't ask," I said simply and she kicked me in the leg.

"That's the part where you cut your losses and turn your attention to another more willing girl, Badge. It's not the green light for kidnap."

"You gave me the green light a long time ago, baby. I'm just trying to figure out how to make you remember that."

"You remember things through Fox-tinted glasses. All I remember was a group of boys who followed me around like a bad smell. I would have cut you all loose eventually." She shrugged and my heart yanked.

"Don't do that," I growled, turning the cruise control on as I turned to her and leaning forward, gripping the edge of the boat either side her. "You can hate me now, hate all of us. But don't pretend the past meant nothing. I was there. It was real. The five of us had something not many people get in life and as fucked as it is now, I still believe some of it is salvageable. At least for four of us."

"That's the first time you've acknowledged that Maverick was important to you once," she whispered, a flicker of pain in her eyes as the first glimmer of the sun peeked over the horizon. My heart was pulled down into a pit of despair that I'd buried a long time ago.

"That's what makes his betrayal worse," I whispered.

"You betrayed him first. Just like you betrayed me first. Did you ever consider I might be here just to rub salt in your wounds? Make sure they never close. Make sure you never forget the hurt you caused me. Maybe I did die in that grave and I came back to haunt you, Fox Harlequin. I'm just a dead girl here to torment you."

"If that's the case then you're doing a good job of it so far, hummingbird. But if you're haunting me then that makes me your unfinished business. And I'm open to you taking your pound of flesh from me first, but after you've got your revenge, you'll find all that's left beneath that venomous need for vengeance is a girl seeking what she lost all those years ago. And I'm it, baby."

I turned away from her, flipping the cruise control off and steering us across the waves in the direction of the cove. The sun was starting to pour light into the world, orange and gold spilling across the horizon like a giant door opening in the sky.

I turned into the cove, slowing as I drove towards the reef. I killed the engine as we passed under the archway of stone everyone around here called Hell's Gateway and dropped the anchor into the water. I pulled Rogue to her feet, her brow creasing as I turned her back to me and held her against my chest. A curse died on her lips as she looked towards the horizon and I rested my chin on her shoulder.

"I missed watching the sunrise with you, remember how much you used to love me waking you at dawn whenever we fell asleep under the pier," I teased and she breathed a laugh.

"I hated that, Badger."

"Only at first, then you'd start looking like you do now. Like you couldn't be angry because it was too fucking beautiful and you knew deep down you didn't really wanna miss it."

"Guess you always thought you knew what I wanted before I did," she said, tossing me a stern look. "And maybe you did once, but not anymore, Fox. I'm not sixteen anymore."

"People don't change. Bad shit just happens that makes them build walls. We can tear them down whenever we want to."

"Have you got walls, Foxy?" she purred as the sun rose higher and her flesh was bathed in gold.

"Not against you." I trailed my fingers across her waist, over her stomach, her tank riding up as I brushed my mouth across her neck, not caring to look at the sky as she watched the night shift into day. She was my sunrise. The one I'd been waiting for for ten years. And I wanted to wake to her every day, watch her light up my morning for as many days as I had left on earth.

Her hand came up to cup the back of my neck as she just gave in for once and her fingers tangled in my hair as my hand slid higher under her top, caressing her silky flesh and making her shiver against me.

"You can't win me with a sunrise," she said breathily.

"No, but maybe I can win you with a thousand," I replied. "Spend the morning with me, Rogue. Pretend we're kids again. Hate me tomorrow."

She said nothing and I pulled away, staring out at the sun gilding the water and wishing I could force it back beneath the horizon again and again until we were sixteen, all of us sitting on the edge of forever, vowing to belong together always. I wanted my brother back as he'd been before our bond had been permanently broken. I wanted Rogue before I'd permanently broken her. I wanted the me back who used to laugh and love my friends with abandon. When the whole world didn't weigh on my shoulders. When we'd convinced ourselves we'd always be together no matter what, and I'd believed it with every scrap of my heart too.

We watched until the sun was full and fat above the water and Rogue turned to me with a sad kind of smile.

I brushed my thumb across her cheek and she leaned into my touch, a possessiveness filling me like a demon.

"Would you go back with me if I could take you there?" I asked and she hesitated before nodding, letting me see into her soul at last. The part of her I knew was there, but she was determined to hide away from me. But we'd written our lives together, the most important years of her youth had been experienced at my side. And I knew her more deeply than she even knew herself.

"Then let's pretend," I growled against her lips then drew away, pulling my shirt off and kicking my shoes off too. I opened the storage box at the back of the boat, taking out snorkels and masks, tossing a set onto the bench for her. I took the knife I kept there in its holster, strapping it to my ankle. I never went anywhere unarmed. My father had drilled that into me and it had saved my life more than once.

"Get changed," I ordered, nodding to my bag and she looked pissed at my command, but her eyes were feasting on my body too.

I pressed my tongue into my cheek before turning and diving overboard.

I swam deep under the cool water, adjusting to the chill that rippled through my skin. I was made for the water. My dad had taught me and Maverick to swim in the pool at Harlequin House. And we'd been surfing almost as long as we'd been walking. Our competitive natures had pushed us both to be the best at everything we did together. We'd thrived on that. But I guessed he thrived on revenge and blood nowadays. *Asshole.*

I surfaced, turning back to the boat and my throat thickened as I found Rogue pulling her pyjama top off with her back to me, the little lilac bikini bottoms framing her ass. She tied the top into place and grabbed the snorkel and mask before diving off of the boat.

I put my mask on and swam toward her, catching her hand as she put hers on too. "You wanna see if that octopus still lives at the bottom of the reef over there?" I pointed to where we'd found it once.

"You mean Inky? He's gotta be dead," she said. "How long can they live?"

"Let's find out." I swam away from her across the water over the reef that lined the rocky wall which arced around the cove.

I took a breath and dove deep, swimming down past the colourful coral, a swarm of silver fish racing beneath me. I reached the bottom, catching hold of a rocky outcrop from the reef to steady myself and Rogue gripped my arm to hold herself down too. We peered into the dark hole in the reef wall and I squinted to catch sight of our old friend. Bubbles slipped from my mouth as we waited, but nothing appeared.

We soon ran out of breath and swam back to the surface. I let the snorkel fall from my mouth as I sucked in a lungful of air and Rogue did the same, a smile spreading across her face.

"Stick your arm in next time," she dared and I laughed.

"Fine, but if I get dragged into that hole, you better come after me, hummingbird," I teased.

"Seems like an easy way to solve all of my problems if an octopus eats your domineering ass," she reasoned.

"I see how it is." I splashed her and she gasped then splashed me back. I grabbed her by the waist, yanking her against my hip and tickling her sides.

"No, Fox!" she yelled and she wrapped her legs around my hips.

I brushed my nose against hers then threw her away from me so she splashed back into the water with a scream. I laughed, diving underwater and powering towards the bottom again. I sensed Rogue following, ready to watch me die by octopus, but there wasn't a creature on earth who'd walk away from Fox Harlequin alive if it tried it.

I made it to the bottom, catching hold of the rocks and pulling myself forward. I reached toward the hole and Rogue gripped my leg, squeezing. I glanced back, finding her shaking her head and I rolled my eyes, stuffing my arm into the hole. Rogue pulled herself along my body until she was holding onto my shoulders, her colourful hair flowing around me as she hugged my back like she was preparing to pull me away from a killer crustacean. Or whatever the fuck octopuses were. All I knew for certain was that they weren't squids.

My fingers brushed the back of the hole, but instead of just letting her know there was no creatures currently lurking in it, I gripped the rock and jerked myself forward, pretending I was being hauled into the hole. Rogue wrapped her legs around my waist, yanking my shoulders furiously as she tried to pull me back and a stream of bubbles left me as I laughed, releasing the rock and swimming for the surface with a little limpet on my back.

My head breached the water and Rogue gripped me tighter, her thighs locking around my waist and her arms clamping around my shoulders.

"Did it get you?" she gasped and I roared a laugh.

"Psych. It was empty."

"You motherfucker," she hissed, but her body vibrated as she laughed.

"I've officially proved you care about me," I said smugly and she took my ear between her teeth, tugging firmly.

"There's another sea monster here who'll end you, Badger," she growled and the cool press of a blade kissed my throat.

A low noise of desire left me and I reached up to grip her hand around the hilt.

"Stealing from me now, are we hummingbird?" I growled.

"Maybe I didn't want the octopus to have the joy of killing you, Foxy. Maybe I'm planning to slit your throat and leave you here for the reef sharks to devour," she warned.

I pressed my throat into the blade. "Are you sure they'll destroy the evidence in time before someone comes looking for me, baby?"

"I'll be long gone before they find me," she whispered.

"Is that what you want?" I asked. "Is that what sixteen year old Rogue wanted?"

She paused, her grip on the blade loosening until she let me pull it from her fingers. "She was an idiot."

"She was perfect," I growled.

"And now I'm ruined," she sighed and I twisted around, pulling her against me as my teeth ground in my mouth. I gripped the back of her head, pressing my forehead to hers and looking her directly in the eyes. "Never."

She melted against me, shaking her head, her mouth grazing mine. "I like pretending we're them."

"We are them," I growled. "Just with scars."

"We can't go back," she whispered, her breath skating against my mouth.

"Pretend," I insisted and she nodded, water droplets running down her face from her hair.

"Old me wouldn't have kissed you," I told her. "He was chicken shit."

"New you steals kisses I don't ask for," she said sternly and I grinned darkly, drawing her closer, her body wrapping around mine as the water lapped against our shoulders.

"But you do ask for them, just not with your mouth," I said cockily.

"Is that what you'll tell the court when I press charges for assault?" she teased and I ran my fingers up her spine, making her quiver.

"Nah, I'll kiss you in front of them and everyone will agree I knew what I was talking about after you melt into a puddle at my feet."

She smacked my shoulder, her features twisting in anger, but her eyes were glittering.

"Remember the last time we climbed up there and jumped?" I nodded to the stone archway and Rogue looked over at it. Sea birds were circling around it where they were nesting in the rocks.

"Chase fell and nearly dashed his head in on the reef," she said with a laugh. There was literally only one place the water was deep enough for jumping into and if you missed, it was game over.

"He climbed up after though and still jumped," I snorted.

"He'd die before he got left out," she mused.

"It's a miracle we're all still breathing after the crazy shit we used to do."

She bit her lip, still looking at Hell's Gateway. "Bet I could still climb up there."

"It's dangerous," I growled immediately, even though I knew how hypocritical that was. But I wasn't an idiot kid now, and I wasn't gonna risk her hurting herself.

"I thought we were sixteen today," she challenged and the mischief in her eyes jabbed the boy in me.

She let go, swimming away from me toward the arch and I cursed as I took chase. She started climbing up the craggy rock before I made it there and I hurried to follow, trying to catch hold of her before she could jump, but the girl was fast.

She made it to the top of the archway and I pushed to my feet as I scaled it too. I was about to demand she get down – for all the good it would do – when she offered her hand to me.

She was dripping wet, her toned body dipped in honey by the sun and the glimmer in her eyes made me feel like I was in front of a goddess who possessed every part of me, right down to my soul. I really was a kid again then, standing in front of the girl he'd loved before he'd even known what love was.

I placed my hand in hers and she smiled at me, giving me this look that felt painfully temporary.

"See you at the bottom," she said, tugging my hand and I jumped over the edge with her, aiming for the darkest water below. My heart soared as we hit the surface and sank deep under the waves, a rush electrifying my body.

When we came up, we swam back to the boat and I climbed up behind her, running my thumb down her spine as I stepped past her to grab bottles of water from my pack. I checked my phone, finding a message from JJ saying all was quiet from The Damned Men, but the fire at Maverick's warehouse had been put out overnight. I didn't think it would be long before he hit back at us, but he'd have the cartel to distract him for a while first. And if we were lucky, they'd kill him for us and end this war for good.

When I turned around to face Rogue again, she was right behind me on her tip-toes and a lump bobbed in my throat.

"This doesn't mean anything," she said, then kissed me hard, clutching the back of my neck. I dropped the water bottles and my phone, gripping her waist and tugging her closer.

I kissed her slow and deep and her tongue moved with mine, tasting of sea salt and my future wife. I was half tempted to get down on one knee right now if I knew she wouldn't kick me in the balls for it. I'd earn that yes from her somehow though. My girl had broken over me once and it was my job to heal her now. I'd find each of her fractured pieces and mend them one at a time. Until she stopped hurting and hating. Until she forgave me for all the bad shit I'd done. Until she realised she'd always been mine and always would be.

CHAPTER TWENTY EIGHT

"Rooooogueeee!"

The mewing cries of my new friends called to me from beyond my thin trailer walls and I groaned, cramming a pillow down over my head and trying to pretend they weren't there.

After giving Fox a morning of pretending and letting myself get altogether too caught up in the idea of being sixteen and the whole world not sucking ass, I'd convinced him to let me come back here for a few days. He'd been checking in near constantly because he was expecting Maverick to strike back after the blow we'd struck against him, but so far all was quiet on the western front. Which apparently should have been concerning me, but I wasn't going to let myself get all worked up about that. If Maverick wanted to come after me for my part in what had happened then I'd deal with that when he did. I'd long since learned not to waste my time worrying about the future. It wasn't guaranteed anyway.

"'S'tooearly," I mumbled back semi loudly, hoping they'd get the hint and leave me to my pit.

I was perhaps a little hungover after partying down on the beach with them last night and trying to drown the whispers about the Harlequins out of my stupid brain. I didn't want to be thinking about them all of the damn time. I'd spent the last ten years doing that as little as humanly possible. And I'd come here with a very clear plan in mind, but so far, that had not come together.

I had upped my key count from one to two now though so maybe I just needed to focus and get my hands on the others. Then I could do what I came here to do and get the fuck out of town. Maverick's key was currently stashed in the vent above my little shower. I would have preferred to keep it on my necklace with my own, but I couldn't risk the others seeing it and realising that I had an actual chance of breaking into that crypt and setting their nightmares loose.

Either way, last night had been a well thought through effort to drink myself into oblivion and forget them, and I was pretty sure it had worked too. I didn't have any memories of dreaming about any of them. Or having nightmares either. Nope. It was nothing but a void of darkness for me last night and I was thinking that I might make it a habit. That said, the pounding in my skull did not agree with me there.

"It isn't early," Lyla called back. "It's past lunchtime and there's a huge party going down at Paradise Lagoon today."

"I'm partied out," I protested.

"Not today you aren't," Di called back. "We got you a job working it and I know your broke ass needs the cash."

I cursed. She was right, my broke ass did need the cash. I may have been so pissed about the fact that Luther was back from the not-so-dead that I'd dumped the cash I'd stolen from Harlequin House in a homeless dude's hat a few nights ago and I'd spent a lot of last night complaining about my need to pay my rent tomorrow with a total of zero funds.

I felt it was totally justified though. I hadn't been driving their stupid car either and I hadn't been spending time at their stupid house. I didn't want anything from them. Least of all their guilt money.

I had seen them though. Mostly Fox, coincidentally hanging out nearby while supposedly giving me space.

I'd told him that I needed a few days back here to just chill out, get my head straight and figure out my options and at the time he'd seemed to be understanding, but I was getting the feeling my time was running low and I was going to be summoned back into the fold soon enough.

"Alright," I called, stumbling out of bed and rubbing my eyes as I headed to the door to open it for them.

Bella was there too, looking fairly lucid for once which meant she also looked kinda sad and was generally being a lot quieter than the other two.

"What's the job then?" I asked, leaving the door open so that I could talk to them while I made coffee and Mutt could go pee.

"Chester and Jolene Granville who run The Dollhouse are putting on this huge party for the rich assholes who have come here on their college spring break this week," Di explained as she came in and took a seat at my little table. "They need escorts filling the place to make sure it's not a total sausage fest."

"I'm not fucking frat boys for cash," I said grumpily, glancing back out onto the porch where Bella and Lyla were sprawled out and making themselves at home.

"That's the beauty of it," Di explained, taking the coffee I handed her. "They need girls to just dance and keep the party going. They'll want you to encourage the assholes to keep spending their money at the bar and to take part in the games, but you don't have to suck any dicks unless you wanna earn the extra. It's a hundred bucks for the day and if you happen to win any of the contests then you can keep the cash prizes too. We basically have to make sure the party goes off and keep them spending."

"That said, I charged fifty bucks per BJ last year and twenty for a handy and I made almost two grand in one day," Lyla said, raising her brows like that might tempt me.

"Fuck me, didn't you get lock jaw?" I laughed and she grinned.

"I could barely even chew solids the next day, but I didn't have to work the whole rest of the month, so I felt like it was a fair trade off." She tossed her blonde hair and winked at me and I could only laugh in response as I tracked down some painkillers and took them for the hangover.

"I bought wrist splints for her in case she needs them tomorrow too," Di cackled and I couldn't help but fall apart with them.

Bella smiled but she had that kinda dead look in her eyes and I frowned as I looked at her.

"If you don't wanna hook up with frat boys for cash I bet JJ would give you more shifts working the bar," I said casually. "I could put in a good word with him if any of you were looking to get out of the sex trade or wanted to have a break for a bit?"

Lyla and Di glanced Bella's way but she just shook her head. "I'll just fuck it up. At least there's not much to get wrong when it comes to fucking. I just have to lay back and wait for it to stop."

"Jesus, Bella, if you hate it that much then why-" Lyla began but Bella waved her off.

"I don't hate it. I don't care," she said and that just made me feel worse for her somehow.

"Honestly, Bella," I said. "JJ would take you on full time, I'm sure of it. I think you could be really good behind the bar and-"

"Nah. Like I said, I'd fuck it up. But thanks." Bella stood up and wandered off, her scarlet hair trailing down her spine as she moved a little way away from my porch, still waiting for us but clearly ending the conversation there.

"I've got it," Lyla said, pushing to her feet and heading after Bella as I frowned, wondering if I'd offended her or something.

"Forget it, Rogue," Di said, moving to stand beside me and giving me a little nudge. "None of us can help Bella until she's ready to help herself."

I shrugged and let it go. I'd certainly never had anyone try to help me fix shit in my life. I knew all too well that it was on each of us to make the best of this life that we could manage and never to make the mistake of relying on anyone else.

"What do I need to wear to this thing then?" I asked, leading the way into my room and Di followed me eagerly.

I let her have a free run at my small closet and took up position on the bed as there wasn't much floor space left.

"Ah-ha!" Di said triumphantly, grabbing the tiniest bikini I owned from my drawer and tossing it at me. It was navy blue with a thong bottom and fitted top which gave the girls some serious boost.

"You're sure no one will assume I'm for sale?" I asked warily as I stripped out of my pyjamas and changed into it. "Because I've got nothing against your line of work, but when I was a kid, this guy tried to-"

"Hey, I get it," Di said. "Your body is your own and you wanna make the choices about who you share it with without any ulterior motives clouding your judgement. If it makes you feel better, these douchebags always have pockets full of cash and get utterly wasted. Stealing from them is like stealing candy from a baby. A sleeping baby. A sleeping baby who's in another room. And they're just rich kids looking to get their dicks wet, most of them aren't even thinking about paying for it until it's offered, so don't worry about having to fight them off."

I laughed, liking the sound of robbing them blind a whole lot more than the idea of sucking strange dick for cash.

"Perfect. But you'll have to give me an alibi if they catch me. Also, where exactly am I supposed to hide all of that cash in this outfit?" I asked.

She tossed me my shortest, most ass-cheek-revealing booty shorts and I caught them in the face before getting up to pull them on. I had to jump a few times to force the denim over my ass, but once I was in, I had to admit that my butt looked good enough to bite and I now had pockets for the cash.

I grabbed my fancy makeup out of the bag I kept in my nightstand and Di hopped up onto the bed behind me as I applied it, combing her fingers through my hair and weaving it into a fishtail braid which she pulled around to hang down over my left shoulder.

"Maybe we need to find you a seashell bra to match your mermaid look," she said as she finished up and I got done painting my lips bubblegum pink.

"I don't think mermaids have asses that hang out of the back of their shorts," I pointed out as I grabbed a white lace cardigan and pulled it over my arms to finish the look.

"No. But they have a tail that guys would chase for miles..." Di raised her eyebrows suggestively and slapped my ass as I laughed again and we headed back out to meet the others.

I paused to leave a bowl of food and water out on the little porch for Mutt and he licked my hands excitedly as he scrambled to get close enough to eat it.

"Be good while I'm gone," I warned him as I locked the door to my trailer, leaving him outside. It was too damn hot for him to be cooped up in there all day and even though he had a home now, Mutt was a street dog born and bred. He much preferred to have the freedom to wander while I was out than to be locked up somewhere and he already had the woman who ran the cafe down on the beach wrapped around his little tail. He'd be begging scraps from her before I even made it to the lagoon no matter how much food I'd just given him.

"Have we got a ride or do you guys wanna go in my car?" I asked as we caught up to Lyla and a decidedly cheerier looking Bella. Though as I took in the width of her pupils, I could hazard a guess as to what had perked her up. I figured I could offer them a ride despite my aversion to using the guilt-Jeep seeing as they'd sorted this job out for me and all.

"I was gonna suggest we walk but I will take you up on that ride in a heartbeat," Lyla announced excitedly.

"Okay, but no promises about being the designated driver for the return trip," I warned them. "I'll get us there, but I'm in the mood to party so I'll probably ditch the car and go get it tomorrow or something when I sober up."

"Sounds good to me. I'll probably finish up the night by letting one of the frat boys pay for the full deal and take me back to his hotel. They always stay up in those fancy ass resorts on the cliffs with the nice pools and free breakfast spreads. I can probably work my way around a few more of them before I even have to leave in the morning and then I'll have enough money for the month and then some," Lyla announced proudly and I could only commend her on her work ethic.

"You're definitely committed to working all those long, hard hours," I teased and she grinned, looking the picture of seduction in her micro skirt and bikini top.

"You know it, baby."

"Last year I ended up spending the whole weekend with this dude who paid me to teach him how to make a woman come so that he could go back and use it on his girlfriend," Di said. "It was so sweet and he worked really hard. I bet that bitch is out there thanking me right now."

"For spending a weekend fucking her boyfriend?" I laughed. "If she is, she's a better woman than me."

"Oh come on, you can't seriously expect me to believe you've never had a dude cheat on you?" Bella asked. "That's just what they do."

"Sure I have," I replied with a shrug, remembering the time I'd come home to find my boyfriend balls deep in my roommate back when I was living in Greendale. "And I packed up my shit to the backing track of him begging me not to go and blaming the girl then walked the fuck out of there and never looked back."

"Wow. I think I love you a little bit for that," Di said. "Were you just stone cold bitch face while he cried?"

"Pretty much," I admitted with the hint of a smirk. That one had hurt a little though if I was being honest. Miguel had been the kind of guy who was always telling me how beautiful I was, always touching, kissing, flirting and promising me the sky. I'd known he was a flirt and a common douchebag, but he'd been growling ti amo into my ear every time he fucked me over and over again for months before I found him cheating. I was just glad I hadn't given in to the urge to try and let myself love him in return for the declarations he'd been making to me, but it had still stung. Even a guy who called me his whole world and professed his love over and over hadn't really wanted me in the end. He'd wanted Linda with her big tits and come fuck me eyes. And that bitch had always drunk my milk. I made sure to go into her room and pour plenty of it on her carpet before I left so that she'd have the joy of that smell lingering alongside the feeling of my ex's dick rutting between her thighs.

"I took his car too," I added. "Sold it for two hundred bucks and a coupon for a free grilled cheese. Best sandwich I've eaten in my entire life. Fact."

We headed out of Rejects Park and around to the parking lot where my shiny new Jeep stood out like a sore thumb and I led the girls over to it.

"You have got to be shitting me," Bella breathed as I unlocked it.

"How is that your car?" Lyla demanded.

"It's not." I shrugged. "It's Fox Harlequin's. He got it for me to drive, but I don't want shit from him so mostly it just sits here."

"Girl, if a man wanted to sugar daddy me this hard, I'd be on my knees worshipping his cock like it was the holy grail, even if he was old enough to be my grandpa and had balls hanging down to his knees," Di announced. "So why the hell are you rejecting all that cash from a guy as hot as him?"

"Yeah, I'd ride Fox for free without him even buying me a car," Lyla added. "He's hot as fuck and he's got that whole dangerous vibe going that says when he was done with me he could just kill me and no one would ever even find my body. I dunno why that's getting me wet, but if you don't want him then I wanna make a play."

"No," I said a little harshly, colour pinking my cheeks as I tried to fight the gut reaction to tell her to back off because he was mine. He wasn't. Hadn't been for a long damn time. "Believe me, that man is much more trouble than he's worth. And I don't wanna hear about you washing up in the bay because he got bored," I added with a grin that said I might be joking. But who knew really? Fox was cut from the same cloth as his father and men like that believed they ruled the damn world. Luther would happily see me dead if he caught me back in town just like Shawn had been more than happy to dispose of me the moment I saw something he hadn't wanted me to. The biggest injustice in all of that was that I hadn't even really heard anything he'd been saying. I'd just seen him talking with some couple I didn't recognise and had been dumb enough to linger by the door to take a closer look at them. The woman had spotted me and before I knew it, I was being choked out, tossed out and forgotten. At least I was used to that last part by now.

We all piled into the Jeep, putting the top down and blasting the music as R.I.P by Sofia Reyes, Rita Ora & Anitta played and we sang along. The girls threw their arms in the air and stood up as we drove down the streets and I laughed at them, real smiles filling my lips in their company which felt pretty damn good.

When we pulled up at the parking lot on the hills outside Paradise Lagoon, we found it full of cars already and the thump of music playing in the distance called us to the party which was clearly already underway. There were narrow footpaths that led down into the natural basin which held the crystal blue water which really did look like a slice of paradise on a normal day. I preferred it when there was hardly anyone here and the sandy beach that surrounded it was undisturbed with the little island at the heart of the water tempting people to swim out and relax on its shore. But I guessed partying here would be cool too.

Right now, however, speakers had been set up to blast music out, there were pop up bars and food joints all around the edge of the lagoon and flashing lights gave the place that tacky, plastic vibe which apparently the rich assholes on spring break just freaking loved.

"Let's go and find Chester and get our passes and cash for showing up," Lyla announced as we made it down to the crowd of partying douchebags and I took in my surroundings.

"Hey, baby, you wanna drink?" some asshole asked, his gaze skimming over all of us as he held a red solo cup out like he hadn't even decided which one of us he was talking to yet.

"No thanks," I brushed him off and Lyla laughed as she led us through the crowd to a large bar that had been set up with a marquee behind it to serve the drinks.

We headed into it and I ignored the couple of gropers who grabbed my ass while mentally preparing to punch a fucker if it kept happening.

Lyla ducked away behind the bar, but the other girls just moved over to grab some drinks and I recognised Carter as he hurried to pour us a row of tequila shots.

"Hey, gorgeous. Are you working today?" he asked and I didn't miss what he meant by 'working' as his freshly healed face morphed into what I was guessing was an attempt at a smoulder and he checked me out super obviously.

"I'm just here to amp up the crowd," I replied, taking my tequila and tossing it back. "I'm not selling anything else."

His smile only grew at that like it was an invitation for him to try his luck and I rolled my eyes. Why was I always attracting guy drama? Though I had to admit it wouldn't be the worst idea for me to find someone a whole lot less Harlequin to get my kicks with if I wanted to survive those boys while I was in town.

Lyla reappeared with a big grin and a handful of hot pink lanyards which she handed out to each of us. The words *ask me for anything* were emblazoned across them in black lettering and I raised an eyebrow at the less than subtle suggestion that anyone wearing one might be up for sale.

But any protests I might have had about wearing it died on my lips as she handed me a crisp hundred dollar bill next and I realised that this was easy money.

"Let's go party then," I suggested, tossing the lanyard over my neck and turned back out to face the sunshine. If someone wanted to pay me to get the party started, then I was all in.

"I'll come find you for a dance when I'm on my break," Carter called behind me and I waved in his vague direction, not really agreeing and not entirely blowing him off.

I strode back out through the crowd, weaving my ass left and right to avoid the pinchers before they got a chance to grab at me while slipping my fingers into unsuspecting pockets and liberating dollar bills to join the feed-the-Rogue fund. Then I headed down the sandy beach towards an area that had been set up with various games and attractions.

My gaze instantly fell on the mechanical rodeo bull in the centre of the attractions on offer where a dude was clinging on by his fingertips as the thing rocked and swung all over the place.

There was a sign hanging above it saying that every hour one rider won fifty dollars and a tray of shots for being the contestant to hold on for the longest. The timer hanging beside it said there was only ten minutes left before this hour was up.

"I'm gonna win me some money," I announced, pointing it out and the girls whooped excitely as we pushed our way through the dude heavy crowd to the front just as the guy currently riding the bull was thrown off of it.

"When you say win, are you actually gonna be able to stay on for longer than six minutes and thirteen seconds?" Lyla asked, pointing at the leader board where a guy called Collin was currently in the top spot.

"Easy," I agreed. Collin was going down.

"Okay, I'm gonna take bets on you then," Lyla announced with a grin and Bella nodded along as she joined her.

"I'm gonna take bets on whether or not your tits will fall out of that bikini top while you're up there," Di added. "We'll split the takings four ways when you win."

"On it," I agreed with a grin, grabbing the elasticated cable which kept the areas around the bull fenced off before jumping up onto the inflatable that surrounded it. "My turn," I called out to the guy running the show just as he was about to call another dude out of the crowd. He took one look at my lanyard and smiled before gesturing for me to climb on up.

I headed over to him first, kicking off my shoes and shrugging out of my cardigan before moving to hop up onto the bull.

There was a rope in front of me between the bull's shoulder blades and I took hold of it with my right hand as I clamped my thighs around its girthy belly. Years ago, when me and the Harlequin boys had first started climbing up to Sinners' Playground, we'd managed to get the mechanical bull there working. It was pretty much the only attraction we'd ever been able to give life to and we'd ridden on that thing more times than I could count before it gave up on life for good. So assuming I hadn't completely forgotten all of the tactics I used to employ to hand the guys their asses with my times, I was pretty sure I had this in the bag.

I looked up as the crowd of rowdy college dudes whooped and cheered and shouted shit about wanting to give me a real ride later and my gaze collided with a pair of very pissed off, very green eyes on the face of one scary bastard of a Badger.

"Rogue!" he yelled, and though the rest of his sentence was lost to me beneath the shouts of the crowd, it was easy enough for me to see he was telling me to get down. My gut lurched as I found him here and my pulse picked up as I wondered if he'd known I was here somehow or if it was just a coincidence. How did he always figure out how to find me? I hadn't even brought my cellphone with me today so he couldn't have tracked that.

I cupped a hand to my ear and shrugged innocently like I had no idea what he was saying and in that moment, the bull began to move beneath me.

I lost sight of Fox's angry ass face as I concentrated on winning some nice green money, rolling my hips and swaying along with the movements of the bull, making sure I didn't lock up and fall on my ass. The trick was to treat it like we were one and the same, me and the bull.

I found myself grinning and even laughing as the crowd whooped and cheered and the bull spun back and forth, jerking left and right and bucking up in an attempt to unseat me.

The longer I managed to stay on, the louder the crowd yelled for me and I managed to pick up the words of a chant. "Tits out! Tits out! Tits out!" I was guessing that was due to Di's little bet, but this bikini top was designer shit that JJ had bought for me and it was made to hold my girls until its dying breath. I wasn't going to be flashing anyone today, but I was willing to bet a certain

Badger might be getting a little antsy at the tone of the crowd.

The bull got faster and faster and I kept rolling with it, clinging on as hard as I could until finally it jerked too hard and I was sent crashing to the inflatable mats beneath me.

I rolled onto my back laughing as I caught my breath, turning my head to look over at the timer and see if I'd managed to do it or not.

But instead of the timer, I found myself looking up at big, pissed off gang leader - oh no, wait, he wasn't the leader was he? Because daddy dearest was still running the show. So he was just a nobody liar.

I made a move to get up, but before I could, Fox grabbed my upper arms and hauled me up to stand before him.

"What the fuck do you think you're doing?" he demanded and I managed to get a look over his shoulder at my time.

Six minutes, twenty-three seconds. *I won!*

I yelled in triumph and managed to shove my way out of his grip before running over to the guy hosting the attraction to claim my fifty bucks.

He handed it over with a grin that died a sudden death as his gaze shifted behind me and I felt Fox moving up close again.

I snatched my prize, grabbed my shoes and cardigan and huffed irritably as I went in search of the other girls who were splitting up the take from the bets and laughing together towards the back of the crowd.

Di threw her arms around me in congratulations as she handed over a fistful of cash and I grinned triumphantly.

"How's your wrestling skills, babe?" Lyla asked. "Because they've got a jello wrestling pit over there and-"

"No fucking way," Fox snapped, catching up to me again and grabbing my wrist.

I squealed in protest as he dragged me away from my friends, carving a path through the crowd and pulling me around one of the huge speakers before shoving me up against the back of it so that I could feel the heavy thump of the bass vibrating through my core.

"What part of *you're mine* are you failing to grasp?" he demanded angrily, his entire body rigid with tension.

"Christ, I was riding a mechanical bull, not a cock. What's your damn problem?" I demanded.

"My problem is the fact that you're half naked. More than half in fact. And every motherfucker in this place is looking at you and wanting to sink his cock into you. And I don't want them looking," he demanded, tugging his tank off and forcing it over my head.

I refused to play ball so my arms were left pinned to my sides as I stood there in the grey material, scowling at him.

"How did you even find me anyway?" I demanded.

"I saw you leave your trailer. I knew those girls would be working this party so it wasn't hard to figure out," he snapped.

"What do you mean, you saw me?" I asked, because there was no way I would have missed his big ass skulking about.

"We're going home," he said forcefully, ignoring my question and making me all kinds of suspicious.

"Bye then," I replied, making a move to step away but he just pushed me back to my spot against the speaker.

"I meant you and me," he growled.

"No. I have a job here today." I forced an arm through his stupid tank and yanked the lanyard out to show him. "I'm not missing out on easy money just because you can't hack the idea of other men looking at me. That's a you problem, not a me problem."

"I'll give you three times the money you're earning here if you want it," he snarled, pulling a roll of cash from his pocket and shoving it into my hand. It had to be at least five hundred dollars in small notes and I scowled down at it for a long moment before schooling my expression and looking back up at him.

"Then what?" I asked, softening my voice as I stepped closer to him. "Can I wear the bikini at home?"

"Yes," he replied, his gaze dipping to look down the front of the shirt he'd forced on me.

"And what if I wanted to earn some more of your money? How much would you give me to fuck me?" I asked.

"What?" he growled.

"Well you seem to want to pay for my time, so I have to assume you

495

think it's for sale. So how much am I worth to you? A grand? Two? Ten?" My fingers balled around the cash he'd given me as his brows knitted together and he didn't seem to grasp my point at all.

Fox hunted for an answer and I slammed my shoulder into him as I forced my way past.

"Wrong answer, dipshit," I snarled as I jogged into the crowd before he could catch me again and threw the handful of cash he'd given me into the air.

The people all around us screamed in excitement and dove for it, making sure he had no chance of catching me as I raced away to the far side of the lagoon.

I yanked his stupid shirt back off, tore it right up the centre and threw that away from me too, only stopping when I made it to the jello wrestling pit where two girls were fighting in the red slime to the mad cheers of the crowd.

I blew out a frustrated breath, turned around abruptly and smacked straight into Chase, knocking his arm hard enough to make him spill the shot he'd been holding onto his bare chest where it ran down over his abs in a trail of golden brown.

"What the fuck, ghost?" he growled.

"Don't tell me you're all stalking me now too?" I snapped in return. "I'm gonna overdose on big dick energy if this goes on much longer."

"What the fuck are you talking about?" Chase grumbled, looking down at his chest like the alcohol on his skin was the biggest problem in the world to him right now. "I'm fucking covered now," he cursed.

I glanced over my shoulder and spotted Fox pushing through the crowd hot on my heels with a face like thunder.

"Well, waste not want not," I said, quickly turning back to Chase and leaning forward to lick the spilled drink off of his skin.

He fell utterly still as I pressed my tongue to the tight muscles at the base of his abdomen, dragging it up between the centre of his abs and tasting the sweetness of his skin beneath the bitterness of the tequila.

I reached up to grip his shoulders as my tongue collected the last drops from his chest and I looked up into his blue eyes with a guilty smirk. His lips were parted in surprise and for once there wasn't a snarky word spilling from his mouth, just heat in his eyes and tension in his Trojan like body.

"Sorry about that, Ace, but I needed a distraction and it looks like you're it." I pressed a kiss to his cheek then darted away right as Fox roared some kind of animalistic threat and slammed straight into him.

Chase managed to keep his feet, shoving Fox back just as hard and he started yelling at Fox to calm the fuck down and calling me a crazy bitch while Fox threatened to rip his balls off if he ever touched me like that again.

I mentally high fived myself for that combination of a brilliant plan and getting myself a free drink and turned to run. But just before I could manage it, a long, taloned hand snatched hold of my wrist and I was whirled around to find Rosie Morgan glaring at me in all her fake haired glory. Yeah, yeah, I was a hypocritical unicorn haired bitch, but who cared?

"Did I just see you trying to get your hooks into my man?" she demanded in a shrill voice, her cheeks inflating like a puffer fish and giving me the desire to smack them to make them pop.

"Err, technically, he just served me a drink in an unorthodox-"

Rosie lunged at me and I jerked back, but before she could actually do anything about the fury etched into her heavily painted features, JJ appeared and caught her around the waist, hauling her back.

"Getting into fights, pretty girl?" he asked me with a grin, ignoring the way Rosie was trying to squirm free and come at me.

"Nah," I replied. "It's just a misunderstanding. Rosie thinks I'm after her boyfriend-"

"I'm not her boyfriend," Chase said as he and Fox finished up their scrap, seeming to have realised that I'd been provoking them and came to loom over me like a pair of sun blocking assholes.

"Chasey!" Rosie shrieked. "You said if I let you do that thing to my ass then you'd marry me-"

"I said, I might be tempted to marry you. I'd need to do it a few more times to be sure," he corrected and I shuddered. Gross. I did not want to hear about that.

Rosie's face fell like she actually had believed he was gonna marry her and I almost felt bad until I remembered what an unsufferable twat she was. "But, Chasey-"

"Why don't you go get yourself a corndog while we deal with getting

Rogue out of here?" he suggested, pulling a roll of cash from his pocket and waving a five dollar bill at her like she was a kid and he was offering her candy money.

"Should I do that thing with it, like-"

"Not today, Rosie," he replied, hiding a smirk. "Just fuck off for a bit, yeah? I'll come find you when I want you."

Rosie shot me a final poisonous look, snatched the five dollars and strutted away.

"Well, I guess I'll be off too," I tried but the three of them surrounded me, blocking my escape and I huffed out a breath.

"Where's my shirt?" Fox demanded.

"I lost it," I replied. "Besides, you've checked out my tits like six times since you caught up to me, so I don't know why you're complaining about my outfit choices."

Chase laughed loudly while JJ grinned and checked them out too.

"Every other girl here is wearing a bikini, Fox," JJ reasoned. "You can't seriously expect her to cover up all the time."

"Yeah," I agreed. "And I'm not the one flashing my nipples at everyone," I added, pointing between Fox and Chase. "JJ is the only one of us with any kind of decency."

"I don't know about that, pretty girl," JJ said in a low voice that had me thinking about the way his body felt against mine and wondering why the hell he was wearing a shirt after all.

"Last call for the raft race!" a voice boomed over the speaker system and I looked up with interest. "This is the biggest competition of the day - winning team gets three hundred and fifty dollars!"

There was a lot of cheering from the crowd as people moved away towards the starting point and I bounced up and down on the balls of my feet eagerly.

"Come on, we can be a team," I suggested. "I'll be the captain and if we win, I'll split the winnings with you. You'll all get five bucks each."

"It's teams of two, not four," Fox replied, seeming like he was actually considering it and I grinned widely.

"See – you're tempted! Please don't drag me out of here. I'm earning my own money and I'm actually having fun," I said, giving him the big eyes.

"You've already been paid for your day promoting. The Granvilles will never even know if you leave now," he replied.

"I'm not talking about *their* money," I said, rolling my eyes and pulling the cash I'd made today from my pocket. I had the bet money from the rodeo bull and about another two hundred dollars which I'd liberated from several pockets.

"You do know you shouldn't be thieving on Harlequin turf without paying us a cut, right?" Fox asked pissily and Chase snorted a laugh.

I sighed dramatically and tugged a single dollar from my take before tucking it down the front of Fox's shorts, making him grunt with a mixture of irritation and surprise.

"Consider my debt paid," I said with a grin and JJ chuckled.

"Fine," Fox conceded. "Let's go do this dumb race then if you're so determined to earn your own money. But if I catch any more guys staring at you, I reserve the right to break their faces."

"Perfect," I said ignoring the face breaking because that was up to him. "You and JJ can be a team. I'm with Chase."

"What?" they all asked simultaneously and I just rolled my eyes as I grabbed Chase's hand and tugged him after me towards the race.

"Everyone knows Chase is the only one who cares about winning this thing as much as I do. You two are dead weight I don't need to carry. If you wanna try and prove me wrong on that then feel free to team up and try to beat us. Just promise me you won't cry over it when we win."

I tugged on Chase's hand harder to make him hurry up, ignoring Fox and JJ's protests and slipping through the crowd before jogging towards the girl who was taking sign ups. She wrote our names down while Chase acted like he didn't want to be here though not making any attempt to leave all the same and she directed us towards the piles of equipment they'd provided to build the rafts.

We moved down the sandy shore to the edge of the lagoon and stopped before a pile which contained four big, blue barrels, six long wooden poles, a bunch of old plastic bottles, other random bits of trash and a long coil of rope.

I bit my lip as I looked over our options, releasing Chase's hand and trying to work out which would be the fastest method of putting a raft together while the other teams all did the same around us.

Thanks to our little run down here, by the time Fox and JJ made it to the line up, they were positioned six places along from us, but of course Fox just made the dudes beside us move with a glower and a death threat.

"I think we should try and make a small raft," I said, glancing over my shoulder and finding Chase placing a cigarette between his lips.

I huffed out a breath of frustration and whirled on him, plucking it from his lips just as he raised his lighter and tossing it away with a growl.

"Get your head in the game, Cohen," I snapped.

"It's a dumb raft and a couple hundred bucks," he said with a frown and a shrug that said he gave no shits about winning this thing, but fuck that. I knew him even if he wanted me to think he'd changed. Chase was the most pettily competitive motherfucker I'd met in my entire life, he just needed a little motivation to remember why he wanted to win so bad.

"No. It's the chance to beat Fox into the dirt and rub our victory in his face."

"And JJ's," Chase added flatly but there was the hint of a smile at the corner of his lips.

I glanced at the douchebags in question and found the two of them discussing their own tactics. Despite their supposed lack of interest in doing this with me, they sure looked like they wanted to try and beat us now.

"Yeah. But we all know you like coming out on top," I taunted.

It might have been a long time since I'd been a part of the way these boys functioned, but I knew that much wouldn't have changed. Chase hated being told what to do and he always went at life like he had a damn point to prove.

"The prize is still bullshit," he muttered, but his gaze had shifted to the equipment we'd been given and I could see those little cogs in his brain working out how we should do this.

"What do you want to win then?" I demanded as the girl announcing the game finished blathering on about rules and started counting down from ten to signal the start of it.

"A favour," he said, his lips pulling up into an evil little smile.

500

"Done. But I'm keeping all the cash." I held my hand out to take his and he snorted a laugh as he slapped his palm against mine.

The whistle blew and we dove into action, grabbing barrels and kicking the empty bottles aside.

We made quick work of lashing two of the barrels between four of the wooden poles and we quickly tied off the ropes while all around us the other teams were working to connect all four of their barrels together.

"You'd better hope that they don't sink under your round ass, little one," Chase teased as the two of us lifted the thing up and ran it down to the edge of the water.

"My ass won't be the issue, macho man," I pointed out. "Perhaps you shouldn't have spent so much time bulking up. You really could have taken the preparation for this race more seriously."

Chase laughed again and it almost seemed like we were having fun together, but I was too damn competitive for that. I'd have fun when we won our prize and not a minute sooner.

"You're gonna fall in!" JJ yelled out behind us as we moved back to grab our oars and he and Fox worked to make their big ass slow raft.

"No chance," I replied determinedly. If we fell in then that was it, we'd be out of the race. The winner had to make it across dry. And I damn well would.

I waded out into the water with Chase right beside me and my heart leapt as his strong hands closed around my waist so that he could lift me up onto the front of our precarious creation.

The whole thing pitched forward with my weight on the front of it and I gasped as I felt it beginning to overbalance, but Chase caught the rear end and stopped it while I fought to stay upright.

He climbed onto the back and suddenly the raft was leaning his way, the nose rising up as the discrepancy in our weight knocked the balance off again.

"Let's get moving," he barked, all bossy and shit like he thought he was team captain and I rolled my eyes over my shoulder at him before I began to paddle. I was team captain, clearly, but there wasn't time to argue the toss about that now.

We were the first onto the water and I set my gaze on the small island in the middle of the lagoon which had been set up with more speakers and lights ready for a celebration party for everyone who made it across.

I also spotted a little plastic trophy placed on the edge of the table where a couple of bar staff were working to fill plastic solo cups and no doubt entice the winner into spending all of their winnings the moment they got it. But not me. All of that green was about to find a nice new home in my pocket.

We paddled in perfect synchronicity and quickly made progress across the lagoon, but the deeper the water beneath our little vessel got, the more the nose lifted into the air until the whole thing lurched with the promise of capsizing.

I cried out in alarm, my arms flying out to balance me and I managed to drop my goddamn oar in the process.

"Shit, Rogue, you're fucking this whole thing up," Chase growled, sounding way too pissed off for a guy who didn't give a crap about winning. *I guess leopards can't change their spots after all, Mr Competitive.*

"I didn't do it on purpose, your big ass is making the boat tip up!" I reminded him, placing my palms flat on the blue barrel between my thighs to steady myself as I leaned forward to try and counter his weight.

"Stop flashing your ass at me and grab that oar," Chase growled and I cursed him beneath my breath as I leaned to my left and tried to reach for the damn thing as it floated just out of reach.

I leaned a little further and the raft lurched to the left, almost flipping up as I began to fall, but Chase caught the back of my shorts and managed to haul me back at the last second.

Adrenaline thundered through my veins and I glanced back to see more teams dragging their rafts towards the water as my heart pounded in my chest.

"We need to move so we're both sitting in the middle to balance it out," Chase commanded. "Then we can grab your oar and win this thing."

"Aye aye, captain," I teased. "Where do you want me then?"

"I'm gonna shift forward and you back up until we meet in the middle," he said.

"So you want me in your lap?" I asked, looking over my shoulder at him with an arched brow.

"Well it'd be more fun if we didn't have clothes on, but maybe I'll get you to do that as your favour to me," he tossed back as he started to inch towards me. "And this position would be ideal too, because I don't have to see your face. Maybe we can add a gag to the mix and-"

"Shut up, dickhead. We need to focus," I snapped. "We can discuss the finer details of you fucking me in the ass while I choke on a ball gag later."

He barked a laugh and I grinned to myself too. Sometimes hating him was kinda fun.

He moved forward and I scooted back until my ass really was pressed against him and he curled a strong arm around my waist to hold onto me while I leaned out over the water to retrieve my oar.

I practically had to stand up, my ass pushing right back into him as I leaned all the way out and he leaned the other way to keep us balanced.

The moment I snagged the oar, Chase tugged me upright again and we started paddling without another word.

The heat of his broad chest behind me and the feeling of his breath on the back of my neck made my skin tingle, but I ignored the sensation in favour of focusing on the island ahead of us and the sound of victory calling my name. And Chase's I guessed. But I was sitting on the front of the raft, so who was really going to be the winner here?

My heart raced with adrenaline at the sound of more rafts getting closer to us, but I kept my eyes on the prize.

The front of the raft finally bumped onto the sandy shore of the island and I yelled out in triumph as I leapt off of it and raced up the beach towards the dude who now stood there holding the little plastic trophy ready to give to the winners.

Chase was right behind me and I threw my arms into the air, leaping on him and whooping our victory to the sky as he was forced to grab hold of my ass to hold me up while I wound my legs around him like a monkey.

"Fuck yes!" I shouted and Chase shook his head at me like he was indulging a child, but he was fighting off a grin too.

"Actually," the dude behind us said a little sheepishly and I glanced at him where he held my trophy out of reach. "The rules said you had to include all four barrels to build the raft, so unfortunately the two of you forfeited the race."

The smile fell from Chase's features in the blink of an eye as my excitement dropped like a stone to the pit of my stomach.

"Bullshit," I said defiantly. "I never heard that rule." Though to be fair, I hadn't been listening to the rules at all, so it was perfectly plausible. *Fucking perfect.*

"Well, then you should have paid more attention," the little jobsworth piped up and I practically snarled at him as Chase set me down on my feet in the sand.

"I'm sorry, what was that you just said?" Chase asked darkly, stalking right up to the guy and taking hold of the front of his bright yellow polo shirt. "Because it sounded like congratulations to me."

"I...what?" the dude gasped.

"I'm pretty sure you were just congratulating my girl and giving her that prize," Chase growled in a deadly tone. And shit, I kinda liked it when his bossy wasn't being directed my way.

"But-"

"Did I fucking stutter?" Chase demanded. "Congratulate her. Now."

"C-congratulations," the guy said, his gaze swivelling to me as he held out the crappy plastic trophy and a little golden envelope which presumably held my winnings.

"Good boy." Chase slapped his cheek a couple of times patronisingly. "Give the asshole a tip, Rogue," he added, glancing at me.

"I suggest you stop being an asshole," I said to the dude who looked mildly tempted to piss his pants.

"That's a damn good tip," Chase said, smirking at me before shoving the douchebag away from him hard enough to knock him on his ass in the sand.

I grinned widely and threw my arms in the air, resuming my victory celebrations as I clutched onto my trophy and kissed it dramatically while shoving the cash into my pocket with the rest.

The guy scrambled away and made it to a microphone where he called out to announce that we were the winners and Chase shook his head as he watched me running victory laps across the sand.

I looked out over the water and my happiness grew as I spotted Fox and JJ yelling at each other while their shitty raft sank beneath them and I could see that Chase was getting a kick from that too.

More of the teams were beginning to arrive on the island and music burst to life as a girl in a red bikini climbed up onto a podium and suddenly started up a foam cannon.

I waved my trophy above my head and ran at Chase again, leaping onto his back as more girls started shooting foam everywhere and the winners' party began.

Chase gripped my thighs and finally gave into the fun, making a game of running towards the cannons so that we were shot over and over again and the fluffy white foam washed over our bodies as we laughed and cheered.

I slid off of Chase's back and he turned towards me, hooking an arm around my waist and tugging me close again.

"Are we even now then, little one?" he taunted. "Does this make you hate me a bit less?"

"No, I still hate you plenty," I assured him as I wound my arms around his neck and pushed my fingers into his dark hair. "But the way you knocked that dude on his ass earned you one day of me pretending I don't."

"What if I enjoy hating you?" he asked, tugging me a little closer as if we were dancing, but we weren't moving enough for that to be the case.

"No worries, Ace. I'm a big girl. I gave up on being loved a long time ago and I don't really care if I'm not liked either."

His brow pinched and he tugged me even closer, leaning down to say something to me just as the sound of Fox yelling my name drew our attention away again.

I let go of Chase, turning towards the others as they appeared through the press of foam covered bodies and I slapped on a taunting grin as JJ and Fox reached us. I waved my trophy in their faces and JJ congratulated me while Fox muttered about JJ's shoddy knot tying skills.

They all began bickering and I tried to fight the smile which wanted to work its way onto my lips at the familiarity of the scene. I closed my eyes and started dancing to the music which was thumping out of the speakers now, letting them get on with it and missing Maverick as I imagined him weighing in to announce some reason why he was the real winner and whispering in my ear that we should just run off and ditch these idiots while they argued it out.

The three of them finally fell silent and I cracked an eye open as I found them all just kinda staring at me like I was a crazy person. But seriously, we were in the middle of a dance floor full of foam while everyone around us partied. They were the only assholes not dancing right now.

JJ cracked a grin and announced that he was going to get us some drinks and I decided to stick to my own decision. One day of pretending I didn't hate them. So I grabbed Chase's hand followed by Fox's and gave them a stern look.

"Dance with me," I commanded and I barrelled on as I saw the start of protests in their eyes. "Let's just dance like we don't hate each other and we can go right on back to it tonight. But I really don't get many days where I smile this much and I don't want it to end yet. So can you both just take your heads out of your asses and have a fucking drink? We can all get shit faced and pretend none of it ever happened. Just for today."

Fox looked pained at my words and Chase looked sceptical, but when JJ re-appeared with a tray full of shots which looked suspiciously like he'd stolen them, they all took a couple and seemed to give in to my request. The burn of the alcohol raced down my throat and we all started dancing in the mess of foam, acting like the carefree kids we'd once been.

Before long we were all coated in slick white suds as the girls with cannons continued to coat everyone. I could hardly even see anyone as the white foam built up all around us and the sound of Break My Heart by Dua Lipa pounded from the speakers and I tried to ignore the words and the meaning they could have held for me and these reckless boys.

I might not have been able to see a whole hell of a lot, but I could feel their hands as the three of them stayed close to me, touching me and pressing nearer as we danced, making sparks of energy race across my skin and my breaths come heavier. I bit my lip on any protests I might have made to the contact and just enjoyed it even though I knew I shouldn't have. It was impossible to be sure whose hand was whose as I was forced to close my eyes against the bubbles repeatedly and the crush of more partiers around us. There was a forbidden kind of thrill to that which I refused to put a name to.

The longer the music went on, the more I actually felt like I was enjoying myself in their company. We used to sneak down to these events when we were teenagers and party like this whenever we could and the familiarity of just having fun with my boys called to me like a warm blanket and the taste of home. It was bittersweet and I knew I'd suffer for it once I came down from this high, but in that moment, I couldn't help but just want to feel it. To pretend that nothing had ever happened to break us; we were still just us and I was happy, whole, unbroken and wanted.

A hand found mine in the gap between songs and I laughed as I was tugged out of the press of bodies, quickly losing sight of the other guys as the crowd closed in on the space we'd been occupying and the sea of white foam made it impossible to recognise anybody amongst it.

When we emerged on the far side of the party, I found JJ smirking at me as he glanced around conspiratorially and tugged me down the side of the marquee which was serving as a bar.

"What are you up to Johnny James?" I asked, my pulse pounding with this wholly new part of our games as he pushed me back against the thick canvas.

"I told Fox we were gonna grab drinks," he said, his eyes burning with heat that made my toes curl and bad ideas scrawl their way through my mind and body alike. "We've got five whole minutes of freedom here before we need to head back. Let's make the most of them."

"I'm still pissed at you for lying to me," I warned but I didn't really feel those words right now, the buzz of the alcohol, the heat of the sun and the beat of the music had swept me away from my anger and I didn't want to visit it again right now.

"Then let me make it up to you," he pressed, shifting into my personal space and taking a kiss before I'd even decided if I was going to offer him one yet.

But the moment his lips found mine, I was a goner. Fire burned beneath my skin and I moaned into his mouth as I pushed my hands beneath his shirt to feel the way the foam slipped over his muscles.

My heart pounded to a heady rhythm and as my palm slid up over his chest, I could feel his own heart meeting it beat for beat. This was crazy and stupid and exhilarating and felt so fucking good that I never wanted it to stop.

JJ growled hungrily as he tugged my bottom lip between his teeth and I gasped as he unbuttoned my shorts, his hand slipping inside them as heat built between my thighs.

"JJ," I breathed, meaning it as a refusal while it came out as a plea.

"Five minutes, pretty girl," he growled. "Let me show you why I charge so damn much for my time."

There were a hundred protests that I should have been making to this insanity, but as JJ's fingers pushed inside me and his mouth covered mine again, I found I'd forgotten them all and I could only surrender to the power he held over me instead.

CHAPTER TWENTY NINE

I was getting a decent buzz after who fucking knew how many beers, but the cigarette between my lips didn't taste half as sweet as what I really wanted in my mouth. Rogue and JJ had disappeared and Fox was off hunting for 'his girl'. Which was bullshit in my humbly honest opinion, but fuck if he'd listen to me on that matter. It wasn't just the fact that she point blank refused his attention on a daily basis, but that he had no right to call her his anything. If she belonged to anyone, she belonged to all of us. But I still thought the best thing we could do for ourselves would be to cut her loose and agree she belonged to no one.

Still…

The beer was giving me ideas that I shouldn't have been entertaining. But after we'd won the race together and she'd smiled at me like she had when we were kids, my dumbass dick was getting ideas. Dirty ideas. The kind that would lead me down a seriously dark path. Because I knew if I allowed myself one taste of Rogue Easton, I wouldn't be able to get enough. I'd keep coming back to drink the poison at her well until I helped fulfil the prophesy of her return destroying us all. A prophesy I'd admittedly made up. But I'd already seen how Fox and JJ were acting now she was back. They were pussy whipped and JJ was either going to have to lose that starry look in his eyes when he was around her or Fox would figure out his feelings were as strong as his own and they'd clash. And JJ and Fox never clashed. It was expected of me, but J was the peacekeeper. If he went up against Fox over this, it was going to be apocalyptic.

I hadn't voiced this to either of them though, partly because they disregarded my fucking opinion on the subject and partly because while they were busy staring at her, I was stealing glances too. And today I could have sworn she'd looked at me with want in her eyes. The alcohol in my bloodstream certainly seemed to think so. What was the harm anyway? I'd promised myself a kiss from her lips if I survived the night destroying Maverick's drug warehouse. Technically I was owed it. Didn't have to be some feelings-filled headfuck, I just wanted to satisfy a craving I'd had when I was a teenager. That was all. And screw what Fox or JJ would think of that.

I dropped my beer bottle into the hands of a waitress then forged a path out of the foam towards the marquee. Maybe Rogue and JJ had headed in there to get more drinks, but as I walked towards the entrance, a lull in the music made my hearing snag on a breathy moan. My heart twitched in recognition and I fell entirely still as Rogue moaned again.

A deep and primal urge to rip apart whoever was touching her filled me and I circled around the side of the marquee, taking a long drag on my cigarette, preparing to spill blood.

Darkness thumped through my veins as I reached the end of it and stepped into the shadowy area behind the marquee that backed onto a group of palm trees.

Smoke coiled up around me as I stopped breathing, taking in Rogue pressed back against a tree with JJ's hand moving beneath her waistband, her shorts' button popped open and his other hand circling beneath her bikini top. Her head was tipped back, her eyes shut, her teeth digging into her lower lip. And JJ watched her like the world began and ended with her fucking pussy.

I was dragged back into the past, standing before the summer house on the Rosewood property, watching as Rogue stood topless in front a very naked Maverick. She'd chosen him and now she'd chosen fucking JJ. Pain rippled through the centre of my chest and anger sent a knife slicing down my spine. I was blinded by rage, stalking forward as I let my smoke fall from my lips, doing what I should have done the day I caught her with Maverick and shoving JJ hard, sending him stumbling away from her.

Rogue's eyes flew open and I dove on JJ as realisation spread across his face. I threw my fist into his gut and snatched his wifebeater in my fist, forcing him back against a thick tree trunk. His knee came up into my side before he slammed a rib-crushing punch into my chest and I growled as I threw another punch of my own.

"Stop it!" Rogue snapped, launching herself onto my back and slapping her hands over my face so I couldn't see.

JJ took the opportunity to sucker punch me and I ripped Rogue's hands from my eyes, lunging at JJ again with a snarl. I tackled him down onto the sand and Rogue tried to heave my shoulders back as I laid into him, then she bit into my fucking neck like a damn vampire.

"Get off me, ghost," I snarled, reaching back and grabbing a fistful of her hair.

JJ slammed another punch into my chest and I rolled over, crushing Rogue beneath me making her curse.

JJ threw himself on top of me and Rogue yelped as our combined weight crushed her into the sand.

"You're hurting her," I snarled, shoving JJ back and he huffed as he stood up, kicking me off of her before pushing his perfect hair back into place.

"Well I'm glad that's dealt with, bro," he said and I smacked his hand away as he offered it to me, pushing to my feet and leaving Rogue in the sand.

JJ moved to help her up and I scowled between them, my breathing growing shallow. I took out my cigarettes, lighting up another one as I broke eye contact with them, figuring out how to play this. Because now my instincts were wearing off, it was hard to cover for the reason I'd just acted like a fucking jealous asshole over him touching the ghost. It wasn't like I gave a shit.

"God, Chase, I landed on a thistle." Rogue rubbed her ass and I shrugged, dragging down smoke into my lungs and avoiding JJ's eye.

"I had a feeling all this anger was an act, dude, thanks for clearing that up," JJ said with a dark smirk, taking Rogue's hand and stepping forward so he was half concealing her from me. The action made me want to rip his eyes out and feed them to a seagull. But that was the point wasn't it? The exact thing I'd been worried about. Rogue had shown up and suddenly she was tearing our group apart just like I'd known she would the moment she picked Maverick. Well fuck that.

I pushed my fingers into my hair, fronting this shit out as Rogue frowned at me. "You're an idiot," I tossed at JJ. "Fox will castrate you and make your balls into a necklace."

"Are you gonna tell him?" JJ growled and I pushed my tongue into my cheek.

"No," I said. "That's on you. Ain't my business."

Rogue scoffed and I glowered at her.

"You kinda made it your business when you twat blocked me and attacked JJ," she snapped. "What gives?"

I took another long drag on my cigarette, ignoring the burning pain in my chest over her and him. "You show up here and fuck with my boys, that's what gives," I snarled then I turned to JJ with venom spreading over my tongue. "She's playing you, man. This is what she wants. When Fox finds out, he'll fucking kill you. I wouldn't be surprised if she tells him herself."

"Watch your mouth," JJ warned and I shook my head at him, unable to believe this shit.

"Goddammit, J. She's got you by the balls. She's gonna fuck us all up, just like I said." I shot her another dark look and she shook off JJ's hand, marching toward me.

"Shut your damn mouth, Cohen. You're just being a jealous bitch right now."

I scoffed. "As if."

"I wasn't born yesterday," she said coolly. "You just laid into your best friend because you couldn't stand seeing his hands on me."

I blew a cloud of smoke into her face and she blinked against it, grimacing, but not moving away. "I wouldn't touch you if your pussy granted eternal life, ghost."

I sneered and she sneered right back, and all the while my heart beat like a drum in my chest and ached like she was squeezing it in her fist.

My gaze shifted to JJ's over her head and he gave me his puppy dog look.

"We're cool right, brother?" he asked intently and I drew away from Rogue.

"Yeah, we're cool." I turned my back on them, feeling Rogue's eyes digging needles into my back as I rounded the marquee and left them to their fuck fest.

Fucking JJ. Didn't he give a shit about what this was gonna do to our group? I mean, fuck Fox for laying a claim on her that he didn't have a right to stake. I would have hate fucked her into next week given the chance, but it looked like JJ had gotten there first. Bitterness filled my gut and I grabbed a shot off of a cocktail waitress's tray before stuffing a dollar bill between her tits, downing four more and heading back toward the party.

I wasn't gonna hate JJ for this. That was the trap Rogue was laying so screw her for trying it. My bond with J and Fox was unbreakable. But Fox was too hot headed, too possessive. If he found out that JJ was messing around with her, I feared what would happen.

I wanted to leave, but then my gaze snagged on Rosie who was dancing with a group of her friends near a couple of bikini clad girls wrestling in a paddling pool filled with jello. I headed over to join them, pulling Rosie against me. She giggled in that high-pitched tone of hers I'd learned to tune out a long time ago and started grinding her ass back against my dick. The music thumped to a repetitive beat in my skull and I went to that deadened place inside me I'd cultivated a long time ago. Thanks to Luther. I had a lot to thank King Harlequin for in fact. Like the body count linked to my name, a healthy bunch of scars and an ice cold heart that made killing as easy as brewing coffee.

My phone buzzed in my pocket and I took it out, my throat tightening as I found a message from my dad. It was a single X. The only thing he ever sent me. An agreement between us that if he ever desperately needed me and no one else in the fucking world could help, he could send me that message. *Fuck.*

I shoved my phone away, unsure if I was going to ignore it or not.

I didn't dance with Rosie, but she sure as shit danced on me. One of her dudebro friends planted a beer in my hand and I gave him a look that told him not to be such a kiss ass before I downed it. My head started spinning and as Rosie openly caressed my dick through my shorts, my gaze hooked on JJ and Rogue returning to the foam party, starting to dance together.

Rogue's eyes swung my way, landing on Rosie with an acidic hate that heated my blood. I smirked at her in a challenge, gripping Rosie's waist and pulling her closer. I'd seen my friend fingering Rogue and now I wanted a little payback. Seemed only fair.

My gaze remained locked with Rogue's as I dipped my head, driving my tongue between Rosie's lips. She tasted of tequila and was vaguely appetising, but the thing that got me rock hard was Rogue watching us, trying to mentally drive daggers into our skulls. JJ tried to pull her away, but she didn't go, just staring as I gripped Rosie's ass and ground her against my cock.

I kissed her the way I'd wanted to kiss Rogue, sliding my hand up and around her throat and squeezing as I drove my tongue into her mouth possessively. My heart splintered with every movement of my tongue, but a twisted satisfaction soothed it too. Rogue was still staring, her eyes full of hurt, confirming that her desire for me hadn't been imagined. And that made me feel like lighting the world on fire just for her. JJ's attention had been snagged by a couple of girls who were getting him to sign their tits, no doubt regulars at his club.

I released Rosie from the kiss and she started sucking on my neck, murmuring *Chasey* into my flesh. She travelled lower, taking the path Rogue had taken earlier when she'd licked her drink off of me and it was all too easy to picture it as her doing it again. Rosie was suddenly on her knees, tugging at my shorts and I looked around, realising we'd gathered a decent audience of spring breakers. Plenty of whom were chanting *suck suck suck suck.*

Rogue's upper lip peeled back as I fisted Rosie's hair, her palm eagerly squeezing my cock through my shorts. *I don't need Rogue Easton. I don't need ghosts who fuck my friends and forget I exist.*

I was drunk enough that I kinda didn't care about a group of college kids watching me get sucked off and I let my eyes fall closed as I imagined Rosie's hair was rainbow coloured before wrapping it in my fist. Just as Rosie started to shimmy my shorts down, she was yanked away from me with a yelp of alarm.

My eyes flew open and I found Rogue there, throwing her fist into Rosie's face and the college kids whooped excitedly.

Rosie stumbled backwards, crashing onto her ass in the paddling pool of jello and the bikini clad girls ran for the hills. My lips parted as Rogue dove in on top of her, beating the living hell out of her as Rosie screamed like a groundhog being mauled by a coyote. I swear I got even harder as Rogue went full savage on the girl and I realised I probably should have been pulling her off of Rosie. But…shit. I was a slave to watching her, her fists pounding into Rosie's gut, her coloured hair flying around her and a snarl on her lips. *Ho-ly fuck, ghost is jealous.*

Fox suddenly appeared like a storm cloud descending on the party, dragging Rogue out of the jello pool which was gathering a seriously excited audience, most of which consisted of catcalling frat boys.

"Are you insane?" Fox snarled at Rogue and she laughed wildly as if to prove that she was. And I liked that a whole fucking hell of a lot. My dick liked it even more, straining against my shorts and tenting them for her.

Rosie scrambled to her feet behind Rogue, dripping jello with tears running down her cheeks. She ran to me, crashing into my chest and I patted her back vaguely as I continued to stare at Rogue.

"Oh man, I turn away for one second and I miss you jello fighting with Rosie." JJ appeared with a pout and Rogue giggled. Fucking *giggled*.

She wants JJ not you.

Venom seeped into my blood and I turned away from them, locking my arm around Rosie's shoulders and marching her out of the party.

"She a-attacked me!" Rosie sobbed, sniffing loudly.

"Yeah," I murmured. "And it was hot as fuck."

"What?" she gasped, looking up at me and I realised I'd said that out loud.

"You were hot as fuck, Rosie," I amended and she nuzzled into me.

"She's a psycho." She sucked in a shaky breath, still crying.

"Yeah," I murmured. *A hot fucking psycho I want to bend over and ram my dick into while she curses me with every colourful word she knows.*

I headed back to the road that led down to the lagoon, whistling at a cab driver who was sunning himself on the hood of his car.

He jumped to attention and I threw a couple of twenties at him before pushing Rosie into the back seat of his cab. "Give us ten minutes."

He nodded, averting his eyes as I followed Rosie into the backseat and let her go to town on my cock to cheer her up. I was a saint like that.

I leaned my head back against the seat as she slurped on my dick like it was a free lollipop and I shut my eyes so I could picture Rogue in her place. Rosie gave a decent blowjob, but her gag reflex was piss poor. When she'd made a song and dance over licking every inch of my shaft, I pushed her head down until she was choking, cursing as I thought of Rogue taking me all the way in and soon spilled myself down her throat. *That's one way to stop a girl crying.*

I pulled up my shorts and pushed Rosie out of the car, whistling for the driver.

Rosie stared in at me through the window in surprise and I took my shades from my pocket, pushing them on before lighting up another cigarette.

"I could come over later, Chasey?" she called through the window and I pretended I couldn't hear her as the driver started the engine and turned the car around, leaving her coughing in a cloud of dust.

Maybe part of me liked punishing Rosie for being a royal dick when she'd lived with Rogue in her group home as kids. Or maybe I was just an asshole and didn't give a flying fuck if I hurt her feelings. She liked sucking my cock, and I liked having my cock sucked. Seemed like a win-win situation to me. Only her pussy was probably collecting cobwebs at this point. I hadn't fucked her since…hmm. Definitely since before I'd fucked her friend Whitney anyway. And certainly since Rogue had returned to town. I hadn't buried myself in anyone's pussy since then. Maybe it was because hers was the only pussy I was craving lately, or maybe it was because sex always turned women into clingy criers. BJs were a halfway house that had clear boundaries. So call me an angel for saving girls' hearts.

"Where are ya heading, my man?" the peppy driver called.

I considered the message I'd gotten from my dad and knew deep down that I was heading there anyway, even if I didn't wanna admit that was the reason I'd left the party.

"Nettle Grove," I said, cracking a window to let the smoke seep out of it, but I was making one hell of an ashy mess back here so it was too late for tapping my cherry on the edge of it. I'd paid him enough for two trips to town though, so he wasn't complaining.

We were soon turning down the quiet road that led toward the beach and he parked up beside the overgrown shithole of a house which was where I'd been born and raised.

"Have a good one." The driver hopped out, opening the door for me like I was some kind of king and I flicked him a thumb's up.

I dropped my cigarette butt to the ground, crushing it beneath my heel before heading through the little gate toward the wooden house which looked a year or two from falling down. Hopefully it would take my dear daddy with it when it fell. Though that was probably too kind of a death for him.

I walked up the steps onto the creaking porch, pushing through the door and wrinkling my nose at the stench of festering trash. The garbage can was overflowing with takeaway boxes and PBR cans littered the floor all the way up to it.

I opened the fridge, finding it full of his beers and nothing else, tutting under my breath before making a slow passage deeper into the house. There were photos of him and my momma on the mantlepiece, but the ones of me had cigarette burns in the eyes or were gone completely. My dad had always blamed me for the bad shit in his life. I was his biggest regret, a mistake he couldn't undo.

"You here, Dylan?" I called.

I'd stopped calling him Dad the moment I'd moved out of this house into Luther's. Momma had hated it, smacking me anytime she heard me say it, but calling him Dad was like calling him an upstanding citizen. He didn't live up to being either.

"Up 'ere," his gruff voice came from somewhere above me and I moved through the grimy living room before marching upstairs.

My gaze settled on him in the bathroom at the far end of the hall, the door wide, revealing the old man on the floor with his pants around his ankles in a puddle of his own piss and possibly shit.

He was clutching his chest, his dirty white tank stained with what looked like several days' worth of food, beer and cigarette ash.

I rubbed my thumb over my chin as I slowly walked toward him, my footfalls heavy against the wooden floorboards.

"Took you long enough," he snapped at me. "You always were a layabout."

I clenched my jaw, moving to stand in the doorway and lighting up another cigarette as I gazed down at my pathetic father as he covered his dick up with a grubby towel.

"What happened?" I questioned, though it was pretty obvious.

"Fucking fell, didn't I? My leg's been givin' me trouble again. Don't just stand there. Help me up, you piece of shit," he snarled.

I took my time contemplating that request, tapping ash onto the bathroom floor in front of him as he glared at me, wheezing. He'd been chain smoking his whole life and that familiar rattle in his chest probably should have been a good enough reason for me to quit the habit. Only I wouldn't be living into old age to wither away like this, all alone. That was not in my fucking future. I'd put a gun to my head before that ever happened.

"Remember when you broke my foot with your baseball bat and told me a real man would walk himself to the hospital?" I mused like it was a heart-warming family memory.

"A waste of space kid like you needed a firm hand," he snapped, trying to use the shower curtain to get up, but only serving to rip it down on top of himself. "You coulda been somethin' worthwhile if you'd listened to the lessons I tried to teach ya. Instead you're some second rate gangbanger who gets bossed around by Fox Harlequin all day long."

It hurt more than I liked and I hated that he still had such a hold on me. But only his words could bruise me these days, not his fists. He'd lost the upper hand with me physically some time ago.

I stamped down on his bad leg, making him roar with pain, a murderous hate filling me as I glared at this bastard who'd made my youth hell. I'd only let him live this long so he could rot away in this house, live out his lonely, pathetic life here missing my momma. She was better off dead than still sleeping in his bed anyways. He'd ruined her life and now I made sure to ruin what was left of his in return.

I leaned down to speak in his ear, the scent of sweat and piss rising under my nose. "I should let you die here in your own shit," I growled, letting him linger with worry for a moment as he sneered at me, wondering if I'd really do it. But I gripped his shoulders, hauling him to his feet and grabbing his cane which had rolled out into the hall. He gripped it tightly with grunts and groans while I yanked his pants up and cursed when my hands came away wet.

"For fuck's sake," I hissed, washing my hands before taking out my phone and shooting a message to Mrs Bevlin who was his on-call carer. My dad was too proud to call for her help. No, when shit like this happened, he summoned his only flesh and blood who he hated with a passion, just so I could pick up the goddamn pieces. But he'd have to suck it up and let Bevlin help him today, because I wasn't going to be washing the ass of a guy who used to beat me black and blue and had never said a good word in my direction. I'd have to stay and make sure he let her help him though. So it looked like my afternoon had gone from shit to shittier.

Dad had always said I was a plague on this house, a curse who brought misery to anyone I touched. I didn't think that was true anymore, but I liked being a plague on him at least.

When Bevlin arrived, I left her to sort my dad out and sat on the porch in the dusty old rocking chair Dylan would have shot me for sitting in once. It was his chair. But since his leg had gotten all twisted up in a fishing boat accident, he didn't sit out here much, preferring the threadbare armchair in the lounge he'd pulled up to the window so he could see the ocean. *Note to self: spray paint that window black.*

My phone buzzed in my pocket and I took it out, finding a message waiting for me.

Fox:

Where did you go?

Chase:

Had to check in on Dylan.

Fox:

I hope you gave him hell.

By the way, we need a fourth member for the boat job next week. As it's your job, I figured you could pick them.

Chase:

Sure did. And will do, brother.

I thought on that and my mind settled on the pretty thief who I wanted there on that job. She'd gotten deep under flesh and it was time to face that truth head on at last. And I wasn't going to give Fox a chance to say no, so he wasn't going to find out about it until it was too late to stop me.

If Rogue Easton wanted to play with me and my friends, then I was going to throw her in at the deep end and watch her drown. *Game on, little one.*

CHAPTER THIRTY

I may have overindulged at the lagoon party. Just a smidge.

I had fuzzy memories of JJ picking lumps of jello out of my hair and of Chase dragging a sobbing, beat down bitch away to deliver her home. But it took me a little longer to figure out how I'd ended up in a soft bed with the scent of cedar wrapped all around me and strong arms coiled around my body.

But as I groaned against the thickness of my tongue and the dull ache in my skull, I remembered Fox tossing me over his shoulder and carrying me back up the path that led out of the lagoon while JJ held my hand where Fox couldn't see him and cracked jokes.

Some guys in a black pick up had come to get us and we'd ridden back here in the back of it. Here being Fox's house of course and if I wasn't mistaken, this was his bed too and his hard body wrapped around me.

"Shit," I mumbled, my mind going to Mutt who I'd left back at Rejects Park as I tried to roll over, but the arms surrounding me just tightened, stopping me from escaping.

"Stay," Fox commanded sleepily and I got the feeling that didn't only refer to the 'in his bed' sense of the word.

"I can't," I grumbled. "Someone kidnapped me and my dog is back home, hungry and locked out all night-"

"We stopped by the tin can you refer to as home and picked him up on our way here," he said, tugging me closer and inhaling deeply as he buried his face against my neck. Warmth tumbled beneath my skin at the contact, but I bit my lip against it.

"He's here?" I asked hopefully, cracking my eyes and sure enough finding myself in Fox's big ass bedroom.

There was light shining in through the closed curtains and the sound of the sea and the gulls crying out to each other carried in to me from beyond them.

A waggy little white tail caught my eye from a nest of blankets that had been tossed on the floor and I spotted my dog as he rolled over to show me his belly, hopeful for a rub as always.

"I can't believe you went and got him for me," I said slowly and Fox sighed against my neck, pressing forward to place a kiss on the sensitive skin there and making a shiver pass through my body.

"He might be a little bastard who likes to use my potted plants as a damn toilet, but I know the fleabag is important to you," he said. "Which makes him important to me too. Got it?"

I swallowed thickly and rolled onto my back so that I could look at him where he laid beside me.

"Thank you," I breathed, drinking in the sight of his blonde hair all messed up against the pillows, the rough edge of stubble which lined his jaw and the roiling storm that lived in his green eyes begging me to dive into it.

"I'd do anything for you, hummingbird," he replied simply. "Always have, always will."

I shifted a little, my bare legs sliding beneath soft sheets and making me wonder about what else had happened last night. "Did we..."

"What?" he asked, shifting beside me so that he could prop his head up on his hand and his leg moved between mine, his thick thigh pressing mine apart to make room for his.

"Well, I'm in your bed and I was pretty wasted, so I can't really remember much but I'm guessing we had sex?" I asked, my heart beating a little faster at the idea of that and the fact that I couldn't remember it.

Fox tsked irritably, knocking my thighs further apart and dropping his hand beneath the sheets before slipping it up the outside of my leg and around the curve of my ass. I just watched him with my heart thumping solidly until I felt him hooking his fingers into the fabric of my bikini bottoms which he pulled wide before releasing to snap back against my hip again.

"I've been waiting for you for my entire adult life. I'm hardly going to fuck you while you're comatose. Even if you were begging me for my cock from the moment I got you in here."

"Liar," I growled, shoving his chest as a weird mixture of relief and disappointment swept through me. Why the fuck was I disappointed? It wasn't like I would have been happy to find out that I'd decided to take another bull for a ride before crashing last night. Especially this particular one.

Fox laughed darkly and rolled on top of me, grabbing my wrist to lift my arm before threading his fingers through mine. He gave me a heated look as he pressed my hand down into the pillow above my head while his weight crushed me into the mattress.

"No, hummingbird," Fox said in a low voice. "I wouldn't lie about that. And I wouldn't do that to you. I don't want to get you wasted and fuck you in the dark so you can't even remember it. When I fuck you there won't be a single forgettable moment."

"Look at you all chivalrous," I murmured, far too much of my attention being stolen by the rigid cock which was currently pressed against my core and begging me to make him put that claim to the test. "I guess it's a shame that my life experience proves that most men aren't as considerate."

"What's that supposed to mean?" he growled, a threat in his tone which promised annihilation to any man who ever might have hurt me or fucked me in the past. I huffed out a breath before trying to roll out from beneath him.

"I want to go have a shower, Fox," I demanded when he didn't move an inch.

"I want an answer to my question," he insisted, his weight pressing down harder.

"And you think that pinning me to your bed and grinding your dick into me is the way to get it?" I hissed, ignoring the heat that said dick was sending flooding through my body as I stubbornly maintained my anger.

Fox shoved himself off of me with a snarl of irritation, rolling to lay back on his bed beside me and letting me get to my feet.

"We told you what happened here when you left," he said, pinning me with those green eyes as I stood before him in my bikini and one of his tanks. "It's time you returned the favour."

"No," I snapped. "I don't owe you any more slices of my tattered soul. You did a good enough job of carving it up the last time I was here. If I let you take another turn at it there won't be anything left."

I turned and stalked out of the room, slamming his door behind me and striding down the corridor to mine with Mutt right on my heels.

I headed into my room and locked the door behind me before stripping out of my clothes and tossing them haphazardly on the floor as I headed for a shower.

The hot water and steam calmed me down a little, but I still felt tender and bruised on the inside from that little altercation when I emerged clean with wet hair dripping down my spine.

I dressed in a pair of black shorts and a white tee with a slogan printed on it in big black letters which said *I hate everyone*. It seemed pretty damn fitting today.

The denim shorts I'd been wearing at the lagoon yesterday were sitting on the chair at the foot of my bed and I quickly searched the pockets, hunting down the crumpled dollar bills I'd left inside them.

I smoothed them out as best I could and made sure I had enough to cover my rent, pleased that at least that much was going alright as I transferred the cash to the pocket of the black shorts I now wore.

I raised my chin and headed back out of the room, down the stairs to the kitchen where I found a row of three Harlequins lined up at the breakfast bar like a row of executioners.

"We need to talk," Fox said, pushing a plate of toast towards me which I accepted purely because I was hungover and in danger of puking if I didn't eat.

"About what?" I asked, taking a savage bite from my breakfast and staying right where I was on the far side of the kitchen island to keep a nice solid barrier between me and those three men.

"About what the fuck you've been doing for the last ten years," Chase growled. "We can't just let some unknown girl live in our house when you could have been up to fuck knows what while-"

"I don't live here," I snapped. "I just keep getting dragged back here."

"This isn't the way we should be having this conversation," JJ interrupted, getting to his feet as he tried to keep the peace. "We're just worried, Rogue. It's been a long time and we can see that a lot has happened to you. But if you won't tell us, then how the hell are we supposed to understand you now?"

I shrugged obnoxiously and took another feral bite of toast. "I'm sure you can figure it out. My story is a pretty common one around here. Just ask any of the girls down at Rejects Park and I'm sure it'll be close enough. Is that all?"

"No, it isn't," Fox growled. "I'm not letting you brush us off with this. You have a story. And we need to hear it."

I looked between the three of them with heat prickling in my veins then shrugged like I didn't give a shit.

"Fine. I'm not promising to tell you all of it, but you can ask me what you want to know and I'll give you some of it," I offered because I could tell they weren't going to let this go.

"Not good enough," Chase snapped, reaching for a cigarette and jamming it into the corner of his lips.

Fox leaned over and snatched it before he could light it, crushing it in his fist and tossing it down before him.

"Start talking, hummingbird. How long did you stay at Sandra's?" Fox asked, taking control of the conversation as always. He was so fucking domineering.

"Your dad's bitch cousin who built a metal shack on the side of her house and calls it a group home?" I questioned. "The one who makes those kids go into school and sell drugs to their friends while keeping all the profits for herself?"

"Dad said you'd be safe there," Fox said heavily. "He said she'd look after you."

I scoffed with disbelief and strode away from him, taking a seat in the big cream armchair beside the patio doors which led out to the pool.

"Well, if dear old Luther said I'd be fine, then of course I understand why you would believe him. Your dad always liked me so much after all. He always did have my best interests at heart," I snarked, my back already up and we'd barely even begun. If I got through this without killing one of them, it would be a damn miracle.

Fox exchanged a glance with JJ, some unspoken bullshit passing between them before they moved to take a seat on the couch opposite me. Chase followed but chose to perch his ass on the arm instead of sitting down properly.

"Okay, so Luther's cousin was a first class dick," Chase said while the others seemed to be considering what to ask me first. "So how long did you even bother to wait to hear from us?"

"Four months," I ground out, deciding to give them the whole truth about that. "Four months of crying for you and aching for you and wondering why you would have abandoned me so thoroughly after all the promises the four of you made me. I understood why you sent me away. I knew you had no choice in that. But why did you destroy my phone? Why didn't any of you even email me just to let me know you gave a shit about me?" I forced myself to stop there but I could have gone on: *Why did you have to be so fucking cold when you told me to go? Why did you all look at me like you didn't even know me? Didn't even fucking care about me at all? Why was it so fucking easy for you to throw me away when you knew that you were all I ever fucking had? When you knew it would kill me.*

"We had a lot of pressure on us that first year after we were initiated into the Harlequins," JJ said, looking down at his hands. "Luther kept a close eye on us, moved me and Chase in here. He got us all new cellphones which we were paranoid he was monitoring and-"

"And we had to become real Harlequins," Chase added in a dark tone. "We had to spill blood and learn how to live with the stains it left on our souls. We had to become soldiers in this army-"

"And I was just the first of all the sacrifices you had to make," I replied bitterly. "Got it. I've come to terms with the fact that that's just who I am, so I don't need to hear you justify it." I turned to look out at the pool, not wanting to look at any of them as the pain of that admission cut into me despite the fact that I'd been living with that truth for ten long years.

"What's just who you are?" Fox demanded and I looked back at him, not really wanting to say it, but we were down the rabbit hole now and maybe it was better to just get all of this out there and let them see it.

"Disposable," I said, holding his eye.

"Like fuck you are," JJ growled, making a move to get up, but Fox slapped a hand against his chest to stop him.

"Says the man who threw me away and forgot about me," I tossed back, shrugging like I didn't care, like it didn't cut me apart to say it out loud, like that empty void inside me didn't seem to stretch and stretch endlessly at the admission that I knew I wasn't ever going to have anyone who loved me, chose me, wanted me in a permanent kind of way.

"That's not how it was!" JJ shouted and this time Fox had to grab his arm and force him back down into his seat while I remained unmoving before him.

"Where did you go when you ran from Sandra's?" Chase asked, his face a perfectly still mask as he hid whatever he felt about this away for only him to experience.

"I hopped on a bus, rode it to the end of the line and ended up in Drayville. I slept on the street for a week then met a guy who asked me to come to a party with him while I was buying myself something to eat one night after spending the day picking pockets. I went because I had nowhere else to go and he liked me even though I didn't talk much or smile at all. I guess what he really liked was my body, but either way, he was the only person I'd met who had offered me anything at all. So, when he suggested I could come stay with him and his friends, I agreed," I told them.

"What friends?" Fox asked, looking like he wanted to rip the guy's throat out just for offering me a place to stay. But if he hadn't, I would have been left on the street. I certainly hadn't had any other options available to me.

"Just a bunch of other teenage runaways who were all squatting in this old house on the edge of town." I shrugged. "A lot of them were hooked on one drug or another but I didn't find any comfort in their vices. If anything, the few times I tried getting high with them I just ended up feeling worse. The only effects it gave me was forcing me to look into the eye of the emptiness inside me and realise how little I had. What little I was worth."

I shifted uncomfortably, caught between the desire to throw all of this heartache at them and let them take responsibility for what they'd caused or to just bury it down deep and pretend it wasn't there. But fuck it, if they wanted to hear it they could, and if they wanted to go on pretending that there was something to be salvaged here afterwards then I really would know how delusional they were.

Fox swiped a hand down his face, his body rigid with tension as he seemed to be forcing himself to remain in his seat.

"So you lived in some dirty squat with a bunch of addicts? For how long?" he asked tensely.

"What did you do for food?" JJ added, his eyes full of what looked like pain for sixteen year old me, but it didn't do me much good now. Where had that concern been when I actually needed it? "Was there water, or-"

"Oh yeah, it was a falling down piece of shit with holes in the roof, but it came with a brand spanking new bathroom with a jacuzzi tub and one of those toilets that squirts water up your asshole and blow-dries it for you. And there was an in-house chef who prepared us gourmet meals three times a day plus snacks," I replied scathingly.

"You don't have to be a dick about it," Chase growled.

"Sorry if the shitty reality of my life makes you uncomfortable, Ace," I sneered at him. "I assumed you all realised what you were throwing me out into when you ditched my ass and sent me off with nothing and no one. I mean, we did all grow up in the same place. There was a reason why none of us ever tried to run from our shitty lives before all of that crap happened with me and Axel. We all knew it could easily be worse."

"If it was that bad you could have reached out," JJ said quietly and I scoffed.

"I think you all made it clear enough that I couldn't do that. And that you didn't want me to and wouldn't have helped me regardless, even if it had crossed my mind. Which I can assure you, it didn't. But if this story is too hard for your sensitive little souls then I'm happy enough not to recount it," I said, scowling between the three of them and folding my arms over my chest.

Mutt growled low in the back of his throat like he was agreeing with me then hopped up into my lap and curled himself against me. At least someone had my back. I was pretty sure that dog was the one and only creature on this planet who I could rely on wholeheartedly. Though he'd probably ditch me in a heartbeat for a cosier home and more expensive dog chow, so it was probably pretty dumb to start relying on that idea.

"So what happened in the squat?" Chase asked, plucking another cigarette from his box and placing it between his lips. This time Fox didn't try to stop him as he lit up.

"I was there for a few months, stealing shit to get by. Then one day I was caught trying to dip my fingers into the pocket of a thug who I should have known better than to attempt to steal from. But I hadn't eaten for two days and it wasn't easy to make the trek to the better parts of town, so I tried my hand despite my better judgement. Luckily for me he thought it was funny. The guy was a fresh signup to The Diamond Cutters Crew and he liked the look of me. Told me he'd forget I tried to rob him if he could take me on a date."

"What was his name?" Fox asked and I had to wonder if he was keeping some little list somewhere of all these names he was so desperate to collect. Maybe he had colour coded pens to rank them in order of importance and a fancy red one to strike their names out once he'd cut their heads off or whatever he had planned.

"Cody. You already know about him," I said.

"That guy you fucked?" Fox growled and the others looked between the two of us like that information seriously interested them.

"You make it sound like there was only the one," I drawled, not giving a shit if it bothered him that I'd been with other men. I wasn't his. I'd told him plenty of fucking times. And I was even less his back then than I was now.

"What was he like?" JJ asked. "Was he nice...did he love you?"

"Would that make it better or worse in your mind?" I asked and they looked between themselves again like they weren't even sure. I decided to give them a vague answer before moving on. "He was nicer to me than anyone else had been since I left this place," I said. "But it was clear enough what he wanted from me. I chose to give him it, be his girl, have somewhere to sleep at night that had running water and shit. He liked me being there a lot because he liked to fuck me a lot. Is that good enough for your curious little minds?" I left out the details about how much I'd hated myself for making that choice. How I'd felt like I'd whored myself out even though I had liked him well enough. He'd been nice to me for the most part and had never made it into any kind of transaction. But I was young and he knew what he wanted. He wasn't gentle with me when he took it even if he didn't force me. The first time we were together, I'd told him I was a virgin right before he'd pushed himself inside me and he'd barked a laugh as he shoved his cock in roughly. *"Not anymore,"* he'd grunted, barely pausing as I gasped with the pain of it before he started moving his hips again, driving in and out of me and groaning my name as he came a few minutes later. At least it hadn't lasted long.

"That was a few months after you left the foster home?" Chase asked. Like the timing was so freaking important to him.

"So what?"

"So you were still sixteen. How old was he?"

"Fuck off, Chase. Who gives a shit?" But he'd hit the nail on the head because even though I hadn't cared at the time, Cody had been twenty one and maybe what had happened between us was a little more fucked up in hindsight than I'd realised at the time.

"I do," Fox said darkly.

"No. You don't," I snapped, refusing to let them see me doubt or question the choices I'd made to survive. They knew full fucking well I'd have to have done plenty of dodgy shit to get by on my own. They just didn't like thinking about it because they knew when it came down to it that it was all on them. "You don't like hearing it, but whether you want to admit it to yourself or not, you already knew all of this. From the second you bothered to ask about me all those years ago and realised I'd run away from that shitty group home. You know exactly what happens to runaway kids on streets like these. So you know I was fucked in every which way you can imagine. You know I had punk ass boyfriends who treated me like shit and you know that I put up with a lot of it. I had a few rules that I stuck by. If they hit me, I left. If they cheated, I left. And sometimes I just left because I was sick of sucking the same old dick. After Cody, I found other gangster douchebags to date because they could offer me security and I could offer them a girlfriend who wouldn't go trying to wife them or baby daddy them or fall in love or any of that bullshit. I moved from town to town whenever I got sick of my surroundings or the people I was hanging out with. I ran with hood rats and gangsters because that was what I knew best and it was the only place I fit, but I never signed up to any gangs and I was always ready to cut my losses and leave. I didn't always have boyfriends because I didn't need anyone to look after me, but as much as you might not like it, I do actually like dick, so when it suited me I did. And don't go thinking I was some poor, helpless girl getting used by a bunch of assholes, because I can assure you that I used them just as much."

"And what about the one who tried to kill you?" Chase growled, sucking on his cigarette like it was a lifeline which he was determined to cling to no matter what.

"What about him?" I asked casually, even though a prickle of unease ran through my body at the mention of Shawn. I wouldn't rest well until that motherfucker was dead.

"How long were you with him?" JJ asked.

"What town were you in?" Fox demanded at the same moment.

I weighed that information in my mind then shrugged. "Just over two years. And I'm not telling you where."

"Two years?" Fox choked out, looking like he wanted to kill the dude even more than he had before.

"This guy was another gangster then?" Chase asked, cutting a little too close to the truths I wasn't willing to share with them. "What gang? One the Harlequins are at peace with? Or one pitched against us?"

"How the fuck am I supposed to know?" I asked. "You don't tell me shit about your little boys' club and he never did either."

"You were with the dude for two years and he never spoke gang business in front of you?" Chase scoffed disbelievingly.

"I'm not a fucking idiot," I snapped at the underlying suggestion that I was some fucking bimbo moron. "I specifically made it clear I wasn't interested in any of that. I didn't want anything to do with his gang and he was happy to keep me out of it."

"His gang?" Fox asked, perking up like a Labrador who'd spotted a ball. "Was he running it?"

My heart leapt as he caught that little nugget of information too damn easily and I cursed myself. If I wasn't careful I'd end up giving them Shawn's identity and they'd take away my right to deal with him myself.

"What part of me not wanting to tell you about him don't you understand?" I asked, my anger rising fast while I was forced to re-live all of this shit. "That motherfucker will meet his end when I'm good and ready to give it to him. It's far too fucking late for you to play the knight in shining armour for me. I haven't been a damsel in distress for a long time. I don't even know why you're so determined to hear about all of this. Were you hoping to find out that I'd been adopted by some kind old dear who sent me to some fancy ass college where I'd fallen in love with a billionaire who had taken my virginity when I was twenty one in the sweetest, gentlest way imaginable before setting me up for life in his palace? You know the world we live in. You know what happens to the people at the bottom of the barrel and the three of you pushed me right down to live amongst the dregs who are just about surviving there."

"Rogue," JJ said, his voice rough as he stood up and moved towards me, but I lurched to my feet, knocking Mutt off in my haste to rise.

"No," I snarled as Mutt ran around my legs and barked to warn him off too. "You were the ones who were so desperate to hear all of this. But I can't possibly tell you all of it in one sitting and I don't care to. I've been used and tossed aside and beaten down so many times and by so many people that I lost count. Life has spent a long fucking time teaching me that I'm not ever going to be rescued and I'm not ever going to be loved and I'm okay with that. I know how to rescue myself and I know what I am willing to sacrifice to survive, and I can promise you it's more than I ever even knew I had to give. But there is one thing I am not and never will be and that is someone's fucking possession. I gave myself to all of you once, with my whole heart and soul and everything I was. I belonged to you. And you taught me exactly what price there was to pay for loving someone like that when you turned your backs on me. So I should thank you really for teaching me my worth and for making me strong enough to survive everything else that I've had to since you destroyed me. Because after that, it wasn't like it could ever get worse, was it? All I had to do was make sure I never gave myself to anyone ever again and that way, when they tossed me aside like everyone does in the end, I could just bounce back up and move the fuck on."

"We did it to save your life!" Fox yelled like that made it okay.

"Well you know what, Fox?!" I screamed in reply. "I wish you hadn't! I wish you'd let me die when I had a life worth fucking living. I wish you'd let Luther kill me and allowed me to go in the belief that I was loved by the four of you. That I might have had something good to live for rather than just throwing me away and letting me fall on my face in the fucking dirt so that I could just go on existing and you could tell yourselves bullshit stories about me being happy somewhere without you."

"We were just a bunch of kids!" Chase shouted, ashing his cigarette aggressively and standing up too. "We did the only thing we could. You should be grateful-"

"No. You just took the easy way out," I spat. "You cut me loose and forgot about me while becoming that motherfucker's little pawns. Well I hope you're all as happy as I am with the outcome because as far as I'm concerned, the decision you all made for me was worse than him killing me. You gutted me, ripped my heart out and stamped on it before sewing me back together and forcing me to go on living without it beating in my chest. And you seriously expect me to thank you for it? Fuck you."

I turned and whirled away from them, heading straight for the garage door to escape from this room and their suffocating presences. I needed to not look at them, not to see the pain in their eyes or the regret in their souls because it was too fucking late for all of that. I'd spent ten years failing to get over them followed by just hating them when I realised I couldn't, and I wasn't going to let them force some bullshit forgiveness on me.

I made it to the door before Fox caught me, grabbing my arm and shoving me against the wall to stop me from leaving.

"You're not running from me again, hummingbird," he snarled, his green eyes blazing.

"If you don't let me get out of here and get some fucking space right now then I swear to you that the next time I can escape you, I'll run and never look back. You'll never see me again," I swore with every ounce of my being, glaring at him and daring him to test me on this because if he didn't get his fucking hands off of me right now then I was going to do it. I'd run and run further away than I'd ever gone before, so far that Sunset Cove wasn't even a shadow in the distance anymore and they'd never stand any chance of finding me again.

Fox seemed to realise I meant it, pain swimming in his green eyes as he released me and forced himself to step back.

"Promise me you're coming back," he breathed, sounding like a broken man as he looked at me with so much emotion in his gaze that it cut into me. But I didn't want to see it, didn't want to hear it.

"Let me go right now and I will," I said, dropping my gaze to his chest because I couldn't take anything else. I didn't even know why I was promising him that, only that I needed to get out of here and I knew it was the only way that he would let me.

He stepped back and I wrenched the door open and headed through it with Mutt on my heels, looking at the keys hanging on the wall and snatching the ones to JJ's GT.

I ran down the stairs, my heart pounding so hard that I couldn't hear anything beyond the pulse in my ears as I raced towards JJ's car and leapt into it. Mutt scampered over my lap into the passenger seat as I sat there with the door wide, trying to pull myself together.

I closed my eyes for half a second, reaching up to touch my cheek with shaking fingers as I felt a tear slip down my skin.

I smacked my head back against the headrest and slammed my hands into the steering wheel as I fought the urge to scream. This couldn't be happening again. I couldn't be letting them gain this power over me again. Because I wouldn't survive them destroying me a second time. I couldn't. It would kill me more thoroughly than a knife to the heart.

"Rogue," JJ's voice jolted me out of my panic and I whirled around to find him leaning in through the open door of the car, reaching out to cup my face in his hand as he tried to pull me to him. "I'm sorry, pretty girl," he said, the pain in his honey brown eyes breaking into my soul and making me ache to just fucking forgive him. To forget about all of it and let him pull me closer, let him take care of me and rely on him and-

"No," I snarled, shoving his hand off of me and forcing back all of that ache and longing and refusing to feel any of it. Because I wasn't going to let him have any part of me that he could hurt. I couldn't. Not again. So I took all of that hate and the pain and the venom in my soul and spat it back at him with as much grit as I could muster. "Stop trying to boyfriend me, JJ. We're fucking. Not falling in love. You don't have to pretend you give a shit about me just because you put your dick in me."

He lurched back like I'd punched him in the face, but instead of getting angry like I hoped he would, he just seemed even fucking sadder.

"You know that's bullshit, Rogue," he said. "You know I'm here for you and I hate what happened between us when-"

"I don't know that!" I yelled. "All I know is that I'm dead inside because you and your friends killed me ten years ago."

"We saved your life," he growled but I was shaking my head, jamming the key into the ignition and starting the engine.

"Thank you so fucking much for the years of misery," I hissed. "Now get out of my way or I'm going to run you down."

JJ didn't get much choice about stepping back and I tried not to feel an inch of guilt at the look he was giving me as I tore away from him.

More tears spilled down my cheeks as I drove, but I was helpless to stop them now, all of the pain and heartache of the memories this place held rearing up in me despite my best attempts to keep them out.

I didn't even realise where I was driving to until I found myself pulling along the street outside Rosewood Manor, the key hanging around my neck feeling hot against my skin as if it knew it was where it belonged.

But I knew why I'd come here the moment I pulled up. This place held the secret that could bring the Harlequin boys to their fucking knees. It was what it would take to truly destroy them and probably me too. But I didn't care about that. I could just run from it, disappear, change my name and become a new ghost in a new town who no one ever thought to give a shit about.

Not them though.

If I set this secret free it would destroy them. Maybe even kill them, though I knew I didn't want it to go that far. What I wanted was to force their hands, make them do what they swore to do ten years ago and run the fuck away from this place. Because that was the only thing they would be able to do if I outed that secret. Run and run and fucking run and hope to hell it never caught up to them. Ten years ago they chose Sunset Cove over me, so I'd gladly take it from them in payment for what they'd done.

For a while I'd begun to doubt whether or not I still wanted to do this, but now my answer was crystal fucking clear.

The Harlequin boys had destroyed my life.

Now I was going to repay the favour.

I just needed to be certain that the instrument of their destruction was still where we'd left it all those years ago. And that meant I needed to get into the grounds of that house, check out the graveyard and make sure the crypt was still locked up tight.

I kept driving down the street, eyeing the new fence with the electric wire running over the top of it to keep people out and I smiled to myself as an idea came to me.

There weren't many houses out this way, but further up the road was a turning onto the highway where a bar filled with bikers and deadbeats sat.

I pulled off of the road into a layby and left the GT with the windows wide as I told Mutt to wait there before continuing on foot through the trees. He could hop out of the car if he really wanted to, but I was hoping he'd just wait quietly while I did the insane part of my plan. Then we could go pay my rent and I could figure out what the fuck I was doing with my life while lying on the beach butt ass naked drinking tequila.

It didn't take me long to make it through the trees to the highway where the bar sat with several old trucks and a group of motorcycles in the parking lot around the back of it as expected.

These dudes were not the kind of men that it was a good idea to steal from even if they weren't the biggest MC in the state.

I was careful as I approached, looking out for any sign of anyone outside the building who might spot me coming and keeping an eye on the windows too.

But the good thing about people who thought they were too terrifying for anyone to steal from them, was that in their arrogance, they tended to do dumb shit like leave their vehicles unlocked.

I slipped out of the shadows at the back of the wooden building, keeping an eye on the door that was wedged open with a brick and thanking my luck that there were no windows out here overlooking the parking lot.

I blew out a long breath as I focused on the task at hand. I wasn't going to let my anger with the Harlequins fuck this up for me.

I darted across the lot and made it past the motorbikes to the cars which were parked up, trying the door handles one after another in the hopes that I was right about these guys thinking they were untouchable.

Sure enough, on my fourth attempt, I found a red pickup with the door unlocked. I smirked to myself as I eased it open and slipped into the footwell, popping open the plastic panel to reveal the wires.

For a moment, I was forcibly reminded of being thirteen and boosting my first car with Chase.

"It's the blue wire," Chase hissed, trying to snatch the wire from my hand as the two of us fought for space in the footwell of the old green Chevy.

"It's not, Ace. Stop crowding me," I growled, slapping his hand away before connecting the two wires I was holding.

The car started up with a reluctant wheeze of the engine and Chase whooped in triumph loud enough to draw the attention of the people inside the store, including Mr Harper, whose car this happened to be.

"Oh fuck," Chase breathed as our Math Teacher came running out of the store yelling at us and I did the only thing I could think of, throwing the car into drive and slamming my foot down on the gas.

Chase started yelling instructions as the car shot off down the street, grabbing the wheel when I forgot about it and looked over my shoulder to see Mr Harper charging after us, screaming out for someone to call the cops.

Between the two of us, we somehow managed to drive the thing all the way out to Gallows Bridge where we crashed it into the trees at the side of the road and fell about laughing as smoke curled out from beneath the hood where it was smashed against a fallen trunk.

"You're a bad influence on me, little one," Chase laughed, as we clambered out of the wreck before wrapping his arms around me and squeezing tight.

"No way. You're the one who said you wanted to get back at him for failing you on that pop quiz," I protested, grinning up at him as his dark curls fell into his eyes.

"I didn't think you were gonna Google how to hotwire a car," he

protested, but the smile on his face was worth a thousand crazy risks. Especially as I glanced at the black eye he was still sporting after his dad had gotten a call from Mr Harper the super dick about that dumb quiz.

"I'd Google how to dispose of a body for you if it'd make you smile like that, Ace," I promised and he gave me a grin so big it lit me up from the inside out. "Now let's get out of here before the cops show up."

He shoved me to get me moving and we both laughed as we started running down the road in the vague direction of the beach. The others would freak when they found out what we'd done. Fox would tell us off, Rick would curse us for leaving him out and JJ would come up with a bunch of targets for us to hit next. And if stealing more cars would make Chase smile like that then I'd happily steal a hundred of them and maybe he'd be able to forget about his asshole dad altogether. At least for a little while.

I got the truck started, blinking off the memories and reminding myself that even though all I'd ever wanted was to see Chase smile, he didn't even feel bad about casting me out of this town and ruining my life. So there was no point reminiscing about old crap like that about him. My love for him had been all consuming, his for me had been optional, disposable, forgettable.

I hopped up into the seat and took off out of the parking lot, keeping an eye on my rear view mirror and smirking to myself when no one appeared from the bar to notice my theft. By the time anyone did, I should be done with this vehicle anyway. I just hoped they weren't too pissed about the condition they'd be getting it back in. But fuck it, I wasn't gonna be hanging around here long anyway so they wouldn't be able to come after me even if they did figure out who took it.

I sped down the road towards Rosewood Manor, snapping my seatbelt into place as I spotted my target and drove on past it for several hundred yards before slamming on the brakes.

I took a deep breath, put the truck in reverse and swivelled in my chair to look out the back window. I lined up the wooden pole holding the electrical power cables which ran into the manor with the rear of the truck before slamming my foot down on the gas.

The truck accelerated fast and I screamed as it slammed into the pole, the impact throwing me into my seatbelt and deploying the airbag in my face.

I coughed as I inhaled the white powder from the airbag and scrambled to get my belt off and get out of the truck, quickly rubbing down anything I'd touched with the hem of my shirt, just in case the cops took enough interest in this to investigate it.

I looked up at the buckled pole and broken power cables with a grin before turning and sprinting towards Rosewood Manor through the trees on the far side of the road.

I skirted the fence as I ran through the undergrowth all the way around the back of the property until I was certain I had to be close to the graveyard.

I kept going until I found a tree with thick branches hanging low enough to climb and hauled myself skyward until I made it up to the top of the fence.

I eyed it warily as I wondered whether there was any chance they had a backup generator. Because if they did, I was about to find out just how powerful the voltage on this thing was.

With a deep breath, I jumped from the tree to the fence, catching hold of it and heaving myself over the top with a grunt of determination.

Luckily, my ass did not get barbecued and I grinned as I lowered myself down on the other side into the graveyard. I glanced around warily, hoping the CCTV was also off the grid now that the power was down before darting between the family graves to the squat stone building in the centre of the fenced off space.

The crypt was just as I remembered it with the stone statue of a weeping angel leaning over the doorway. His wing was draping forward to create a small archway that I could stand beneath as I reached out to trace my fingers over the ring of keyholes set into the stone door.

I knew whose was whose. The locks that matched the four boys' keys surrounding my own in the centre.

I took my key from my neck and slowly pushed it into the lock, my heart thundering as I slid it into place and resisted the urge to turn it. My breaths came more heavily as I stood there, feeling how solid the stone was, appreciating the fact that this was still here, our secrets still concealed within. And one secret in particular which I was going to lay claim to to exact my revenge on the boys who had destroyed me.

It didn't even feel like a choice anymore. More like the desperate plea of my heart to seek retribution for what they'd stolen from me before I could ever even consider the idea of trying to find happiness again.

In fact, I was certain I wouldn't be finding any of that.

But maybe I could find a little peace if I could just make them hurt the way they'd hurt me. And maybe that would have to be enough.

CHAPTER THIRTY ONE

I hunted the whole of Sunset Cove before I finally found my car parked up on the curb near Sinners' Playground. Someone had tossed three ice cream cones on the hood which a bunch of seagulls were currently tearing into and leaving scratches on my fucking new paintwork. And by someone, I meant Rogue. And by tossing one look at the shady looking ice cream vendor down the street who was giving me the side eye, I also meant him.

I didn't even care to try and chase the birds away as I started running down onto the beach toward the pier. I was just relieved she hadn't skipped town already. Maybe it was a weak hope to think she might not still be planning to go though. Maybe she'd dumped my car and jacked herself a new ride somewhere along the seafront, but my gut told me she was in our old stomping ground. And I had to see her. I didn't know if I could convince her to stay because I couldn't erase every shitty thing that had happened to her because of us. But I'd fucking try.

I climbed the beam up to the railing on the pier, swinging my leg over and dropping into the park. I strode between the old shops, casinos, checking through the windows to make sure she wasn't there. My heart was thrashing like a wild beast in my chest and I knew it wouldn't rest until I found her again.

Please be here, pretty girl.

"Rogue!" I called, figuring if she wanted to run from me I wasn't going to stop her anyway.

But maybe if she knew I was here, I could convince her to talk to me. Convince her that…fuck, I didn't even know. That I wasn't an asshole? I was. That I hadn't meant for any of that bad shit to happen to her? Well fucking duh, but how did that make it any better? She was right. When we'd exiled her from Sunset Cove, there wasn't a chance she was going anywhere good. But staying had equalled death. And we'd only meant for it to be temporary. She wasn't meant to run. We were supposed to contact her, find her. But when we'd tried…hell, I hated to even think of it now. The long and short of it was, Luther would have killed her if we'd run to her too soon. And by the time we finally searched, it was too late. She was gone.

"Rogue!" I bellowed, frightening a flock of gulls which took off into the sky from the top of the arcade with indignant squawks.

"Go home, JJ!" her reply came and the air rushed out of my lungs. She hadn't left. She was here. And my heart beat more solidly as it urged me toward her.

I moved through the maze of old rides, searching for her among them. "Where are you?" I growled, desperate to see her.

"I'm a ghost remember?" she said bitterly.

"You're not dead," I snarled, rounding the dodgems and hunting each car for her. "If you come out here, I'll show you how real you are."

"Is the wind alive, J?" she called, her voice now drifting off somewhere ahead of me. I caught sight of a tanned leg before it disappeared around an old candy cart and I started jogging after her. "The wind can move and howl and you can feel it against your skin, but it's still just a ghost. Like me."

"Stop it," I growled, running around the next corner and finding her sitting on a golden horse on the old carousel. Her hair was being pulled to and fro in the wind and her little dog was sitting obediently at her feet, a pious follower of this heartbreakingly beautiful goddess. Just like I was.

Her eyes were red, but it looked like her tears had long since dried. I didn't think she'd ever looked so captivating as she did now with her mascara smudged and strength burning in her eyes. A smile didn't compare to that deep and endless sea that lived in her gaze. Not even one as perfect as hers.

I walked towards her, looking up at her on the horse as she gazed impatiently at me like anything I said would be a waste of time. And she was probably right about that.

"I know my apologies are worthless," I said darkly, reaching out to grip her calf and her throat bobbed as she gazed at me. "And I'm not here to drag you home."

"Why are you here then, Johnny James?" she asked icily, tugging her leg out of my grip and Mutt jumped up, growling at me as he got the silent message from his master that she didn't want me here.

I stepped up onto the carousal, stuffing my hands into my pockets and shaking my head. "Because once upon a time, I would have followed you anywhere. And then I lost you and now…I guess I've done what I couldn't do back then."

"What's that?" she asked bitterly.

"I found you," I said with a boyish shrug before stepping closer to her again. She tipped her head to the side as she watched me approaching like I was a lion in the long grass.

"Maybe I want to be lost, JJ," she sighed. "Maybe I was lost for so long that it started feeling good."

"Nothing feels as good as having a home, sweetheart. And this is your home," I said firmly. "Are you really going to leave again?" My throat seized up as I prepared myself for the answer. Because if she chose to go, I'd have to accept it. I knew I couldn't chase her to eternity when she didn't want me in her shadow. I'd have to let her go. But I wasn't ready. I'd never be ready. Not after going so long without her only to have her back for nothing but a few short weeks. I had so much I wanted to give her, but I didn't know how. These past years had fucked me up too and now we were finding each other broken instead of whole and it wasn't anything like I'd wanted it to be.

"I'm still thinking about it," she said, twisting the key at her throat between her fingers.

I nodded, looking out in the direction of the bright blue sea. "This isn't an excuse but…Luther never would have let us come find you."

She scoffed. "I don't wanna hear it, J. You could have found a way. I would always have found a way for you guys."

I nodded, guilt tugging at my chest as I thought back on one of the days me, Fox and Chase had all been trying to locate her.

"Maybe if you hadn't smashed her fucking phone when we sent her away, this wouldn't be so hard," Chase growled as we stood in Fox's room.

"As if my father would have let her keep it anyway," Fox said, stalking back and forth in front of the balcony doors.

Luther was out on a job and we did what we always did whenever we had some time away from him. We planned how to find Rogue. But this time it was more than that, we were going to fucking do something about it. It had been two months since she'd left and Luther hadn't mentioned her in weeks.

"I had to prove my loyalty to him so he'd trust us," Fox hissed, getting up in Chase's face.

I groaned, knocking my head back against the wall. "Just stop fighting. We need to do this now.*"*

"Fine," Fox snarled, stalking to the door and opening it. We followed him into the hall, heading toward Luther's office and Fox knelt down in front of the door as he took a couple of picks from his pocket.

I moved to stand guard by the stairs while Chase threw me an anxious look. The house was quiet. Luther probably wouldn't be back for hours, but he had plenty of armed men crawling about outside.

Fox had been practising picking locks for a few weeks now and as a click sounded, I turned and found him pushing his dad's office door open with a smug grin.

I gasped and Chase pumped his fist in victory. I jogged across the hall, following them into the office and Fox ran around the huge desk, taking Luther's iPad out of a drawer.

"Three five nine nine," I breathed. I'd watched Luther unlock it over breakfast a few days ago and my heart hammered as Fox tapped in the number.

We all held our breath then my heart leapt as the screen unlocked. I hurried around the desk, my shoulder pressing against Fox's, and Chase crushed in close on the other side. Fox brought up Luther's emails, typing in the name of his cousin in Fairfax. Nothing came up.

"Shit," Fox swore, typing in Fairfax, then Rogue Easton, anything he

could think of that might seek out an email.

"Forget it, check his contacts for Sandra," Chase hissed and Fox nodded as he switched onto them, hunting through them for her name. He found it, tapping on her details and nothing but a phone number sat beneath it. No address, no email. Fuck.

"Write it down," Fox growled and I grabbed a pen and paper, scribbling the number down as Fox started checking Luther's browser history.

A door slammed downstairs and my heart lurched as Fox nearly dropped the iPad.

"Put it away," I hissed and Fox quickly locked it, tossing it back into the drawer and we all ran for the exit.

We slipped out into the hall and shut the door. Fox dropped down, fumbling with his picks as he worked to lock it again.

I scrambled over to the stairs, peering down them, fear crashing through me as I expected Luther to appear at any second.

"Hurry," Chase urged and Fox cursed as he worked.

Footsteps pounded this way downstairs just as a click sounded behind me and relief rushed through my chest as Fox jumped up. We jogged back to his room as quietly as possible, our breaths coming heavily between us.

Fox fell down on his bed, switching on the tv and Chase and I dropped down beside him, kicking up our feet as solid footfalls thumped upstairs. I shoved my hand under Fox's pillow, stashing the number there as my throat thickened with fear.

A loud knock came at the door and I shared a worried look with my friends before the door pushed open.

Luther stood there, blood flecking his cheeks and staining his golden hair red. My heart bunched up in my chest as his murderous gaze slid over all of us before settling on Fox.

"The motion sensor camera in my office was just triggered." He held up his phone, showing a video of the three of us at his desk and the world closed in on me, choking out all the air from my lungs.

"I tried," I told Rogue.

"It's not good enough," she breathed and I nodded, stepping closer to her.

"But it's something, right?" I asked, knowing I was an asshole for it, but I just needed her to stop looking at me like that.

"It doesn't change anything."

"I know, pretty girl," I sighed, staring at her up there looking like a dark queen and falling back on my instincts. If I couldn't make her forgive me, I could at least make her smile. I took out a roll of cash from my pocket and held it up to her. "A thousand dollars to sit with the lady?"

She snorted, shaking her head as she fought to keep her expression flat. "No."

"Alright two thousand, but I want some firm, over the pants stroking for that."

"Oh, I've just figured out why you keep following me everywhere. This is all a long ploy to get me to work at your club, isn't it J?" she taunted, a smirk pulling at the corner of her mouth. *Fuck yes.*

"Yeah," I played along, stepping closer again and laying my hand on the golden horse's head. "You'd bring in top dollar, pretty girl. I have a problem though…"

"What's that?" she asked as my hand ran down the horse's neck onto the saddle between her thighs.

I looked up at her, my smile dropping away as I brushed her inner thigh with my fingertips. "I want to keep you all to myself."

I thought of Chase's reaction when he'd found me with her and knew this shit was getting messy fast. He'd shown his cards and I'd shown mine. I wasn't going to stop him from making his move on her if that was what he wanted, but I sure as fuck was going to try and lock her down before that could happen. The bigger problem was Fox. Because fuck my life, he was going to shoot me dead if he found me with her. But I just couldn't stop myself.

Her lips parted as I painted a circle on her skin and she released a ragged breath. "I told you-"

"You don't belong to anyone. I know," I said, cocking my head to one side. "You're not for sale…but I am. And I've got an offer on right now that might interest you."

"Oh yeah?" She quirked an eyebrow.

"I'm free to any girl with hair the colour of the rainbow." I smirked and she released a breathy laugh.

"Not too many of those around here."

"It's a very limited offer," I agreed and she cracked a smile that made my heart tug.

I reached up to brush her lips with my thumb, tracing the curve at the corner. "Let me make that smile last longer, sweetheart. It looks far too temporary."

"Where'd you learn to talk like that, J? And how many times have you used it to get a girl to suck your dick?" She knocked my hand away from her face and a low noise left my throat that was entirely animal.

"I'm not playing you, Rogue," I growled.

"You didn't answer my question." She swung her leg over the horse so she was side-saddling it with her back to me, her attention falling to her chipped nail polish.

"Anything that comes out of my mouth around you is real, sweetheart. I could talk a straight guy into blushing for me for the right price, but with you I wanna do it because it makes me feel good to make *you* feel good."

"Uhuh," she said disinterestedly, clearly not believing me. I pushed her and she fell off the horse, turning to me with a shocked expression as she landed on her feet.

I gripped the pole rising up from its back and used it to swing myself around the horse toward her like I was doing a bit in one of my shows. "I pushed you about when we were kids, don't go telling me the rules have changed, pretty girl."

"It's hardly fair now I can't beat you in a fight with all those stupid muscles."

"They're less stupid once you're wrapped up in them. C'mere, lemme show you."

She backed away, slipping between a dolphin and a shark and I hounded after her around the carousel while Mutt yipped at me in warning.

"I'm good," she said lightly, still retreating, her eyes scraping down my body.

"Why are you eye fucking me then?" I taunted and her gaze snapped back up to mine as I called her out.

"No harm in looking," she said, fronting it out and my grin widened.

"No harm in touching either, or sucking, or licking, or fuck-"

"I'm not going to make that mistake again," she said and the smile fell from my face, a blade twisting in my chest as she confirmed what I'd thought anyway. I was just a bad decision. The dick for hire, only good for one thing. But at least that meant I could offer her something.

"Alright," I conceded as I trapped her inside a large sea turtle which had a bench in the centre of it. "I'm good for talking too. I heard what you said loud and clear. And I'm here to call bullshit."

She folded her arms, glaring at me and I hated that. I hated it so fucking much I wanted to just grab her and kiss her until she stopped looking at me like that. Like I'd fucked up everything in her life. Which I had, I knew I fucking had.

"On what?" she deadpanned.

"The little miss disposable act," I said, stepping into the turtle so she either had to climb out or face me. "You are the least disposable person I've ever known. And for the record, I know what it's like to be disposable. But you, sweetheart, you're a fucking blood diamond. Rare as hell, wanted by everyone."

"I'm wanted by no one," she hissed, her blue eyes watering and I could see the depth of her belief in those words. Nothing I said right now would change that. But I could try and prove it. I didn't know how, but I'd figure it out.

"I want you," I swore. "I want you more than I've ever wanted anything, Rogue. I'll never be done with you."

"You're a liar," she breathed, but her resolve was fading, her gaze falling to my mouth as I closed the distance between us.

"No, but I'm a thief, an escort, a dirty fucker with a black heart. But you like that about me, don't you?" I tracked my thumb across her chin and she swallowed hard, her pupils dilating.

"I liked the old JJ."

"He's got nothing on the new one," I promised, leaning down to brush my mouth along her jaw. "He couldn't have done this to you."

She shivered, tilting her head to the side as I dragged my lips up to her ear and her body arched into me.

"Or this." I slid my hand up her top, slowly running my fingers up to her breasts, waiting for her to tell me no, but her moan told me to continue.

I pushed my hand into her bra, finding her nipple hard and waiting for me as I pinched and caressed it. She dropped her head against my shoulder as she moaned again, like she was trying to hide from her own desires, but there was no fucking chance I was going to let her. I may have been a bad decision, but if she wanted to make it again, I'd always be here for her to do so.

I moved my mouth to her ear as her hand fisted in my shirt and I could sense the rage in her from the tension in her posture.

"Hate me, pretty girl," I growled. "But have me too."

I'd been used by hundreds of women, but Rogue was the first I really wanted to use me for nothing in return. She'd owned me a long time ago, my heart bought with her smiles and endless days in the sun at her side. She could use me until I was ruined, because my only wish in my whole life had been that this girl wanted me the way I wanted her. But if I couldn't have that, then she could have whatever pieces of me she liked and discard the rest. My body might have been leant to others, but my heart had never been touched by anyone but her. And she would always have that claim on me.

"I'm so fucking angry," she growled into my chest, her hands tracking down my body until she was tugging at my shorts. My cock was already iron hard for her. I had to jack myself off for ten solid minutes pre-show sometimes to get it up, but for Rogue I was amped and ready to go with a single look.

"I know, pretty girl," I murmured. "Be angry. Just don't leave. Promise you won't leave."

"I can't do that." She grasped my dick through my shorts and I hissed through my teeth.

I wasn't sure if I was about to be castrated or have the best fuck of my life, but I was pretty sure I was going to enjoy it either way. So long as her hands were on me like that, I couldn't *not* enjoy it.

She started jerking me off through the material, her hand squeezing and yanking my cock in this brutal way which I fucking loved. I scored my thumb across her nipple again, getting as rough with her as she was with me as I squeezed her breast hard and growled into her hair.

"Come on then, Rogue, take it out on me. You're holding back."

She shoved her hand into my shorts, grabbing my balls and squeezing them until I gasped.

"*Motherfucker*," I hissed and she looked up at me with a grin that said she was enjoying this, but I had better ideas of how to make her smile.

I tugged her hand off of my balls, wrapping her palm around my bare cock and groaning as I made her pump it. I smirked at her as she was forced to pleasure me, but before she could get mouthy about it, I pushed my free hand into her panties and sought out her burning hot pussy. I kicked her legs wider, shoving two fingers into her soaking heat and she cried out as I pumped them furiously in and out of her. I released her fist on my cock and she continued to give me the hand job of fury and wrath as I pushed a hand into my pocket and took out a condom.

She snatched it from me, tugged my hand out of her panties and climbed away over the turtle's head. I groaned, climbing after her and trying to catch her.

"This is torture enough, pretty girl," I growled as she weaved between the animals.

She ran out of sight and I jogged after her around the carousal with a grunt of frustration, my gaze landing on her shirt on the ground. I smirked as I slowed my pace, striding past a horse with her bra hanging on its ear. As I hounded after her, I found her shorts on the back of a crab, her sneakers discarded on the floor and finally her little yellow panties on the fin of a dolphin.

I hooked them off of it onto my finger, finding the seat of them wet against my palm and my dick got even harder - if that was even possible right now. I tucked them into my pocket and moved after her, rounding a large starfish seat and finding her sitting on the back of the same golden horse I'd found her on before. Her legs were spread either side of it, her back pressed against the pole behind her as she teased her clit with one hand while massaging her breast with the other.

I bit down on my fist, groaning as I approached her. "Where's the condom?" I gritted out and she shrugged innocently, but her eyes darted sideways and I found it stretched over a swordfish's face, the tip of it ripped open on the point.

I pushed my tongue into my cheek, approaching her at a predator's pace as she lifted her chin in a challenge.

"Fuck you, Johnny James," she said breathily, her tone drawing me in instead of pushing me away.

"Yeah, fuck me, pretty girl," I ordered as I reached the rear end of the horse.

I grabbed her hips, yanking her closer to me. She gasped as I shoved her hand away from her pussy, running my tongue up the centre of her and her thighs trembled against my hold as I pushed them even wider.

Her hands fisted in my hair and she ground her clit against my mouth as I sucked and teased her mercilessly. I wanted her coming on my tongue fucking pronto and I wasn't going to be a gentleman about what I did next.

She gasped and moaned and her dog yapped at us in alarm, the poor fucker probably thinking I was eating his mistress for lunch. Which, technically, I was.

"Look away, Mutt," Rogue demanded before she gasped, quivering against me as I circled my tongue over her little bundle of fun.

The sound of scampering feet told me the dog had run off and I looked up at my girl with a wicked grin. "He might come running back when I make you howl."

"Stop talking," she gasped, pushing my head back down between her thighs and I laughed into her pussy before driving my tongue into her tight hole.

She bucked her hips, gasping and moaning as I gave her clit all of my attention next, sucking and kissing before starting up a rhythm with my tongue that had her spilling curses I'd never even heard before.

Her thighs locked around the horse as she moaned loudly, coming beautifully on my tongue and I drank in the flavour of the rainbow with hungry licks.

Her body melted like hot candle wax and I pulled her down off of the horse, smirking at the wet patch she left on its back as I carried her to the sea turtle, placing her down on her feet facing away from me. She stumbled shakily and I slapped her ass hard.

"Fuck, J," she cursed and I laughed as I pushed her forward to bend over the turtle's head.

She found her strength again, pushing her ass back against me with a growl. "Dammit, why did I destroy the condom?"

I barked a laugh, taking another one from my wallet and tearing open the wrapper with my teeth like a porn star. I'd made an art out of making contraception look sexy a long time ago and I was bringing my A game for my girl. "You could destroy ten and I'd still pull one from my hair or my sock or my ass or my-"

"Get inside me, Johnny James," she growled and I clenched my jaw, splaying my hand on her tanned back and tugging my shorts down.

I lined myself up with her wet entrance then shoved myself inside her fully, making her cry out. If a pod of dolphins were hanging out below the pier, they were definitely getting an earful right now.

I growled at the perfect tightness of her pussy before driving myself in and out of her with powerful thrusts, taking everything I needed from her and giving her everything I had. She clutched onto the turtle's head, her clit grinding against its face as I took her forcefully and kept her down beneath me.

"I hate you," she moaned and I rolled my hips, making her gasp as I rubbed her g-spot before pounding into it, grinding her into the turtle's face who was definitely smiling around about now as I rubbed my girl's pussy against it.

My hands gripped her tightly and my gaze ran over the angel wings which decorated her back as they flexed and rippled with every thrust that drew our bodies together.

She cursed and moaned and said completely unintelligible things as I fucked her so good that she was soon coming hard on my cock, squeezing me and making a shudder of pleasure run down my spine. I held her still as I claimed my own release from her, pumping in and out of her a few more furious times before finishing deep inside her.

"Fuck," I rasped as ecstasy made my head spin and I sighed her name as I held her down a moment longer. "You don't hate me," I growled, drawing myself out of her and taking the condom off, tying a knot in it.

She stood up, pushing a hand through her hair and my gaze followed the curves of her body. *I am one lucky, lucky fuck.*

She batted her long lashes, stepping toward me and giving me a devil's smile. She didn't answer me, instead slipping her fingers into my pocket and pulling out the panties which were poking out of it.

"These are mine, thief," she purred and I gave her a puppy dog look.

"I thought they were a gift," I said innocently.

She snorted, pulling them on and brushing past me to collect the rest of her clothes while I tossed the condom into the booth in the middle of the carousel. I sighed as I watched her perky ass go, feeling like I had far too many stupid things I wanted to say which would probably make her run for the hills. I settled on the only thing that mattered, figuring anything else I said would just be fucking dumb.

"Are you going to stay in town?" I trailed after her as she pulled on the last of her clothes and tugged her hair out from under the hem of her shirt.

"Maybe."

I grabbed her hand, wheeling her around to face me. "I need a yes, sweetheart." My heart beat out of rhythm and she frowned at me, shaking her hand out of mine. And there it was. The rejection every girl gave me when they were done with me. The retreating, the cold wall in their eyes, the look that said *can you go now?*

I stepped back and hardened my heart, looking away from her. I was used to this, it never usually hurt. But with her it was gutting.

"I guess I'm not quite done with this town. Not yet anyway."

A heavy breath of relief left me and she frowned.

"I'll stay for now. But not for you," she said and I nodded, the relief bittersweet after the sting of her withdrawing from me. I should have expected it anyway. I was a good distraction from a shitty situation. But I wanted to be more than that, I just didn't know how to be.

"Fox will probably be camped out in a bush outside your trailer right about now," I mused, burying the pain in my chest and slapping on a smile. "I can deal with him for you if you want to go there?"

"You sure?" she asked hopefully.

"Course, pretty girl." I took out my phone, shooting a text to Fox.

JJ:

I found her. But she's gonna skip town if you don't get out of her trailer and leave her in peace there for a while.

Fox:

Fine. I'll give her a day.

JJ:

Three.

Fox:

Two.

JJ:

Done.

"You've got two days of peace," I told her brightly and she pursed her lips.

"Aren't you doing the boat job tomorrow?" she asked with a frown.

"Yeah, why?" I asked as we stepped off of the carousel.

"Just wondering." She shrugged. "How much is it worth again?"

"I don't recall me ever telling you," I taunted and she smirked.

"Well I'm asking now."

"Eighty grand. Half goes to Luther's empire of course, but the rest is split evenly between the four of us who pull off the job. It'll be a tidy ten grand each."

"Four?" she questioned.

"Yeah, Chase is picking the fourth. There's armed guards and the best way to pull the job is to come at the boat from both sides so we have a back up escape plan if needed. It's safer to go in pairs, we can watch each other's backs."

"Well don't die, Johnny James," she said.

"I think that's the nicest thing you've said to me since you got back to town," I said with a teasing grin and she jabbed her elbow into my side.

"Just don't, 'kay?"

I slung my arm around her shoulders, drawing her close, unable to resist the urge to hold onto her just a little longer. "'Kay, pretty girl."

I met Fox down by the marina dressed in my fisherman gear, cap and all, looking real authentic. Fox was matching me, waiting on the small fishing boat along the dock and I jumped onto it with a grin.

"Well ahoy there, seaman," I said brightly and he rolled his eyes. "Where's our other fellow seaman?"

"Stop saying seaman like that," Fox said sternly, taking out his phone and checking it for messages from Chase.

I dumped my bag of tools down in the back of the boat and glanced around at the other fishermen preparing their boats. It was early morning and we had fifteen minutes before the ferry left the shore. I could just make out the large white side of it further down the dock, La Mujer Bonita written in swirling red writing near the front. There wouldn't be many people heading out on it this early, the tourist season was only just beginning so I was banking on a quiet vessel, but the armed guards were going to be our biggest problem. We'd had a tip off about them a couple of weeks back and tweaked our plans to accommodate them. They were there to protect the cargo from any shady passengers though. They wouldn't be expecting anyone shady to climb aboard and rob them blind.

It sounded like there were more than those Cartier watches being transported now, but whatever valuables they were guarding we weren't interested in them. Fox wanted the watches and nothing else. We could take them right out of the box with the code we'd all memorised and the police would never be able to figure out when they went missing. We had to get on the ferry, down to the hold and back off of it again without anyone ever realising

561

we were there. It was going to be quick and dirty and I couldn't fucking wait.

The minutes crept by and Fox tried calling Chase several times to no reply.

Anxiety bled into me and I pressed my hand to his arm as La Mujer Bonita sounded its horn and started pulling out of the dock.

"We've gotta go," I hissed and Fox looked to me with fury etched into his face.

"Fucking Chase. This *his* goddamn job," he snarled.

"Can we do it alone?" I asked and he ran his tongue over his teeth as he considered it.

Fox's phone buzzed in his hand and I leaned closer so I could read the message from Chase.

Chase:

On my way. Get going. We'll meet you on the water.

"This isn't the plan," Fox snarled.

"Come on, let's go. If he says he'll be there, he'll be there," I said and Fox nodded, giving in and moving to start up the engine. We had no choice anyway. The ferry was leaving and this was our one shot.

We were soon out on the water, trailing behind La Mujer Bonita and my heart skipped and danced with excitement as we rode the waves behind it, holding back enough so as not to cause any suspicion.

I gazed across the sea as I hunted for any sign of Chase. There weren't as many boats out on the water as there could have been and I smirked at our good luck. So long as our brother made it here, we'd all be celebrating back at the house before ten am.

We were heading out into the deep blue waters that stretched between the mainland and Ballena Island and I hunted left and right for my boy. *Come on, asshole, where are you?*

A glint of white caught my attention up ahead and I spotted Chase driving a speedboat, cutting through the waves. Beside him, Rogue stood with a long, brown wig over her hair and my heart clenched in shock as Fox straightened beside me.

"*No*," Fox spat, but it was too late now. Chase had chosen the fourth member of our party and if we didn't roll with it, we weren't going to pull off this job.

"It's too late," I muttered to Fox as my heart hammered out of control. "She's in."

CHAPTER THIRTY TWO

I bit my lip as I caught sight of Fox looking mad enough to shit a brick dressed up like a fisherman in a really bad porno. Like what would his bit even be? *Let me come plunder your trout? I need to inspect your sea cave...* No. Pass. I'd stick with the cover story me and Chase had come up with thanks. Billionaire newlyweds on our honeymoon.

"Looks like Foxy isn't too pleased with my choice of crew member," Chase said, smirking at me as he drove the speedboat in a wide arc around to the far side of the ferry. He was such a dick sometimes. Why did I like that so much? I guessed I was probably a dick too.

He'd let me style him as part of my agreement to join in with this shit – because clearly the ten grand pay out wasn't enough incentive for me – and he was currently wearing a pair of cream chinos and a white linen shirt with half the buttons undone. And freaking navy boat shoes with white stitching. I cracked up every time I looked at him and he was smirking too despite his best attempts not to. He looked so fucking fancy, I just couldn't take it.

In return, I was wearing a pair of flouncy white and blue patterned harem pants with a matching crop top that had a French label in it with a designer name I couldn't even pronounce. I'd coupled it with a long, brunette wig to cover up my rainbow hair and Chase had even stolen a pair of wedding bands for us to wear. Though I was pretty sure the addition of the rings was just to piss Fox off. Far be it from me to miss the chance to badger the Badger though, so I was happily wearing mine.

When Chase had shown up at my trailer yesterday afternoon to offer me this job, it had seemed like I should just tell him to get fucked. But he'd pulled the stupid favour card on me without bothering to try and apologise or make me feel anything I didn't want to, so I'd found it easy enough to agree in the end. I'd have been dumb to turn down that much cash anyway. So as I stood at his side and stole the cigarette from the corner of his lips to take a deep drag on it, I didn't even care when he narrowed his eyes on me.

"I bet you didn't think you'd end up marrying me, did you, Ace?" I teased, watching the way the glow of the cigarette reflected in his dark blue eyes as he looked down at me.

"Well it's pretty obvious I wouldn't be your first choice, isn't it, little one?" he asked icily, taking the cigarette back to stub it out as we pulled around to the rear of the ferry, following in its wake.

"What's wrong, Ace?" I asked. "Are you really pissed because you think I'm gonna drive a wedge between Fox and JJ or is it something else?"

"Like what?" he growled, his gaze running over me in my fancy pants clothes and enough unspoken words hanging between us to make the air thick.

But before I could answer, the ferry's engine fell quiet and the huge boat slowly stopped moving forward ahead of us.

"That's our cue," Chase said, forgetting our conversation in favour of the more important task at hand as he directed the boat over to the side of the ferry. "Paulo has taken the ferry out of action, but we only have twenty minutes before they'll get her up and running again and we need to be back on this boat by then."

My heart pounded as I looked up at the top deck, watching for anyone looking back our way as Chase moved the speedboat close enough to tie it off on the railings that lined the edge of the lower deck of the ferry.

The moment it was done, I climbed up onto the edge of the speedboat and grabbed hold of the railing so that I could pull myself up. Apparently, I wasn't moving fast enough for Mr Grouchy though because he placed a hand on my ass and shoved.

I cursed him as I made my way up onto the deck and Chase followed right behind me, ignoring my offer of help as I held my hand out to him. He brushed past me before leading the way up a set of narrow maintenance stairs to the top deck and I followed while internally cussing him out.

When we made it to the open space on top of the boat, we found Fox and JJ already waiting for us and Fox strode forward looking seriously pissed as he glanced around to make sure that there wasn't anyone about to see us up here.

"I should just call this whole thing off," Fox growled, glowering at Chase. "Go back down to the boat, Rogue. We can do this without you."

"Fuck off, Fox. You need four people and you got me, so suck it up."

Fox looked inclined to flip out, but JJ caught his arm. "Come on man, we don't have the time to waste like this."

"What the fuck are you wearing anyway?" I teased, smirking at the olive green waders the two of them were dressed in.

"We're fishermen, because the only time anyone will see us during this job is out on the water," Fox snapped. "What are you supposed to be?"

"Newlyweds," Chase said, grabbing my wrist and showing Fox the ring with a taunting smirk. "Seems like we might actually have a reason to be on a passenger ferry, unlike a pair of fishermen-"

"No one will see us," Fox cut me off impatiently.

"Let's go," JJ insisted while Fox looked like he wanted to rip the ring right off of my finger despite the fact that he knew it was bullshit.

I moved to follow JJ towards the front of the boat as we hunted for the stairs which led down to the hold and the others fell into step with us too.

"I'm half tempted to say we should cut our losses now," Fox growled as the four of us crept across the deck of the ferry.

We headed between the shipping containers that had been placed up here for transportation before peeking out towards the part of the deck where the passengers were allowed to congregate.

"Seems a bit dumb to me," I commented. "Because you'd just be cutting yourself out of the take."

"If I decide to call it off, we'll *all* be leaving," he snarled, grabbing my wrist and tugging sharply to make me stop walking.

"You don't hold any power over me, Fox," I hissed. "Not unless you lay your hands on me and force me to your will. Which is something you seem pretty damn fond of doing, might I add."

My gaze dropped to my wrist where he was gripping me tightly and he blew out an aggravated breath.

"Can we just get on with it?" Chase suggested, looking like this whole thing was boring him, but he had to have known the way Fox would react to him bringing me here.

"Don't try to make out that I'm like that creep who tried to kill you," Fox said in a low tone, ignoring Chase entirely. "Every time I make you do something you don't like, it's for your own good. And don't go pretending that you don't like the feeling of my hands on your body. You have that built in detection system after all."

He reached out with his free hand and placed it over my heart against the thin fabric of my flouncy shirt. As he'd been hoping to, he found my heart racing beneath his palm, but I just narrowed my eyes.

"I get off on the adrenaline rush of pulling jobs like this. Not your company. So if you want to get my heart pounding, I suggest you take your hands off of me and we all go steal some shit."

JJ chuckled beneath his breath from his position to our right where he was keeping a lookout for any of the guards who were onboard. Luckily, for such a big boat carrying such expensive cargo, the security crew wasn't all that large. They were relying on their CCTV systems to keep them informed of anything important and Fox knew where all the cameras were so that we could avoid them.

"Look, we're here now. Let's have this dumb little argument back at the house after we get our hands on those watches," Chase suggested.

"Agreed," I said and Fox cursed as he released me.

"Stay with me," he said, his gaze boring into mine as he swiped a palm over his face.

We moved on, slipping out onto the upper deck which was thankfully abandoned due to the chilly morning breeze and heading towards the stairs that led down to the hold.

My heart was pounding in the most delicious way as we went, my body tingling with the knowledge that we shouldn't be here, that we were doing something wrong. And it felt oh so fucking right.

I swear, pulling high risk jobs felt better than sex when my adrenaline was flooding my limbs like this and my skin felt all hot and prickly. It was like the rush of an oncoming orgasm like no other. And pulling it off would always end in the most satisfying flood of ecstasy too.

A hand slid over the small of my back and I had to stifle a gasp as I looked up at JJ beside me, his honey brown eyes twinkling with knowledge as he smirked at me like he could tell how worked up I was feeling and was getting ideas about how to help me release some of that tension.

Okay, so pulling jobs like this felt better than *most* sex. But with him, that was a different story all together. Maybe we could celebrate together when we got back to dry land and have the best of both experiences one after the other...

Once we were out of sight on the stairs, Fox passed out ski mass to all of us and I accepted mine with a grin as my pulse continued to pound, watching the guys as they pulled them on to conceal their features.

Aside from the differing clothes hugging their muscular forms, there was hardly any way to tell the three of them apart, though I knew there was no way I'd ever get them mixed up. Still, there was something weirdly thrilling about the anonymity of the ski masks. The fact that they could almost be anyone beneath them. And it just brought to light how dangerous these men really were, too. Who they were to anyone on the outside. Something about that just made me like it even more.

Fox and Chase moved ahead to check beyond the next corner and I pushed up on my tiptoes to whisper in JJ's ear.

"You wanna keep that mask on when you sneak into my trailer tonight, Johnny James?" I asked him seductively and he groaned with longing, his hand grabbing my ass and squeezing tight for a brief moment as he dropped his mouth beside my ear too.

"How about I tie you up and make you scream for mercy as well?" he suggested, diving into this fantasy headfirst without so much as the slightest flicker of hesitation.

Fuck, that sounded crazy hot. I was definitely up for that and the look in his eyes said he could tell.

I bit my lip, forcing myself not to turn my head and kiss him as I drew back. JJ Brooks was a mistake that I'd decided I was gonna just keep making over and over again until I left this place. He felt too damn good to deny myself and I was perfectly alright with some mutually beneficial using.

Fox's low, sharp whistle forced us to move on, the two of us carefully keeping enough distance between our bodies to be sure that we wouldn't be tempted to act on the energy pulsing between us while we focused on what we came here to do.

We made it to a dark doorway and Fox moved me back against the cold metal of the wall beside it with a hand on my hip, his fingers digging in just enough to make sure I didn't move while he poked his head through to get a look. My stomach knotted as the pressure of his hand on me increased and I had to wonder if he was holding me still because he didn't trust me to pull this off without constant supervision or if he was trying to protect me. Though knowing Fox, it was probably a combination of both things.

When the coast was clear, Fox and Chase led the way into the hold and darted towards the left of the room where the shadows were thickest.

I sped after them, my footsteps as silent as a cat's as I hurried across the metal floor.

The space surrounding us was wide open, crates and boxes of every size and shape filling it and making it impossible to tell what was housed in each of them. My sticky little fingers itched with the urge to hunt for more things to steal, but I had to force that desire aside, knowing we needed to keep this job clean to make sure there wasn't too much heat on us once the robbery was discovered.

But Fox clearly knew exactly where we were headed as he moved through the darkened space and led the way between the closely stacked cargo as he began jogging towards the rear of the boat.

I found myself beside Chase who tossed me a look I couldn't read as we kept pace with one another.

Fox paused, raising a hand to stop all of us from proceeding and pointed ahead, placing a finger to his lips. I leaned around a tall box and peeked out, spotting a closed door ahead of us which seemed to be locked up tight. Chase had given me a rundown of the plan so I was guessing that was the door we needed to bust through.

"I'm gonna have to pick it," Fox breathed so low that I barely caught the words. "You three keep watch."

He didn't wait for us to agree before heading on towards the door and the three of us spread out across the room to look out for the guards who were patrolling the vessel.

The minutes ticked by as Fox worked on the lock, the odd soft curse spilling from his lips, letting me know that it was causing him trouble.

I slipped away from the others, spying a low light down a corridor which led away from the hold area.

I probably should have held back, but I always was a curious duck and as a man started laughing somewhere ahead of me, I just couldn't help but creep closer.

A little way down the corridor, I found a small room with the door ajar and two guards sitting at a table smoking inside. Their backs were to me and they were leaning together as they watched something on one of their phones. I eyed the security cameras behind them, taking note of their guard uniforms before my gaze caught on a set of keys hanging on a hook by the door.

Jackpot.

I reached out carefully and took the keys from the hook, holding them tightly in my hand so that they didn't make a sound before backing away again.

I crept towards Fox and as fast as I could while keeping silent, my heart pounding with the rush of danger as I moved behind him and he cursed as I touched his shoulder.

"I almost had it then," Fox growled irritably, like I was the reason he was struggling.

"Oh, Foxy, why do you always have to do things the hard way?" I teased, hanging the keys from my finger and dangling them before his face.

He gaped at me for a moment before the surprise in his gaze turned to excitement and he got to his feet, taking the keys from my hand and pressing me back against the door as he turned the right one in the lock.

"I forgot how much I enjoyed getting into trouble with you, hummingbird," he said as he pressed his body right up against mine until the door fell open behind me and I would have fallen if his arm hadn't locked tight around me to hold me up.

"So are you glad Chase brought me along?" I asked.

"Fuck no. But I'll enjoy it while it lasts because there's no way in hell it'll be happening again." He released me abruptly and the others hurried over as we headed into the room where the valuables were kept. *Dick.*

"Here it is," Fox announced in a whisper, leading us to the rear wall of the space where several safes and lockboxes were lined up.

He made a beeline for them, starting with the biggest, strongest looking bastard in the row as he hunted for the one which held the watches and I turned away from him to keep a look out as Chase moved to help him.

The kids I'd grown up with couldn't crack safes. Hell, I had no idea where you even learned to do something like that. I'd stolen my fair share of shit over the years, but I liked to do it the easy way - pickpocketing, shoplifting or breaking and entering if I was really desperate. The only safe I'd ever broken into was one where some dumbass had left his lock combination written down somewhere that I could find. And that was only one of those little hotel things where the take hadn't been all that much anyway.

If we pulled this off, I was going to get more money from my cut than I'd earned in the last year. It was almost enough to make me reconsider using the secret in that crypt to destroy these motherfuckers and to just stay here earning like this forever. Almost. But not quite. There were a few things I wouldn't ever sell in this lifetime and one of them was my heart. There may not have been much of it left, but I wasn't going to allow what there was to be destroyed again. And I knew that that was what would happen if I stayed in this town with these boys. I'd barely been here a month and it hurt too much already. There was no two ways about it.

The sound of heavy footsteps made my heart leap and I exchanged a concerned look with JJ as we ducked down, hidden behind the door that should have been locked.

"Hurry up," Chase hissed so low that I barely caught the words and I glanced over my shoulder just as Fox found the lockbox he was looking for and opened it using a passcode. *So much for crazy safe cracking skills then.*

The two of them started grabbing the watches out, filling their bags and cursing as the sound of footsteps drew nearer.

"He's gonna find us," I breathed, exchanging a look of fear with JJ.

"Quick," he said, moving to help the others as they piled the watches into their bags.

I shifted toward them too, but I knew it wasn't going to be enough to just grab the shit faster. The guard was gonna catch us. There was no two ways about it. And for this job to go off without a hitch, we needed to be sure they never knew we were here. My heart drummed against my chest and the thrill in my veins turned to fear for a moment. We needed to do something fast.

Chase finished filling his bag first, tossing it over his shoulder and catching my eye just as I made my decision.

I knew Fox would stop me if I told him what I was going to do, so I just jerked my head away from our group to tell Chase my plan. His eyebrows rose in surprise but that was all I had time for as I turned and scampered away.

I pushed the door open carefully and darted through it, scrambling to the end of the closest row of boxes, my heart leaping as I found Chase right on my heels.

But he only gave me a look of solidarity as we made it far enough from the others to buy them some time and I shoved a tall crate as hard as I could.

The thing began to fall and we sprinted away just as the crash rang out, echoing in the hollow space.

The guard yelled something and my gut plummeted as another guard called out from somewhere ahead of us too.

The distraction would keep them away from the others, but if we didn't move our asses then they were going to find us in about three seconds flat. Fox and JJ were going to have to lock that door and figure out what to do with the keys to cover our asses. It was on them now.

I spotted a narrow space between two huge crates and darted into it, dragging Chase behind me and wriggling into the shadows as the pounding footsteps drew closer.

We fell still, pressed together in the dark while my heart slammed into my ribcage with painful, thundering beats.

Chase's hand found my cheek, his palm cupping it through the material of my ski mask as I looked up into his sea blue eyes.

"It's okay, little one," he breathed, making my throat thicken with the use of that old nickname. "Five more seconds to let them move beyond us and we sprint for the exit. Got it?"

I nodded mutely, not trusting my voice in that moment as the sound of the guards finding the upturned crate reached me and suddenly, Chase's hand had left my face and he was forcing his way back out of our hiding place.

"Can you keep up?" he murmured softly as he caught my wrist and tugged.

"I'm not the one the cops caught stealing those beers from the liquor store when we were thirteen," I hissed, drawing a low chuckle from him in response.

"Let's see if you can still run like the wind then, shall we?"

I threw a glance in the direction the others were then turned to follow him as he broke into a sprint. We couldn't wait for them here. We just needed to get back to the boats and everything would be okay.

We ran on and fear knotted in my gut as we left the others behind. I hated to admit that I even gave a shit about Fox and JJ, but in that moment, I couldn't deny the terror racing through me at the idea of them getting caught. But that was why we had to run. We needed to be ready to draw the guards' attention away again if it was necessary.

I had to believe it would be okay.

And as Chase grabbed my hand while we sprinted up the stairs towards the upper deck, it felt like maybe it really would be.

CHAPTER THIRTY THREE

I kept Rogue's hand in mine as we ran upstairs and slipped onto the upper deck, my heart thumping against my ribcage. My phone buzzed in my pocket as we rounded the corner and I tugged it out, finding a message from Fox.

Fox:

Get to your boat and get away from here. We'll meet you at the car.

I shot him a reply agreeing to that then stuffed my phone away and guided Rogue along the walkway out on the deck. The sound of footfalls marched this way and I tugged open the nearest door, shoving her inside it and pulling it closed behind us. We were in some sort of storage closet which was barely big enough for the two of us and Rogue was crushed between my body and the wall.

My heart was thrashing out of control, my gut twisting as I looked down at this girl who had once possessed every inch of my being. She gazed back at me through her ski mask as voices sounded close by and I breathed in the coconut laced scent of her, a scent I had never forgotten in all the time she'd been away. In all the time I'd secretly missed her, drinking and smoking and fucking her out of me. But she'd never really left. No poison on earth could kill the part of me who still adored her.

"Did you see someone up here?" a voice growled just beyond the door and my body stiffened.

I slid the bag of watches from my back, quietly passing them to Rogue and taking a knife from my belt. She clutched my arm as a shadow beyond the door blotted out the light around the rim. Tension coiled in my muscles as I waited to pounce, but then the voices moved away.

I sighed, turning back to Rogue as she shouldered the bag, but I didn't draw away, caging her in with my arms and resting my forehead to hers. The girl who would never be mine. Who would choose Maverick and JJ before me. And no doubt Fox too. Had I ever even been an option?

I tugged her ski mask off so that I could look at her properly in the dim light that made it into the closet before reaching up to tug mine off too.

I dragged my thumb over her cheek and her lips parted, her sea blue eyes full of light and dark, twisting together. She was the one thing on earth I could never earn myself. And the one thing capable of destroying everything I'd earned besides her.

My cellphone buzzed in my pocket again and I pulled it out to look.

Fox:

We're back on our boat. Are you clear?
Make sure Rogue doesn't leave your sight.

It was just down to me and her. I pushed my phone back into my pocket without answering the message, my brain turning over what we needed to do to get out of here. What I had to do.

"I think they're gone," she breathed and I nodded, pulling back from her but she wrapped her hands in my shirt, tugging me close again.

"We've got a honeymoon to get to, sugar," she taunted and I mustered a laugh, but it came out dark and bitter. My dad had once told me I was good for nothin' and nobody. And he pitied any woman who might be stupid enough to marry me one day. But it looked like the only one I'd ever wanted was as smart as a whip.

"Fate's calling, little one," I growled.

"I thought you didn't believe in that shit?" she whispered and I shrugged then pushed the door open, tugging her after me. *I do when I'm the one paving the path of it.*

We jogged toward the back of the ferry, crossing into the cargo area and ignoring the sign that said members of the public weren't allowed back here. Then we slipped into a maintenance stairway, circling down toward the lower levels so that we could get back to our boat.

Heavy footfalls sounded below us, coming this way and my gut lurched as we turned tail, having nowhere to go but back up the stairs.

"Hey! You're not allowed back here!" a man barked behind us and Rogue gasped in alarm, her eyes widening as she looked up at me.

"Come on, Ace," she hissed, making my throat tighten as she tugged me back the way we'd come. We raced up the stairs, taking them two at a time as the sound of pursuit came from below.

Rogue turned off sharply into the corridor to our right. She grabbed my sleeve to pull me after her and I followed for a few steps before she let go as she broke into a sprint, clearly thinking I was following.

I stalled, staring after her, my feet rooted to the spot while the guard's footsteps pounded up the stairs behind me and I realised this was my chance.

My heart crushed in my chest and I tried to tear out the piece of it who loved her and leave it here to rot. *It has to be done. It's the only way.*

I took a deep breath, stealing myself to go through with this shit, then I forced myself to keep running up the stairs. Leaving her behind. *Fuck.*

My teeth gritted and I fought the nausea in my gut as I made it to the top deck with the guards closing in.

I set my gaze on the railing, the thundering beat of my pulse drowning out the sound of my second thoughts and I gritted my teeth as I forced myself to stick to this fucking decision. It was the only way. She was going to destroy us if she stayed with us. I had no fucking choice.

Do it, motherfucker.

I ran to the edge of the ferry, vaulted over the railing and dove off of it before I had a chance to change my fucking mind, hitting the water and sinking in deep. I held my breath, staying under and swimming beneath the waves in the direction of the speedboat we'd brought here. I came up for air at the rear of the ferry, my heart cleaving in two as shouts of pursuit sounded somewhere on the boat above me. But they weren't following me. They were following her.

Fuck fuck fuck.

I swam for the speedboat, hauling myself up into it and releasing the rope fixing it to the ferry. My throat thickened as I switched the engine on and took off, turning it around and making a wide arc toward the shore. One glance back at the ferry confirmed JJ and Fox's boat was already gone and the finality of what I'd done hit me like a tsunami.

My breaths came unevenly and I grabbed my smokes up from where I'd left them on the bench, jamming one between my lips and lighting it up with a shaking hand.

Life was better without her.
I can't let her fuck with my boys again.
This is the right thing to do.
The cops will take her away.
She'll never come back.
She'll never want *to come back.*
We'll be okay again.
She won't tear us apart.

I fisted my hair, hating myself, sickened by what I'd done, but I'd made a vow to get rid of her. Protect my boys from her. I wasn't going to let her ruin us. Even if I had to break all over again. But it was better it happened now while her claws weren't in too deep. The longer it went on the worse it would be. This was better. It had to be better.

When I was halfway to shore, I killed the engine, left the keys in the ignition, abandoned my smokes and dove overboard. I kicked off my shoes, swimming for the mainland, my gaze set for home.

I had a long way to go, but I could make it. I just had to figure out what I was going to tell my brothers, because Fox and JJ could never find out what I'd done. I'd have to live with it and let this secret decay inside my chest until it hollowed out my heart and numbed me to the bone.

She was the only girl my heart had been worth giving to anyway. So if it was cast in flame, seared and burned and reduced to ashes after this, who gave a fuck? She'd already done half the job ten years ago, so now I was just finishing off the rest before she got a chance to do it herself.

It hurt like a bitch already, but I'd swallow the pain of my betrayal, let it drag me into the dark and eventually I'd find peace again. Just the three of us and our empire. Never to be torn apart by Rogue Easton ever again.

Rejects Park

ROGUE

CHAPTER THIRTY FOUR

I raced down corridor after corridor as the sound of thundering footsteps followed me and my heart broke with panic for Chase. He'd been right behind me. What the hell had happened? I'd almost gotten away when I realised he wasn't with me anymore and now I'd had to turn back for him because I couldn't leave him behind. There was no fucking way I was going to accept the idea of him getting caught.

This couldn't be happening. There was no freaking way it was happening. We'd been so close to getting away clean.

I turned another corner, pulse racing and fear coursing through my limbs as if I could feel the walls closing in around me.

I'd totally lost track of where I was, let alone where I'd last seen him. I needed to get back to the speedboat and hope he was there, and if not then I'd have to search the whole fucking ferry until I found him. Because even if he was caught he would still be onboard and I'd find a way to break him out of wherever he was being held no matter what it took to do it.

I'd lost my way among the maze of corridors on the middle deck of the ferry, but I knew all I needed was to make it to the speedboat where either Chase would be waiting for me or I'd find Fox and JJ at their fishing boat instead. And if Chase wasn't there then I knew between me and the others we'd figure out how to get him back.

I snatched my stupid cellphone from my pocket and tried switching it on for the twentieth time, but the damn thing was dead. I hadn't been bothering to charge it much because Fox kept fucking badgering me on it, but now I wished I'd made sure it had juice more than anything in the fucking world so that I could call on them and figure out what the hell I should be doing…and make sure they were all okay too. Because as much as I knew I should hate them, my heart couldn't bear the idea of anything happening to them either. And as fucked up and broken and damaged as I knew that made me, I just needed to know they were alright. They *had* to be alright.

I gasped in relief as I finally found a staircase and I darted up it towards the top deck, the sounds of the guards who were hounding me drawing closer behind me as I ran. But I didn't have time to waste worrying about them.

The cool morning air kissed my skin as I finally emerged on the top deck, finding myself close to the cargo area of the ferry and sprinting towards the large containers sitting there.

I ran between two of the huge containers, shrouded in the shadows between them with my heart thrumming to the beat of a war drum.

Shit, why didn't I have a fucking gun when I needed one?

The sound of the guards' shouts filled the air and a voice sounded that made my heart leap in terror.

"Stop!" a man yelled from somewhere way too close to my hiding place. "There's nowhere to run to up here!"

But he was wrong. I could see the railing at the rear of the ferry now. I knew the boys' boats were down there. All I had to do was run and jump and they'd be waiting to pull me to safety.

A gunshot rang out as I failed to slow, but I just ran faster, weaving from side to side and ignoring the yells of the men at my back while the weight of the bag full of watches weighed me down. Not that I was tempted to give up our prize though.

I was almost at the railing now. I could dive over the edge and one of my boys would pluck me out of the water before these assholes ever even got the chance to chase us.

We'd be back on dry land before the cops made it out here.

I just had to jump.

My hands hit the cold metal railing at the rear of the boat and I jumped up onto it, about to do just that - dive overboard and swim to the speedboat lashed to the back of it in a leap of faith.

But as my heart soared in anticipation of the dive, I stumbled to a halt, a breath catching in my throat as my eyes widened in horror.

The boats weren't there.

Neither of them.

There was nothing to the rear of the ferry or the sides or anywhere to be seen in the dark blue water all around us either.

"No," I breathed as the weight of that fact hit me like a tonne of bricks. *"No."*

Strong hands grabbed me from behind and I cried out as I was wrenched away from the railing and my view of the sea was stolen.

But it didn't matter. I'd seen it clear enough. They'd gone. Left me. Abandoned me all over again when I was relying on them. When I'd put my trust in them like a fucking fool and put myself in the perfect position to be forgotten all over again.

I'd set myself up for this without ever even realising it.

And now I was going to pay the price for ever trusting the Harlequin boys to do anything for me. I'd been so caught up in guarding my heart from them that I hadn't even considered the fact that I'd been placing my life in their hands by agreeing to come on this job with them. They hadn't needed a fourth member to help them watch their backs - they'd needed a fucking fall guy to sacrifice if everything went wrong.

Pain splintered through my chest as I realised they'd abounded me to this. To the guards who had shoved me to my knees and were pushing and pulling at my body, tearing the bag away from me, shoving their hands into my pockets and checking what I had on me.

The guard in front of me reached down and ripped the dark wig from my head, making a cascade of rainbow coloured hair tumble over my shoulders as he released a low whistle of surprise.

"Well shit, she's a looker," he said and his buddies chuckled as I was tugged upright between them.

I should have been fighting, but what was the point? We were out in the ocean and no one was coming to help me. I had nowhere to go and no hope of getting onto another boat even if I could fight my way out of their hold. I was utterly fucked and I knew it just as well as the men who had abandoned me here to get screwed.

"You wanna tell us where your boyfriend ran off to?" another one asked, patting me down roughly and making me recoil towards the guy holding me.

"He's not my boyfriend," I snarled in response. "He's nothing to me."

None of them are.

The guards dragged me away from the railing towards the front of the ferry, but I could hardly hear the words they were saying or even see where we were going.

My limbs were trembling with hurt and betrayal and fucking rage unlike anything I'd ever known.

I'd let the Harlequin boys force their way back into my life and this was the thanks I got for it. Abandoned again. Rejected again. Forgotten again.

They'd proven every single thing I'd already known they thought about me. When it came down to it, that was just what I was to them.

Disposable.

And it hurt so fucking bad that I could barely even breathe. How had I let this happen again? How could I have been so fucking stupid?

My broken heart was tearing open and haemorrhaging freely in my chest as tears burned my eyes like acid and the hurt of this betrayal carved into me, making my scars crack and bleed again after I'd worked so hard to make sure they never could.

And as I was hauled away to meet my fate with the cops, it was easy enough for me to solidify the oath I'd been aiming to keep since the moment I came back to this godforsaken place.

I was going to tear them down and bring them low and leave them bleeding out in the dirt behind me when I ran. Whatever it took, I wasn't going to let them get away with this. Not again. I was done holding back. And the Harlequins were about to find what happened when I decided to fight dirty.

CHAPTER THIRTY FIVE

We waited and waited until my soul couldn't take it any longer. An hour. A whole fucking hour and they hadn't shown up.

JJ had forced me to get in the car and leave when red and blue lights had flashed further up the street, and I knew in the darkest regions of my heart, my girl was in trouble. Real fucking trouble.

Chase's phone went to voicemail every time I called and Rogue's did the same. I needed to know what was happening. I couldn't deal with not knowing.

"We just need to go home," JJ said firmly. "Maybe they split and headed there. Maybe they couldn't get back here, maybe they got lost or-"

"Then why haven't either of them called?" I snarled at JJ as he drove the car down the roads at high speed.

He shook his head, worry etched into his features and I dragged my fingers through my hair as I sent text after text, getting no reply from either of them.

We soon sped through the gates of Harlequin House and I leapt out of the car before JJ had even pulled on the parking brake in the garage, tearing up the stairs into the house and shoving the door wide.

Before I could take a single step into the hallway, Chase crashed into me, throwing his arms around me, smelling of the sea, his clothes dripping wet and his hair damp.

"Fox, fuck, I couldn't help her," he croaked, clutching onto me and dread seeped through my blood.

"What happened?" I demanded as JJ joined us, wrapping his arms around Chase too until he was crushed between us.

"We got split up on the ferry. I had to hide, but I tried to search for her. I couldn't find her. And when I did…they had her. The guards got her with the bag of watches. Fuck, I'm so sorry." He pulled away from us, clutching his chest like he was in pain. And I felt that pain too, slicing through my insides like a meat cleaver.

"She was locked in a room and they had guns. I heard them calling ahead to the cops on the mainland…there was nothing I could do," he said heavily, shaking his head. "I eventually got back to where my boat should have been, but the rope had come loose. It was fucking gone, so I just jumped and swam for home. I lost my phone. I lost…everything." His shoulders shuddered and JJ pressed a hand to his back as he shared a horrified look with me.

My jaw pulsed and a thousand furious thoughts crashed through my head. *Rogue. They have my girl. The fucking cops have her and she'll go down for this. For our crime. A crime she never should have been involved in.*

I launched myself at Chase, tearing him away from JJ and slamming my fist into his gut. I punched and punched, my fury ripping through me like an earthquake as I shoved him against the wall. But then I saw the hurt in his eyes and realised he hadn't even fought back, like he wanted this. Like he wanted me to make him pay for it.

"You brought her on that job," I hissed and he nodded, dropping his gaze from mine.

"I know,' he rasped. "I know what I've done. I'm sorry."

"Leave him, brother," JJ urged, clutching my arm to get my attention and I looked to him as my world tore apart. "We'll get her back. We'll figure it out."

"It's too late," Chase said darkly and I shot him a glare, venom spilling through my veins.

"It's *never* too late. I'll fight my way into the underworld for that girl and destroy any demon who tries to keep her from me," I spat and Chase shook his head at me.

"Even Fox Harlequin isn't above the law," he murmured. "She's gone."

"She's not gone!" I bellowed, storming away from him, ripping a picture from the wall and launching it down the hall. Glass smashed everywhere and my boots crunched over it as I made it to the kitchen and grabbed one of the stools by the island, throwing it at the wall and smashing it so that it clattered back to the floor in pieces.

Mutt started barking upstairs and my heart bunched up in my chest, aching with the force of a hammer slamming into it over and over.

I'll come for you, hummingbird.

I'll bring you home.

I swear on every tarnished piece of my soul, I will never abandon you again.

CHAPTER THIRTY SIX

I sat alone in a cell with my gaze on my feet and an echo resounding through my skull that bounced between the hurt of the Harlequins' betrayal and the pure, fucking fury I was feeling in my soul.

I felt like I was going to burn apart with so much of it consuming me. Like I was teetering on the edge of falling one way or another and there was nothing left in me to give anymore.

I clawed my hands into my hair and let myself scream.

I hadn't said a single word since I'd been hauled into the station here on Ballena Island. I wouldn't either. Though they had my prints on record from some crimes I'd committed when I was kid. But as they hadn't ever arrested me for them, they'd never put a name to those records and they were still working on trying to figure out who the hell I was. But I'd never been caught before and I wasn't planning on giving them my identity.

They could only hold me for two days without charging me but as they'd caught me red handed with thousands of dollars worth of stolen watches, I was willing to bet they would charge me pretty damn soon. I was going to go down for this. There was no two ways about it. No way out of it.

There was nothing I could do. It was hopeless. I just had to wait this out.

Wait for the inevitable and find out what followed.

"Rogue Easton?" a gruff voice asked and I flinched upright at the sound of my name.

How the fuck had they found that out? I was nothing. No one. I didn't even have any forms of ID to link me to my birth name. I'd been a ghost since my boys had cut me loose ten years ago. Hell, I hadn't even used my real surname since I'd run away and left this place.

I lifted my chin but didn't say anything as I tried to figure out what I was supposed to do.

"Are you Rogue Easton or not?" the cop asked in a flat tone that said I was pissing him off. "Because some big motherfucker just strode in here saying you're his girl. He paid your bail if that's your name. If not...well, maybe we'll have to keep you a little longer."

Relief spilled into me before I could help it, quickly followed by outrage as I realised just who would have done that for me.

Fucking Fox. Of course he'd buy my freedom. It was the perfect way to own me in a real, tangible way. Just another knife to drive into my back before he ripped it free and left me to bleed out for good.

"I'm not his girl," I snarled and the cop shrugged.

"I don't give a shit if he's your ballet instructor and the two of you are off to perform Swan Lake naked on the beach. His money says you're his problem, so you can either confirm your name and fuck off or stay in here pouting. I assume you can't pay your own bail considering you came in here with jack shit on you – aside from the stolen merchandise of course."

My upper lip curled back at the idea of accepting anything from that asshole, but I wanted out of here and I wanted to know why the fuck they'd abandoned me on that damn ferry.

I didn't really care what excuses he came up with though. There was a time when we'd made the concept of ride or die seem tame. None of us ever would have left another behind, no matter what the reason. Not willingly. I would have fought tooth and nail for any of them and would have died before abandoning them. So whatever dumb reason they had for leaving me behind, it sure as fuck wasn't good enough.

Still, if Fox wanted to waste his money on my bail then I wasn't gonna say no. But he'd be losing it when I ran from this fucking town, so I hoped they'd set it damn high.

"That's me," I grunted, getting to my feet and approaching the doors as the cop unlocked my cell.

I swiped my hands across my cheeks, hoping to fix some of the evidence of my tears, though I was sure my eyes were red and puffy enough to give it away no matter what I did.

"Alrighty then." The cop led me down a long corridor to the front desk and I signed the paperwork he needed to release me while looking around for Fox out in the reception area. But I couldn't see much through the frosted glass in the doors that divided me from it and the cop kept prattling on about how damn lucky I was which was setting my teeth on edge.

Once everything was done, the cop led me through to the reception and pointed me towards the darkness beyond the glass doors at the front of the building. Then he turned away to file the paperwork without seeming to give a shit about me anymore at all. I eyed him suspiciously, suddenly free and not entirely sure if I wanted to be.

How was I even making bail before I was charged? Why hadn't they charged me already anyway? I may not have been arrested before, but I understood the concept of being caught red handed with stolen goods and the way things went with clear evidence like that. So why was I being cut loose?

I took the plastic bag of my personal possessions which held my dead cellphone and my necklace with the key on it and quickly looped the leather back over my head before pocketing the pink monstrosity.

I frowned at the cop's back as he walked away from me then turned to the door, glancing at the clock and seeing that it was almost one in the morning. I'd been here all day and half the night. But now I was free – or at least free enough.

I stepped out into the warm night air and looked across the dark space outside the police station. A single figure stood leaning against a motorcycle in the middle of the empty parking lot, the whole world seeming to hold its breath around him.

The bottom dropped out of my stomach and I fell entirely still as my eyes met the gaze of the man who was waiting for me. The corner of his mouth lifted into a wicked smirk that seemed to say *check mate*.

"Hey, baby," he said, his voice cruel and taunting, lilting in a mockery of the way I'd answered his call the night I'd escaped his island. He was wearing a leather jacket and black jeans, his jaw rough with stubble and his eyes dark with a thirst for vengeance.

"Maverick?" I breathed, glancing around and wondering if there was any chance that I could outrun him because holy fuck, this was bad.

The last time I'd seen this particular psychopath, I'd been stealing from him and running the fuck away from his wrath while helping to orchestrate the destruction of thousands of dollars worth of stock he'd been managing for the cartel. I'd helped to place a target on his back and had aligned myself with the men he'd made into his enemies. We weren't friends. Hell, I doubted hatred even came close to what he felt for me right about now. And I sure as fuck wasn't getting on his bike.

"You didn't think I just forgot about you robbing me and helping those pricks destroy my warehouse, did you?" he asked casually, pushing himself to stand upright and making a lump form in my throat.

Shit. This was so much worse than bad. This was catastrophic - an end of the world annihilation of an utterly agonising kind.

"It was a misunderstanding," I said lamely and the darkness in his eyes seemed to deepen, but he didn't grace that bullshit with a response.

"Hop on, beautiful, I don't have all night," Maverick growled, patting the back of the bike like he seriously expected me to get on it. I'd sooner climb up onto a set of gallows and tighten a noose around my own neck.

"Erm, I'm cool just catching a bus or something," I hedged, glancing around in the hope of spotting someone who might be able to help me. Shouldn't this place have been crawling with cops? Where the fuck was everyone? Maybe I should just run back inside the building? But then what? I could hardly explain who Maverick was or why I was certain he'd want to kill me.

There was a row of palm trees to the left of the parking lot with a low fence just beyond them. A motorcycle couldn't follow me there. Maybe if I just ran for it, hopped the fence then raced away as fast as I could he wouldn't be able to catch up. It didn't seem like the best plan in the world, but it definitely beat going willingly.

"I already told you once. I'm prepared to do whatever it takes to destroy the Harlequins. And it just so happens that I've got a particular taste for taking down Fox. I plan on destroying him in every way I can." Maverick smiled callously as he took a single step towards me. "So that means I'm gonna destroy *you.*"

"I'm not coming with you," I growled, preparing to bolt and his eyes flashed hungrily like he was hoping I would.

"Yeah," he purred in a deadly tone which left no room for questions. "You are."

Murder swam in his eyes and I hunted for the boy I'd once known, trying to find him in the sea of darkness waiting for me there. But as I backed up a step and he stalked forward like a hunter, I was sure there was nothing left of that boy. This man was a monster who bled his enemies dry, and after what I'd done to him, I was now one of them.

My eyes flicked left and right as he reached for me, knowing I couldn't let him get his hands on me. That if he did, I was dead. Or worse. Far fucking worse.

I jerked right to throw him off and he lunged that way as I'd hoped while I spun on my heel and fled in the opposite direction. His heavy footfalls followed as I sprinted across the tarmac, my gaze set on the fence beyond the palms.

I just had to run. If there was one thing in this world that I was good for then it was fucking running. I could do this. I *had* to do this.

I raced over the grass at the edge of the lot into the shadows beneath the trees, but his footsteps said he was getting closer and I cursed as my foot hit a dark ditch hidden in the grass.

I stumbled, my stomach cartwheeling, my pulse jack-hammering in my skull, screaming at me to keep going and never look back. But the momentary stumble had cost me too damn much.

Strong hands grasped my arms and Maverick's cold laughter filled the air as he dragged me back against his iron body.

I tried to jerk free, kicking my legs, throwing my elbows back and screaming despite the fact that no one was here to help me. And no one had ever cared about me enough to come to my aid even if they had.

Maverick clamped his arms around me tighter, immobilising me with brute strength and his mouth fell to my ear as furious pants left my lungs and tears burned my eyes, desperation, terror and loss tangling inside me.

He was going to make good on that promise. I knew it like I knew my own shattered soul. I'd seen it in the shadows in his eyes. Ten years ago he'd been broken just as thoroughly as I had, and the ghosts of our past were finally colliding again to fulfil the oaths we'd made in honour of the people we'd once been. Maverick was set on the path of vengeance, his thirst for it as blinding as it was consuming. He'd vowed to destroy the Harlequins and I knew he was going to use me to do it in any and every way he could, no matter what it cost him, no matter what it cost *me*.

When he spoke, his voice was filled with dark oaths that crept under my skin and tried to break my will, claiming me in ways I never wanted to be claimed, owning me as surely as he had when we were kids. But that future held promises which could never be fulfilled now. Because now his intentions were anything but good and I'd fallen prey to the monster in him without ever having the chance to escape. "You're mine now, beautiful. Don't fight the inevitable. It'll only hurt more if you do."

———————————

AUTHOR'S NOTE

Well hello there…how are you doing? Isn't it nice when you get to start off a series and just get to enjoy all of the nice squishy get to know you vibes? Did you like the way we eased you into this world like you were sinking into a warm bath with a nice relaxing glass of vino?

I mean, there might have been a teeny weeny bit of heartache there (Washer Pun not intended (btw you can read Zodiac Academy if this means nothing to you and you wanna meet a fun teacher with a penchant for wearing speedos and squeezing into your heart and other interesting places)).

Anyway, where was I? Oh yeah, we were discussing how Rogue and her boys are living their best lives right about now and it's all sunshine and rainbows in the cove and you're praising us for the feel good vibes and errr…

Okay, yeah, we were dicks with this one.

But honestly, it wasn't intentional. We were like oh noooo sad backstory, waaah, what a road to recovery this shall beee, but then, like a wet salmon slapping us on the ass, we were hit with the reality of the Harlequin Crew and the dark, dark world they live in. I mean, who would have thought that being part of a gang run by a monster of a man wouldn't be fun all the time? Not I, good sir. But, turns out living that kind of life can fuck you up a bit. Or a lot.

Anyway, we've got a few books to go, so I'm sure they'll figure it out in the end. Fox will suddenly decide that sharing is caring. JJ will realise that the best dick you can give is the dick you give for free. Maverick will stop being utterly awful. And Chase will actually turn out to be really cool and not a backstabbing son of a bitch butt sucker after all.

Hmm. Seems like a tall order come to think of it so maybe we'll just focus on Shawn getting what's coming to him. Fucking Shawn. You haven't even met him yet and you just know he's the worst, don't you? So yeah, let's hope he dies easily and without causing any drama. Seems reasonable.

Ahem.

On a more serious note, we really want to thank you so much for reading this story (as well as any others of ours that we may have hooked you into) and let you know how much we appreciate you. Not just the collective you either. I mean YOU as you're reading this rambling nonsense that you've been sucked into after finishing the actual book. We love you. It's true. You are the foundation that our dreams are built on and the reason that we are getting to live them every day. Sorry for getting all weird and poetic there, but what I'm trying to say is that by reading our books you are making it possible for us to keep on writing and writing and writing. And I'm sorry that in payment for that we reach into your chest and squeeze your heart a little too roughly and that our characters aren't gentle when they creep into your mind and shake everything up, but hopefully you're enjoying the ride – even if it gets a little bit bumpy sometimes. Or all of the time. I blame Shawn. Fucking Shawn.

But if you feel the need to curse us then we graciously accept it and can provide locks of hair for use in voodoo dolls, drops of blood to add to magical potions or even our full names so that you can write them on a spelled piece of parchment to burn. All we ask is that you send payment in the form of a bottle of your saltiest reading tears and join our reader group where you can shout at us to your heart's content and meet a group of the best people we know who love all things fictional just as much as you do.

The world is kind of sucking right now, but you know what readers have that non-readers don't? Endless gateways into thousands of worlds where we can escape to at any moment with nothing more than the turn of a page. So take that Corona and stick it up your ass (not the beer bottle kind, unless you're into that type of thing). When we've vaccinated the shit out of you, you'll be nothing but a fuzzy memory of a time when we got to do lots of great reading and hold our families closer.

In the meantime, you'll find us with our heads in a book,

Love Susanne and Caroline x

ALSO BY
CAROLINE PECKHAM
&
SUSANNE VALENTI

Brutal Boys of Everlake Prep
(Complete Reverse Harem Bully Romance Contemporary Series)
Kings of Quarantine
Kings of Lockdown
Kings of Anarchy
Queen of Quarantine
**

Dead Men Walking
(Reverse Harem Dark Romance Contemporary Series)
The Death Club
Society of Psychos
**

The Harlequin Crew
(Reverse Harem Mafia Romance Contemporary Series)
Sinners Playground
Dead Man's Isle
Carnival Hill
Paradise Lagoon

Harlequinn Crew Novellas
Devil's Pass
**

Dark Empire
(Dark Mafia Contemporary Standalones)

Beautiful Carnage

Beautiful Savage

**

The Ruthless Boys of the Zodiac

(Reverse Harem Paranormal Romance Series - Set in the world of Solaria)

Dark Fae

Savage Fae

Vicious Fae

Broken Fae

Warrior Fae

Zodiac Academy

(M/F Bully Romance Series- Set in the world of Solaria, five years after Dark Fae)

The Awakening

Ruthless Fae

The Reckoning

Shadow Princess

Cursed Fates

Fated Thrones

Heartless Sky

The Awakening - As told by the Boys

Zodiac Academy Novellas

Origins of an Academy Bully

The Big A.S.S. Party

Darkmore Penitentiary

(Reverse Harem Paranormal Romance Series - Set in the world of Solaria, ten years after Dark Fae)

Caged Wolf

Alpha Wolf

Feral Wolf

**

The Age of Vampires

(Complete M/F Paranormal Romance/Dystopian Series)

Eternal Reign

Eternal Shade

Eternal Curse

Eternal Vow

Eternal Night

Eternal Love

**

Cage of Lies

(M/F Dystopian Series)

Rebel Rising

**

Tainted Earth

(M/F Dystopian Series)

Afflicted

Altered

Adapted

Advanced

**

The Vampire Games

(Complete M/F Paranormal Romance Trilogy)

V Games

V Games: Fresh From The Grave

V Games: Dead Before Dawn

*

The Vampire Games: Season Two

(Complete M/F Paranormal Romance Trilogy)

Wolf Games

Wolf Games: Island of Shade

Wolf Games: Severed Fates

*

The Vampire Games: Season Three

Hunter Trials

*

The Vampire Games Novellas

A Game of Vampires

**

The Rise of Issac

(Complete YA Fantasy Series)

Creeping Shadow

Bleeding Snow

Turning Tide

Weeping Sky

Failing Light

Printed in the USA
CPSIA information can be obtained
at www.ICGtesting.com
LVHW012154250324
775503LV00029B/672